NAILBITER

THE MURDER EDITION VOL. 1

JOSHUA WILLIAMSON
writer

MIKE HENDERSON
artist

ADAM GUZOWSKI
colorist

JOHN J. HILL
letterer & designer

ROB LEVIN
editor

IMAGE COMICS, INC.

Robert Kirkman - Chief Operating Officer   **Erik Larsen** - Chief Financial Officer
Todd McFarlane - President   **Marc Silvestri** - Chief Executive Officer   **Jim Valentino** - Vice-President
Eric Stephenson - Publisher   **Corey Murphy** - Director of Sales   **Jeff Boison** - Director of Publishing Planning & Book Trade Sales
Jeremy Sullivan - Director of Digital Sales   **Kat Salazar** - Director of PR & Marketing   **Emily Miller** - Director of Operations
Branwyn Bigglestone - Senior Accounts Manager   **Sarah Mello** - Accounts Manager   **Drew Gill** - Art Director   **Jonathan Chan** - Production Manager
Meredith Wallace - Print Manager   **Briah Skelly** - Publicity Assistant   **Sasha Head** - Sales & Marketing Production Designer
Randy Okamura - Digital Production Designer   **David Brothers** - Branding Manager   **Ally Power** - Content Manager   **Addison Duke** - Production Artist
Vincent Kukua - Production Artist   **Tricia Ramos** - Production Artist   **Jeff Stang** - Direct Market Sales Representative
Emilio Bautista - Digital Sales Associate   **Leanna Caunter** - Accounting Assistant   **Chloe Ramos-Peterson** - Administrative Assistant

IMAGECOMICS.COM

FOREWORD

Congratulations on being awesome. The comic industry is a fun little pocket of the
entertainment world. This pocket, which we all love, is dominated by nostalgia.
More than any other form of entertainment, comics is dominated by ideas and
characters and storylines that are decades and, in some cases, nearly a century old.
Comic books seem to be an industry dominated by the familiar.

That's why you, dear reader, in my humble opinion, qualify as awesome. You're
trying something new. That's not the easiest thing to do. You could have bought the
newest tale of Batman fighting the same villains he has for decades. Or you could
have picked up a slew of Star Wars comics to try and recapture that feeling from your
childhood. You could have at least picked up a Walking Dead comic because you
watched the show and think it's neat, but you didn't... you decided to step into the
unknown and seek out something unfamiliar, something completely new.

Bravo. You should be rewarded for your efforts, and you will as soon as you stop
wasting time reading this boring introduction and page through to the good stuff.
Because let me tell you, NAILBITER is great and you're in for a treat.

Still with me? Shame.

So if you're awesome for picking up this book, what does that make the people who
made this? I know comics are fun and all, but I don't think people realize how serious
this business really is. Especially for the creators.

Joshua Williamson and Mike Henderson, creators of this fine series, both put a lot
of blood, sweat and tears into this work. NAILBITER is a great comic, getting a lot
of attention, and their stars are only going to rise. But these guys have been kicking
around the industry for at least a decade working their way up the popularity ladder,
honing their craft, moving from project to project until settling in for this fine series.
That's a journey, and it's a hard one.

The thing is, they could be taking the easy road, working as a gun-for-hire on some
time tested formulaic corporate series. The creator equivalent of a reader who will
never see these words because they'd never take a risk on something new. No,
Joshua and Mike, they're diving in, rolling their sleeves up and getting their hands
dirty crafting a new world.

Sure, Joshua dabbles in corporate comics, but his dedication to creator-owned comics
is clear. He's not one of those fair weather creators, clearly focusing all his attention
on his corporate work, only publishing his creator-owned books when he can be
bothered to muster up the effort to detach from the corporate teat.

What's happening here is important. Don't discount what I'm saying because it may
sound ridiculous at first. There's a relationship being formed here, between reader
and creator... an agreement being made, that will pay off for both parties more than
anyone could imagine. You're agreeing to step through a door into the unknown,
venturing into a new world to experience new things. Joshua and Mike are agreeing
to give this series their all, to devote countless hours toward building this new world,
keeping it interesting and compelling, making something downright magical for you to
experience.

That's the lifeblood of this industry. Not the decades old corporate mascots that limp
along year after year catering to an audience not ready to admit to themselves how
bored they really are.

Theses guys are creating something NEW and you're supporting that new thing.
That's something special... that's something that makes you awesome.

So what are you waiting around for? It's time to claim your reward! Enjoy it as much
as I did... and know, there's much more where that came from.

ROBERT KIRKMAN
Backwoods, CA
2016

ONE

"You're the only one I can trust."

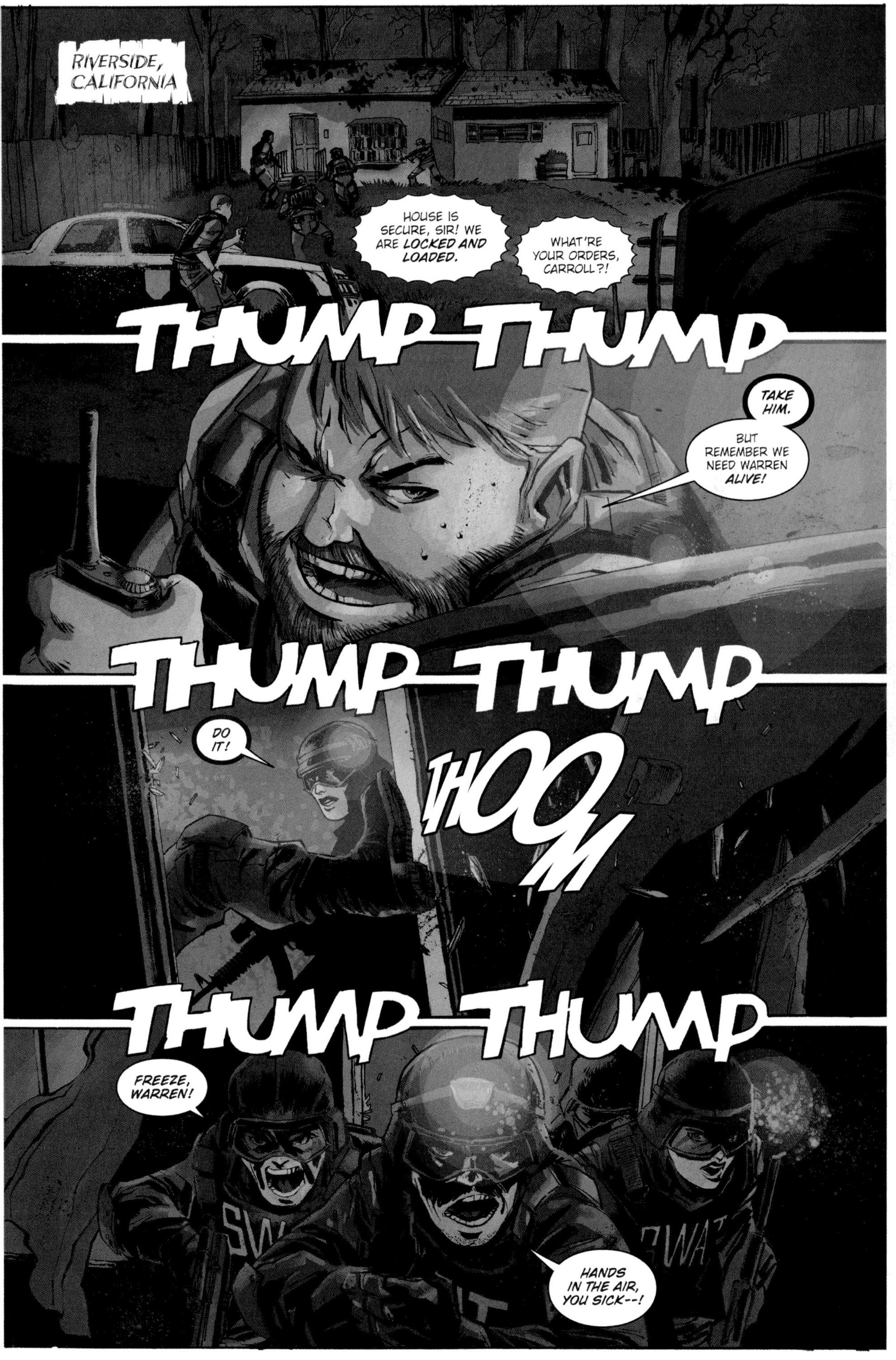

RIVERSIDE, CALIFORNIA
HOUSE IS SECURE, SIR! WE ARE LOCKED AND LOADED.
WHAT'RE YOUR ORDERS, CARROLL?!
THUMP THUMP
TAKE HIM.
BUT REMEMBER WE NEED WARREN ALIVE!
THUMP THUMP
DO IT!
THOOM
THUMP THUMP
FREEZE, WARREN!
HANDS IN THE AIR, YOU SICK--!

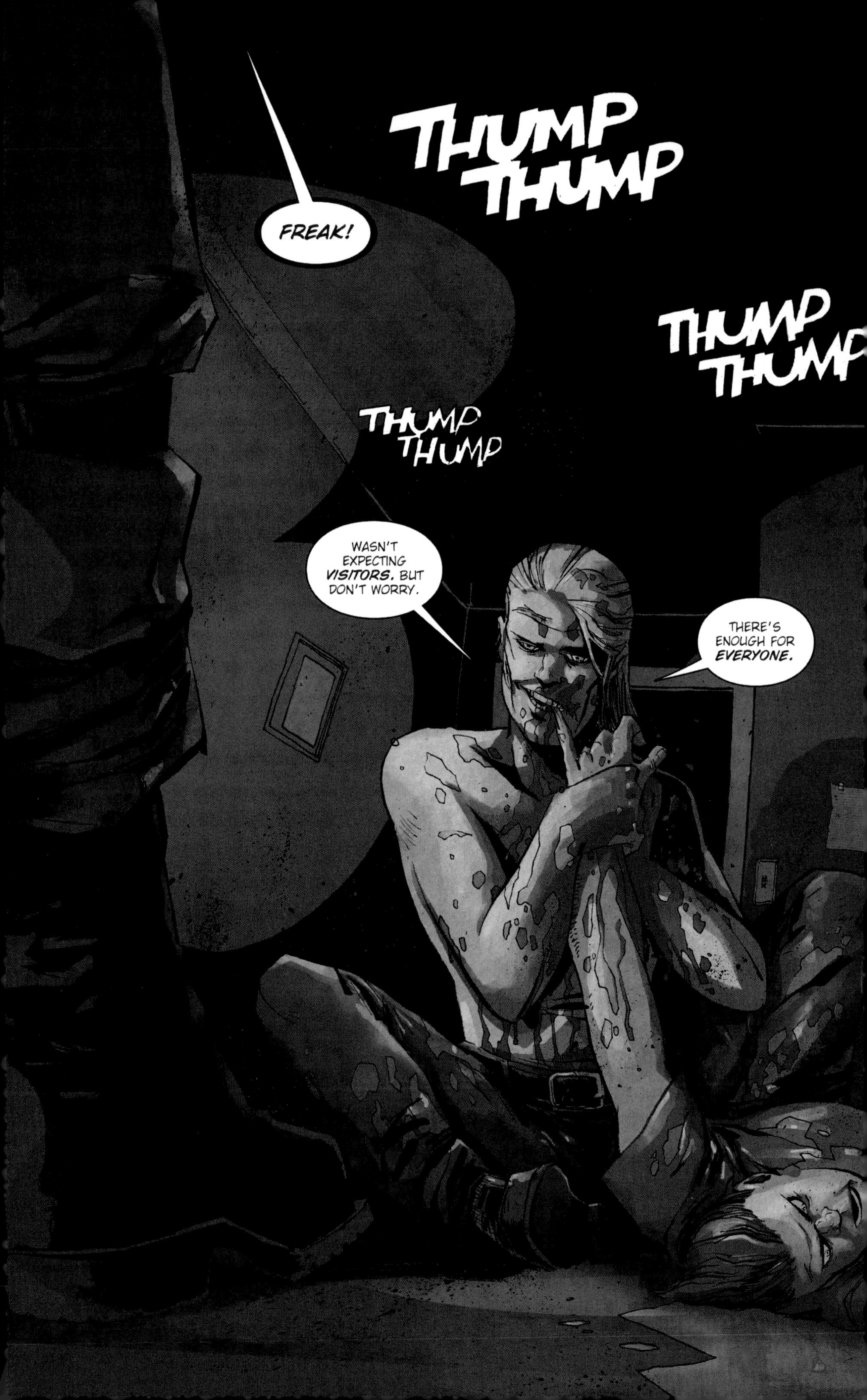
THUMP THUMP
FREAK!
THUMP THUMP
THUMP THUMP
WASN'T EXPECTING VISITORS. BUT DON'T WORRY.
THERE'S ENOUGH FOR EVERYONE.

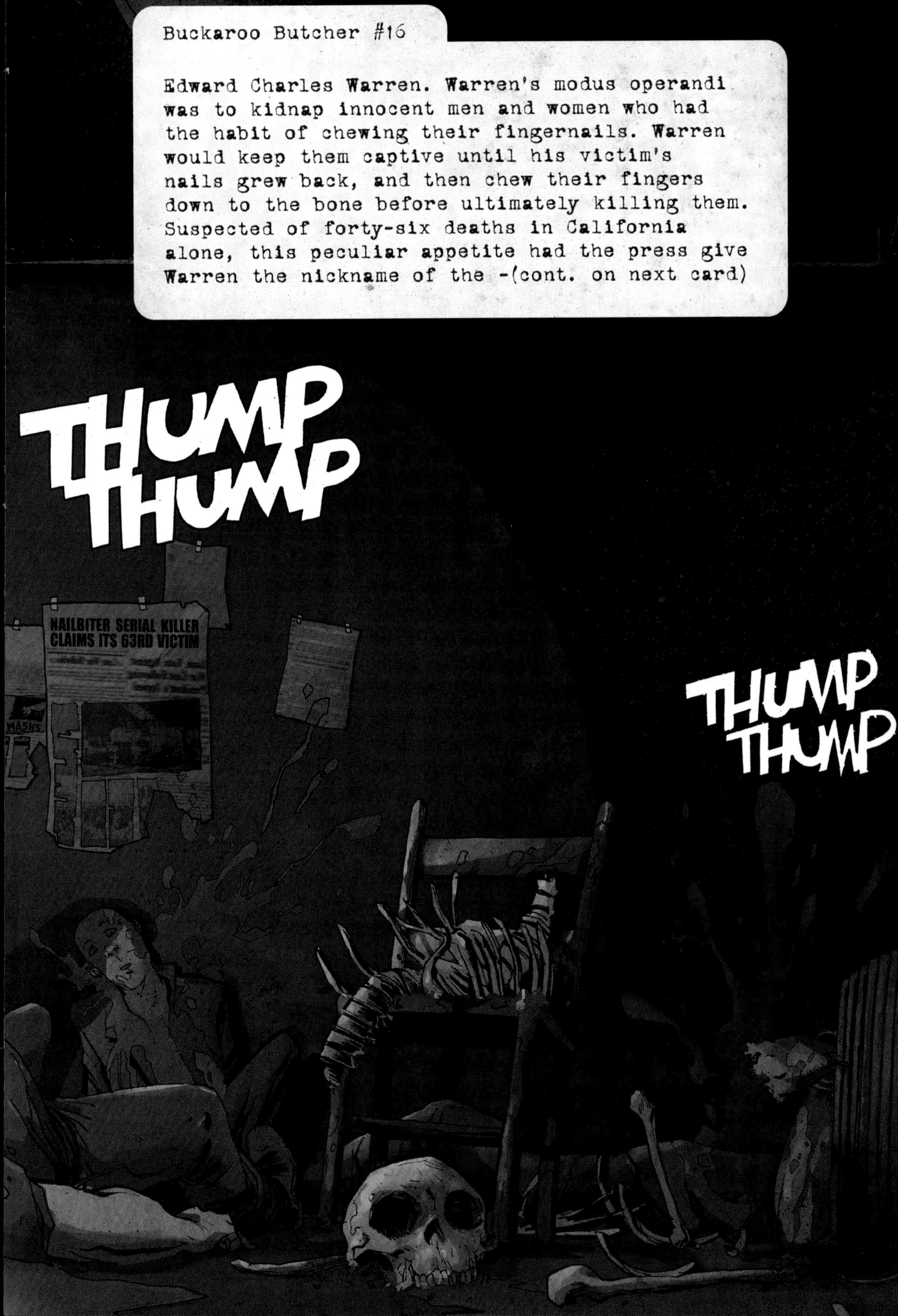
Buckaroo Butcher #16
Edward Charles Warren. Warren's modus operandi was to kidnap innocent men and women who had the habit of chewing their fingernails. Warren would keep them captive until his victim's nails grew back, and then chew their fingers down to the bone before ultimately killing them. Suspected of forty-six deaths in California alone, this peculiar appetite had the press give Warren the nickname of the -(cont. on next card)
THUMP THUMP
NAILBITER SERIAL KILLER CLAIMS ITS 63RD VICTIM
MASKS
THUMP THUMP

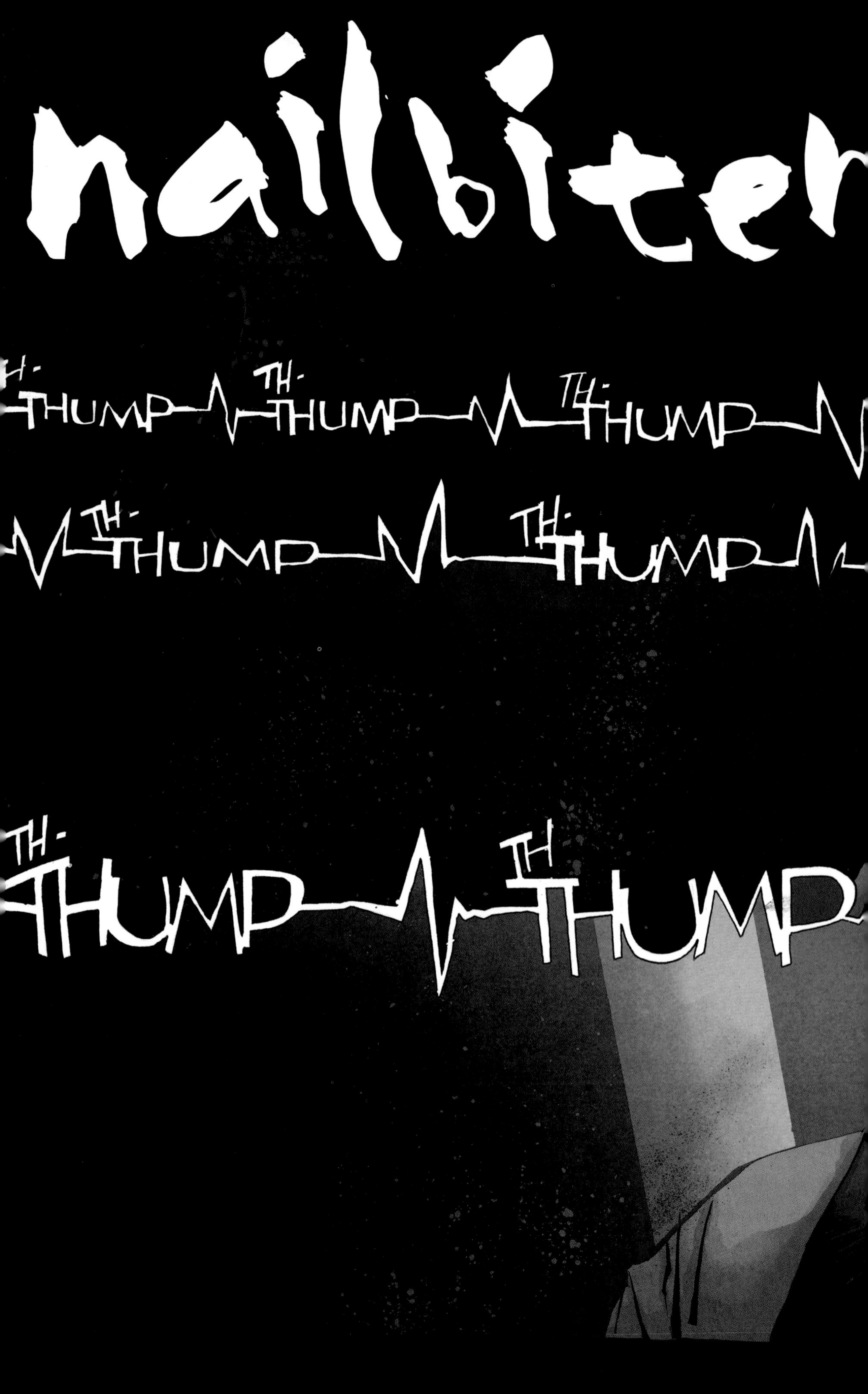
nailbiter
H-THUMP
TH-THUMP
TH-THUMP
TH-THUMP
TH-THUMP
TH-THUMP
TH THUMP

chapter One

“there will be blood”

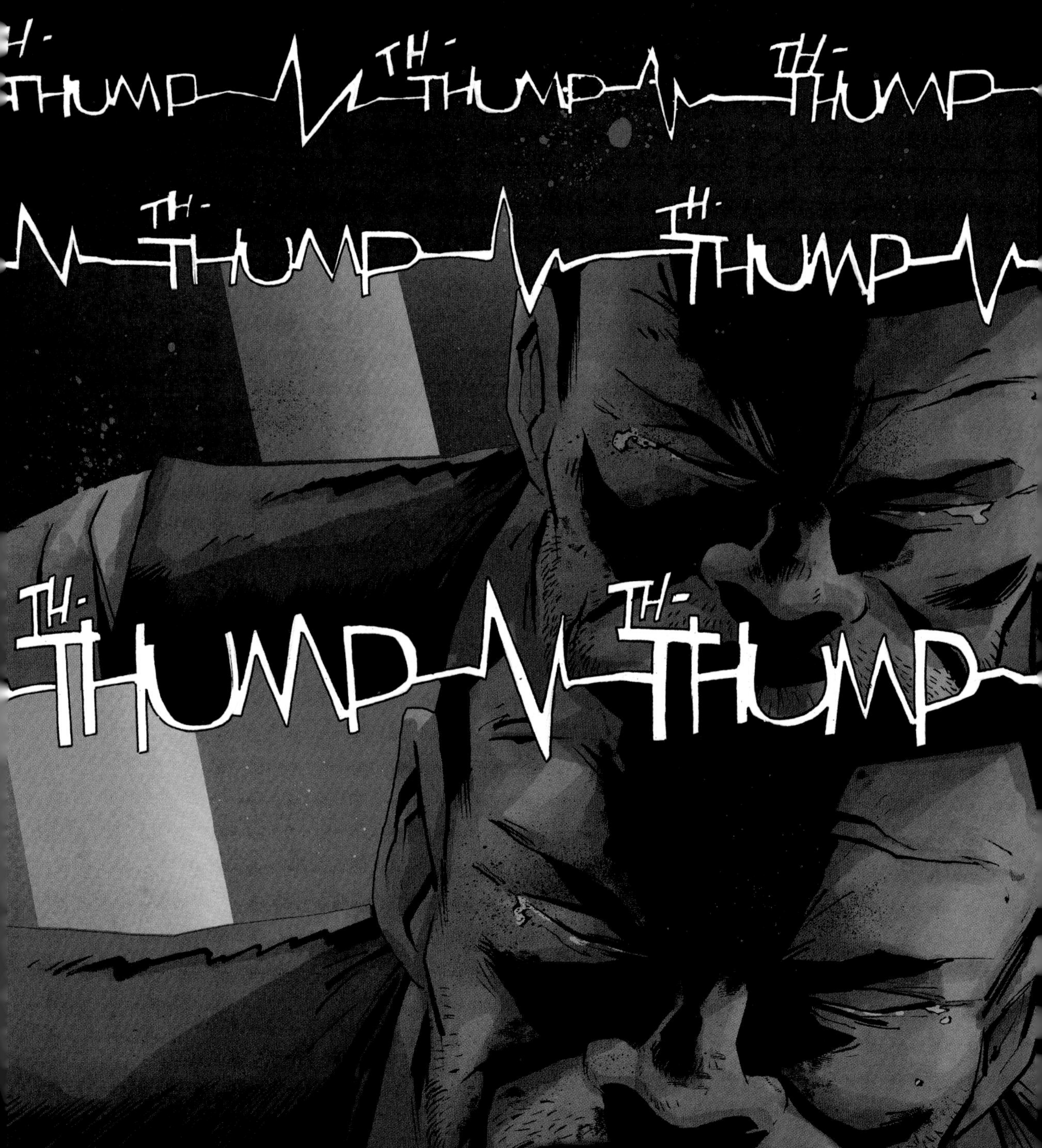
TH-THUMP
TH-THUMP
TH-THUMP
TH-THUMP
TH-THUMP
TH-THUMP
TH-THUMP

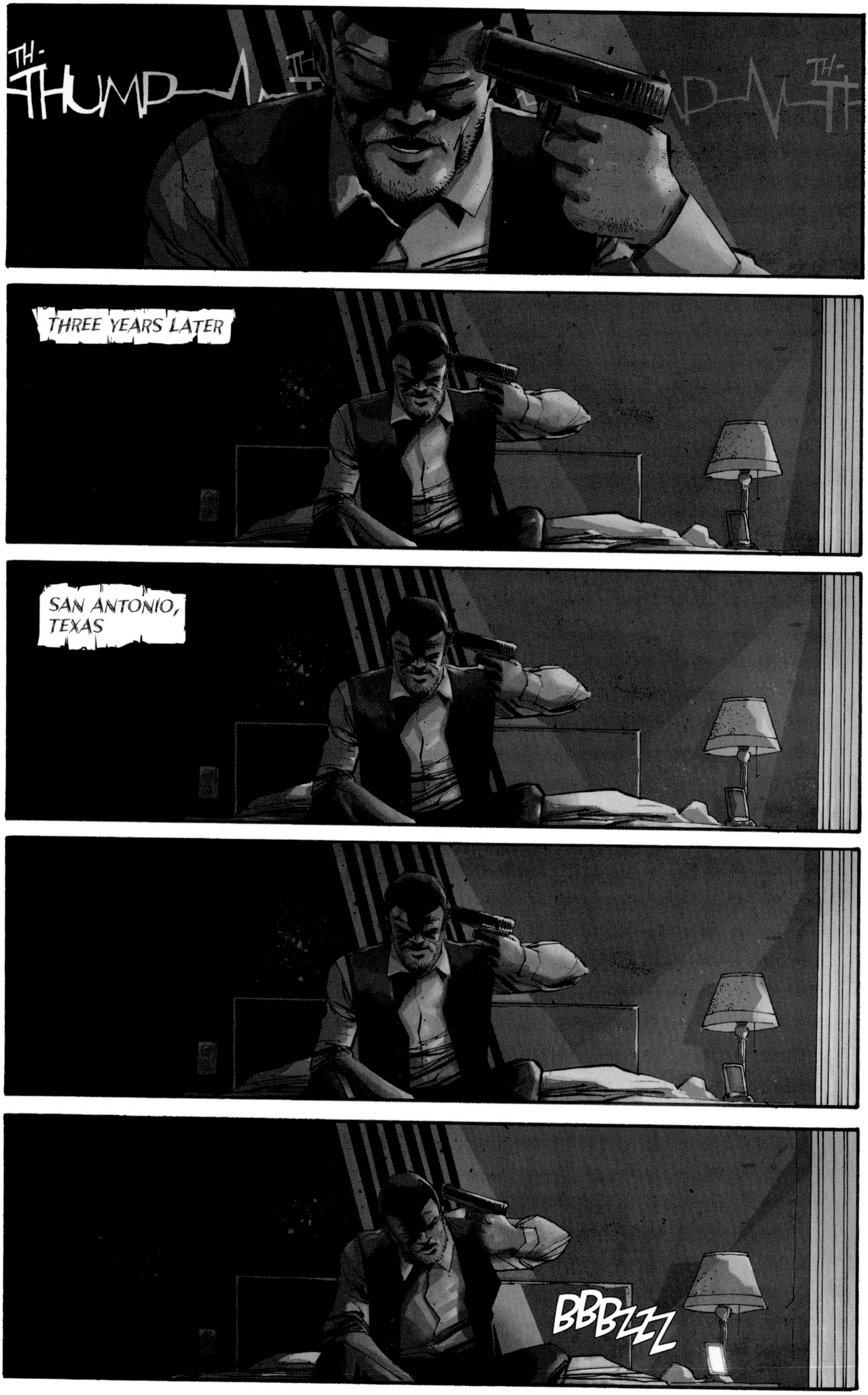
TH-THUMP
TH-
THREE YEARS LATER
SAN ANTONIO, TEXAS
BBBZZZ

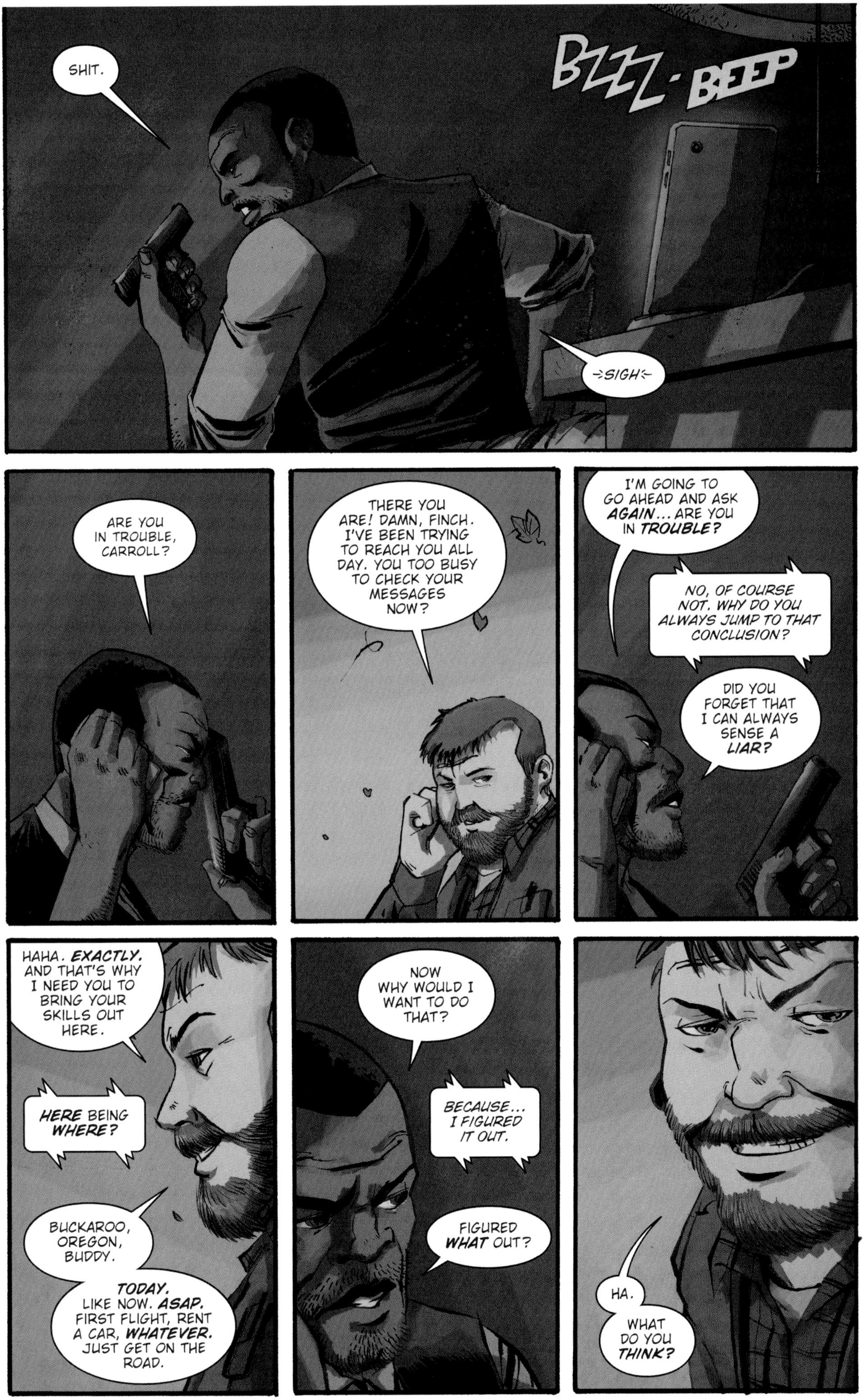
SHIT.
BZZZ-BEEP
>SIGH<
ARE YOU IN TROUBLE, CARROLL?
THERE YOU ARE! DAMN, FINCH. I'VE BEEN TRYING TO REACH YOU ALL DAY. YOU TOO BUSY TO CHECK YOUR MESSAGES NOW?
I'M GOING TO GO AHEAD AND ASK AGAIN... ARE YOU IN TROUBLE?
NO, OF COURSE NOT. WHY DO YOU ALWAYS JUMP TO THAT CONCLUSION?
DID YOU FORGET THAT I CAN ALWAYS SENSE A LIAR?
HAHA. EXACTLY. AND THAT'S WHY I NEED YOU TO BRING YOUR SKILLS OUT HERE.
HERE BEING WHERE?
BUCKAROO, OREGON, BUDDY.
TODAY. LIKE NOW. ASAP. FIRST FLIGHT, RENT A CAR, WHATEVER. JUST GET ON THE ROAD.
NOW WHY WOULD I WANT TO DO THAT?
BECAUSE... I FIGURED IT OUT.
FIGURED WHAT OUT?
HA.
WHAT DO YOU THINK?

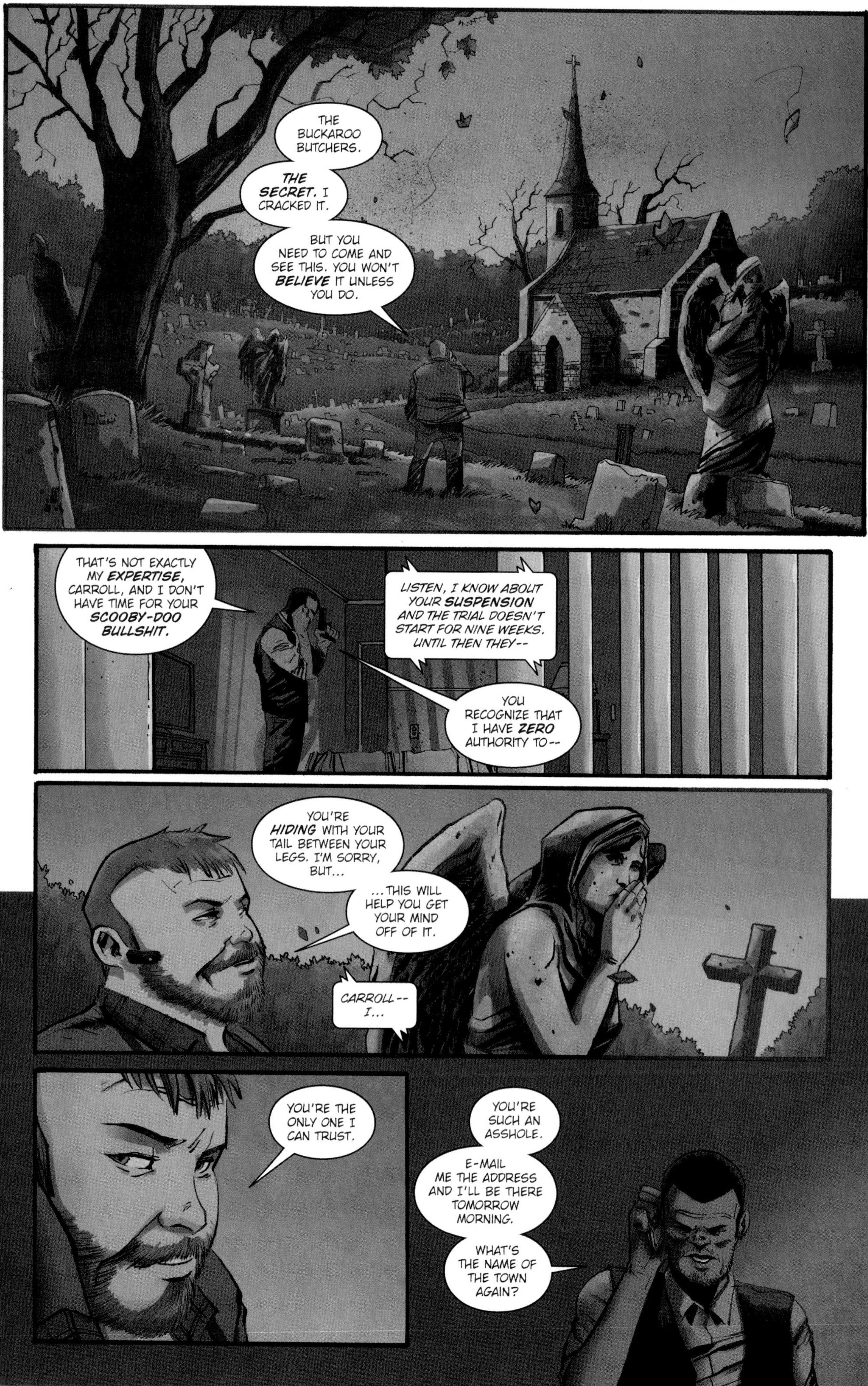

THE BUCKAROO BUTCHERS.
THE SECRET. I CRACKED IT.
BUT YOU NEED TO COME AND SEE THIS. YOU WON'T BELIEVE IT UNLESS YOU DO.
THAT'S NOT EXACTLY MY EXPERTISE, CARROLL, AND I DON'T HAVE TIME FOR YOUR SCOOBY-DOO BULLSHIT.
LISTEN, I KNOW ABOUT YOUR SUSPENSION AND THE TRIAL DOESN'T START FOR NINE WEEKS. UNTIL THEN THEY--
YOU RECOGNIZE THAT I HAVE ZERO AUTHORITY TO--
YOU'RE HIDING WITH YOUR TAIL BETWEEN YOUR LEGS. I'M SORRY, BUT...
...THIS WILL HELP YOU GET YOUR MIND OFF OF IT.
CARROLL-- I...
YOU'RE THE ONLY ONE I CAN TRUST.
YOU'RE SUCH AN ASSHOLE.
E-MAIL ME THE ADDRESS AND I'LL BE THERE TOMORROW MORNING.
WHAT'S THE NAME OF THE TOWN AGAIN?

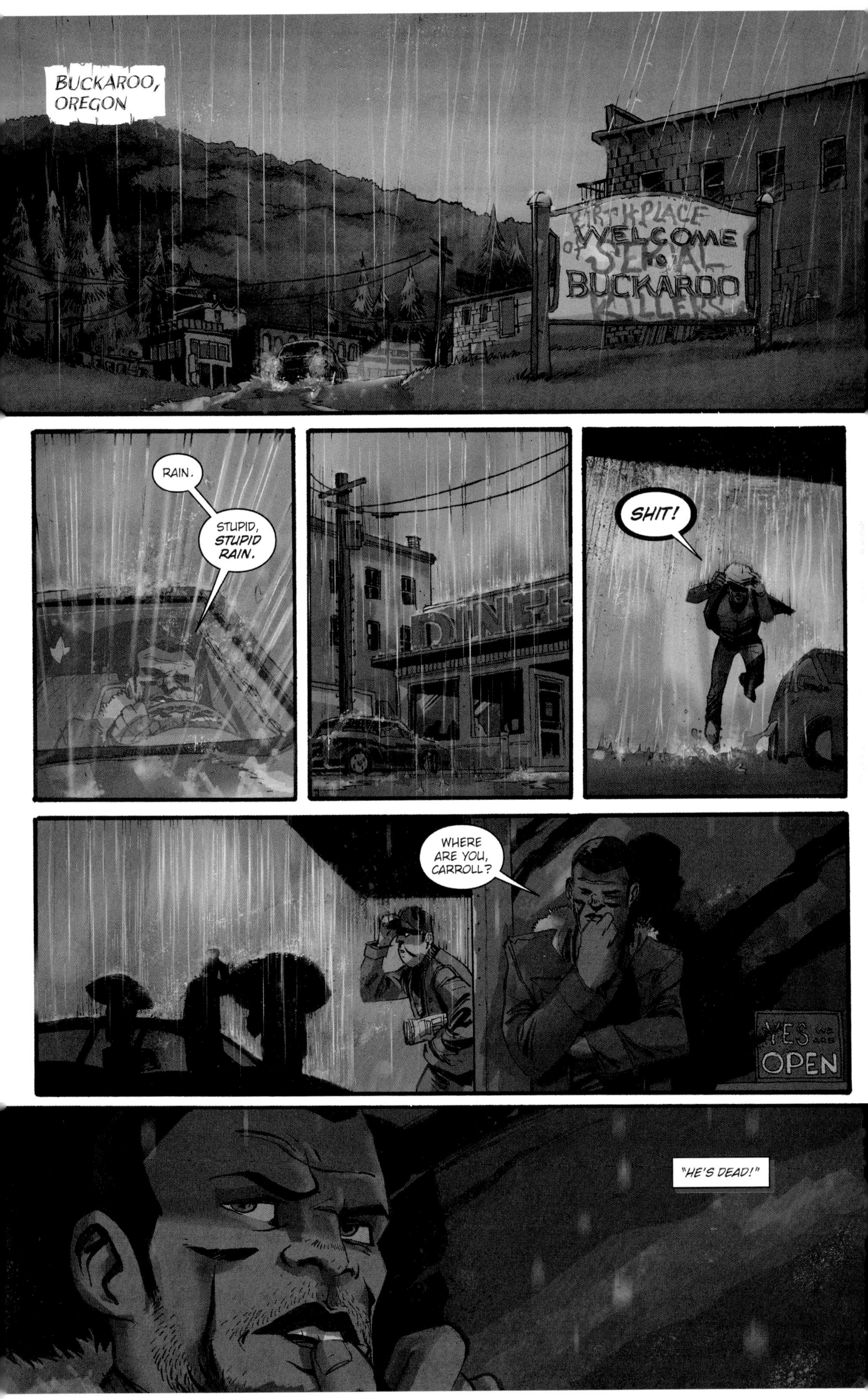
BUCKAROO, OREGON
WELCOME to BUCKAROO
RAIN.
STUPID, *STUPID RAIN.*
SHIT!
WHERE ARE YOU, CARROLL?
YES WE ARE OPEN
"HE'S DEAD!"

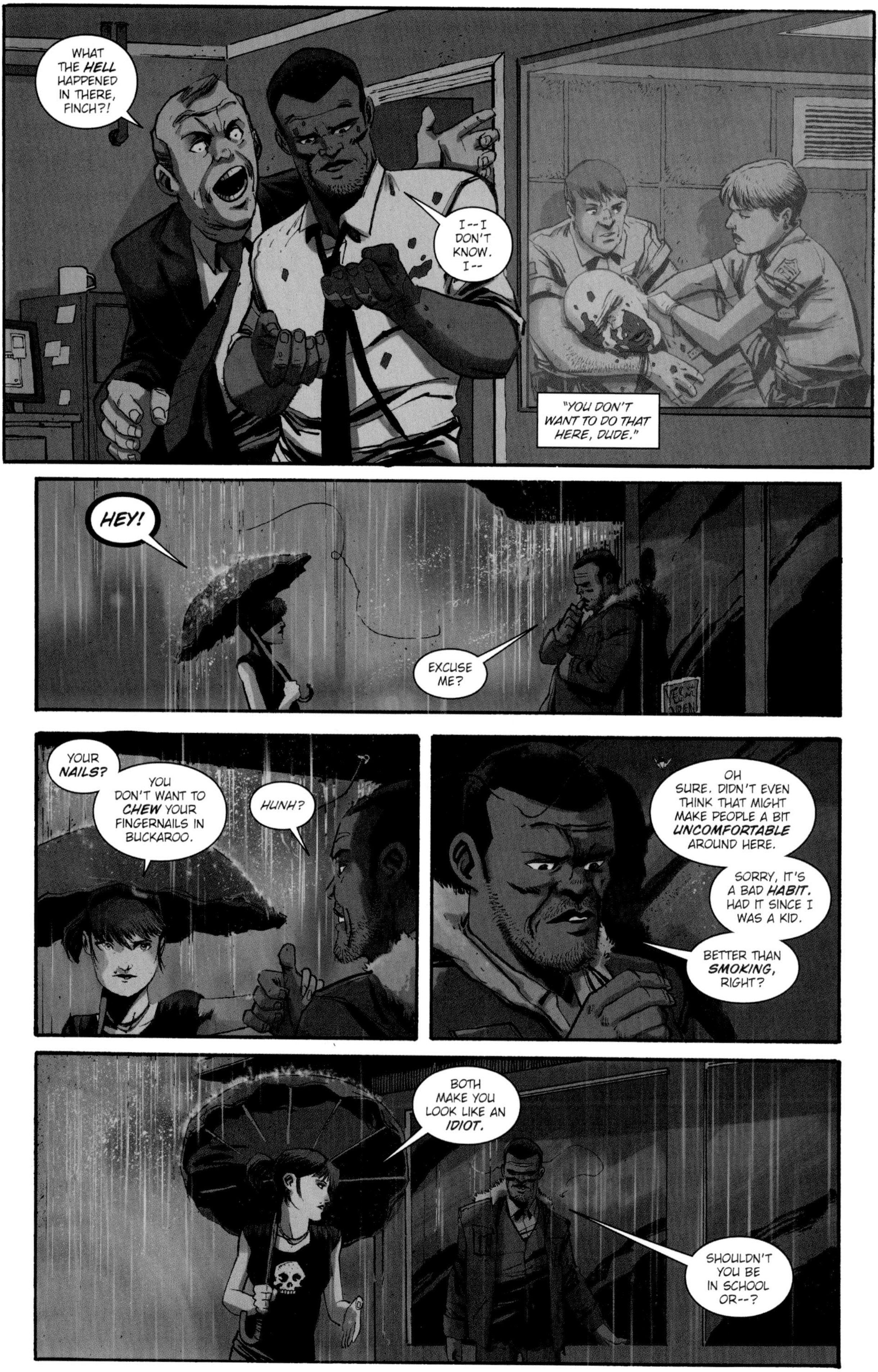
WHAT THE HELL HAPPENED IN THERE, FINCH?!
I--I DON'T KNOW. I--
"YOU DON'T WANT TO DO THAT HERE, DUDE."
HEY!
EXCUSE ME?
YOUR NAILS?
YOU DON'T WANT TO CHEW YOUR FINGERNAILS IN BUCKAROO.
HUNH?
OH SURE. DIDN'T EVEN THINK THAT MIGHT MAKE PEOPLE A BIT UNCOMFORTABLE AROUND HERE.
SORRY, IT'S A BAD HABIT. HAD IT SINCE I WAS A KID.
BETTER THAN SMOKING, RIGHT?
BOTH MAKE YOU LOOK LIKE AN IDIOT.
SHOULDN'T YOU BE IN SCHOOL OR--?

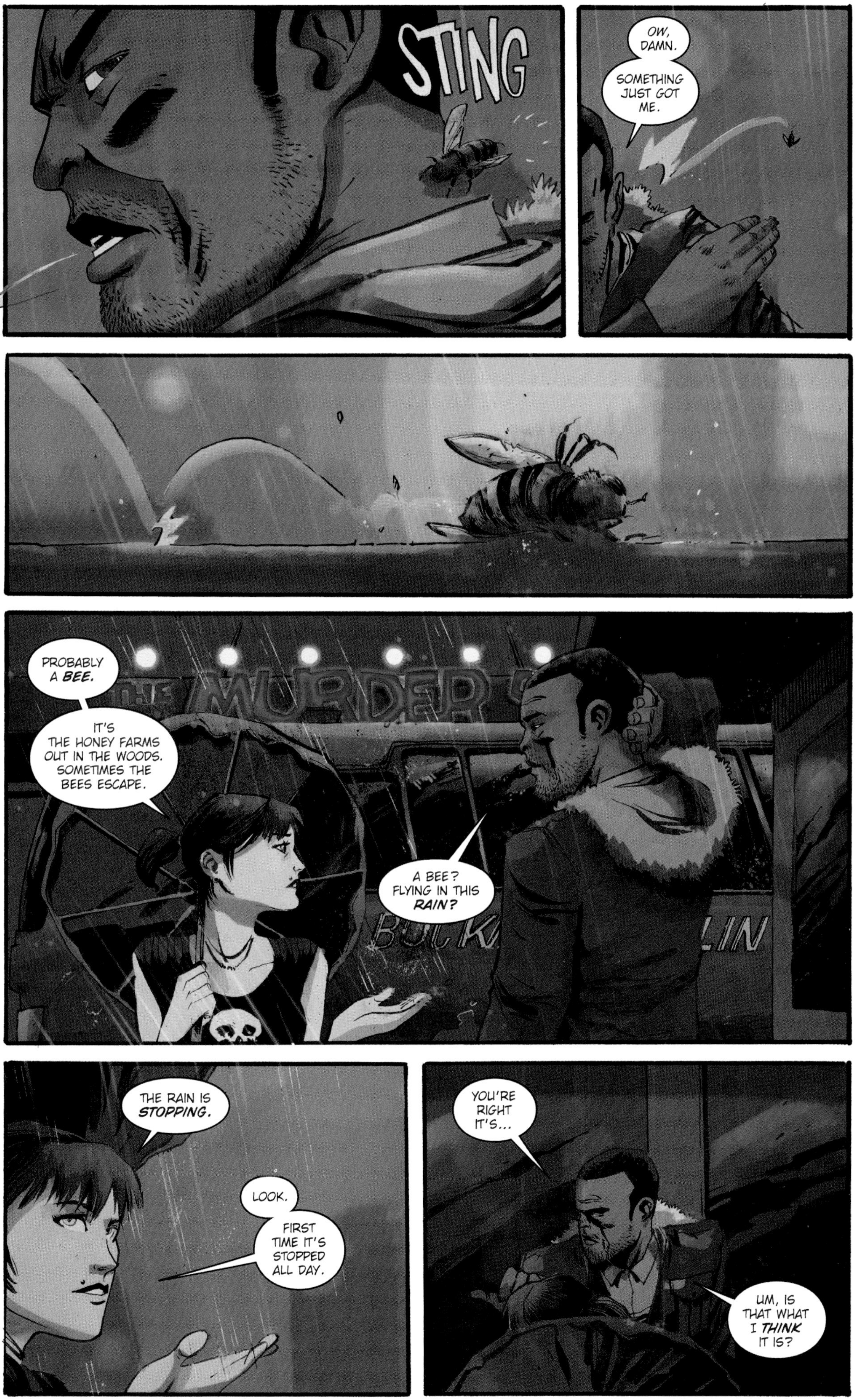
STING
OW, DAMN.
SOMETHING JUST GOT ME.
PROBABLY A BEE.
IT'S THE HONEY FARMS OUT IN THE WOODS. SOMETIMES THE BEES ESCAPE.
THE MURDER
A BEE? FLYING IN THIS RAIN?
THE RAIN IS STOPPING.
LOOK.
FIRST TIME IT'S STOPPED ALL DAY.
YOU'RE RIGHT IT'S...
UM, IS THAT WHAT I THINK IT IS?

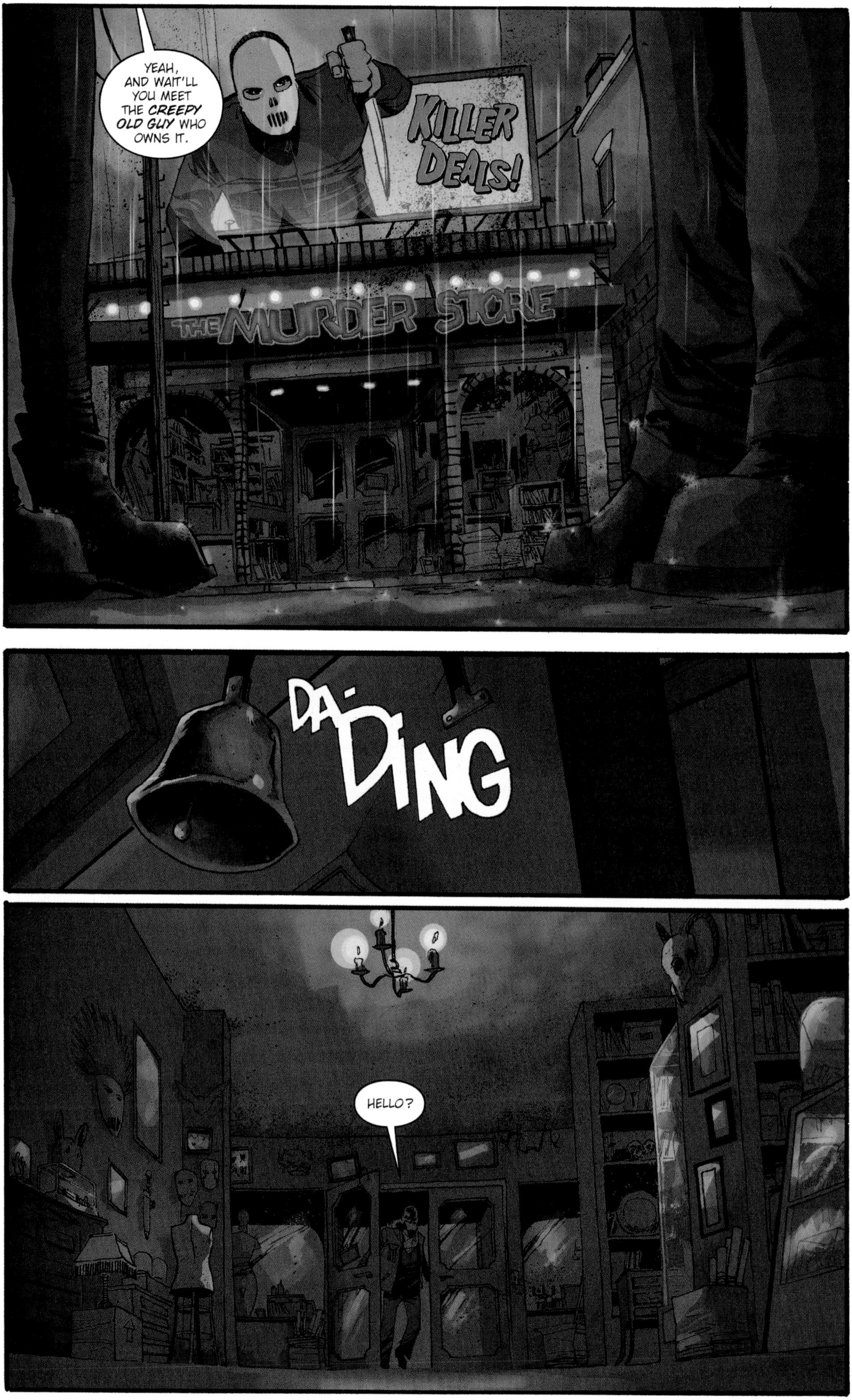
YEAH, AND WAIT'LL YOU MEET THE **CREEPY OLD GUY** WHO OWNS IT.
KILLER DEALS!
THE MURDER STORE
DA-DING
HELLO?

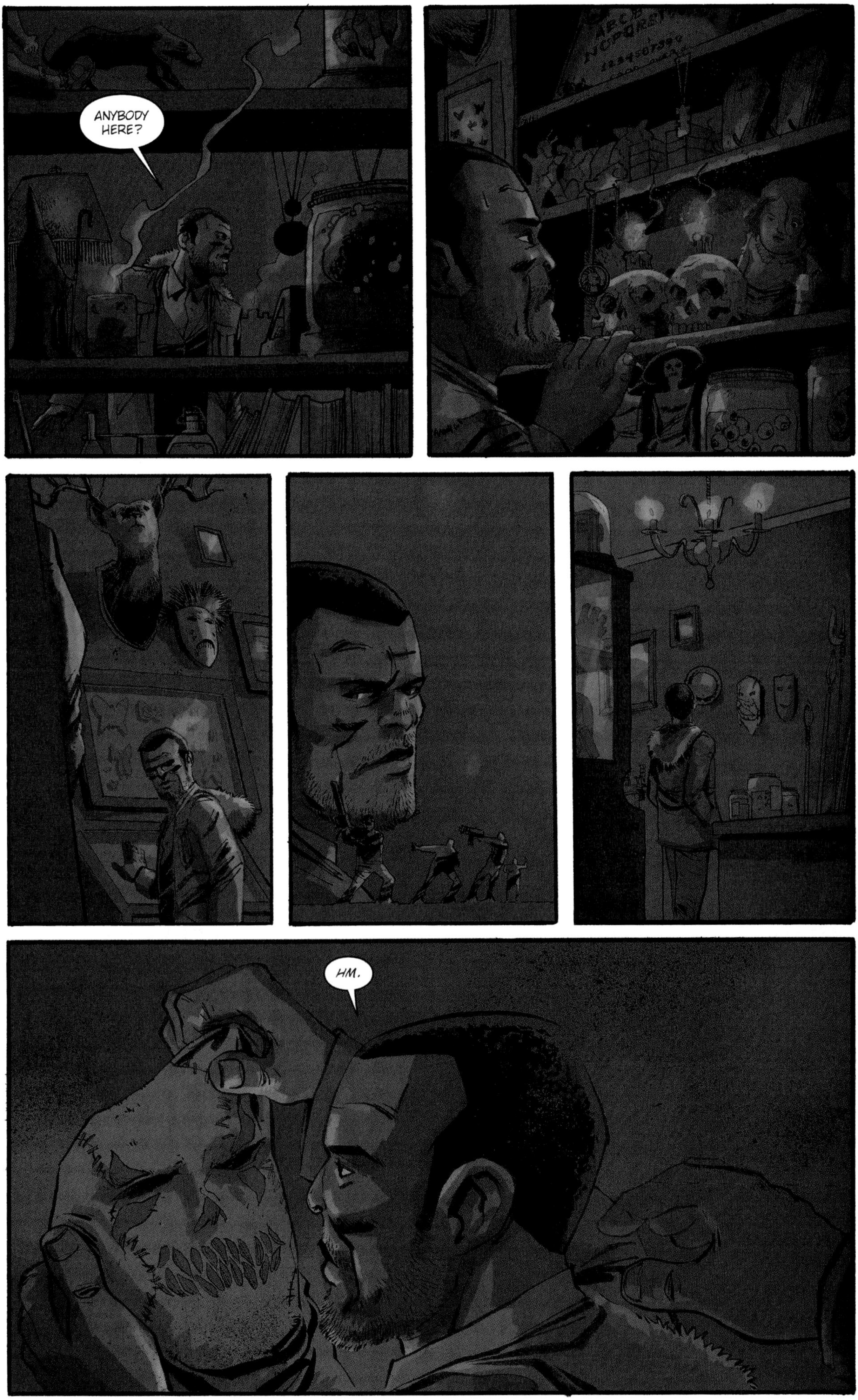
ANYBODY HERE?
HM.

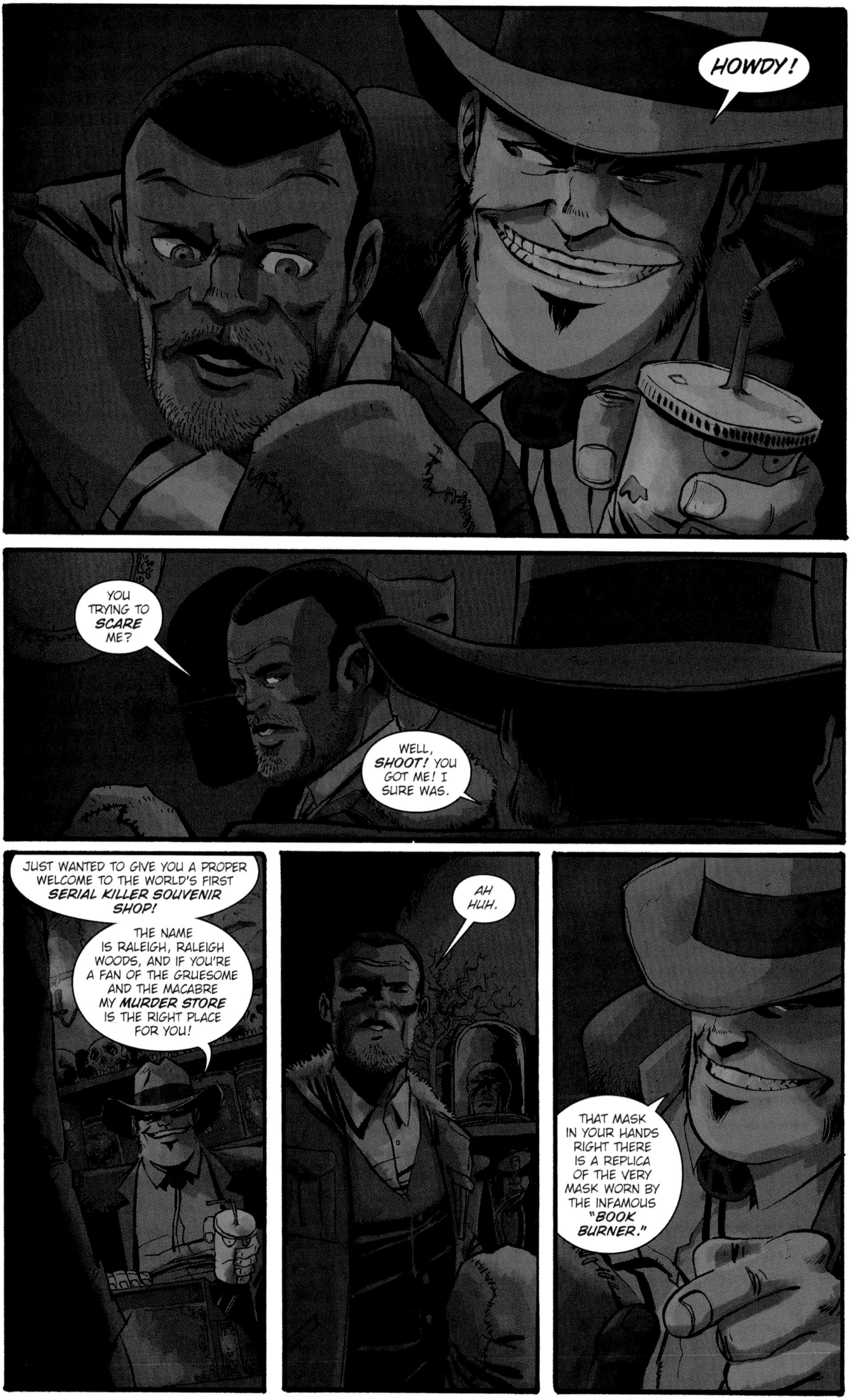
HOWDY!
YOU TRYING TO SCARE ME?
WELL, SHOOT! YOU GOT ME! I SURE WAS.
JUST WANTED TO GIVE YOU A PROPER WELCOME TO THE WORLD'S FIRST SERIAL KILLER SOUVENIR SHOP!
THE NAME IS RALEIGH, RALEIGH WOODS, AND IF YOU'RE A FAN OF THE GRUESOME AND THE MACABRE MY MURDER STORE IS THE RIGHT PLACE FOR YOU!
AH HUH.
THAT MASK IN YOUR HANDS RIGHT THERE IS A REPLICA OF THE VERY MASK WORN BY THE INFAMOUS "BOOK BURNER."

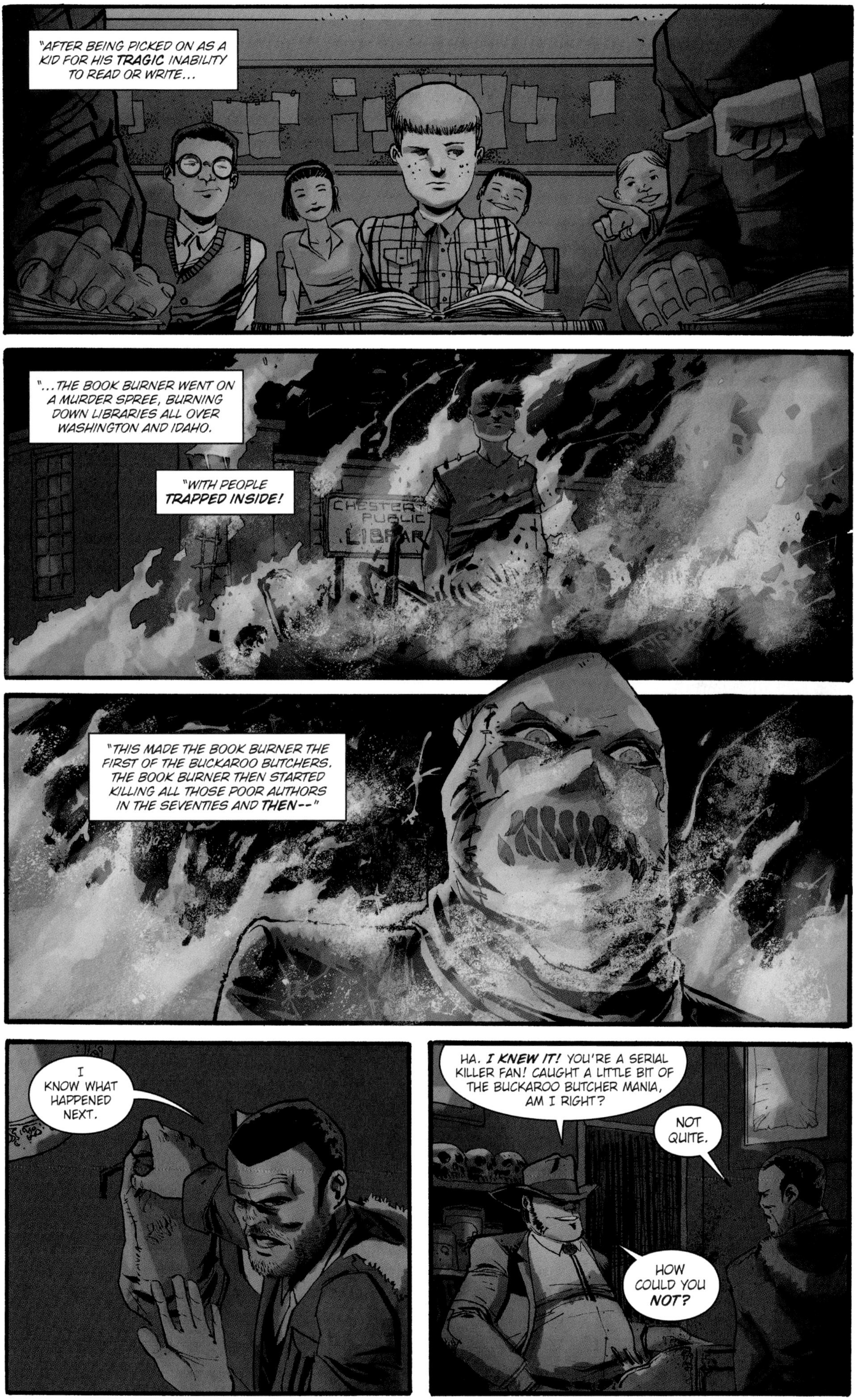

"AFTER BEING PICKED ON AS A KID FOR HIS **TRAGIC** INABILITY TO READ OR WRITE...
"...THE BOOK BURNER WENT ON A MURDER SPREE, BURNING DOWN LIBRARIES ALL OVER WASHINGTON AND IDAHO.
"WITH PEOPLE **TRAPPED INSIDE!**
"THIS MADE THE BOOK BURNER THE FIRST OF THE BUCKAROO BUTCHERS. THE BOOK BURNER THEN STARTED KILLING ALL THOSE POOR AUTHORS IN THE SEVENTIES AND **THEN**--"
I KNOW WHAT HAPPENED NEXT.
HA. ***I KNEW IT!*** YOU'RE A SERIAL KILLER FAN! CAUGHT A LITTLE BIT OF THE BUCKAROO BUTCHER MANIA, AM I RIGHT?
NOT QUITE.
HOW COULD YOU ***NOT?***

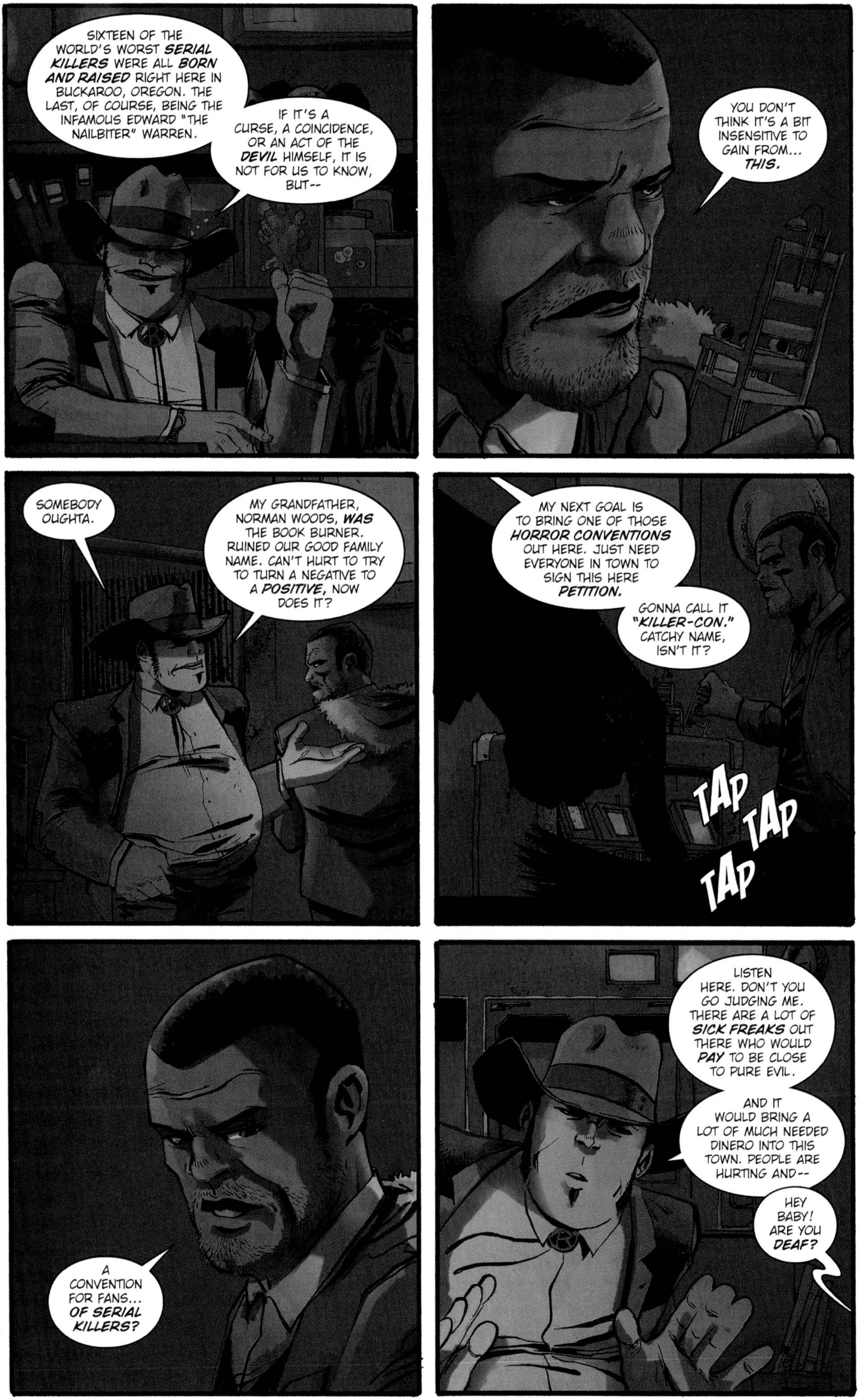
SIXTEEN OF THE WORLD'S WORST SERIAL KILLERS WERE ALL BORN AND RAISED RIGHT HERE IN BUCKAROO, OREGON. THE LAST, OF COURSE, BEING THE INFAMOUS EDWARD "THE NAILBITER" WARREN.
IF IT'S A CURSE, A COINCIDENCE, OR AN ACT OF THE DEVIL HIMSELF, IT IS NOT FOR US TO KNOW, BUT--
YOU DON'T THINK IT'S A BIT INSENSITIVE TO GAIN FROM... THIS.
SOMEBODY OUGHTA.
MY GRANDFATHER, NORMAN WOODS, WAS THE BOOK BURNER. RUINED OUR GOOD FAMILY NAME. CAN'T HURT TO TRY TO TURN A NEGATIVE TO A POSITIVE, NOW DOES IT?
MY NEXT GOAL IS TO BRING ONE OF THOSE HORROR CONVENTIONS OUT HERE. JUST NEED EVERYONE IN TOWN TO SIGN THIS HERE PETITION.
GONNA CALL IT "KILLER-CON." CATCHY NAME, ISN'T IT?
TAP TAP TAP
A CONVENTION FOR FANS... OF SERIAL KILLERS?
LISTEN HERE. DON'T YOU GO JUDGING ME. THERE ARE A LOT OF SICK FREAKS OUT THERE WHO WOULD PAY TO BE CLOSE TO PURE EVIL.
AND IT WOULD BRING A LOT OF MUCH NEEDED DINERO INTO THIS TOWN. PEOPLE ARE HURTING AND--
HEY BABY! ARE YOU DEAF?

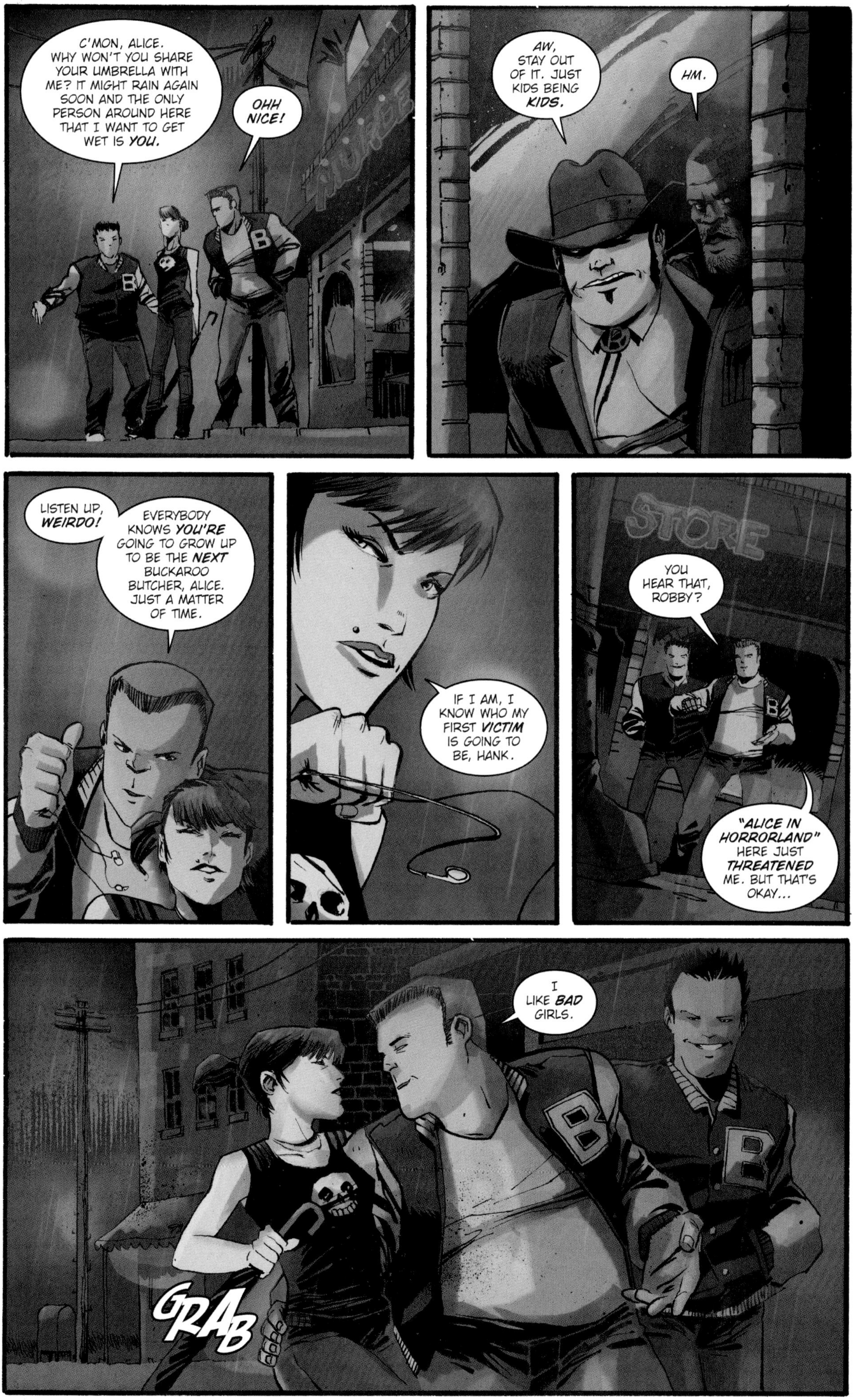
C'MON, ALICE. WHY WON'T YOU SHARE YOUR UMBRELLA WITH ME? IT MIGHT RAIN AGAIN SOON AND THE ONLY PERSON AROUND HERE THAT I WANT TO GET WET IS YOU.
OHH NICE!
AW, STAY OUT OF IT. JUST KIDS BEING KIDS.
HM.
LISTEN UP, WEIRDO!
EVERYBODY KNOWS YOU'RE GOING TO GROW UP TO BE THE NEXT BUCKAROO BUTCHER, ALICE. JUST A MATTER OF TIME.
IF I AM, I KNOW WHO MY FIRST VICTIM IS GOING TO BE, HANK.
STORE
YOU HEAR THAT, ROBBY?
"ALICE IN HORRORLAND" HERE JUST THREATENED ME. BUT THAT'S OKAY...
I LIKE BAD GIRLS.
GRAB

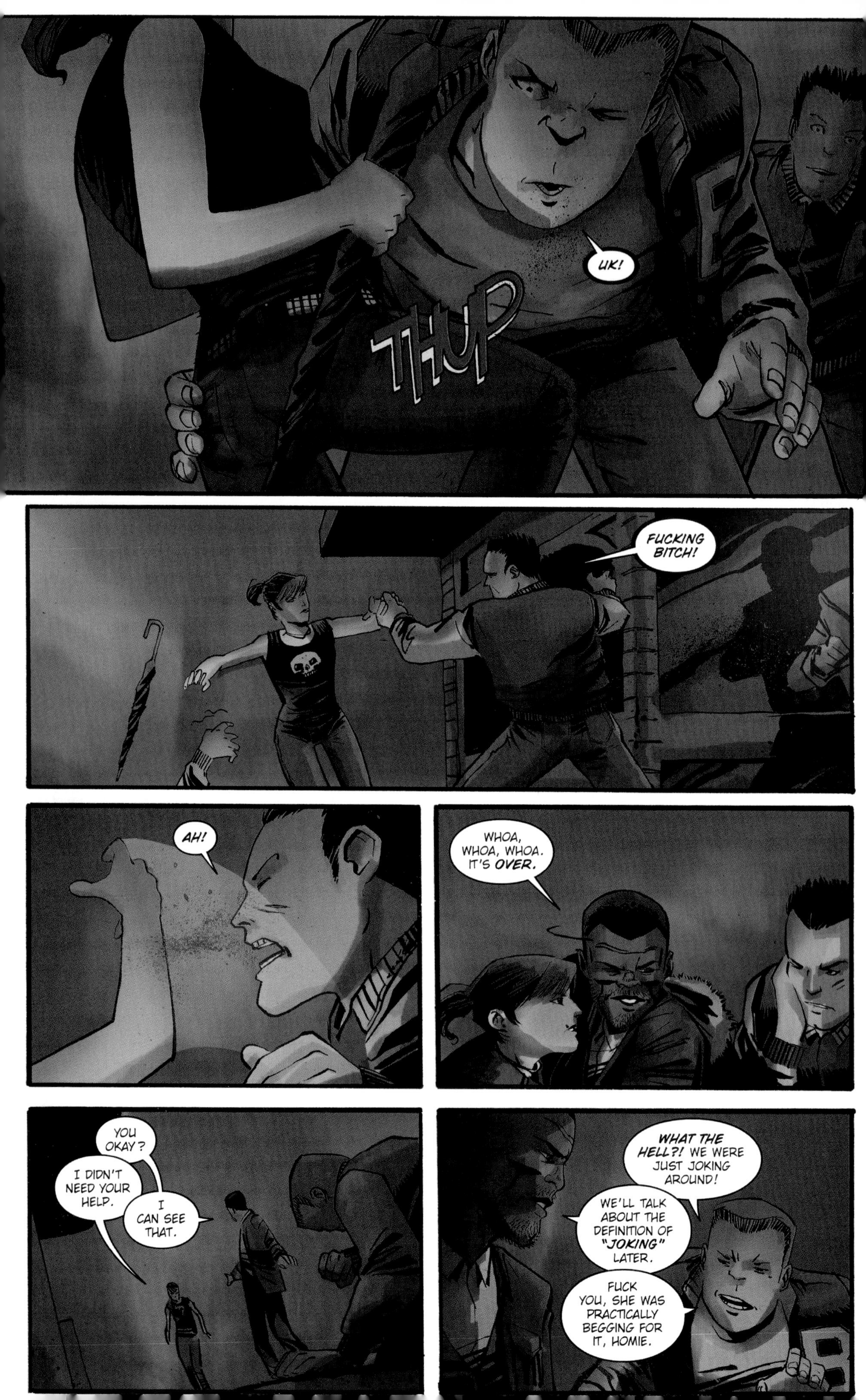
UK!
THUP
FUCKING BITCH!
AH!
WHOA, WHOA, WHOA. IT'S *OVER.*
YOU OKAY?
I DIDN'T NEED YOUR HELP.
I CAN SEE THAT.
WHAT THE HELL?! WE WERE JUST JOKING AROUND!
WE'LL TALK ABOUT THE DEFINITION OF *"JOKING"* LATER.
FUCK YOU, SHE WAS PRACTICALLY BEGGING FOR IT, HOMIE.

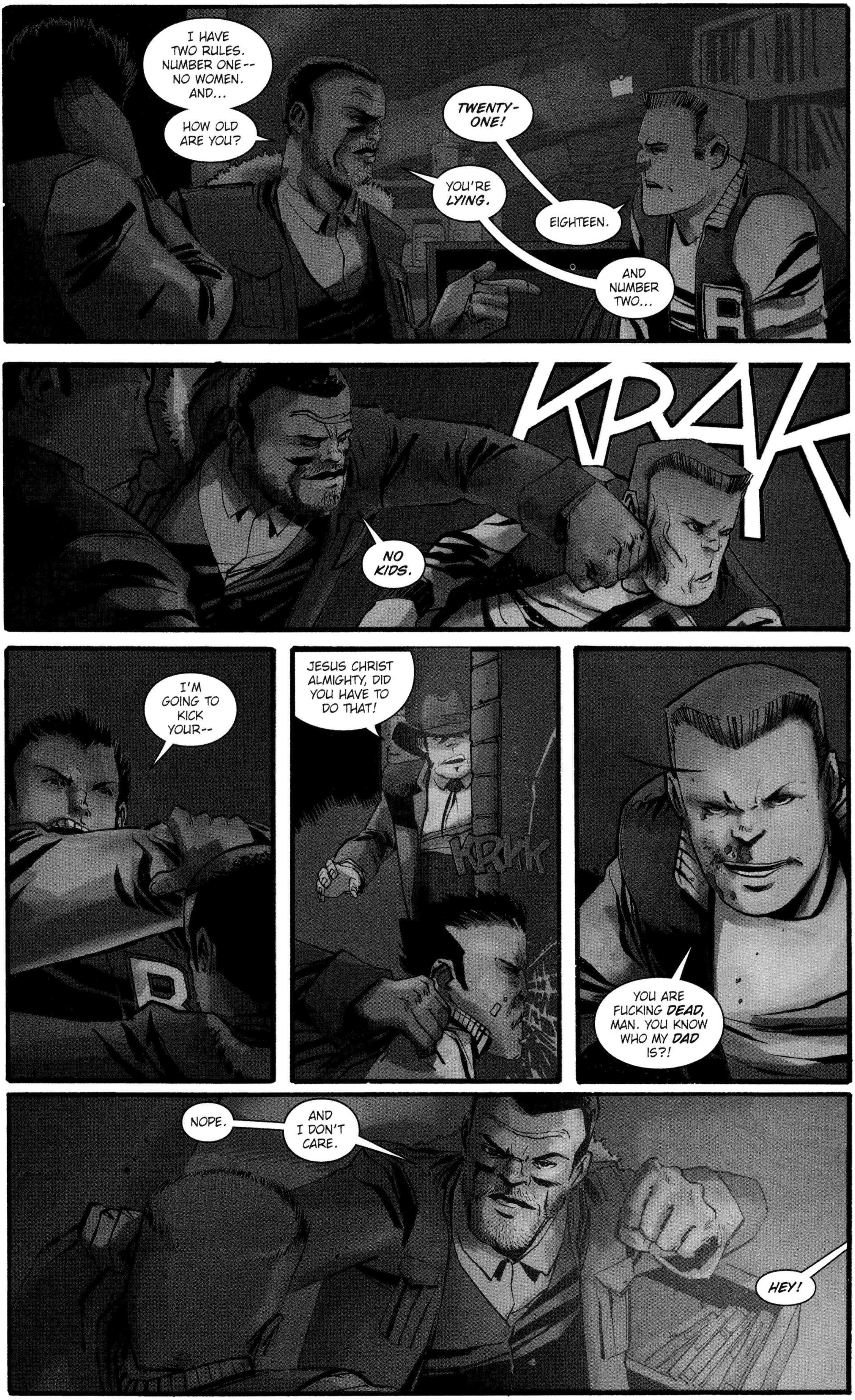
I HAVE TWO RULES. NUMBER ONE-- NO WOMEN. AND...
HOW OLD ARE YOU?
TWENTY-ONE!
YOU'RE LYING.
EIGHTEEN.
AND NUMBER TWO...
KRAK
NO KIDS.
I'M GOING TO KICK YOUR--
JESUS CHRIST ALMIGHTY, DID YOU HAVE TO DO THAT!
KRKK
YOU ARE FUCKING DEAD, MAN. YOU KNOW WHO MY DAD IS?!
NOPE.
AND I DON'T CARE.
HEY!

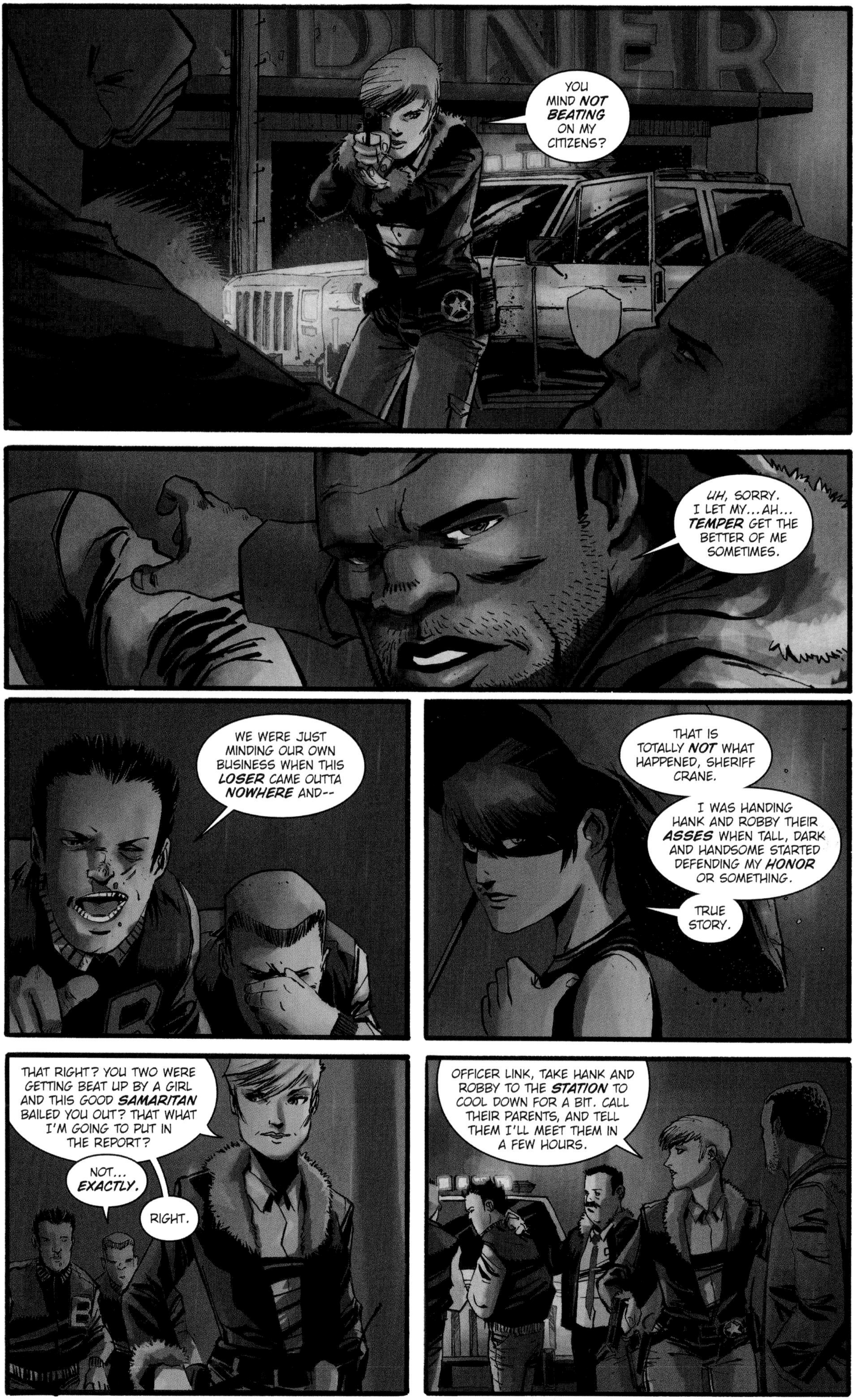
YOU MIND NOT BEATING ON MY CITIZENS?
UH, SORRY. I LET MY...AH... TEMPER GET THE BETTER OF ME SOMETIMES.
WE WERE JUST MINDING OUR OWN BUSINESS WHEN THIS LOSER CAME OUTTA NOWHERE AND--
THAT IS TOTALLY NOT WHAT HAPPENED, SHERIFF CRANE.
I WAS HANDING HANK AND ROBBY THEIR ASSES WHEN TALL, DARK AND HANDSOME STARTED DEFENDING MY HONOR OR SOMETHING.
TRUE STORY.
THAT RIGHT? YOU TWO WERE GETTING BEAT UP BY A GIRL AND THIS GOOD SAMARITAN BAILED YOU OUT? THAT WHAT I'M GOING TO PUT IN THE REPORT?
NOT... EXACTLY.
RIGHT.
OFFICER LINK, TAKE HANK AND ROBBY TO THE STATION TO COOL DOWN FOR A BIT. CALL THEIR PARENTS, AND TELL THEM I'LL MEET THEM IN A FEW HOURS.

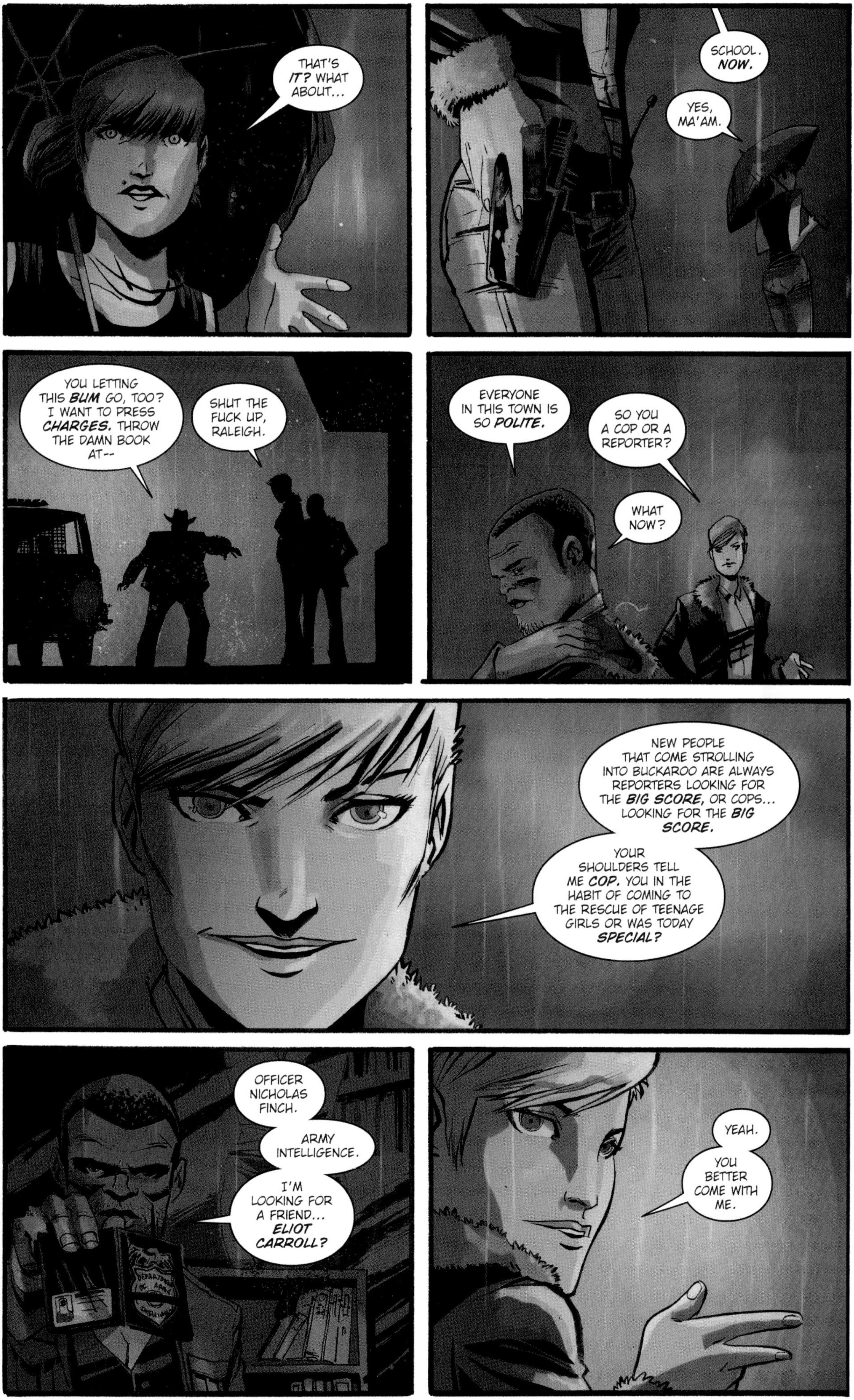
THAT'S IT? WHAT ABOUT...
SCHOOL. NOW.
YES, MA'AM.
YOU LETTING THIS BUM GO, TOO? I WANT TO PRESS CHARGES. THROW THE DAMN BOOK AT--
SHUT THE FUCK UP, RALEIGH.
EVERYONE IN THIS TOWN IS SO POLITE.
SO YOU A COP OR A REPORTER?
WHAT NOW?
NEW PEOPLE THAT COME STROLLING INTO BUCKAROO ARE ALWAYS REPORTERS LOOKING FOR THE BIG SCORE, OR COPS... LOOKING FOR THE BIG SCORE.
YOUR SHOULDERS TELL ME COP. YOU IN THE HABIT OF COMING TO THE RESCUE OF TEENAGE GIRLS OR WAS TODAY SPECIAL?
OFFICER NICHOLAS FINCH.
ARMY INTELLIGENCE.
I'M LOOKING FOR A FRIEND... ELIOT CARROLL?
YEAH.
YOU BETTER COME WITH ME.

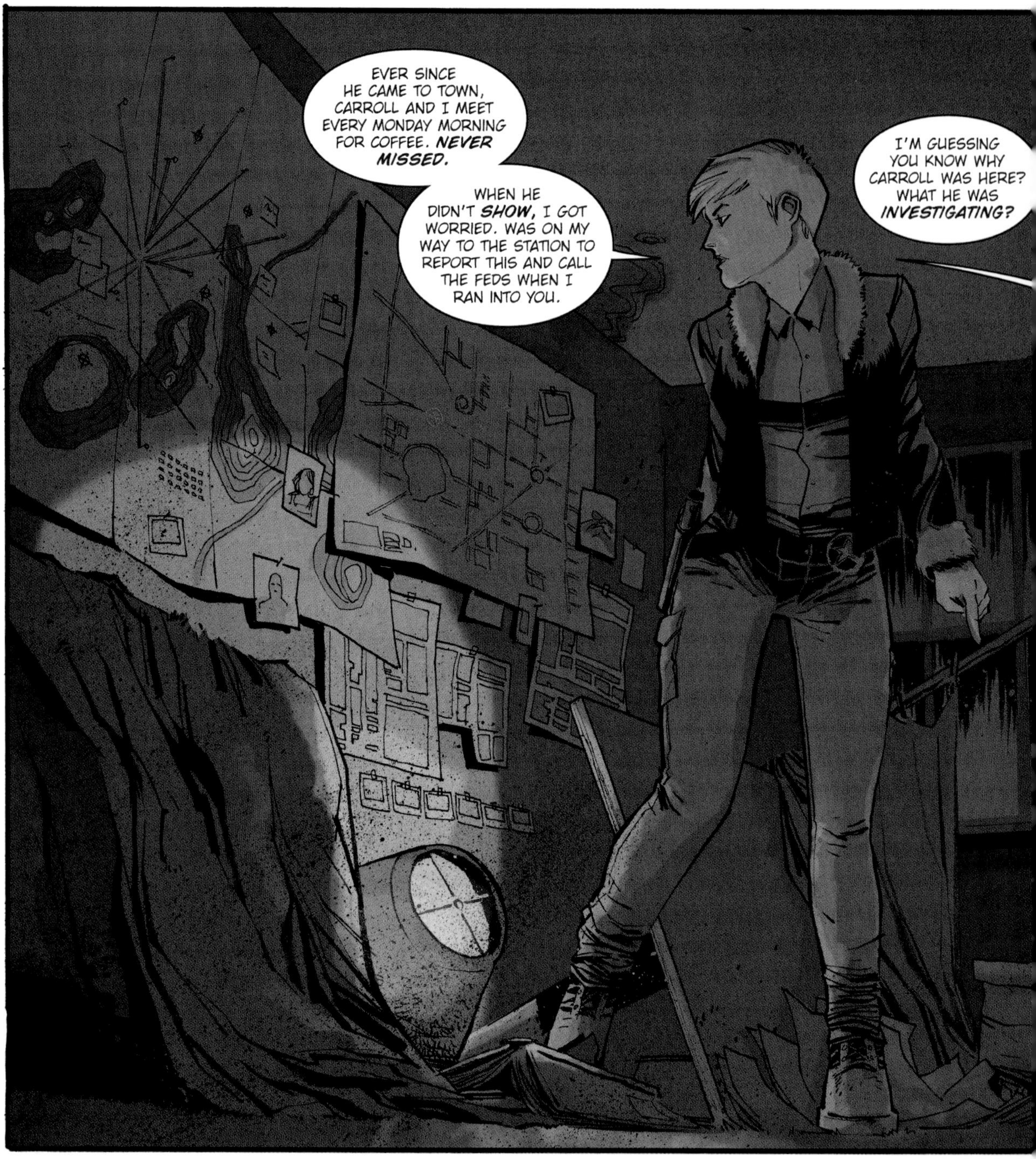
EVER SINCE HE CAME TO TOWN, CARROLL AND I MEET EVERY MONDAY MORNING FOR COFFEE. **NEVER MISSED.**
WHEN HE DIDN'T **SHOW,** I GOT WORRIED. WAS ON MY WAY TO THE STATION TO REPORT THIS AND CALL THE FEDS WHEN I RAN INTO YOU.
I'M GUESSING YOU KNOW WHY CARROLL WAS HERE? WHAT HE WAS **INVESTIGATING?**

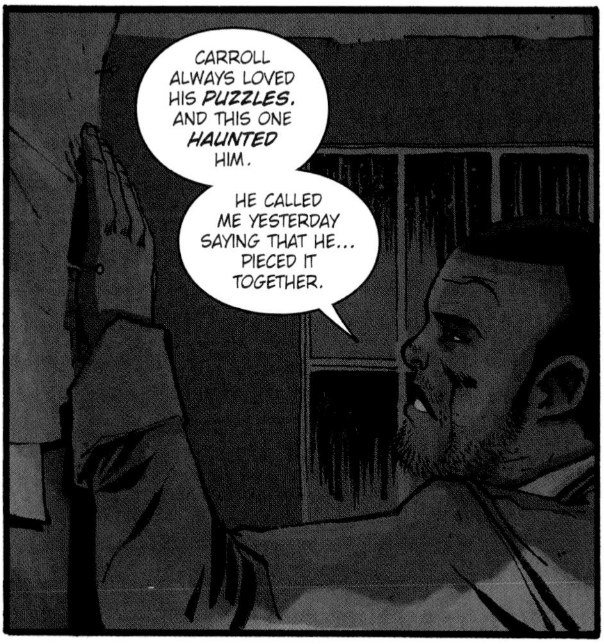
CARROLL ALWAYS LOVED HIS **PUZZLES.** AND THIS ONE **HAUNTED** HIM.
HE CALLED ME YESTERDAY SAYING THAT HE... PIECED IT TOGETHER.

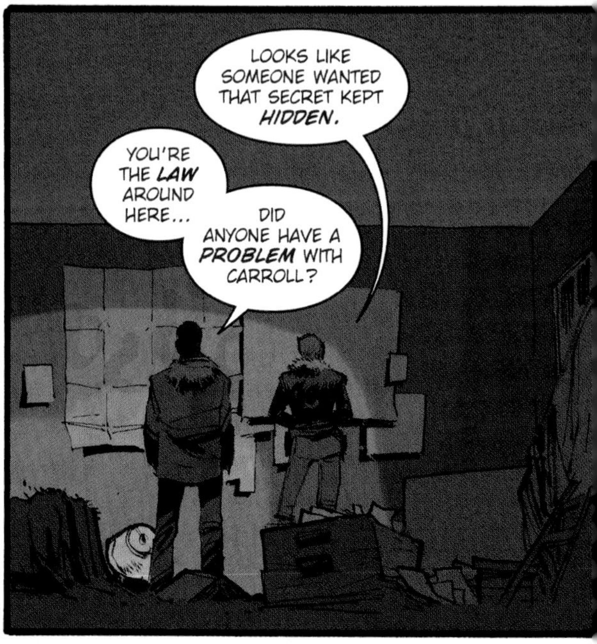
LOOKS LIKE SOMEONE WANTED THAT SECRET KEPT **HIDDEN.**
YOU'RE THE **LAW** AROUND HERE...
DID ANYONE HAVE A **PROBLEM** WITH CARROLL?

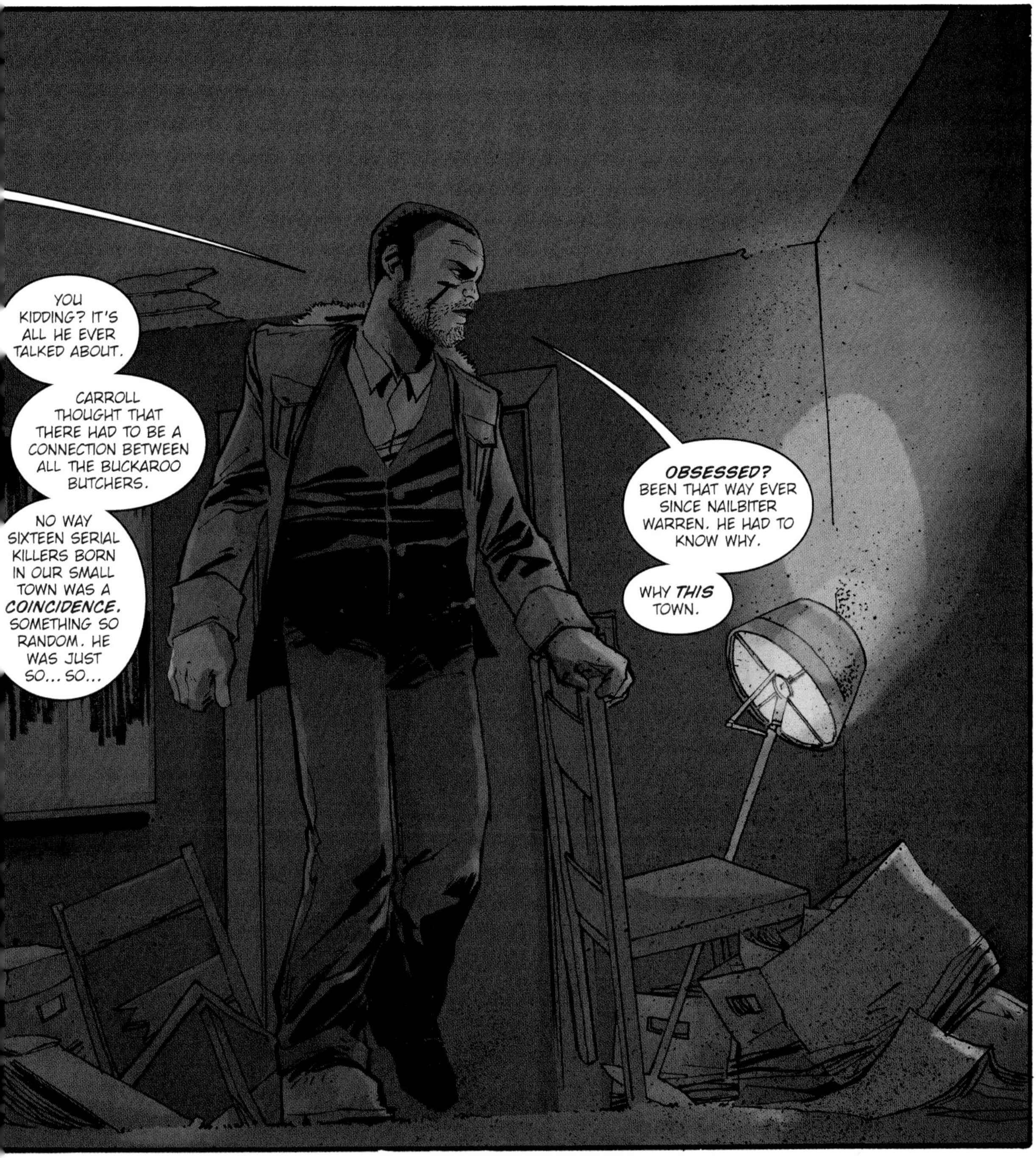
YOU KIDDING? IT'S ALL HE EVER TALKED ABOUT.
CARROLL THOUGHT THAT THERE HAD TO BE A CONNECTION BETWEEN ALL THE BUCKAROO BUTCHERS.
NO WAY SIXTEEN SERIAL KILLERS BORN IN OUR SMALL TOWN WAS A *COINCIDENCE.* SOMETHING SO RANDOM. HE WAS JUST SO... SO...
OBSESSED? BEEN THAT WAY EVER SINCE NAILBITER WARREN. HE HAD TO KNOW WHY.
WHY *THIS* TOWN.

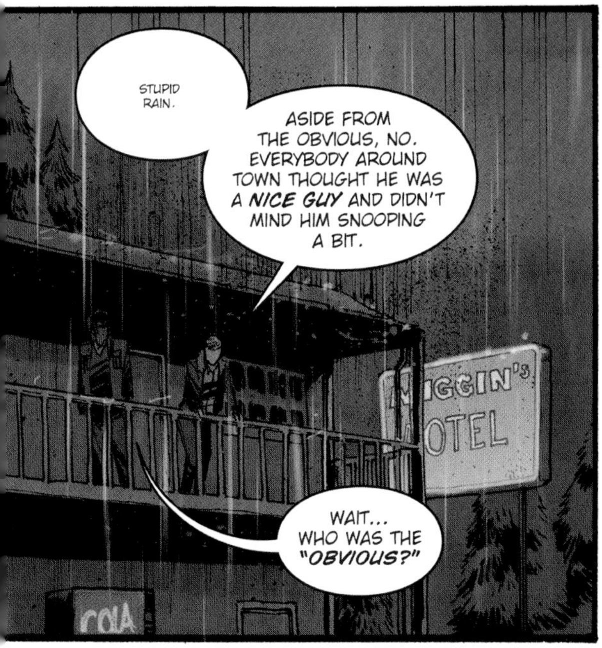
STUPID RAIN.
ASIDE FROM THE OBVIOUS, NO. EVERYBODY AROUND TOWN THOUGHT HE WAS A *NICE GUY* AND DIDN'T MIND HIM SNOOPING A BIT.
WAIT... WHO WAS THE *"OBVIOUS?"*

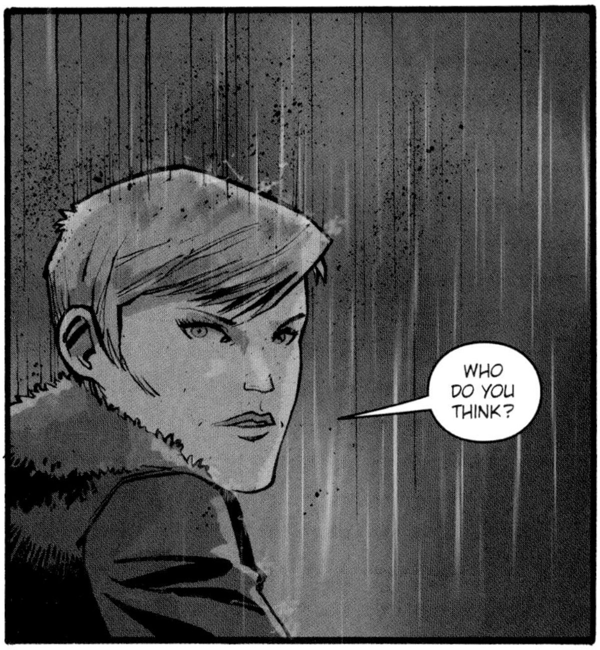
WHO DO YOU THINK?

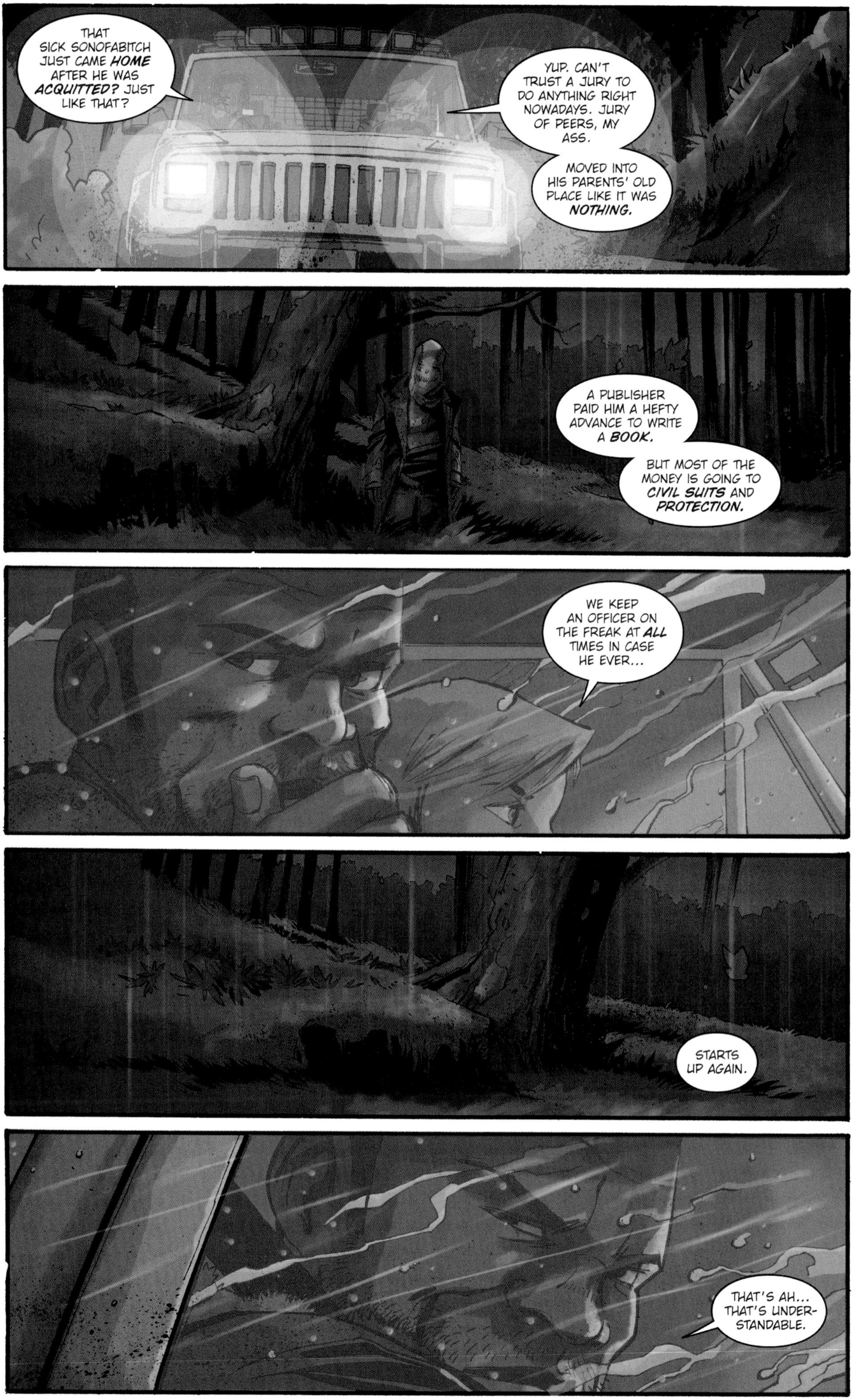
THAT SICK SONOFABITCH JUST CAME **HOME** AFTER HE WAS **ACQUITTED?** JUST LIKE THAT?
YUP. CAN'T TRUST A JURY TO DO ANYTHING RIGHT NOWADAYS. JURY OF PEERS, MY ASS.
MOVED INTO HIS PARENTS' OLD PLACE LIKE IT WAS **NOTHING.**
A PUBLISHER PAID HIM A HEFTY ADVANCE TO WRITE A **BOOK.**
BUT MOST OF THE MONEY IS GOING TO **CIVIL SUITS** AND **PROTECTION.**
WE KEEP AN OFFICER ON THE FREAK AT **ALL** TIMES IN CASE HE EVER...
STARTS UP AGAIN.
THAT'S AH... THAT'S UNDER-STANDABLE.

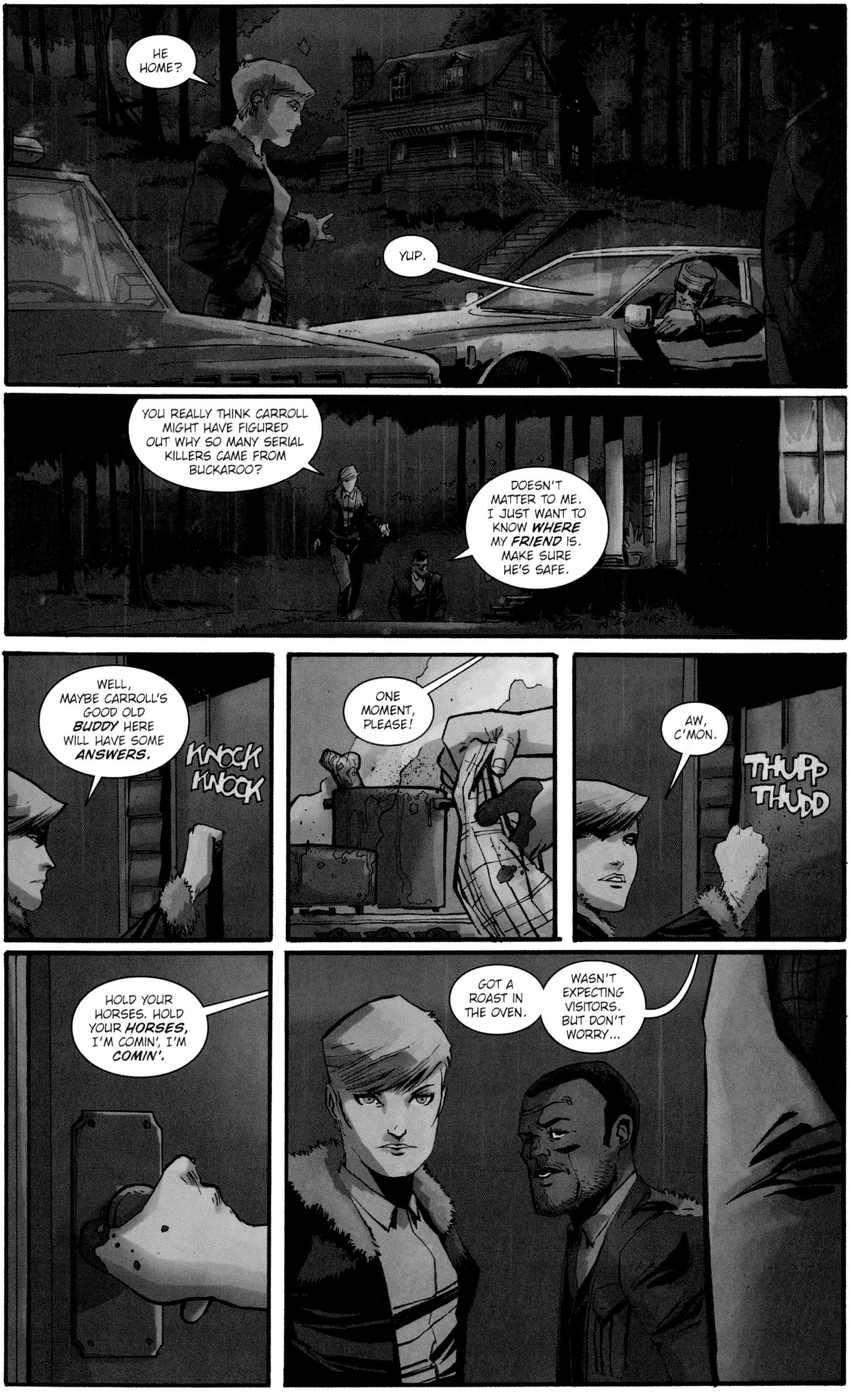
HE HOME?
YUP.
YOU REALLY THINK CARROLL MIGHT HAVE FIGURED OUT WHY SO MANY SERIAL KILLERS CAME FROM BUCKAROO?
DOESN'T MATTER TO ME. I JUST WANT TO KNOW WHERE MY FRIEND IS. MAKE SURE HE'S SAFE.
WELL, MAYBE CARROLL'S GOOD OLD BUDDY HERE WILL HAVE SOME ANSWERS.
KNOCK KNOCK
ONE MOMENT, PLEASE!
AW, C'MON.
THUPP THUDD
HOLD YOUR HORSES. HOLD YOUR HORSES, I'M COMIN', I'M COMIN'.
GOT A ROAST IN THE OVEN.
WASN'T EXPECTING VISITORS. BUT DON'T WORRY...

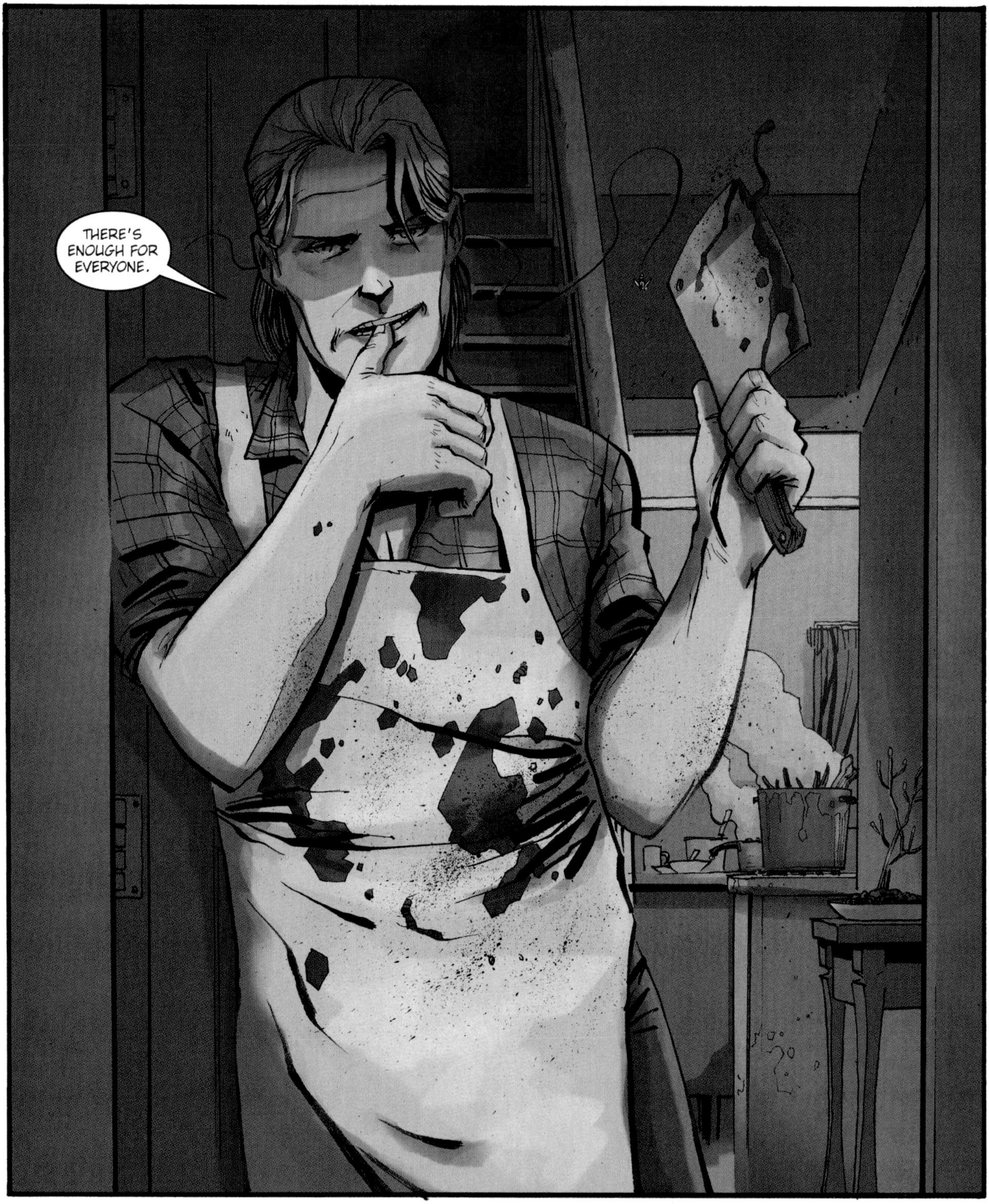
THERE'S ENOUGH FOR EVERYONE.

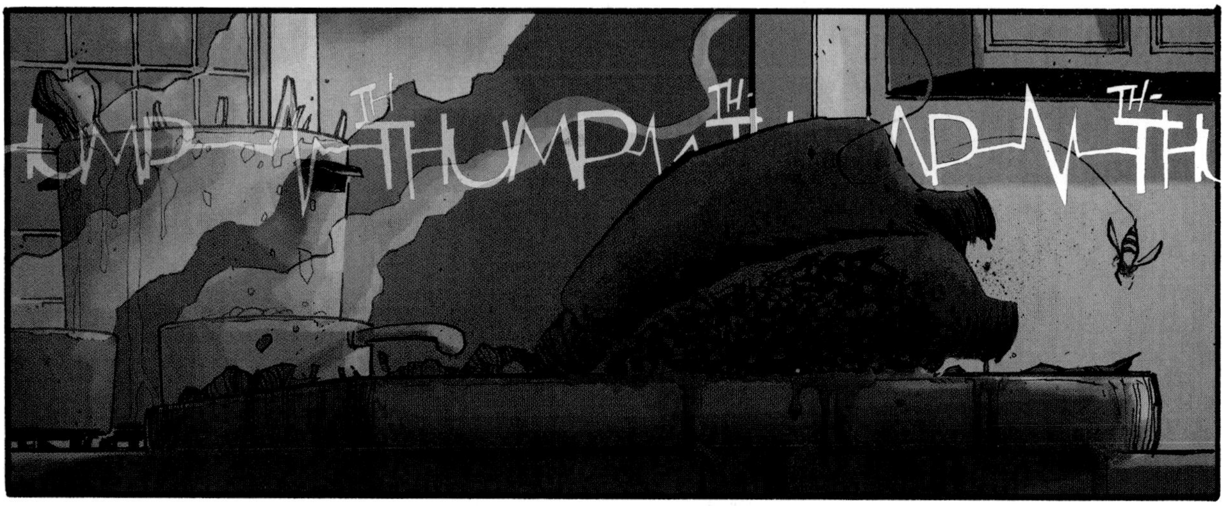
TH-
THUMP
TH-
TH-

TWO

"He was my prom date."

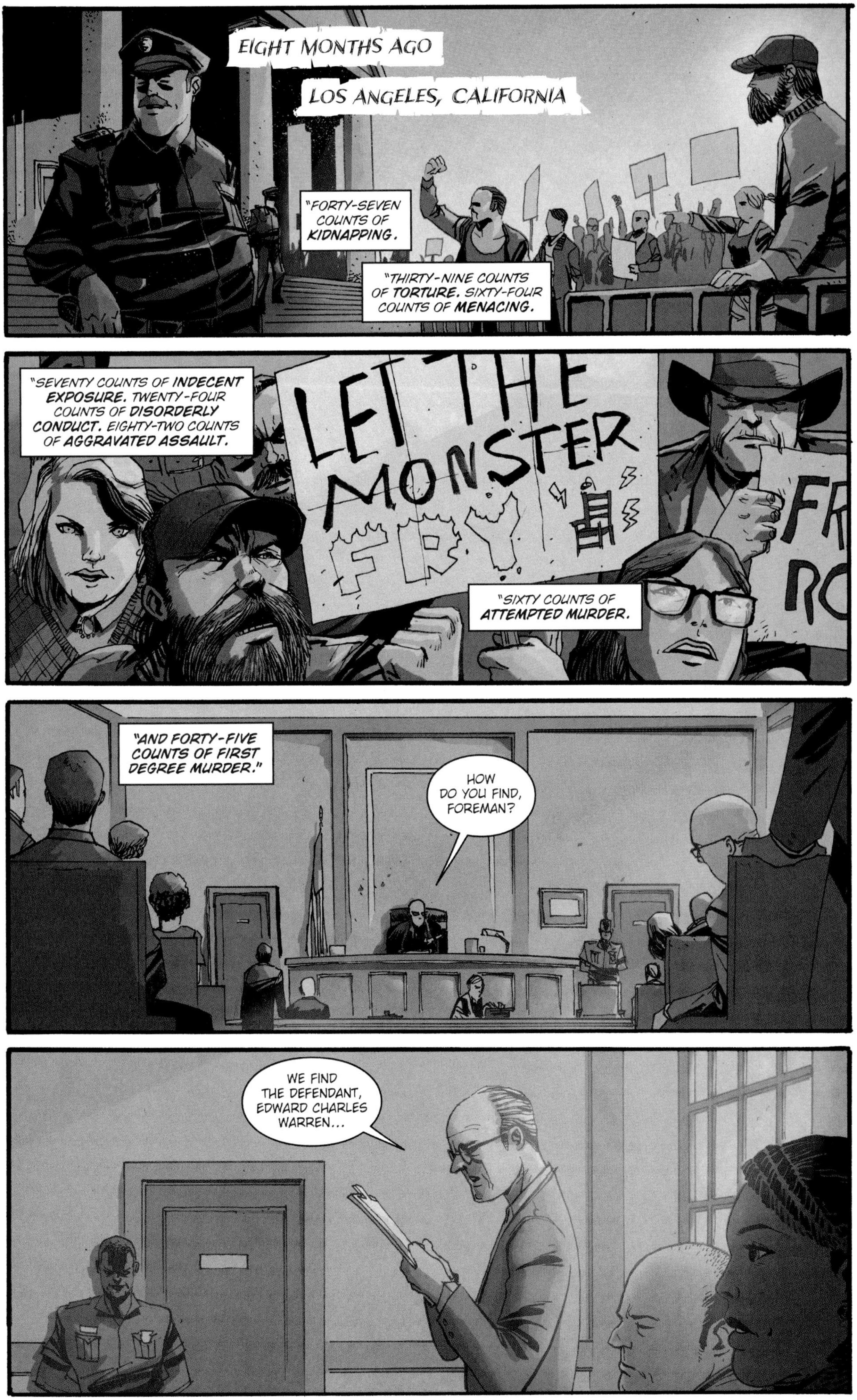

EIGHT MONTHS AGO
LOS ANGELES, CALIFORNIA
"FORTY-SEVEN COUNTS OF KIDNAPPING.
"THIRTY-NINE COUNTS OF TORTURE. SIXTY-FOUR COUNTS OF MENACING.
"SEVENTY COUNTS OF INDECENT EXPOSURE. TWENTY-FOUR COUNTS OF DISORDERLY CONDUCT. EIGHTY-TWO COUNTS OF AGGRAVATED ASSAULT.
LET THE MONSTER FRY
"SIXTY COUNTS OF ATTEMPTED MURDER.
"AND FORTY-FIVE COUNTS OF FIRST DEGREE MURDER."
HOW DO YOU FIND, FOREMAN?
WE FIND THE DEFENDANT, EDWARD CHARLES WARREN...

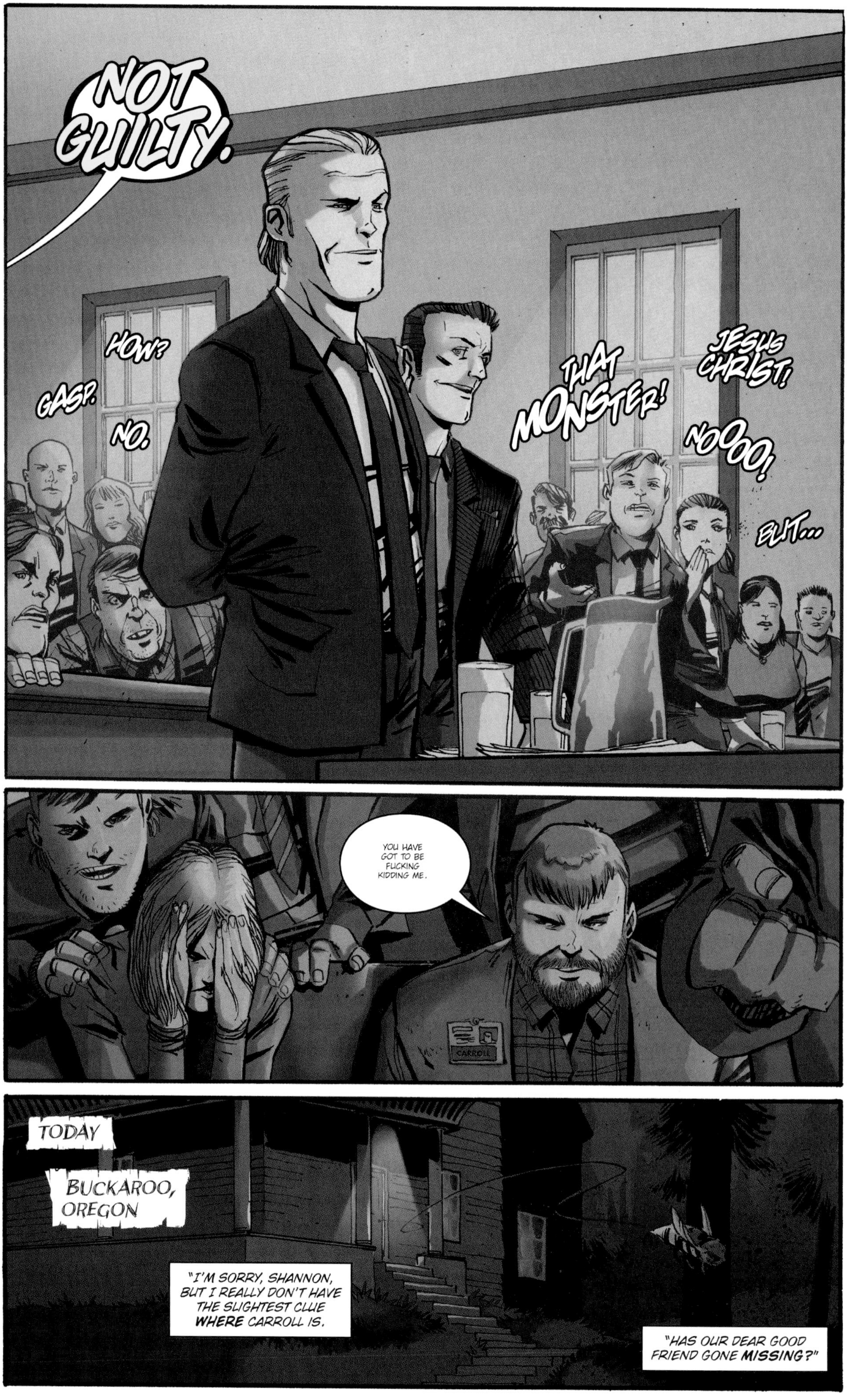
NOT GUILTY.
HOW?
GASP.
NO.
THAT MONSTER!
JESUS CHRIST!
NOOOO!
BUT...
YOU HAVE GOT TO BE FUCKING KIDDING ME.
CARROLL
TODAY
BUCKAROO, OREGON
"I'M SORRY, SHANNON, BUT I REALLY DON'T HAVE THE SLIGHTEST CLUE WHERE CARROLL IS.
"HAS OUR DEAR GOOD FRIEND GONE MISSING?"

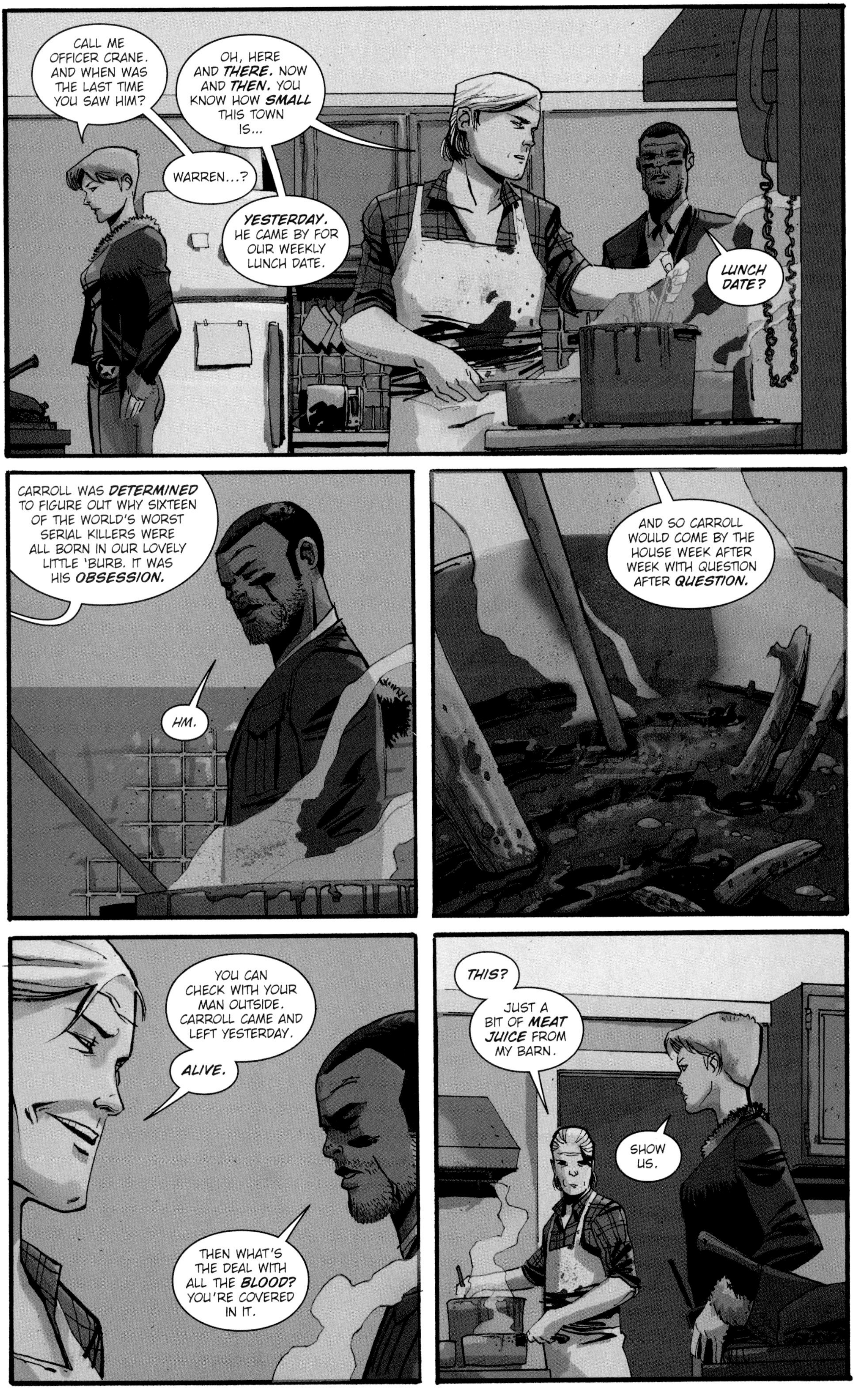
CALL ME OFFICER CRANE. AND WHEN WAS THE LAST TIME YOU SAW HIM?
WARREN...?
OH, HERE AND THERE. NOW AND THEN. YOU KNOW HOW SMALL THIS TOWN IS...
YESTERDAY. HE CAME BY FOR OUR WEEKLY LUNCH DATE.
LUNCH DATE?
CARROLL WAS DETERMINED TO FIGURE OUT WHY SIXTEEN OF THE WORLD'S WORST SERIAL KILLERS WERE ALL BORN IN OUR LOVELY LITTLE 'BURB. IT WAS HIS OBSESSION.
HM.
AND SO CARROLL WOULD COME BY THE HOUSE WEEK AFTER WEEK WITH QUESTION AFTER QUESTION.
YOU CAN CHECK WITH YOUR MAN OUTSIDE. CARROLL CAME AND LEFT YESTERDAY.
ALIVE.
THEN WHAT'S THE DEAL WITH ALL THE BLOOD? YOU'RE COVERED IN IT.
THIS?
JUST A BIT OF MEAT JUICE FROM MY BARN.
SHOW US.

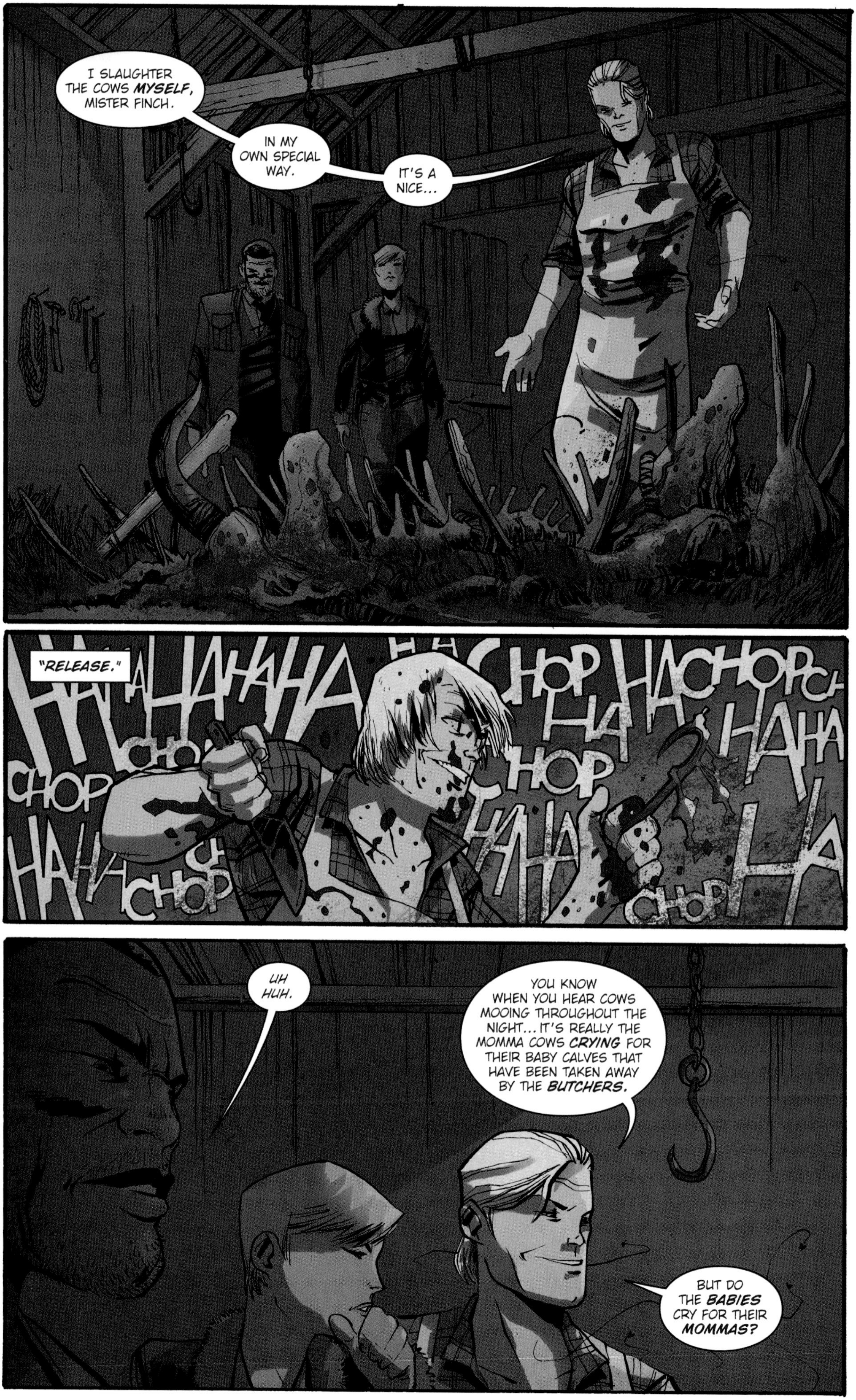
I SLAUGHTER THE COWS MYSELF, MISTER FINCH.
IN MY OWN SPECIAL WAY.
IT'S A NICE...
"RELEASE."
HAHAHAHA
HA
CHOP
HACHOP
CHOP
HA
HAHA
CHOP
CHOP
HAHA
HAHACHOP
HA
CHOP
HA
UH HUH.
YOU KNOW WHEN YOU HEAR COWS MOOING THROUGHOUT THE NIGHT... IT'S REALLY THE MOMMA COWS CRYING FOR THEIR BABY CALVES THAT HAVE BEEN TAKEN AWAY BY THE BUTCHERS.
BUT DO THE BABIES CRY FOR THEIR MOMMAS?

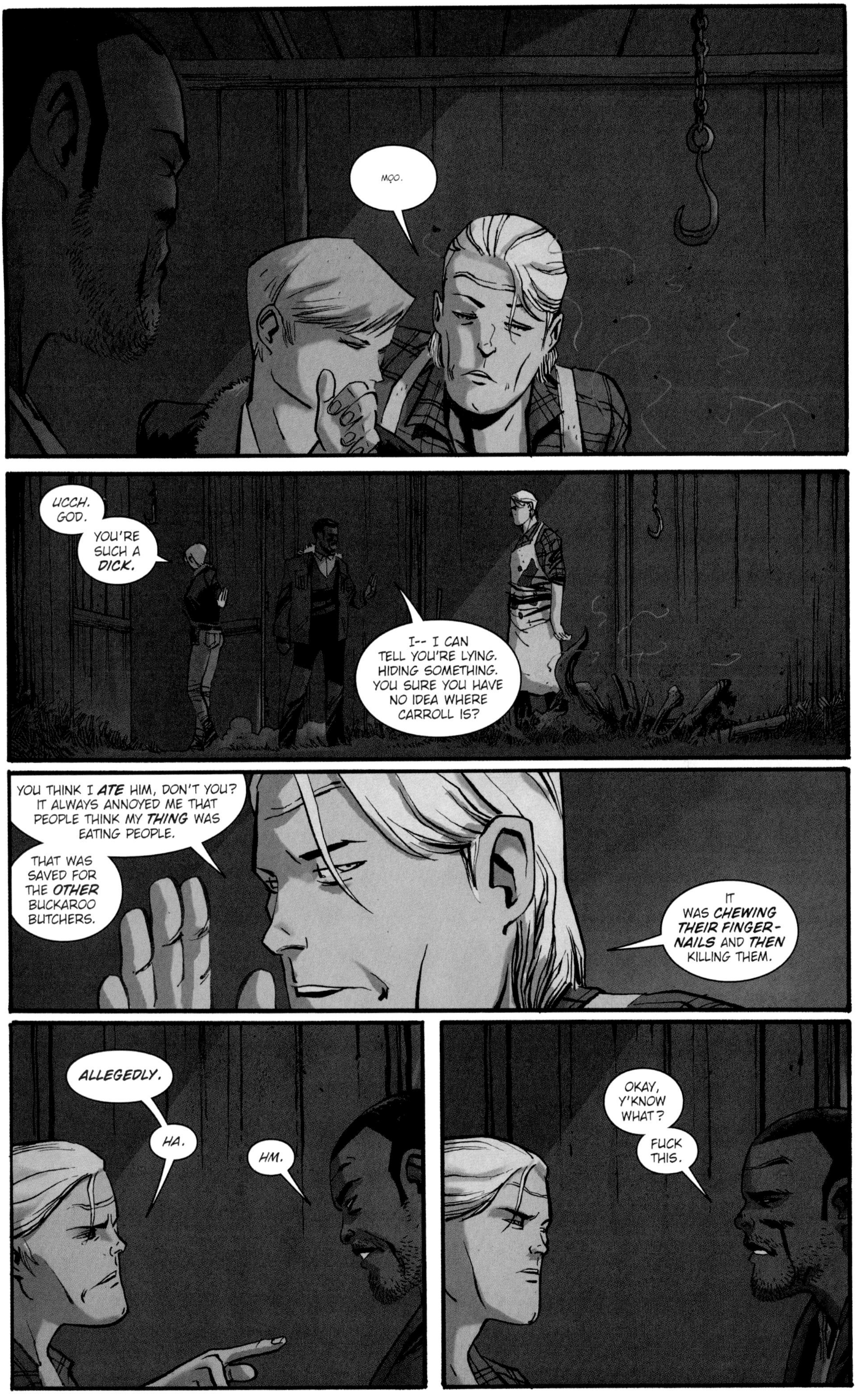
MOO.
UCCH. GOD.
YOU'RE SUCH A DICK.
I-- I CAN TELL YOU'RE LYING. HIDING SOMETHING. YOU SURE YOU HAVE NO IDEA WHERE CARROLL IS?
YOU THINK I ATE HIM, DON'T YOU? IT ALWAYS ANNOYED ME THAT PEOPLE THINK MY THING WAS EATING PEOPLE.
THAT WAS SAVED FOR THE OTHER BUCKAROO BUTCHERS.
IT WAS CHEWING THEIR FINGER-NAILS AND THEN KILLING THEM.
ALLEGEDLY.
HA.
HM.
OKAY, Y'KNOW WHAT?
FUCK THIS.

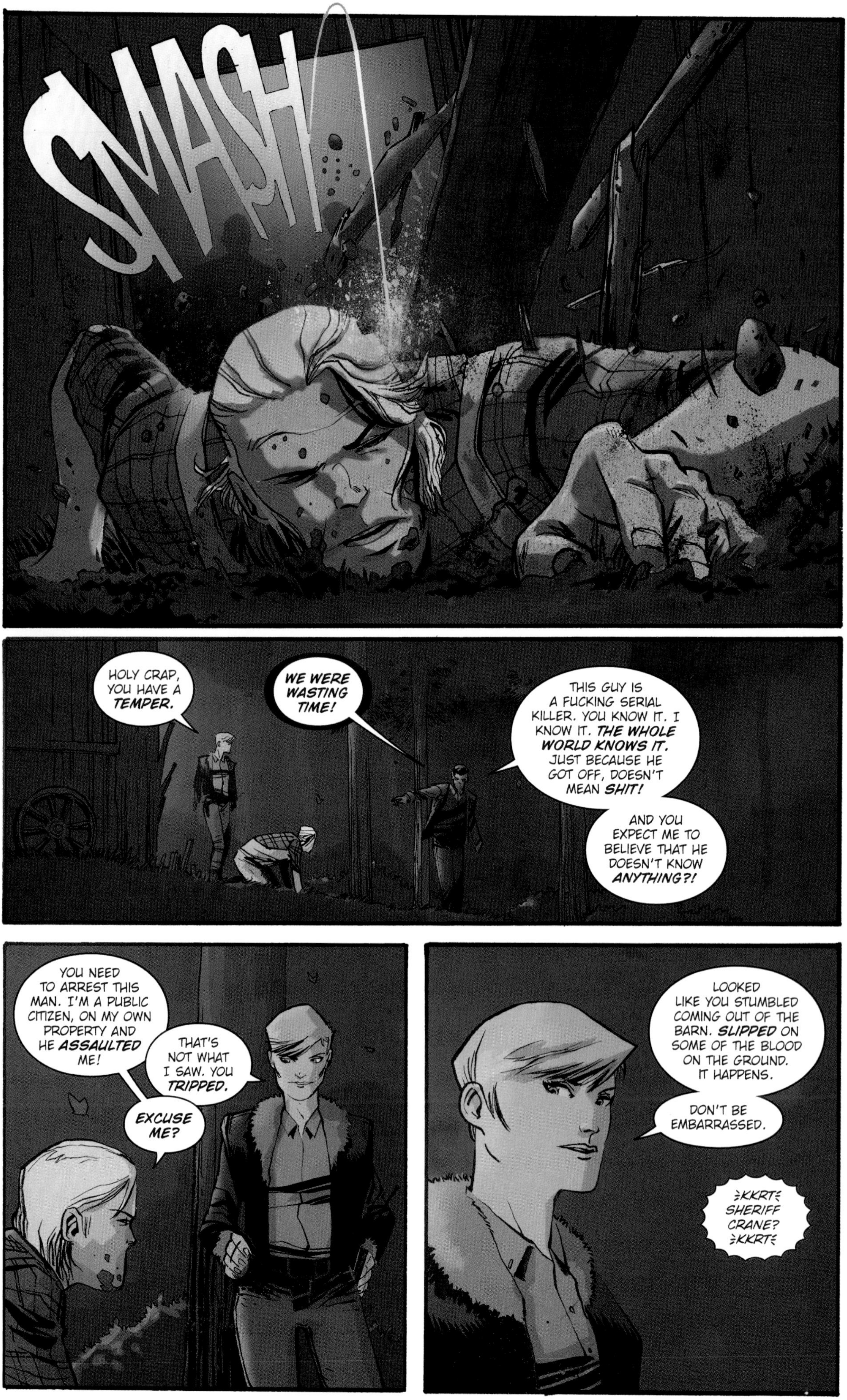
SMASH
HOLY CRAP, YOU HAVE A TEMPER.
WE WERE WASTING TIME!
THIS GUY IS A FUCKING SERIAL KILLER. YOU KNOW IT. I KNOW IT. THE WHOLE WORLD KNOWS IT. JUST BECAUSE HE GOT OFF, DOESN'T MEAN SHIT!
AND YOU EXPECT ME TO BELIEVE THAT HE DOESN'T KNOW ANYTHING?!
YOU NEED TO ARREST THIS MAN. I'M A PUBLIC CITIZEN, ON MY OWN PROPERTY AND HE ASSAULTED ME!
THAT'S NOT WHAT I SAW. YOU TRIPPED.
EXCUSE ME?
LOOKED LIKE YOU STUMBLED COMING OUT OF THE BARN. SLIPPED ON SOME OF THE BLOOD ON THE GROUND. IT HAPPENS.
DON'T BE EMBARRASSED.
KKRT SHERIFF CRANE? KKRT

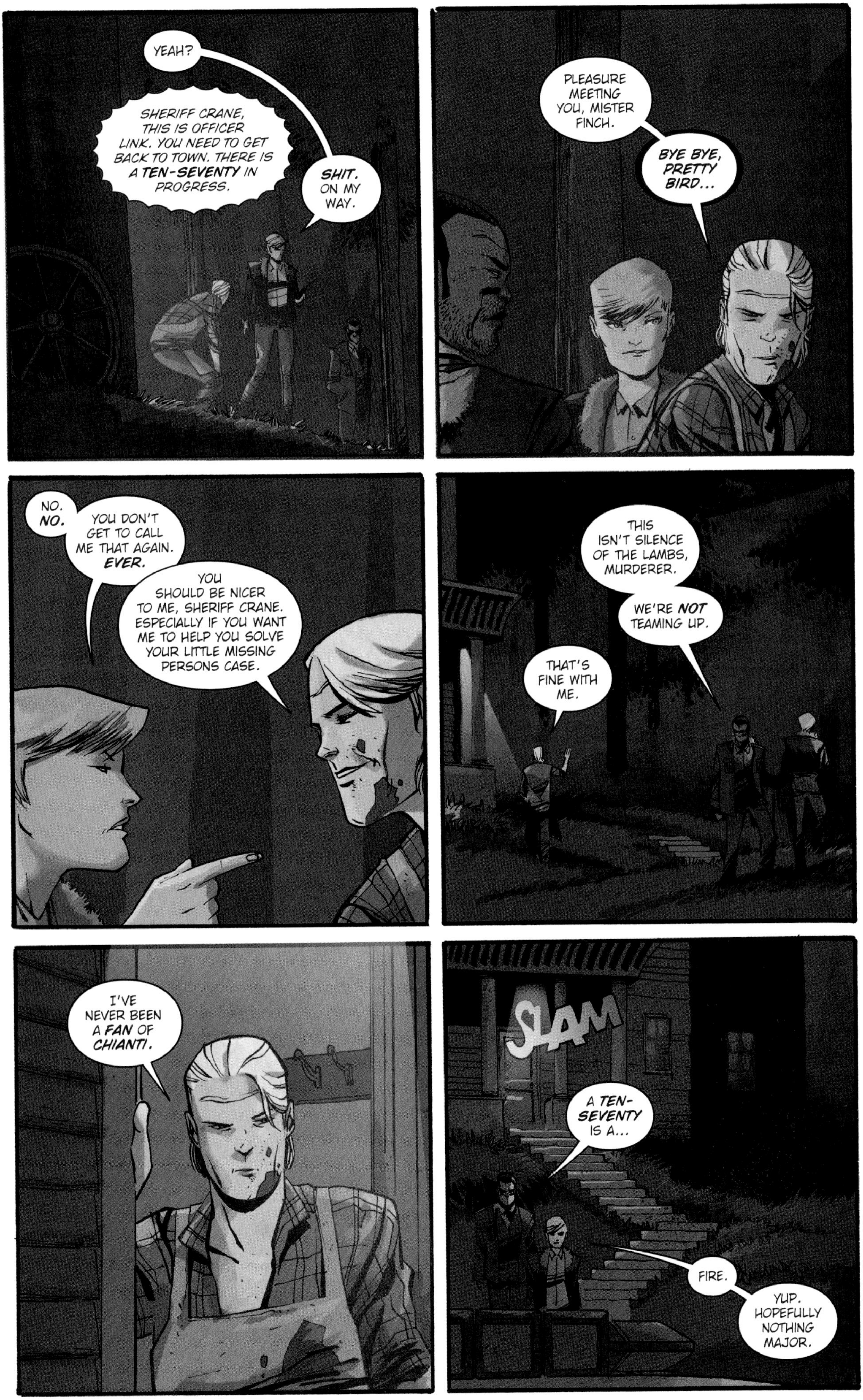
YEAH?
SHERIFF CRANE, THIS IS OFFICER LINK. YOU NEED TO GET BACK TO TOWN. THERE IS A TEN-SEVENTY IN PROGRESS.
SHIT. ON MY WAY.
PLEASURE MEETING YOU, MISTER FINCH.
BYE BYE, PRETTY BIRD...
NO. NO.
YOU DON'T GET TO CALL ME THAT AGAIN. EVER.
YOU SHOULD BE NICER TO ME, SHERIFF CRANE. ESPECIALLY IF YOU WANT ME TO HELP YOU SOLVE YOUR LITTLE MISSING PERSONS CASE.
THIS ISN'T SILENCE OF THE LAMBS, MURDERER.
WE'RE NOT TEAMING UP.
THAT'S FINE WITH ME.
I'VE NEVER BEEN A FAN OF CHIANTI.
SLAM
A TEN-SEVENTY IS A...
FIRE.
YUP. HOPEFULLY NOTHING MAJOR.

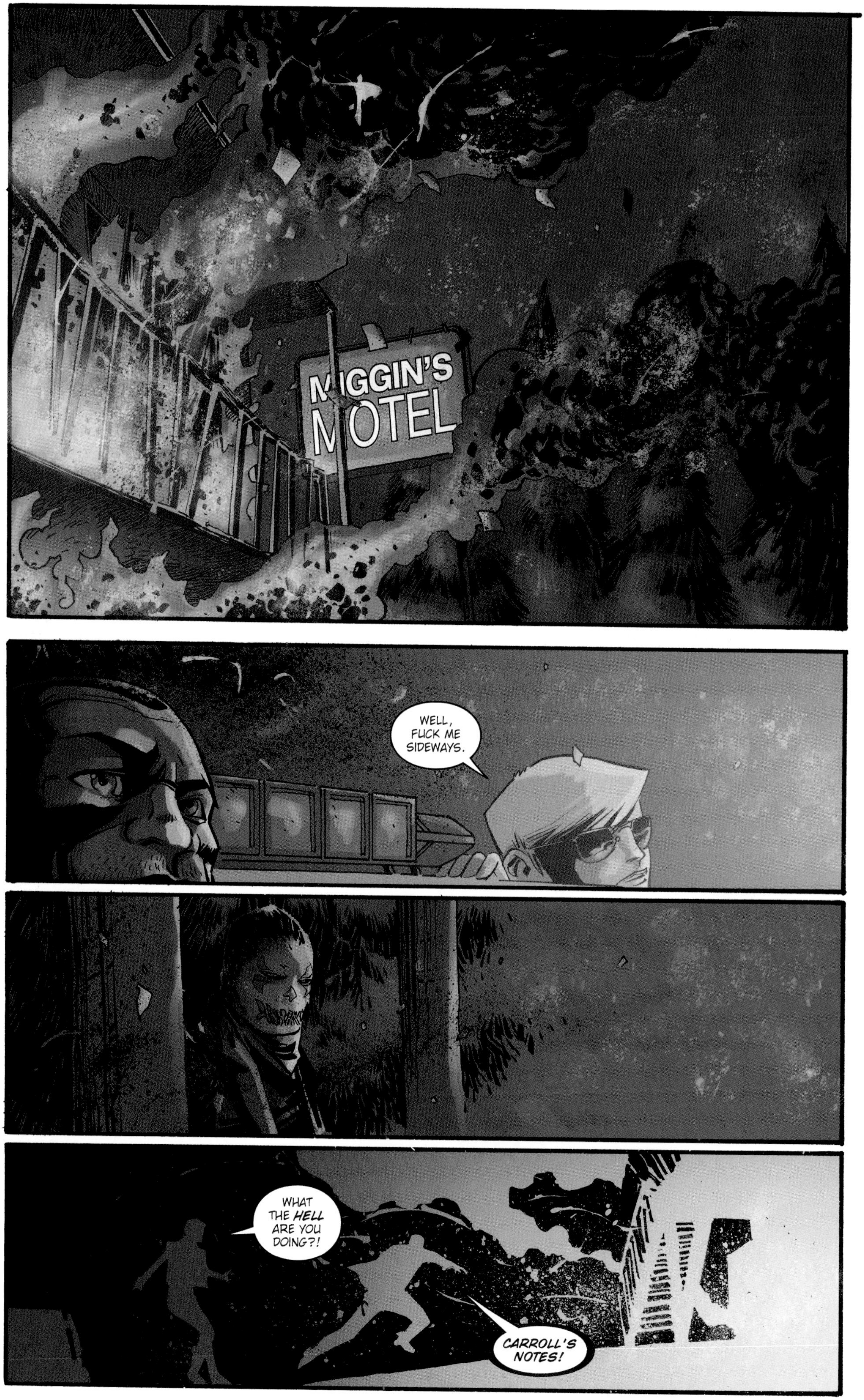
MIGGIN'S MOTEL
WELL, FUCK ME SIDEWAYS.
WHAT THE HELL ARE YOU DOING?!
CARROLL'S NOTES!

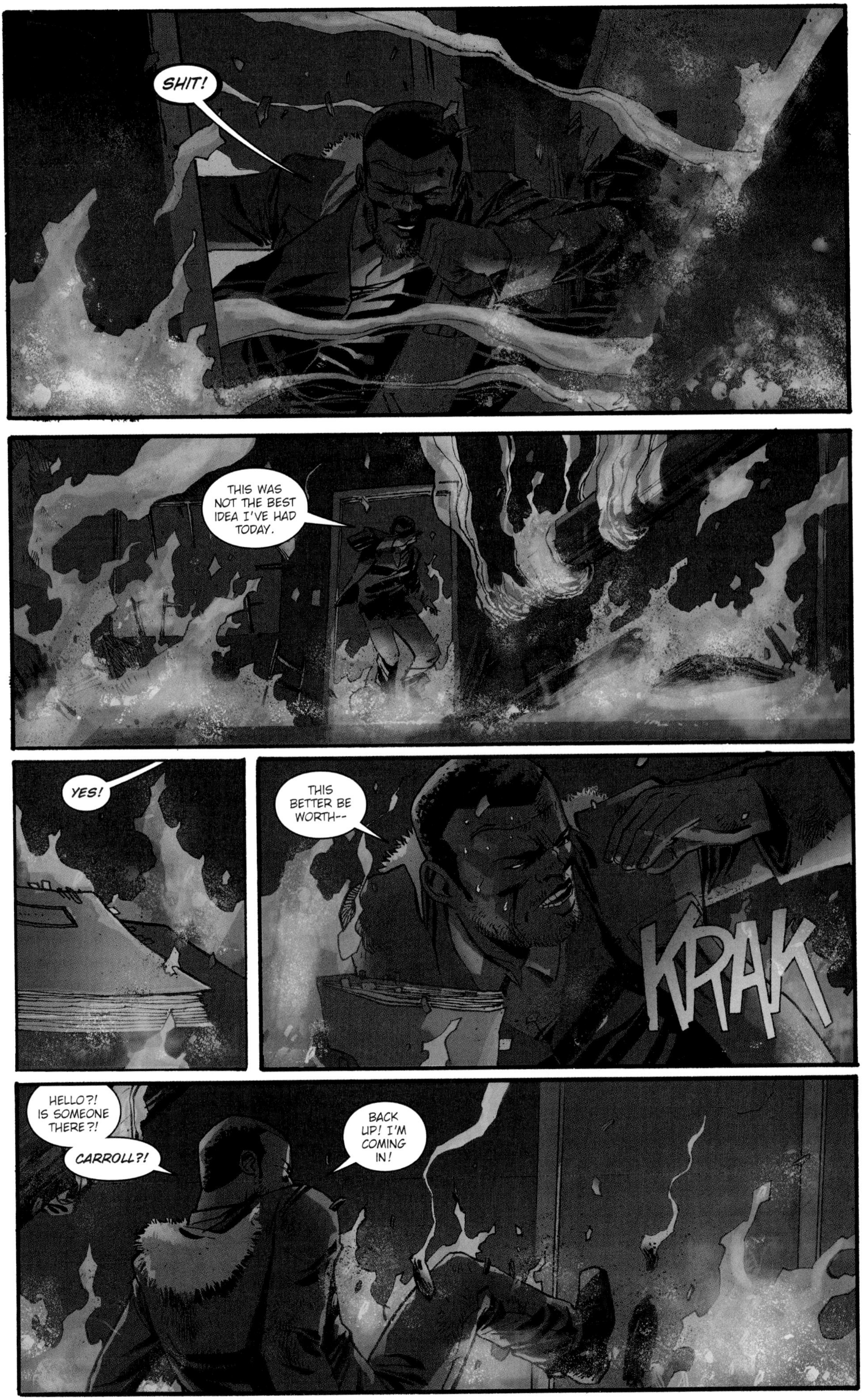
SHIT!
THIS WAS NOT THE BEST IDEA I'VE HAD TODAY.
YES!
THIS BETTER BE WORTH--
KRAK
HELLO?! IS SOMEONE THERE?!
CARROLL?!
BACK UP! I'M COMING IN!

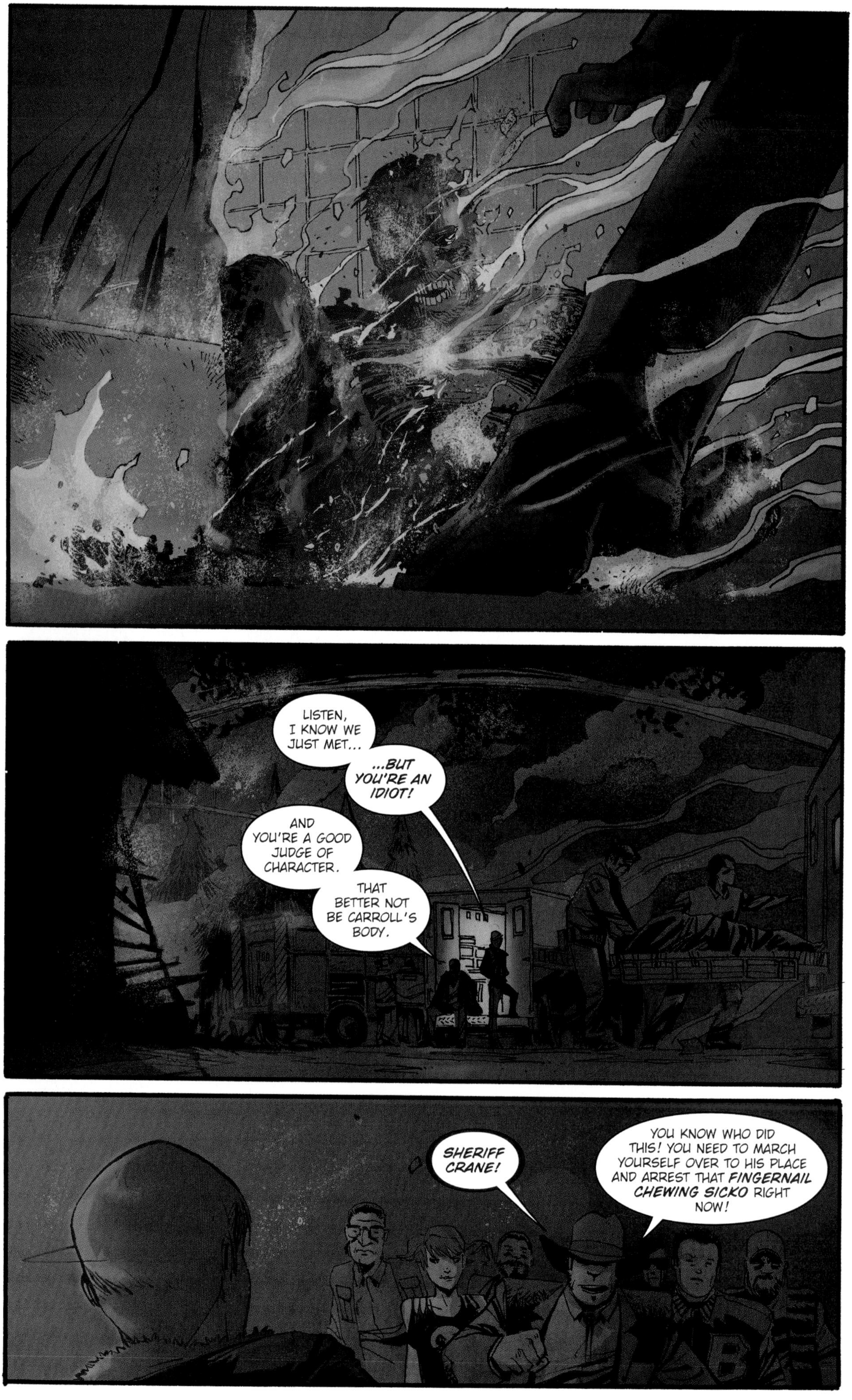
LISTEN, I KNOW WE JUST MET...
...BUT YOU'RE AN IDIOT!
AND YOU'RE A GOOD JUDGE OF CHARACTER.
THAT BETTER NOT BE CARROLL'S BODY.
SHERIFF CRANE!
YOU KNOW WHO DID THIS! YOU NEED TO MARCH YOURSELF OVER TO HIS PLACE AND ARREST THAT *FINGERNAIL CHEWING SICKO* RIGHT NOW!

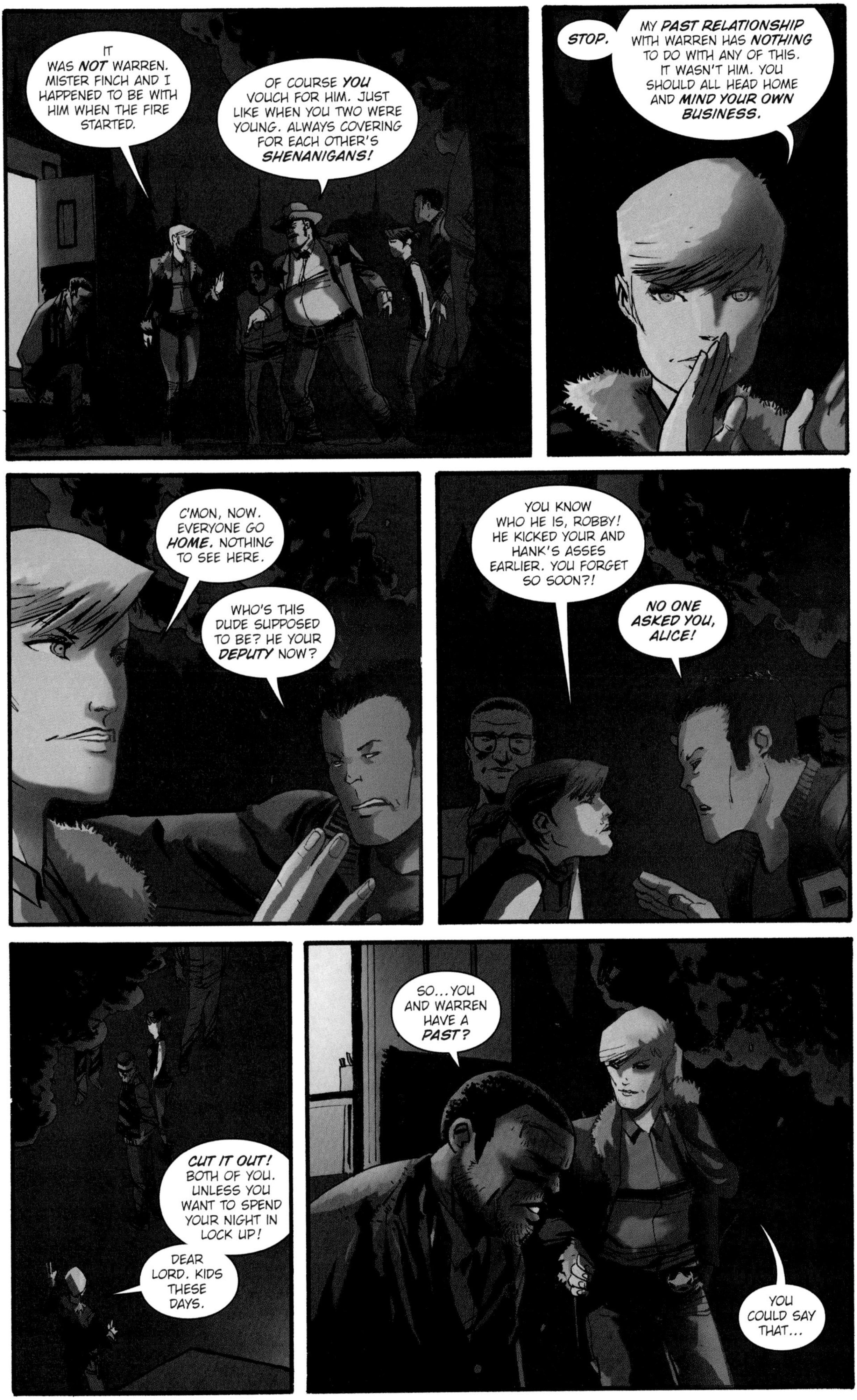
IT WAS **NOT** WARREN. MISTER FINCH AND I HAPPENED TO BE WITH HIM WHEN THE FIRE STARTED.
OF COURSE **YOU** VOUCH FOR HIM. JUST LIKE WHEN YOU TWO WERE YOUNG. ALWAYS COVERING FOR EACH OTHER'S **SHENANIGANS!**
STOP.
MY **PAST RELATIONSHIP** WITH WARREN HAS **NOTHING** TO DO WITH ANY OF THIS. IT WASN'T HIM. YOU SHOULD ALL HEAD HOME AND **MIND YOUR OWN BUSINESS.**
C'MON, NOW. EVERYONE GO **HOME.** NOTHING TO SEE HERE.
WHO'S THIS DUDE SUPPOSED TO BE? HE YOUR **DEPUTY** NOW?
YOU KNOW WHO HE IS, ROBBY! HE KICKED YOUR AND HANK'S ASSES EARLIER. YOU FORGET SO SOON?!
NO ONE ASKED YOU, ALICE!
CUT IT OUT! BOTH OF YOU. UNLESS YOU WANT TO SPEND YOUR NIGHT IN LOCK UP!
DEAR LORD. KIDS THESE DAYS.
SO...YOU AND WARREN HAVE A **PAST?**
YOU COULD SAY THAT...

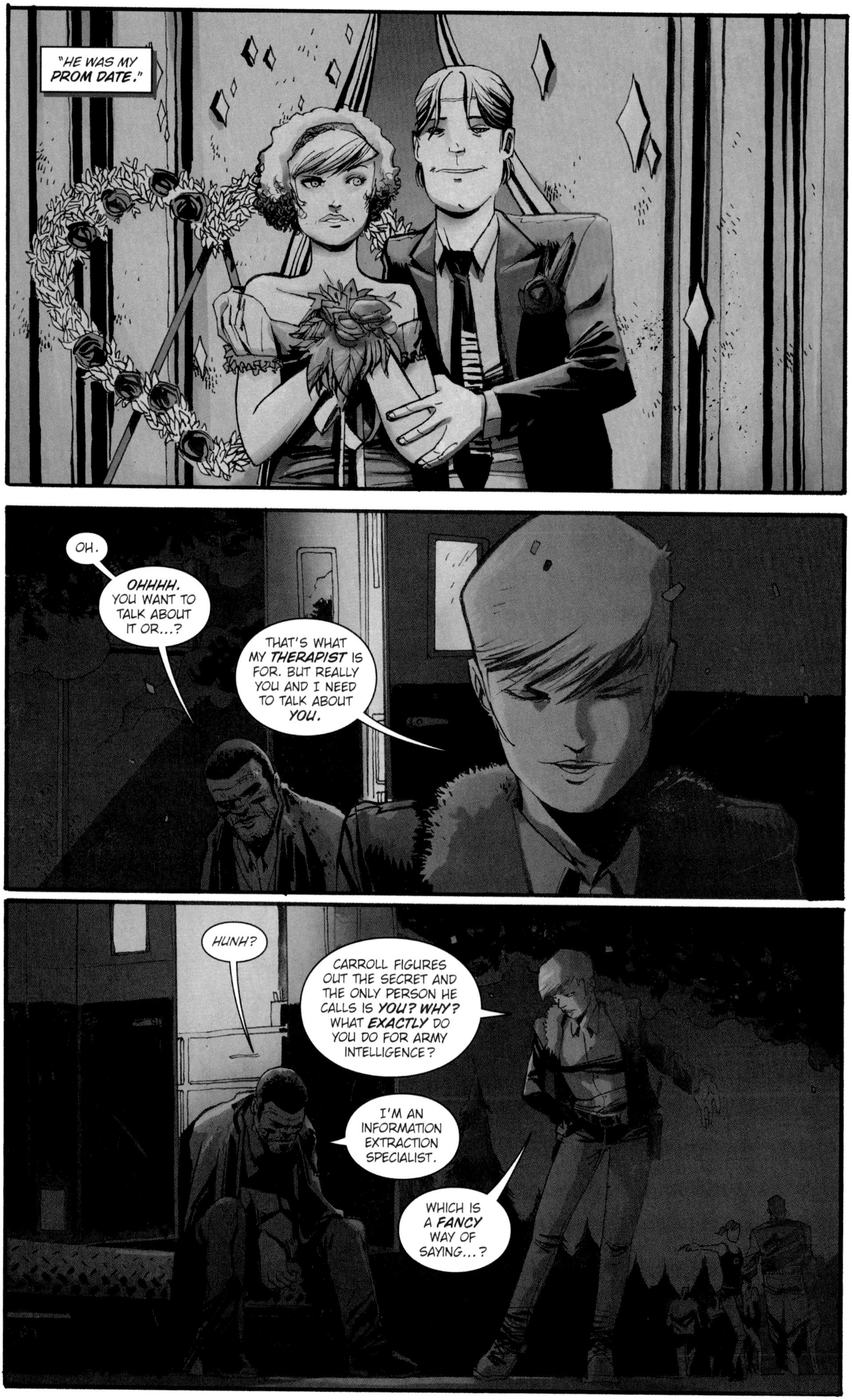
"HE WAS MY PROM DATE."
OH.
OHHHH. YOU WANT TO TALK ABOUT IT OR...?
THAT'S WHAT MY THERAPIST IS FOR. BUT REALLY YOU AND I NEED TO TALK ABOUT YOU.
HUNH?
CARROLL FIGURES OUT THE SECRET AND THE ONLY PERSON HE CALLS IS YOU? WHY? WHAT EXACTLY DO YOU DO FOR ARMY INTELLIGENCE?
I'M AN INFORMATION EXTRACTION SPECIALIST.
WHICH IS A FANCY WAY OF SAYING...?

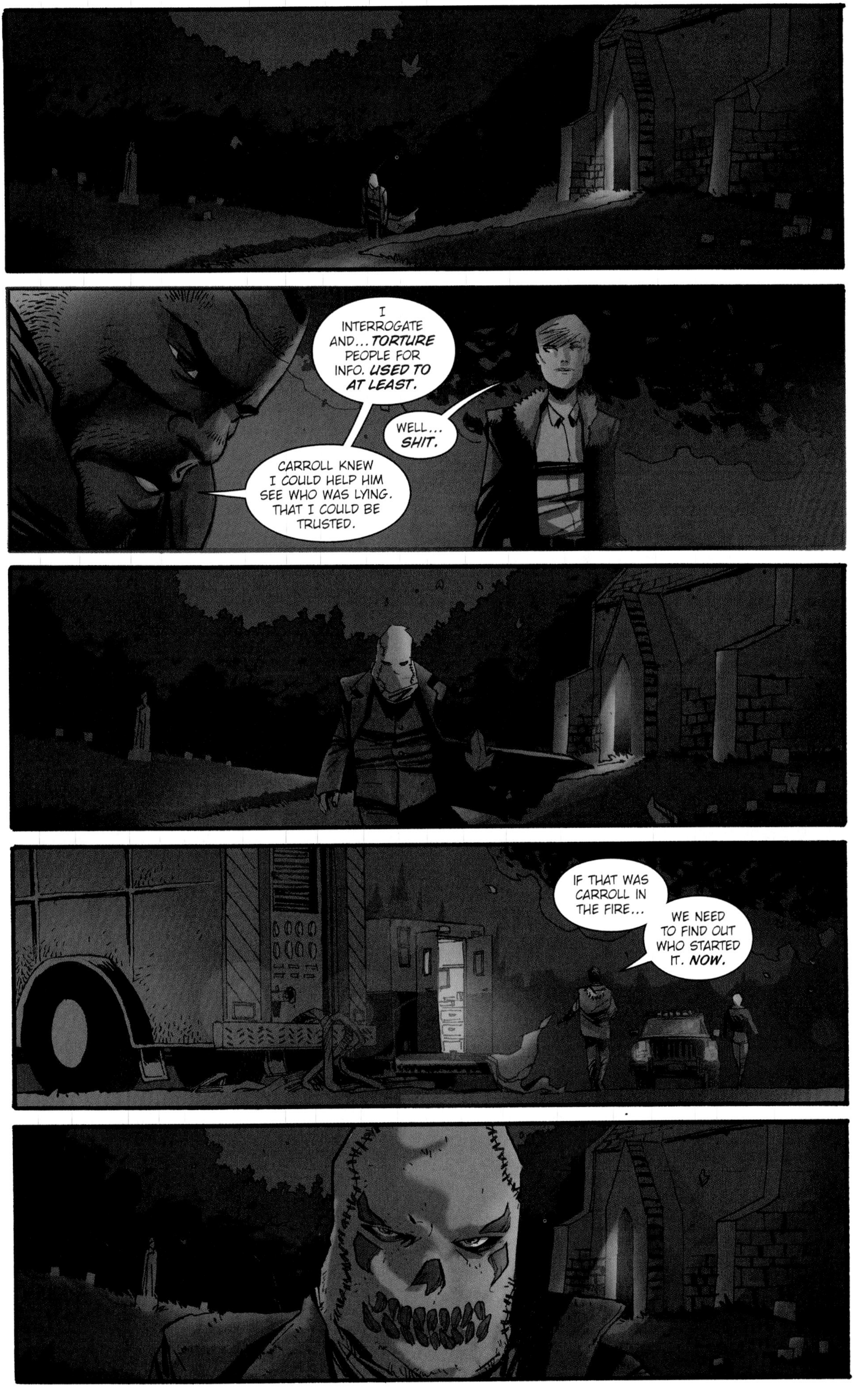
I INTERROGATE AND... **TORTURE** PEOPLE FOR INFO. ***USED TO AT LEAST.***
CARROLL KNEW I COULD HELP HIM SEE WHO WAS LYING. THAT I COULD BE TRUSTED.
WELL... ***SHIT.***
IF THAT WAS CARROLL IN THE FIRE...
WE NEED TO FIND OUT WHO STARTED IT. ***NOW.***

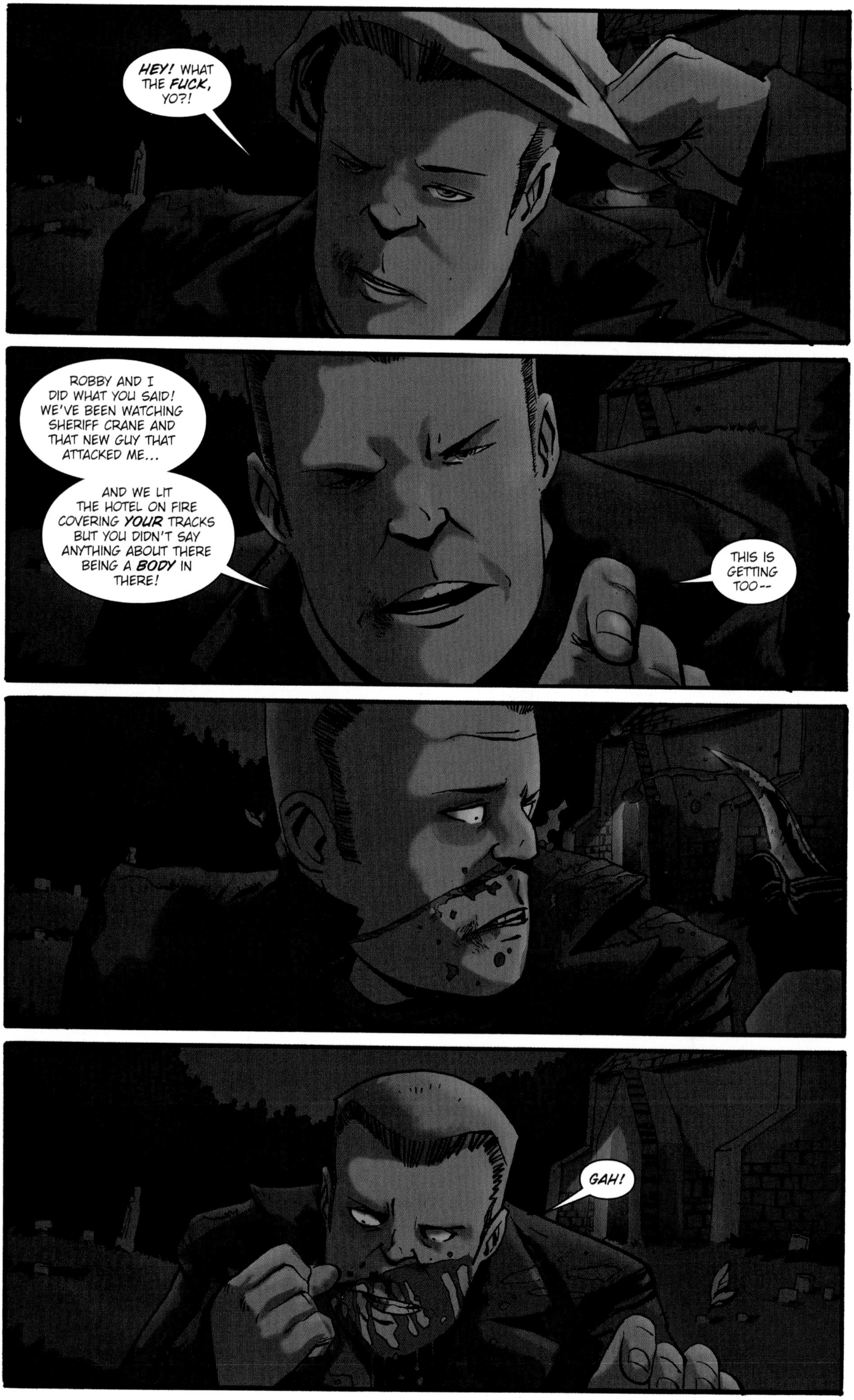

HEY! WHAT THE FUCK, YO?!
ROBBY AND I DID WHAT YOU SAID! WE'VE BEEN WATCHING SHERIFF CRANE AND THAT NEW GUY THAT ATTACKED ME...
AND WE LIT THE HOTEL ON FIRE COVERING YOUR TRACKS BUT YOU DIDN'T SAY ANYTHING ABOUT THERE BEING A BODY IN THERE!
THIS IS GETTING TOO--
GAH!

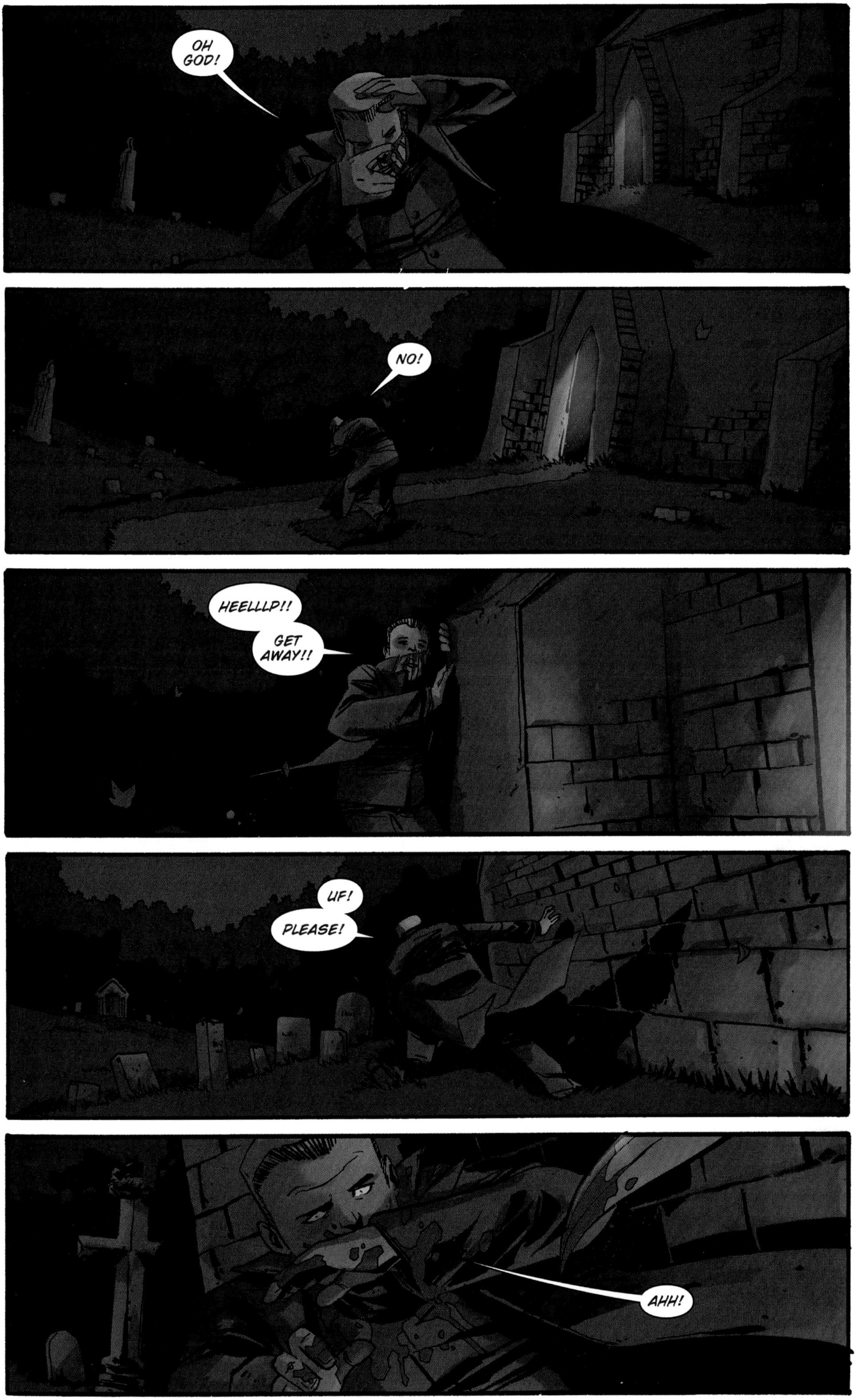
OH GOD!
NO!
HEELLLP!!
GET AWAY!!
UF!
PLEASE!
AHH!

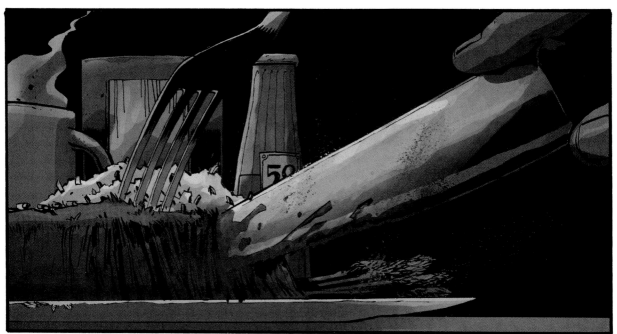

MHHH HMMM.

BEEN A LONG TIME SINCE I'VE HAD A STEAK.

BUT KNOWING *THIS* TOWN, THIS IS PROBABLY SOME POOR SOUL ONE OF YOU PSYCHOS *COOKED UP.*

DON'T EVEN *JOKE* ABOUT THAT.

FOLKS AROUND HERE *HATE* WHEN OUT-OF-TOWNERS EVEN *HINT* THAT THEY MIGHT BE ONE OF THE BUTCHERS.

WHAT'RE YOU GOING TO DO IF THAT BODY ISN'T CARROLL'S? WHAT THEN?

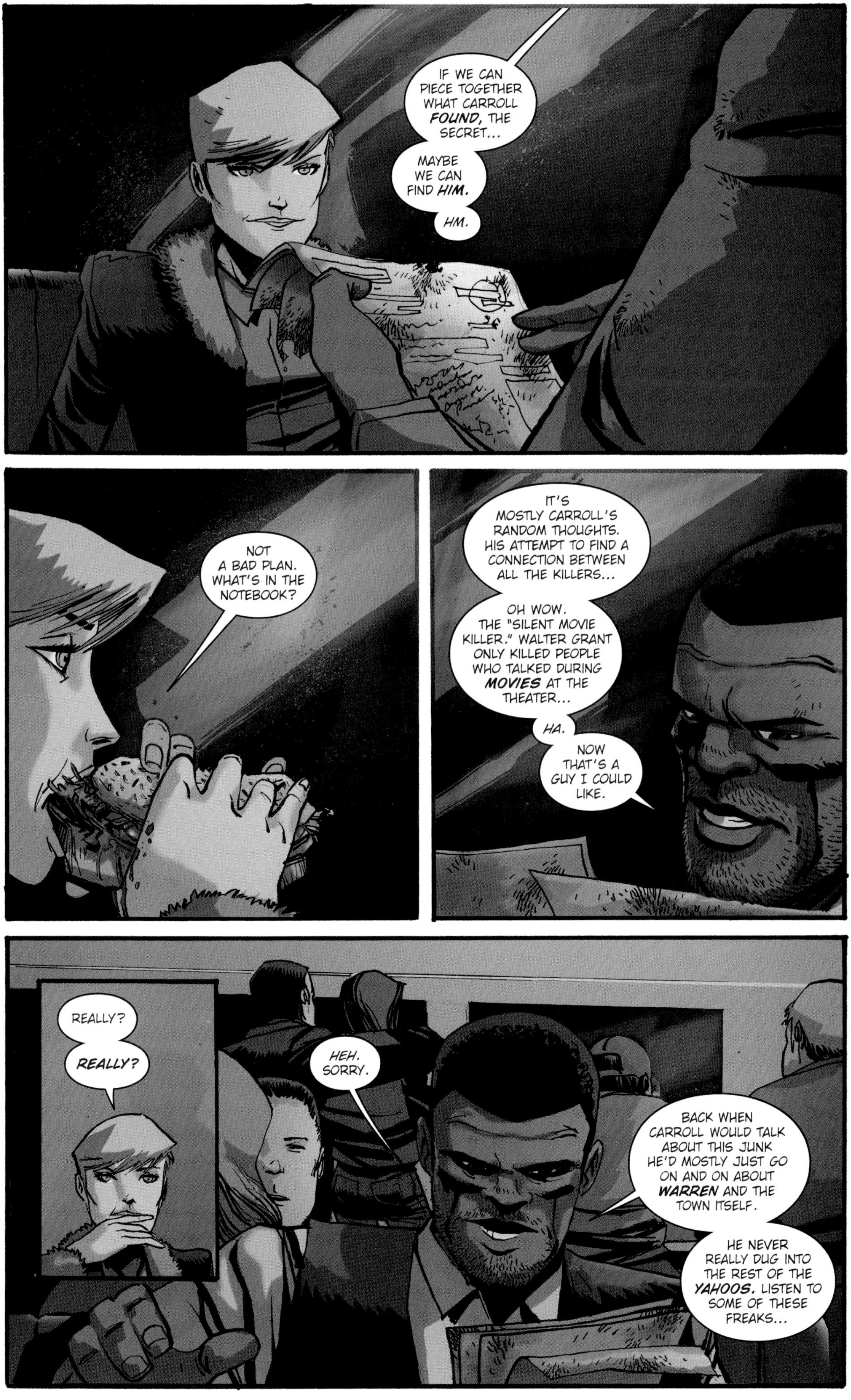

IF WE CAN PIECE TOGETHER WHAT CARROLL *FOUND*, THE SECRET...
MAYBE WE CAN FIND *HIM.*
HM.
NOT A BAD PLAN. WHAT'S IN THE NOTEBOOK?
IT'S MOSTLY CARROLL'S RANDOM THOUGHTS. HIS ATTEMPT TO FIND A CONNECTION BETWEEN ALL THE KILLERS...
OH WOW. THE "SILENT MOVIE KILLER." WALTER GRANT ONLY KILLED PEOPLE WHO TALKED DURING *MOVIES* AT THE THEATER...
HA.
NOW THAT'S A GUY I COULD LIKE.
REALLY?
REALLY?
HEH. SORRY.
BACK WHEN CARROLL WOULD TALK ABOUT THIS JUNK HE'D MOSTLY JUST GO ON AND ON ABOUT *WARREN* AND THE TOWN ITSELF.
HE NEVER REALLY DUG INTO THE REST OF THE *YAHOOS.* LISTEN TO SOME OF THESE FREAKS...

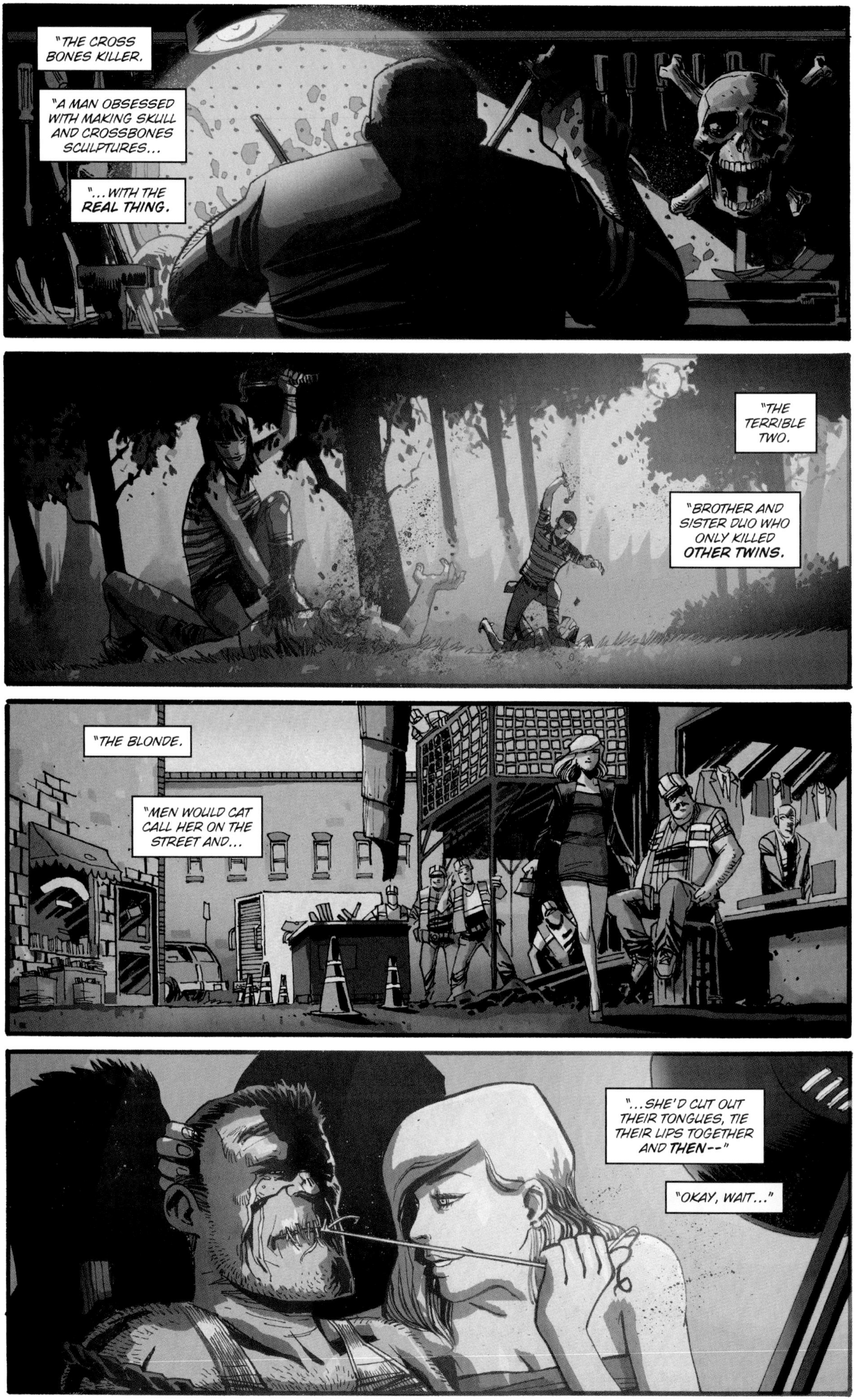
"THE CROSS BONES KILLER.
"A MAN OBSESSED WITH MAKING SKULL AND CROSSBONES SCULPTURES...
"...WITH THE REAL THING.
"THE TERRIBLE TWO.
"BROTHER AND SISTER DUO WHO ONLY KILLED OTHER TWINS.
"THE BLONDE.
"MEN WOULD CAT CALL HER ON THE STREET AND...
"...SHE'D CUT OUT THEIR TONGUES, TIE THEIR LIPS TOGETHER AND THEN--"
"OKAY, WAIT..."

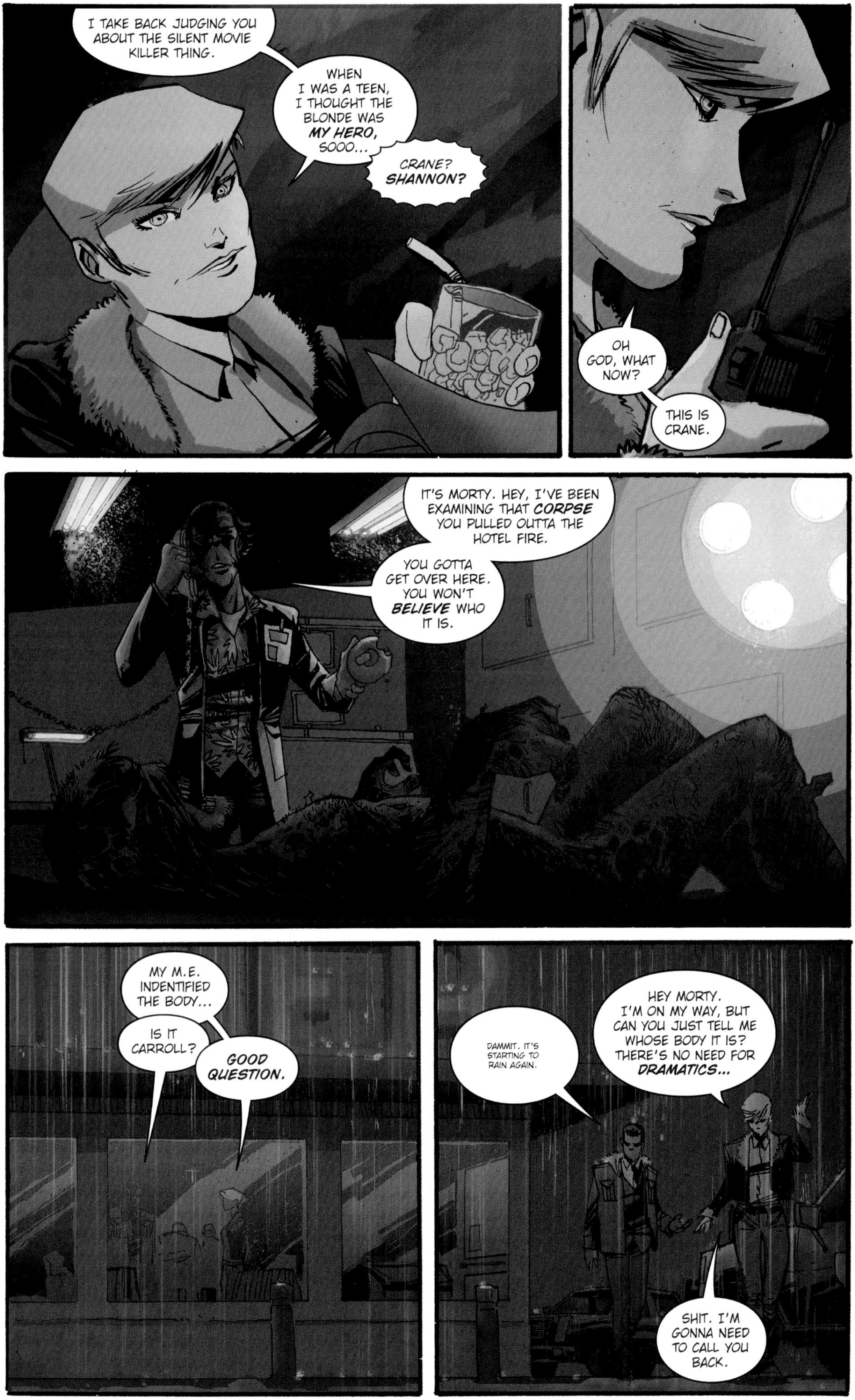
I TAKE BACK JUDGING YOU ABOUT THE SILENT MOVIE KILLER THING.
WHEN I WAS A TEEN, I THOUGHT THE BLONDE WAS MY HERO, SOOO...
CRANE? SHANNON?
OH GOD, WHAT NOW?
THIS IS CRANE.
IT'S MORTY. HEY, I'VE BEEN EXAMINING THAT CORPSE YOU PULLED OUTTA THE HOTEL FIRE.
YOU GOTTA GET OVER HERE. YOU WON'T BELIEVE WHO IT IS.
MY M.E. INDENTIFIED THE BODY...
IS IT CARROLL?
GOOD QUESTION.
DAMMIT. IT'S STARTING TO RAIN AGAIN.
HEY MORTY. I'M ON MY WAY, BUT CAN YOU JUST TELL ME WHOSE BODY IT IS? THERE'S NO NEED FOR DRAMATICS...
SHIT. I'M GONNA NEED TO CALL YOU BACK.

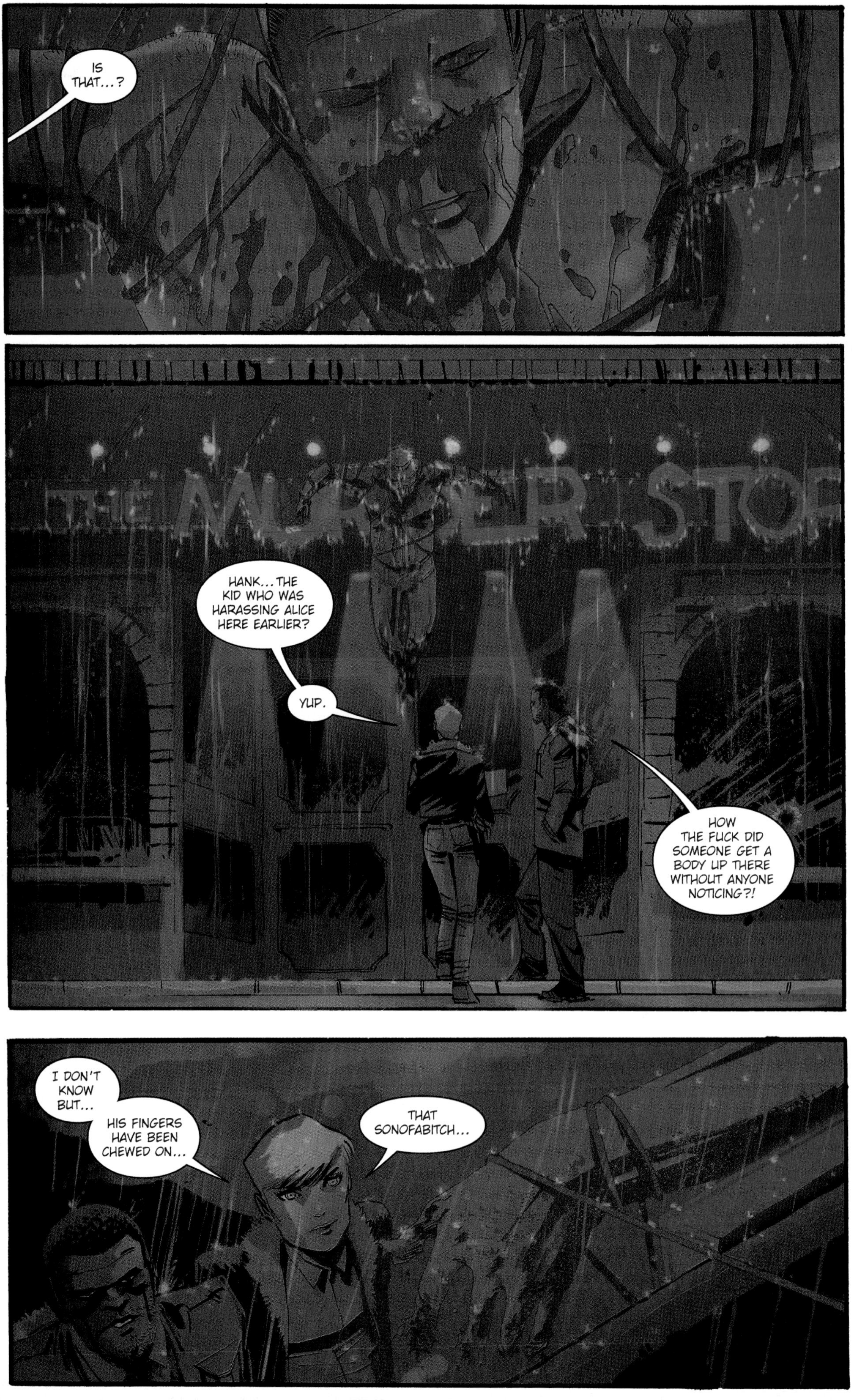
IS THAT...?
HANK...THE KID WHO WAS HARASSING ALICE HERE EARLIER?
YUP.
HOW THE FUCK DID SOMEONE GET A BODY UP THERE WITHOUT ANYONE NOTICING?!
I DON'T KNOW BUT...
HIS FINGERS HAVE BEEN CHEWED ON...
THAT SONOFABITCH...

THREE

"Seems like every new person
I meet lately is related to one
of those serial killers."

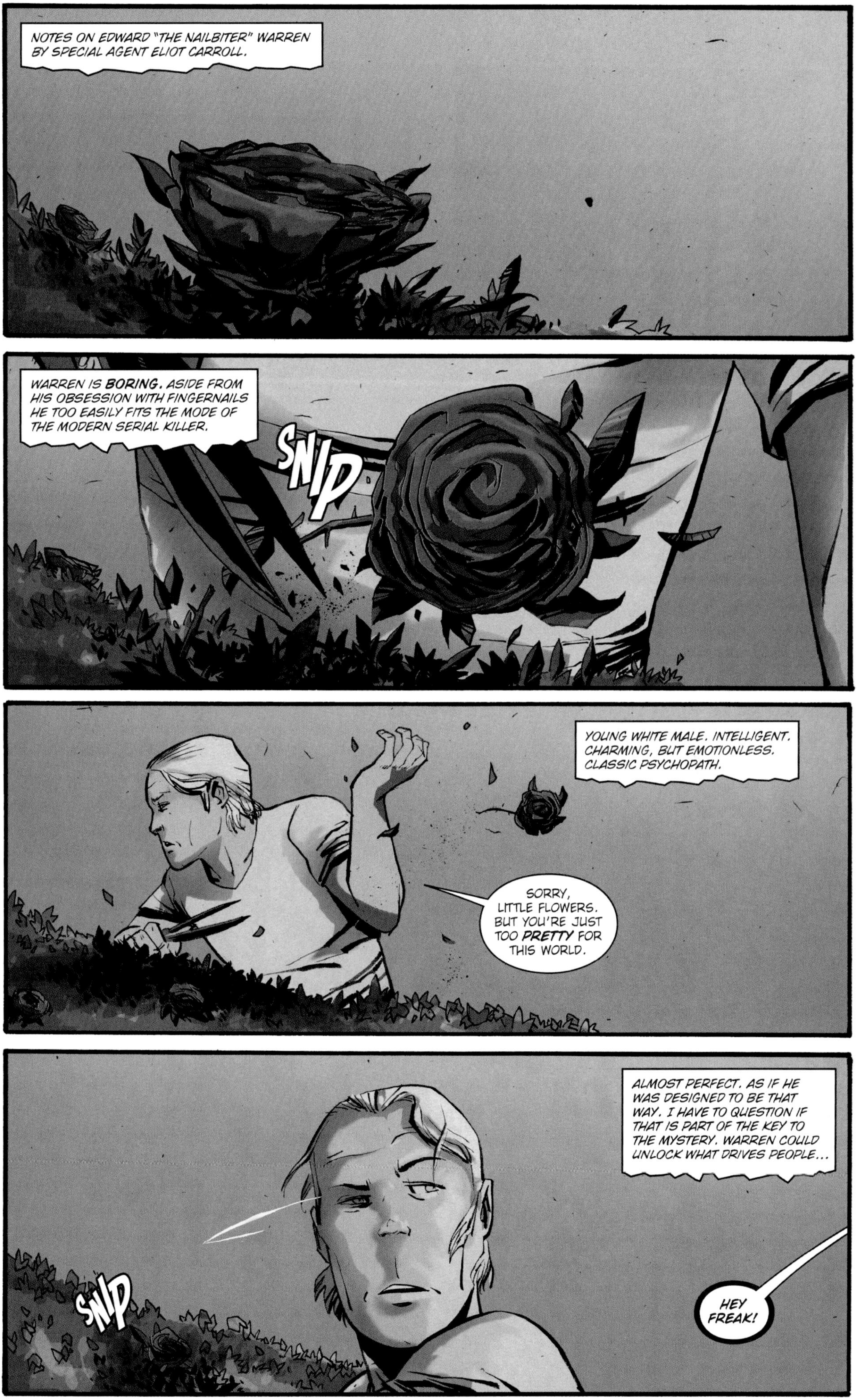
NOTES ON EDWARD "THE NAILBITER" WARREN BY SPECIAL AGENT ELIOT CARROLL.
WARREN IS **BORING.** ASIDE FROM HIS OBSESSION WITH FINGERNAILS HE TOO EASILY FITS THE MODE OF THE MODERN SERIAL KILLER.
SNIP
YOUNG WHITE MALE. INTELLIGENT. CHARMING, BUT EMOTIONLESS. CLASSIC PSYCHOPATH.
SORRY, LITTLE FLOWERS. BUT YOU'RE JUST TOO **PRETTY** FOR THIS WORLD.
ALMOST PERFECT. AS IF HE WAS DESIGNED TO BE THAT WAY. I HAVE TO QUESTION IF THAT IS PART OF THE KEY TO THE MYSTERY. WARREN COULD UNLOCK WHAT DRIVES PEOPLE...
SNIP
HEY FREAK!

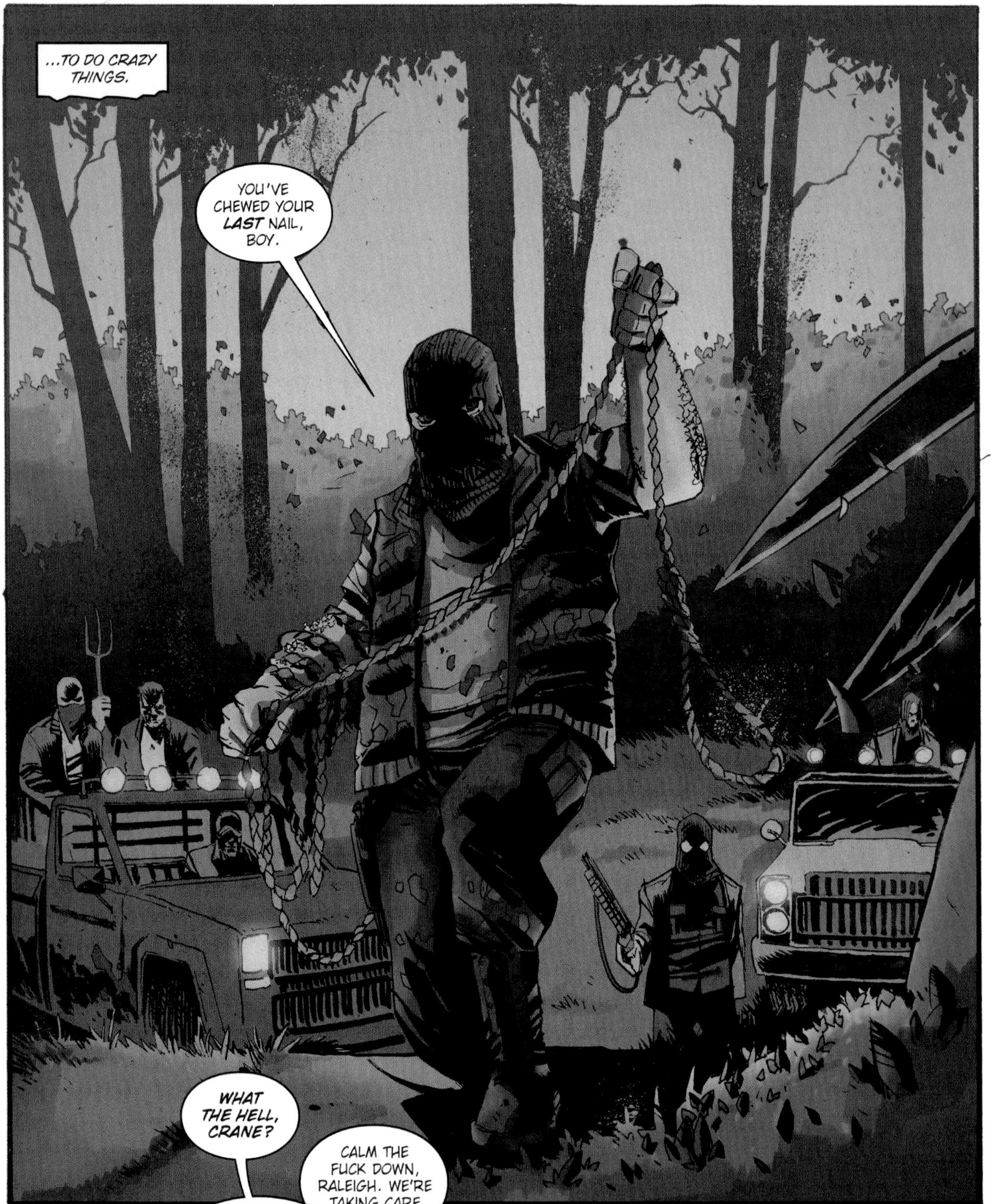
...TO DO CRAZY THINGS.
YOU'VE CHEWED YOUR LAST NAIL, BOY.
WHAT THE HELL, CRANE?
CALM THE FUCK DOWN, RALEIGH. WE'RE TAKING CARE OF--

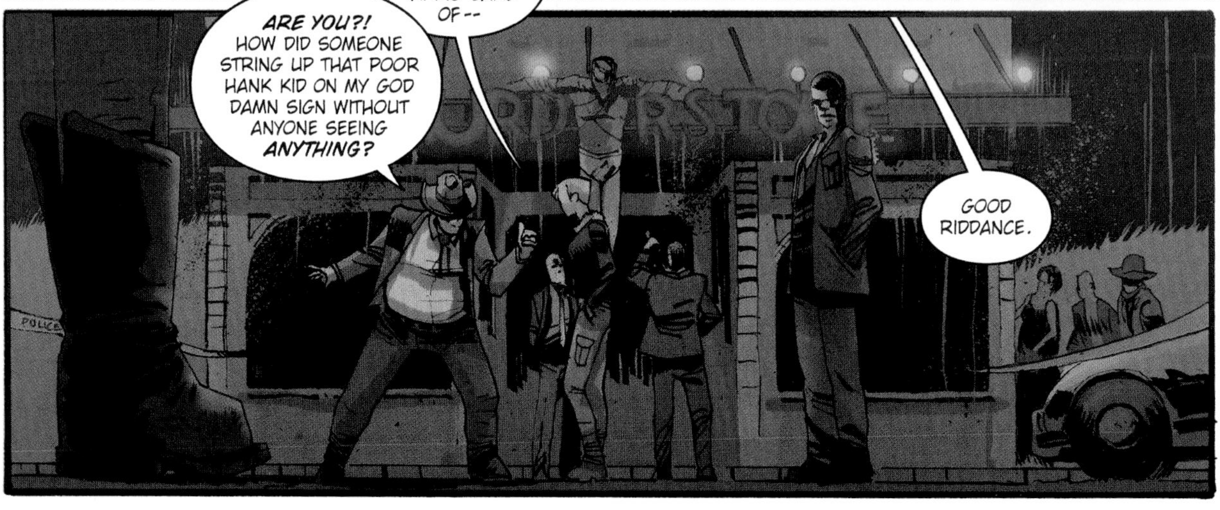
ARE YOU?! HOW DID SOMEONE STRING UP THAT POOR HANK KID ON MY GOD DAMN SIGN WITHOUT ANYONE SEEING ANYTHING?
GOOD RIDDANCE.
POLICE

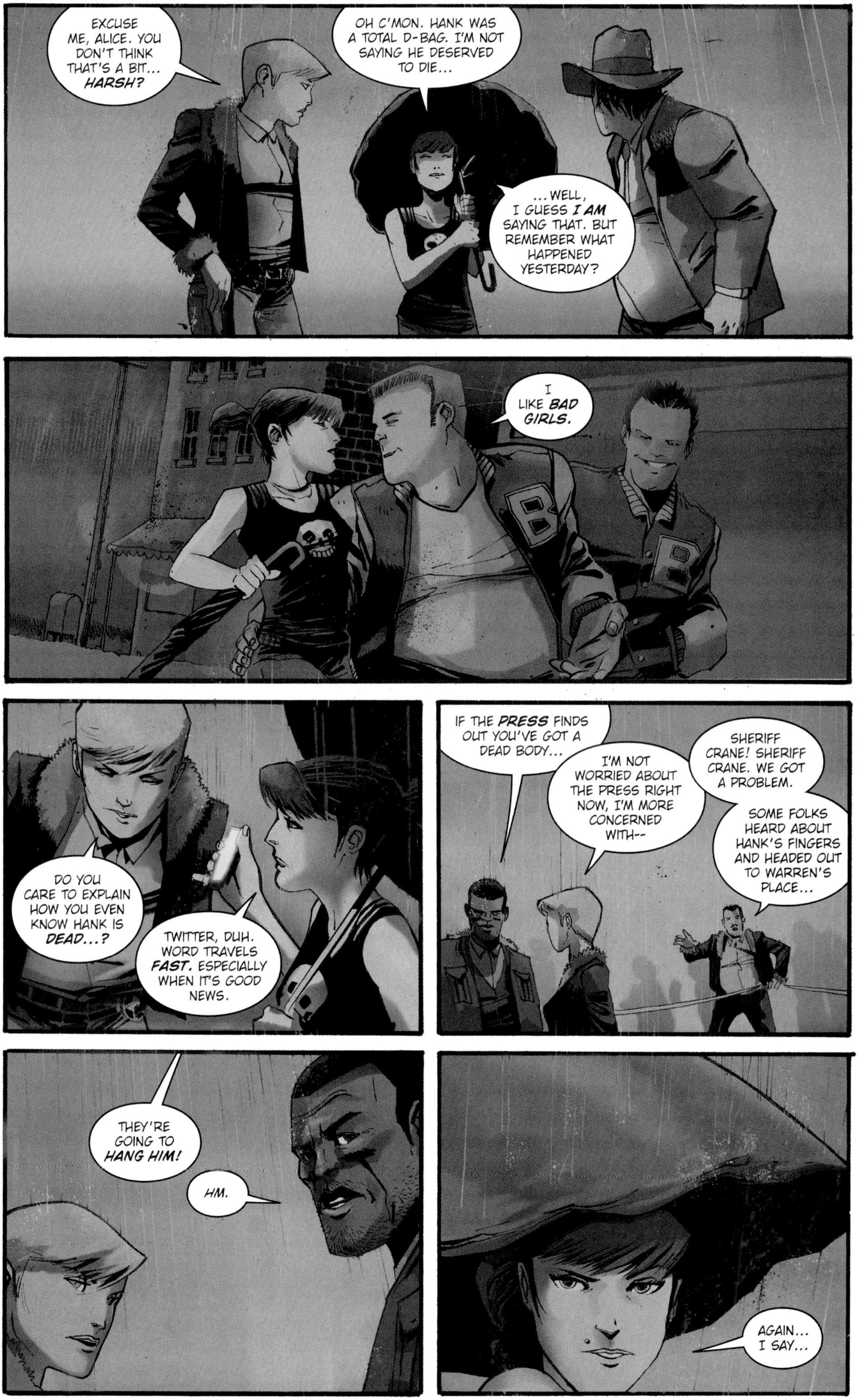
EXCUSE ME, ALICE. YOU DON'T THINK THAT'S A BIT... HARSH?
OH C'MON. HANK WAS A TOTAL D-BAG. I'M NOT SAYING HE DESERVED TO DIE...
...WELL, I GUESS I AM SAYING THAT. BUT REMEMBER WHAT HAPPENED YESTERDAY?
I LIKE BAD GIRLS.
DO YOU CARE TO EXPLAIN HOW YOU EVEN KNOW HANK IS DEAD...?
TWITTER, DUH. WORD TRAVELS FAST. ESPECIALLY WHEN IT'S GOOD NEWS.
IF THE PRESS FINDS OUT YOU'VE GOT A DEAD BODY...
I'M NOT WORRIED ABOUT THE PRESS RIGHT NOW, I'M MORE CONCERNED WITH--
SHERIFF CRANE! SHERIFF CRANE. WE GOT A PROBLEM.
SOME FOLKS HEARD ABOUT HANK'S FINGERS AND HEADED OUT TO WARREN'S PLACE...
THEY'RE GOING TO HANG HIM!
HM.
AGAIN... I SAY...

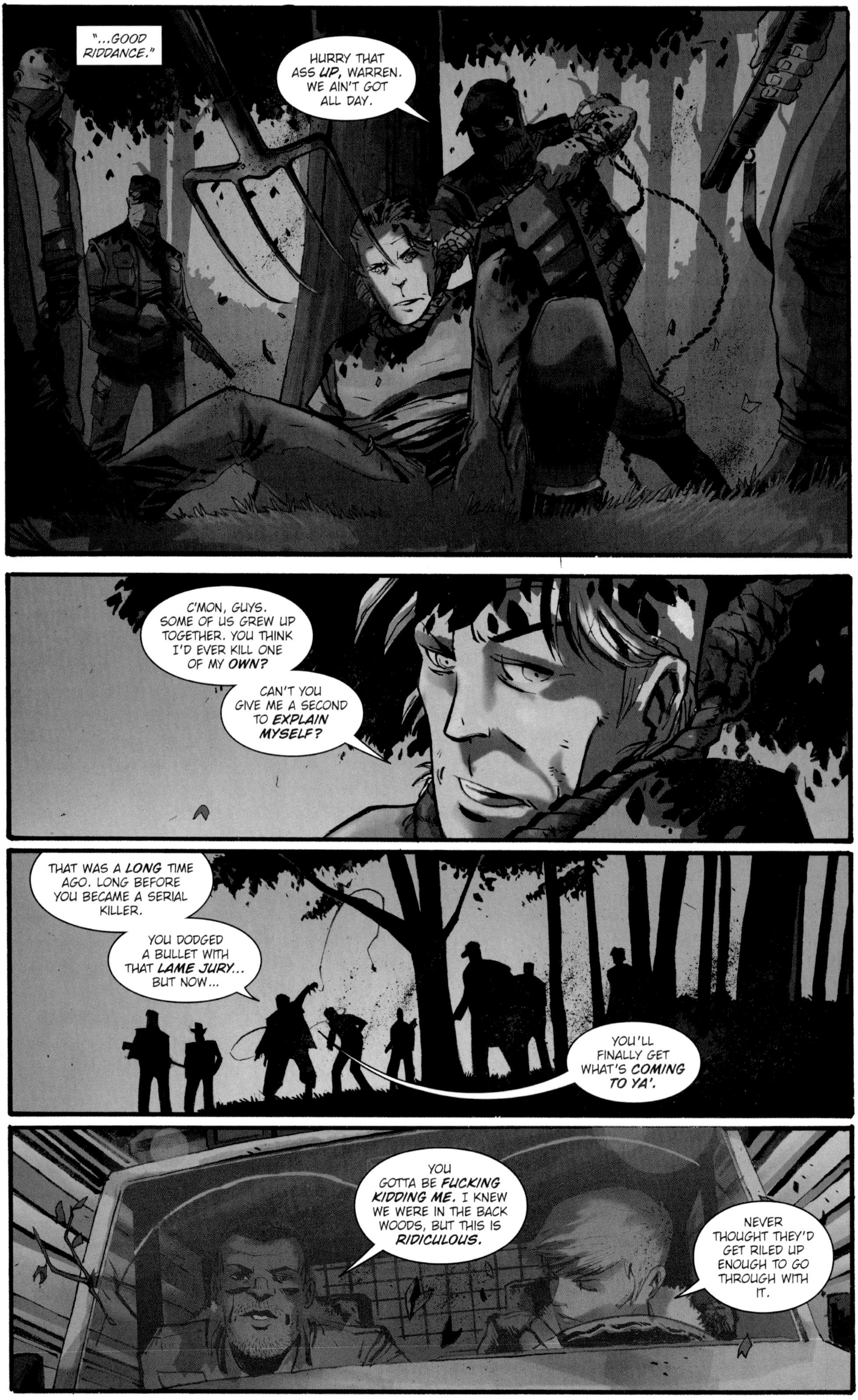
"...GOOD RIDDANCE."
HURRY THAT ASS UP, WARREN. WE AIN'T GOT ALL DAY.
C'MON, GUYS. SOME OF US GREW UP TOGETHER. YOU THINK I'D EVER KILL ONE OF MY OWN?
CAN'T YOU GIVE ME A SECOND TO EXPLAIN MYSELF?
THAT WAS A LONG TIME AGO. LONG BEFORE YOU BECAME A SERIAL KILLER.
YOU DODGED A BULLET WITH THAT LAME JURY... BUT NOW...
YOU'LL FINALLY GET WHAT'S COMING TO YA'.
YOU GOTTA BE FUCKING KIDDING ME. I KNEW WE WERE IN THE BACK WOODS, BUT THIS IS RIDICULOUS.
NEVER THOUGHT THEY'D GET RILED UP ENOUGH TO GO THROUGH WITH IT.

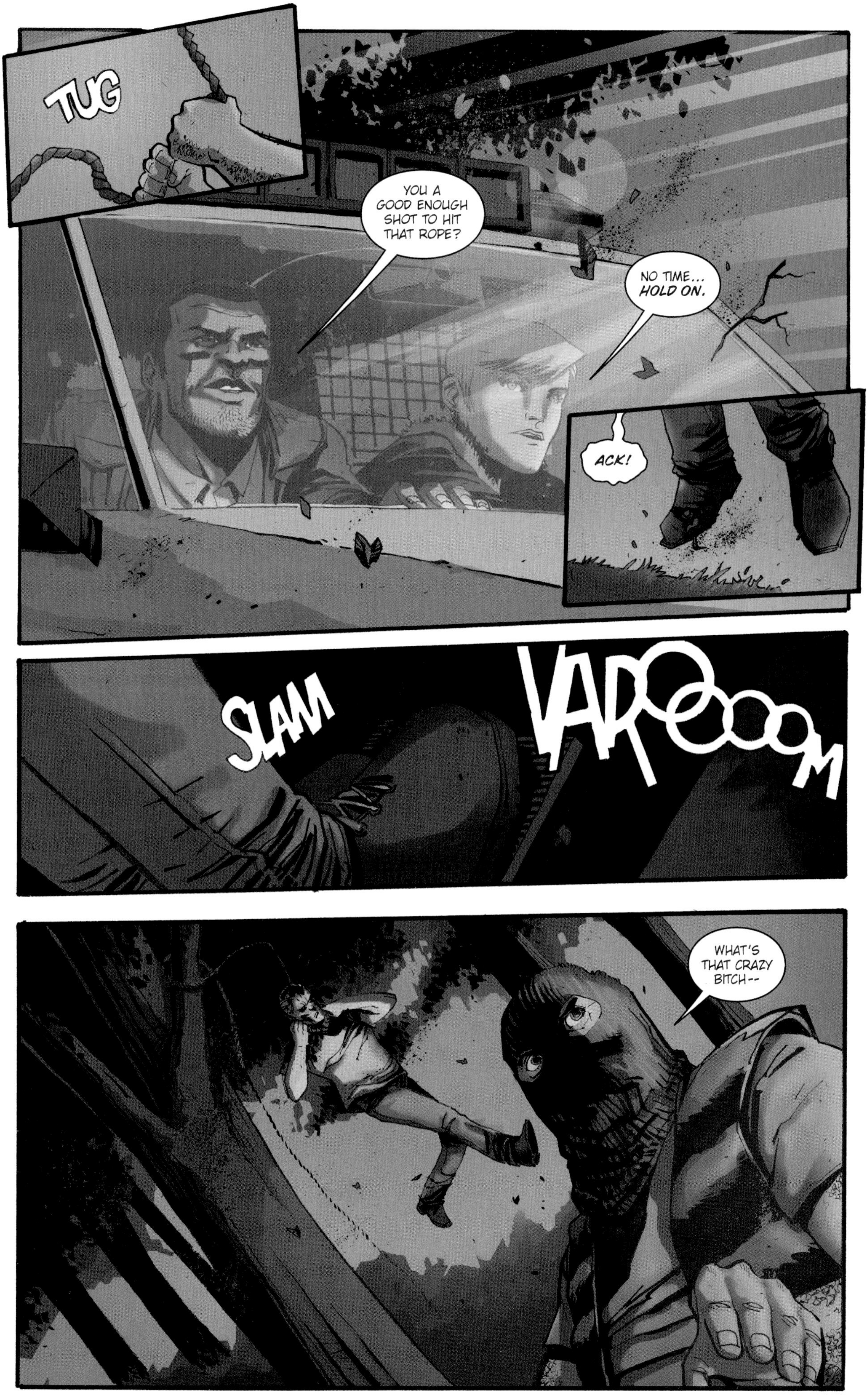
TUG
YOU A GOOD ENOUGH SHOT TO HIT THAT ROPE?
NO TIME... HOLD ON.
ACK!
SLAM
VAROOOOM
WHAT'S THAT CRAZY BITCH--

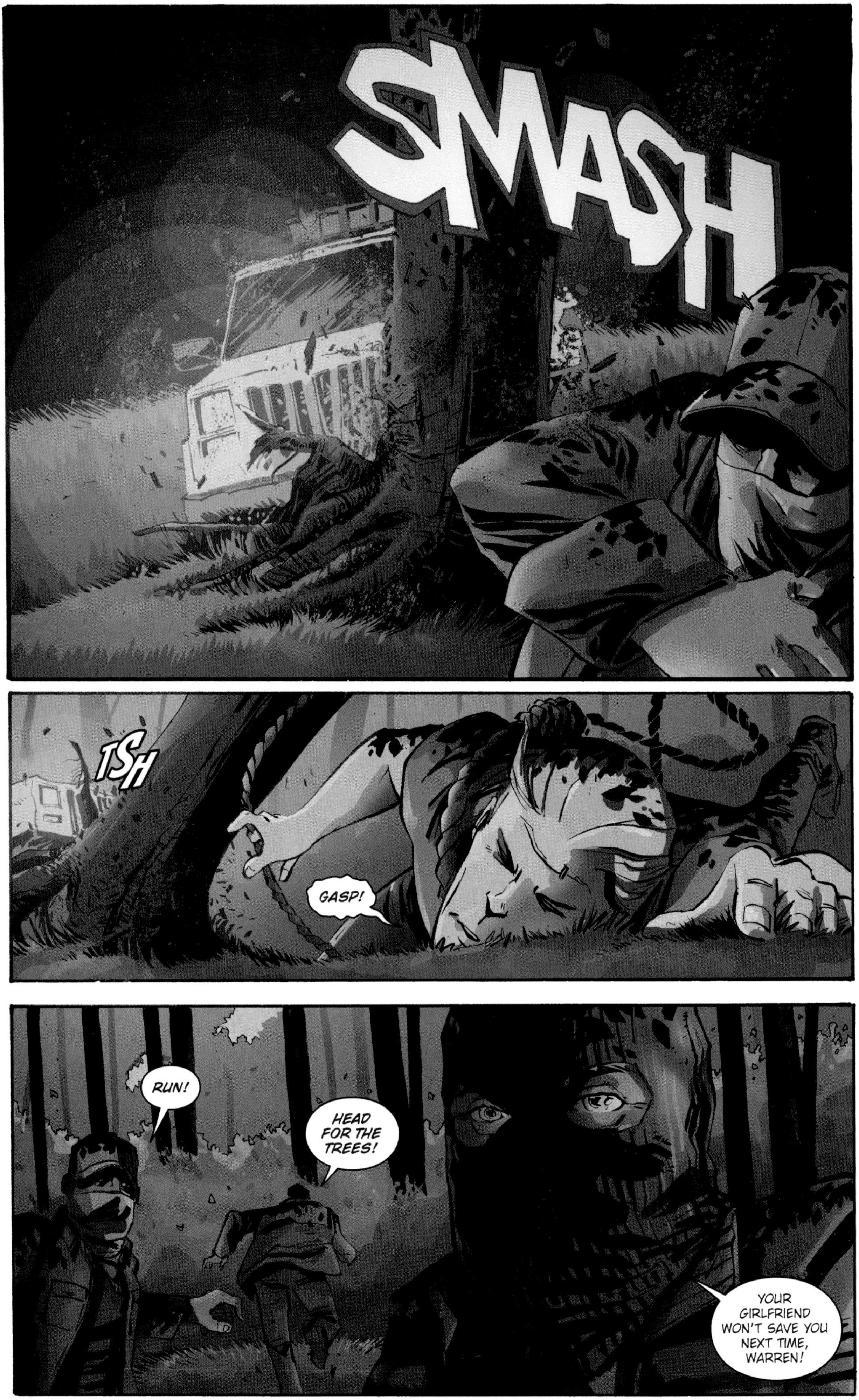
SMASH
TSH
GASP!
RUN!
HEAD FOR THE TREES!
YOUR GIRLFRIEND WON'T SAVE YOU NEXT TIME, WARREN!

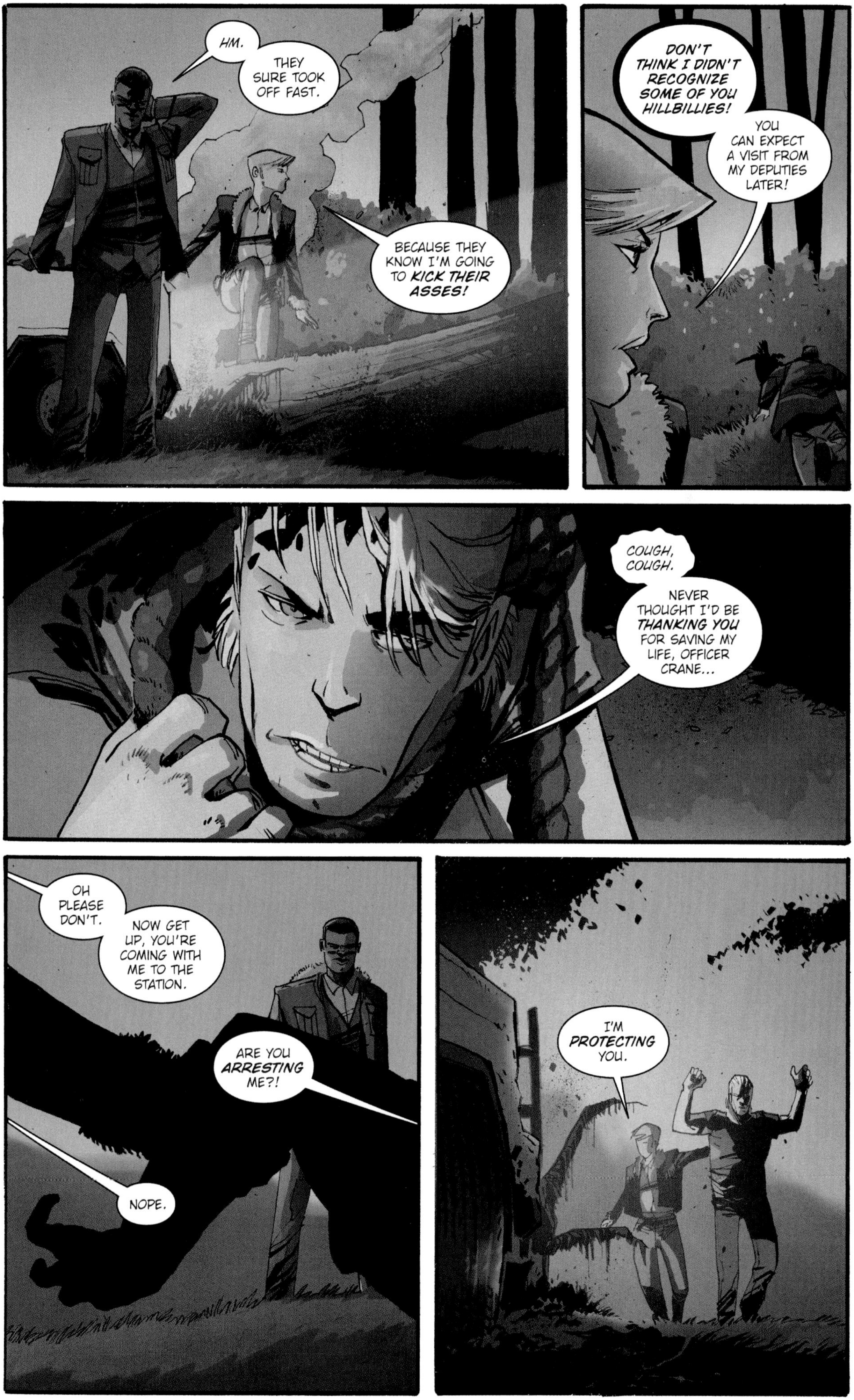
HM.
THEY SURE TOOK OFF FAST.
BECAUSE THEY KNOW I'M GOING TO KICK THEIR ASSES!
DON'T THINK I DIDN'T RECOGNIZE SOME OF YOU HILLBILLIES!
YOU CAN EXPECT A VISIT FROM MY DEPUTIES LATER!
COUGH, COUGH.
NEVER THOUGHT I'D BE THANKING YOU FOR SAVING MY LIFE, OFFICER CRANE...
OH PLEASE DON'T.
NOW GET UP, YOU'RE COMING WITH ME TO THE STATION.
ARE YOU ARRESTING ME?!
NOPE.
I'M PROTECTING YOU.

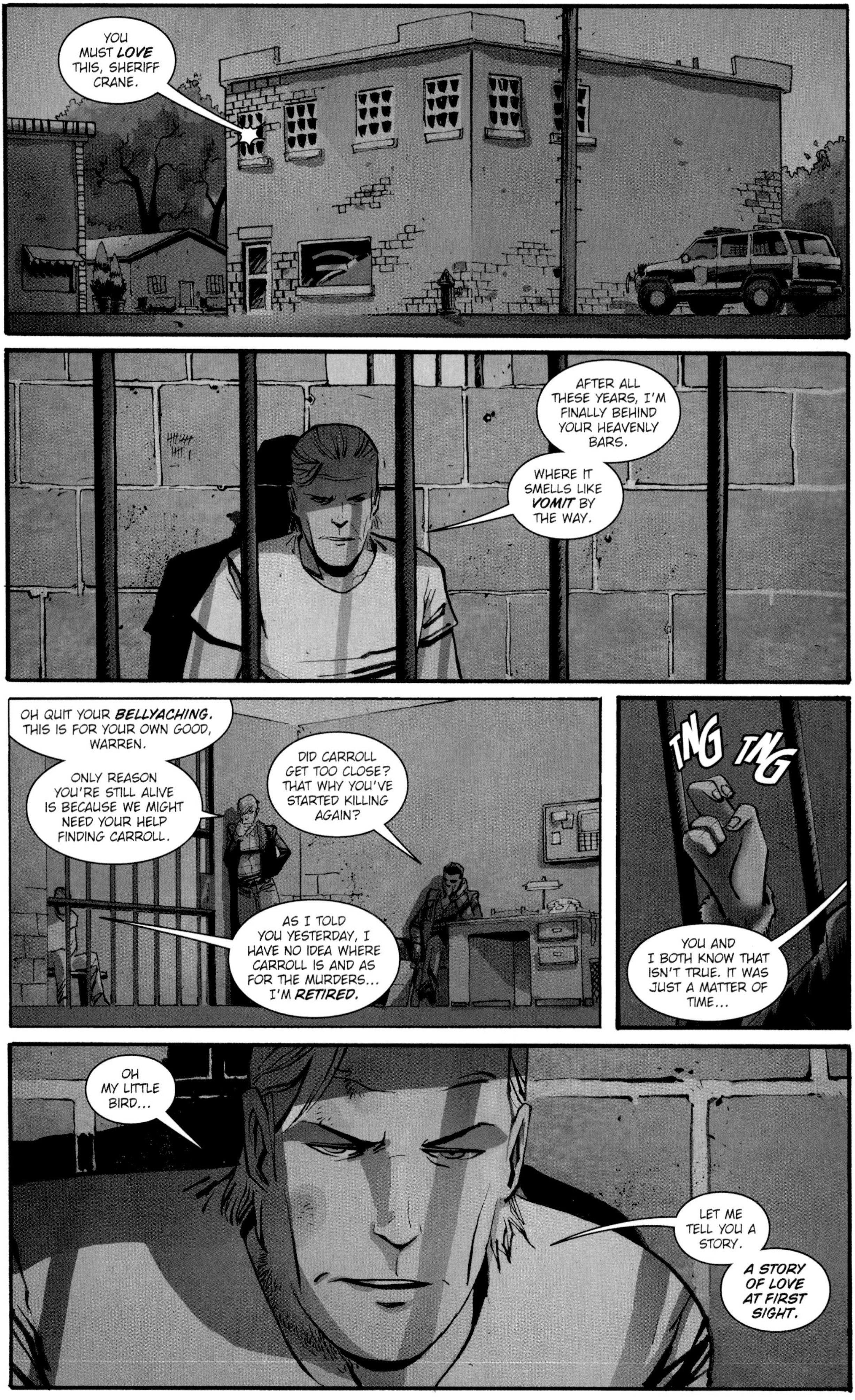
YOU MUST LOVE THIS, SHERIFF CRANE.
AFTER ALL THESE YEARS, I'M FINALLY BEHIND YOUR HEAVENLY BARS.
WHERE IT SMELLS LIKE VOMIT BY THE WAY.
OH QUIT YOUR BELLYACHING. THIS IS FOR YOUR OWN GOOD, WARREN.
ONLY REASON YOU'RE STILL ALIVE IS BECAUSE WE MIGHT NEED YOUR HELP FINDING CARROLL.
DID CARROLL GET TOO CLOSE? THAT WHY YOU'VE STARTED KILLING AGAIN?
AS I TOLD YOU YESTERDAY, I HAVE NO IDEA WHERE CARROLL IS AND AS FOR THE MURDERS... I'M RETIRED.
TNG TNG
YOU AND I BOTH KNOW THAT ISN'T TRUE. IT WAS JUST A MATTER OF TIME...
OH MY LITTLE BIRD...
LET ME TELL YOU A STORY.
A STORY OF LOVE AT FIRST SIGHT.

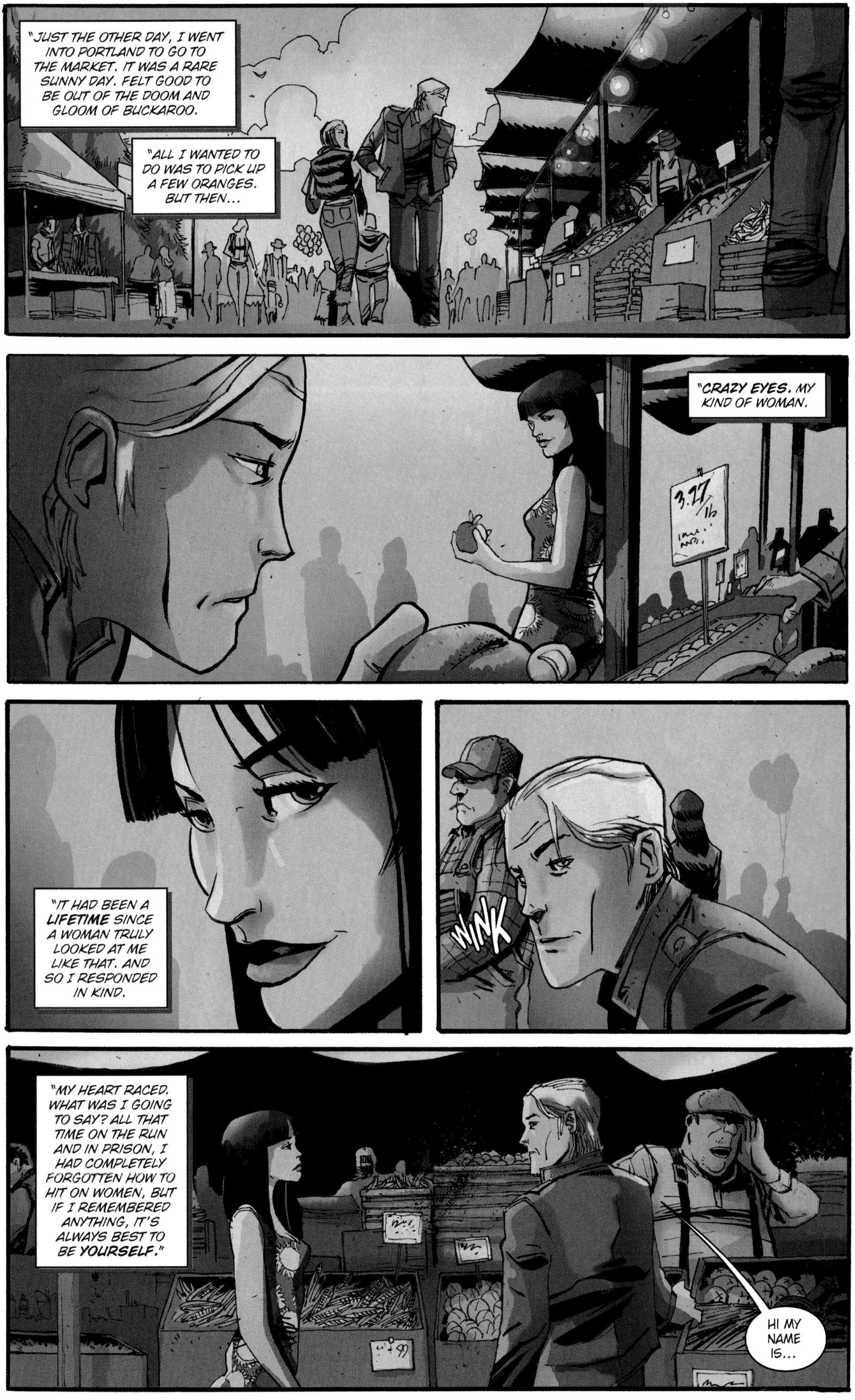
"JUST THE OTHER DAY, I WENT INTO PORTLAND TO GO TO THE MARKET. IT WAS A RARE SUNNY DAY. FELT GOOD TO BE OUT OF THE DOOM AND GLOOM OF BUCKAROO.
"ALL I WANTED TO DO WAS TO PICK UP A FEW ORANGES. BUT THEN...
"CRAZY EYES. MY KIND OF WOMAN.
3.27 /lb
"IT HAD BEEN A LIFETIME SINCE A WOMAN TRULY LOOKED AT ME LIKE THAT. AND SO I RESPONDED IN KIND.
WINK
"MY HEART RACED. WHAT WAS I GOING TO SAY? ALL THAT TIME ON THE RUN AND IN PRISON, I HAD COMPLETELY FORGOTTEN HOW TO HIT ON WOMEN, BUT IF I REMEMBERED ANYTHING, IT'S ALWAYS BEST TO BE YOURSELF."
HI MY NAME IS...

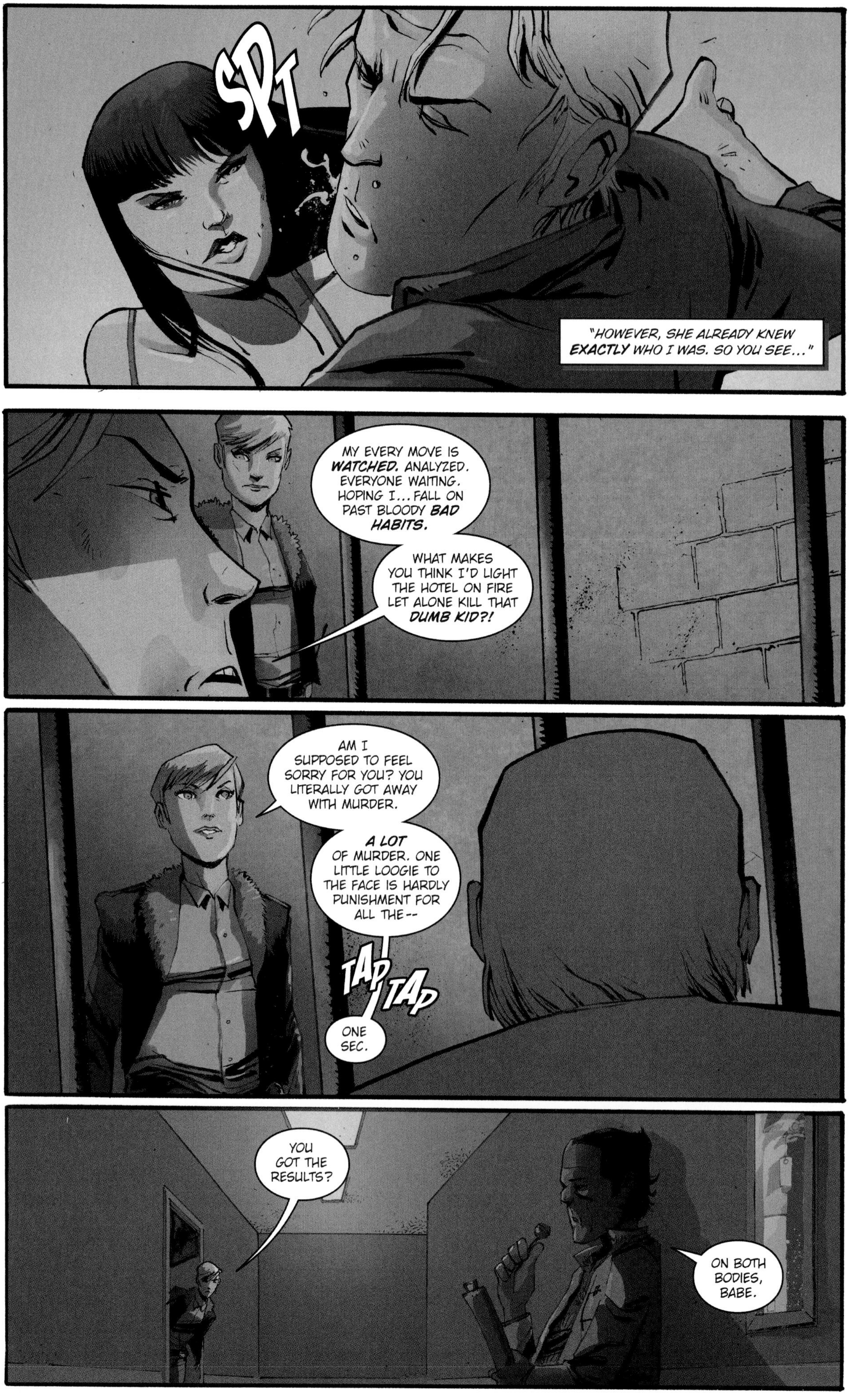
SPT
"HOWEVER, SHE ALREADY KNEW EXACTLY WHO I WAS. SO YOU SEE..."
MY EVERY MOVE IS WATCHED. ANALYZED. EVERYONE WAITING. HOPING I... FALL ON PAST BLOODY BAD HABITS.
WHAT MAKES YOU THINK I'D LIGHT THE HOTEL ON FIRE LET ALONE KILL THAT DUMB KID?!
AM I SUPPOSED TO FEEL SORRY FOR YOU? YOU LITERALLY GOT AWAY WITH MURDER.
A LOT OF MURDER. ONE LITTLE LOOGIE TO THE FACE IS HARDLY PUNISHMENT FOR ALL THE--
TAP TAP
ONE SEC.
YOU GOT THE RESULTS?
ON BOTH BODIES, BABE.

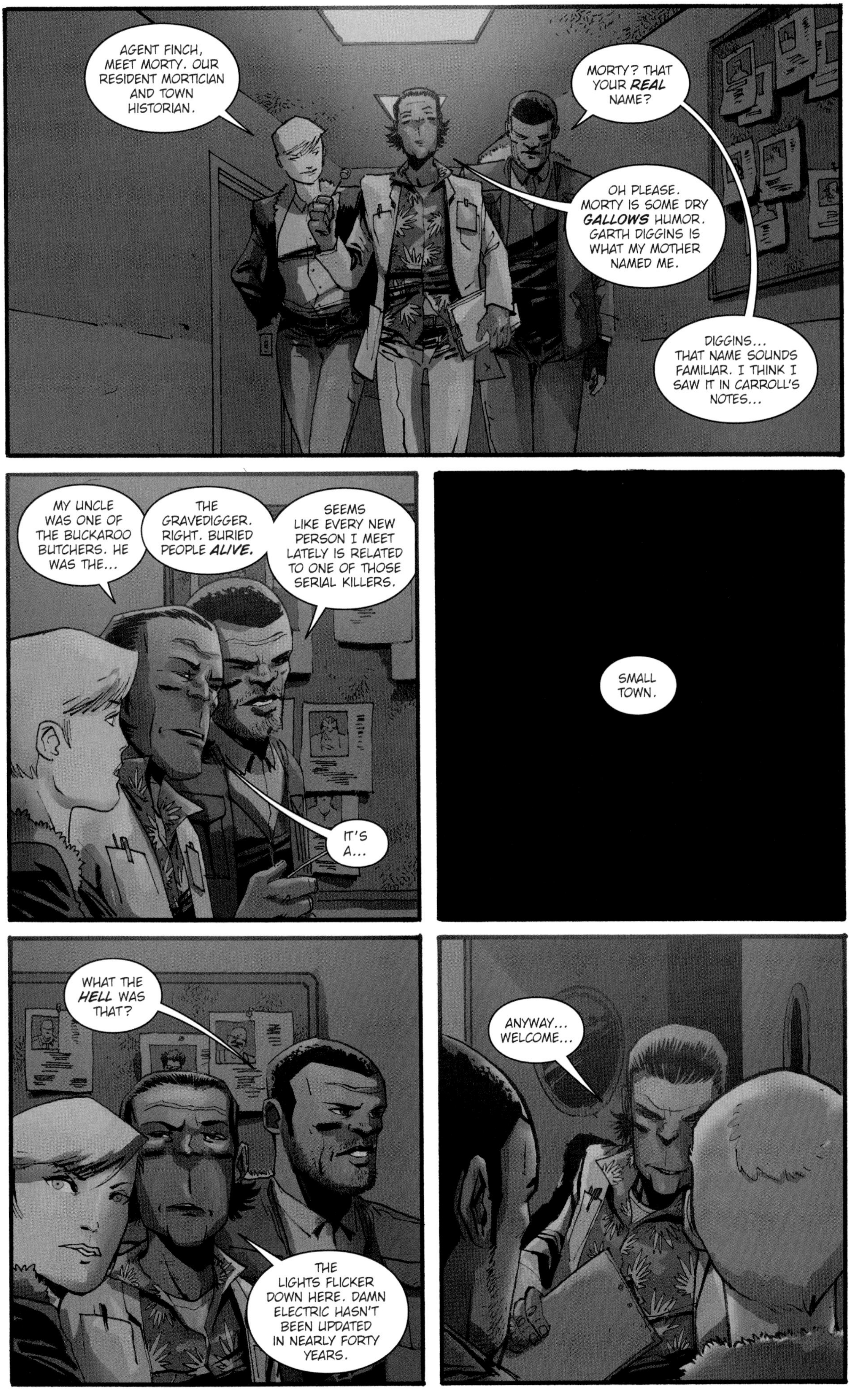
AGENT FINCH, MEET MORTY. OUR RESIDENT MORTICIAN AND TOWN HISTORIAN.
MORTY? THAT YOUR REAL NAME?
OH PLEASE. MORTY IS SOME DRY GALLOWS HUMOR. GARTH DIGGINS IS WHAT MY MOTHER NAMED ME.
DIGGINS... THAT NAME SOUNDS FAMILIAR. I THINK I SAW IT IN CARROLL'S NOTES...
MY UNCLE WAS ONE OF THE BUCKAROO BUTCHERS. HE WAS THE...
THE GRAVEDIGGER. RIGHT. BURIED PEOPLE ALIVE.
SEEMS LIKE EVERY NEW PERSON I MEET LATELY IS RELATED TO ONE OF THOSE SERIAL KILLERS.
IT'S A...
SMALL TOWN.
WHAT THE HELL WAS THAT?
THE LIGHTS FLICKER DOWN HERE. DAMN ELECTRIC HASN'T BEEN UPDATED IN NEARLY FORTY YEARS.
ANYWAY... WELCOME...

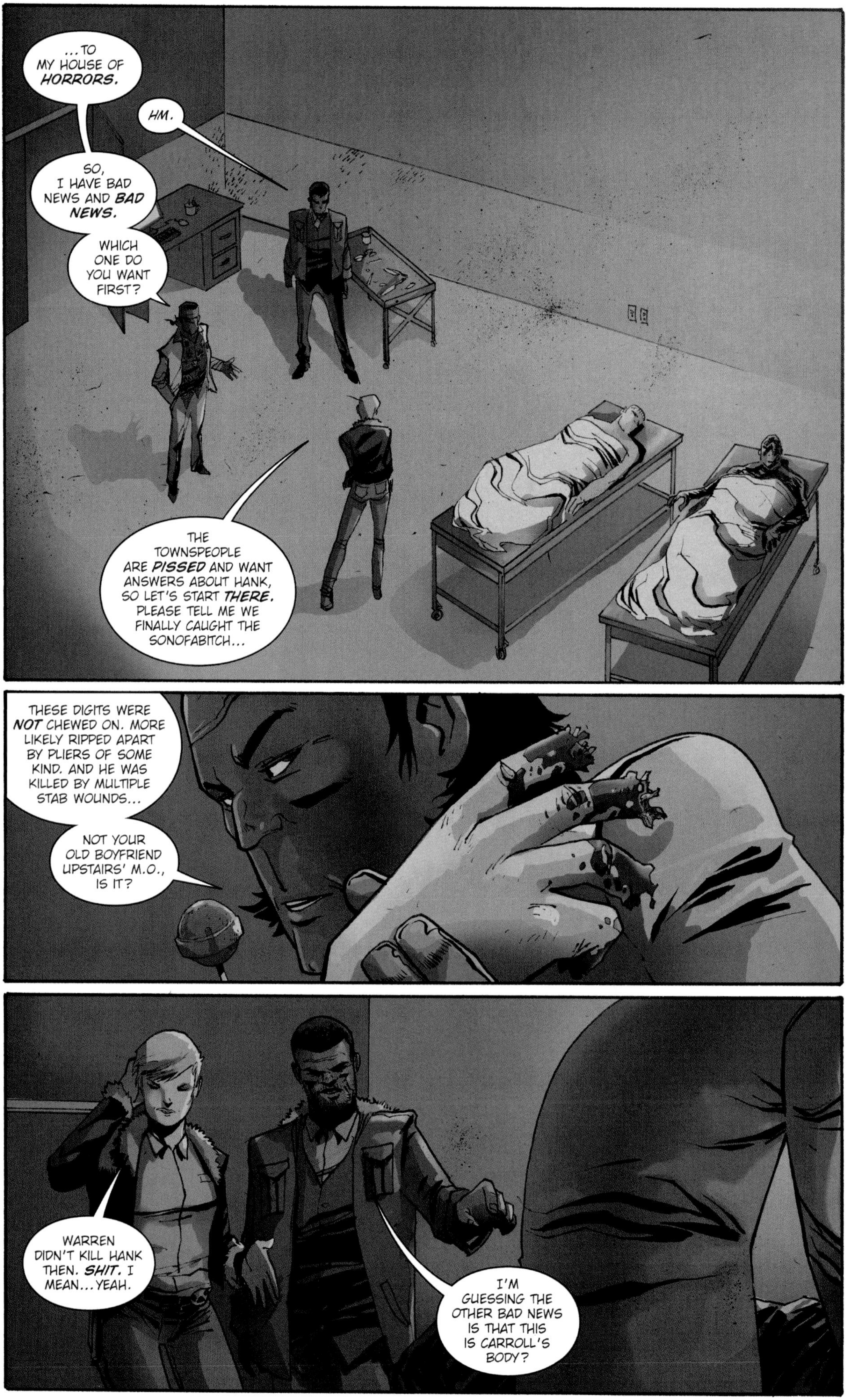
...TO MY HOUSE OF HORRORS.
HM.
SO, I HAVE BAD NEWS AND BAD NEWS.
WHICH ONE DO YOU WANT FIRST?
THE TOWNSPEOPLE ARE PISSED AND WANT ANSWERS ABOUT HANK, SO LET'S START THERE. PLEASE TELL ME WE FINALLY CAUGHT THE SONOFABITCH...
THESE DIGITS WERE NOT CHEWED ON. MORE LIKELY RIPPED APART BY PLIERS OF SOME KIND. AND HE WAS KILLED BY MULTIPLE STAB WOUNDS...
NOT YOUR OLD BOYFRIEND UPSTAIRS' M.O., IS IT?
WARREN DIDN'T KILL HANK THEN. SHIT. I MEAN...YEAH.
I'M GUESSING THE OTHER BAD NEWS IS THAT THIS IS CARROLL'S BODY?

THAT'S WHAT I CALLED YOU FOR LAST NIGHT.
ISN'T YOUR FRIEND.
DAMN LIGHTS. AS I WAS SAYING...
THE LEVEL OF DECOMP SHOWS THAT THIS BODY WAS DEAD LONG, LONG BEFORE IT WAS IN THAT FIRE.
JESUS, WELL THAT'S A RELIEF.
NO, NO IT ISN'T. WE STILL HAVE AN UNIDENTIFIED DEAD BODY ON OUR HANDS THAT WAS IN CARROLL'S HOTEL ROOM.
OH, I KNOW EXACTLY WHOSE BODY IT IS.
AND?
IT'S...
...AH SHIT.

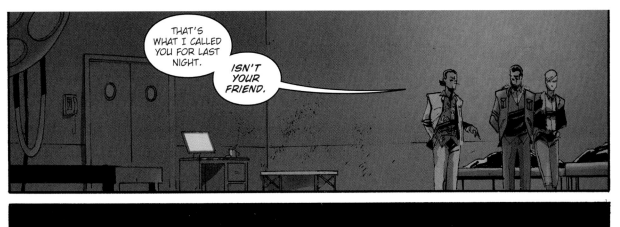

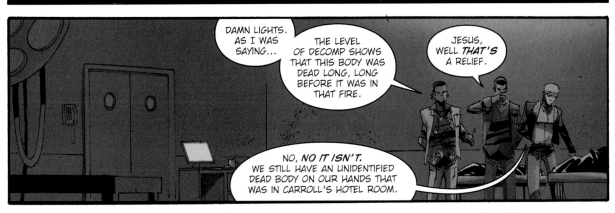

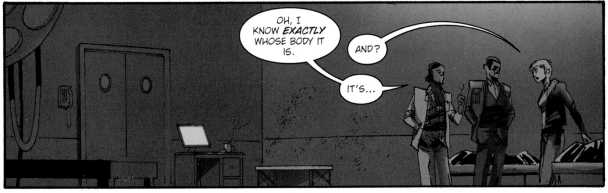

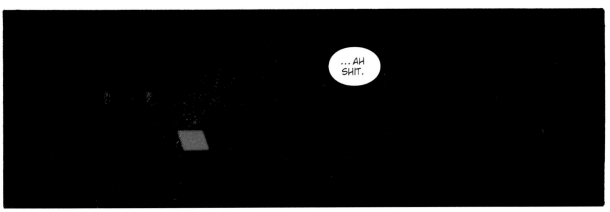

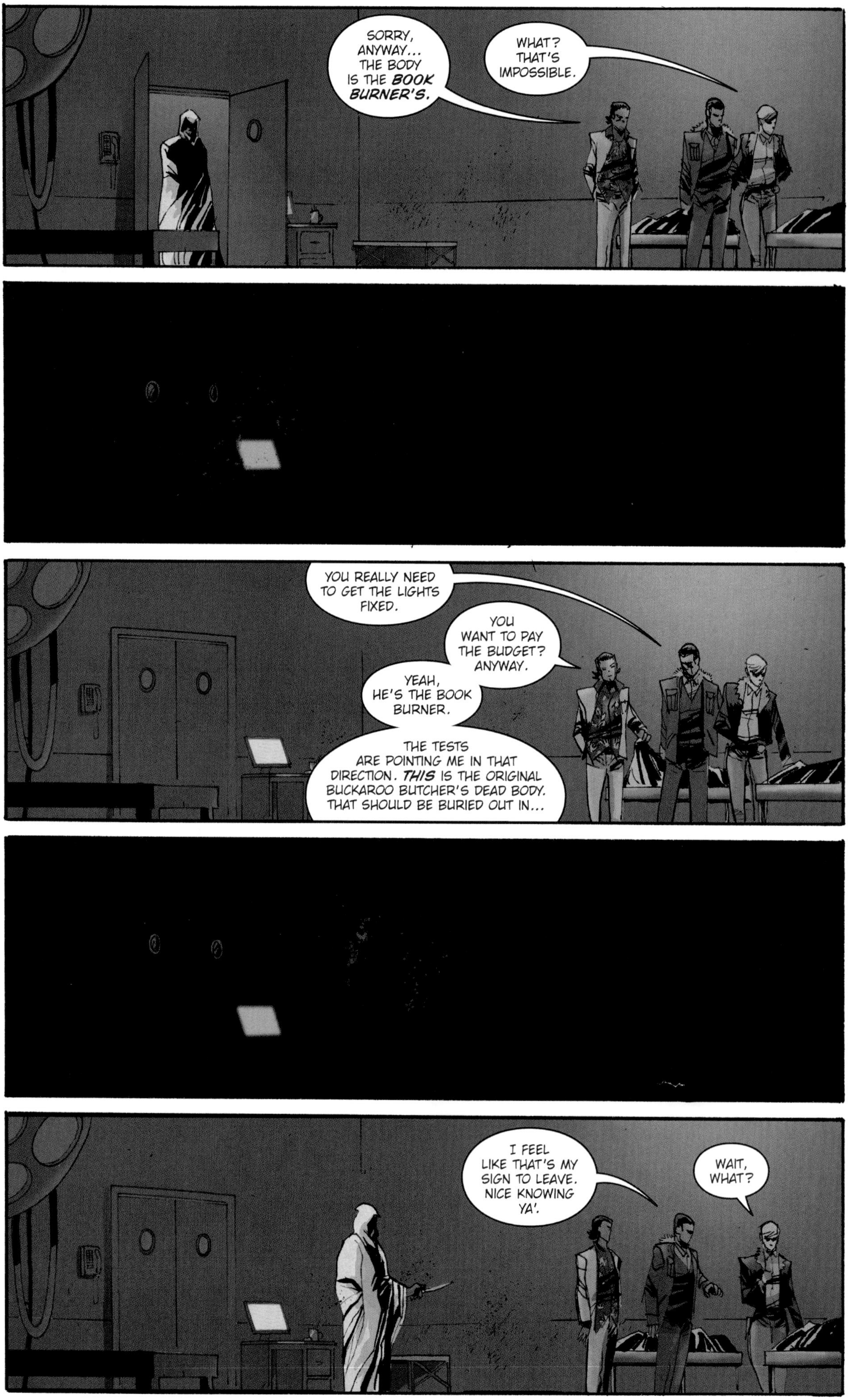

SORRY, ANYWAY... THE BODY IS THE BOOK BURNER'S.
WHAT? THAT'S IMPOSSIBLE.
YOU REALLY NEED TO GET THE LIGHTS FIXED.
YOU WANT TO PAY THE BUDGET? ANYWAY.
YEAH, HE'S THE BOOK BURNER.
THE TESTS ARE POINTING ME IN THAT DIRECTION. THIS IS THE ORIGINAL BUCKAROO BUTCHER'S DEAD BODY. THAT SHOULD BE BURIED OUT IN...
I FEEL LIKE THAT'S MY SIGN TO LEAVE. NICE KNOWING YA'.
WAIT, WHAT?

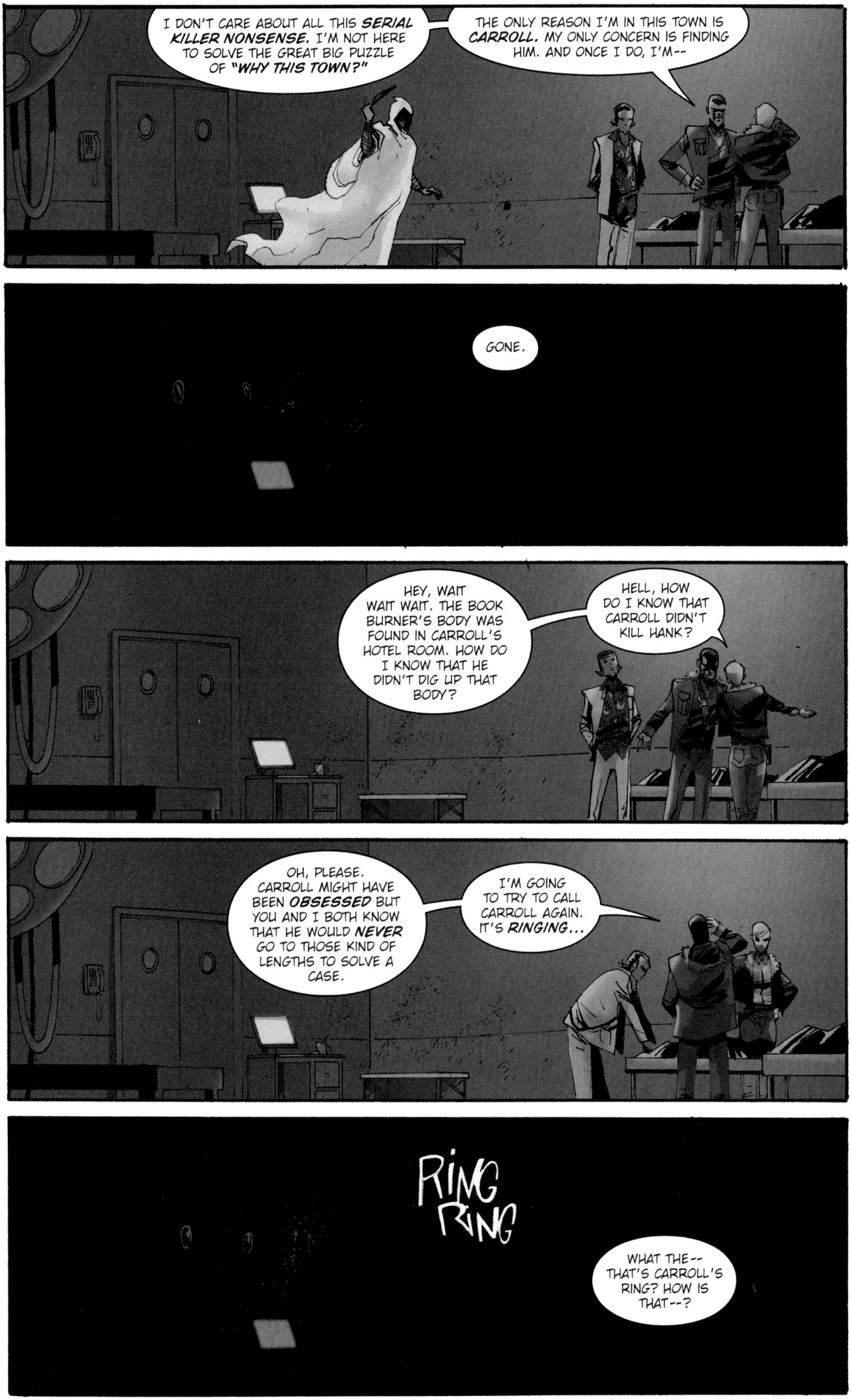
I DON'T CARE ABOUT ALL THIS **SERIAL KILLER NONSENSE.** I'M NOT HERE TO SOLVE THE GREAT BIG PUZZLE OF **"WHY THIS TOWN?"**
THE ONLY REASON I'M IN THIS TOWN IS **CARROLL.** MY ONLY CONCERN IS FINDING HIM. AND ONCE I DO, I'M--
GONE.
HEY, WAIT WAIT WAIT. THE BOOK BURNER'S BODY WAS FOUND IN CARROLL'S HOTEL ROOM. HOW DO I KNOW THAT HE DIDN'T DIG UP THAT BODY?
HELL, HOW DO I KNOW THAT CARROLL DIDN'T KILL HANK?
OH, PLEASE. CARROLL MIGHT HAVE BEEN **OBSESSED** BUT YOU AND I BOTH KNOW THAT HE WOULD **NEVER** GO TO THOSE KIND OF LENGTHS TO SOLVE A CASE.
I'M GOING TO TRY TO CALL CARROLL AGAIN. IT'S **RINGING...**
RING RING
WHAT THE-- THAT'S CARROLL'S RING? HOW IS THAT--?

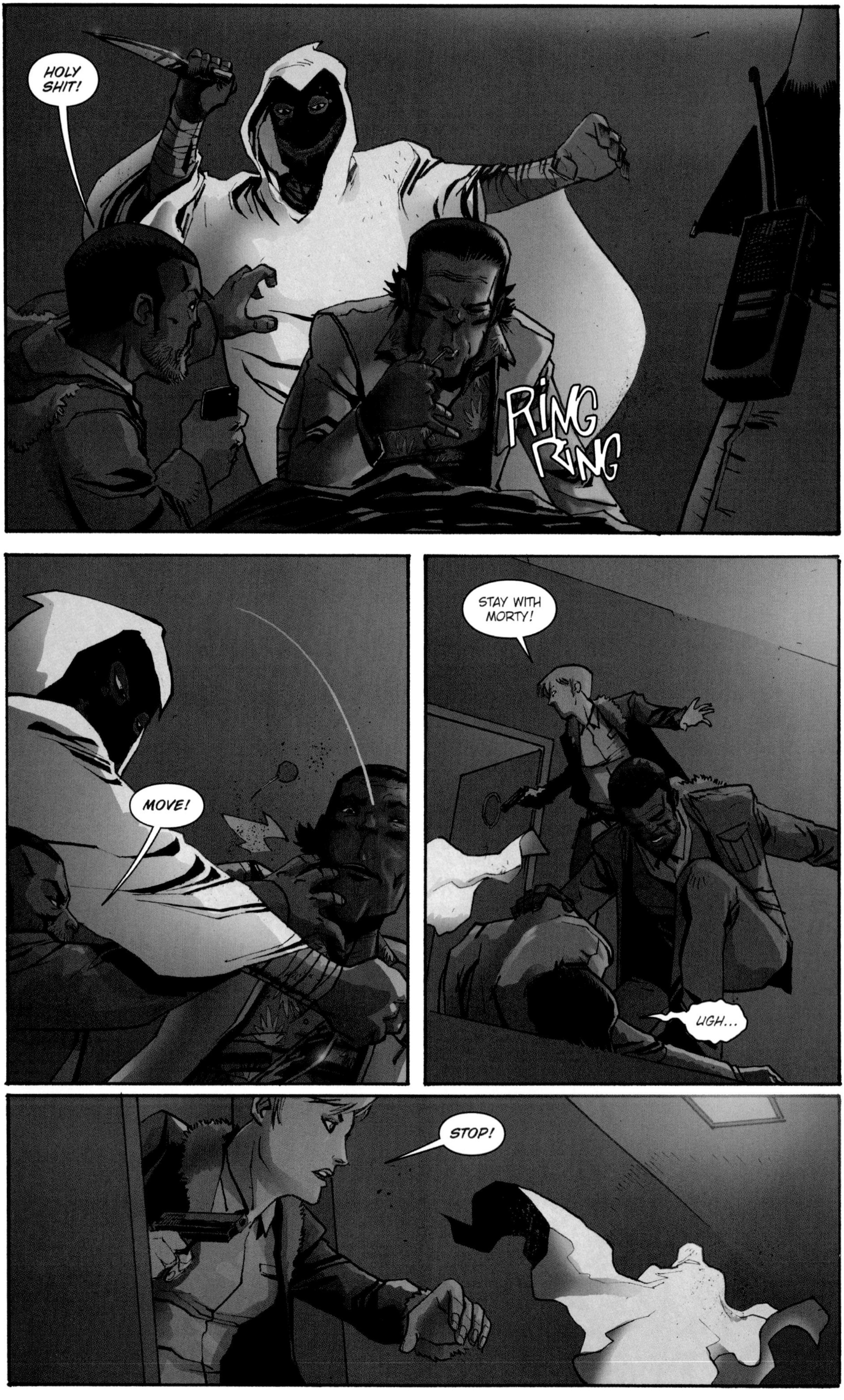

HOLY SHIT!
RING RING
MOVE!
STAY WITH MORTY!
UGH...
STOP!

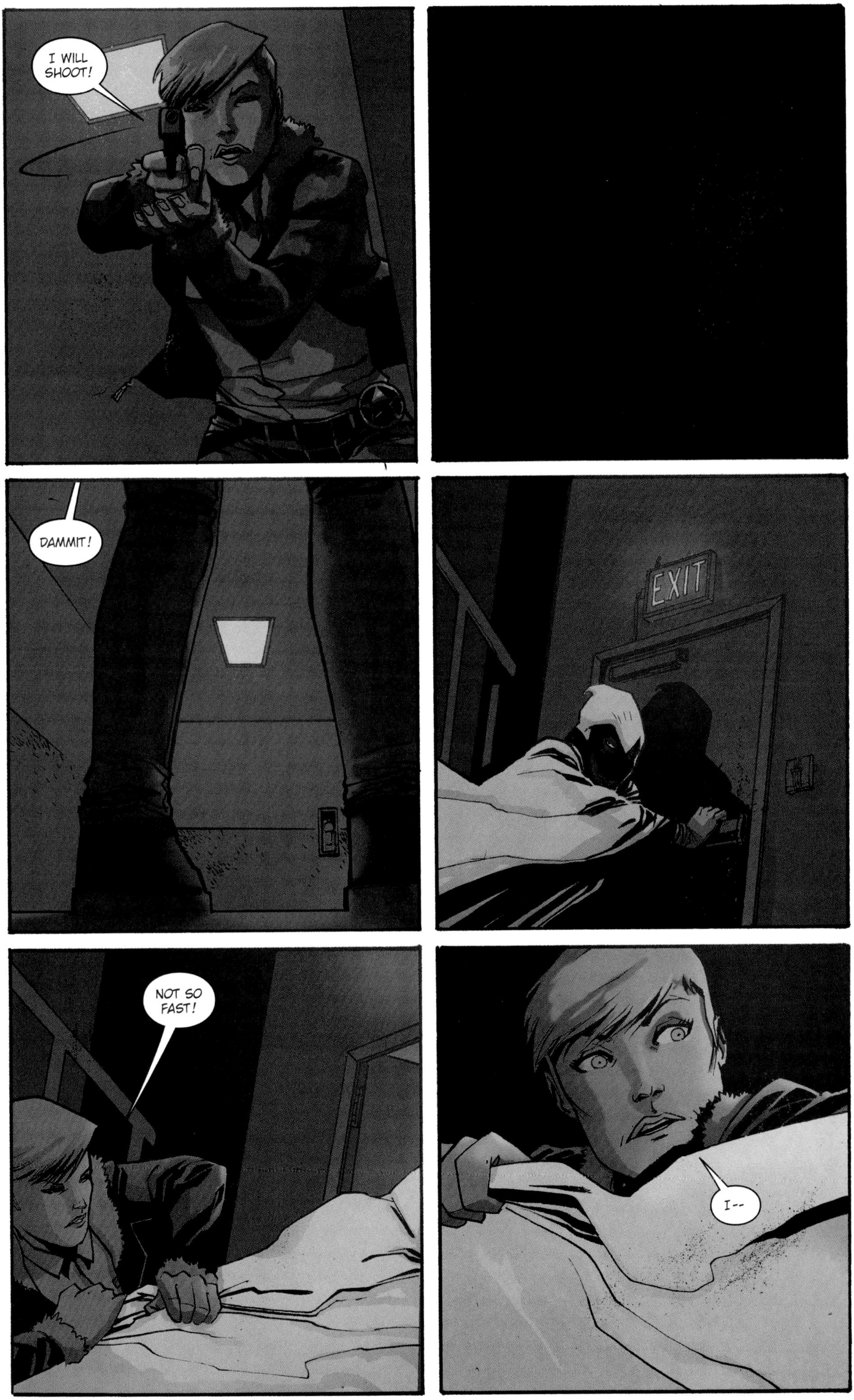
I WILL SHOOT!
DAMMIT!
NOT SO FAST!
I--

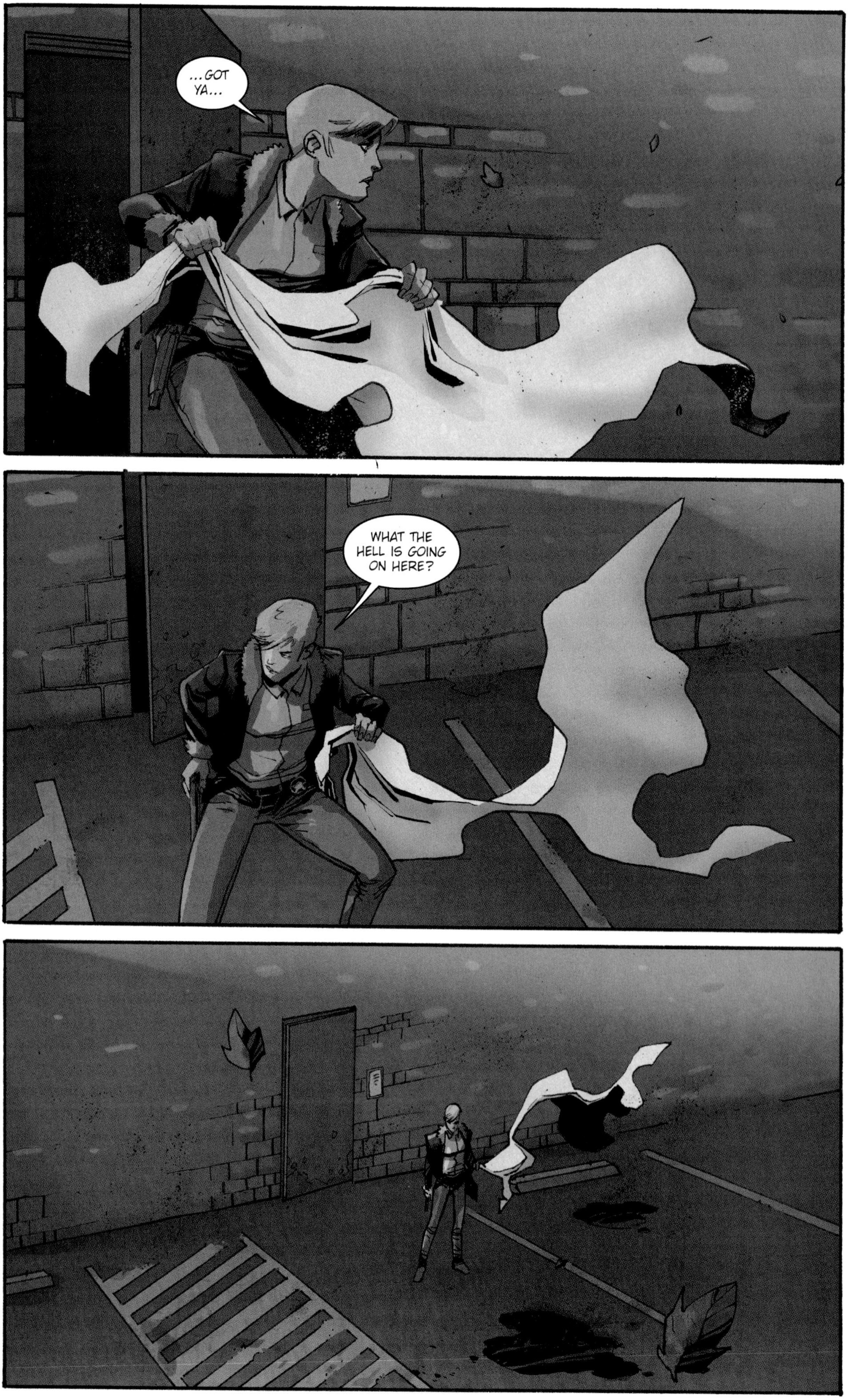
...GOT YA...
WHAT THE HELL IS GOING ON HERE?

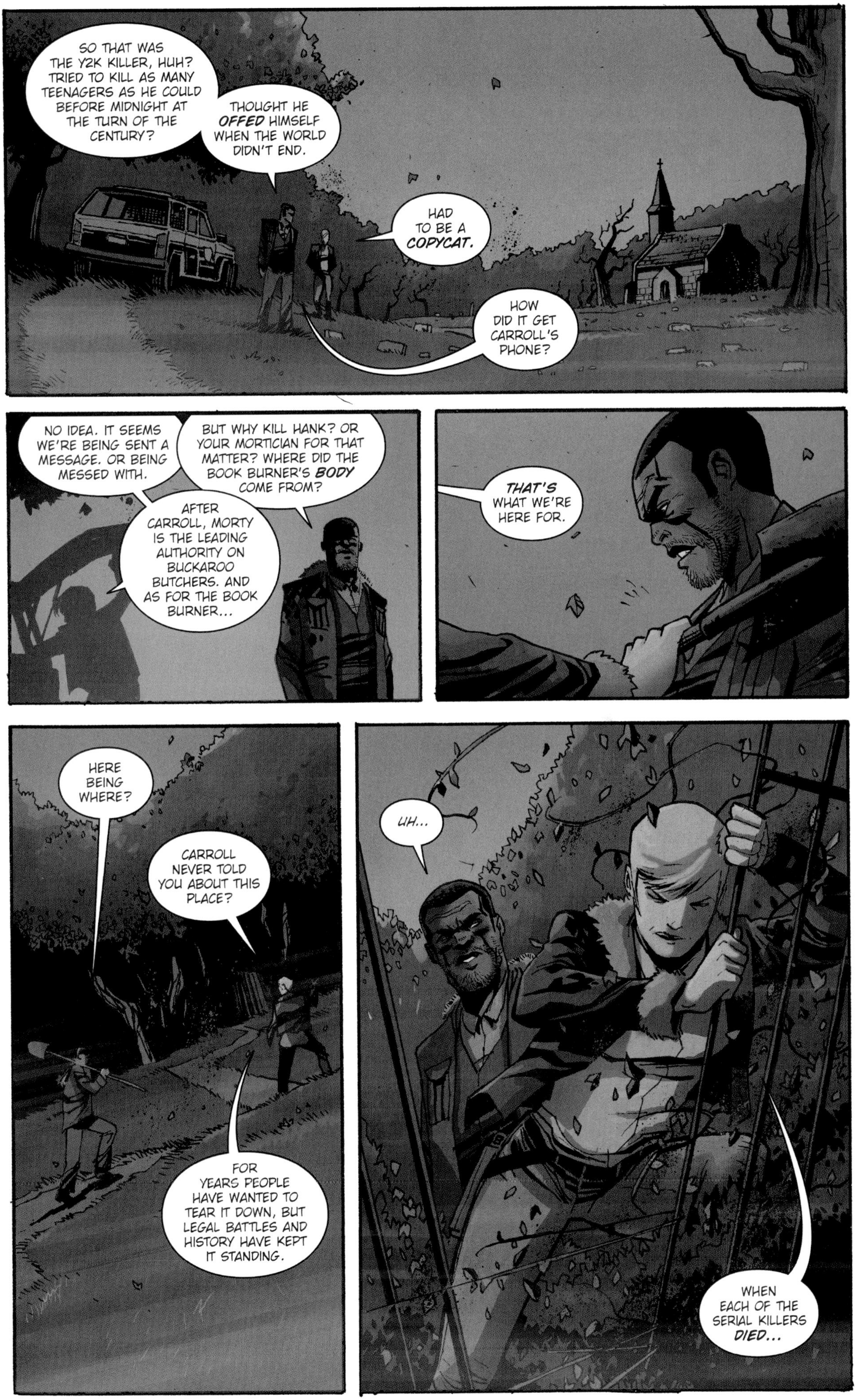
SO THAT WAS THE Y2K KILLER, HUH? TRIED TO KILL AS MANY TEENAGERS AS HE COULD BEFORE MIDNIGHT AT THE TURN OF THE CENTURY?
THOUGHT HE **OFFED** HIMSELF WHEN THE WORLD DIDN'T END.
HAD TO BE A **COPYCAT.**
HOW DID IT GET CARROLL'S PHONE?
NO IDEA. IT SEEMS WE'RE BEING SENT A MESSAGE. OR BEING MESSED WITH.
BUT WHY KILL HANK? OR YOUR MORTICIAN FOR THAT MATTER? WHERE DID THE BOOK BURNER'S **BODY** COME FROM?
AFTER CARROLL, MORTY IS THE LEADING AUTHORITY ON BUCKAROO BUTCHERS. AND AS FOR THE BOOK BURNER...
THAT'S WHAT WE'RE HERE FOR.
HERE BEING WHERE?
CARROLL NEVER TOLD YOU ABOUT THIS PLACE?
FOR YEARS PEOPLE HAVE WANTED TO TEAR IT DOWN, BUT LEGAL BATTLES AND HISTORY HAVE KEPT IT STANDING.
UH...
WHEN EACH OF THE SERIAL KILLERS **DIED...**

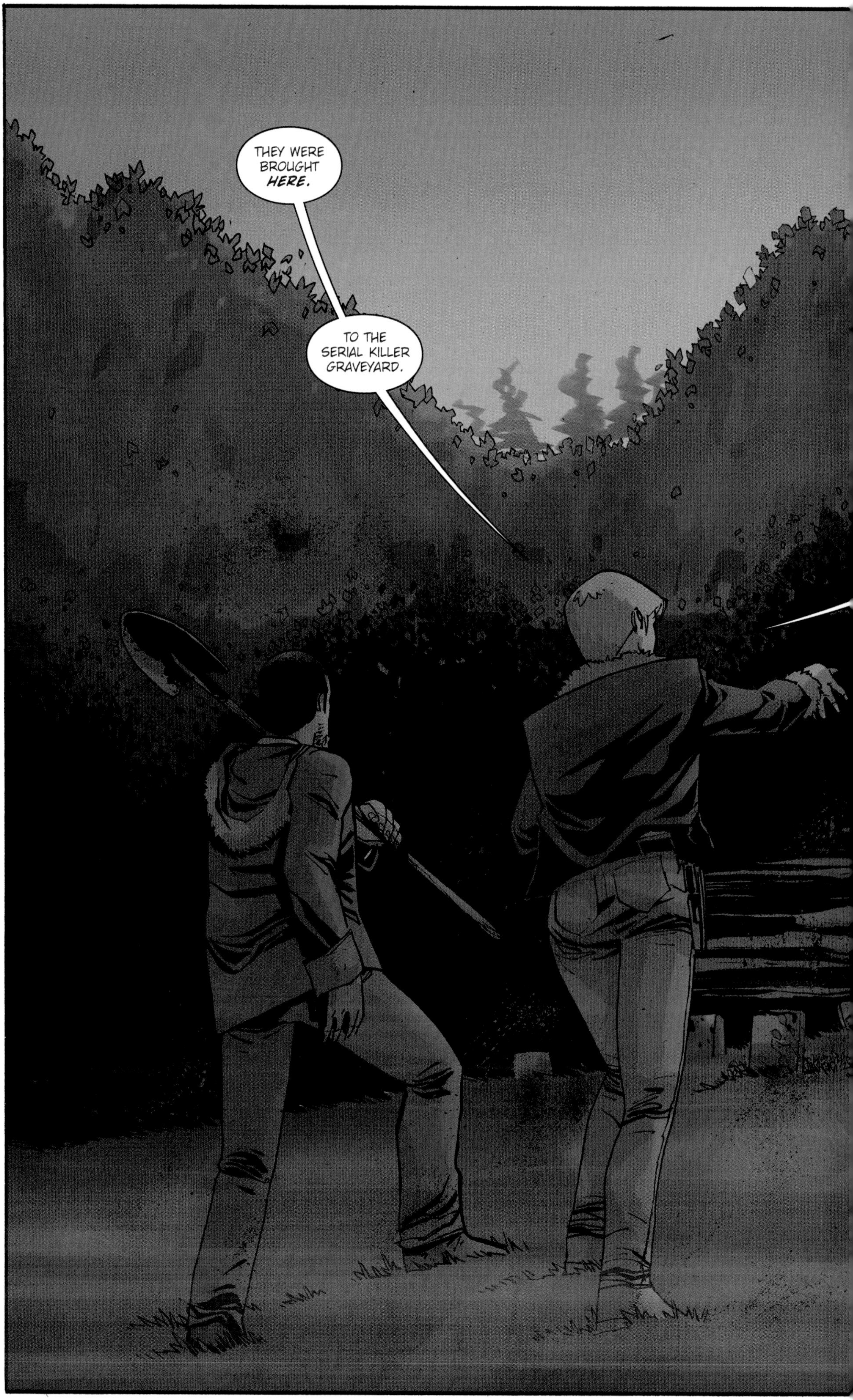
THEY WERE BROUGHT HERE.
TO THE SERIAL KILLER GRAVEYARD.

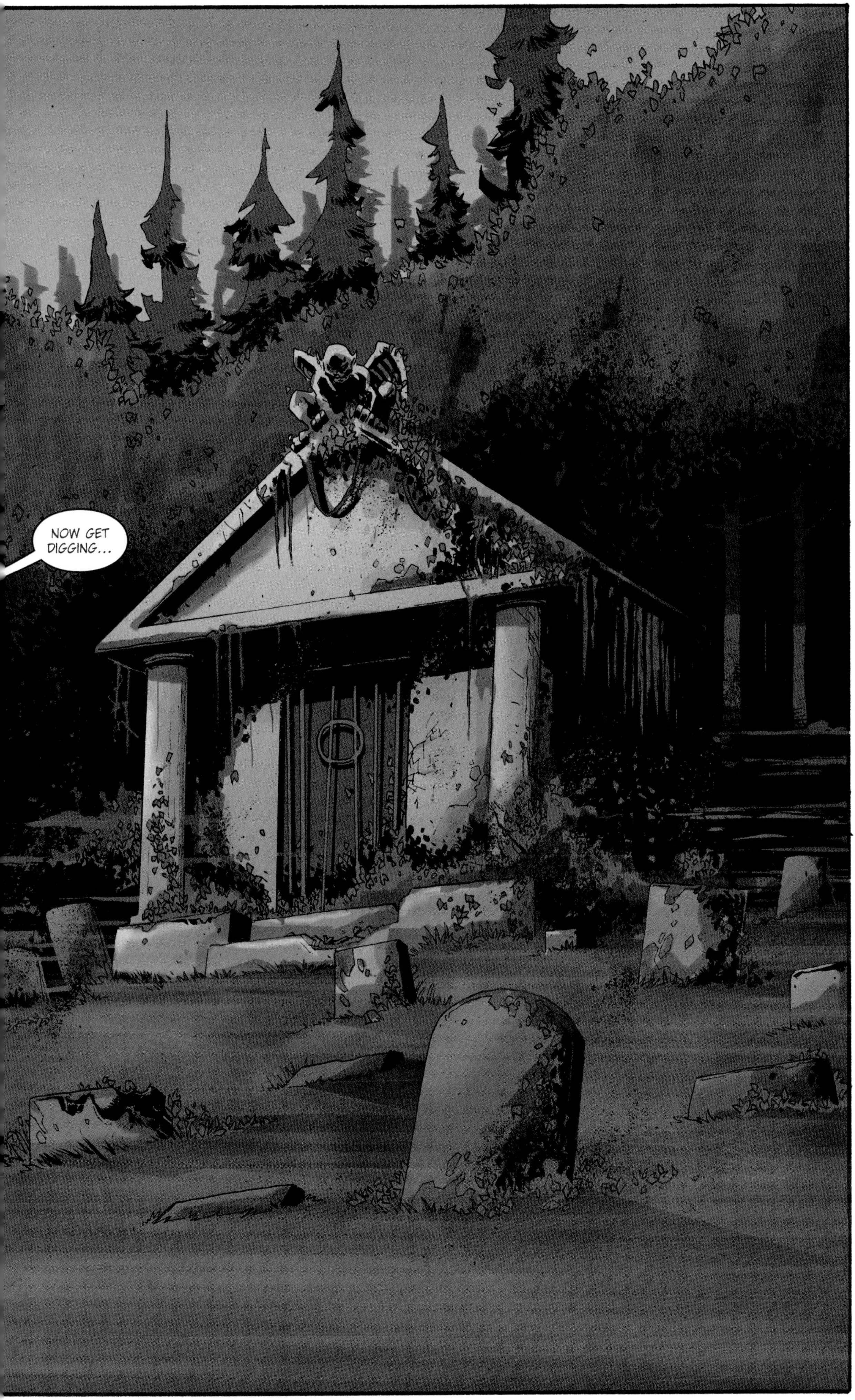
NOW GET DIGGING...

FOUR

"I did it for the town."

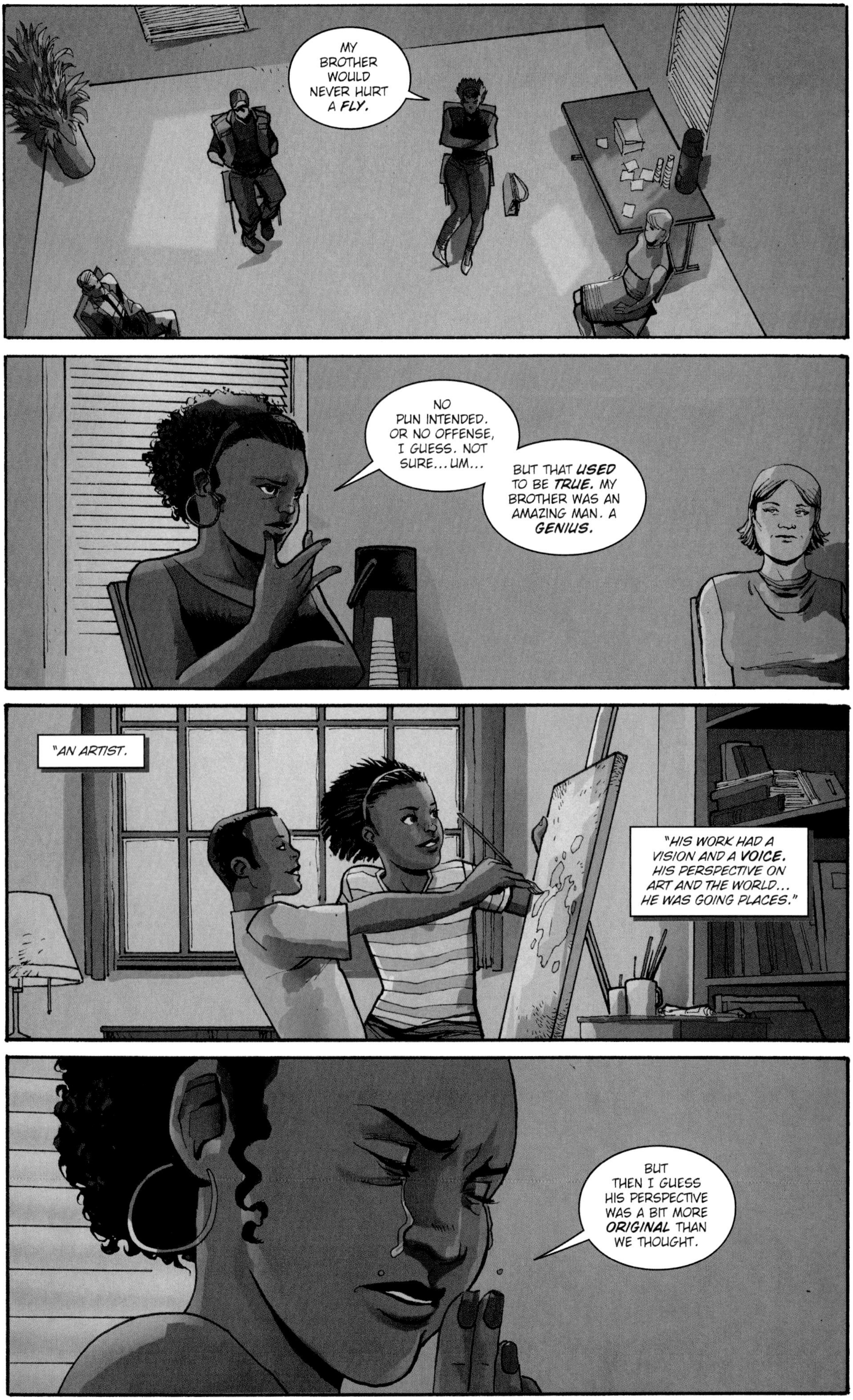
MY BROTHER WOULD NEVER HURT A FLY.
NO PUN INTENDED. OR NO OFFENSE, I GUESS. NOT SURE... UM...
BUT THAT USED TO BE TRUE. MY BROTHER WAS AN AMAZING MAN. A GENIUS.
"AN ARTIST.
"HIS WORK HAD A VISION AND A VOICE. HIS PERSPECTIVE ON ART AND THE WORLD... HE WAS GOING PLACES."
BUT THEN I GUESS HIS PERSPECTIVE WAS A BIT MORE ORIGINAL THAN WE THOUGHT.

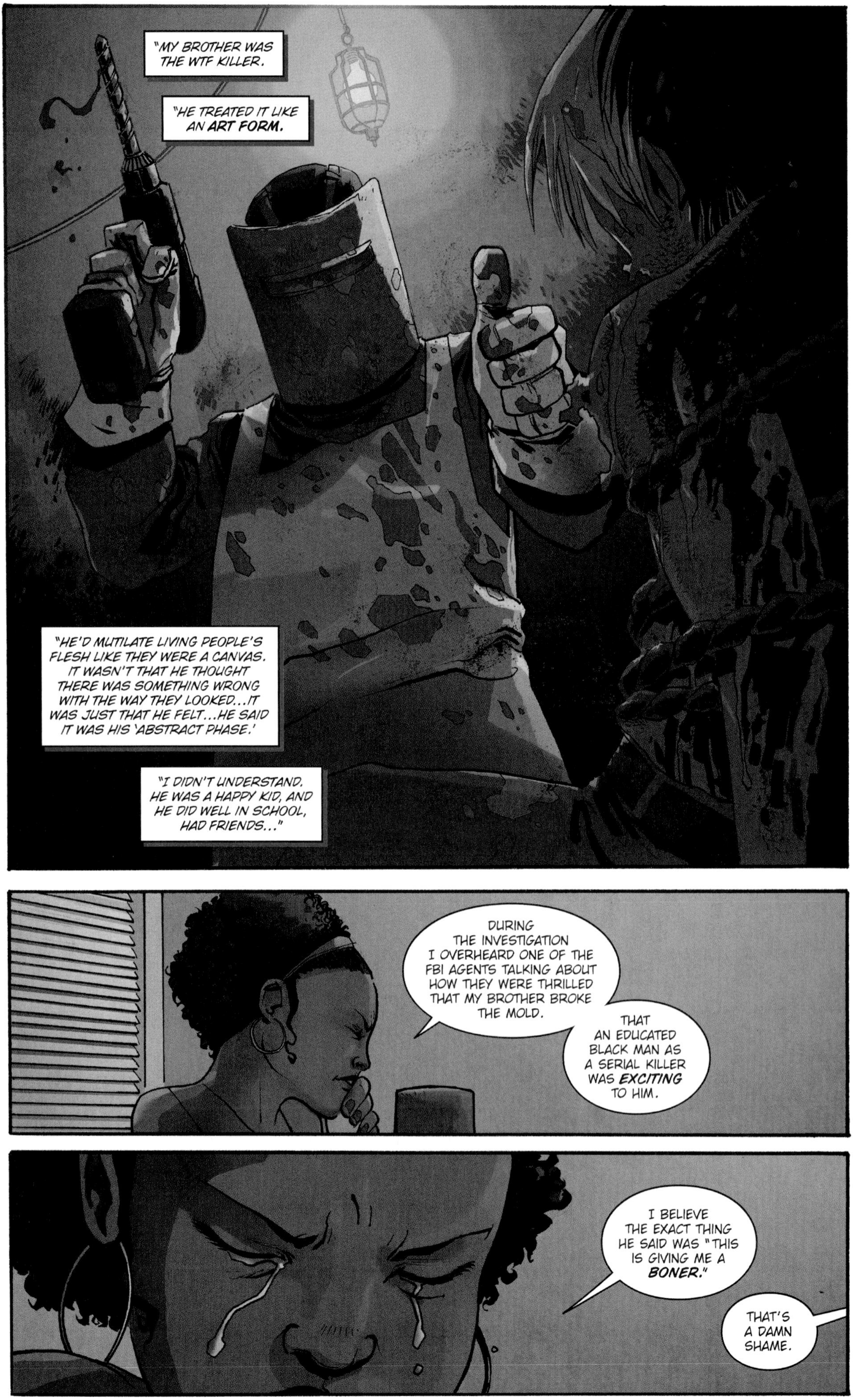
"MY BROTHER WAS THE WTF KILLER.
"HE TREATED IT LIKE AN ART FORM.
"HE'D MUTILATE LIVING PEOPLE'S FLESH LIKE THEY WERE A CANVAS. IT WASN'T THAT HE THOUGHT THERE WAS SOMETHING WRONG WITH THE WAY THEY LOOKED...IT WAS JUST THAT HE FELT...HE SAID IT WAS HIS 'ABSTRACT PHASE.'
"I DIDN'T UNDERSTAND. HE WAS A HAPPY KID, AND HE DID WELL IN SCHOOL, HAD FRIENDS..."
DURING THE INVESTIGATION I OVERHEARD ONE OF THE FBI AGENTS TALKING ABOUT HOW THEY WERE THRILLED THAT MY BROTHER BROKE THE MOLD.
THAT AN EDUCATED BLACK MAN AS A SERIAL KILLER WAS EXCITING TO HIM.
I BELIEVE THE EXACT THING HE SAID WAS "THIS IS GIVING ME A BONER."
THAT'S A DAMN SHAME.

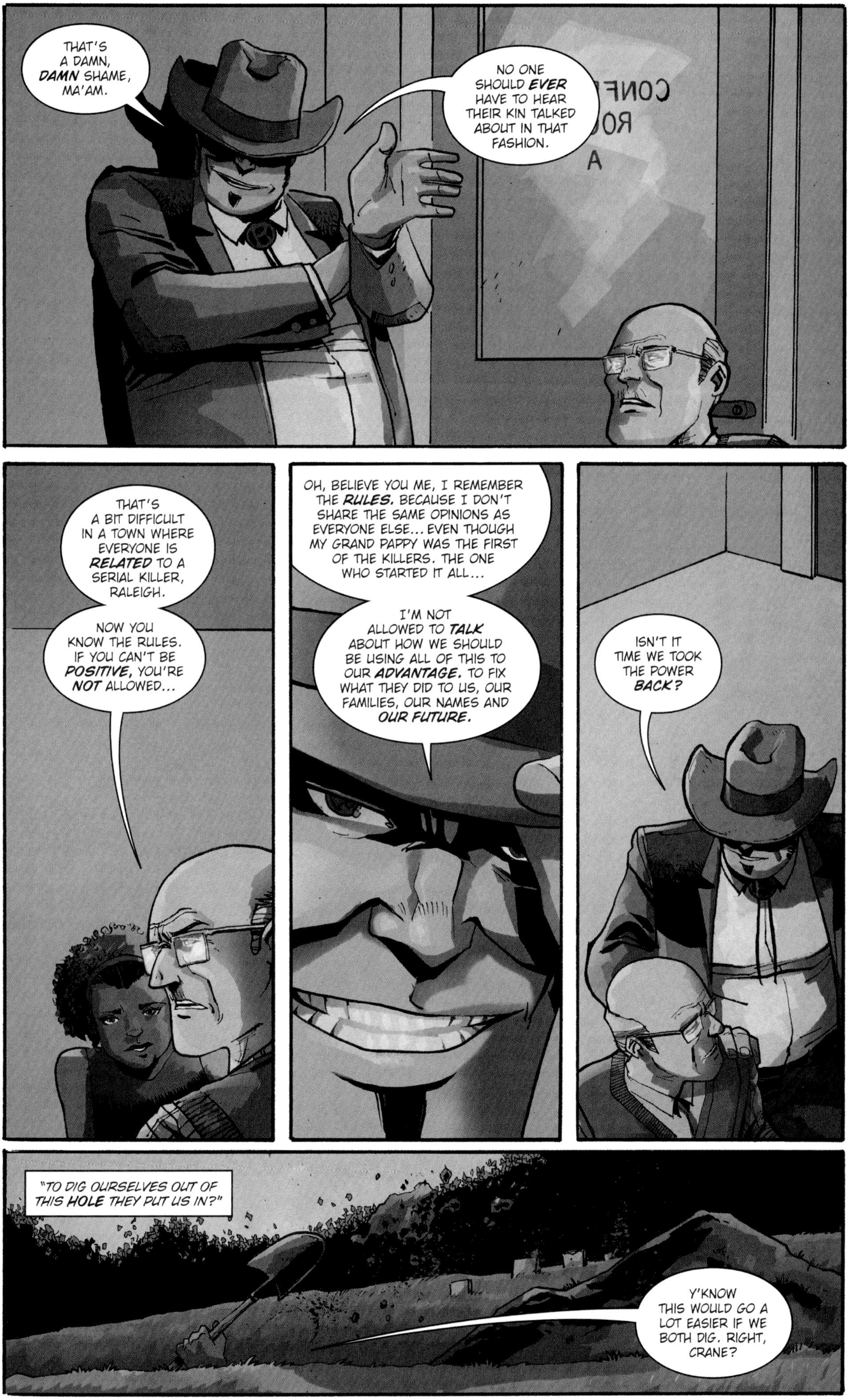
THAT'S A DAMN, DAMN SHAME, MA'AM.
NO ONE SHOULD EVER HAVE TO HEAR THEIR KIN TALKED ABOUT IN THAT FASHION.
CONF RO A
THAT'S A BIT DIFFICULT IN A TOWN WHERE EVERYONE IS RELATED TO A SERIAL KILLER, RALEIGH.
NOW YOU KNOW THE RULES. IF YOU CAN'T BE POSITIVE, YOU'RE NOT ALLOWED...
OH, BELIEVE YOU ME, I REMEMBER THE RULES. BECAUSE I DON'T SHARE THE SAME OPINIONS AS EVERYONE ELSE... EVEN THOUGH MY GRAND PAPPY WAS THE FIRST OF THE KILLERS. THE ONE WHO STARTED IT ALL...
I'M NOT ALLOWED TO TALK ABOUT HOW WE SHOULD BE USING ALL OF THIS TO OUR ADVANTAGE. TO FIX WHAT THEY DID TO US, OUR FAMILIES, OUR NAMES AND OUR FUTURE.
ISN'T IT TIME WE TOOK THE POWER BACK?
"TO DIG OURSELVES OUT OF THIS HOLE THEY PUT US IN?"
Y'KNOW THIS WOULD GO A LOT EASIER IF WE BOTH DIG. RIGHT, CRANE?

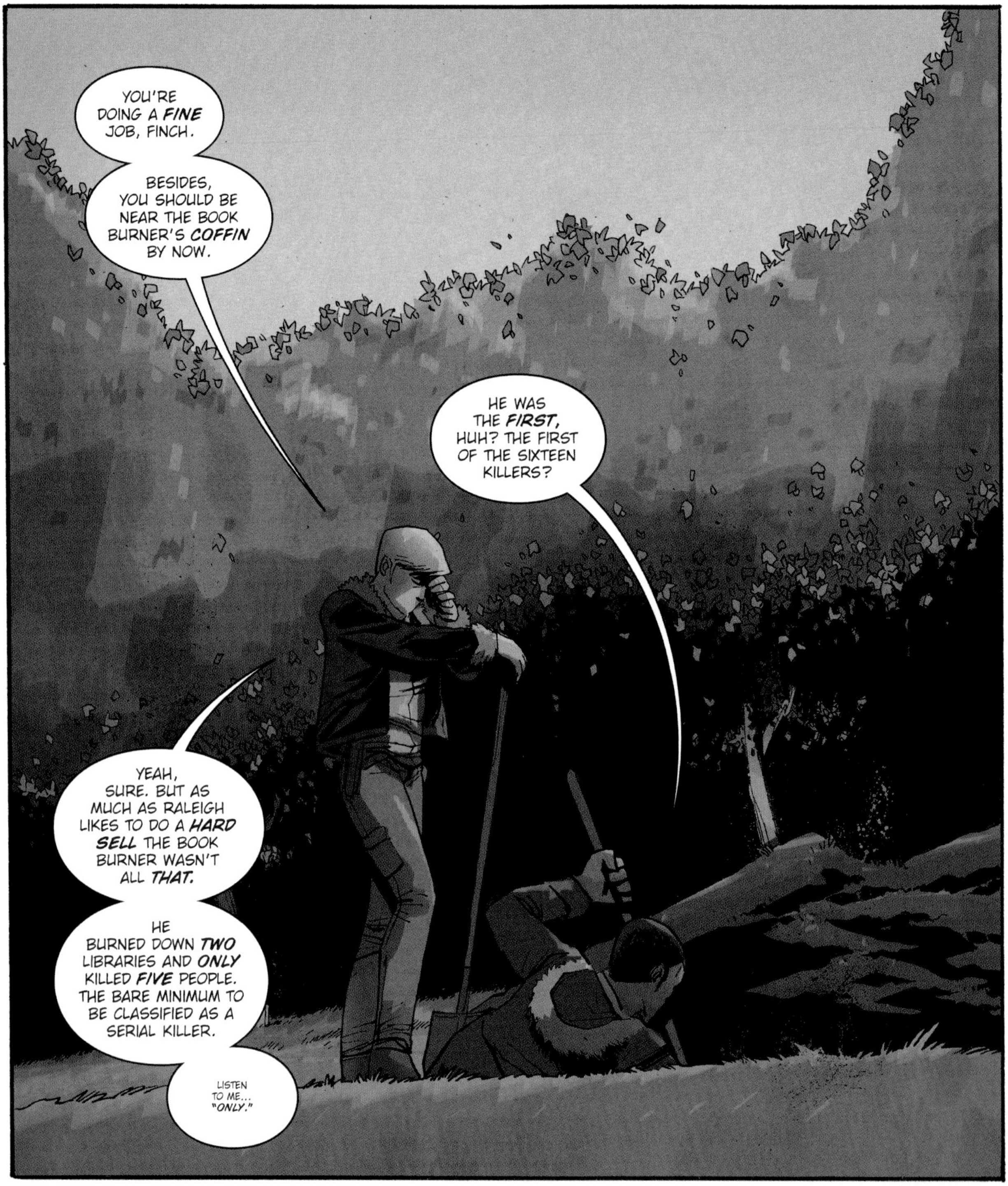
YOU'RE DOING A FINE JOB, FINCH.
BESIDES, YOU SHOULD BE NEAR THE BOOK BURNER'S COFFIN BY NOW.
HE WAS THE FIRST, HUH? THE FIRST OF THE SIXTEEN KILLERS?
YEAH, SURE. BUT AS MUCH AS RALEIGH LIKES TO DO A HARD SELL THE BOOK BURNER WASN'T ALL THAT.
HE BURNED DOWN TWO LIBRARIES AND ONLY KILLED FIVE PEOPLE. THE BARE MINIMUM TO BE CLASSIFIED AS A SERIAL KILLER.
LISTEN TO ME... "ONLY."

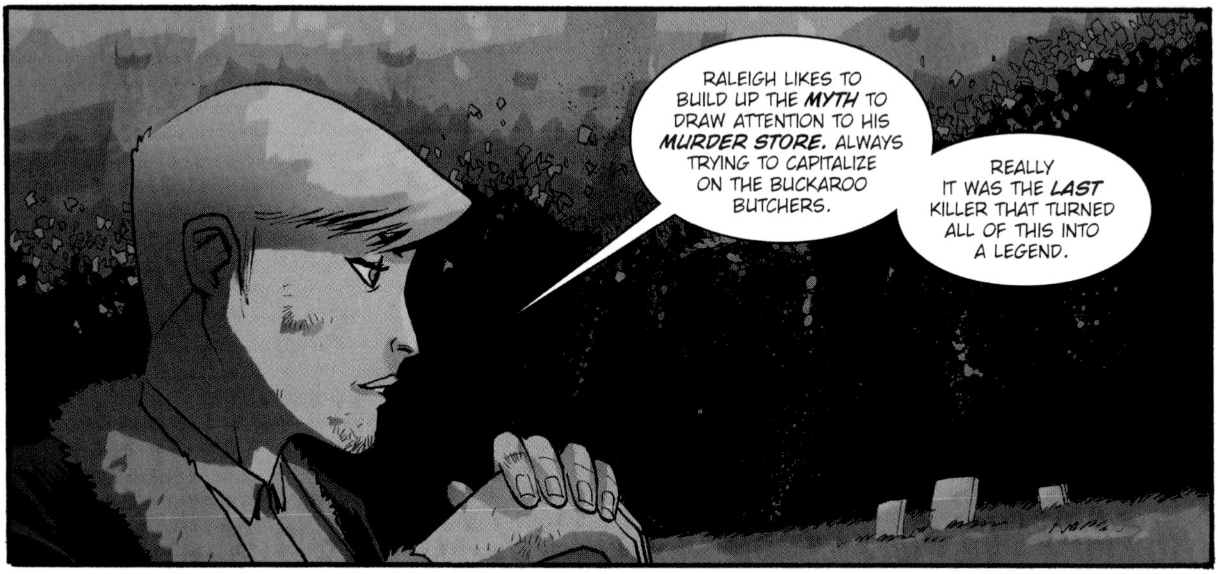
RALEIGH LIKES TO BUILD UP THE MYTH TO DRAW ATTENTION TO HIS MURDER STORE. ALWAYS TRYING TO CAPITALIZE ON THE BUCKAROO BUTCHERS.
REALLY IT WAS THE LAST KILLER THAT TURNED ALL OF THIS INTO A LEGEND.

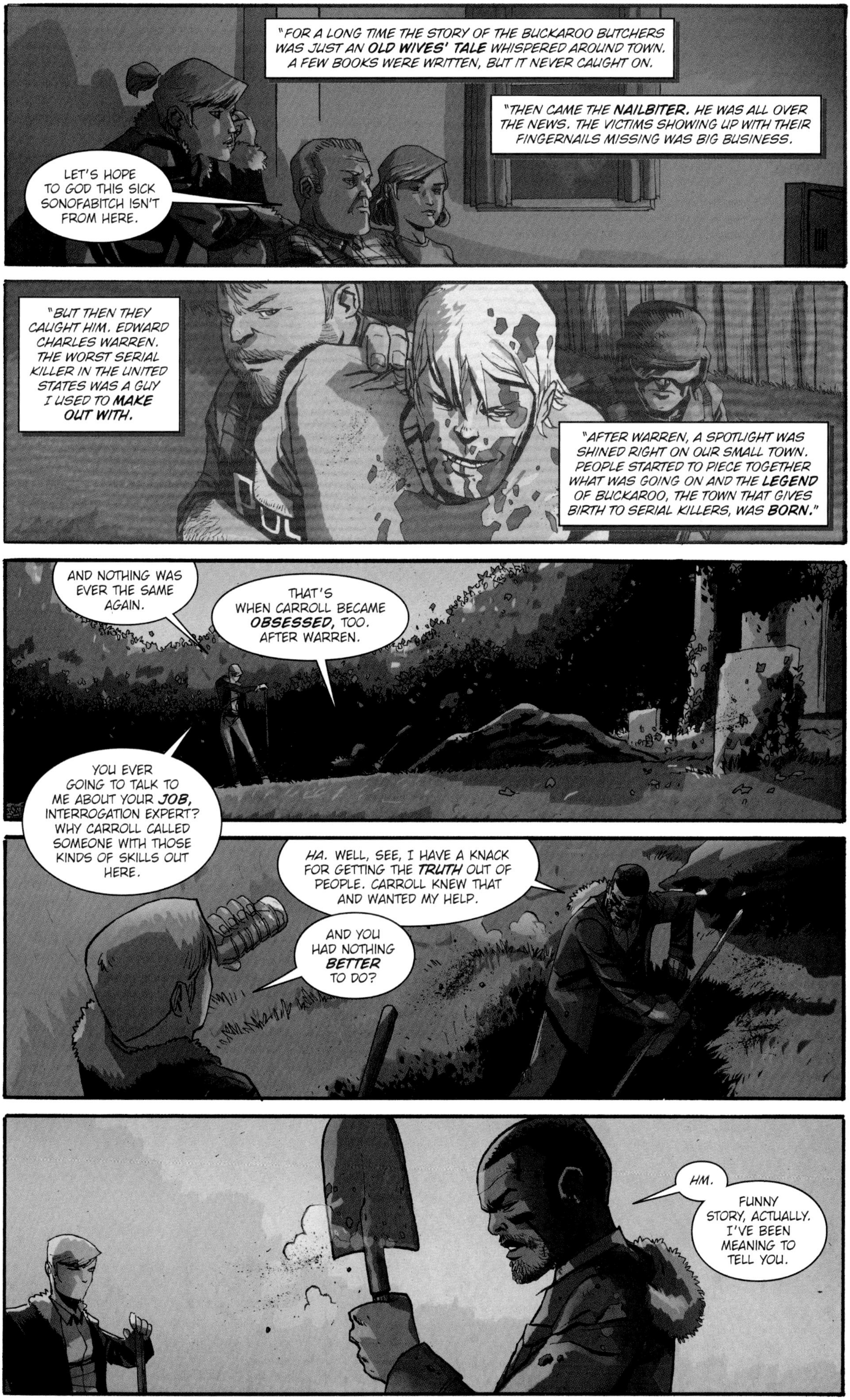
"FOR A LONG TIME THE STORY OF THE BUCKAROO BUTCHERS WAS JUST AN **OLD WIVES' TALE** WHISPERED AROUND TOWN. A FEW BOOKS WERE WRITTEN, BUT IT NEVER CAUGHT ON.
"THEN CAME THE **NAILBITER.** HE WAS ALL OVER THE NEWS. THE VICTIMS SHOWING UP WITH THEIR FINGERNAILS MISSING WAS BIG BUSINESS.
LET'S HOPE TO GOD THIS SICK SONOFABITCH ISN'T FROM HERE.
"BUT THEN THEY CAUGHT HIM. EDWARD CHARLES WARREN. THE WORST SERIAL KILLER IN THE UNITED STATES WAS A GUY I USED TO **MAKE OUT WITH.**
"AFTER WARREN, A SPOTLIGHT WAS SHINED RIGHT ON OUR SMALL TOWN. PEOPLE STARTED TO PIECE TOGETHER WHAT WAS GOING ON AND THE **LEGEND** OF BUCKAROO, THE TOWN THAT GIVES BIRTH TO SERIAL KILLERS, WAS **BORN.**"
AND NOTHING WAS EVER THE SAME AGAIN.
THAT'S WHEN CARROLL BECAME ***OBSESSED,*** TOO. AFTER WARREN.
YOU EVER GOING TO TALK TO ME ABOUT YOUR ***JOB,*** INTERROGATION EXPERT? WHY CARROLL CALLED SOMEONE WITH THOSE KINDS OF SKILLS OUT HERE.
HA. WELL, SEE, I HAVE A KNACK FOR GETTING THE ***TRUTH*** OUT OF PEOPLE. CARROLL KNEW THAT AND WANTED MY HELP.
AND YOU HAD NOTHING ***BETTER*** TO DO?
HM.
FUNNY STORY, ACTUALLY. I'VE BEEN MEANING TO TELL YOU.

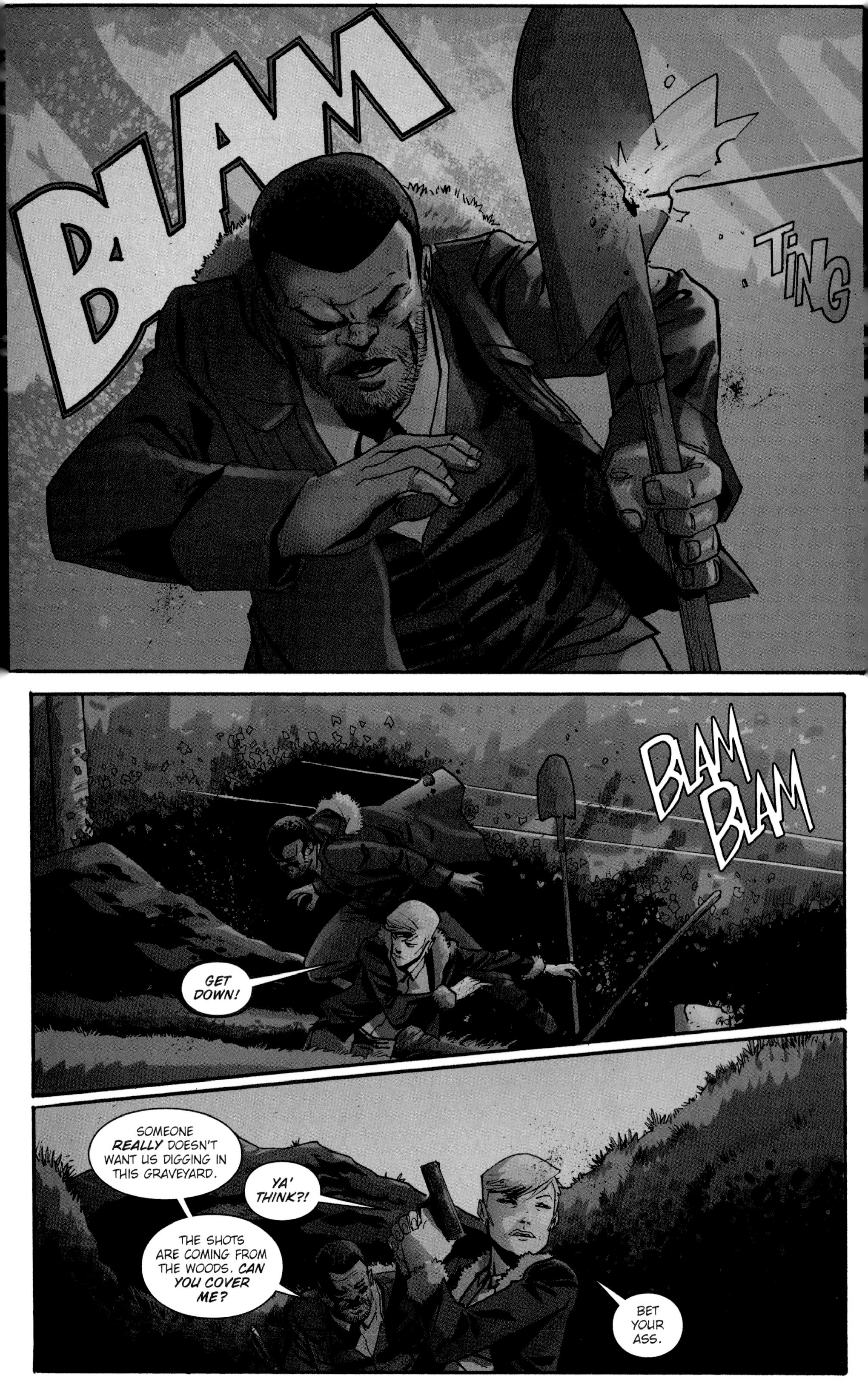
BLAM
TING
BLAM BLAM
GET DOWN!
SOMEONE REALLY DOESN'T WANT US DIGGING IN THIS GRAVEYARD.
YA' THINK?!
THE SHOTS ARE COMING FROM THE WOODS. CAN YOU COVER ME?
BET YOUR ASS.

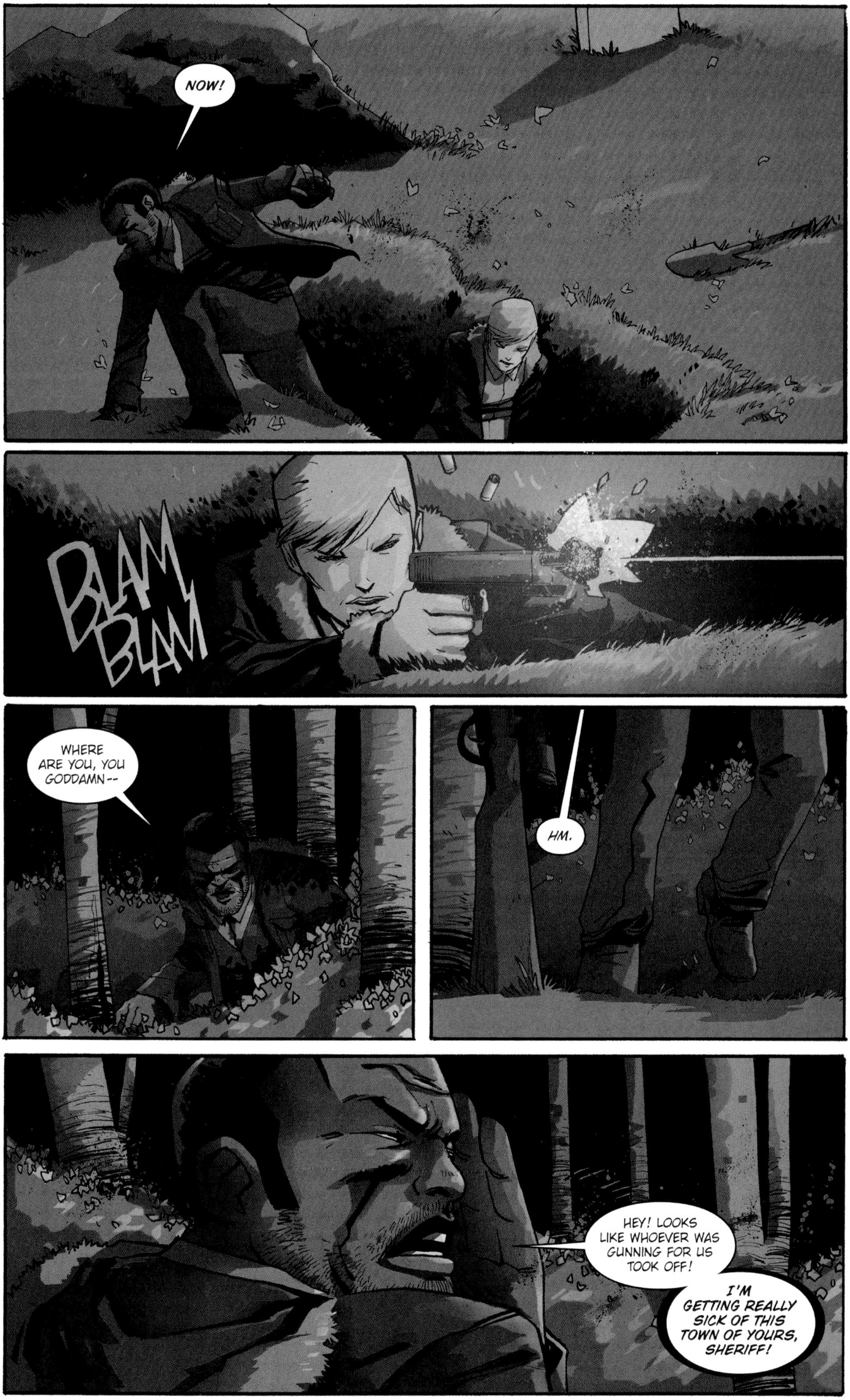
NOW!
BLAM BLAM
WHERE ARE YOU, YOU GODDAMN--
HM.
HEY! LOOKS LIKE WHOEVER WAS GUNNING FOR US TOOK OFF!
I'M GETTING REALLY SICK OF THIS TOWN OF YOURS, SHERIFF!

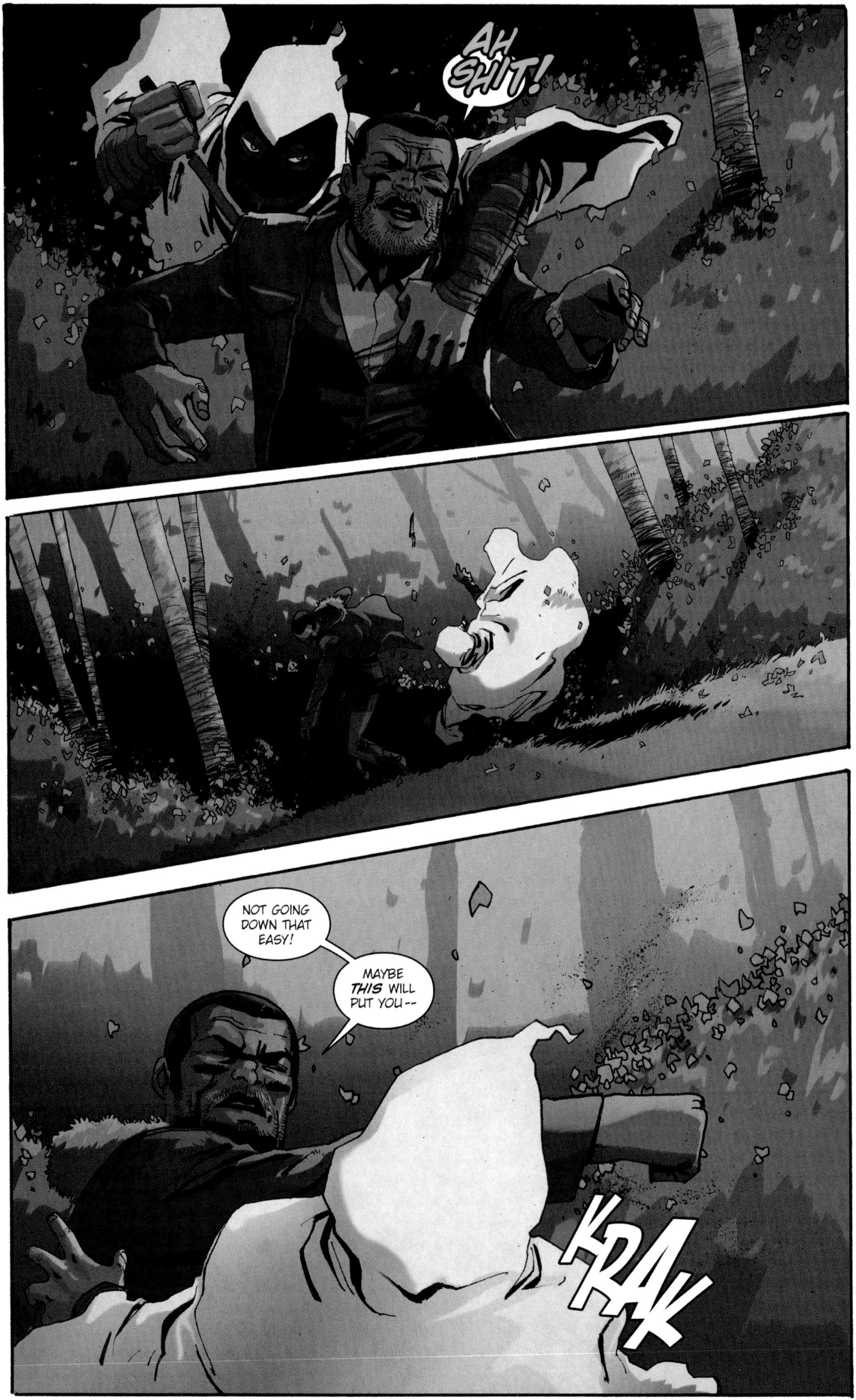
AH SHIT!
NOT GOING DOWN THAT EASY!
MAYBE THIS WILL PUT YOU--
KRAK

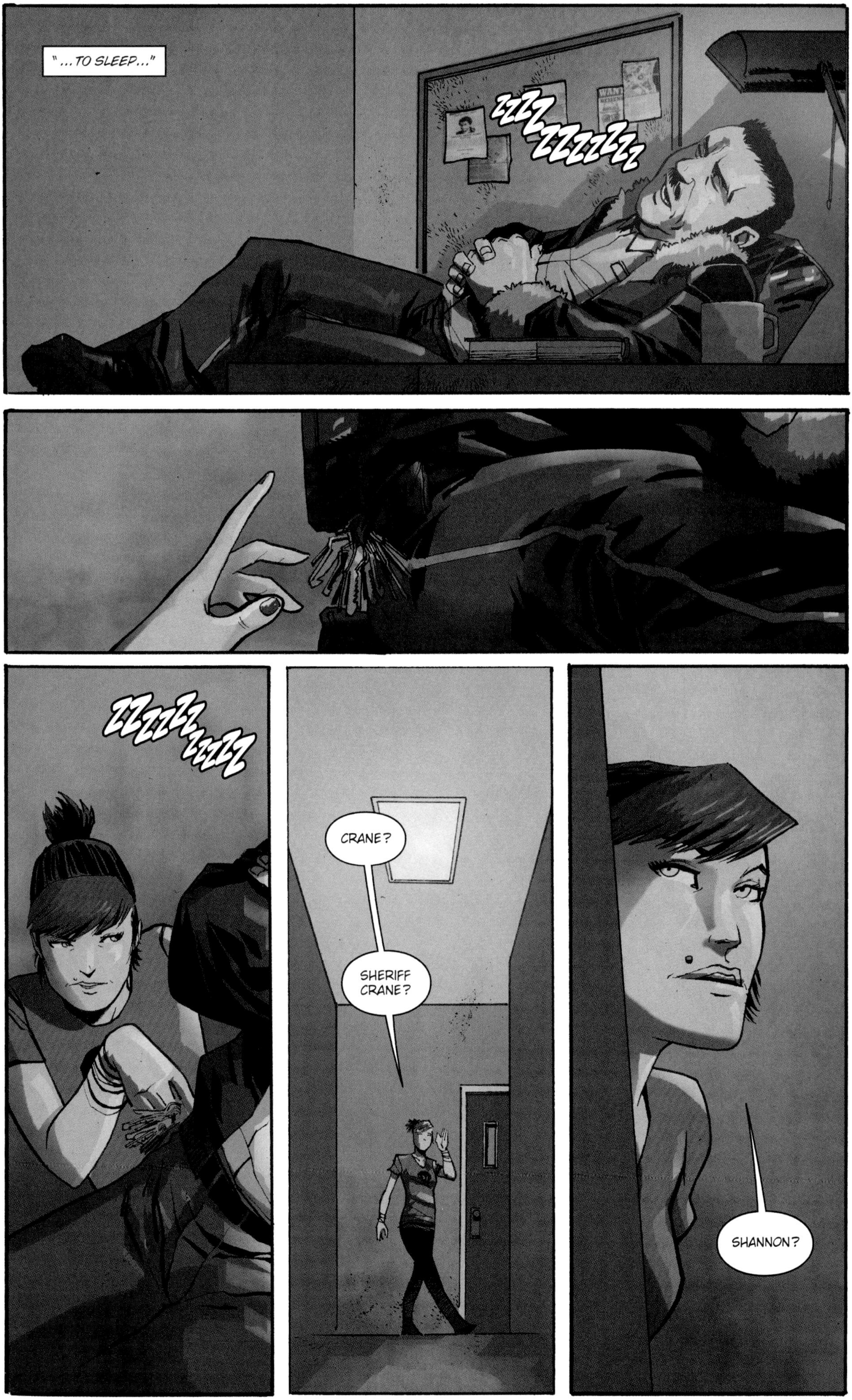
"...TO SLEEP..."
ZZZZZZZZZZZZ
ZZZZZZZZZZ
CRANE?
SHERIFF CRANE?
SHANNON?

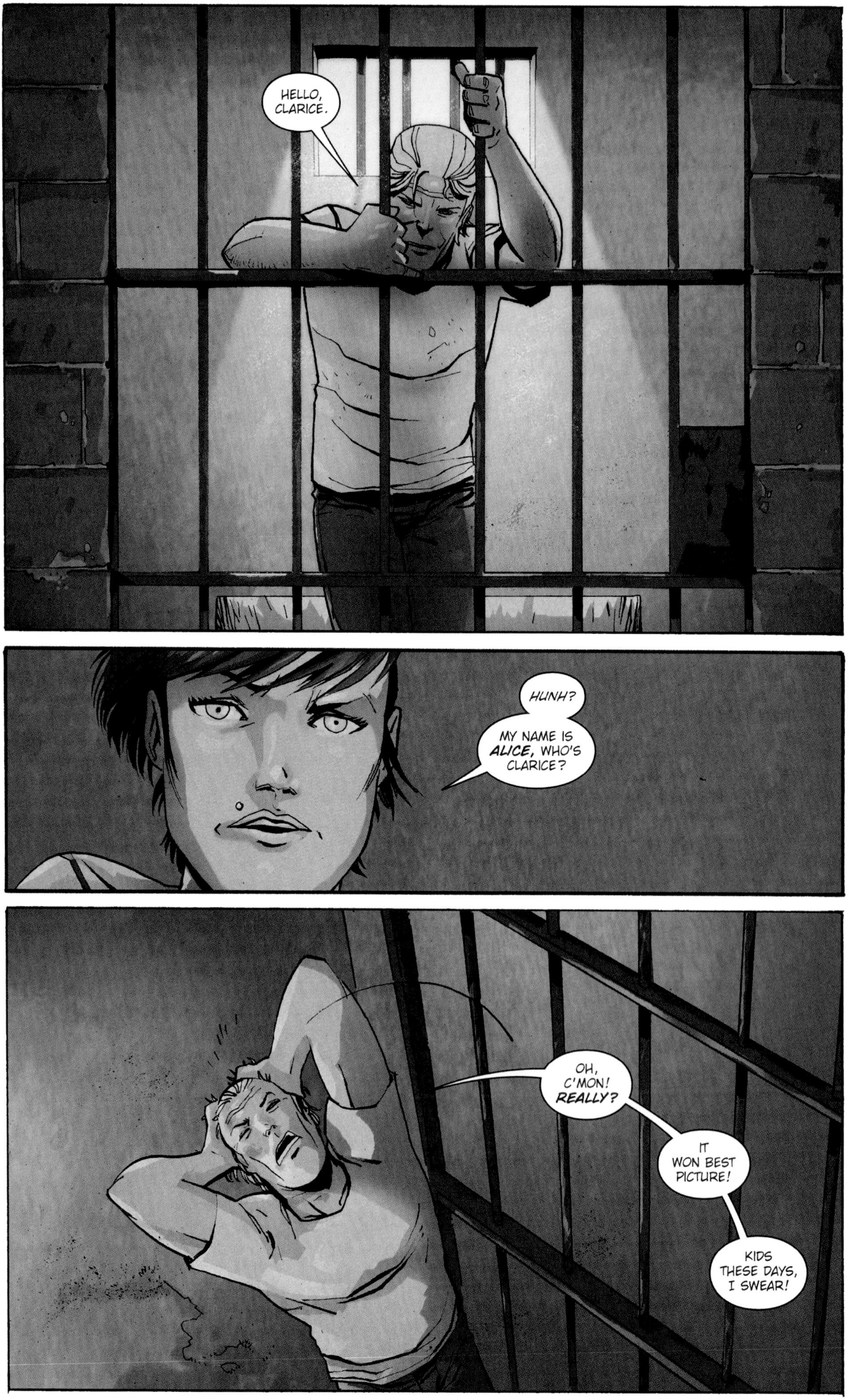
HELLO, CLARICE.
HUNH?
MY NAME IS ALICE, WHO'S CLARICE?
OH, C'MON! REALLY?
IT WON BEST PICTURE!
KIDS THESE DAYS, I SWEAR!

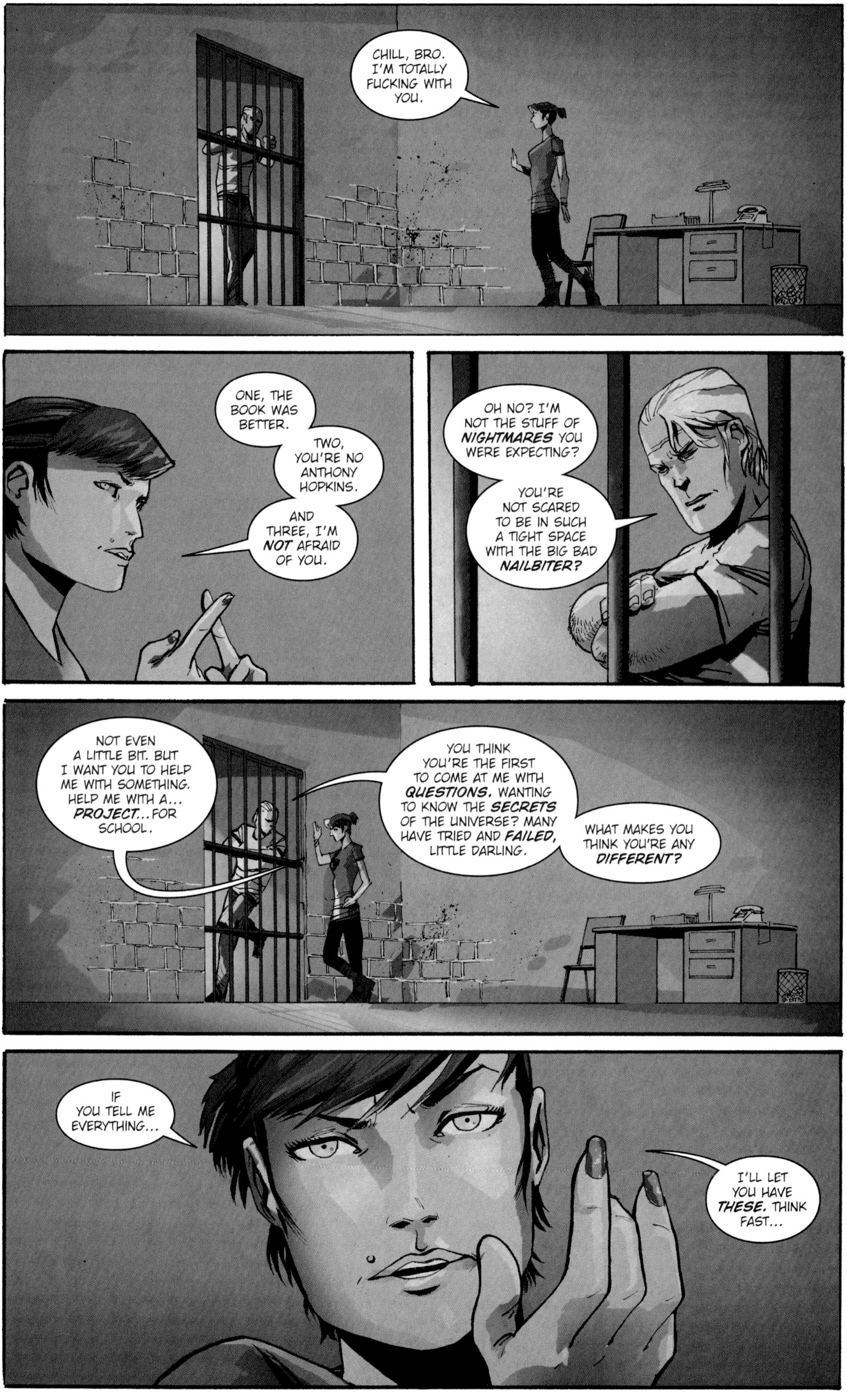
CHILL, BRO. I'M TOTALLY FUCKING WITH YOU.
ONE, THE BOOK WAS BETTER.
TWO, YOU'RE NO ANTHONY HOPKINS.
AND THREE, I'M NOT AFRAID OF YOU.
OH NO? I'M NOT THE STUFF OF NIGHTMARES YOU WERE EXPECTING?
YOU'RE NOT SCARED TO BE IN SUCH A TIGHT SPACE WITH THE BIG BAD NAILBITER?
NOT EVEN A LITTLE BIT. BUT I WANT YOU TO HELP ME WITH SOMETHING. HELP ME WITH A... PROJECT... FOR SCHOOL.
YOU THINK YOU'RE THE FIRST TO COME AT ME WITH QUESTIONS. WANTING TO KNOW THE SECRETS OF THE UNIVERSE? MANY HAVE TRIED AND FAILED, LITTLE DARLING.
WHAT MAKES YOU THINK YOU'RE ANY DIFFERENT?
IF YOU TELL ME EVERYTHING...
I'LL LET YOU HAVE THESE. THINK FAST...

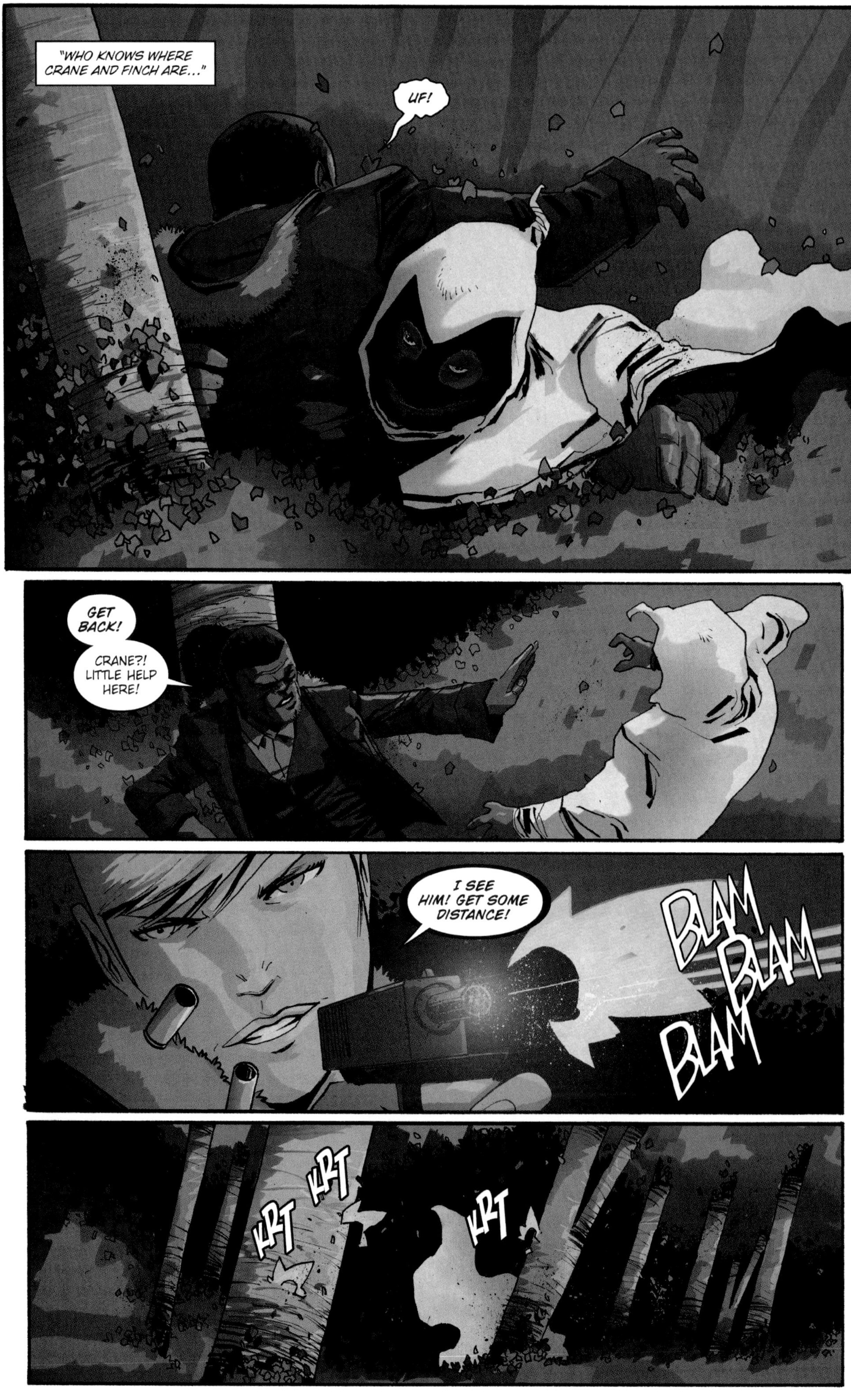
"WHO KNOWS WHERE CRANE AND FINCH ARE..."
UF!
GET BACK!
CRANE?! LITTLE HELP HERE!
I SEE HIM! GET SOME DISTANCE!
BLAM BLAM BLAM
KRT KRT
KRT

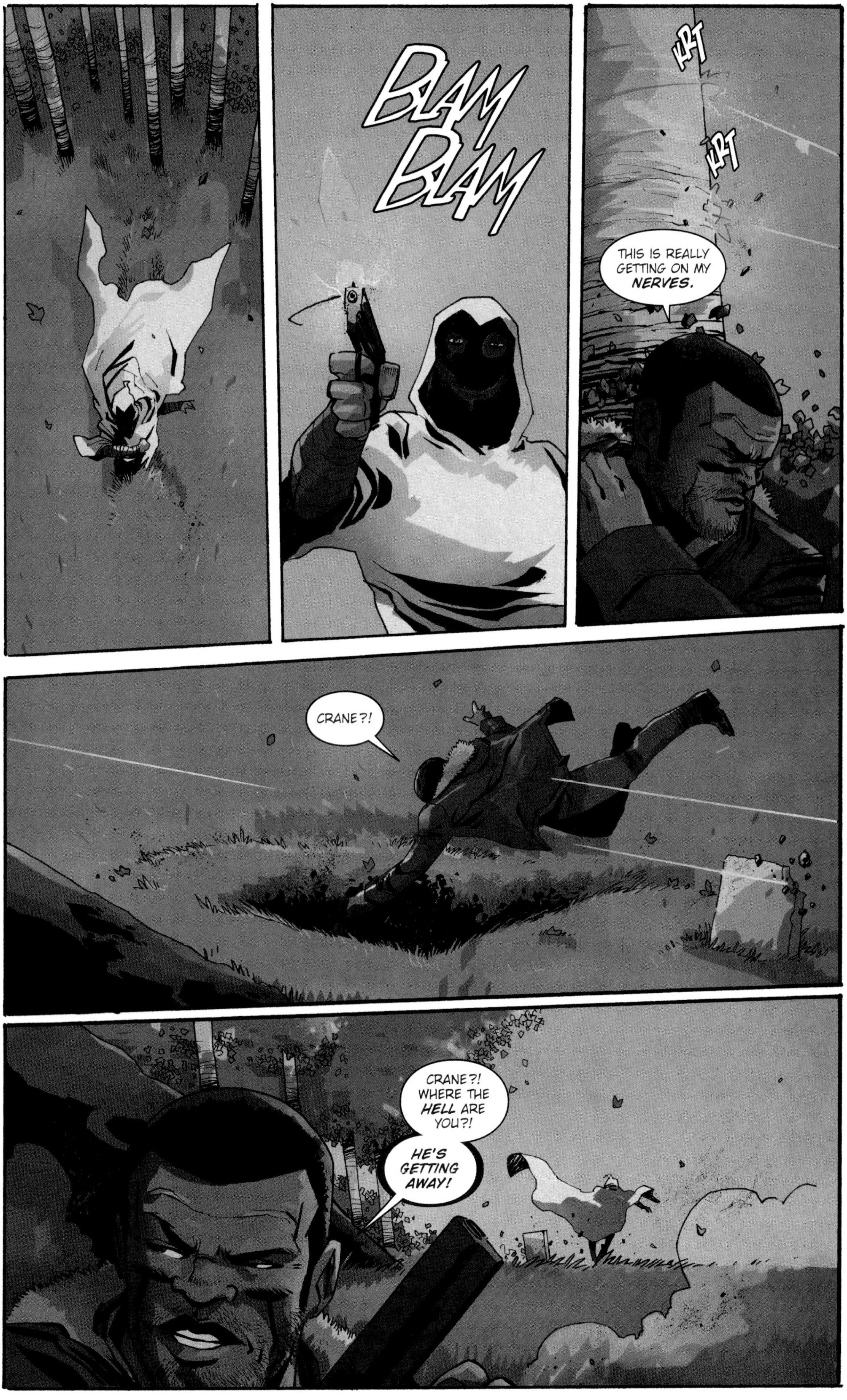
BLAM
BLAM
KRT
KRT
THIS IS REALLY GETTING ON MY NERVES.
CRANE?!
CRANE?! WHERE THE HELL ARE YOU?!
HE'S GETTING AWAY!

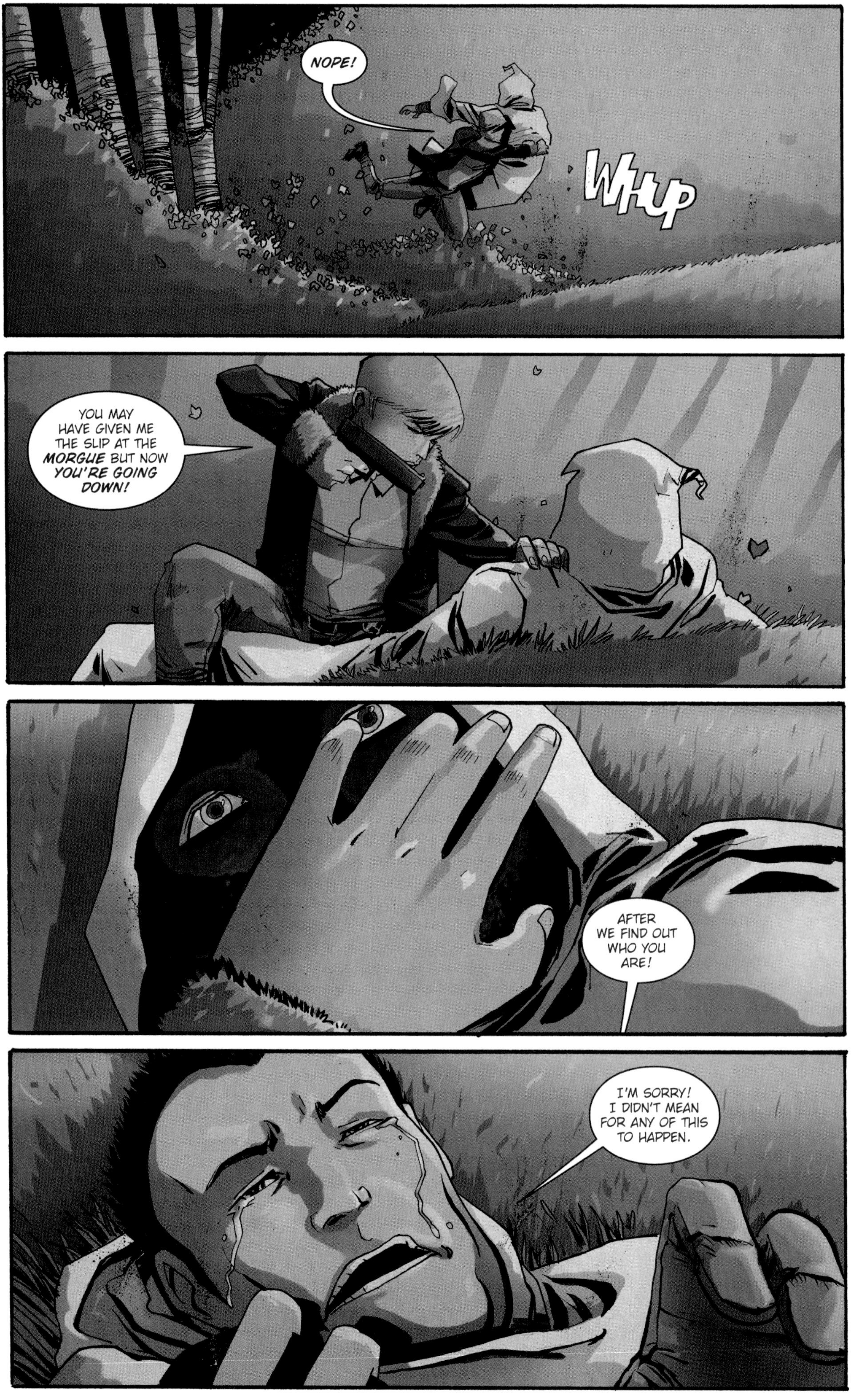
NOPE!
WHUP
YOU MAY HAVE GIVEN ME THE SLIP AT THE MORGUE BUT NOW YOU'RE GOING DOWN!
AFTER WE FIND OUT WHO YOU ARE!
I'M SORRY! I DIDN'T MEAN FOR ANY OF THIS TO HAPPEN.

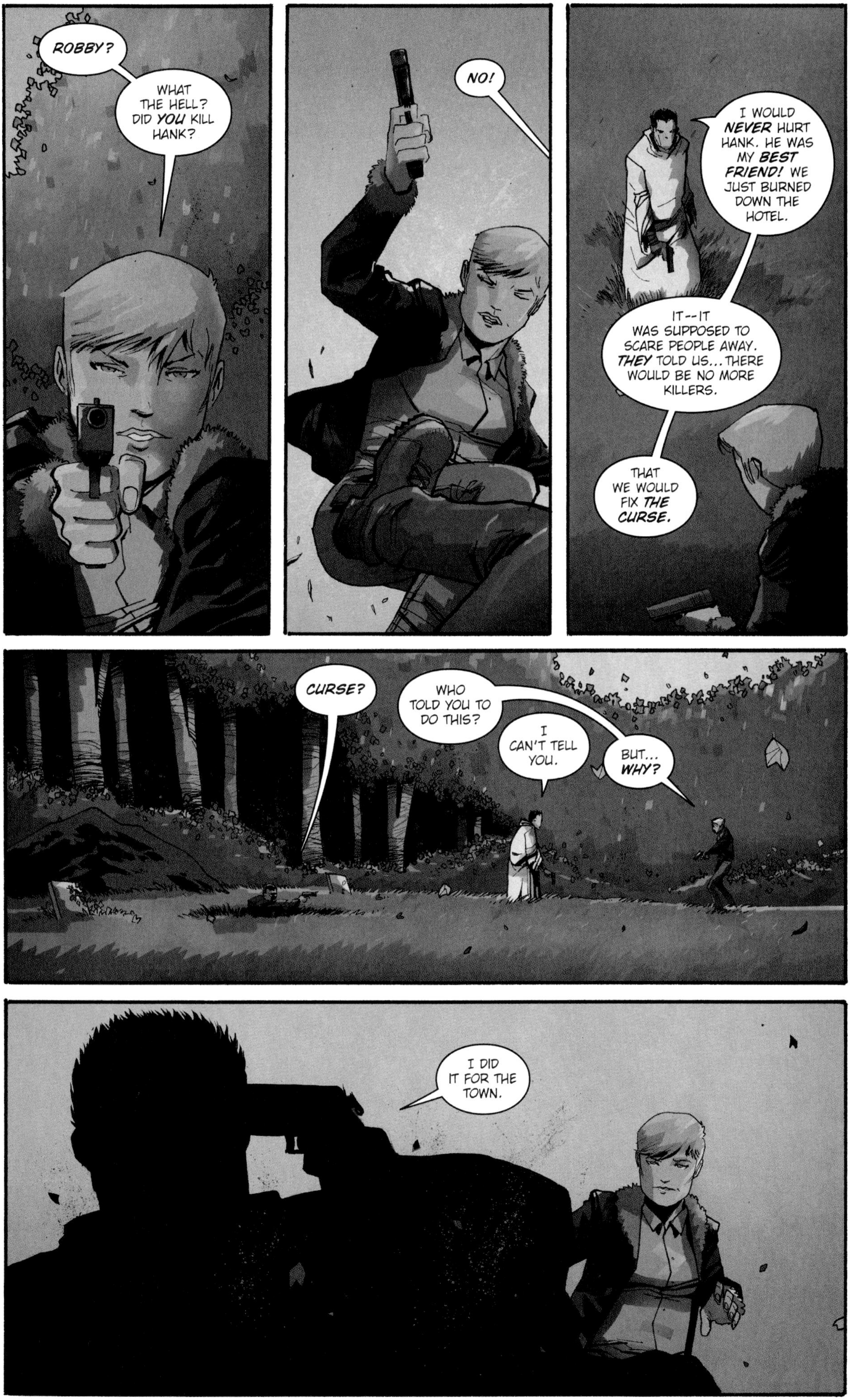
ROBBY?
WHAT THE HELL? DID YOU KILL HANK?
NO!
I WOULD NEVER HURT HANK. HE WAS MY BEST FRIEND! WE JUST BURNED DOWN THE HOTEL.
IT--IT WAS SUPPOSED TO SCARE PEOPLE AWAY. THEY TOLD US... THERE WOULD BE NO MORE KILLERS.
THAT WE WOULD FIX THE CURSE.
CURSE?
WHO TOLD YOU TO DO THIS?
I CAN'T TELL YOU.
BUT... WHY?
I DID IT FOR THE TOWN.

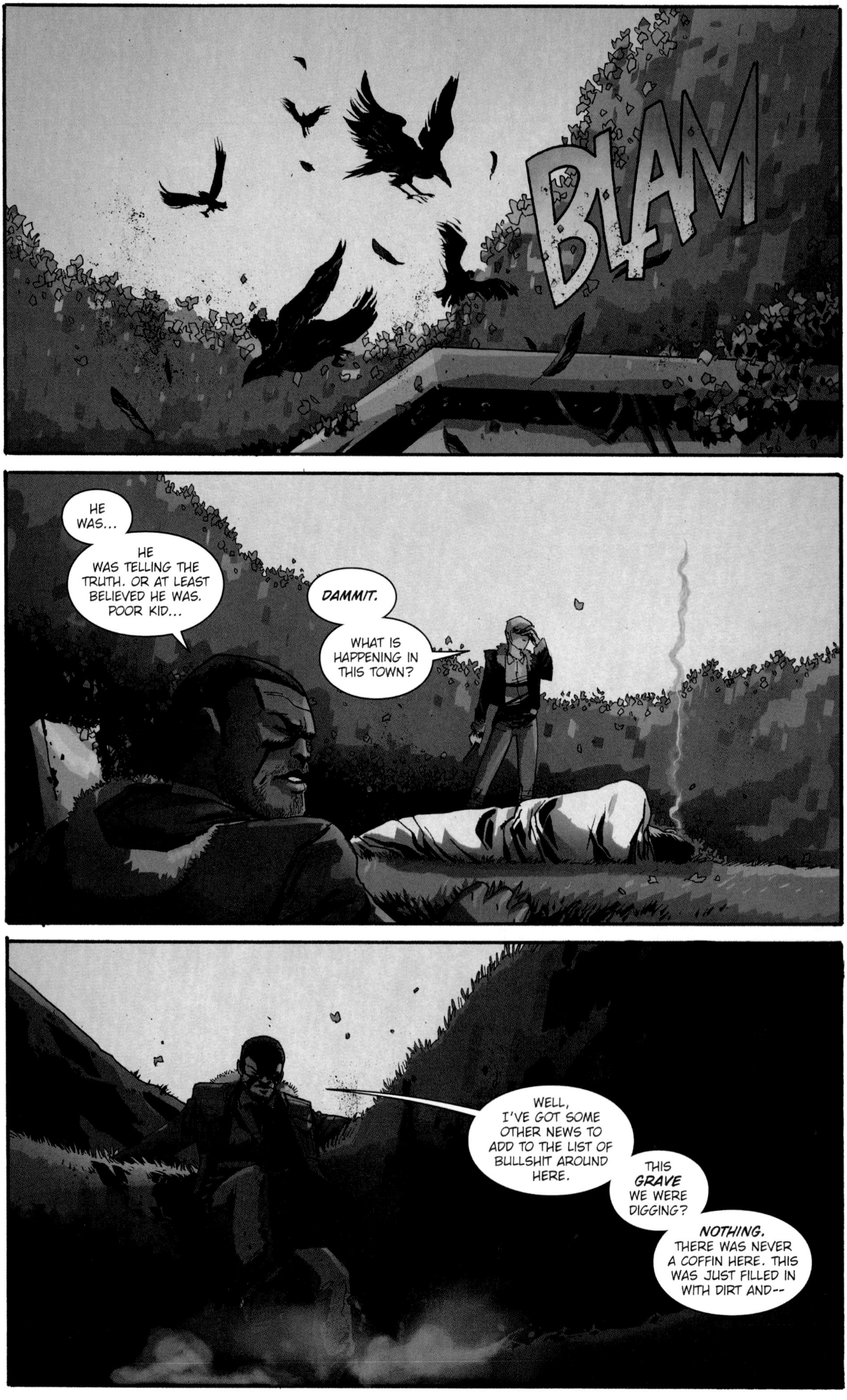
BLAM
HE WAS...
HE WAS TELLING THE TRUTH. OR AT LEAST BELIEVED HE WAS. POOR KID...
DAMMIT.
WHAT IS HAPPENING IN THIS TOWN?
WELL, I'VE GOT SOME OTHER NEWS TO ADD TO THE LIST OF BULLSHIT AROUND HERE.
THIS GRAVE WE WERE DIGGING?
NOTHING. THERE WAS NEVER A COFFIN HERE. THIS WAS JUST FILLED IN WITH DIRT AND--

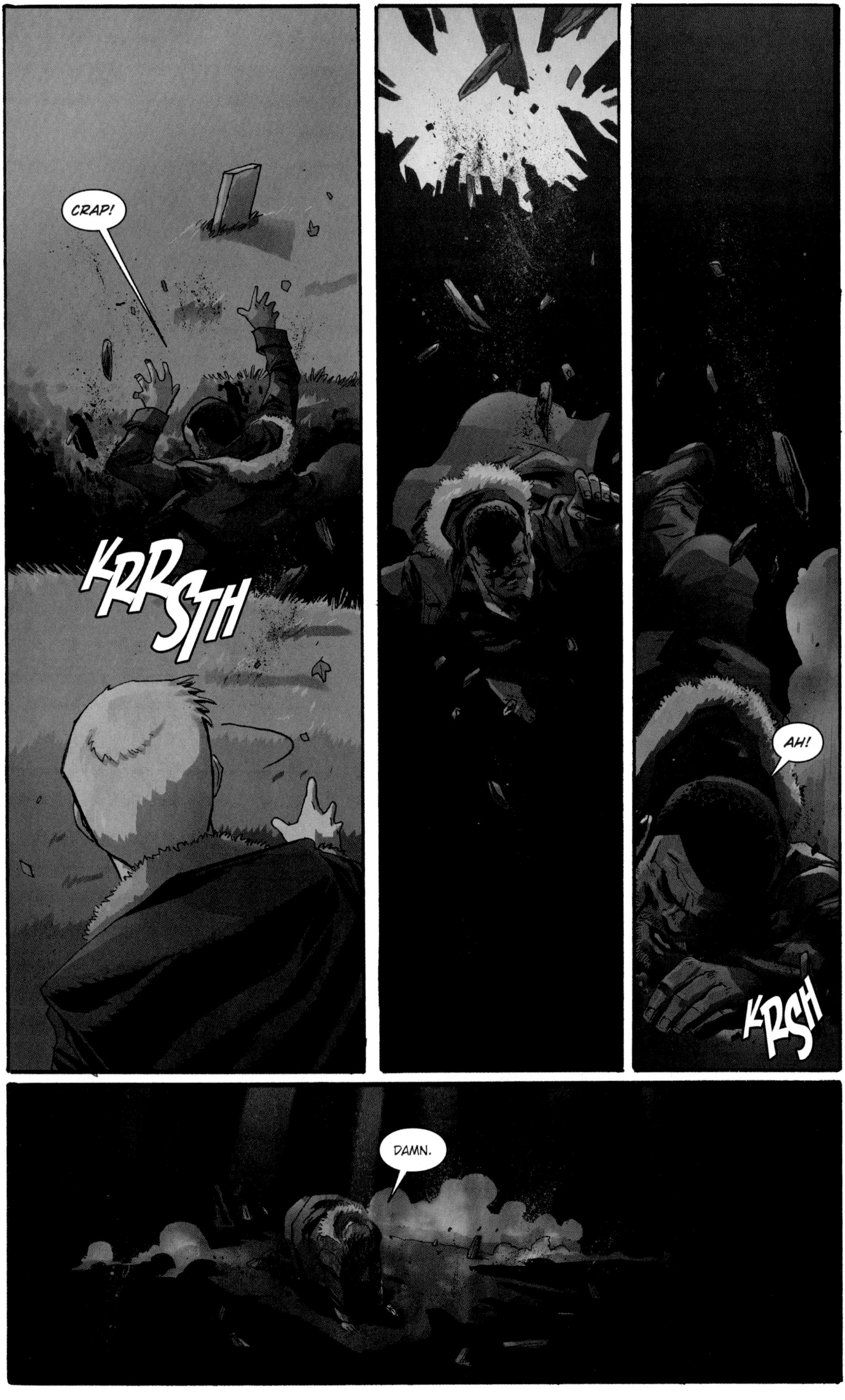
CRAP!
KRRSTH
AH!
KRSH
DAMN.

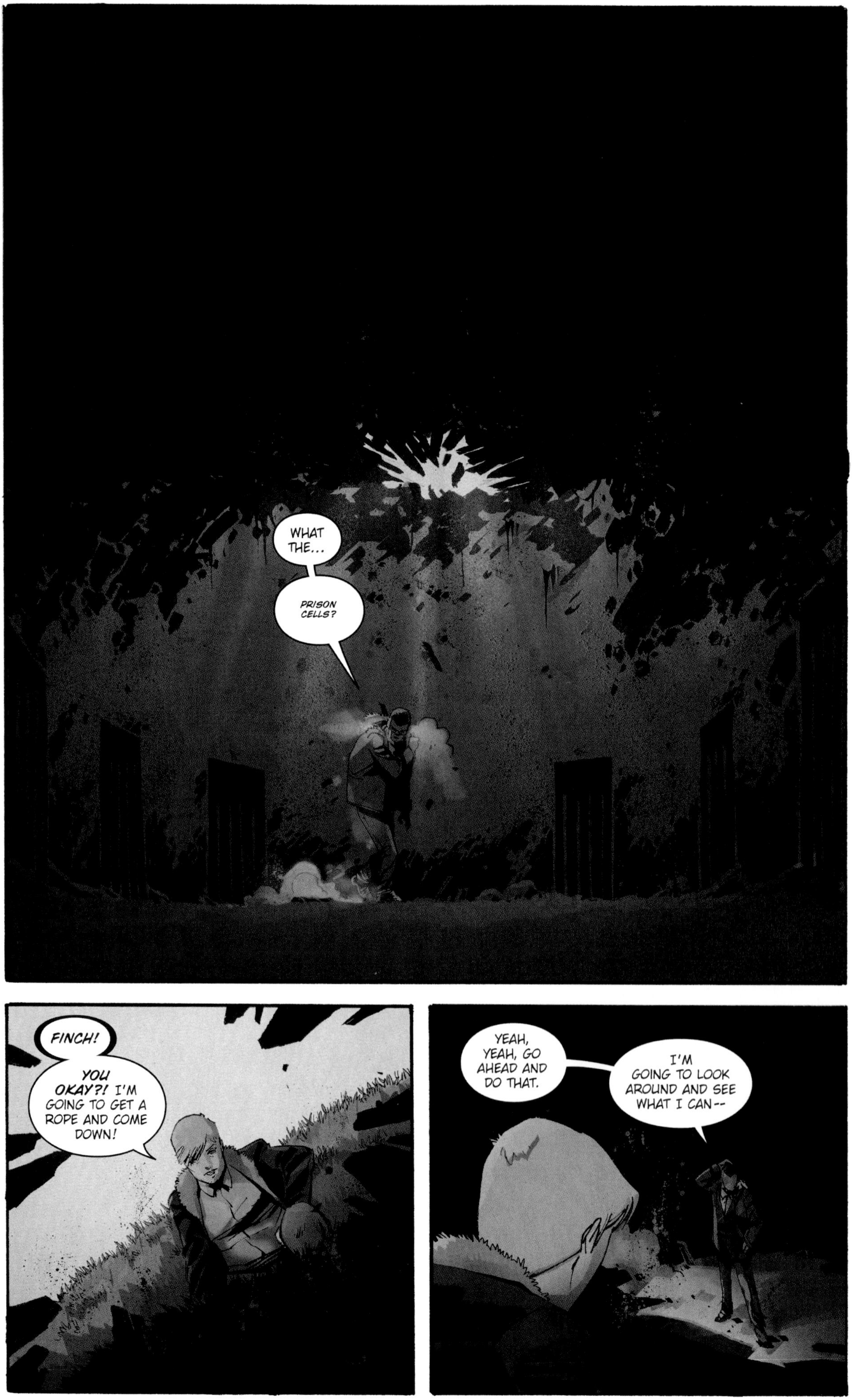
WHAT THE...
PRISON CELLS?
FINCH!
YOU OKAY?! I'M GOING TO GET A ROPE AND COME DOWN!
YEAH, YEAH, GO AHEAD AND DO THAT.
I'M GOING TO LOOK AROUND AND SEE WHAT I CAN--

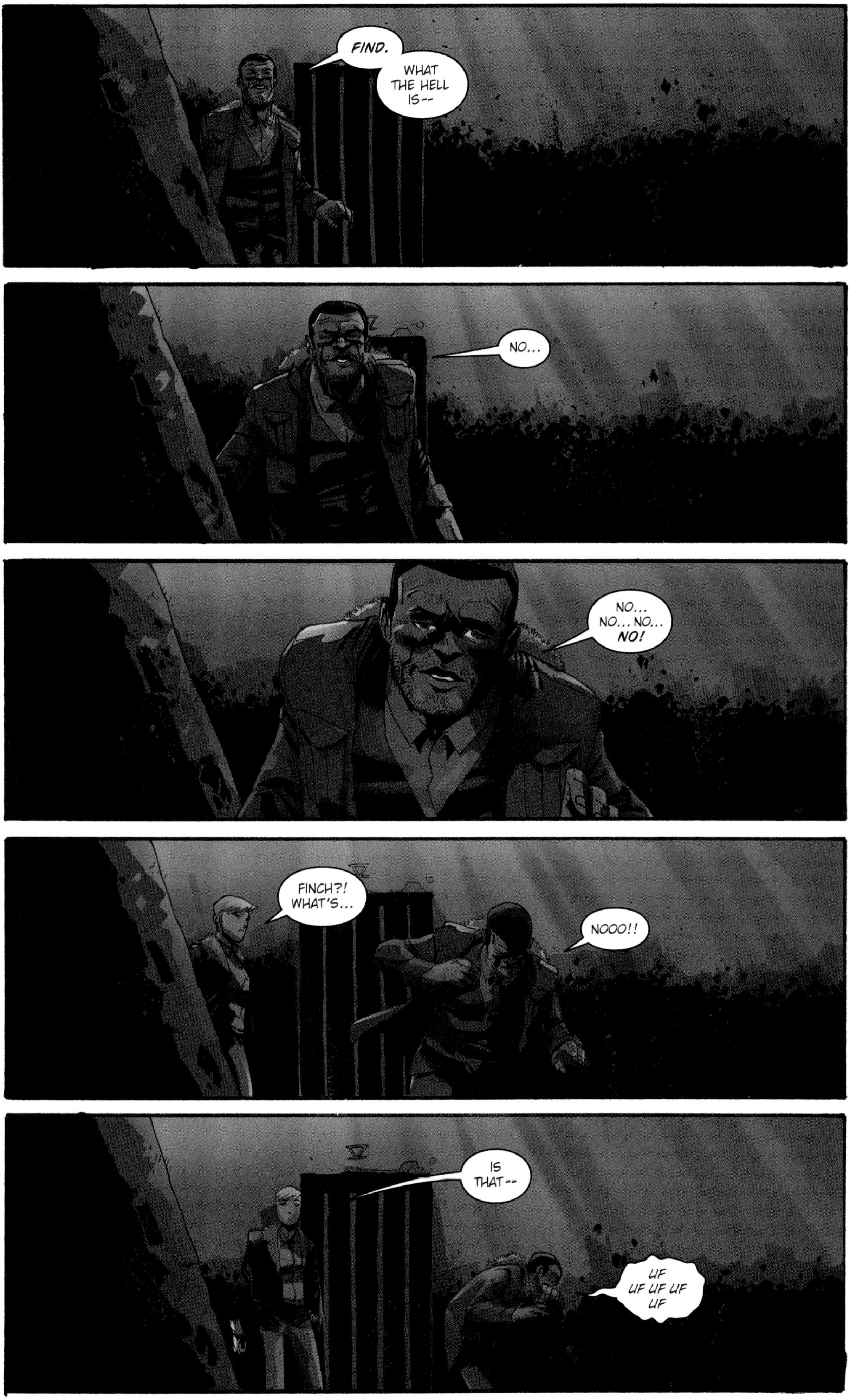
FIND.
WHAT THE HELL IS--
NO...
NO... NO... NO... NO!
FINCH?! WHAT'S...
NOOO!!
IS THAT--
UF UF UF UF UF

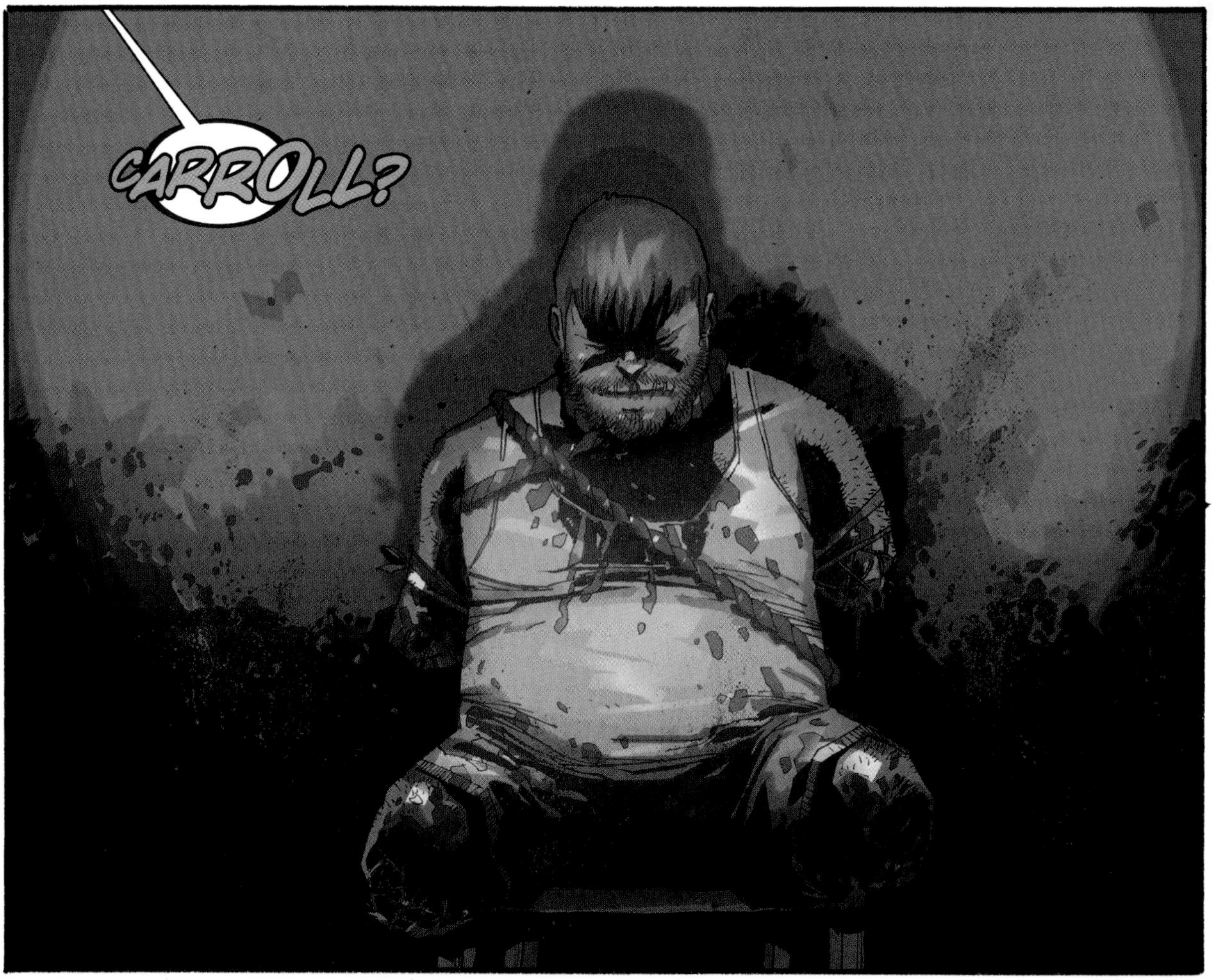
CARROLL?

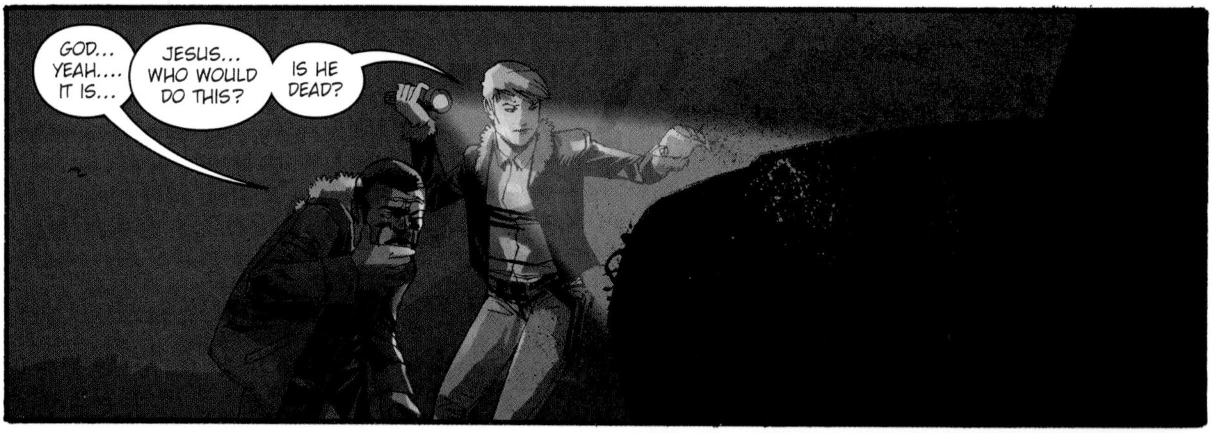
GOD... YEAH.... IT IS...
JESUS... WHO WOULD DO THIS?
IS HE DEAD?

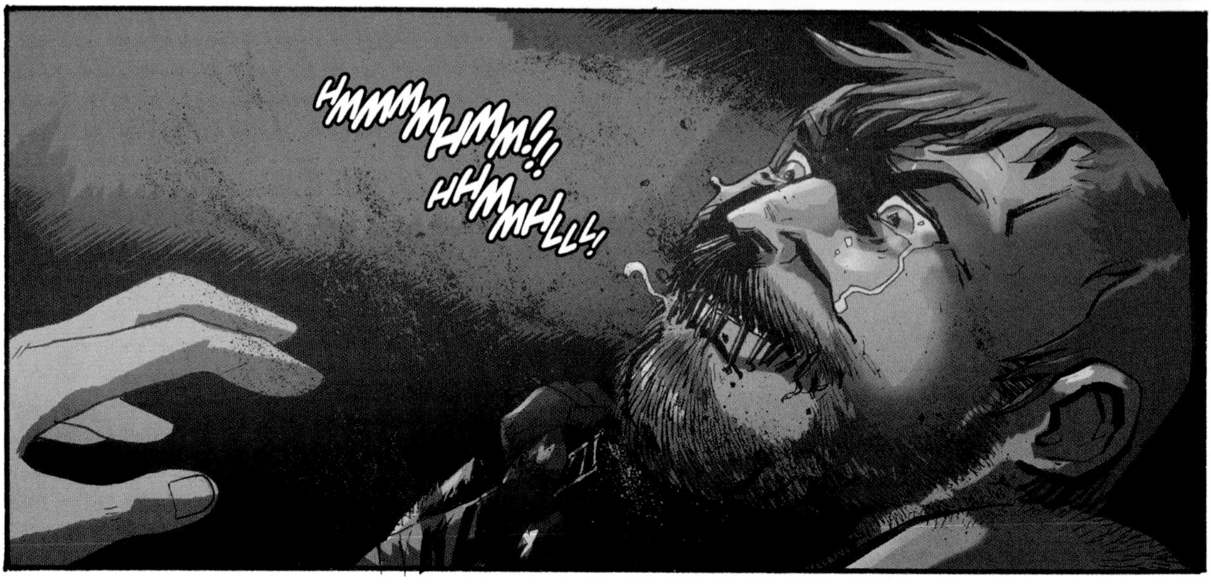
HMMMHMM!!
HHMMHLL!

FIVE

*"If you keep digging into this...
it's going to cost you."*

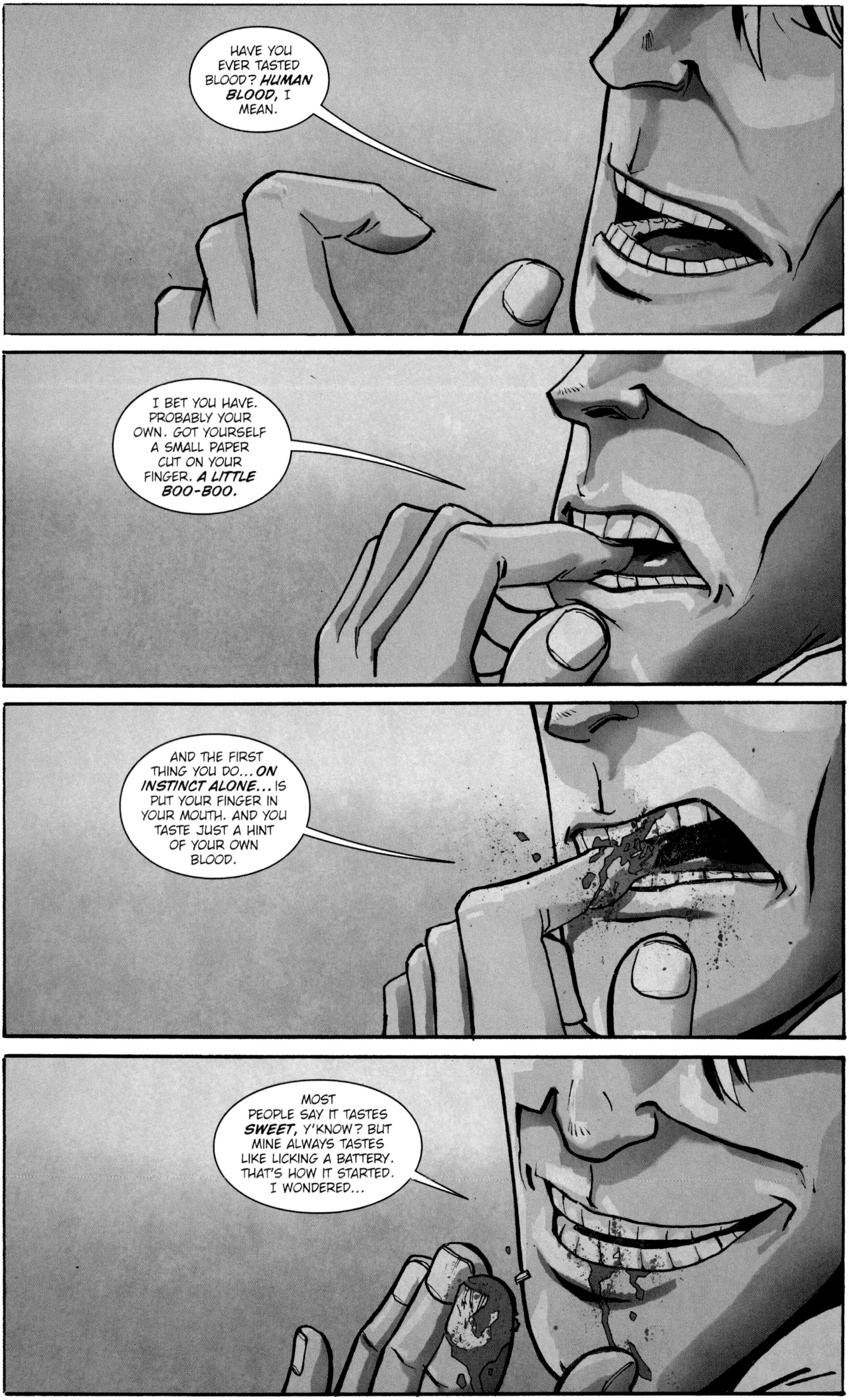
HAVE YOU EVER TASTED BLOOD? HUMAN BLOOD, I MEAN.
I BET YOU HAVE. PROBABLY YOUR OWN. GOT YOURSELF A SMALL PAPER CUT ON YOUR FINGER. A LITTLE BOO-BOO.
AND THE FIRST THING YOU DO... ON INSTINCT ALONE... IS PUT YOUR FINGER IN YOUR MOUTH. AND YOU TASTE JUST A HINT OF YOUR OWN BLOOD.
MOST PEOPLE SAY IT TASTES SWEET, Y'KNOW? BUT MINE ALWAYS TASTES LIKE LICKING A BATTERY. THAT'S HOW IT STARTED. I WONDERED...

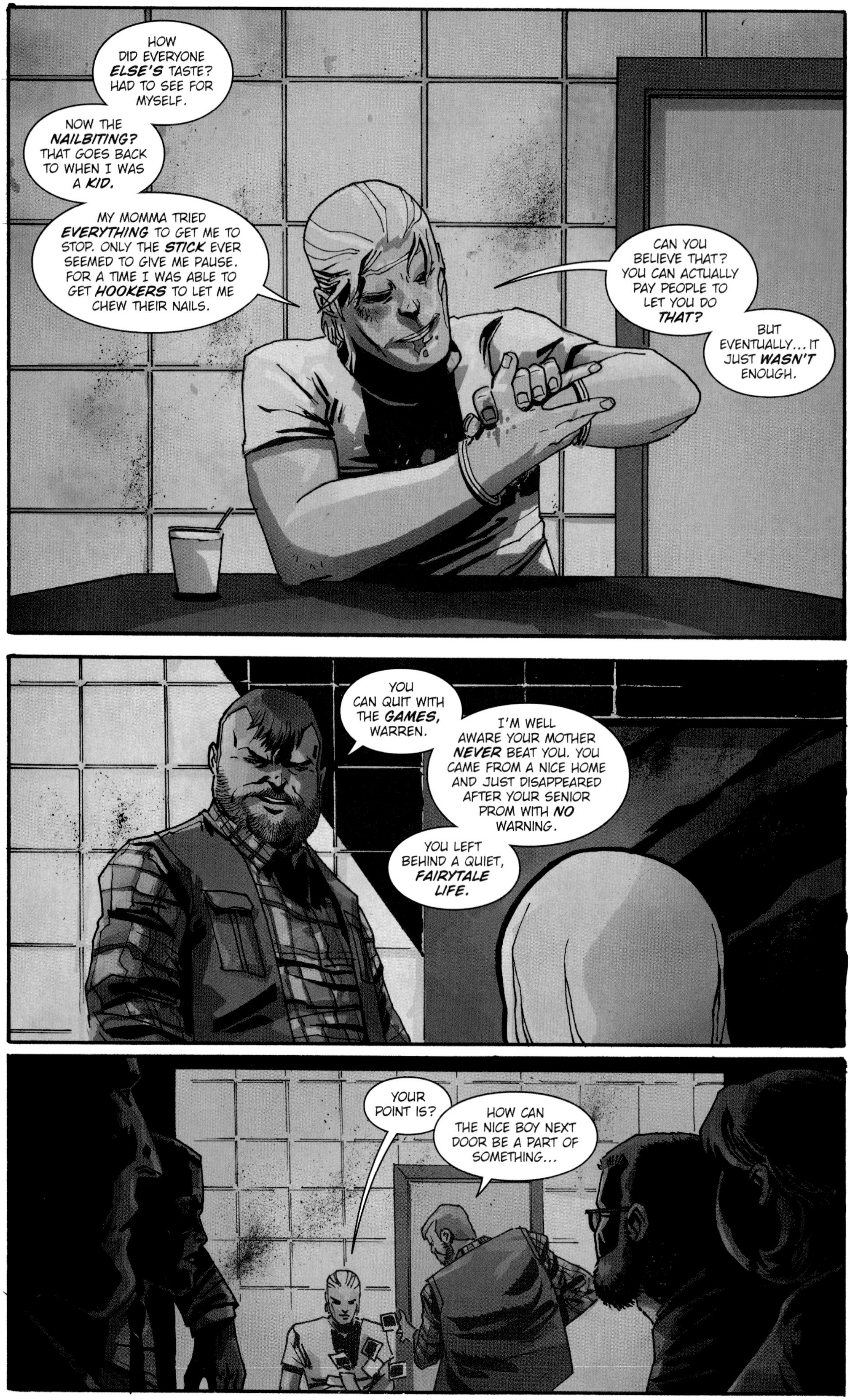
HOW DID EVERYONE ELSE'S TASTE? HAD TO SEE FOR MYSELF.
NOW THE NAILBITING? THAT GOES BACK TO WHEN I WAS A KID.
MY MOMMA TRIED EVERYTHING TO GET ME TO STOP. ONLY THE STICK EVER SEEMED TO GIVE ME PAUSE. FOR A TIME I WAS ABLE TO GET HOOKERS TO LET ME CHEW THEIR NAILS.
CAN YOU BELIEVE THAT? YOU CAN ACTUALLY PAY PEOPLE TO LET YOU DO THAT?
BUT EVENTUALLY... IT JUST WASN'T ENOUGH.
YOU CAN QUIT WITH THE GAMES, WARREN.
I'M WELL AWARE YOUR MOTHER NEVER BEAT YOU. YOU CAME FROM A NICE HOME AND JUST DISAPPEARED AFTER YOUR SENIOR PROM WITH NO WARNING.
YOU LEFT BEHIND A QUIET, FAIRYTALE LIFE.
YOUR POINT IS?
HOW CAN THE NICE BOY NEXT DOOR BE A PART OF SOMETHING...

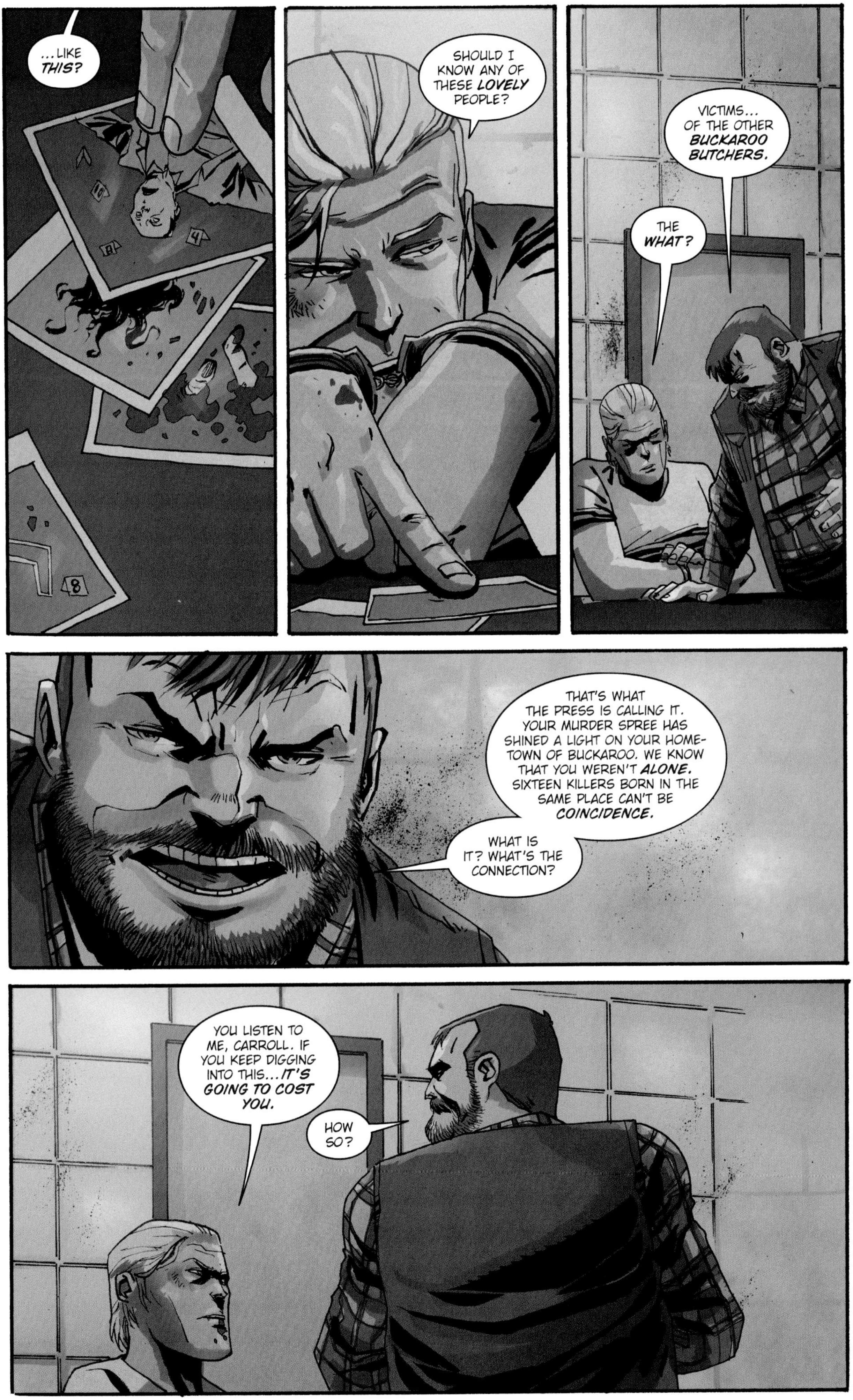

...LIKE THIS?
SHOULD I KNOW ANY OF THESE LOVELY PEOPLE?
VICTIMS... OF THE OTHER BUCKAROO BUTCHERS.
THE WHAT?
THAT'S WHAT THE PRESS IS CALLING IT. YOUR MURDER SPREE HAS SHINED A LIGHT ON YOUR HOME-TOWN OF BUCKAROO. WE KNOW THAT YOU WEREN'T ALONE. SIXTEEN KILLERS BORN IN THE SAME PLACE CAN'T BE COINCIDENCE.
WHAT IS IT? WHAT'S THE CONNECTION?
YOU LISTEN TO ME, CARROLL. IF YOU KEEP DIGGING INTO THIS...IT'S GOING TO COST YOU.
HOW SO?

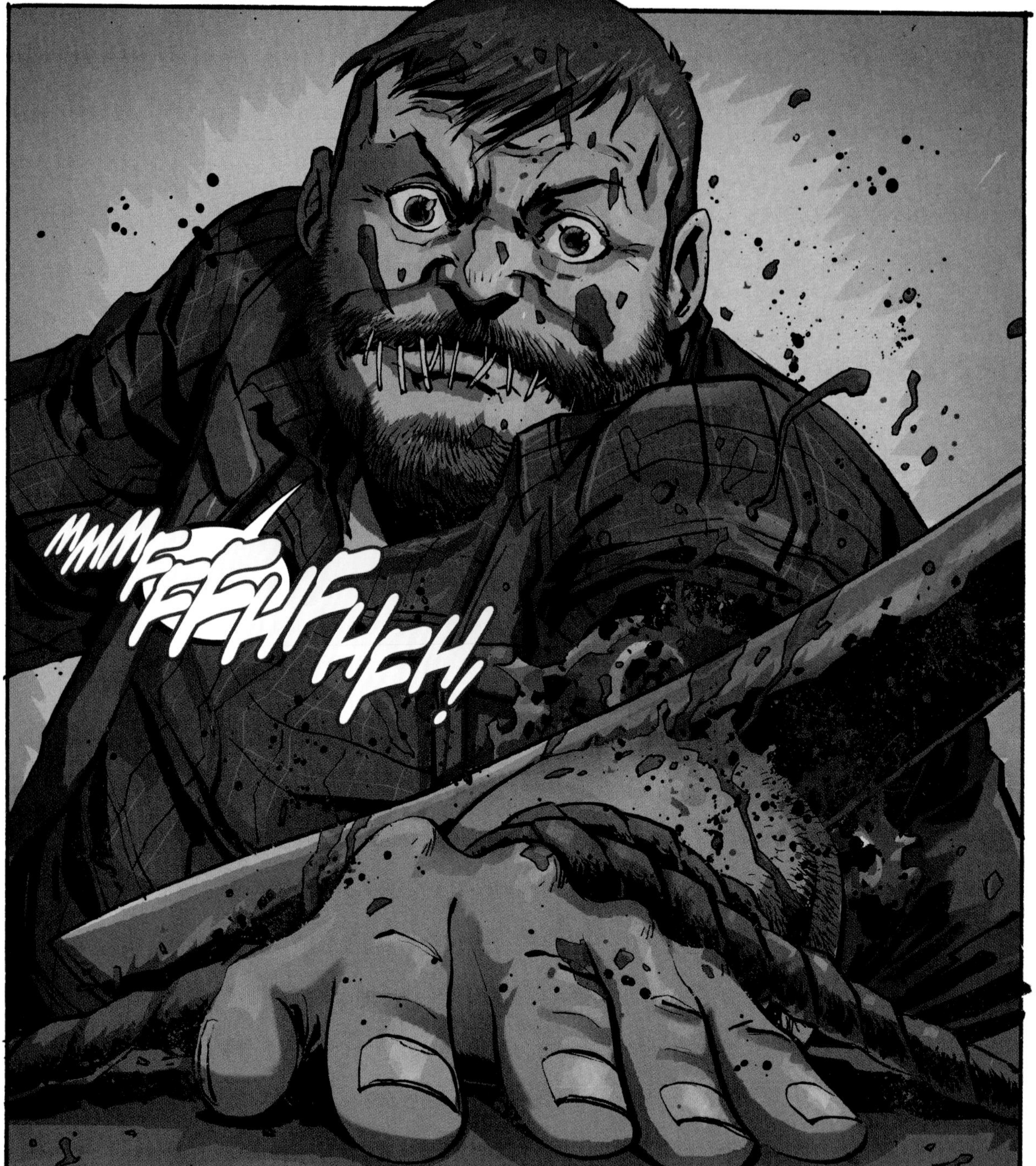
MMMFFFUHFHFH!

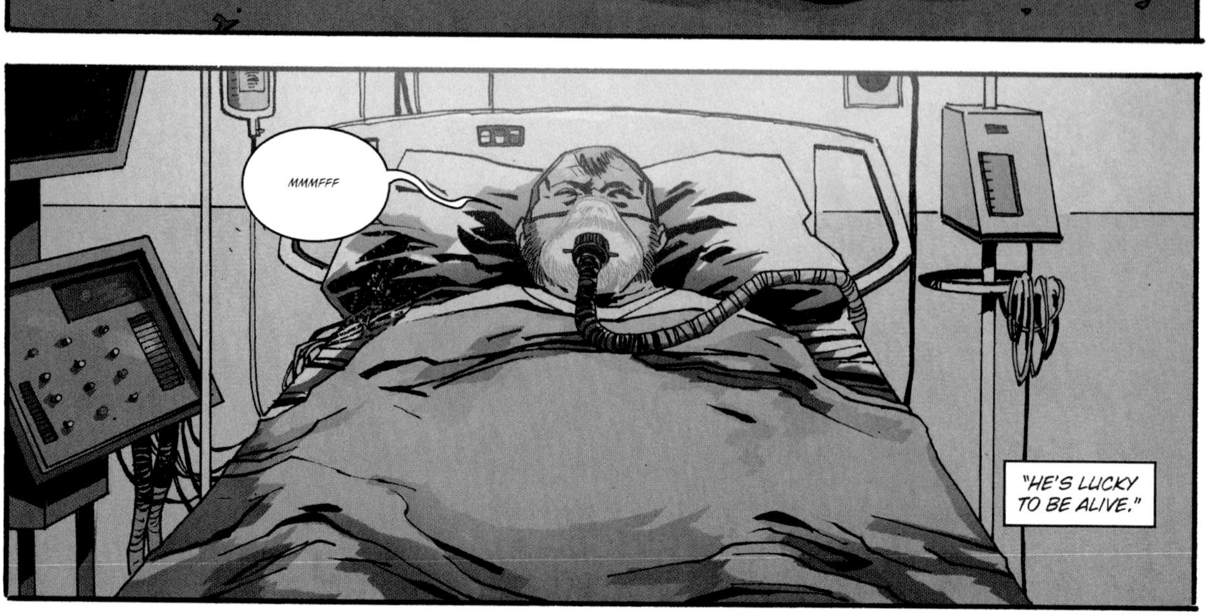
MMMFFF
"HE'S LUCKY TO BE ALIVE."

THE FACT THAT HE SURVIVED BEING LEFT IN THE GRAVEYARD OVERNIGHT IN HIS CONDITION IS *REMARKABLE*, SHERIFF.

DON'T HAVE TO TELL YOU HIS INJURIES ARE SUBSTANTIAL, BUT HE LOST A LOT OF BLOOD. YOU JUST FOUND HIM...

LYING IN THE GRASS IN THE GRAVEYARD, YEAH.

IS HE GOING TO WAKE UP?

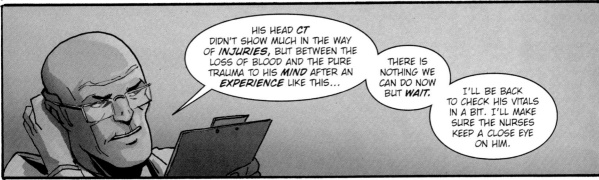

HIS HEAD *CT* DIDN'T SHOW MUCH IN THE WAY OF *INJURIES*, BUT BETWEEN THE LOSS OF BLOOD AND THE PURE TRAUMA TO HIS *MIND* AFTER AN *EXPERIENCE* LIKE THIS...

THERE IS NOTHING WE CAN DO NOW BUT *WAIT*.

I'LL BE BACK TO CHECK HIS VITALS IN A BIT. I'LL MAKE SURE THE NURSES KEEP A CLOSE EYE ON HIM.

YOU *LIED*, CRANE.

YOU TOLD THEM WE FOUND CARROLL IN THE GRAVEYARD?

WE DID. SORT OF. WE KEEP THOSE CAVES BETWEEN US UNTIL I KNOW WHAT THEY ARE, FINCH.

THE MEDIA PROBABLY ALREADY KNOWS ABOUT THE *DEATHS* AND ONCE THEY HEAR ABOUT CARROLL IT'S GOING TO BE A CIRCUS. *BUT* SECRET *CAVES* UNDER THE SERIAL KILLER GRAVEYARD...? THAT'S A WAY BIGGER PROBLEM.

YOU GOT SOME KIND OF *PLAN* THEN, I TAKE IT? TWO DEAD KIDS, AND *NO IDEA* WHY ISN'T LOOKING GOOD.

WE GO TALK TO OUR FINGERNAIL-CHEWING BUDDY AND LET HIM KNOW THE GOOD NEWS.

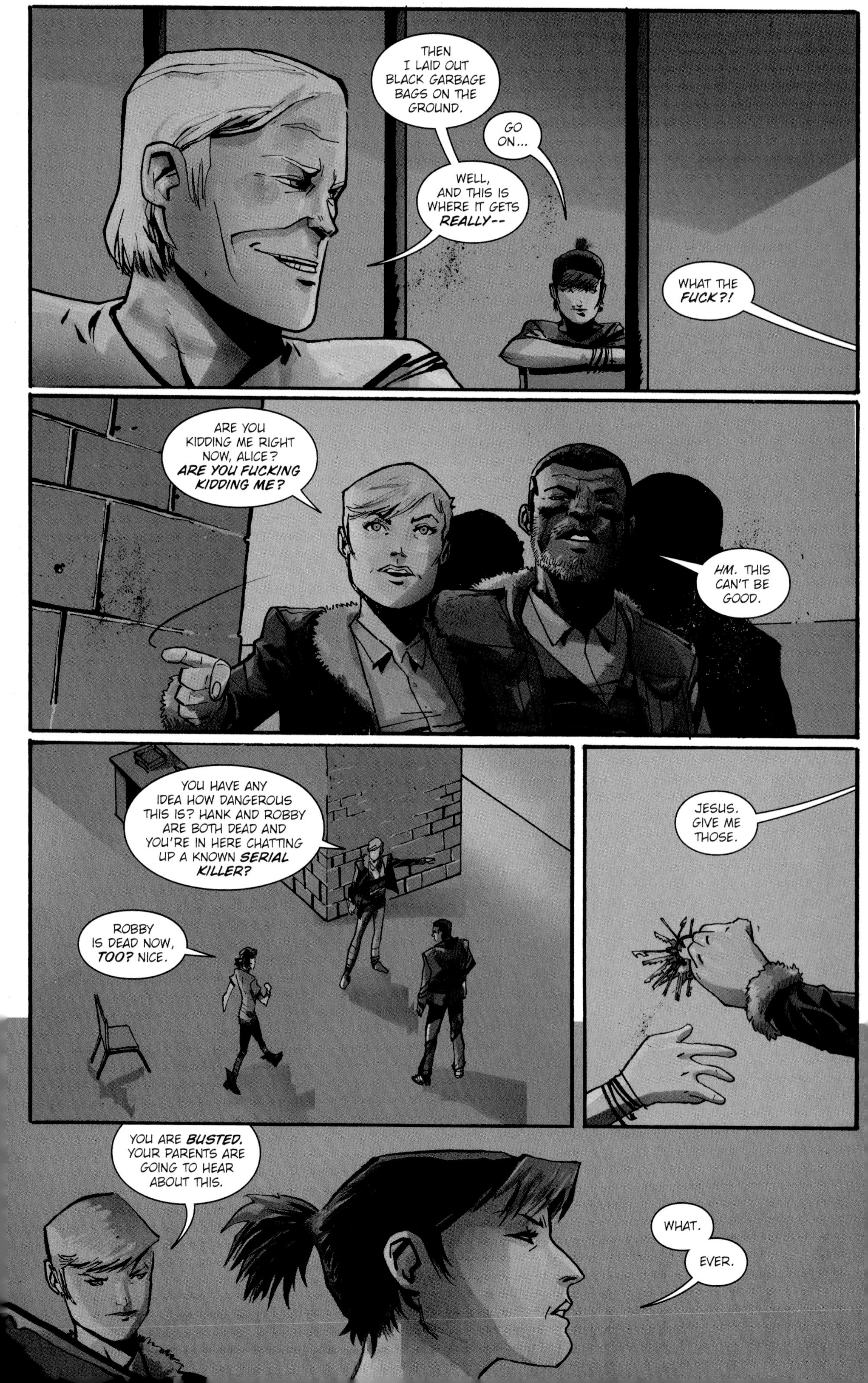
THEN I LAID OUT BLACK GARBAGE BAGS ON THE GROUND.
GO ON...
WELL, AND THIS IS WHERE IT GETS *REALLY--*
WHAT THE *FUCK?!*
ARE YOU KIDDING ME RIGHT NOW, ALICE? ***ARE YOU FUCKING KIDDING ME?***
HM. THIS CAN'T BE GOOD.
YOU HAVE ANY IDEA HOW DANGEROUS THIS IS? HANK AND ROBBY ARE BOTH DEAD AND YOU'RE IN HERE CHATTING UP A KNOWN ***SERIAL KILLER?***
ROBBY IS DEAD NOW, ***TOO?*** NICE.
JESUS. GIVE ME THOSE.
YOU ARE ***BUSTED.*** YOUR PARENTS ARE GOING TO HEAR ABOUT THIS.
WHAT.
EVER.

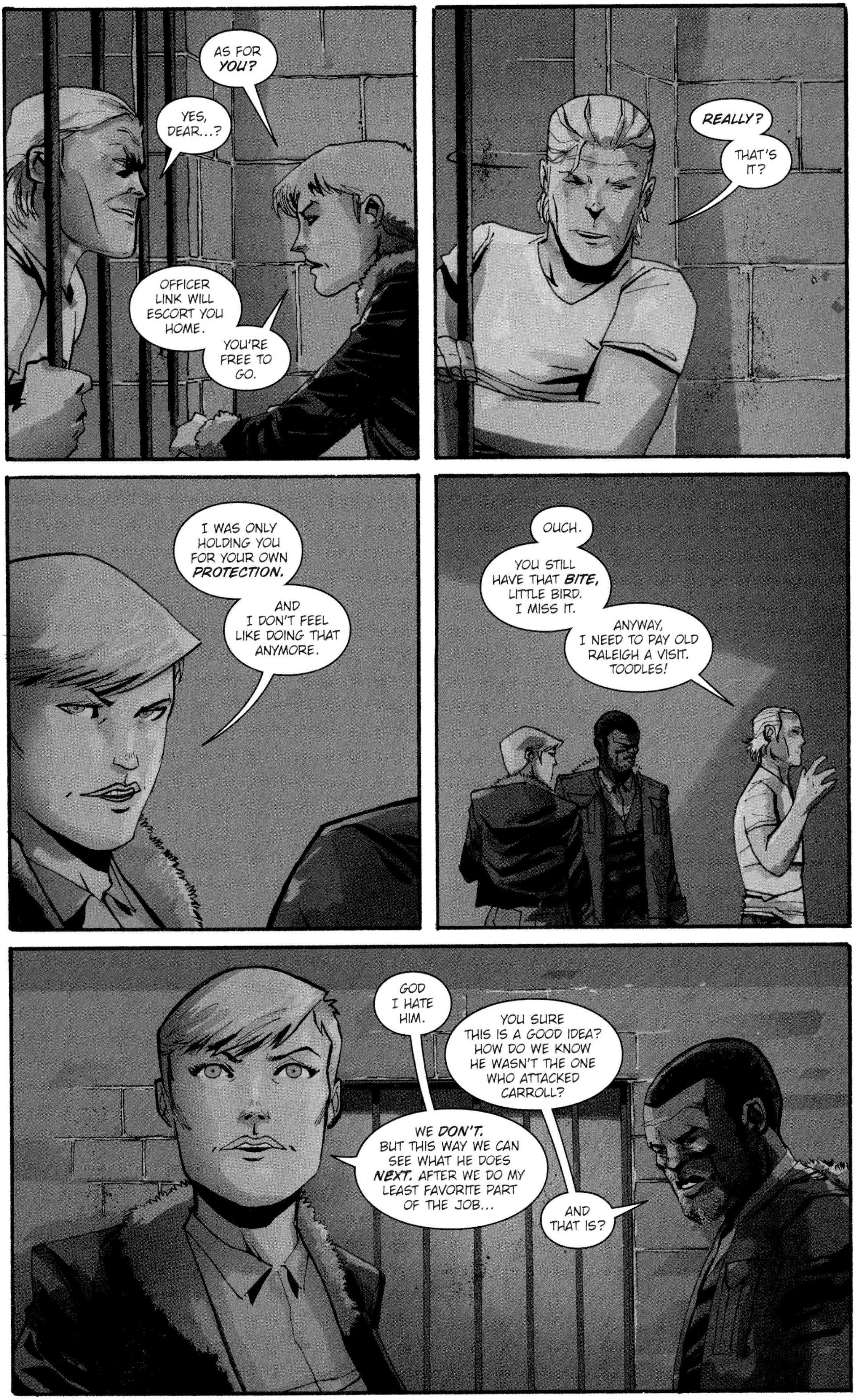

AS FOR *YOU?*
YES, DEAR...?
OFFICER LINK WILL ESCORT YOU HOME.
YOU'RE FREE TO GO.
REALLY?
THAT'S IT?
I WAS ONLY HOLDING YOU FOR YOUR OWN *PROTECTION.*
AND I DON'T FEEL LIKE DOING THAT ANYMORE.
OUCH.
YOU STILL HAVE THAT *BITE,* LITTLE BIRD. I MISS IT.
ANYWAY, I NEED TO PAY OLD RALEIGH A VISIT. TOODLES!
GOD I HATE HIM.
YOU SURE THIS IS A GOOD IDEA? HOW DO WE KNOW HE WASN'T THE ONE WHO ATTACKED CARROLL?
WE *DON'T.* BUT THIS WAY WE CAN SEE WHAT HE DOES *NEXT.* AFTER WE DO MY LEAST FAVORITE PART OF THE JOB...
AND THAT IS?

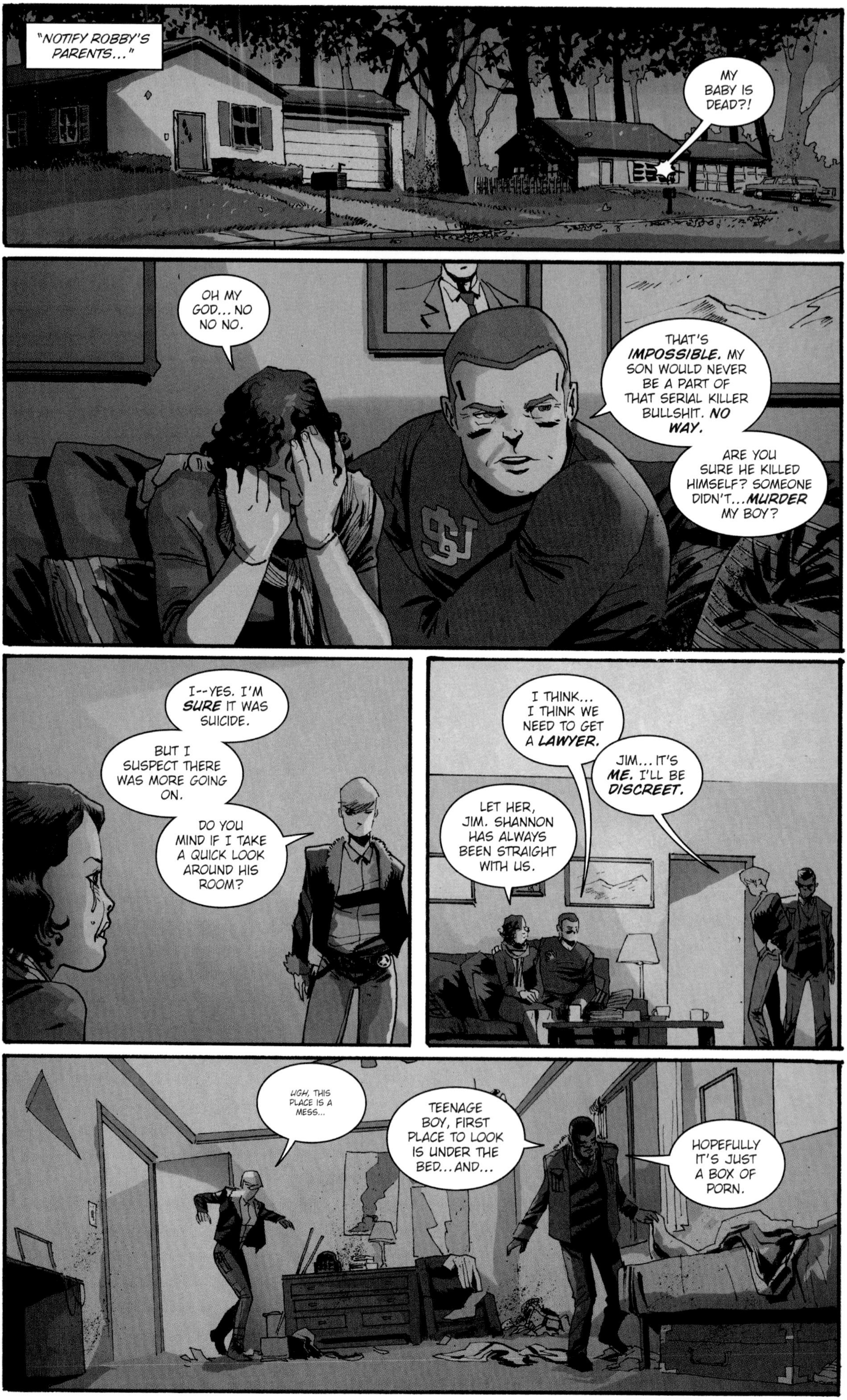
"NOTIFY ROBBY'S PARENTS..."
MY BABY IS DEAD?!
OH MY GOD... NO NO NO.
THAT'S IMPOSSIBLE. MY SON WOULD NEVER BE A PART OF THAT SERIAL KILLER BULLSHIT. NO WAY.
ARE YOU SURE HE KILLED HIMSELF? SOMEONE DIDN'T...MURDER MY BOY?
I--YES. I'M SURE IT WAS SUICIDE.
BUT I SUSPECT THERE WAS MORE GOING ON.
DO YOU MIND IF I TAKE A QUICK LOOK AROUND HIS ROOM?
I THINK... I THINK WE NEED TO GET A LAWYER.
JIM... IT'S ME. I'LL BE DISCREET.
LET HER, JIM. SHANNON HAS ALWAYS BEEN STRAIGHT WITH US.
UGH, THIS PLACE IS A MESS...
TEENAGE BOY, FIRST PLACE TO LOOK IS UNDER THE BED...AND...
HOPEFULLY IT'S JUST A BOX OF PORN.

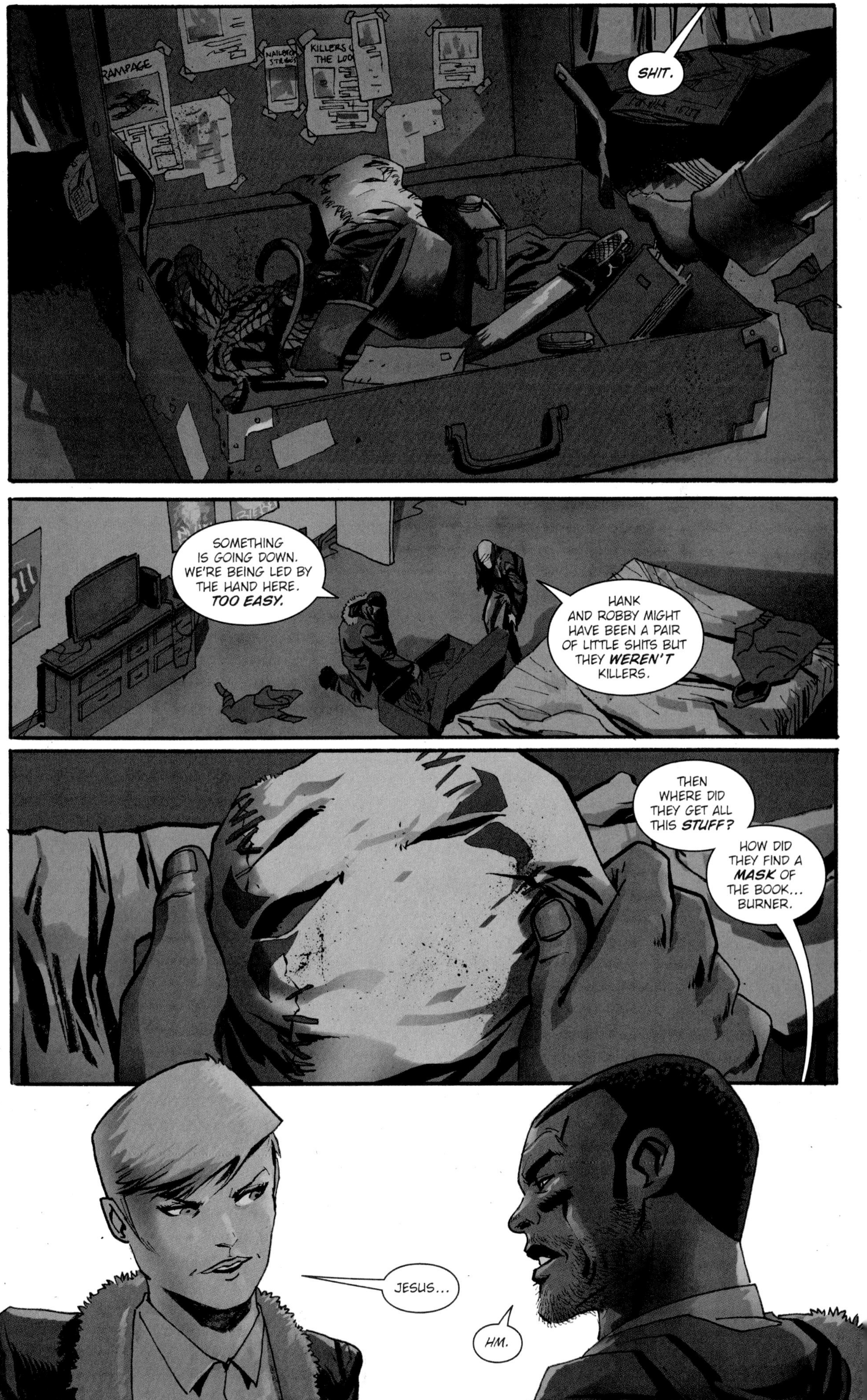
RAMPAGE
SHIT.
SOMETHING IS GOING DOWN. WE'RE BEING LED BY THE HAND HERE. TOO EASY.
HANK AND ROBBY MIGHT HAVE BEEN A PAIR OF LITTLE SHITS BUT THEY WEREN'T KILLERS.
THEN WHERE DID THEY GET ALL THIS STUFF?
HOW DID THEY FIND A MASK OF THE BOOK... BURNER.
JESUS...
HM.

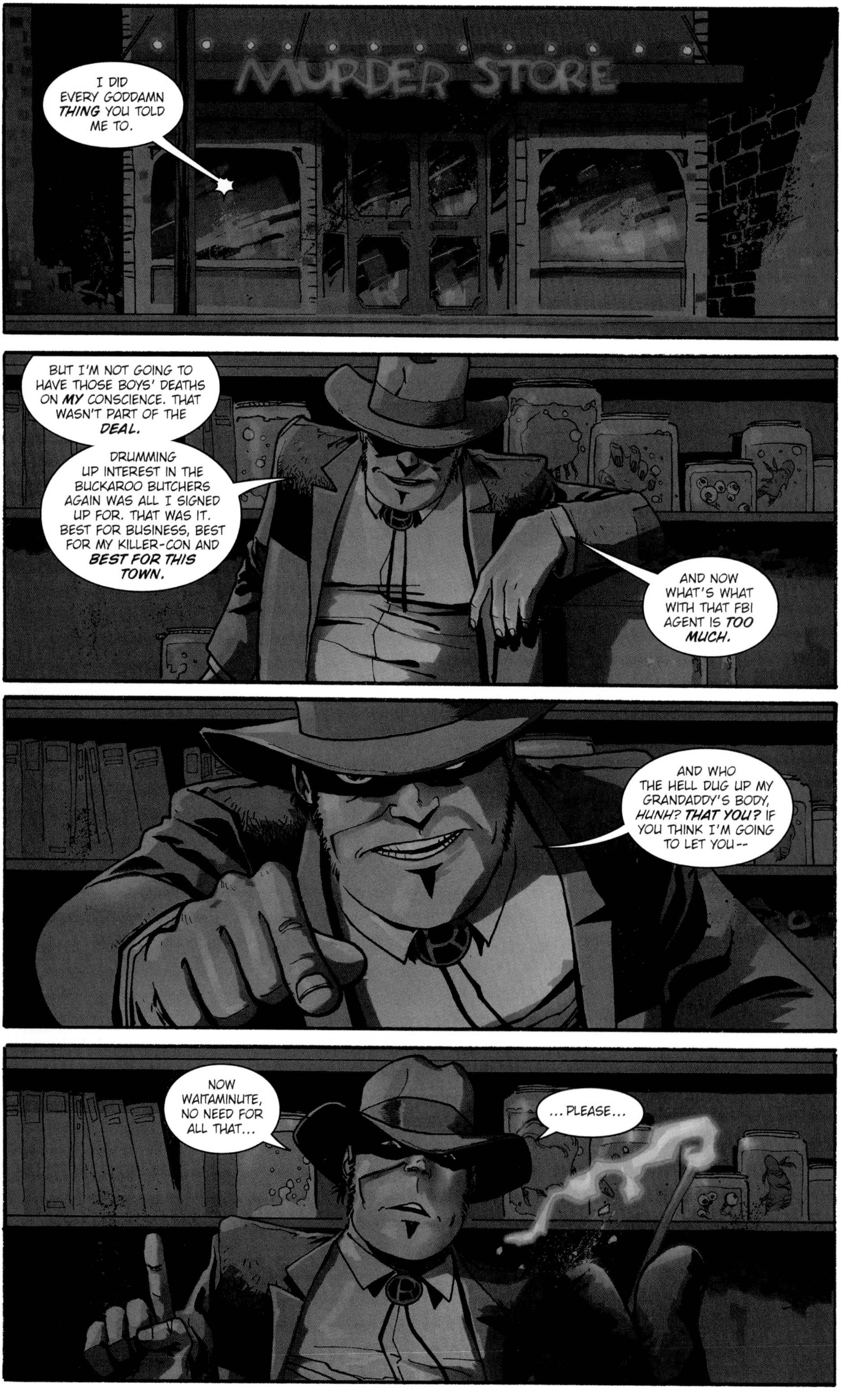
MURDER STORE
I DID EVERY GODDAMN THING YOU TOLD ME TO.
BUT I'M NOT GOING TO HAVE THOSE BOYS' DEATHS ON MY CONSCIENCE. THAT WASN'T PART OF THE DEAL.
DRUMMING UP INTEREST IN THE BUCKAROO BUTCHERS AGAIN WAS ALL I SIGNED UP FOR. THAT WAS IT. BEST FOR BUSINESS, BEST FOR MY KILLER-CON AND BEST FOR THIS TOWN.
AND NOW WHAT'S WHAT WITH THAT FBI AGENT IS TOO MUCH.
AND WHO THE HELL DUG UP MY GRANDADDY'S BODY, HUNH? THAT YOU? IF YOU THINK I'M GOING TO LET YOU--
NOW WAITAMINUTE, NO NEED FOR ALL THAT...
...PLEASE...

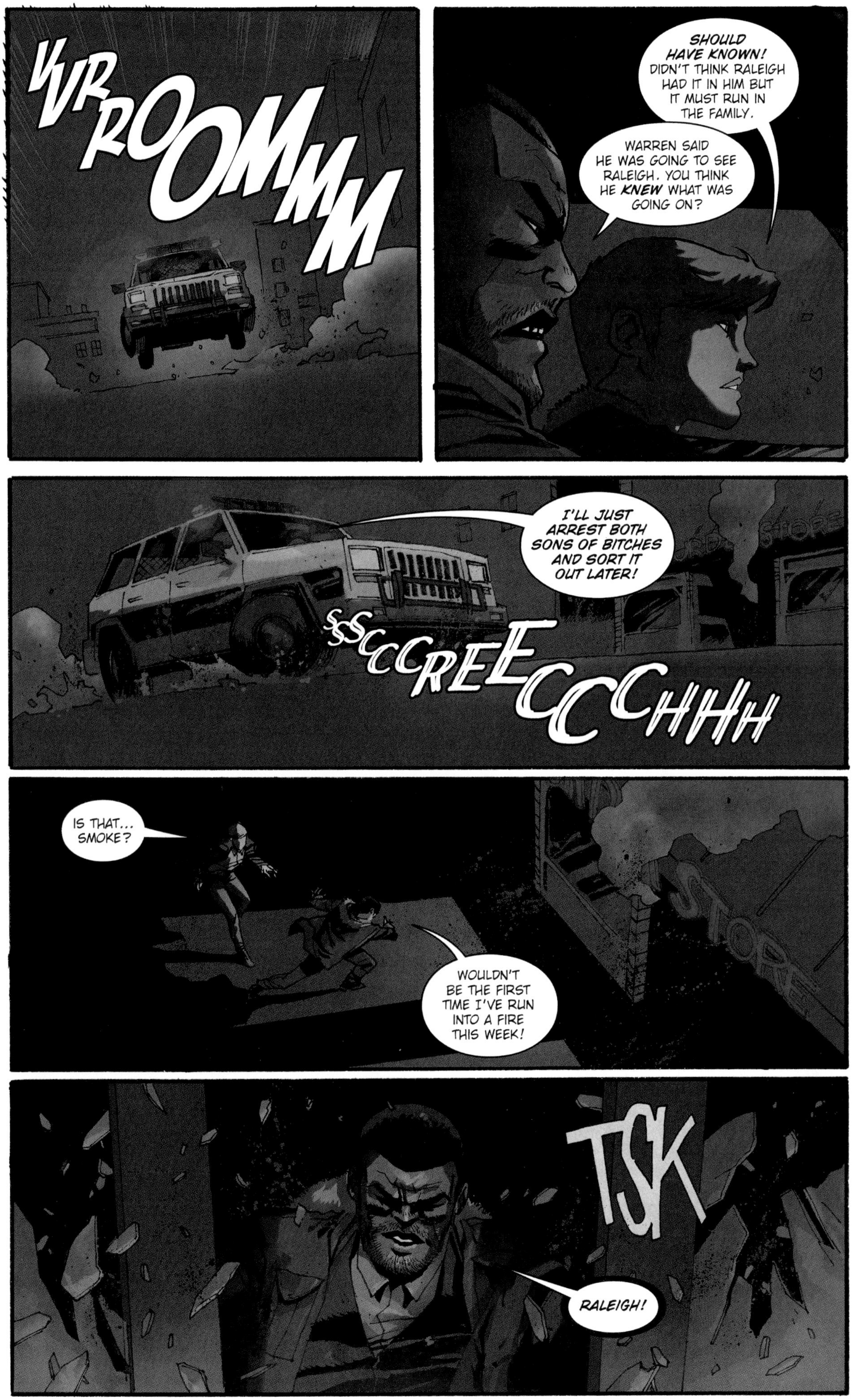
VVROOMMMM
SHOULD HAVE KNOWN! DIDN'T THINK RALEIGH HAD IT IN HIM BUT IT MUST RUN IN THE FAMILY.
WARREN SAID HE WAS GOING TO SEE RALEIGH. YOU THINK HE KNEW WHAT WAS GOING ON?
I'LL JUST ARREST BOTH SONS OF BITCHES AND SORT IT OUT LATER!
SSSCCCREEECCCCHHHH
IS THAT... SMOKE?
WOULDN'T BE THE FIRST TIME I'VE RUN INTO A FIRE THIS WEEK!
TSK
RALEIGH!

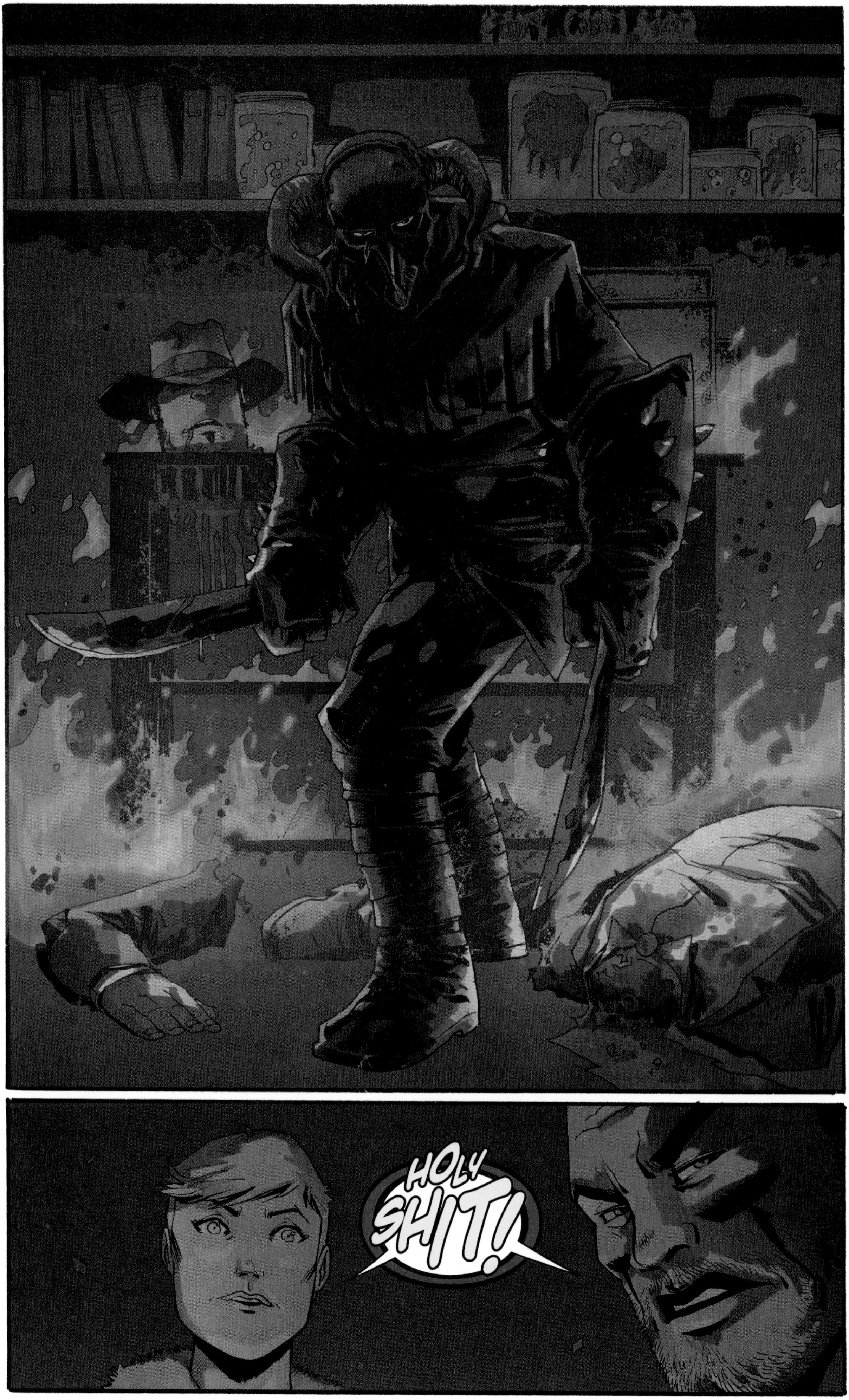
HOLY SHIT!

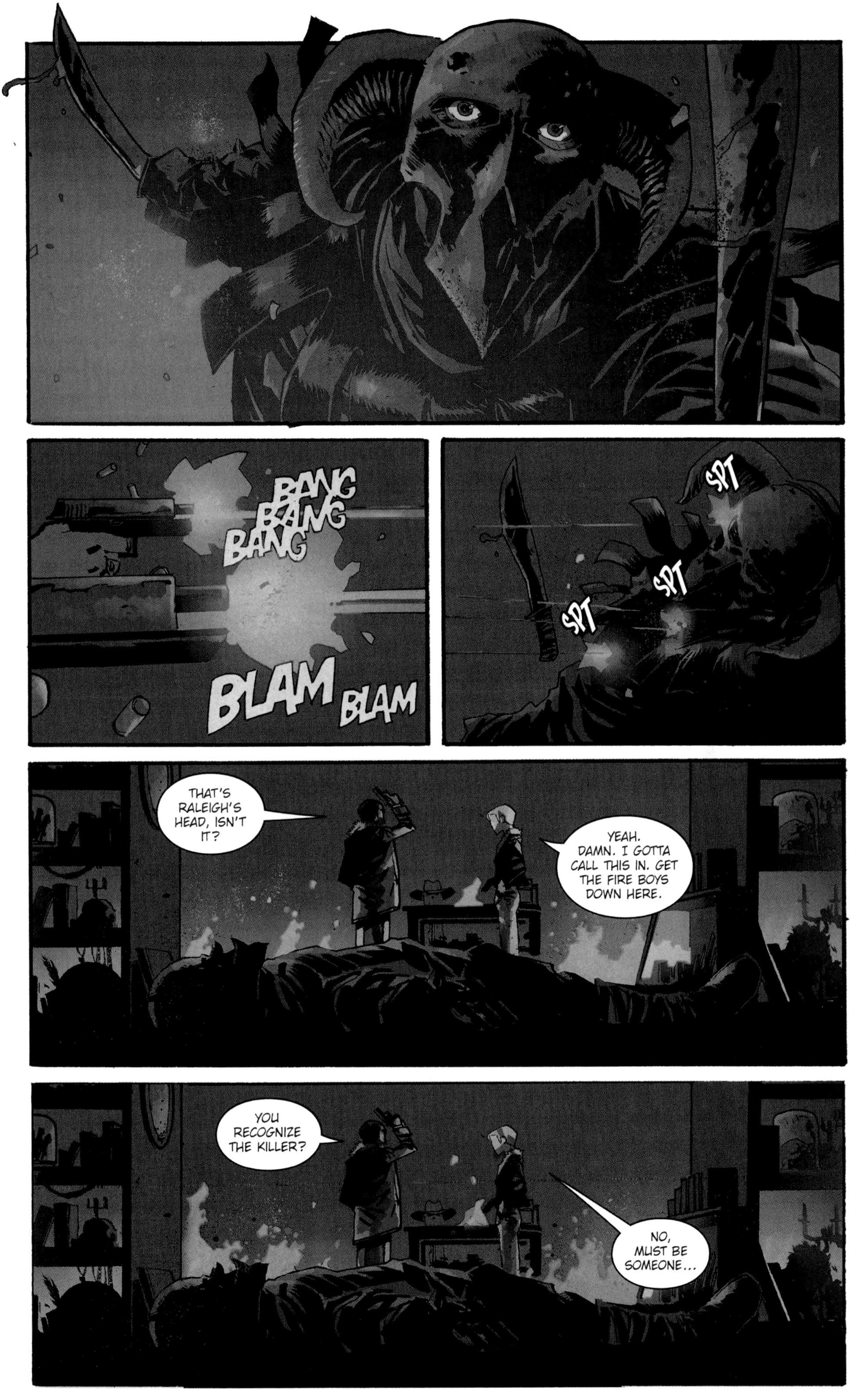
BANG
BANG
BANG
BLAM
BLAM
SPT
SPT
SPT
THAT'S RALEIGH'S HEAD, ISN'T IT?
YEAH. DAMN. I GOTTA CALL THIS IN. GET THE FIRE BOYS DOWN HERE.
YOU RECOGNIZE THE KILLER?
NO, MUST BE SOMEONE...

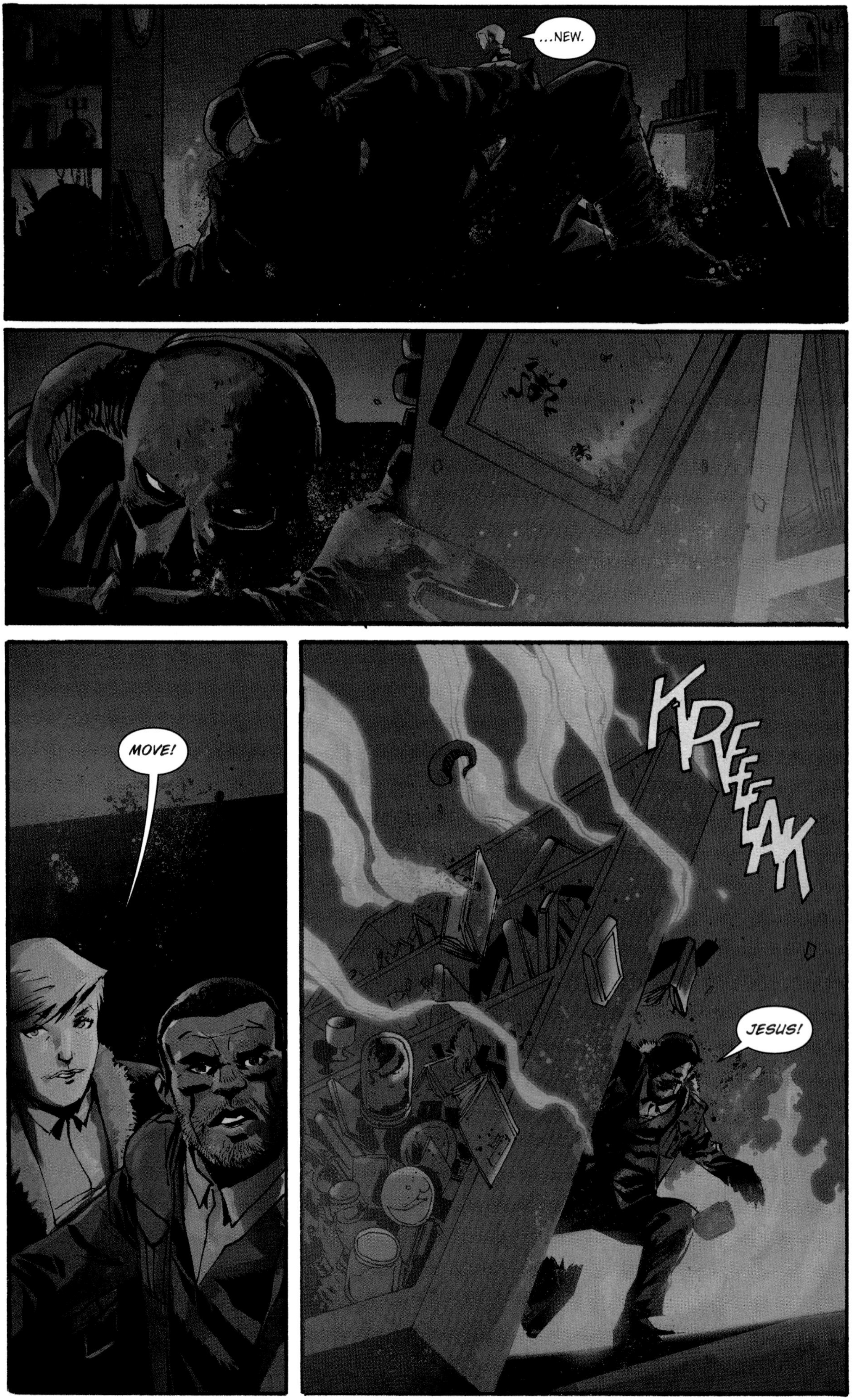
...NEW.
MOVE!
KREEEAK
JESUS!

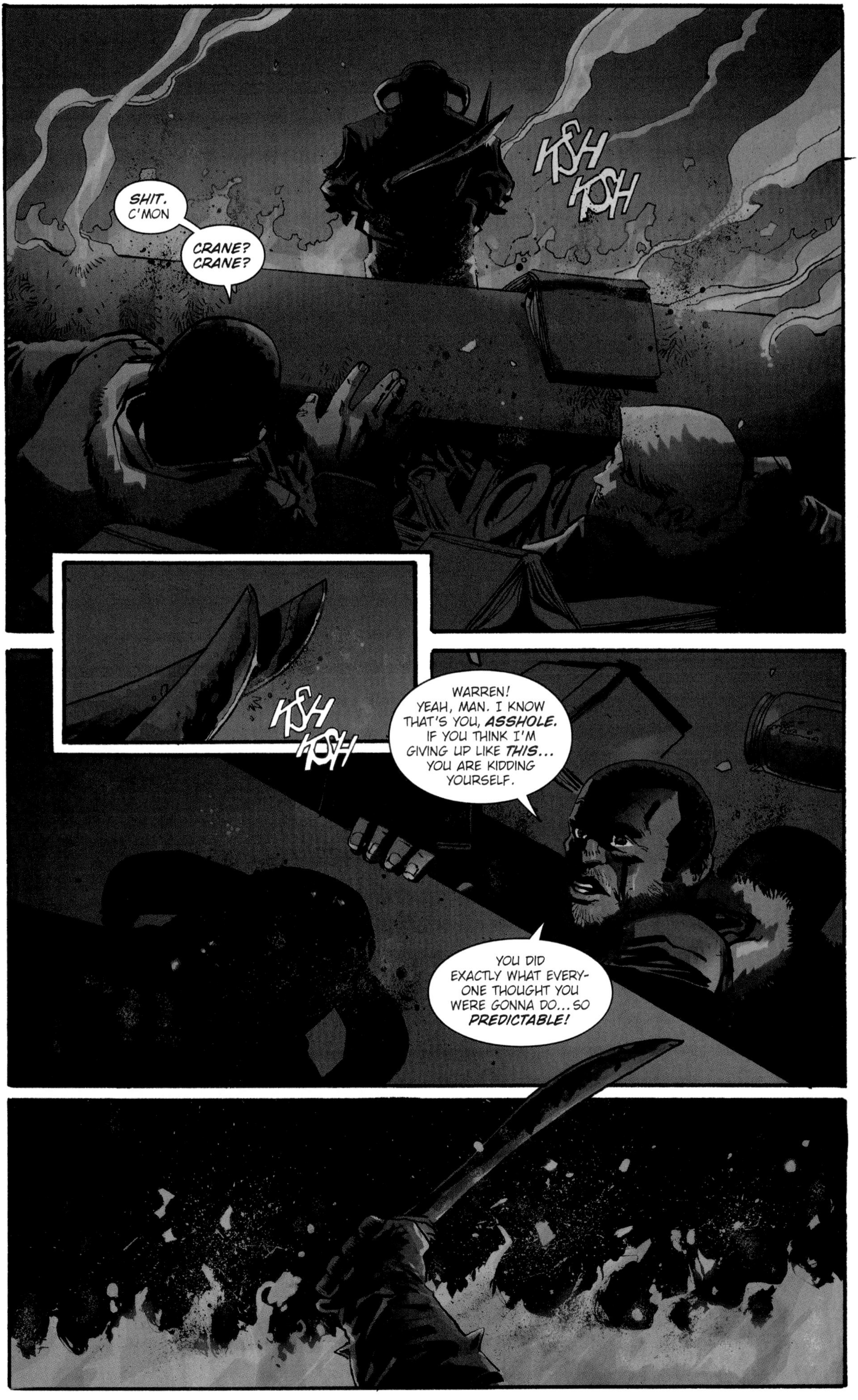
KSH KSH
SHIT. C'MON
CRANE? CRANE?
KSH KSH
WARREN! YEAH, MAN. I KNOW THAT'S YOU, ASSHOLE. IF YOU THINK I'M GIVING UP LIKE THIS... YOU ARE KIDDING YOURSELF.
YOU DID EXACTLY WHAT EVERY-ONE THOUGHT YOU WERE GONNA DO...SO PREDICTABLE!

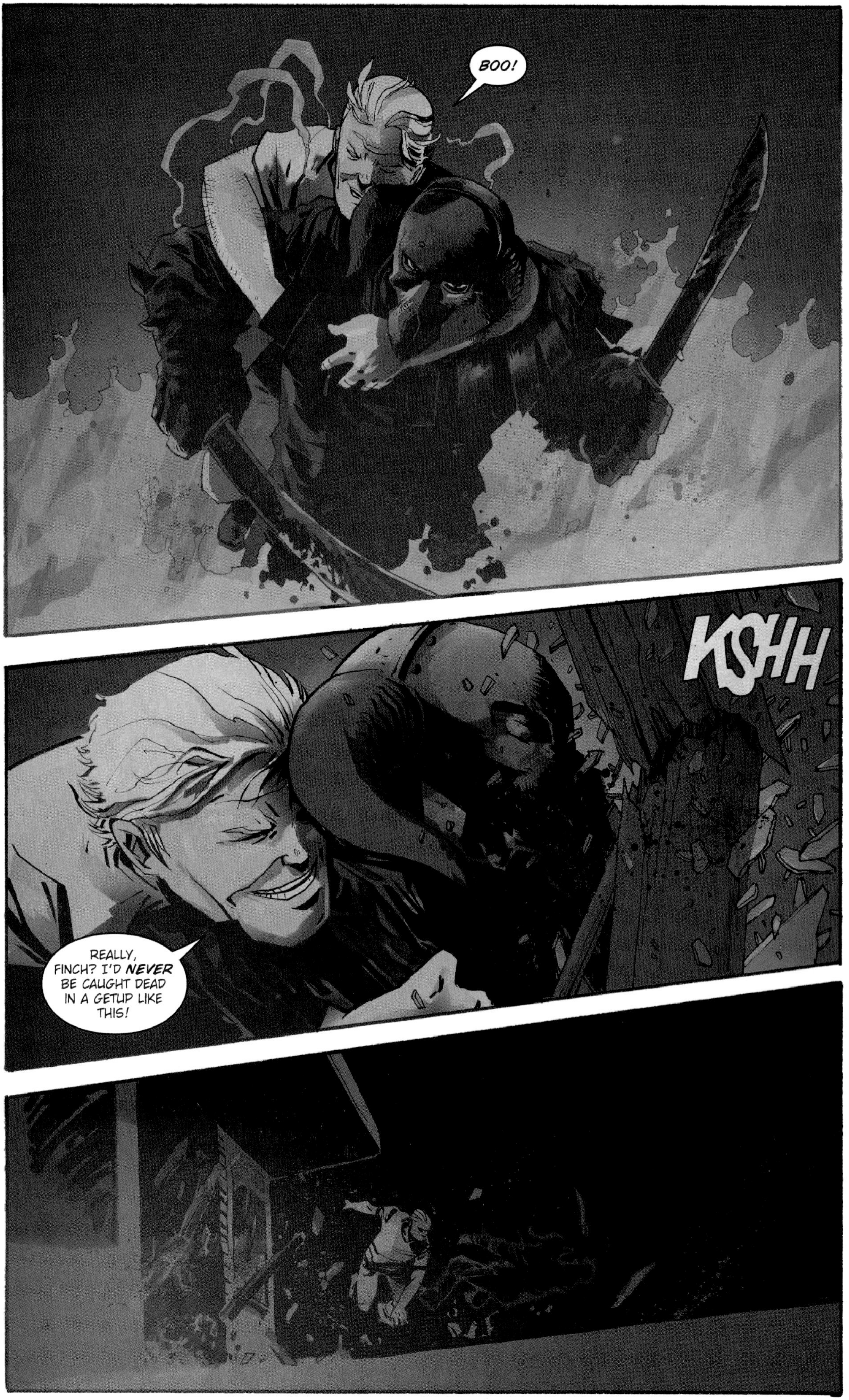
BOO!
KSHH
REALLY, FINCH? I'D NEVER BE CAUGHT DEAD IN A GETUP LIKE THIS!

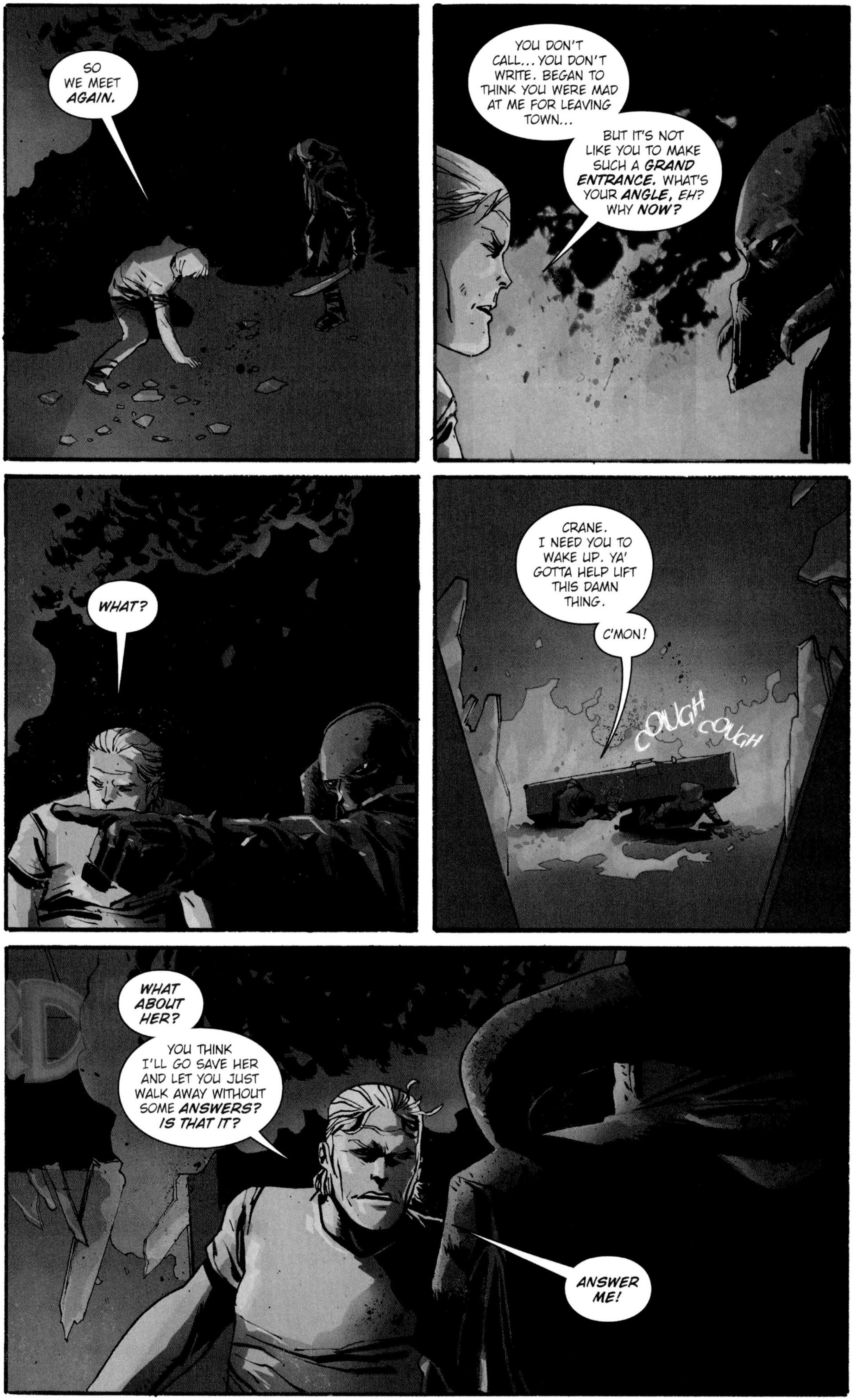
SO WE MEET AGAIN.
YOU DON'T CALL... YOU DON'T WRITE. BEGAN TO THINK YOU WERE MAD AT ME FOR LEAVING TOWN...
BUT IT'S NOT LIKE YOU TO MAKE SUCH A GRAND ENTRANCE. WHAT'S YOUR ANGLE, EH? WHY NOW?
WHAT?
CRANE. I NEED YOU TO WAKE UP. YA' GOTTA HELP LIFT THIS DAMN THING.
C'MON!
COUGH COUGH
WHAT ABOUT HER?
YOU THINK I'LL GO SAVE HER AND LET YOU JUST WALK AWAY WITHOUT SOME ANSWERS? IS THAT IT?
ANSWER ME!

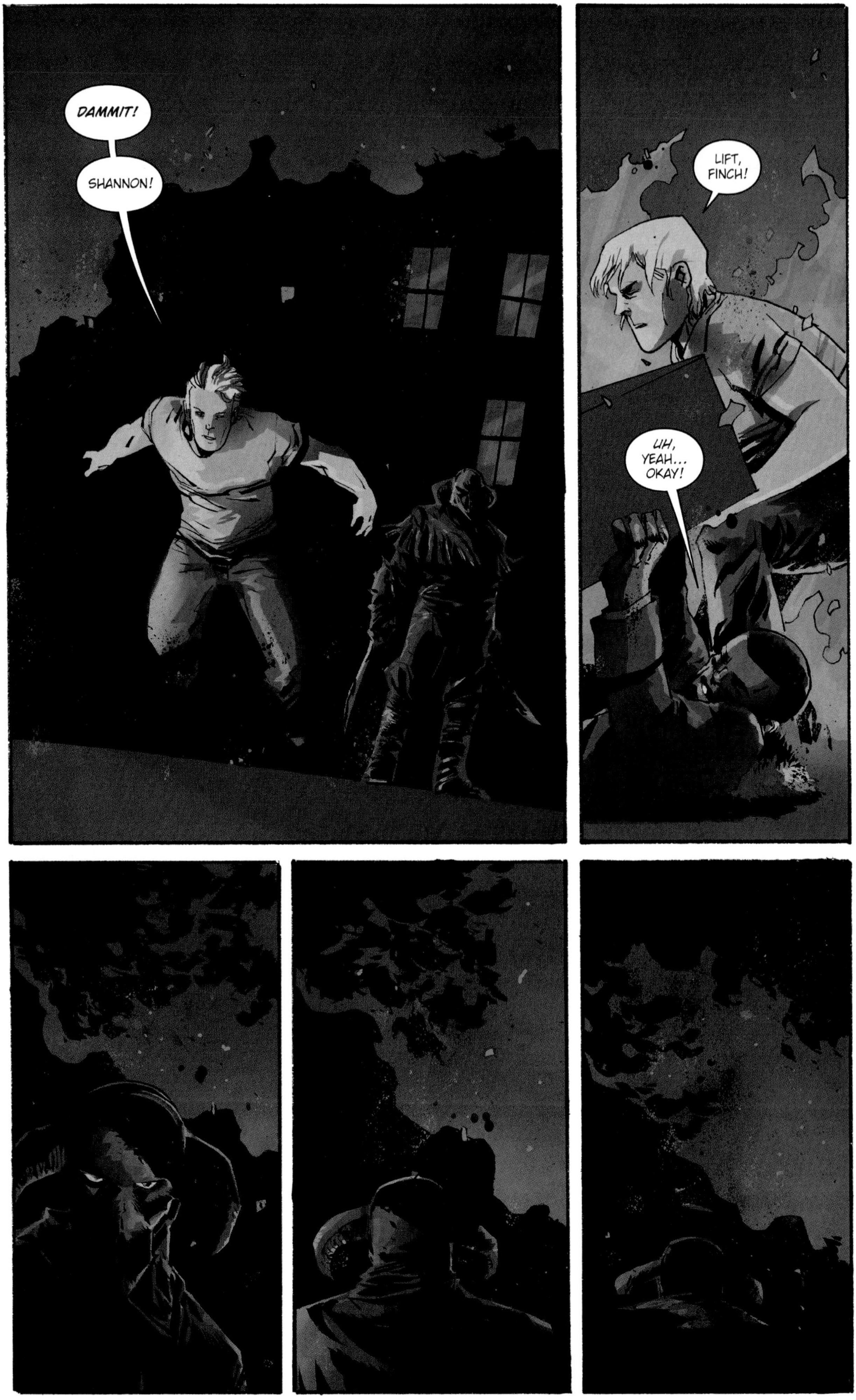
DAMMIT!
SHANNON!
LIFT, FINCH!
UH, YEAH... OKAY!

SHIT... THANKS. I GUESS.

AND NOW THAT YOU'RE FREE IT'S MY TURN TO JET BEFORE THE WHOLE TOWN GETS HERE AND SOMEHOW BLAMES *ME* FOR THIS MESS.

WAIT! WHAT THE HELL HAPPENED? *WHERE IS THAT GUY WITH THE KNIVES?*

NO IDEA, LITTLE BIRD. MUST BE THE *NEWEST BUTCHER.* I CAN ALREADY SEE THE HEADLINES...

WHY WERE YOU COMING TO SEE RALEIGH?

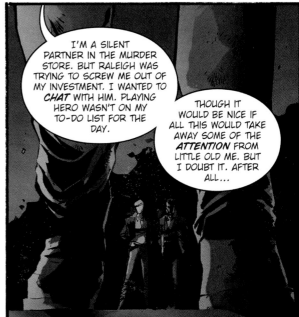

I'M A SILENT PARTNER IN THE MURDER STORE. BUT RALEIGH WAS TRYING TO SCREW ME OUT OF MY INVESTMENT. I WANTED TO *CHAT* WITH HIM. PLAYING HERO WASN'T ON MY TO-DO LIST FOR THE DAY.

THOUGH IT WOULD BE NICE IF ALL THIS WOULD TAKE AWAY SOME OF THE *ATTENTION* FROM LITTLE OLD ME. BUT I DOUBT IT. AFTER ALL...

I'M THE STAR.

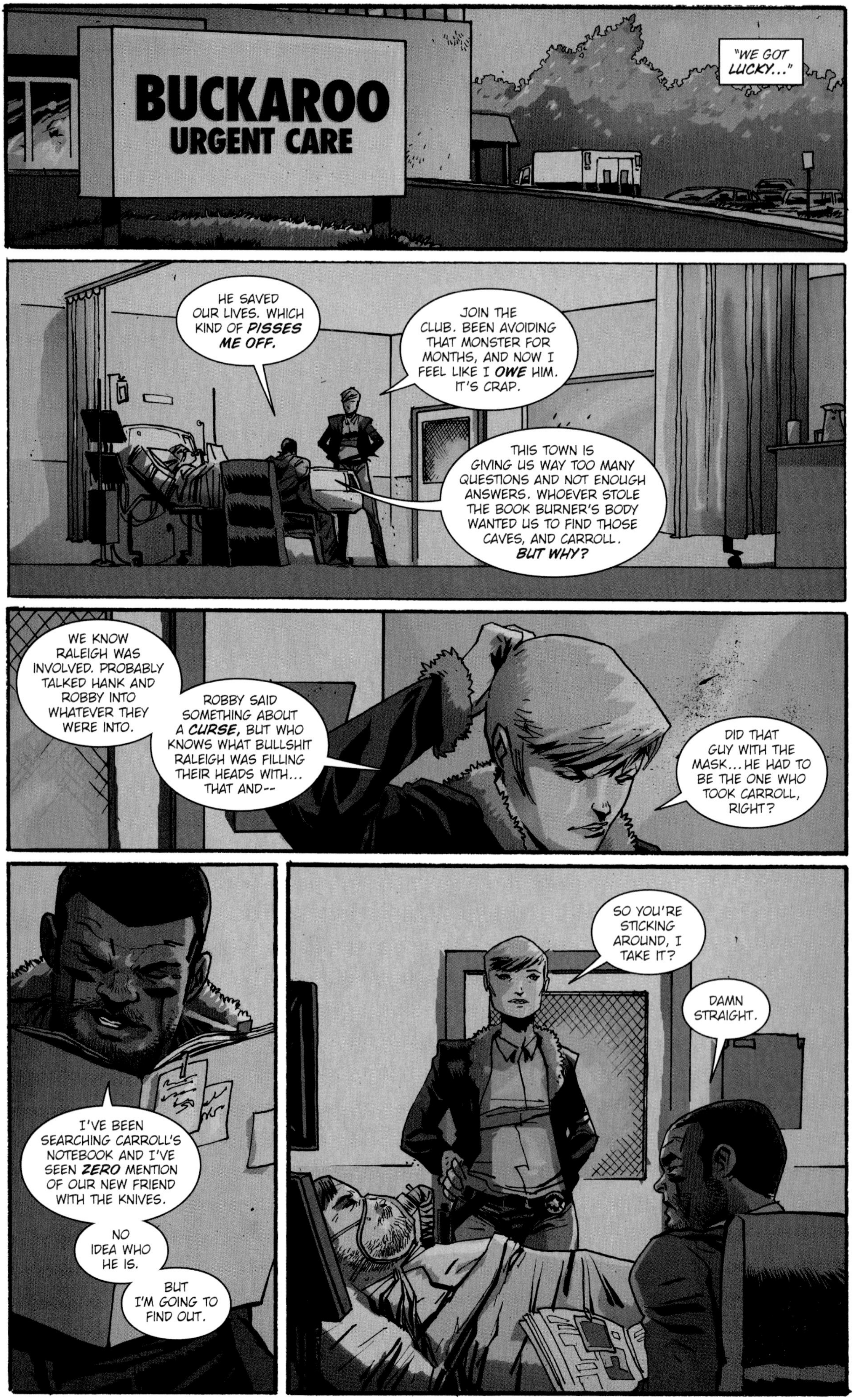
BUCKAROO URGENT CARE
"WE GOT LUCKY..."
HE SAVED OUR LIVES. WHICH KIND OF PISSES ME OFF.
JOIN THE CLUB. BEEN AVOIDING THAT MONSTER FOR MONTHS, AND NOW I FEEL LIKE I OWE HIM. IT'S CRAP.
THIS TOWN IS GIVING US WAY TOO MANY QUESTIONS AND NOT ENOUGH ANSWERS. WHOEVER STOLE THE BOOK BURNER'S BODY WANTED US TO FIND THOSE CAVES, AND CARROLL. BUT WHY?
WE KNOW RALEIGH WAS INVOLVED. PROBABLY TALKED HANK AND ROBBY INTO WHATEVER THEY WERE INTO.
ROBBY SAID SOMETHING ABOUT A CURSE, BUT WHO KNOWS WHAT BULLSHIT RALEIGH WAS FILLING THEIR HEADS WITH... THAT AND--
DID THAT GUY WITH THE MASK... HE HAD TO BE THE ONE WHO TOOK CARROLL, RIGHT?
I'VE BEEN SEARCHING CARROLL'S NOTEBOOK AND I'VE SEEN ZERO MENTION OF OUR NEW FRIEND WITH THE KNIVES.
NO IDEA WHO HE IS.
BUT I'M GOING TO FIND OUT.
SO YOU'RE STICKING AROUND, I TAKE IT?
DAMN STRAIGHT.

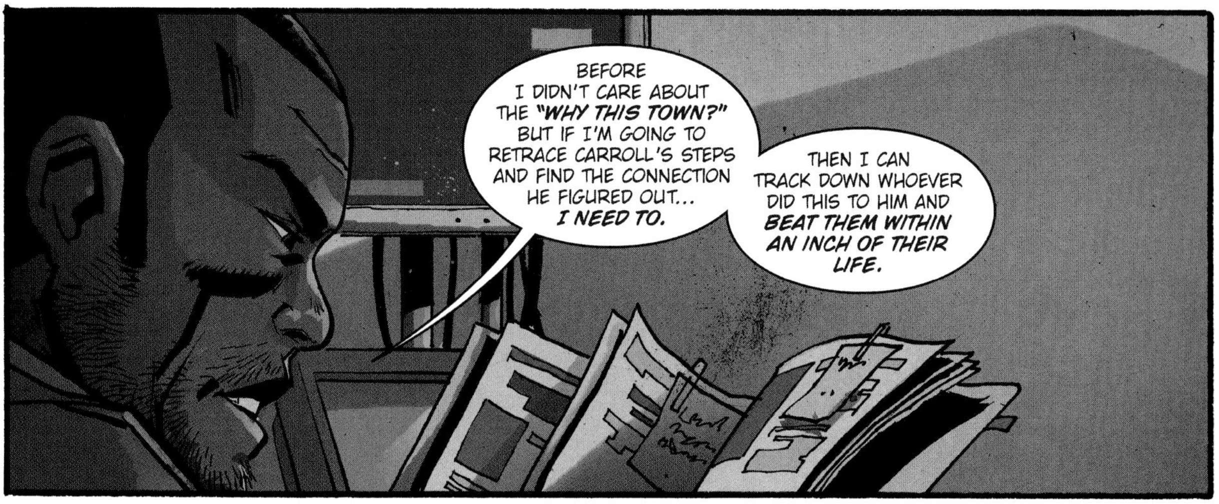
BEFORE I DIDN'T CARE ABOUT THE "WHY THIS TOWN?" BUT IF I'M GOING TO RETRACE CARROLL'S STEPS AND FIND THE CONNECTION HE FIGURED OUT... I NEED TO.
THEN I CAN TRACK DOWN WHOEVER DID THIS TO HIM AND BEAT THEM WITHIN AN INCH OF THEIR LIFE.

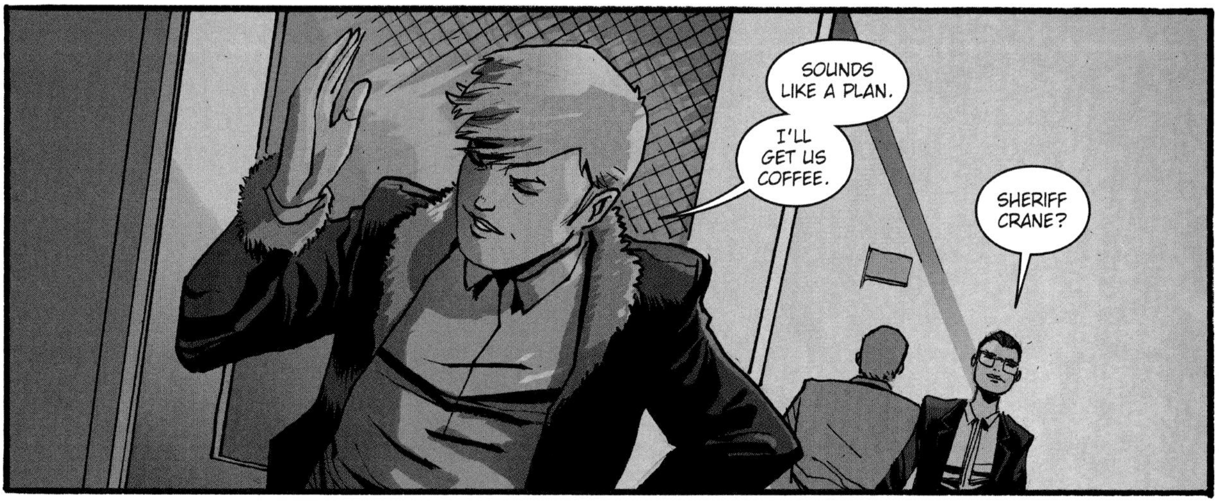
SOUNDS LIKE A PLAN.
I'LL GET US COFFEE.
SHERIFF CRANE?

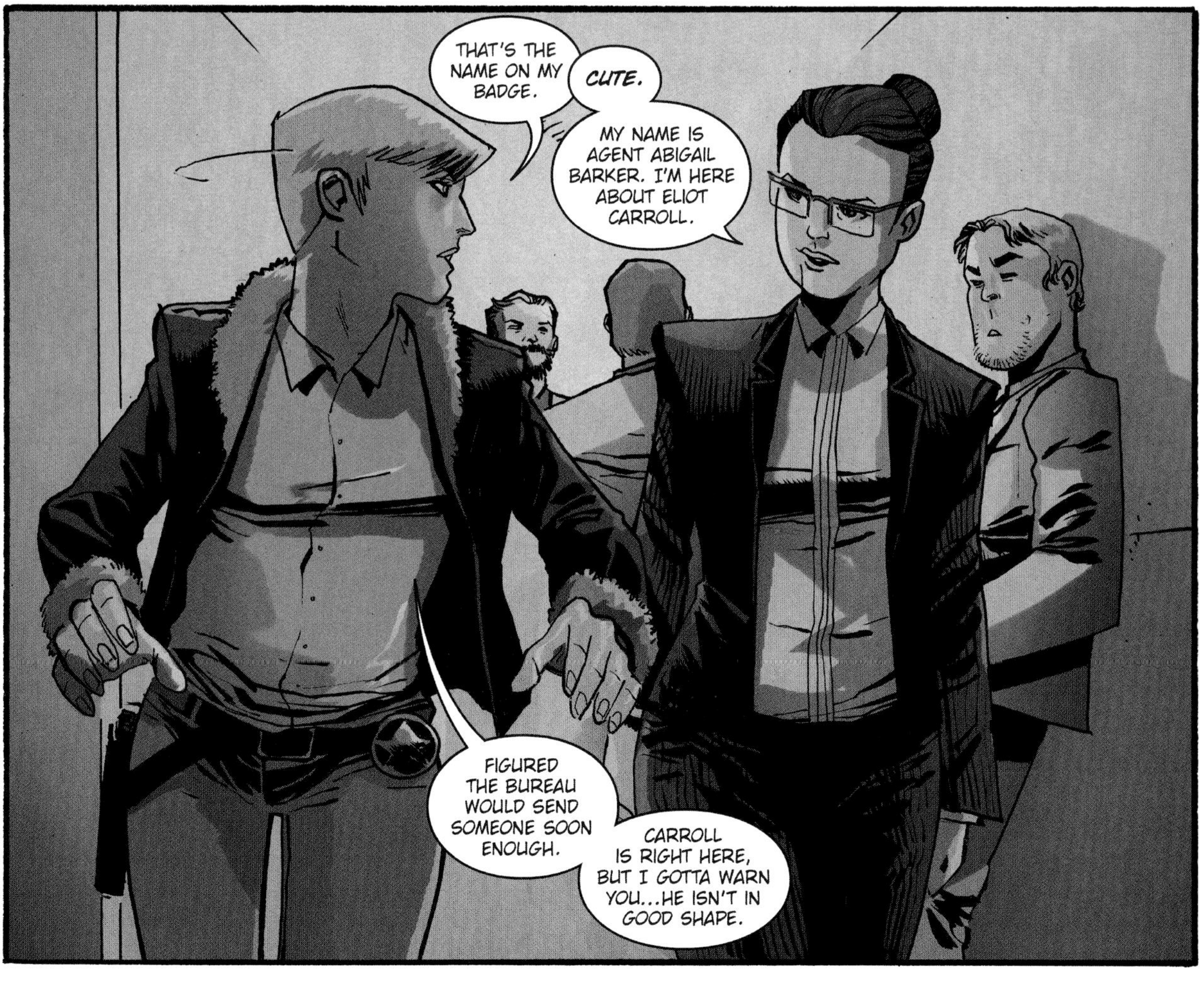
THAT'S THE NAME ON MY BADGE.
CUTE.
MY NAME IS AGENT ABIGAIL BARKER. I'M HERE ABOUT ELIOT CARROLL.
FIGURED THE BUREAU WOULD SEND SOMEONE SOON ENOUGH.
CARROLL IS RIGHT HERE, BUT I GOTTA WARN YOU...HE ISN'T IN GOOD SHAPE.

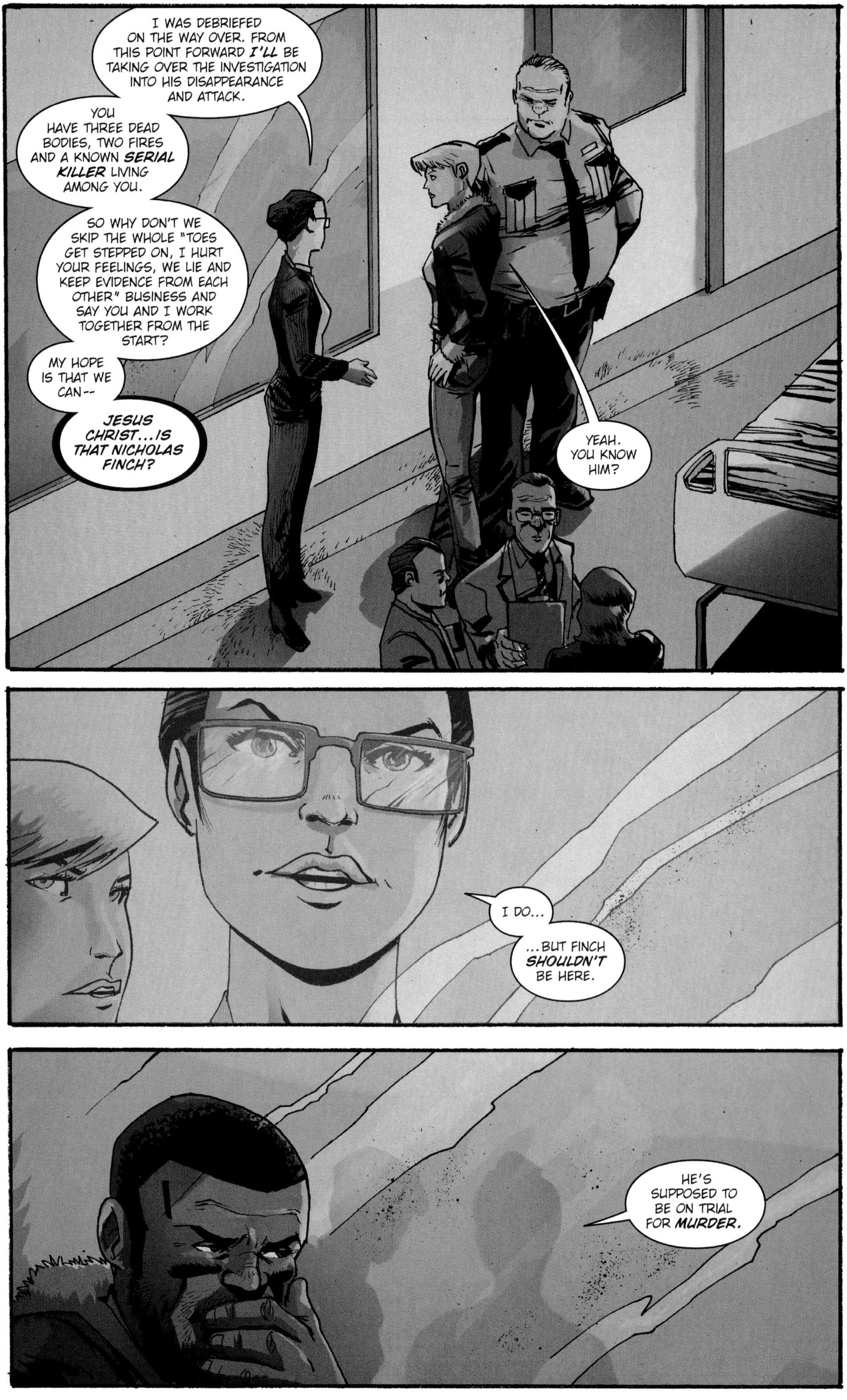
I WAS DEBRIEFED ON THE WAY OVER. FROM THIS POINT FORWARD I'LL BE TAKING OVER THE INVESTIGATION INTO HIS DISAPPEARANCE AND ATTACK.
YOU HAVE THREE DEAD BODIES, TWO FIRES AND A KNOWN SERIAL KILLER LIVING AMONG YOU.
SO WHY DON'T WE SKIP THE WHOLE "TOES GET STEPPED ON, I HURT YOUR FEELINGS, WE LIE AND KEEP EVIDENCE FROM EACH OTHER" BUSINESS AND SAY YOU AND I WORK TOGETHER FROM THE START?
MY HOPE IS THAT WE CAN--
JESUS CHRIST...IS THAT NICHOLAS FINCH?
YEAH. YOU KNOW HIM?
I DO...
...BUT FINCH SHOULDN'T BE HERE.
HE'S SUPPOSED TO BE ON TRIAL FOR MURDER.

FROM THE JOURNAL OF ELIOT CARROLL:

MY COLLEAGUES TELL ME I'M OBSESSED.

THEY TELL ME THIS AS IF I DON'T ALREADY KNOW. AS IF I DON'T SEE MY LIFE SLIPPING AWAY INTO NOTHING. AS IF I CAN'T TELL THIS HAS GONE WELL BEYOND TUNNEL VISION.

BUT I CANNOT REST UNTIL I SOLVE THIS PUZZLE. UNTIL I KNOW WHAT CHANGES THE CITIZENS OF THIS TOWN INTO SERIAL KILLERS. ARE THEY BORN HERE... OR MADE HERE?

I'M GOING DOWN TO THE BASEMENT TO DO MY HOMEWORK. OKAY, MOM?

SHUT UP, DUMMY! OUR SHOW'S ON!

BUT MY COLLEAGUES DON'T UNDERSTAND...MY GOAL IS NOT JUST TO SAVE THE LIVES OF FUTURE VICTIMS.

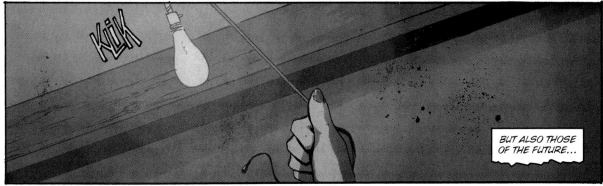

KLIK

BUT ALSO THOSE OF THE FUTURE...

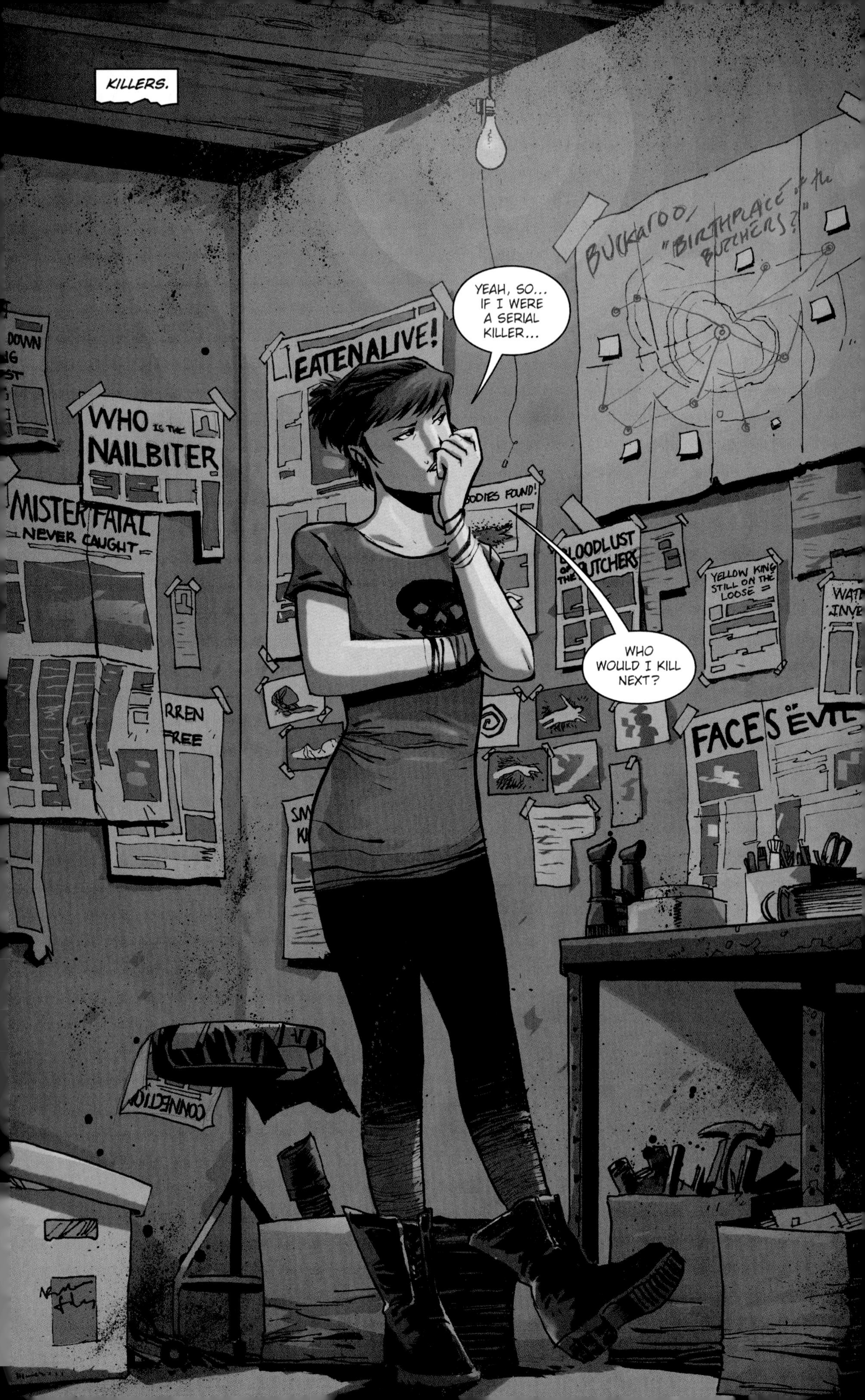

KILLERS.
YEAH, SO... IF I WERE A SERIAL KILLER...
WHO WOULD I KILL NEXT?
WHO IS THE NAILBITER
MISTER FATAL NEVER CAUGHT
EATEN ALIVE!
YELLOW KING STILL ON THE LOOSE
FACES OF EVIL

SIX

"No one should ever have to do this alone."

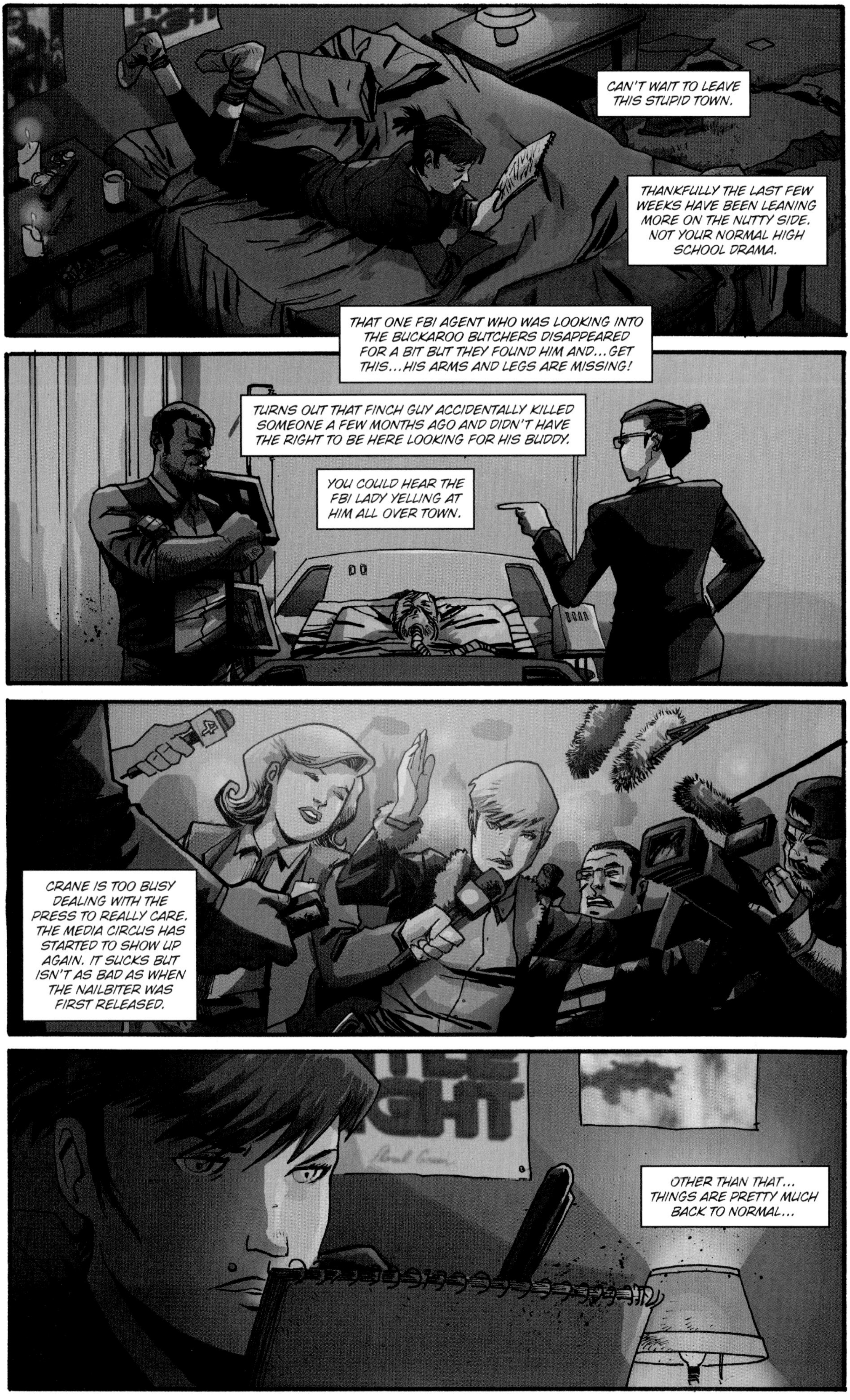
CAN'T WAIT TO LEAVE THIS STUPID TOWN.
THANKFULLY THE LAST FEW WEEKS HAVE BEEN LEANING MORE ON THE NUTTY SIDE. NOT YOUR NORMAL HIGH SCHOOL DRAMA.
THAT ONE FBI AGENT WHO WAS LOOKING INTO THE BUCKAROO BUTCHERS DISAPPEARED FOR A BIT BUT THEY FOUND HIM AND...GET THIS...HIS ARMS AND LEGS ARE MISSING!
TURNS OUT THAT FINCH GUY ACCIDENTALLY KILLED SOMEONE A FEW MONTHS AGO AND DIDN'T HAVE THE RIGHT TO BE HERE LOOKING FOR HIS BUDDY.
YOU COULD HEAR THE FBI LADY YELLING AT HIM ALL OVER TOWN.
CRANE IS TOO BUSY DEALING WITH THE PRESS TO REALLY CARE. THE MEDIA CIRCUS HAS STARTED TO SHOW UP AGAIN. IT SUCKS BUT ISN'T AS BAD AS WHEN THE NAILBITER WAS FIRST RELEASED.
OTHER THAN THAT... THINGS ARE PRETTY MUCH BACK TO NORMAL...

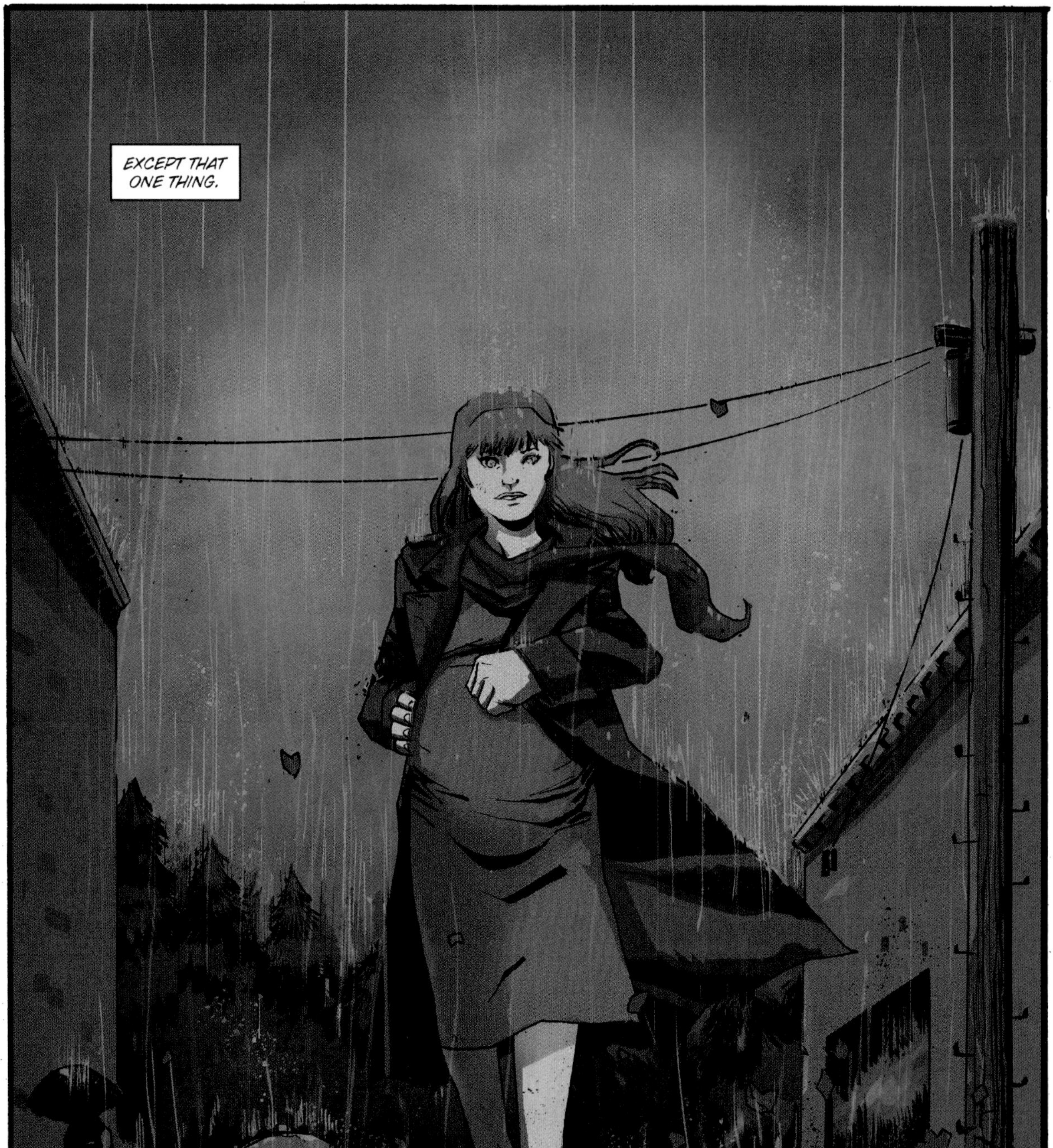
EXCEPT THAT ONE THING.

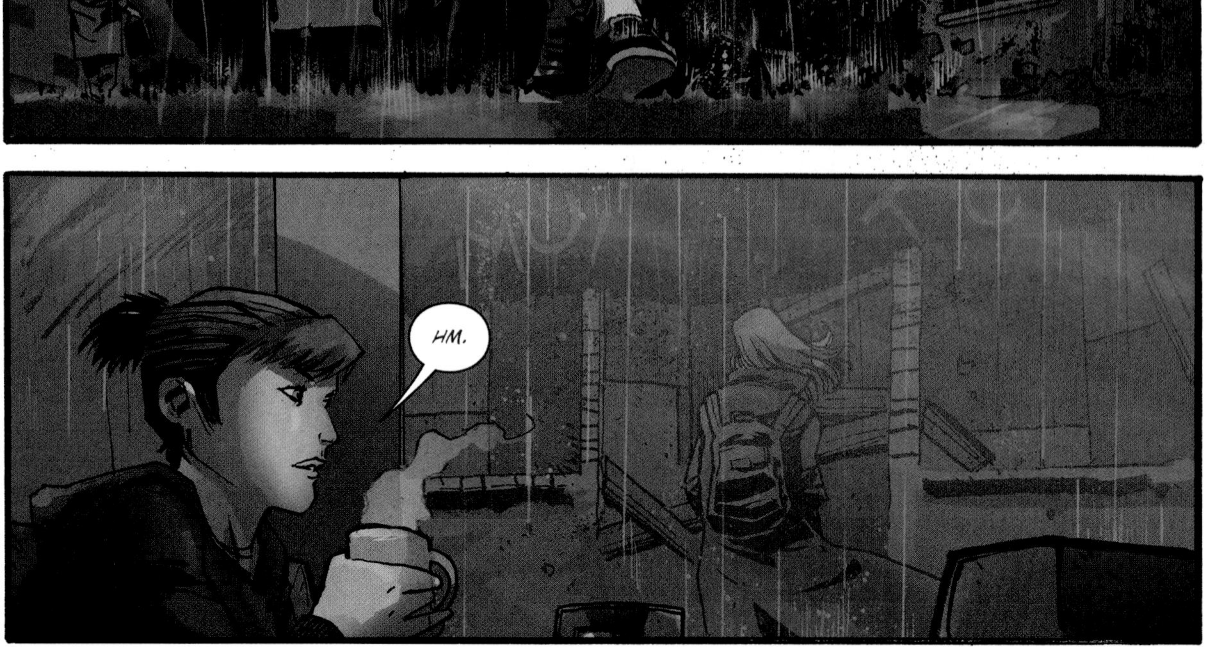
HM.

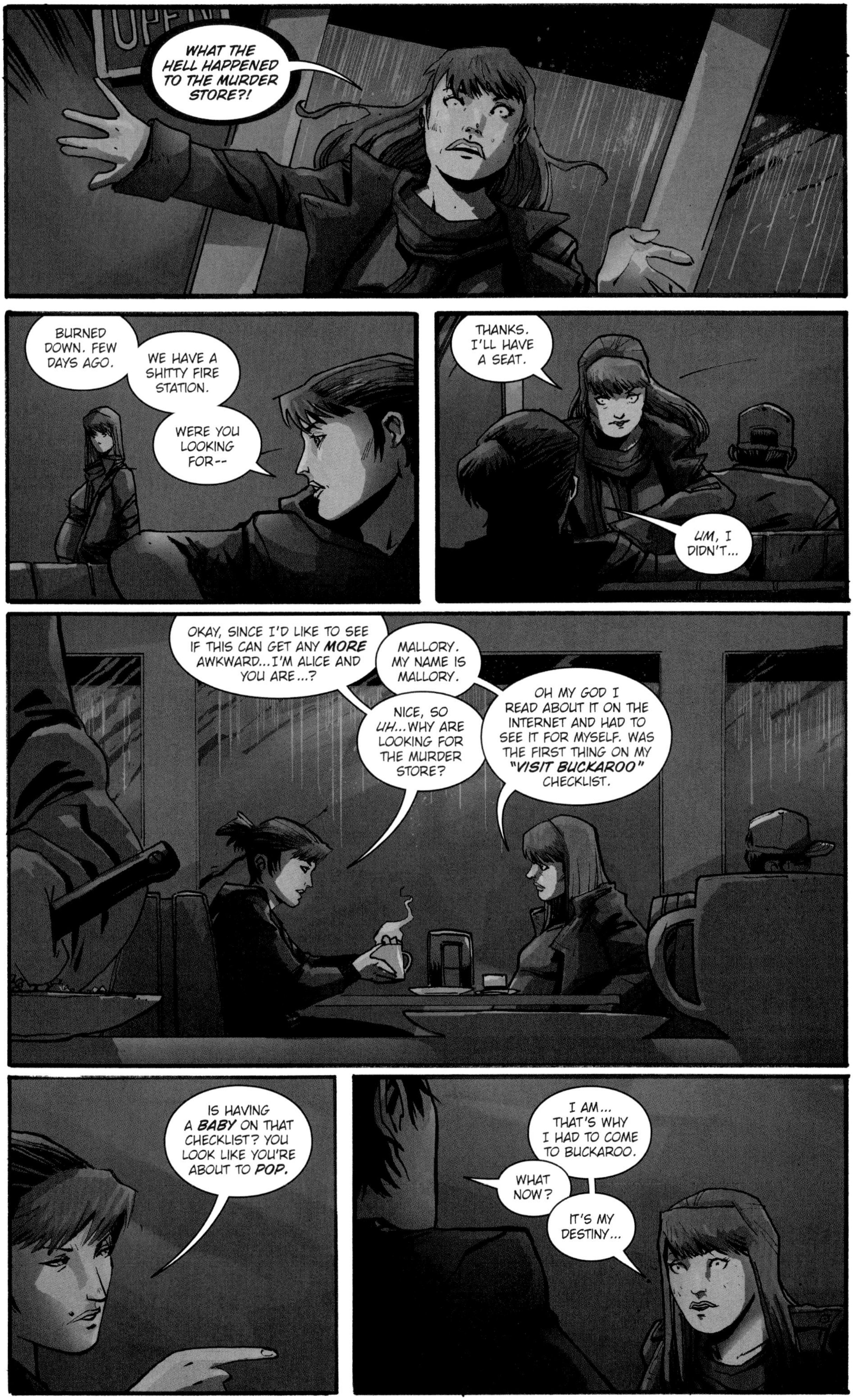

WHAT THE HELL HAPPENED TO THE MURDER STORE?!
BURNED DOWN. FEW DAYS AGO.
WE HAVE A SHITTY FIRE STATION.
WERE YOU LOOKING FOR--
THANKS. I'LL HAVE A SEAT.
UM, I DIDN'T...
OKAY, SINCE I'D LIKE TO SEE IF THIS CAN GET ANY MORE AWKWARD...I'M ALICE AND YOU ARE...?
MALLORY. MY NAME IS MALLORY.
NICE, SO UH...WHY ARE LOOKING FOR THE MURDER STORE?
OH MY GOD I READ ABOUT IT ON THE INTERNET AND HAD TO SEE IT FOR MYSELF. WAS THE FIRST THING ON MY "VISIT BUCKAROO" CHECKLIST.
IS HAVING A BABY ON THAT CHECKLIST? YOU LOOK LIKE YOU'RE ABOUT TO POP.
I AM... THAT'S WHY I HAD TO COME TO BUCKAROO.
WHAT NOW?
IT'S MY DESTINY...

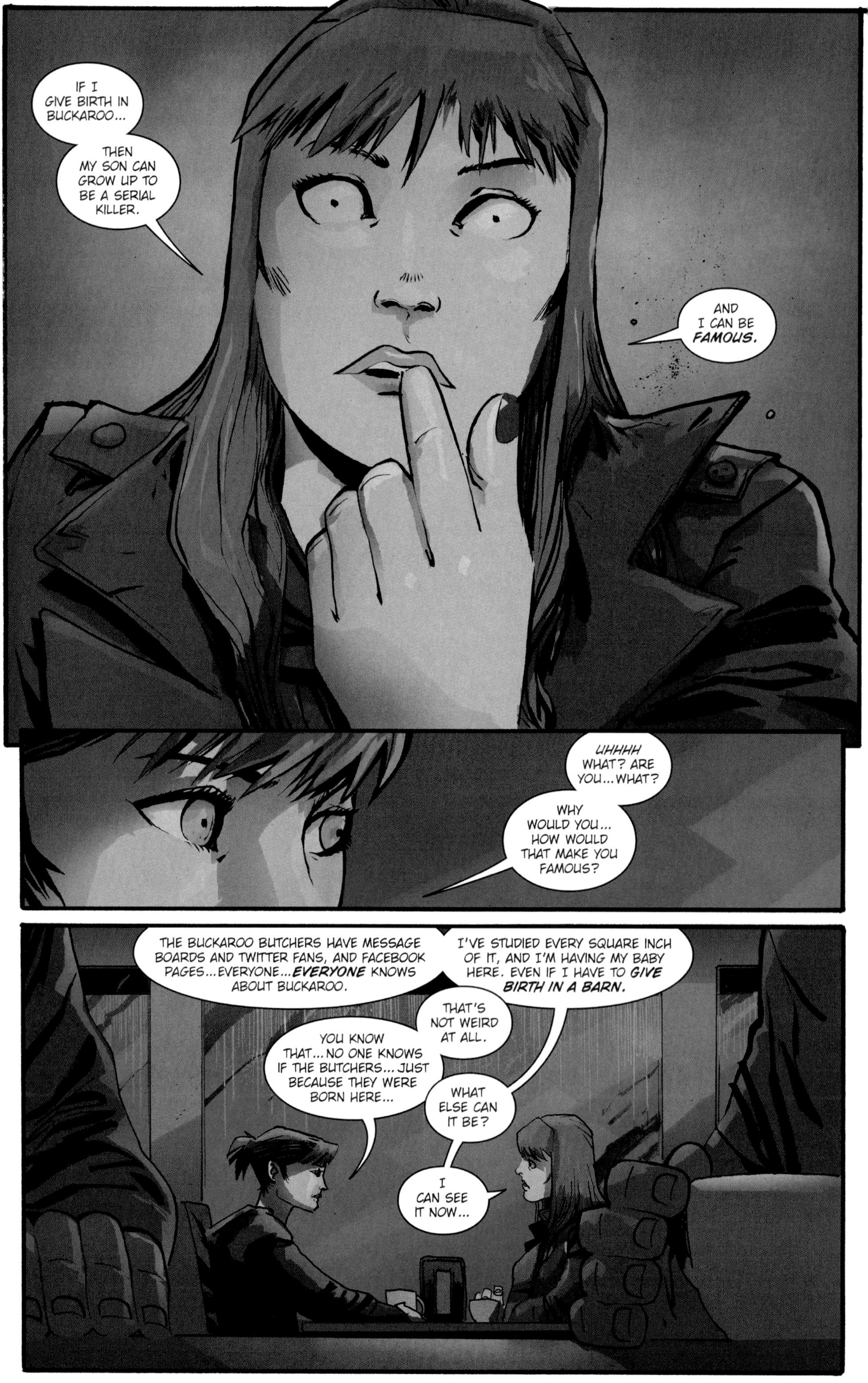
IF I GIVE BIRTH IN BUCKAROO...
THEN MY SON CAN GROW UP TO BE A SERIAL KILLER.
AND I CAN BE *FAMOUS.*
UHHHH WHAT? ARE YOU... WHAT?
WHY WOULD YOU... HOW WOULD THAT MAKE YOU FAMOUS?
THE BUCKAROO BUTCHERS HAVE MESSAGE BOARDS AND TWITTER FANS, AND FACEBOOK PAGES... EVERYONE... ***EVERYONE*** KNOWS ABOUT BUCKAROO.
I'VE STUDIED EVERY SQUARE INCH OF IT, AND I'M HAVING MY BABY HERE. EVEN IF I HAVE TO ***GIVE BIRTH IN A BARN.***
THAT'S NOT WEIRD AT ALL.
YOU KNOW THAT... NO ONE KNOWS IF THE BUTCHERS... JUST BECAUSE THEY WERE BORN HERE...
WHAT ELSE CAN IT BE?
I CAN SEE IT NOW...

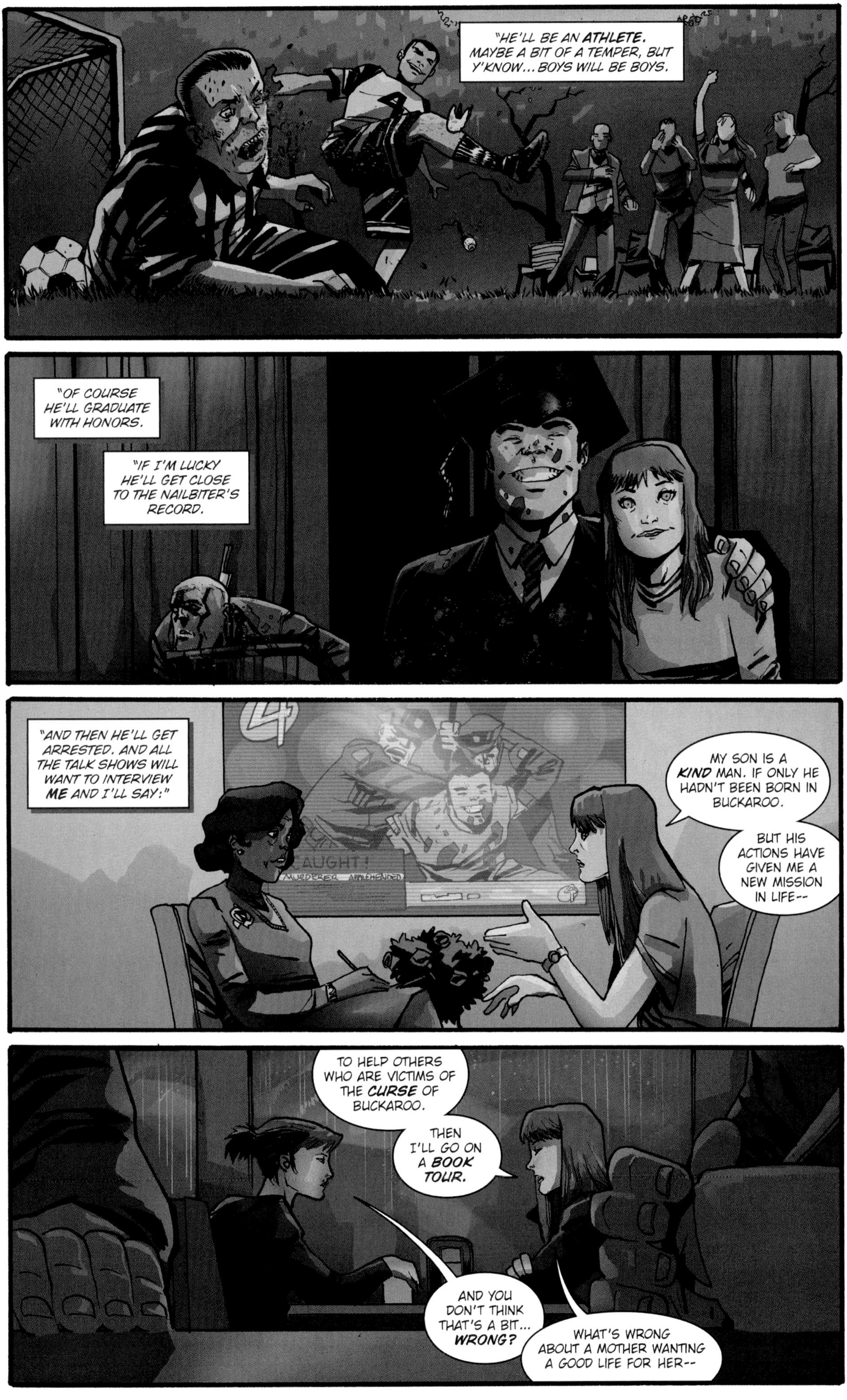
"HE'LL BE AN ATHLETE. MAYBE A BIT OF A TEMPER, BUT Y'KNOW... BOYS WILL BE BOYS.
"OF COURSE HE'LL GRADUATE WITH HONORS.
"IF I'M LUCKY HE'LL GET CLOSE TO THE NAILBITER'S RECORD.
"AND THEN HE'LL GET ARRESTED. AND ALL THE TALK SHOWS WILL WANT TO INTERVIEW ME AND I'LL SAY:"
MY SON IS A KIND MAN. IF ONLY HE HADN'T BEEN BORN IN BUCKAROO.
BUT HIS ACTIONS HAVE GIVEN ME A NEW MISSION IN LIFE--
TO HELP OTHERS WHO ARE VICTIMS OF THE CURSE OF BUCKAROO.
THEN I'LL GO ON A BOOK TOUR.
AND YOU DON'T THINK THAT'S A BIT... WRONG?
WHAT'S WRONG ABOUT A MOTHER WANTING A GOOD LIFE FOR HER--

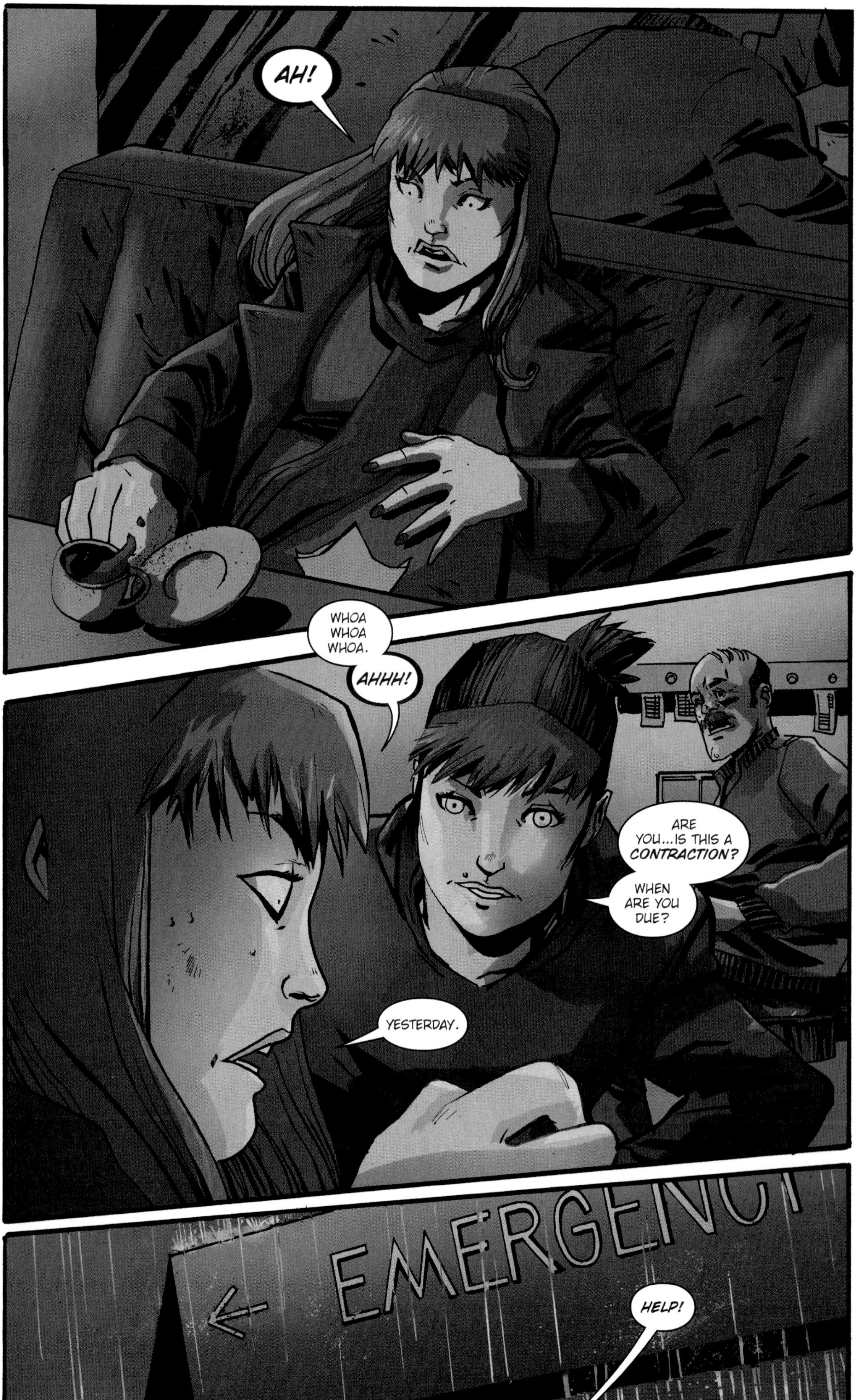
AH!
WHOA WHOA WHOA.
AHHH!
ARE YOU...IS THIS A CONTRACTION?
WHEN ARE YOU DUE?
YESTERDAY.
EMERGENCY
HELP!

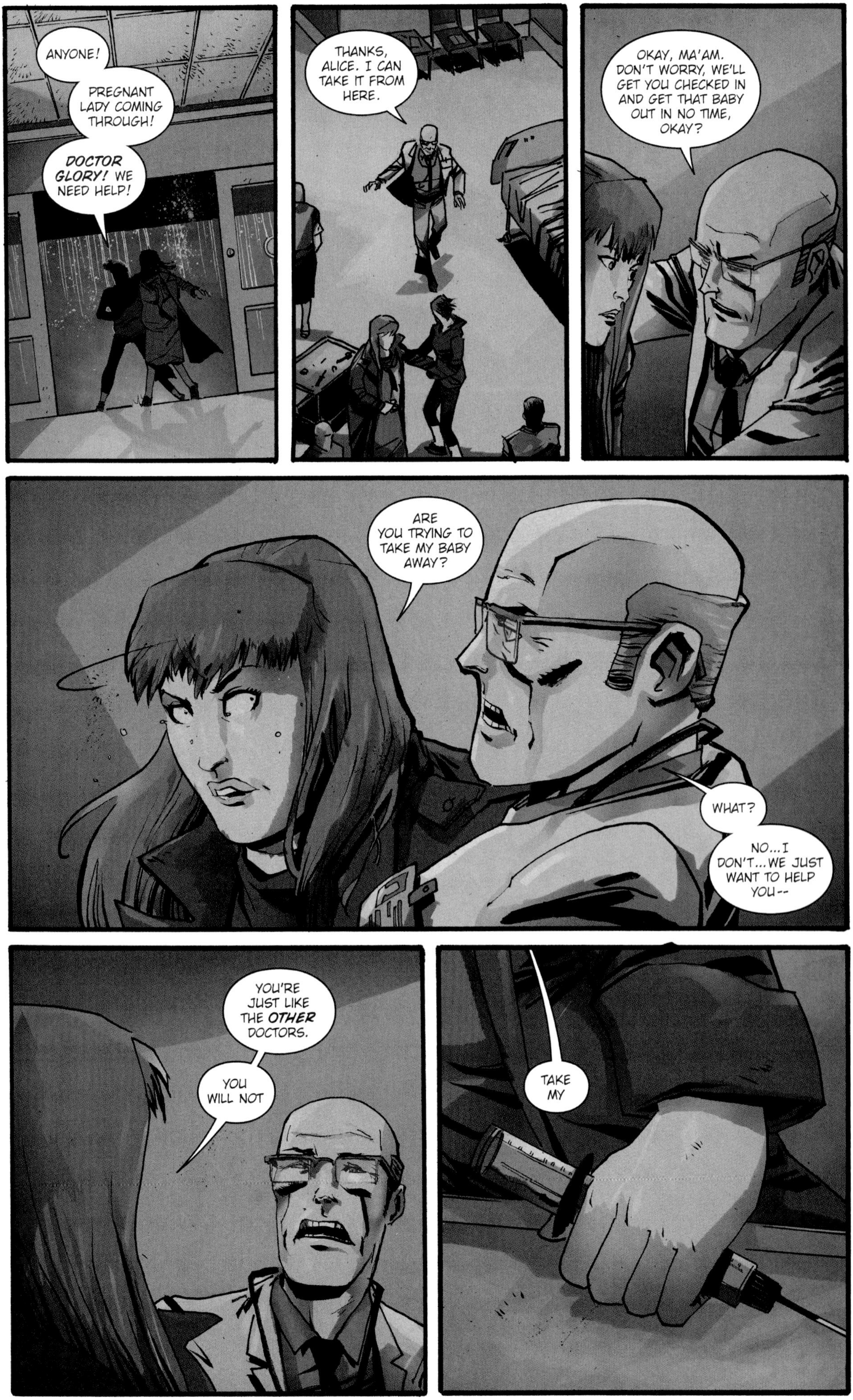
ANYONE!
PREGNANT LADY COMING THROUGH!
DOCTOR GLORY! WE NEED HELP!
THANKS, ALICE. I CAN TAKE IT FROM HERE.
OKAY, MA'AM. DON'T WORRY, WE'LL GET YOU CHECKED IN AND GET THAT BABY OUT IN NO TIME, OKAY?
ARE YOU TRYING TO TAKE MY BABY AWAY?
WHAT?
NO...I DON'T...WE JUST WANT TO HELP YOU--
YOU'RE JUST LIKE THE OTHER DOCTORS.
YOU WILL NOT
TAKE MY

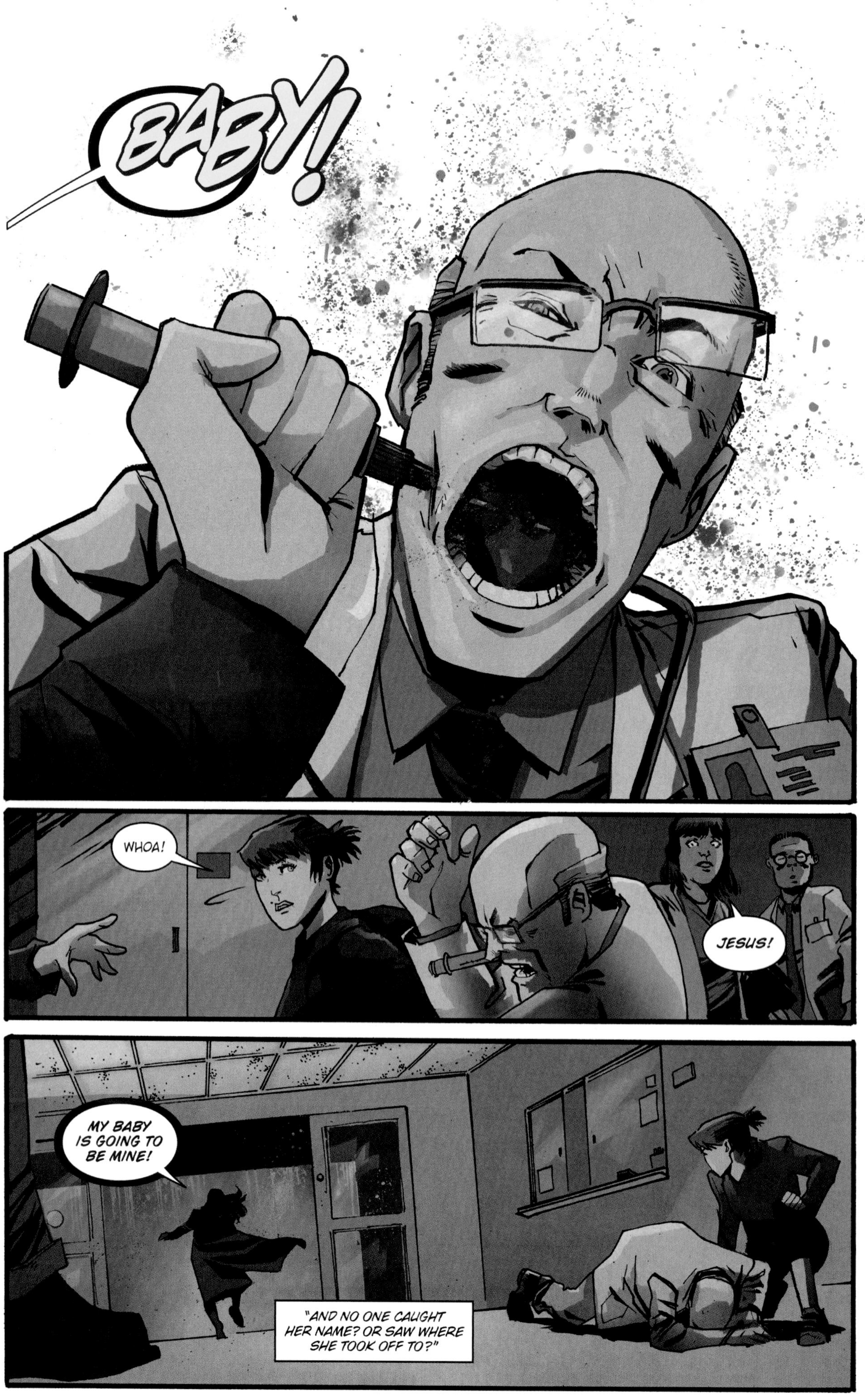
BABY!
WHOA!
JESUS!
MY BABY IS GOING TO BE MINE!
"AND NO ONE CAUGHT HER NAME? OR SAW WHERE SHE TOOK OFF TO?"

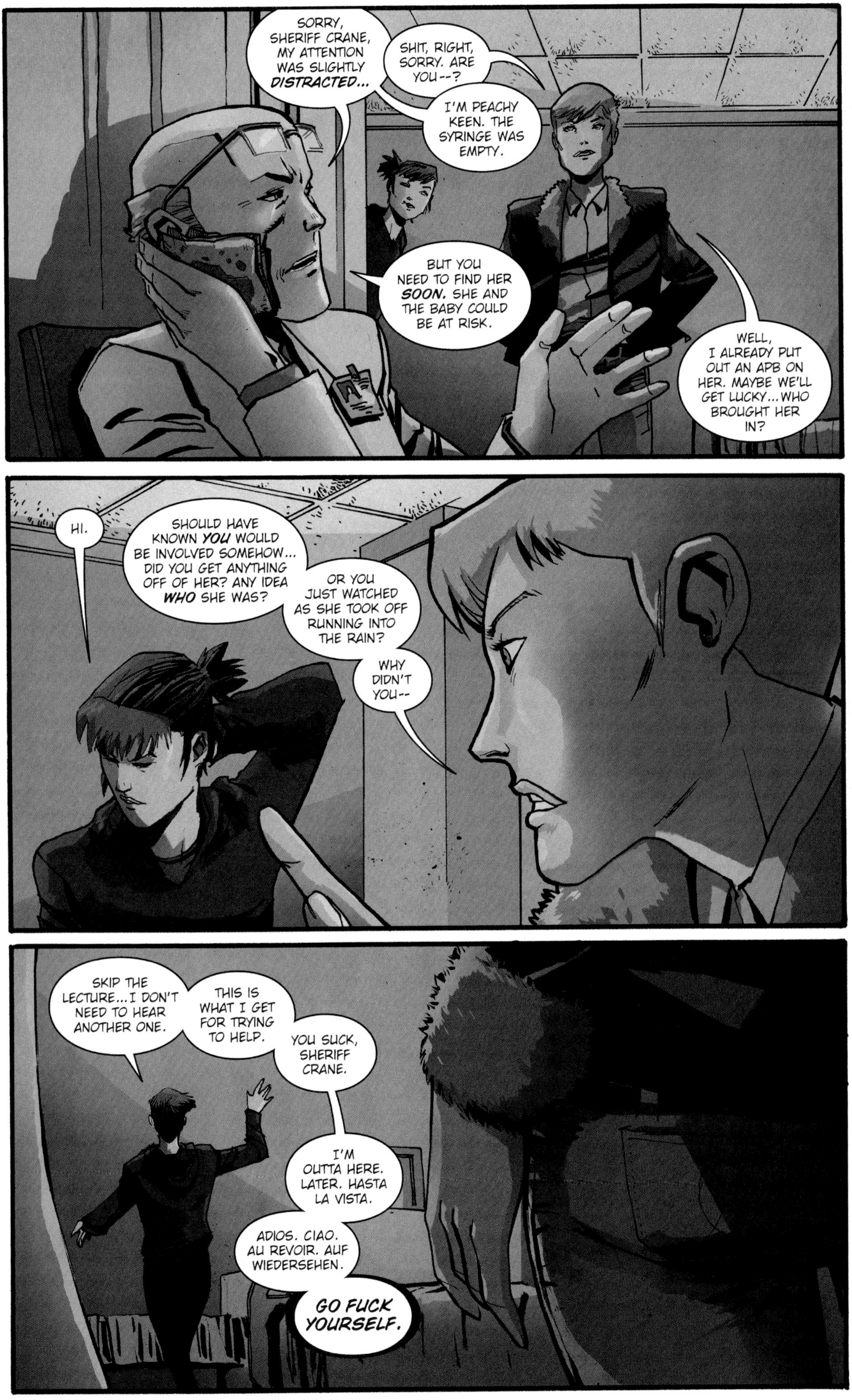
SORRY, SHERIFF CRANE, MY ATTENTION WAS SLIGHTLY DISTRACTED...
SHIT, RIGHT, SORRY. ARE YOU--?
I'M PEACHY KEEN. THE SYRINGE WAS EMPTY.
BUT YOU NEED TO FIND HER SOON. SHE AND THE BABY COULD BE AT RISK.
WELL, I ALREADY PUT OUT AN APB ON HER. MAYBE WE'LL GET LUCKY...WHO BROUGHT HER IN?
HI.
SHOULD HAVE KNOWN YOU WOULD BE INVOLVED SOMEHOW... DID YOU GET ANYTHING OFF OF HER? ANY IDEA WHO SHE WAS?
OR YOU JUST WATCHED AS SHE TOOK OFF RUNNING INTO THE RAIN?
WHY DIDN'T YOU--
SKIP THE LECTURE...I DON'T NEED TO HEAR ANOTHER ONE.
THIS IS WHAT I GET FOR TRYING TO HELP.
YOU SUCK, SHERIFF CRANE.
I'M OUTTA HERE. LATER. HASTA LA VISTA.
ADIOS. CIAO. AU REVOIR. AUF WIEDERSEHEN.
GO FUCK YOURSELF.

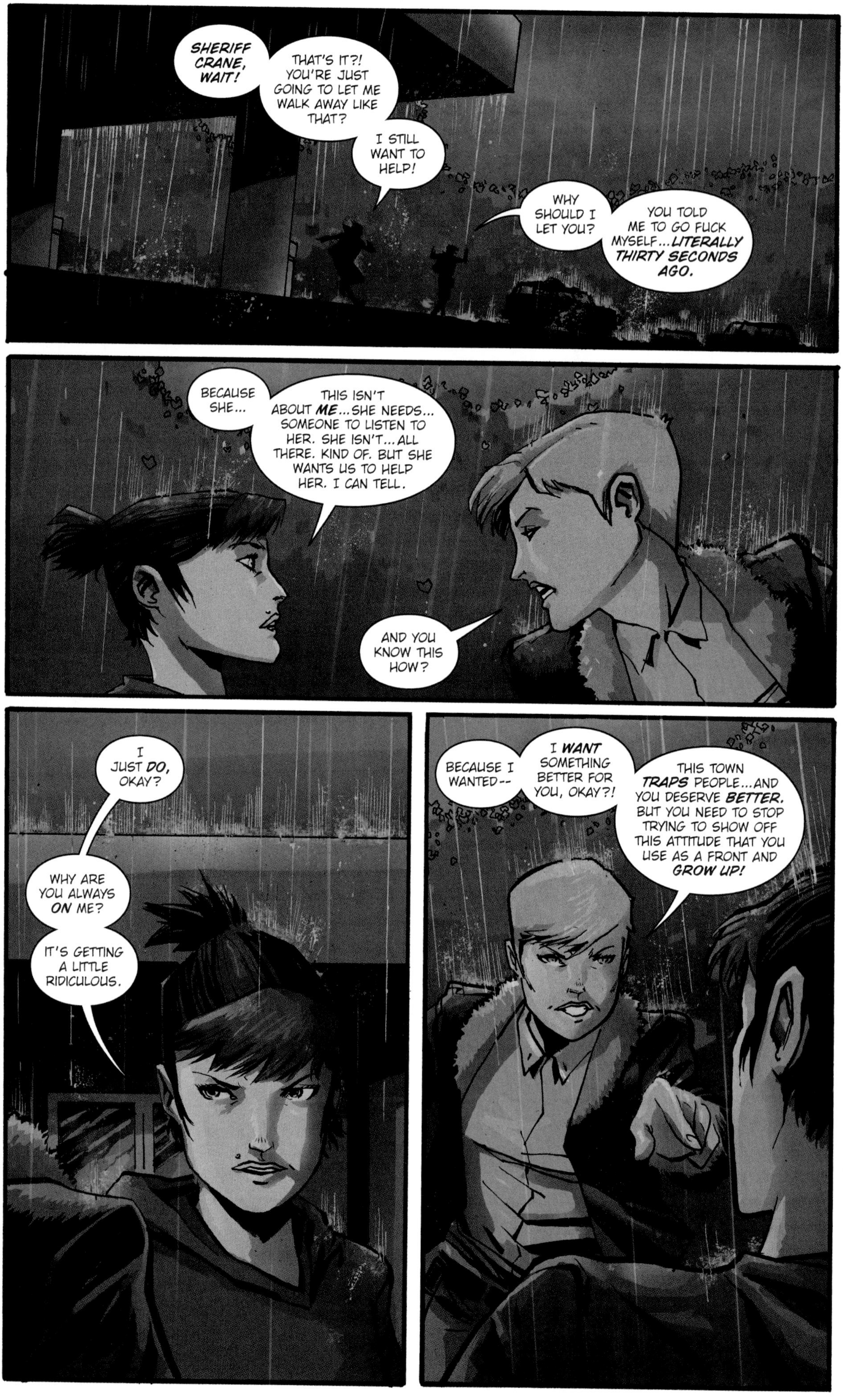
SHERIFF CRANE, WAIT!
THAT'S IT?! YOU'RE JUST GOING TO LET ME WALK AWAY LIKE THAT?
I STILL WANT TO HELP!
WHY SHOULD I LET YOU?
YOU TOLD ME TO GO FUCK MYSELF... LITERALLY THIRTY SECONDS AGO.
BECAUSE SHE...
THIS ISN'T ABOUT ME... SHE NEEDS... SOMEONE TO LISTEN TO HER. SHE ISN'T... ALL THERE. KIND OF. BUT SHE WANTS US TO HELP HER. I CAN TELL.
AND YOU KNOW THIS HOW?
I JUST DO, OKAY?
WHY ARE YOU ALWAYS ON ME?
IT'S GETTING A LITTLE RIDICULOUS.
BECAUSE I WANTED--
I WANT SOMETHING BETTER FOR YOU, OKAY?!
THIS TOWN TRAPS PEOPLE... AND YOU DESERVE BETTER. BUT YOU NEED TO STOP TRYING TO SHOW OFF THIS ATTITUDE THAT YOU USE AS A FRONT AND GROW UP!

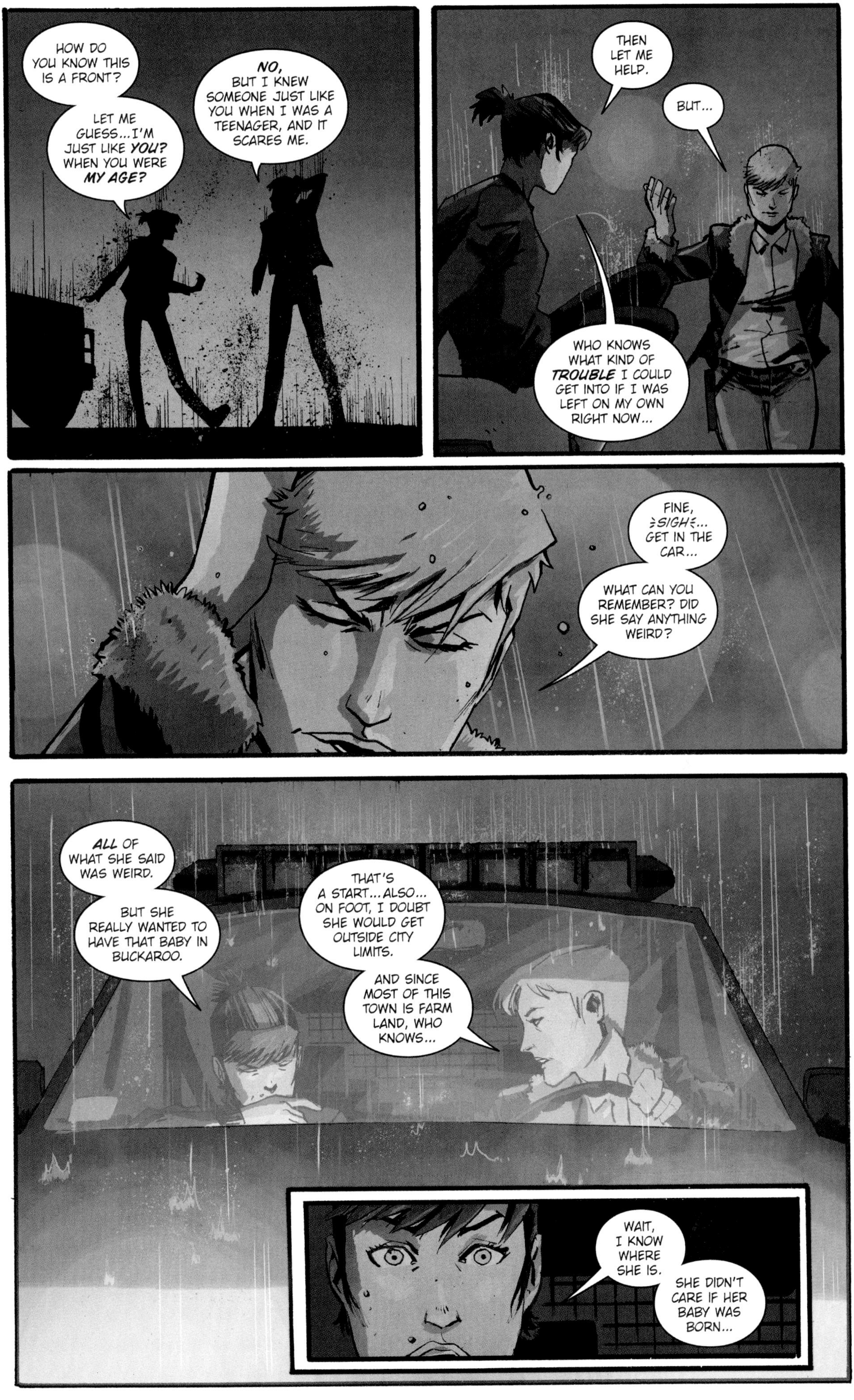
HOW DO YOU KNOW THIS IS A FRONT?
LET ME GUESS...I'M JUST LIKE *YOU?* WHEN YOU WERE *MY AGE?*
NO, BUT I KNEW SOMEONE JUST LIKE YOU WHEN I WAS A TEENAGER, AND IT SCARES ME.
THEN LET ME HELP.
BUT...
WHO KNOWS WHAT KIND OF *TROUBLE* I COULD GET INTO IF I WAS LEFT ON MY OWN RIGHT NOW...
FINE, *SIGH*... GET IN THE CAR...
WHAT CAN YOU REMEMBER? DID SHE SAY ANYTHING WEIRD?
ALL OF WHAT SHE SAID WAS WEIRD.
BUT SHE REALLY WANTED TO HAVE THAT BABY IN BUCKAROO.
THAT'S A START...ALSO... ON FOOT, I DOUBT SHE WOULD GET OUTSIDE CITY LIMITS.
AND SINCE MOST OF THIS TOWN IS FARM LAND, WHO KNOWS...
WAIT, I KNOW WHERE SHE IS.
SHE DIDN'T CARE IF HER BABY WAS BORN...

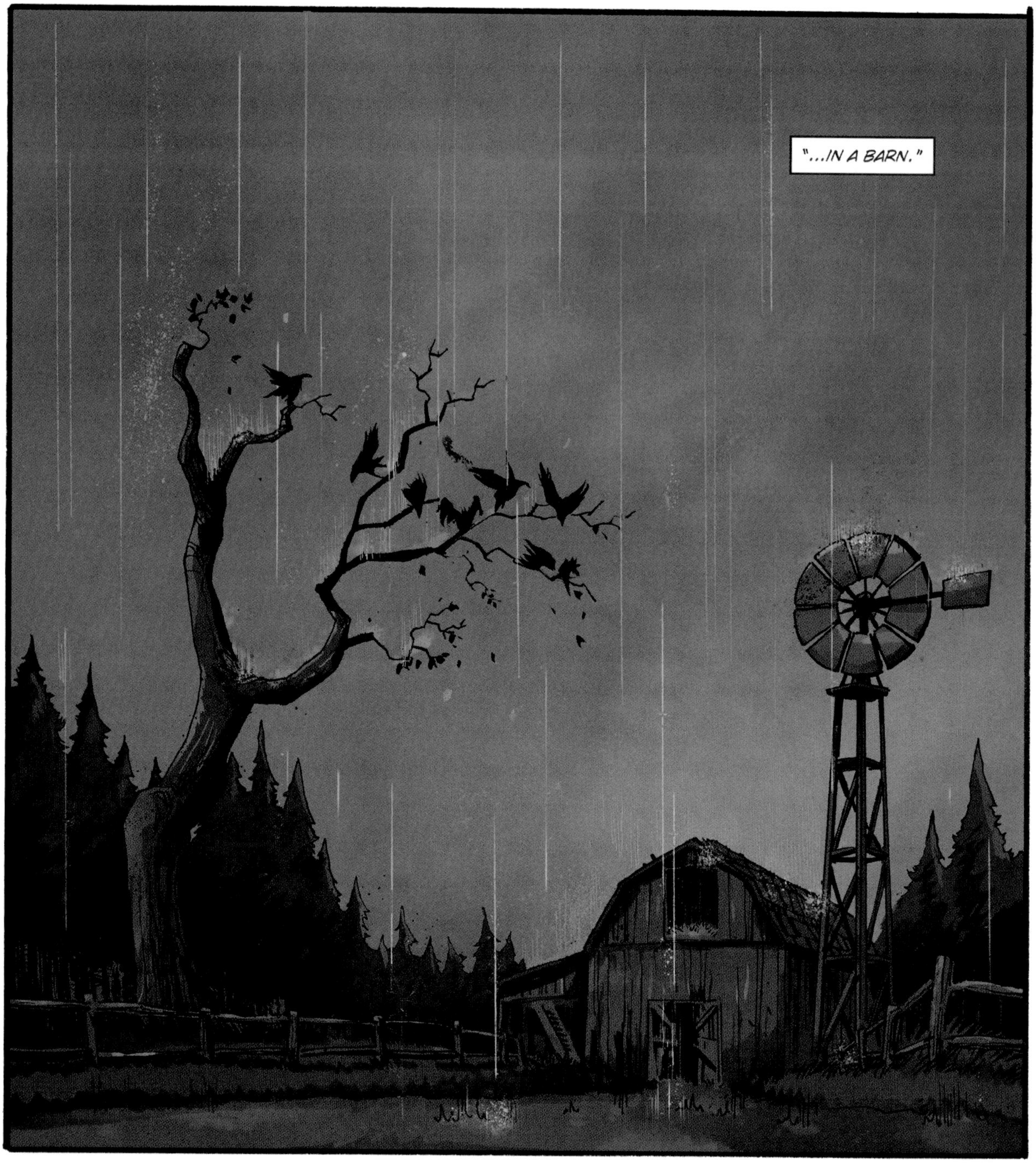
"...IN A BARN."

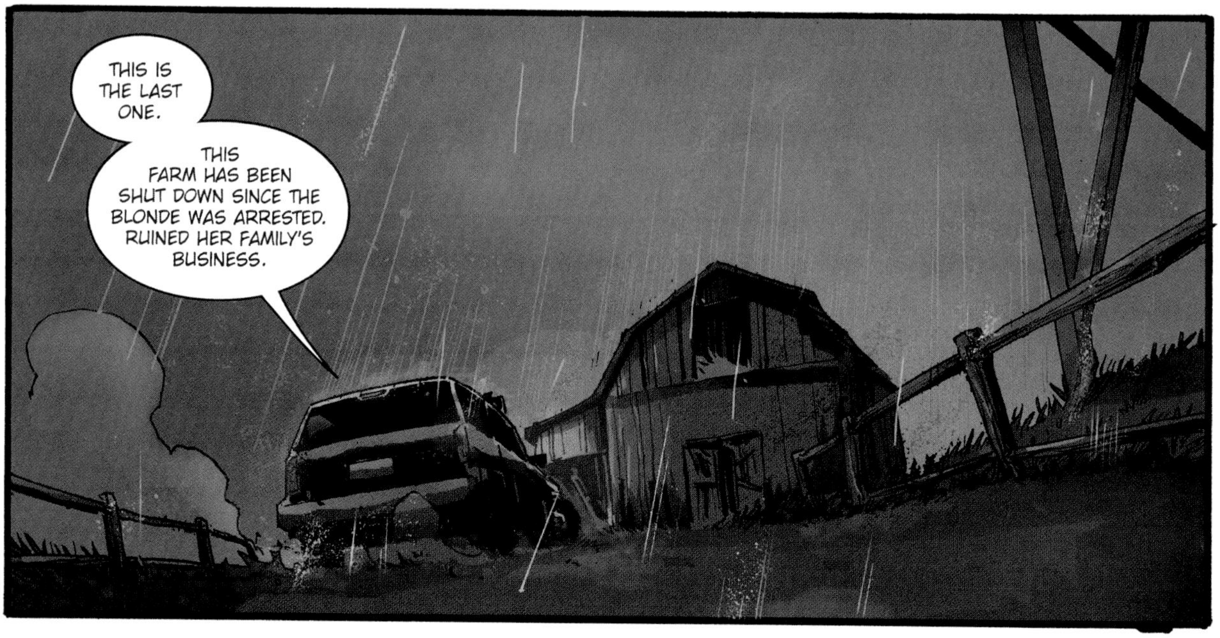
THIS IS THE LAST ONE.
THIS FARM HAS BEEN SHUT DOWN SINCE THE BLONDE WAS ARRESTED. RUINED HER FAMILY'S BUSINESS.

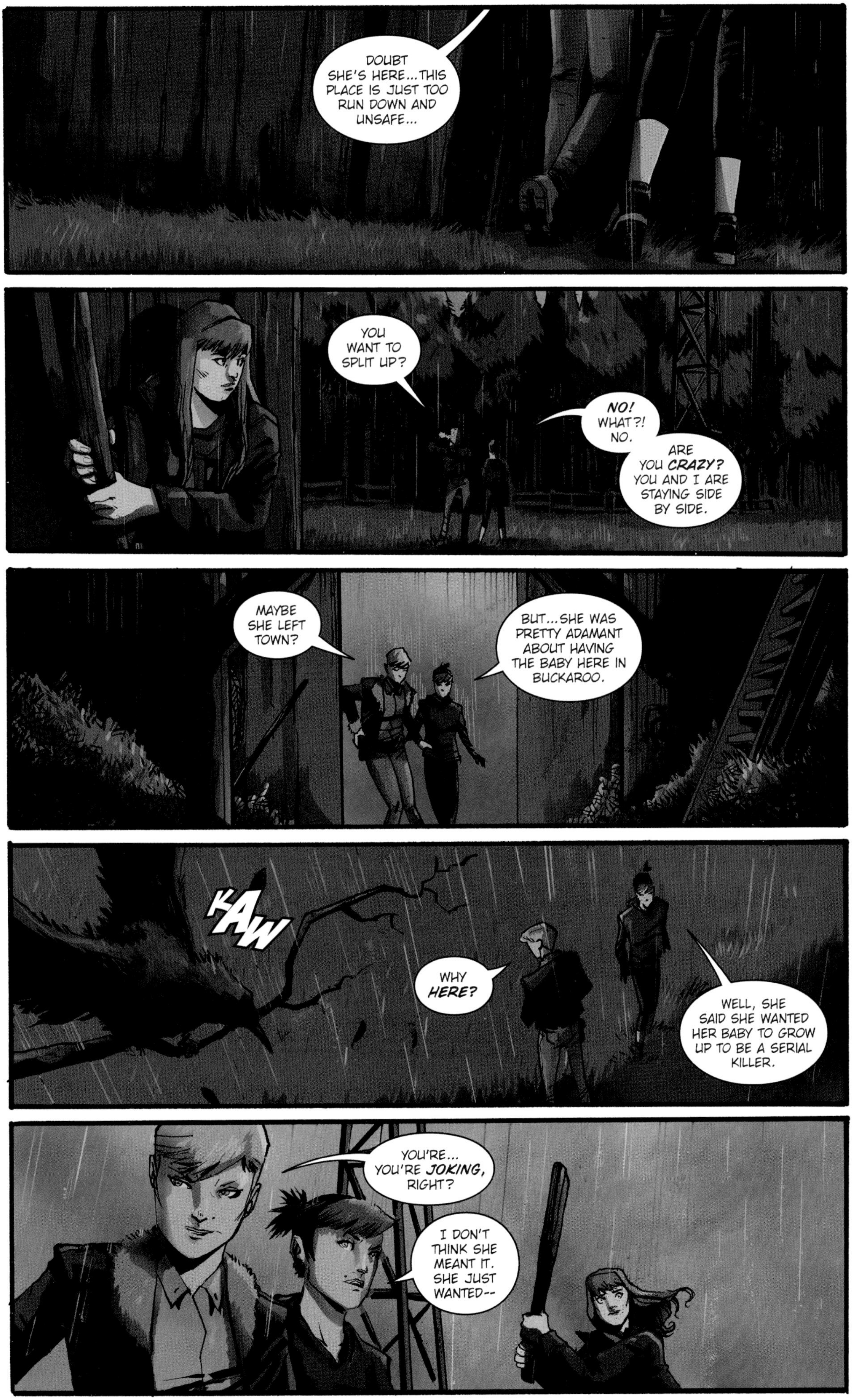
DOUBT SHE'S HERE...THIS PLACE IS JUST TOO RUN DOWN AND UNSAFE...
YOU WANT TO SPLIT UP?
NO! WHAT?! NO.
ARE YOU CRAZY? YOU AND I ARE STAYING SIDE BY SIDE.
MAYBE SHE LEFT TOWN?
BUT...SHE WAS PRETTY ADAMANT ABOUT HAVING THE BABY HERE IN BUCKAROO.
KAW
WHY HERE?
WELL, SHE SAID SHE WANTED HER BABY TO GROW UP TO BE A SERIAL KILLER.
YOU'RE... YOU'RE JOKING, RIGHT?
I DON'T THINK SHE MEANT IT. SHE JUST WANTED--

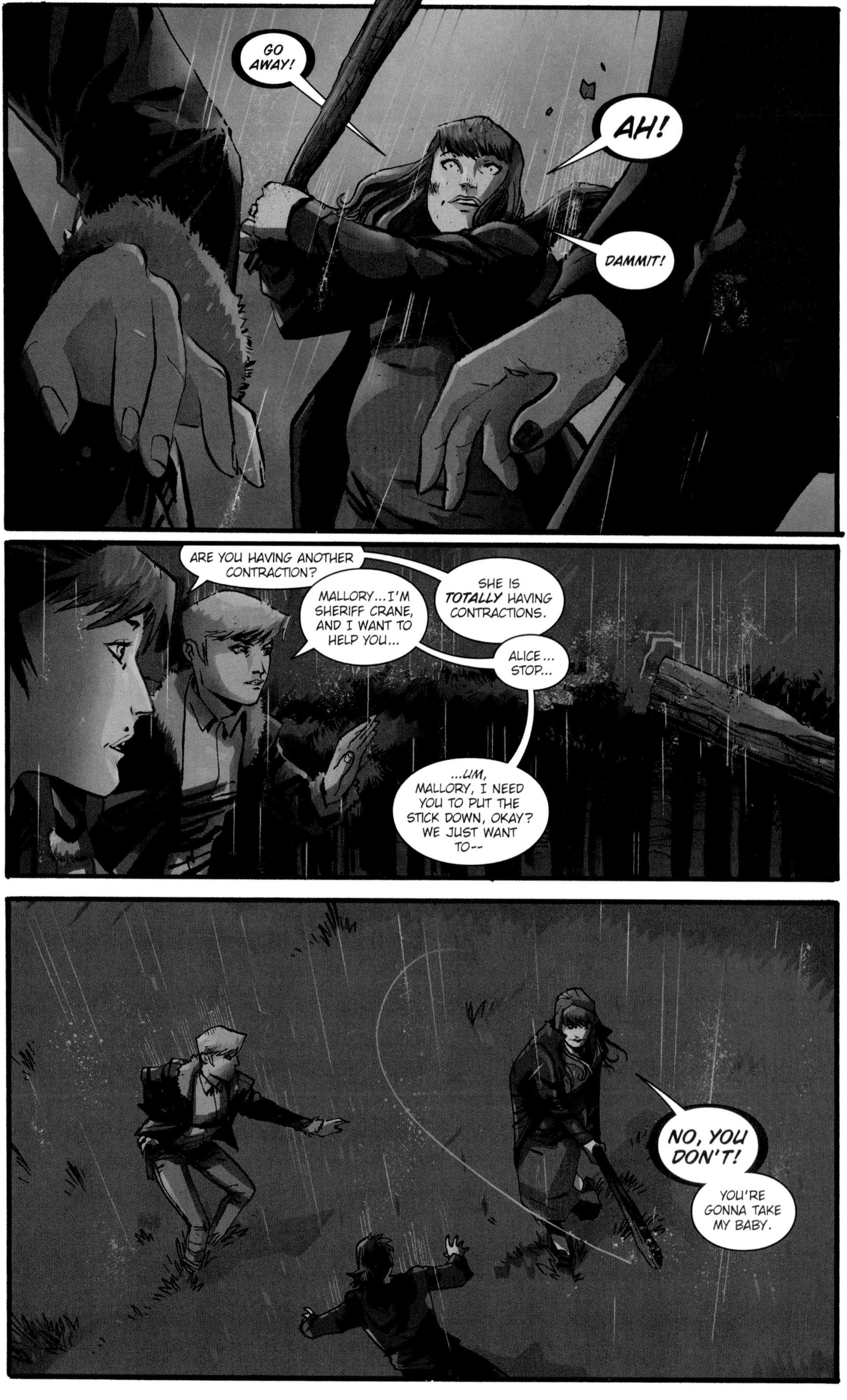
GO AWAY!
AH!
DAMMIT!
ARE YOU HAVING ANOTHER CONTRACTION?
MALLORY...I'M SHERIFF CRANE, AND I WANT TO HELP YOU...
SHE IS TOTALLY HAVING CONTRACTIONS.
ALICE... STOP...
...UM, MALLORY, I NEED YOU TO PUT THE STICK DOWN, OKAY? WE JUST WANT TO--
NO, YOU DON'T!
YOU'RE GONNA TAKE MY BABY.

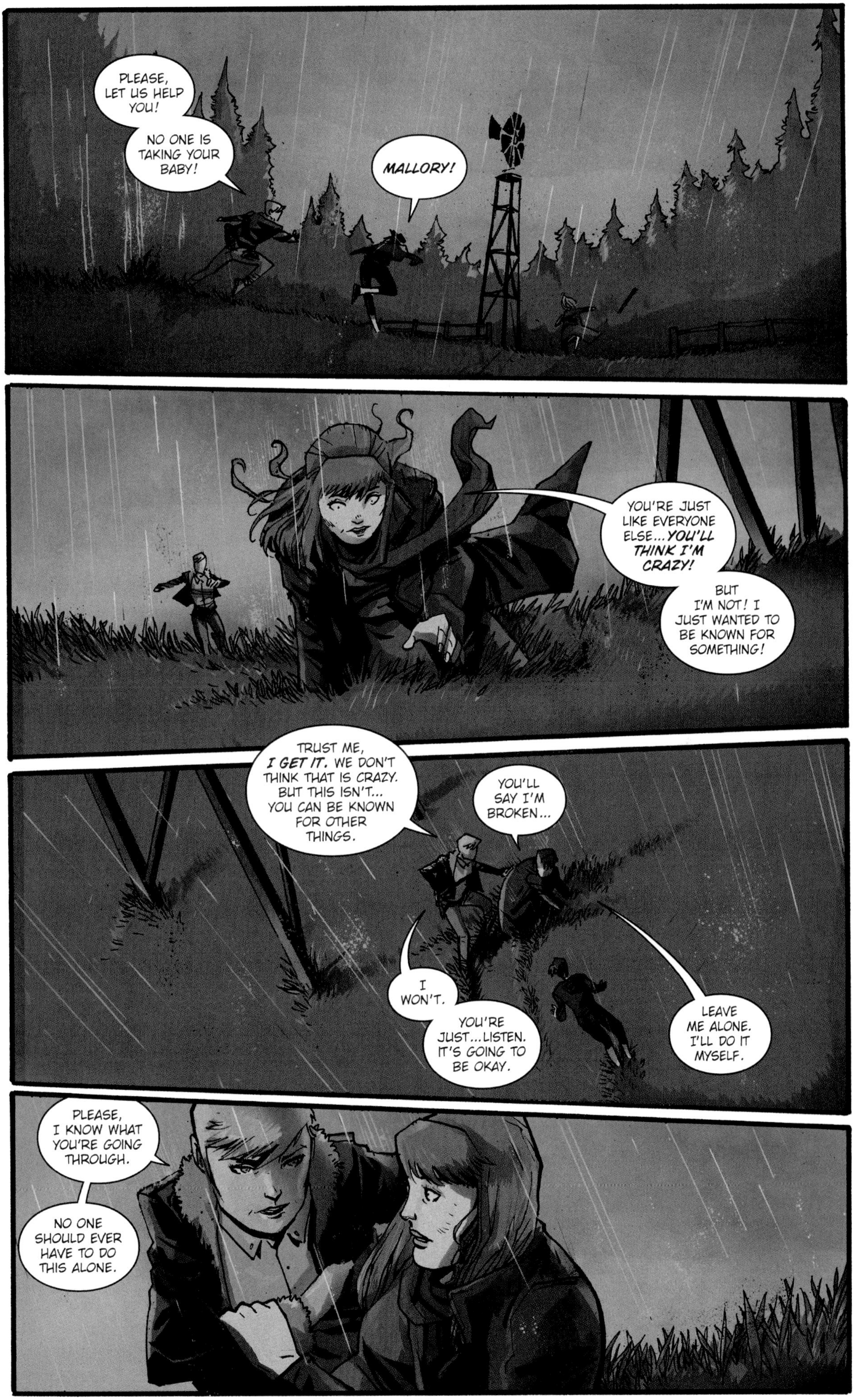
PLEASE, LET US HELP YOU!
NO ONE IS TAKING YOUR BABY!
MALLORY!
YOU'RE JUST LIKE EVERYONE ELSE... YOU'LL THINK I'M CRAZY!
BUT I'M NOT! I JUST WANTED TO BE KNOWN FOR SOMETHING!
TRUST ME, I GET IT. WE DON'T THINK THAT IS CRAZY. BUT THIS ISN'T... YOU CAN BE KNOWN FOR OTHER THINGS.
YOU'LL SAY I'M BROKEN...
I WON'T.
YOU'RE JUST...LISTEN. IT'S GOING TO BE OKAY.
LEAVE ME ALONE. I'LL DO IT MYSELF.
PLEASE, I KNOW WHAT YOU'RE GOING THROUGH.
NO ONE SHOULD EVER HAVE TO DO THIS ALONE.

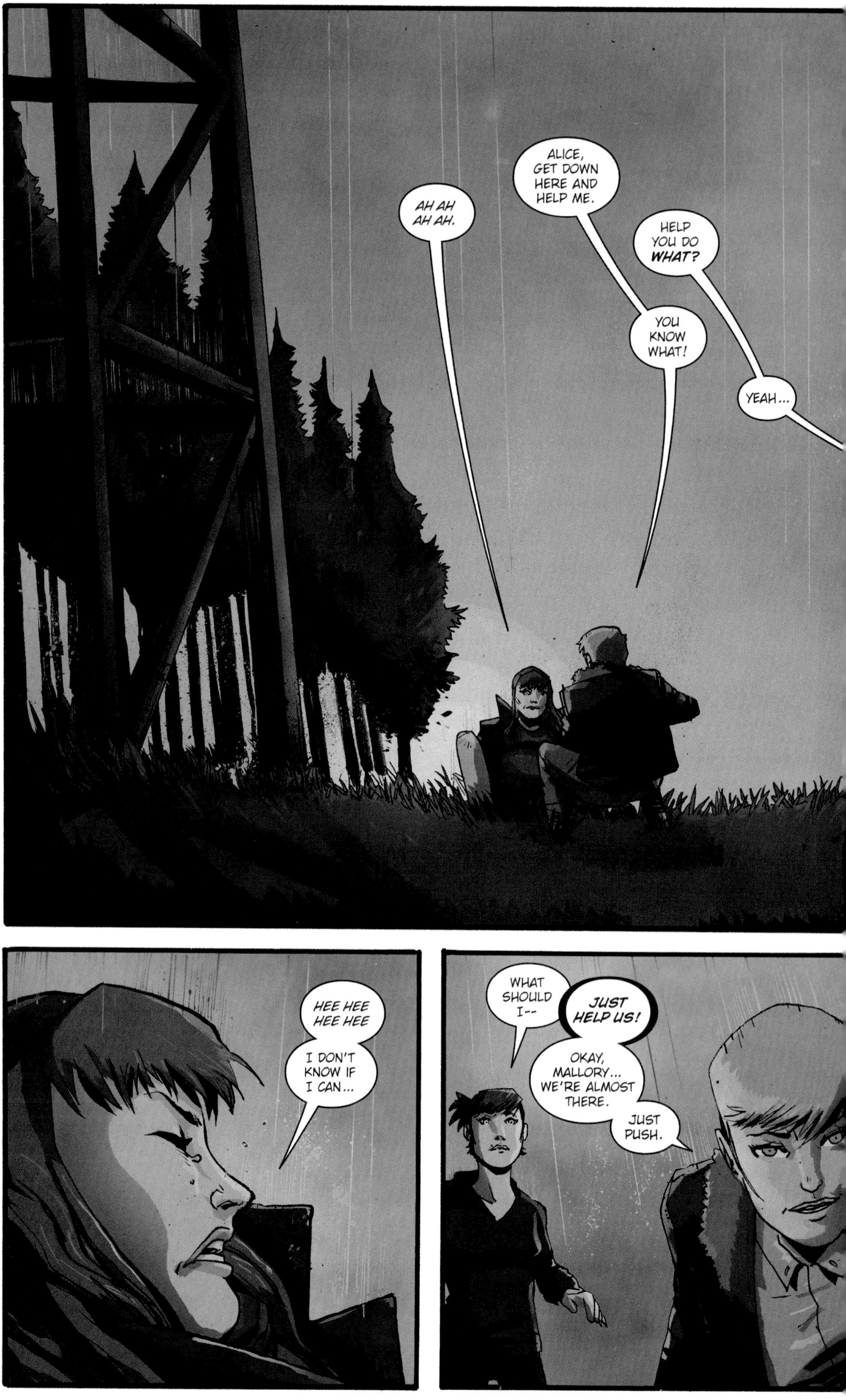
AH AH AH AH.
ALICE, GET DOWN HERE AND HELP ME.
HELP YOU DO **WHAT?**
YOU KNOW WHAT!
YEAH...
HEE HEE HEE HEE
I DON'T KNOW IF I CAN...
WHAT SHOULD I--
JUST HELP US!
OKAY, MALLORY... WE'RE ALMOST THERE.
JUST PUSH.

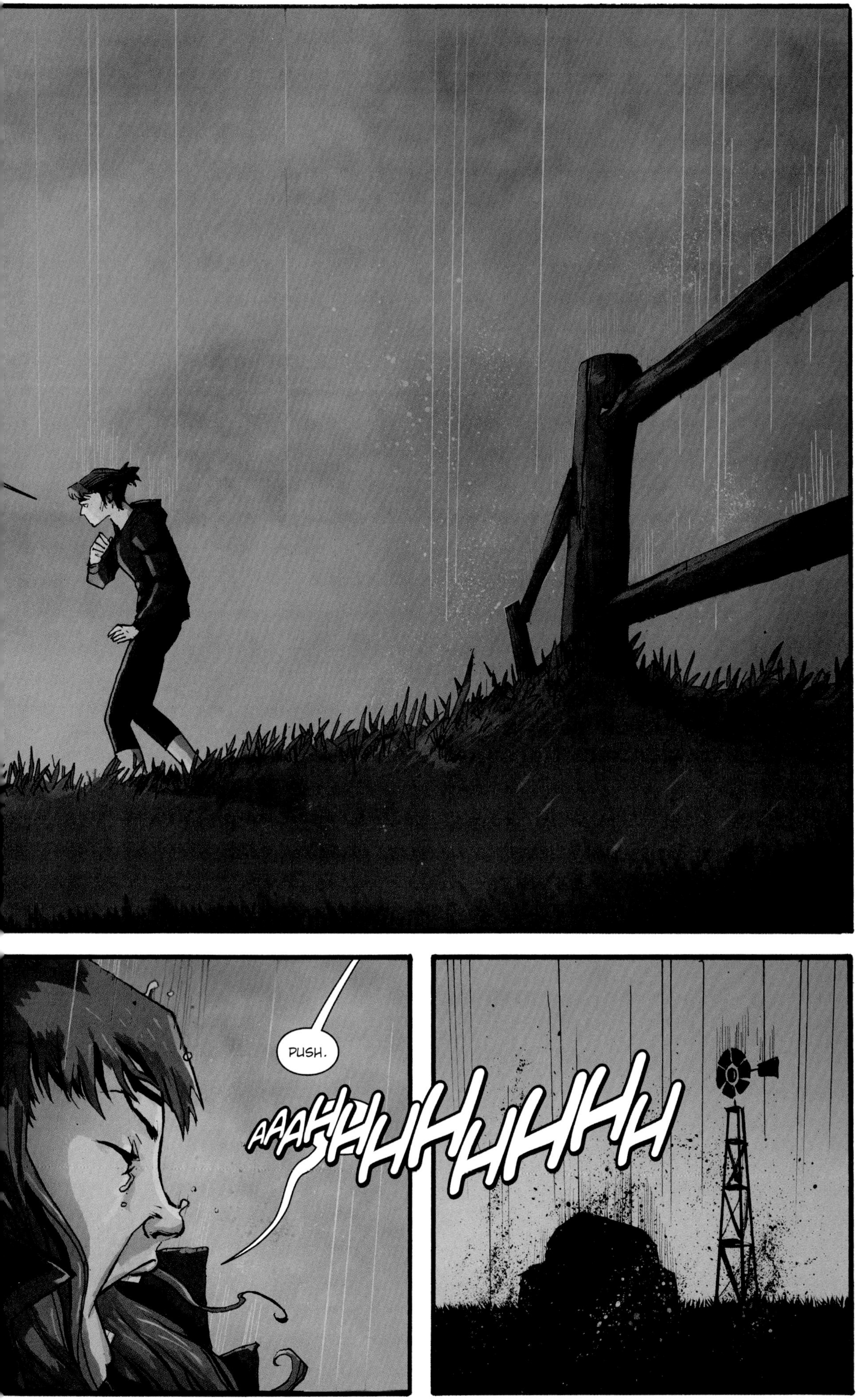
PUSH.
AAAHHHHHHHHHH

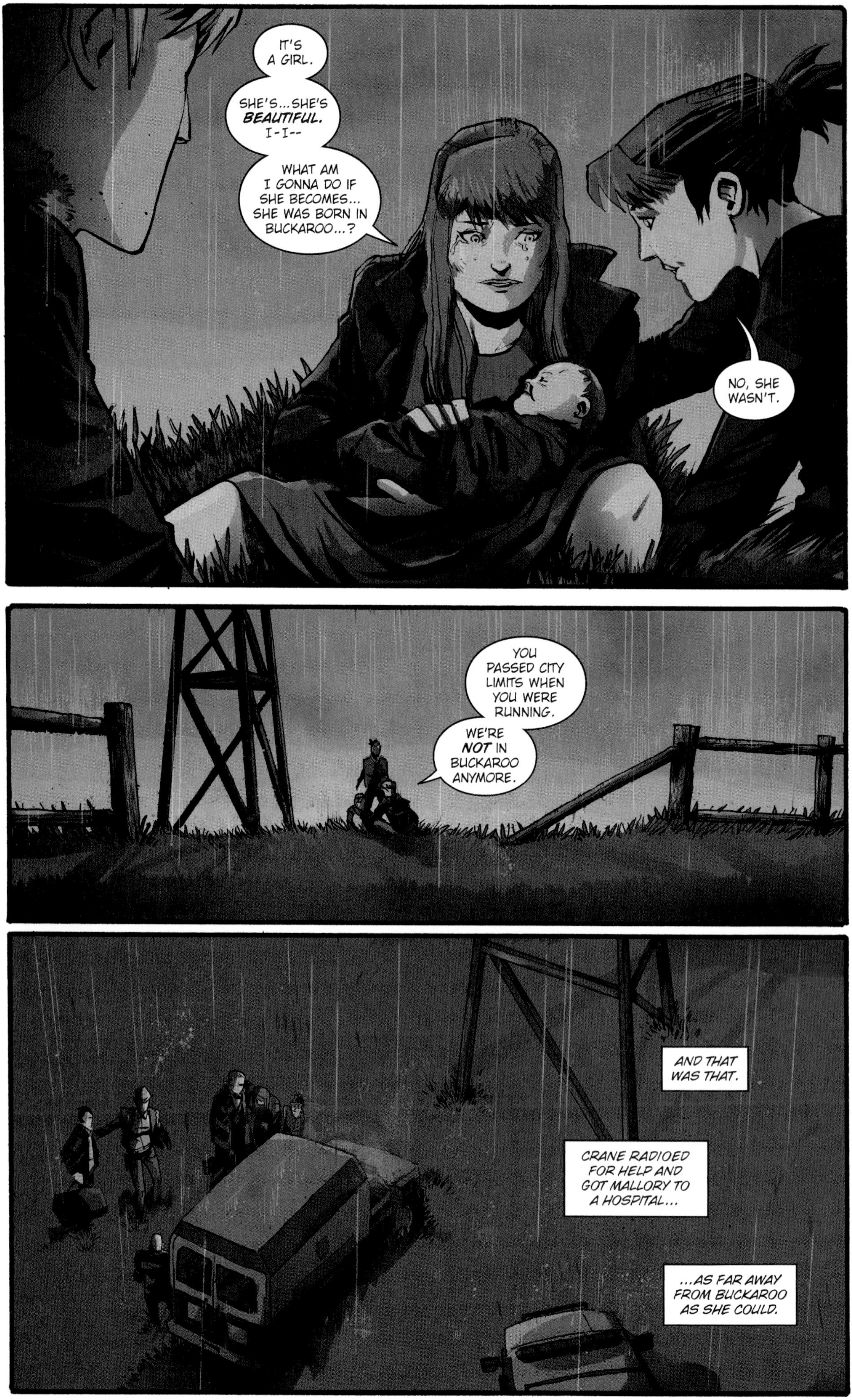
IT'S A GIRL.
SHE'S... SHE'S **BEAUTIFUL.** I-I--
WHAT AM I GONNA DO IF SHE BECOMES... SHE WAS BORN IN BUCKAROO...?
NO, SHE WASN'T.
YOU PASSED CITY LIMITS WHEN YOU WERE RUNNING.
WE'RE **NOT** IN BUCKAROO ANYMORE.
AND THAT WAS THAT.
CRANE RADIOED FOR HELP AND GOT MALLORY TO A HOSPITAL...
...AS FAR AWAY FROM BUCKAROO AS SHE COULD.

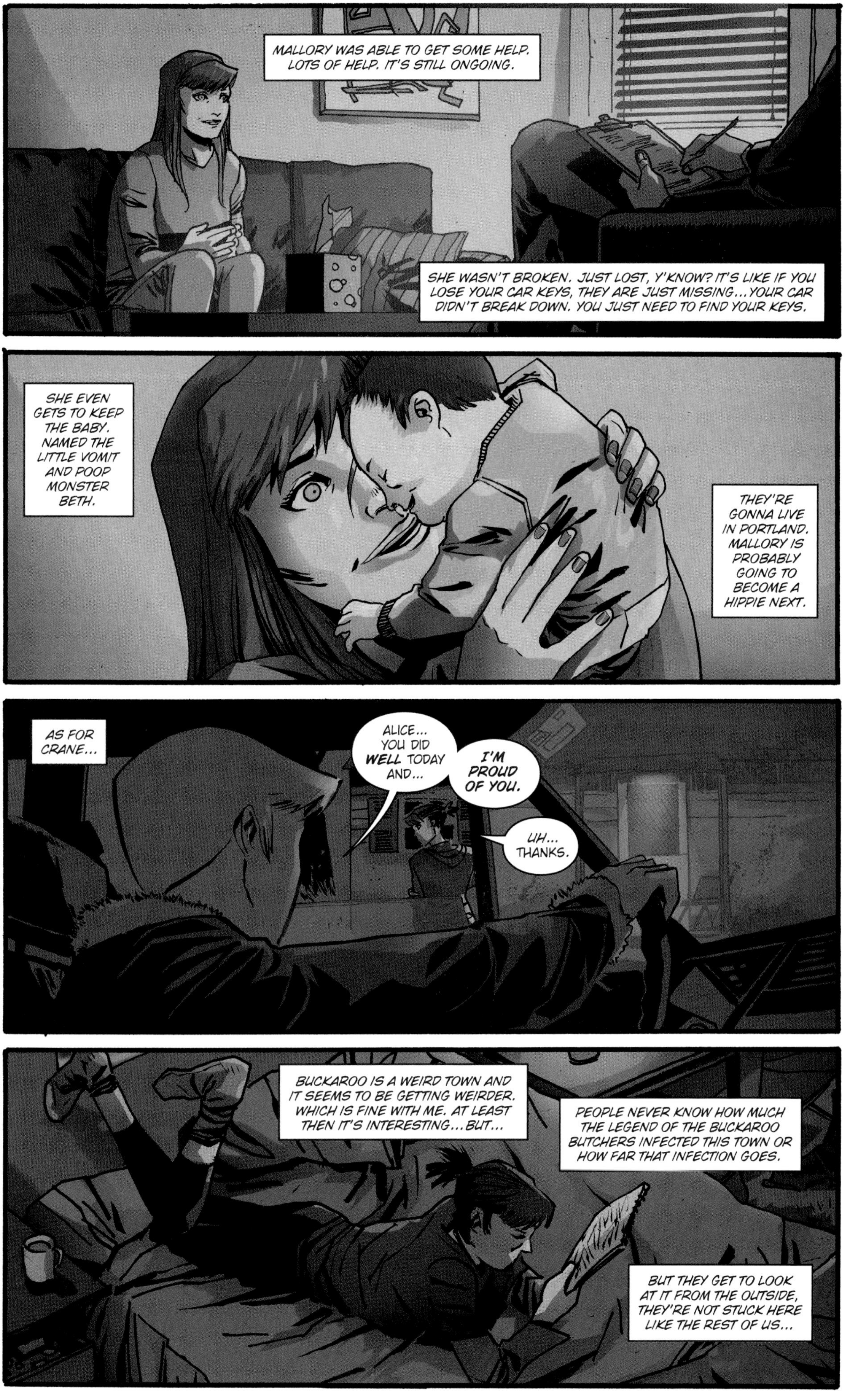
MALLORY WAS ABLE TO GET SOME HELP. LOTS OF HELP. IT'S STILL ONGOING.
SHE WASN'T BROKEN. JUST LOST, Y'KNOW? IT'S LIKE IF YOU LOSE YOUR CAR KEYS, THEY ARE JUST MISSING... YOUR CAR DIDN'T BREAK DOWN. YOU JUST NEED TO FIND YOUR KEYS.
SHE EVEN GETS TO KEEP THE BABY. NAMED THE LITTLE VOMIT AND POOP MONSTER BETH.
THEY'RE GONNA LIVE IN PORTLAND. MALLORY IS PROBABLY GOING TO BECOME A HIPPIE NEXT.
AS FOR CRANE...
ALICE... YOU DID **WELL** TODAY AND...
I'M PROUD OF YOU.
UH... THANKS.
BUCKAROO IS A WEIRD TOWN AND IT SEEMS TO BE GETTING WEIRDER. WHICH IS FINE WITH ME. AT LEAST THEN IT'S INTERESTING... BUT...
PEOPLE NEVER KNOW HOW MUCH THE LEGEND OF THE BUCKAROO BUTCHERS INFECTED THIS TOWN OR HOW FAR THAT INFECTION GOES.
BUT THEY GET TO LOOK AT IT FROM THE OUTSIDE, THEY'RE NOT STUCK HERE LIKE THE REST OF US...

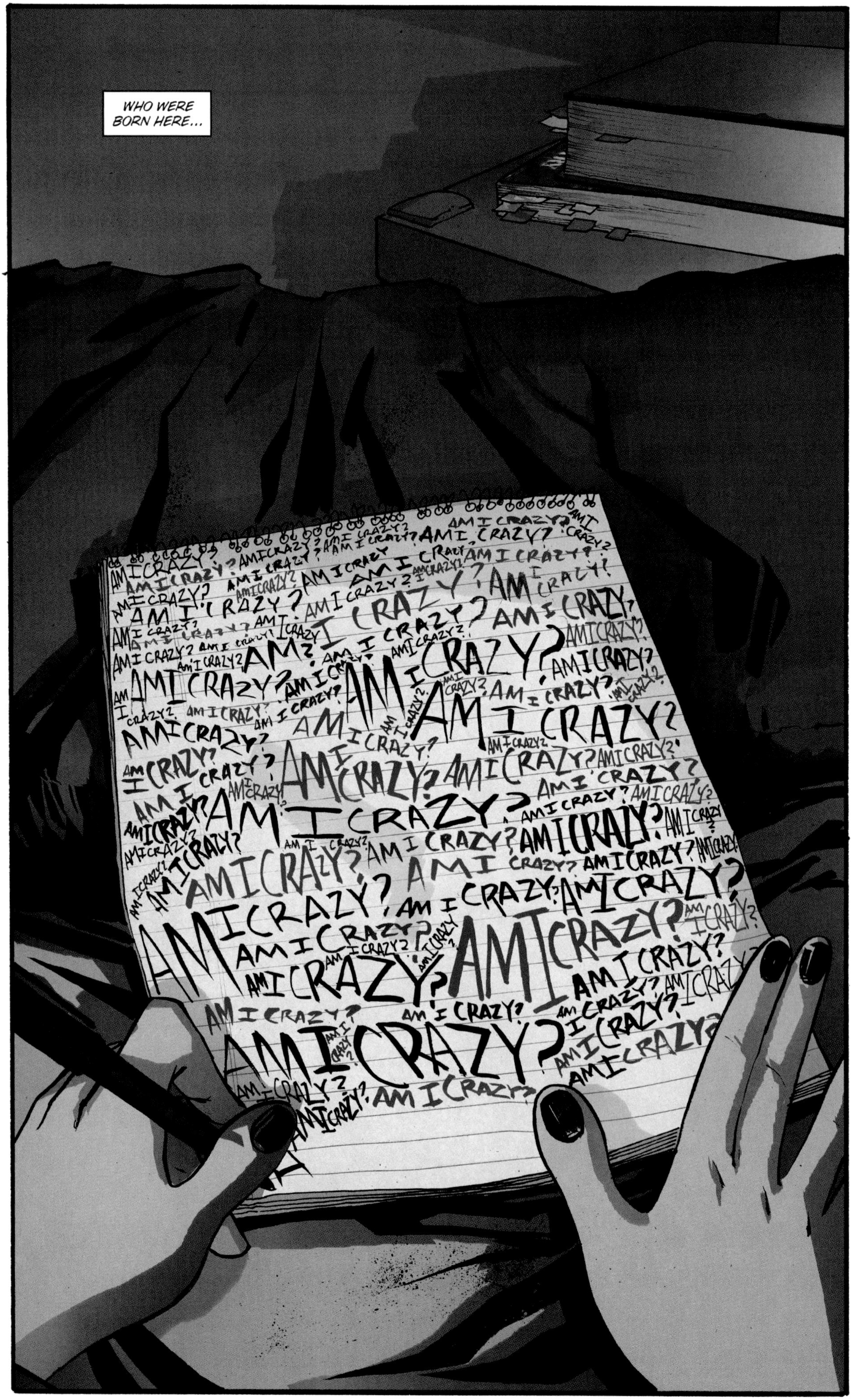
WHO WERE BORN HERE…
AM I CRAZY?

SEVEN

"I'm a big fan."

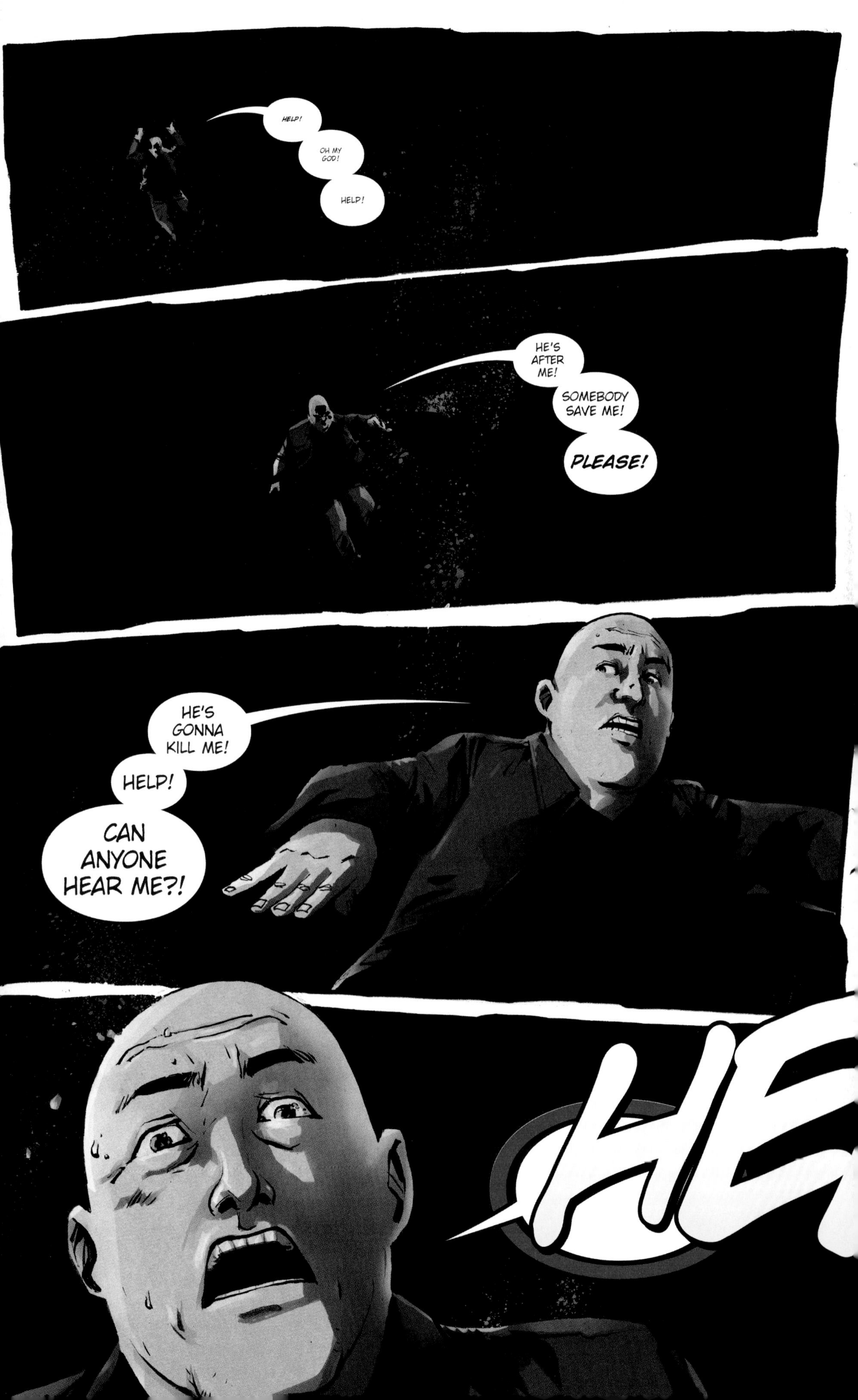

HELP!
OH MY GOD!
HELP!
HE'S AFTER ME!
SOMEBODY SAVE ME!
PLEASE!
HE'S GONNA KILL ME!
HELP!
CAN ANYONE HEAR ME?!

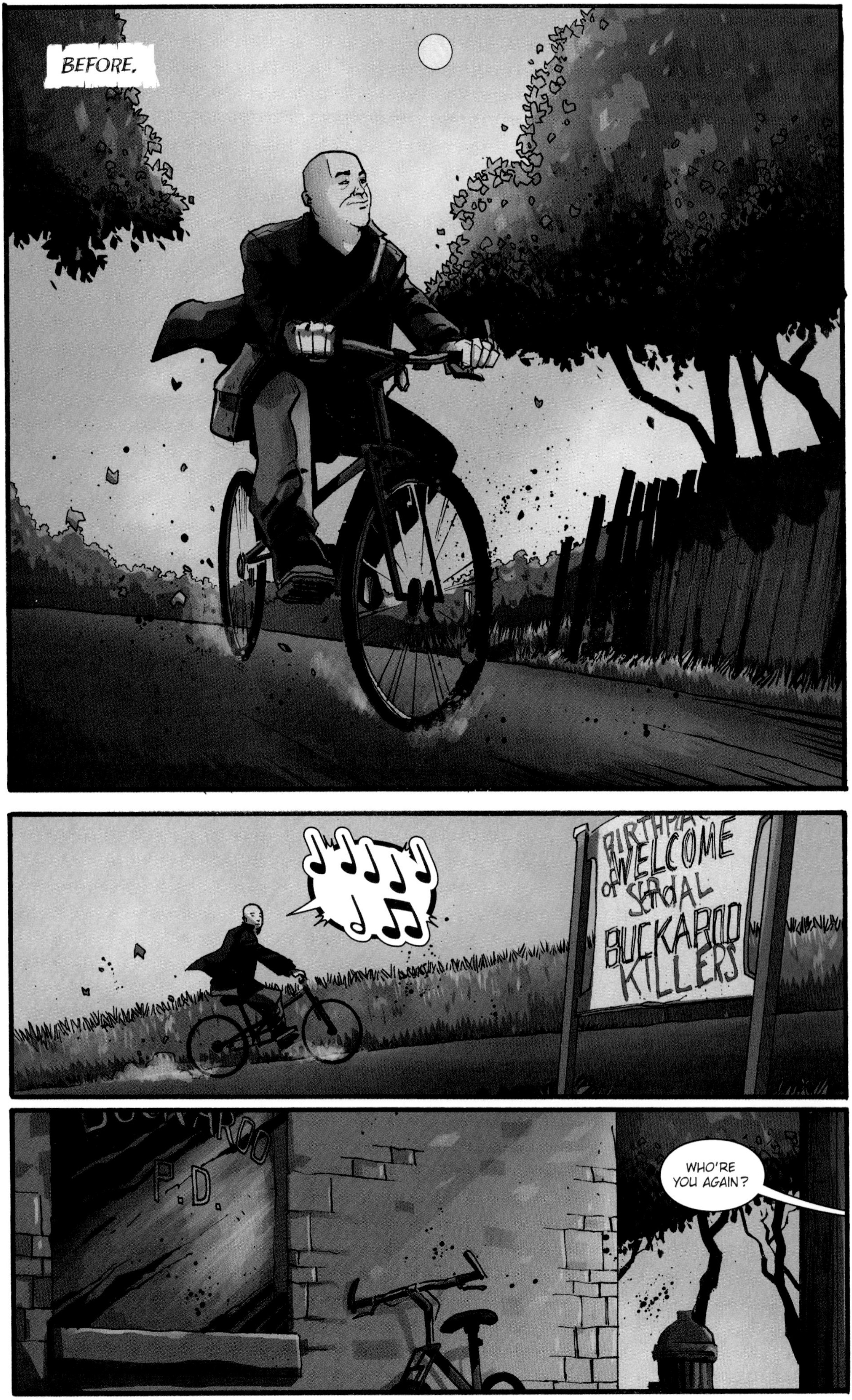
BEFORE.
WELCOME
BUCKAROO
KILLERS
P.D.
WHO'RE YOU AGAIN?

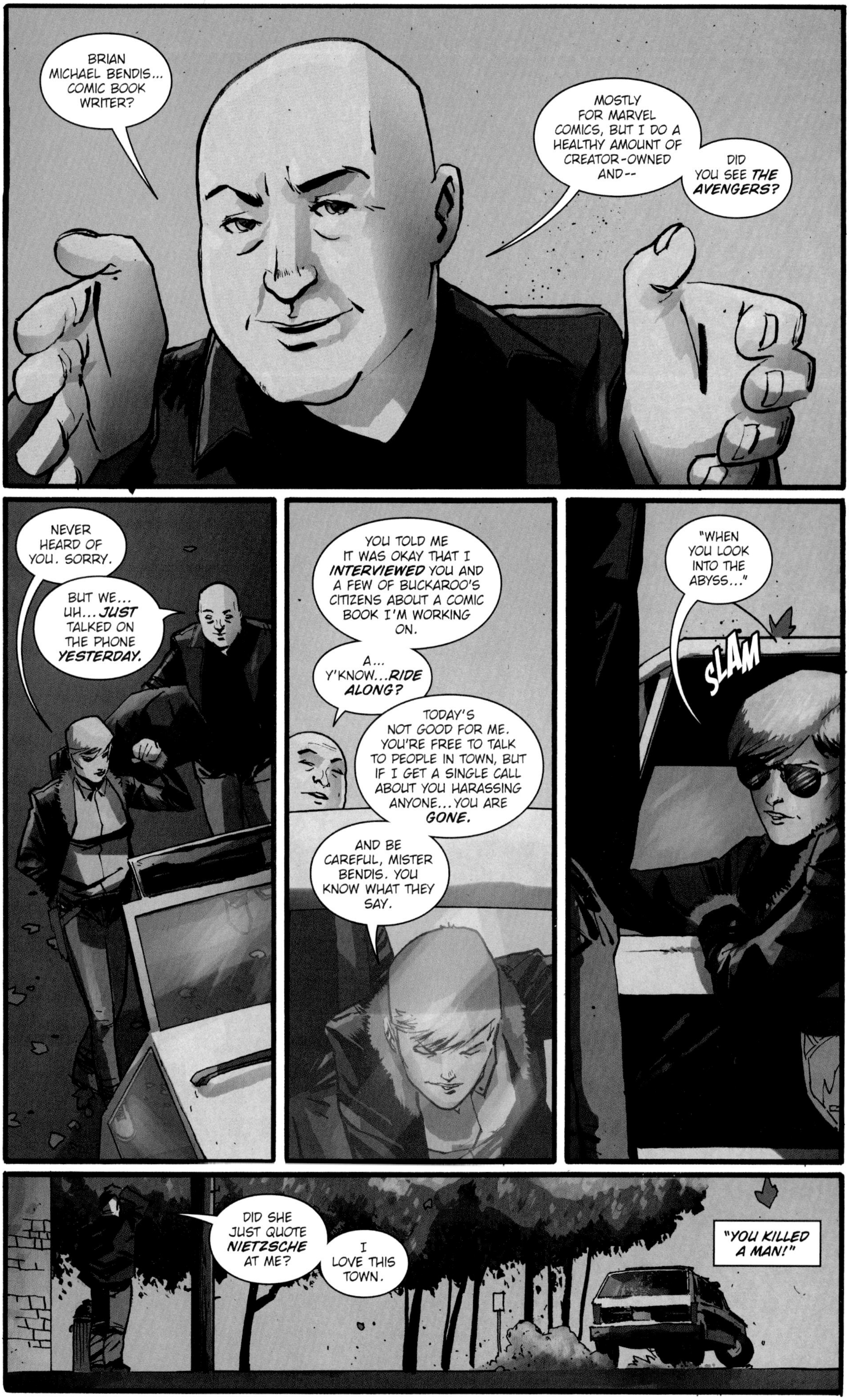

BRIAN MICHAEL BENDIS... COMIC BOOK WRITER?
MOSTLY FOR MARVEL COMICS, BUT I DO A HEALTHY AMOUNT OF CREATOR-OWNED AND--
DID YOU SEE *THE AVENGERS?*
NEVER HEARD OF YOU. SORRY.
BUT WE... UH... *JUST* TALKED ON THE PHONE *YESTERDAY.*
YOU TOLD ME IT WAS OKAY THAT I *INTERVIEWED* YOU AND A FEW OF BUCKAROO'S CITIZENS ABOUT A COMIC BOOK I'M WORKING ON.
A... Y'KNOW... *RIDE ALONG?*
TODAY'S NOT GOOD FOR ME. YOU'RE FREE TO TALK TO PEOPLE IN TOWN, BUT IF I GET A SINGLE CALL ABOUT YOU HARASSING ANYONE... YOU ARE *GONE.*
AND BE CAREFUL, MISTER BENDIS. YOU KNOW WHAT THEY SAY.
"WHEN YOU LOOK INTO THE ABYSS..."
SLAM
DID SHE JUST QUOTE *NIETZSCHE* AT ME?
I LOVE THIS TOWN.
"YOU KILLED A MAN!"

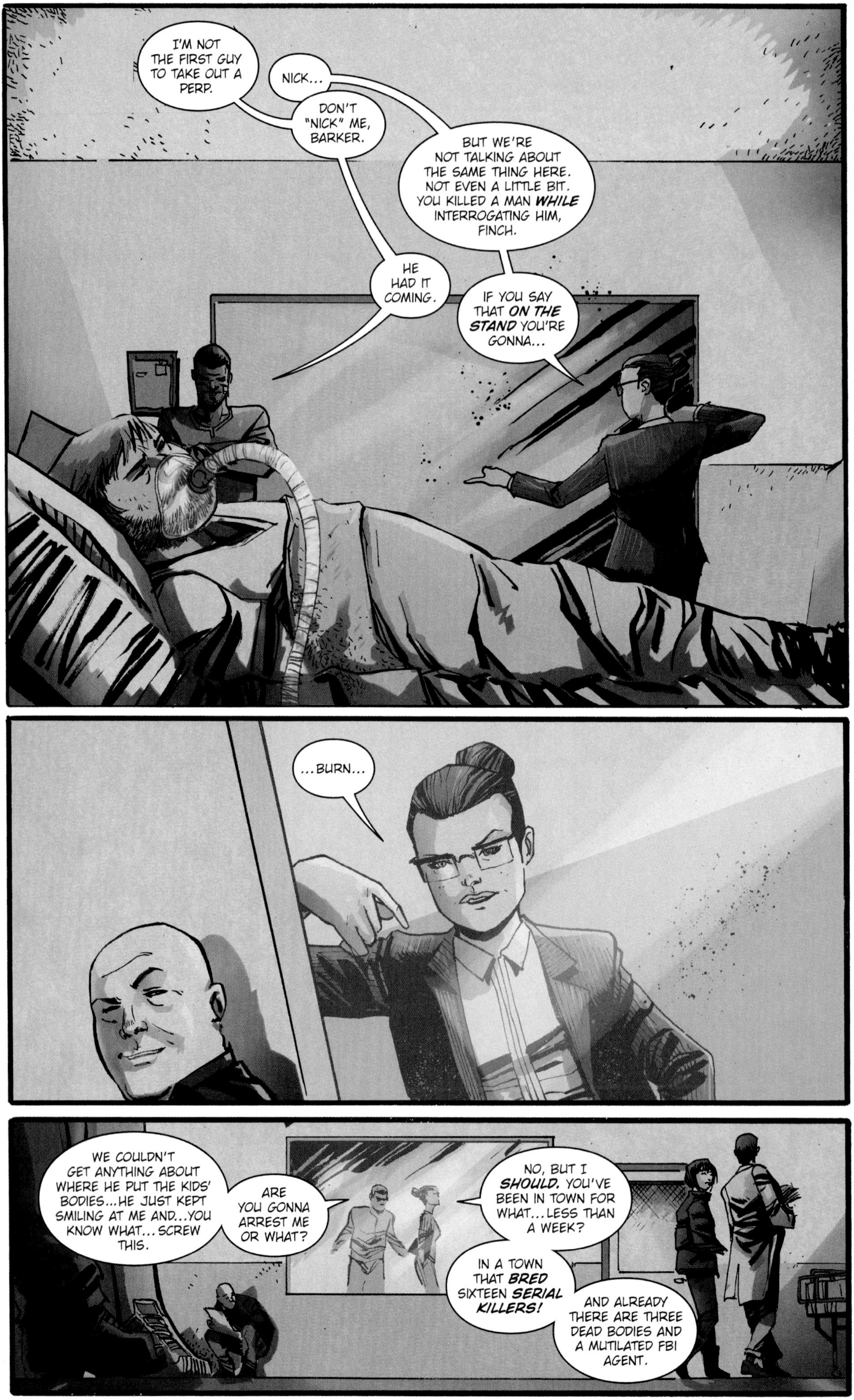
I'M NOT THE FIRST GUY TO TAKE OUT A PERP.
NICK...
DON'T "NICK" ME, BARKER.
BUT WE'RE NOT TALKING ABOUT THE SAME THING HERE. NOT EVEN A LITTLE BIT. YOU KILLED A MAN ***WHILE*** INTERROGATING HIM, FINCH.
HE HAD IT COMING.
IF YOU SAY THAT ***ON THE STAND*** YOU'RE GONNA...
...BURN...
WE COULDN'T GET ANYTHING ABOUT WHERE HE PUT THE KIDS' BODIES...HE JUST KEPT SMILING AT ME AND...YOU KNOW WHAT... SCREW THIS.
ARE YOU GONNA ARREST ME OR WHAT?
NO, BUT I ***SHOULD.*** YOU'VE BEEN IN TOWN FOR WHAT... LESS THAN A WEEK?
IN A TOWN THAT ***BRED*** SIXTEEN ***SERIAL KILLERS!***
AND ALREADY THERE ARE THREE DEAD BODIES AND A MUTILATED FBI AGENT.

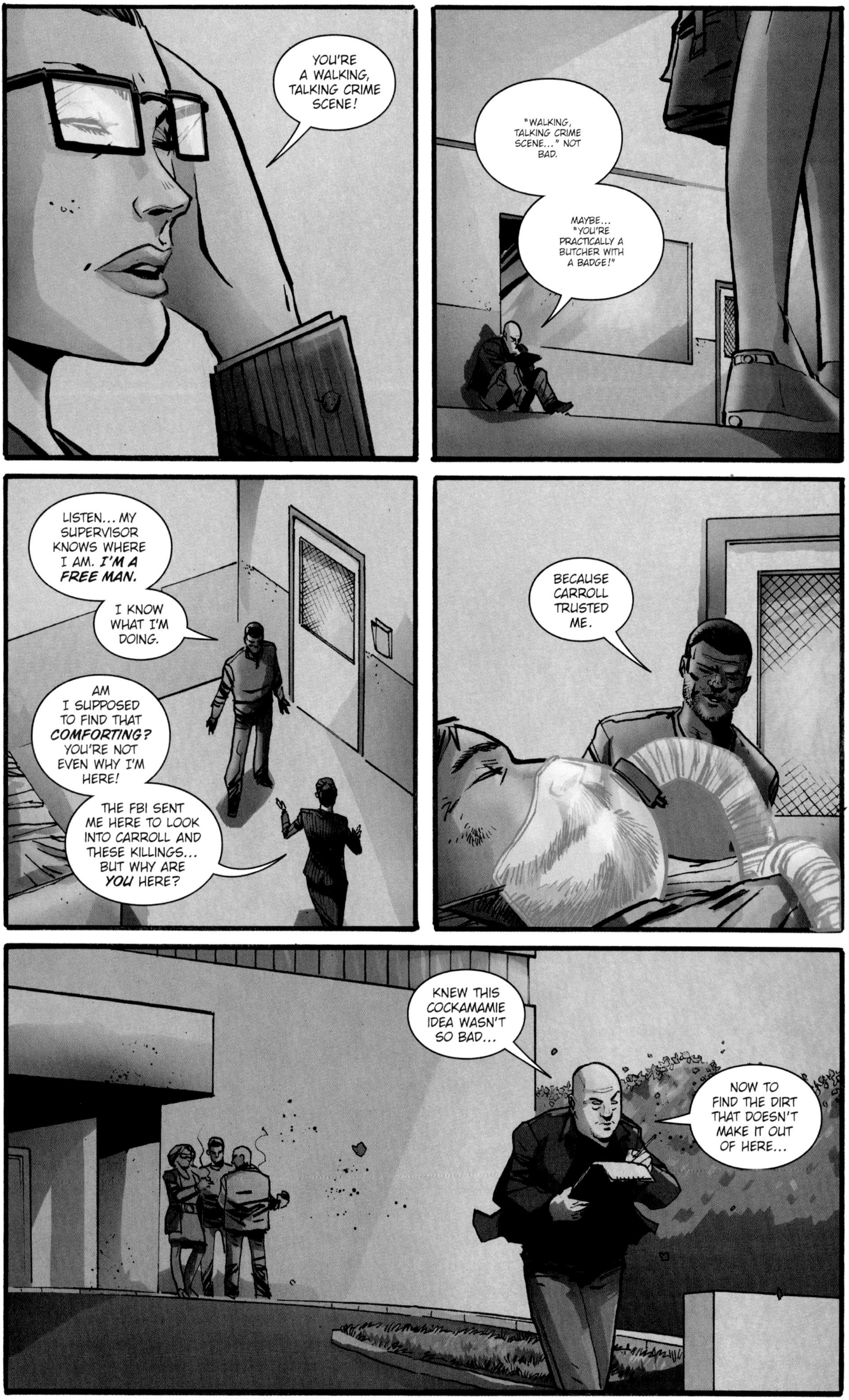
YOU'RE A WALKING, TALKING CRIME SCENE!
"WALKING, TALKING CRIME SCENE..." NOT BAD.
MAYBE... "YOU'RE PRACTICALLY A BUTCHER WITH A BADGE!"
LISTEN... MY SUPERVISOR KNOWS WHERE I AM. I'M A FREE MAN.
I KNOW WHAT I'M DOING.
AM I SUPPOSED TO FIND THAT COMFORTING? YOU'RE NOT EVEN WHY I'M HERE!
THE FBI SENT ME HERE TO LOOK INTO CARROLL AND THESE KILLINGS... BUT WHY ARE YOU HERE?
BECAUSE CARROLL TRUSTED ME.
KNEW THIS COCKAMAMIE IDEA WASN'T SO BAD...
NOW TO FIND THE DIRT THAT DOESN'T MAKE IT OUT OF HERE...

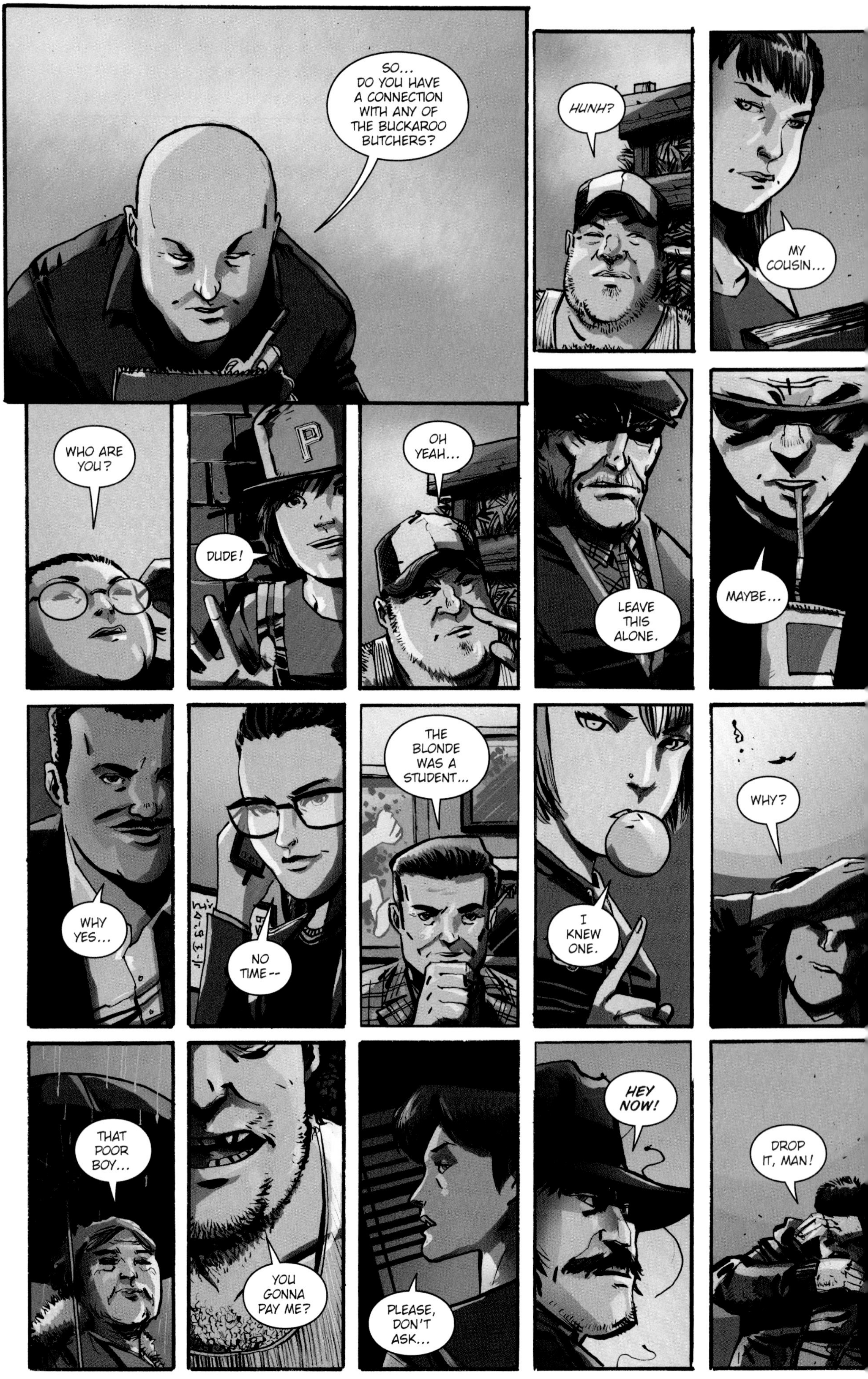
SO... DO YOU HAVE A CONNECTION WITH ANY OF THE BUCKAROO BUTCHERS?
HUNH?
MY COUSIN...
WHO ARE YOU?
DUDE!
OH YEAH...
LEAVE THIS ALONE.
MAYBE...
WHY YES...
NO TIME--
THE BLONDE WAS A STUDENT...
I KNEW ONE.
WHY?
THAT POOR BOY...
YOU GONNA PAY ME?
PLEASE, DON'T ASK...
HEY NOW!
DROP IT, MAN!

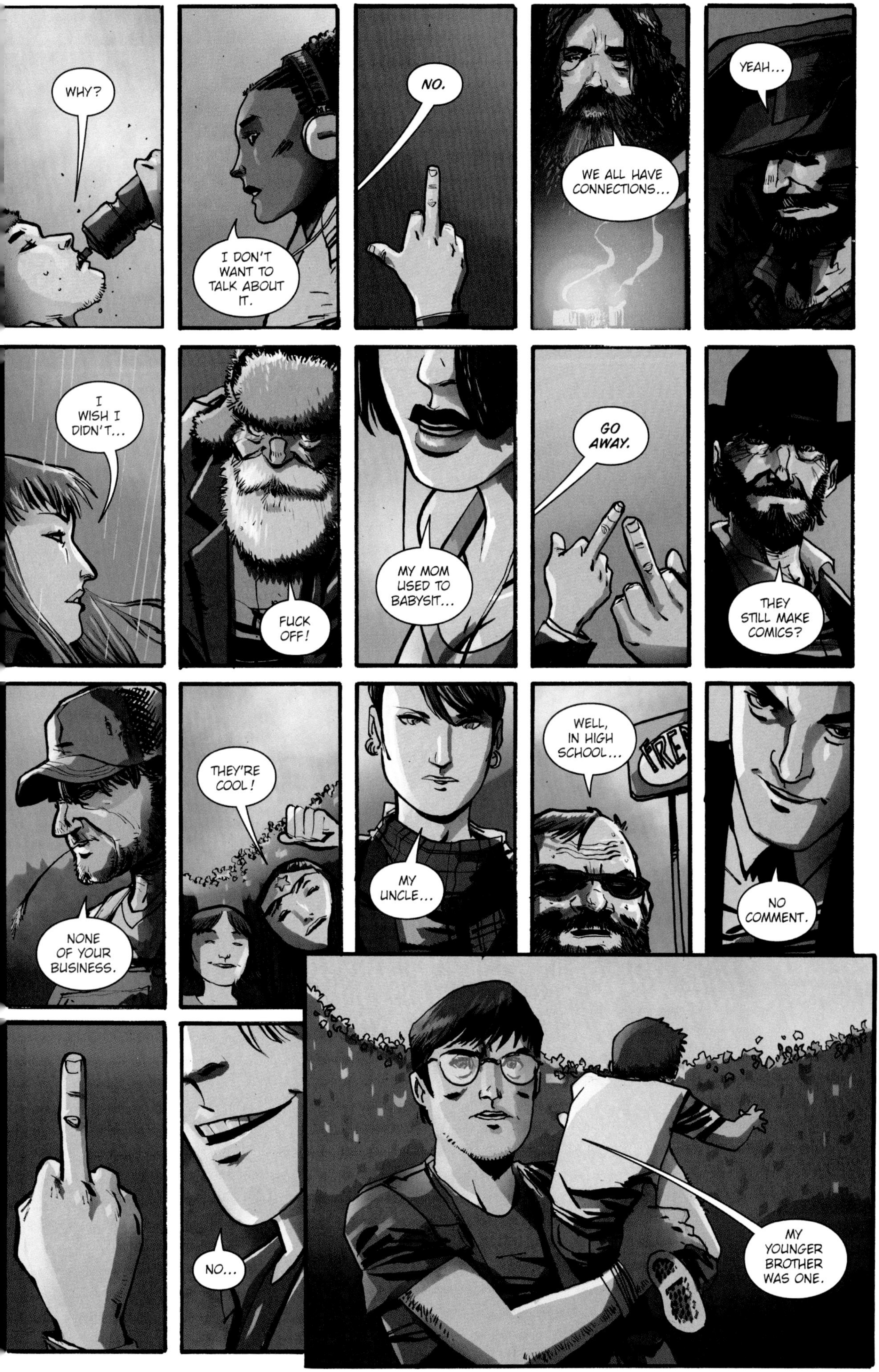
WHY?
I DON'T WANT TO TALK ABOUT IT.
NO.
WE ALL HAVE CONNECTIONS...
YEAH...
I WISH I DIDN'T...
FUCK OFF!
MY MOM USED TO BABYSIT...
GO AWAY.
THEY STILL MAKE COMICS?
NONE OF YOUR BUSINESS.
THEY'RE COOL!
MY UNCLE...
WELL, IN HIGH SCHOOL...
NO COMMENT.
NO...
MY YOUNGER BROTHER WAS ONE.

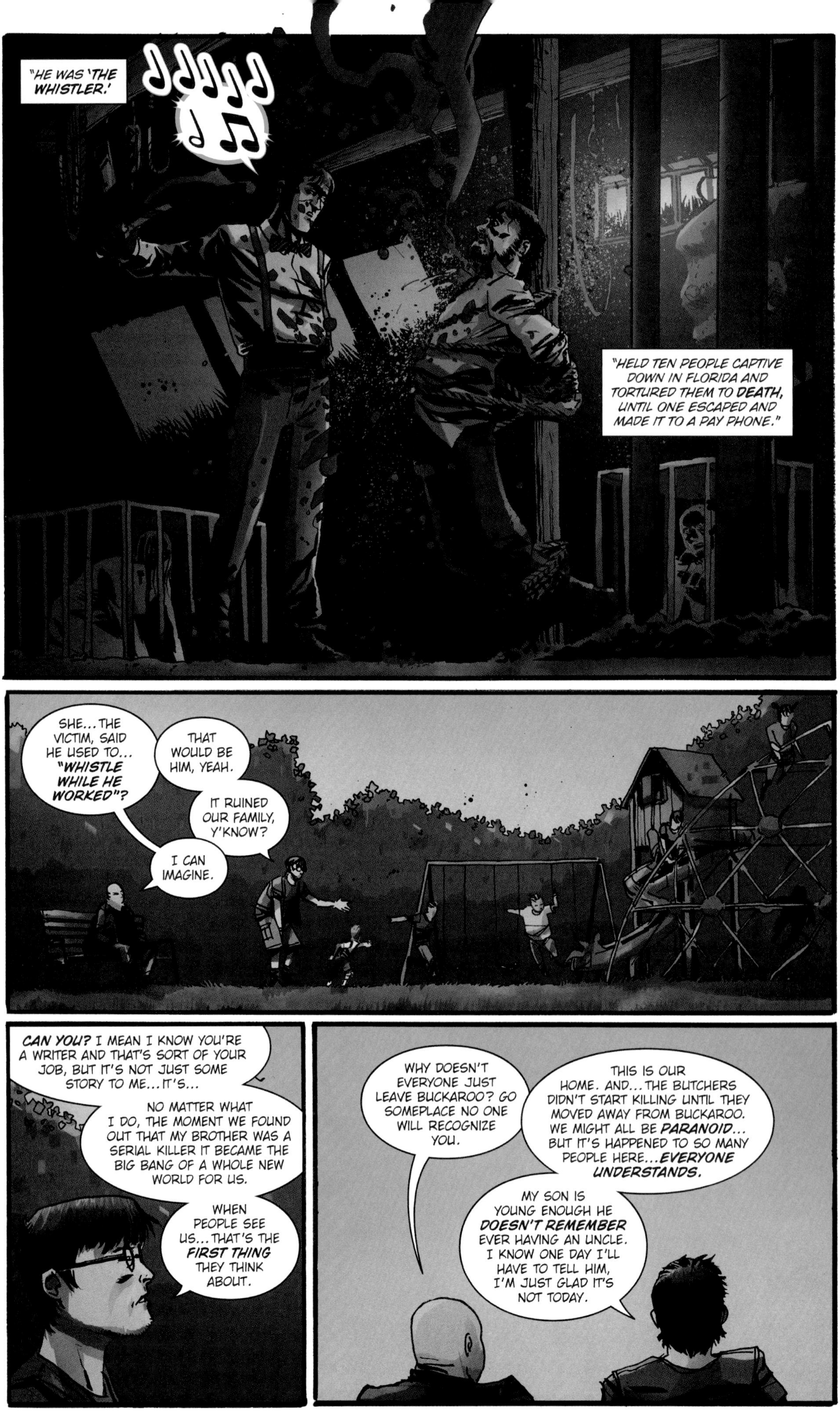
"HE WAS 'THE WHISTLER.'
"HELD TEN PEOPLE CAPTIVE DOWN IN FLORIDA AND TORTURED THEM TO DEATH, UNTIL ONE ESCAPED AND MADE IT TO A PAY PHONE."
SHE... THE VICTIM, SAID HE USED TO... "WHISTLE WHILE HE WORKED"?
THAT WOULD BE HIM, YEAH.
IT RUINED OUR FAMILY, Y'KNOW?
I CAN IMAGINE.
CAN YOU? I MEAN I KNOW YOU'RE A WRITER AND THAT'S SORT OF YOUR JOB, BUT IT'S NOT JUST SOME STORY TO ME... IT'S...
NO MATTER WHAT I DO, THE MOMENT WE FOUND OUT THAT MY BROTHER WAS A SERIAL KILLER IT BECAME THE BIG BANG OF A WHOLE NEW WORLD FOR US.
WHEN PEOPLE SEE US... THAT'S THE FIRST THING THEY THINK ABOUT.
WHY DOESN'T EVERYONE JUST LEAVE BUCKAROO? GO SOMEPLACE NO ONE WILL RECOGNIZE YOU.
THIS IS OUR HOME. AND... THE BUTCHERS DIDN'T START KILLING UNTIL THEY MOVED AWAY FROM BUCKAROO. WE MIGHT ALL BE PARANOID... BUT IT'S HAPPENED TO SO MANY PEOPLE HERE... EVERYONE UNDERSTANDS.
MY SON IS YOUNG ENOUGH HE DOESN'T REMEMBER EVER HAVING AN UNCLE. I KNOW ONE DAY I'LL HAVE TO TELL HIM, I'M JUST GLAD IT'S NOT TODAY.

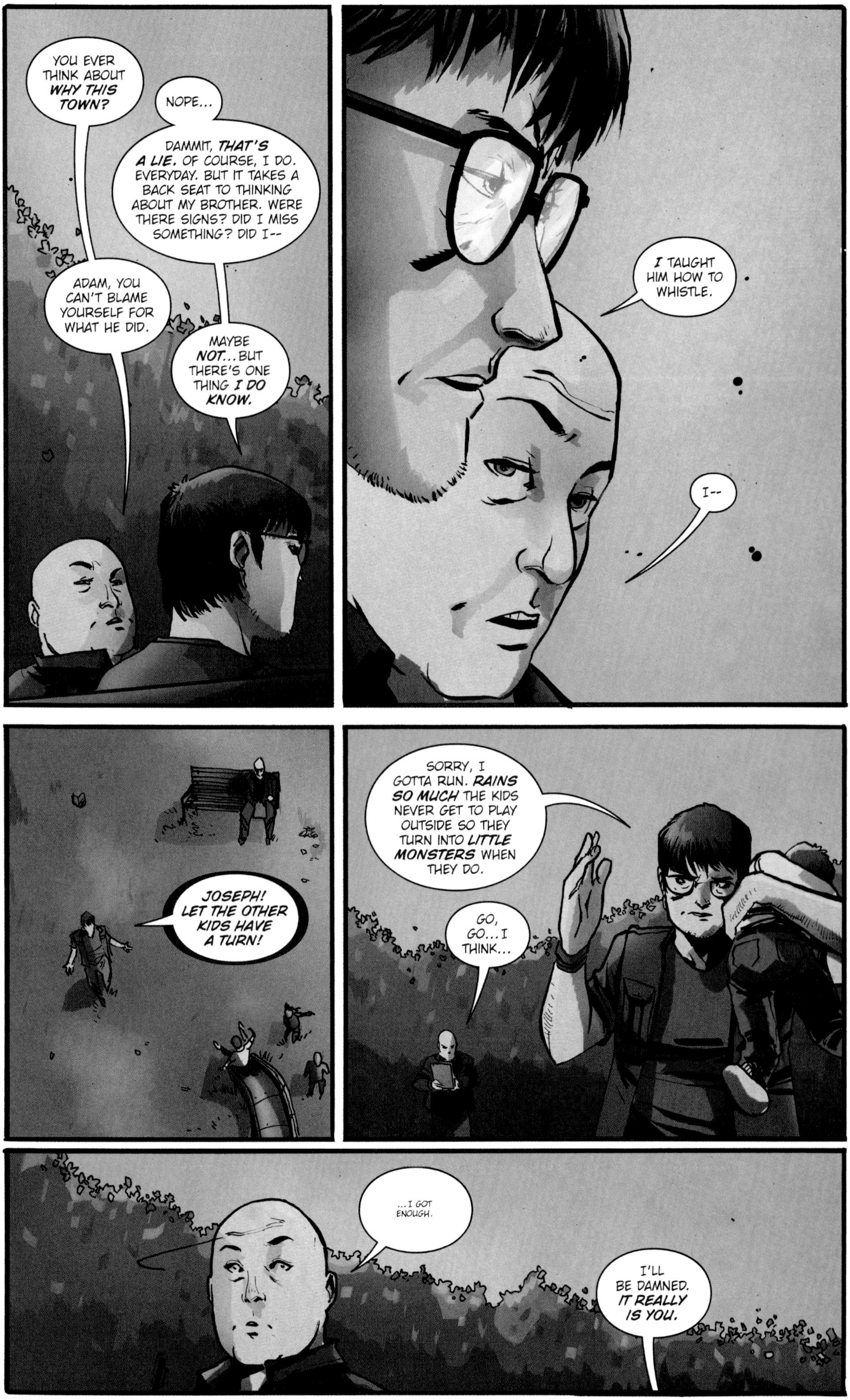
YOU EVER THINK ABOUT WHY THIS TOWN?
NOPE...
DAMMIT, THAT'S A LIE. OF COURSE, I DO. EVERYDAY. BUT IT TAKES A BACK SEAT TO THINKING ABOUT MY BROTHER. WERE THERE SIGNS? DID I MISS SOMETHING? DID I--
ADAM, YOU CAN'T BLAME YOURSELF FOR WHAT HE DID.
MAYBE NOT...BUT THERE'S ONE THING I DO KNOW.
I TAUGHT HIM HOW TO WHISTLE.
I--
JOSEPH! LET THE OTHER KIDS HAVE A TURN!
SORRY, I GOTTA RUN. RAINS SO MUCH THE KIDS NEVER GET TO PLAY OUTSIDE SO THEY TURN INTO LITTLE MONSTERS WHEN THEY DO.
GO, GO...I THINK...
...I GOT ENOUGH.
I'LL BE DAMNED. IT REALLY IS YOU.

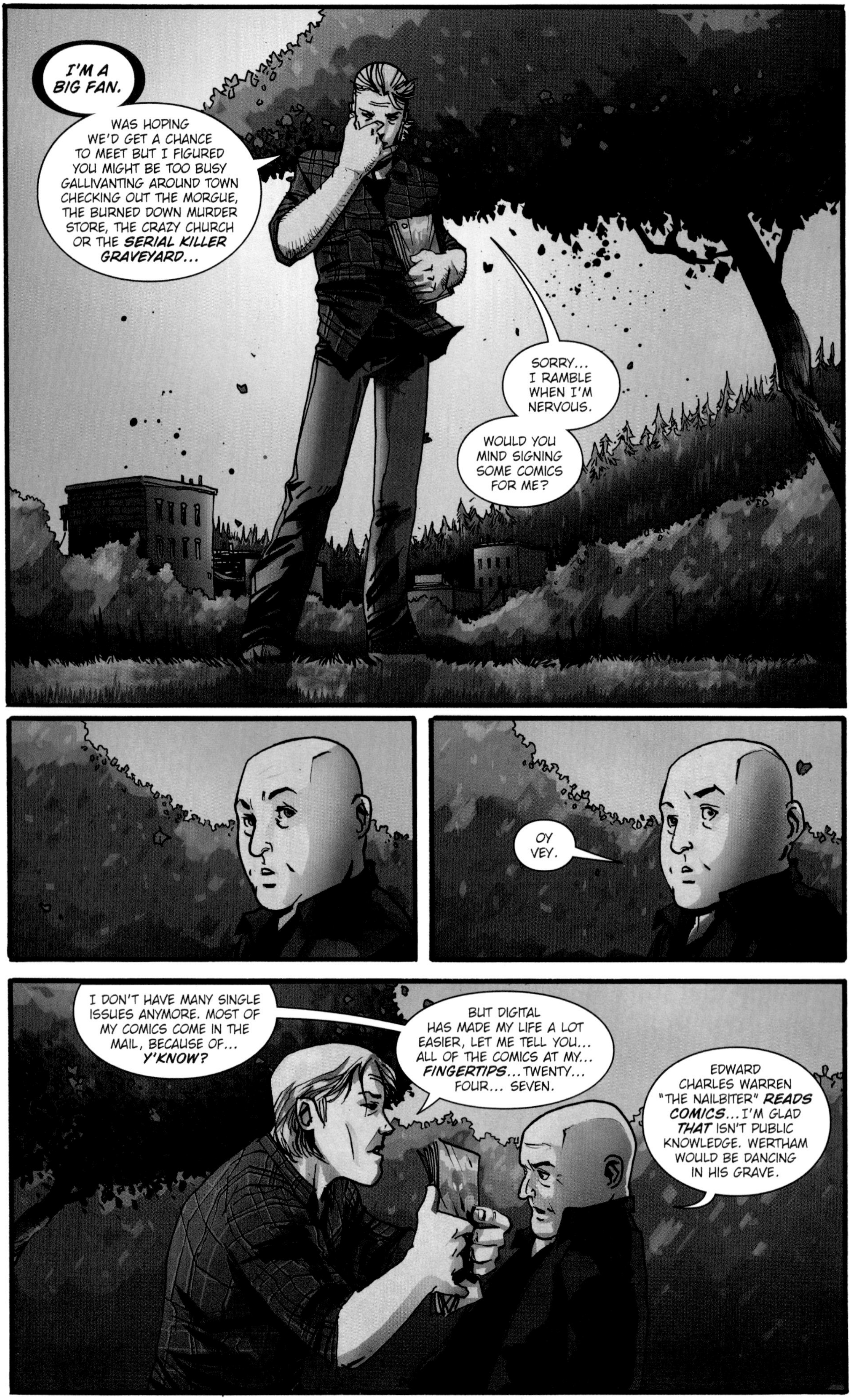
I'M A BIG FAN.
WAS HOPING WE'D GET A CHANCE TO MEET BUT I FIGURED YOU MIGHT BE TOO BUSY GALLIVANTING AROUND TOWN CHECKING OUT THE MORGUE, THE BURNED DOWN MURDER STORE, THE CRAZY CHURCH OR THE SERIAL KILLER GRAVEYARD...
SORRY... I RAMBLE WHEN I'M NERVOUS.
WOULD YOU MIND SIGNING SOME COMICS FOR ME?
OY VEY.
I DON'T HAVE MANY SINGLE ISSUES ANYMORE. MOST OF MY COMICS COME IN THE MAIL, BECAUSE OF... Y'KNOW?
BUT DIGITAL HAS MADE MY LIFE A LOT EASIER, LET ME TELL YOU... ALL OF THE COMICS AT MY... FINGERTIPS... TWENTY... FOUR... SEVEN.
EDWARD CHARLES WARREN "THE NAILBITER" READS COMICS... I'M GLAD THAT ISN'T PUBLIC KNOWLEDGE. WERTHAM WOULD BE DANCING IN HIS GRAVE.

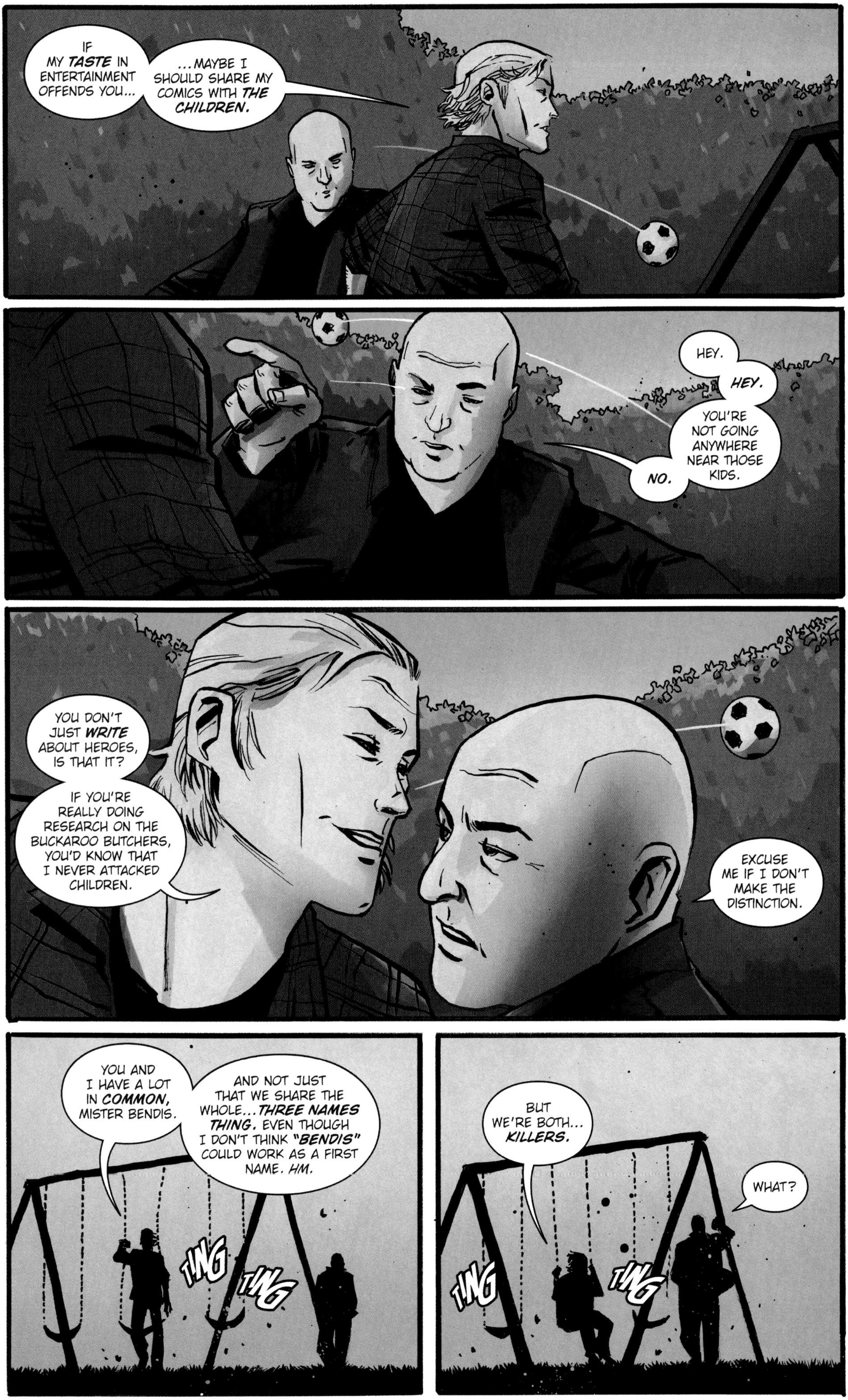

IF MY TASTE IN ENTERTAINMENT OFFENDS YOU...
...MAYBE I SHOULD SHARE MY COMICS WITH THE CHILDREN.
HEY.
HEY.
NO.
YOU'RE NOT GOING ANYWHERE NEAR THOSE KIDS.
YOU DON'T JUST WRITE ABOUT HEROES, IS THAT IT?
IF YOU'RE REALLY DOING RESEARCH ON THE BUCKAROO BUTCHERS, YOU'D KNOW THAT I NEVER ATTACKED CHILDREN.
EXCUSE ME IF I DON'T MAKE THE DISTINCTION.
YOU AND I HAVE A LOT IN COMMON, MISTER BENDIS.
AND NOT JUST THAT WE SHARE THE WHOLE...THREE NAMES THING. EVEN THOUGH I DON'T THINK "BENDIS" COULD WORK AS A FIRST NAME. HM.
TING
TING
BUT WE'RE BOTH... KILLERS.
WHAT?
TING
TING

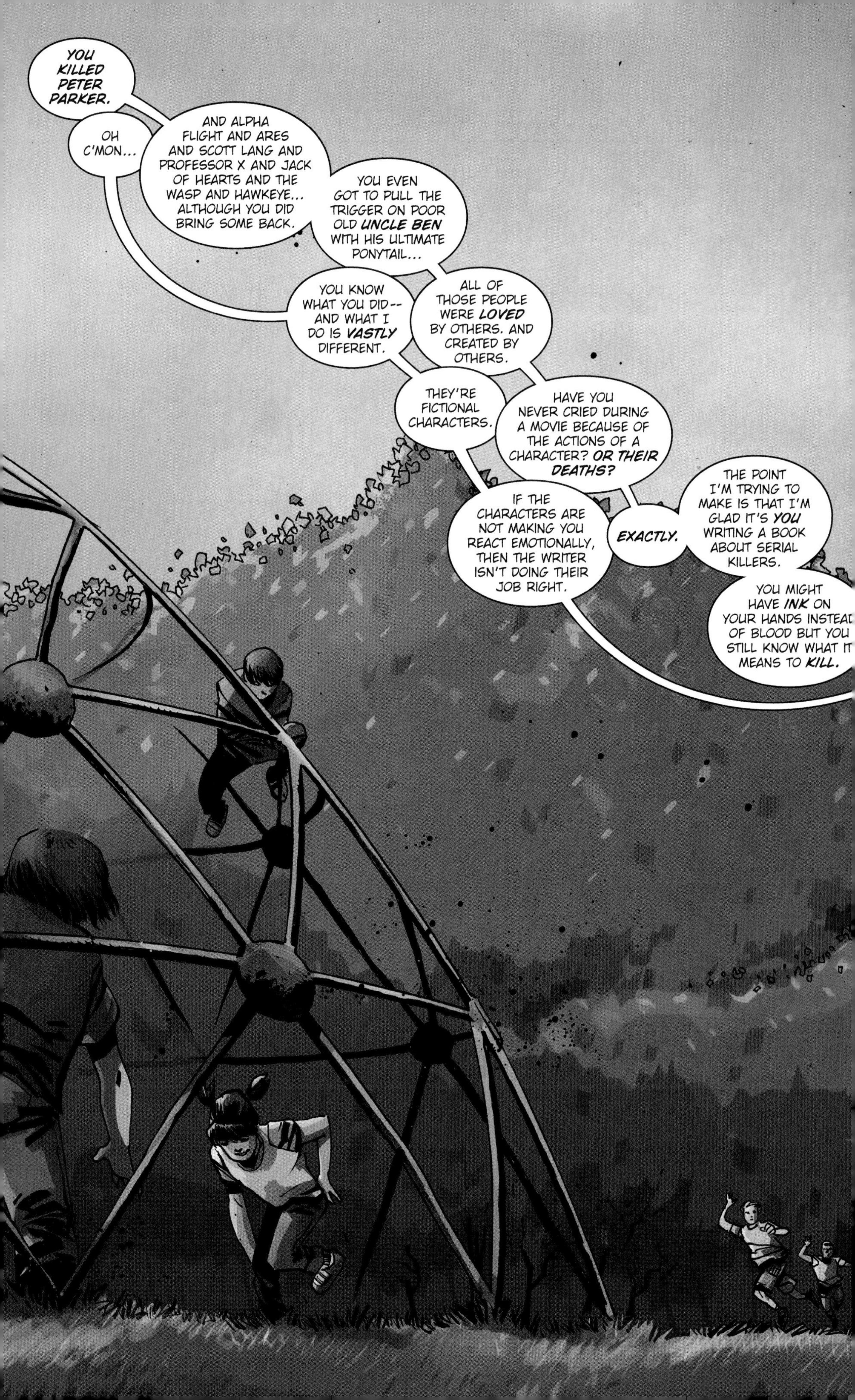
YOU KILLED PETER PARKER.
OH C'MON...
AND ALPHA FLIGHT AND ARES AND SCOTT LANG AND PROFESSOR X AND JACK OF HEARTS AND THE WASP AND HAWKEYE... ALTHOUGH YOU DID BRING SOME BACK.
YOU EVEN GOT TO PULL THE TRIGGER ON POOR OLD UNCLE BEN WITH HIS ULTIMATE PONYTAIL...
YOU KNOW WHAT YOU DID-- AND WHAT I DO IS VASTLY DIFFERENT.
ALL OF THOSE PEOPLE WERE LOVED BY OTHERS. AND CREATED BY OTHERS.
THEY'RE FICTIONAL CHARACTERS.
HAVE YOU NEVER CRIED DURING A MOVIE BECAUSE OF THE ACTIONS OF A CHARACTER? OR THEIR DEATHS?
IF THE CHARACTERS ARE NOT MAKING YOU REACT EMOTIONALLY, THEN THE WRITER ISN'T DOING THEIR JOB RIGHT.
EXACTLY.
THE POINT I'M TRYING TO MAKE IS THAT I'M GLAD IT'S YOU WRITING A BOOK ABOUT SERIAL KILLERS.
YOU MIGHT HAVE INK ON YOUR HANDS INSTEAD OF BLOOD BUT YOU STILL KNOW WHAT IT MEANS TO KILL.

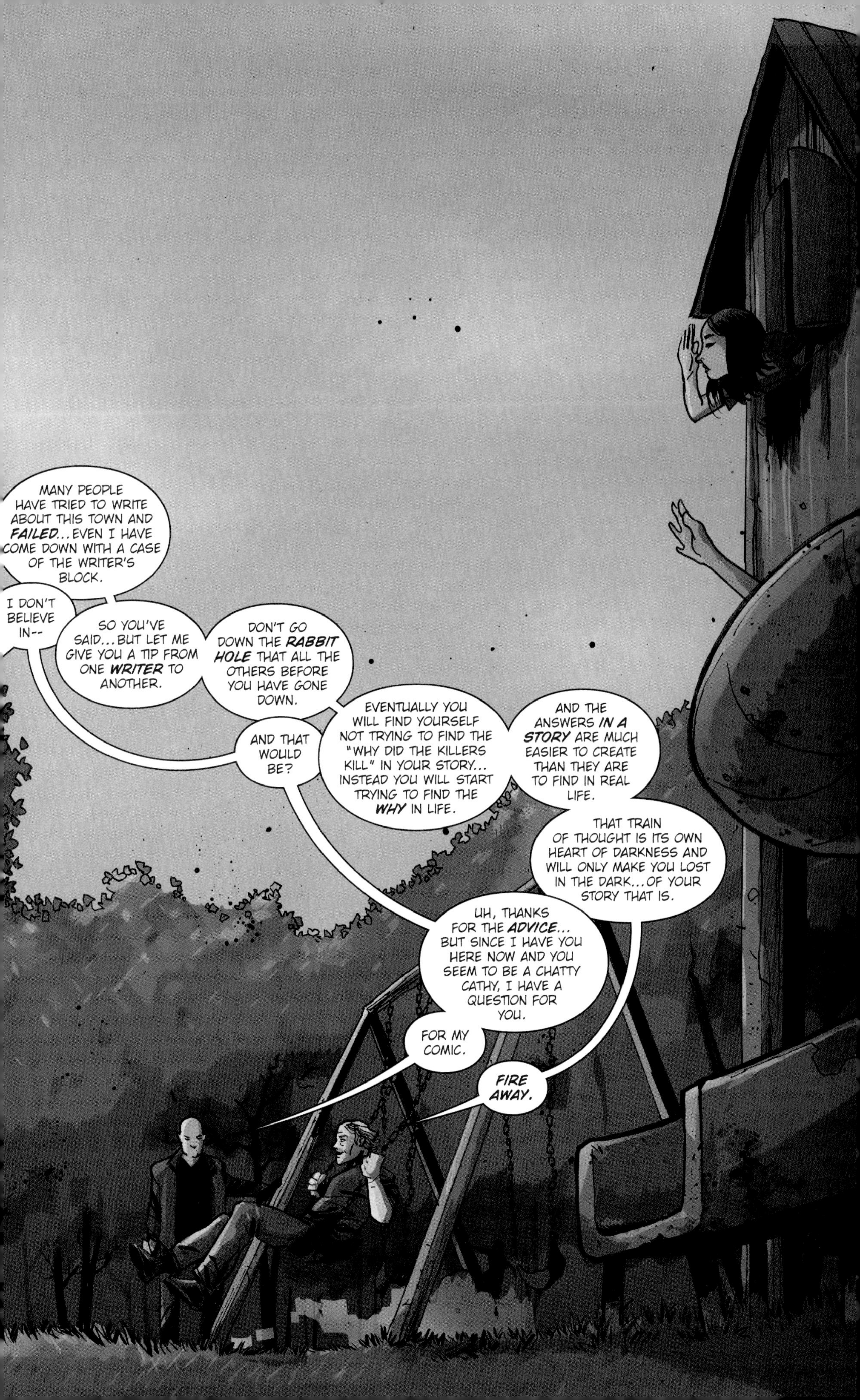
MANY PEOPLE HAVE TRIED TO WRITE ABOUT THIS TOWN AND FAILED... EVEN I HAVE COME DOWN WITH A CASE OF THE WRITER'S BLOCK.
I DON'T BELIEVE IN--
SO YOU'VE SAID... BUT LET ME GIVE YOU A TIP FROM ONE WRITER TO ANOTHER.
DON'T GO DOWN THE RABBIT HOLE THAT ALL THE OTHERS BEFORE YOU HAVE GONE DOWN.
AND THAT WOULD BE?
EVENTUALLY YOU WILL FIND YOURSELF NOT TRYING TO FIND THE "WHY DID THE KILLERS KILL" IN YOUR STORY... INSTEAD YOU WILL START TRYING TO FIND THE WHY IN LIFE.
AND THE ANSWERS IN A STORY ARE MUCH EASIER TO CREATE THAN THEY ARE TO FIND IN REAL LIFE.
THAT TRAIN OF THOUGHT IS ITS OWN HEART OF DARKNESS AND WILL ONLY MAKE YOU LOST IN THE DARK... OF YOUR STORY THAT IS.
UH, THANKS FOR THE ADVICE... BUT SINCE I HAVE YOU HERE NOW AND YOU SEEM TO BE A CHATTY CATHY, I HAVE A QUESTION FOR YOU.
FOR MY COMIC.
FIRE AWAY.

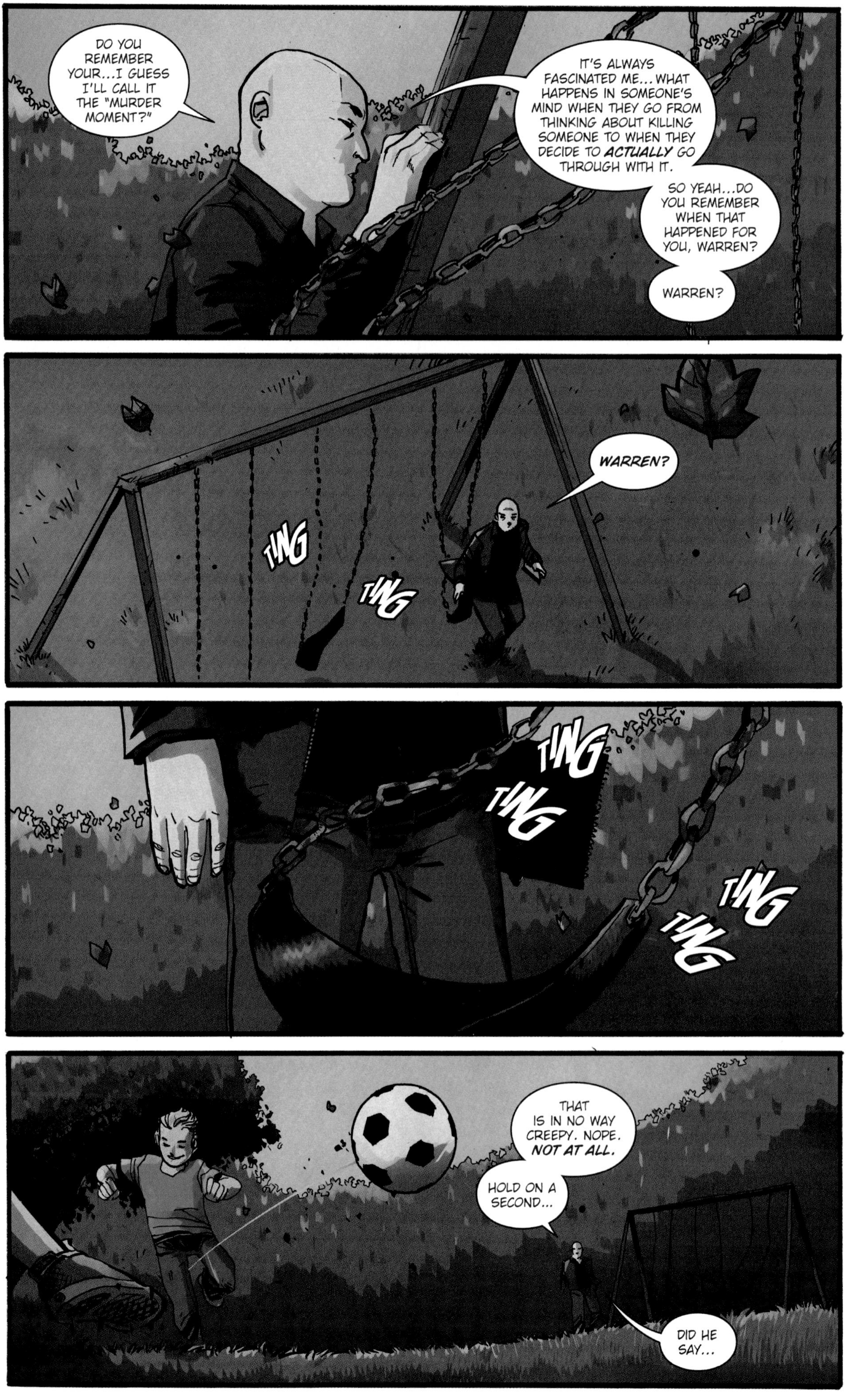
DO YOU REMEMBER YOUR...I GUESS I'LL CALL IT THE "MURDER MOMENT?"
IT'S ALWAYS FASCINATED ME... WHAT HAPPENS IN SOMEONE'S MIND WHEN THEY GO FROM THINKING ABOUT KILLING SOMEONE TO WHEN THEY DECIDE TO ACTUALLY GO THROUGH WITH IT.
SO YEAH...DO YOU REMEMBER WHEN THAT HAPPENED FOR YOU, WARREN?
WARREN?
WARREN?
TING
TING
TING
TING
TING
TING
THAT IS IN NO WAY CREEPY. NOPE. NOT AT ALL.
HOLD ON A SECOND...
DID HE SAY...

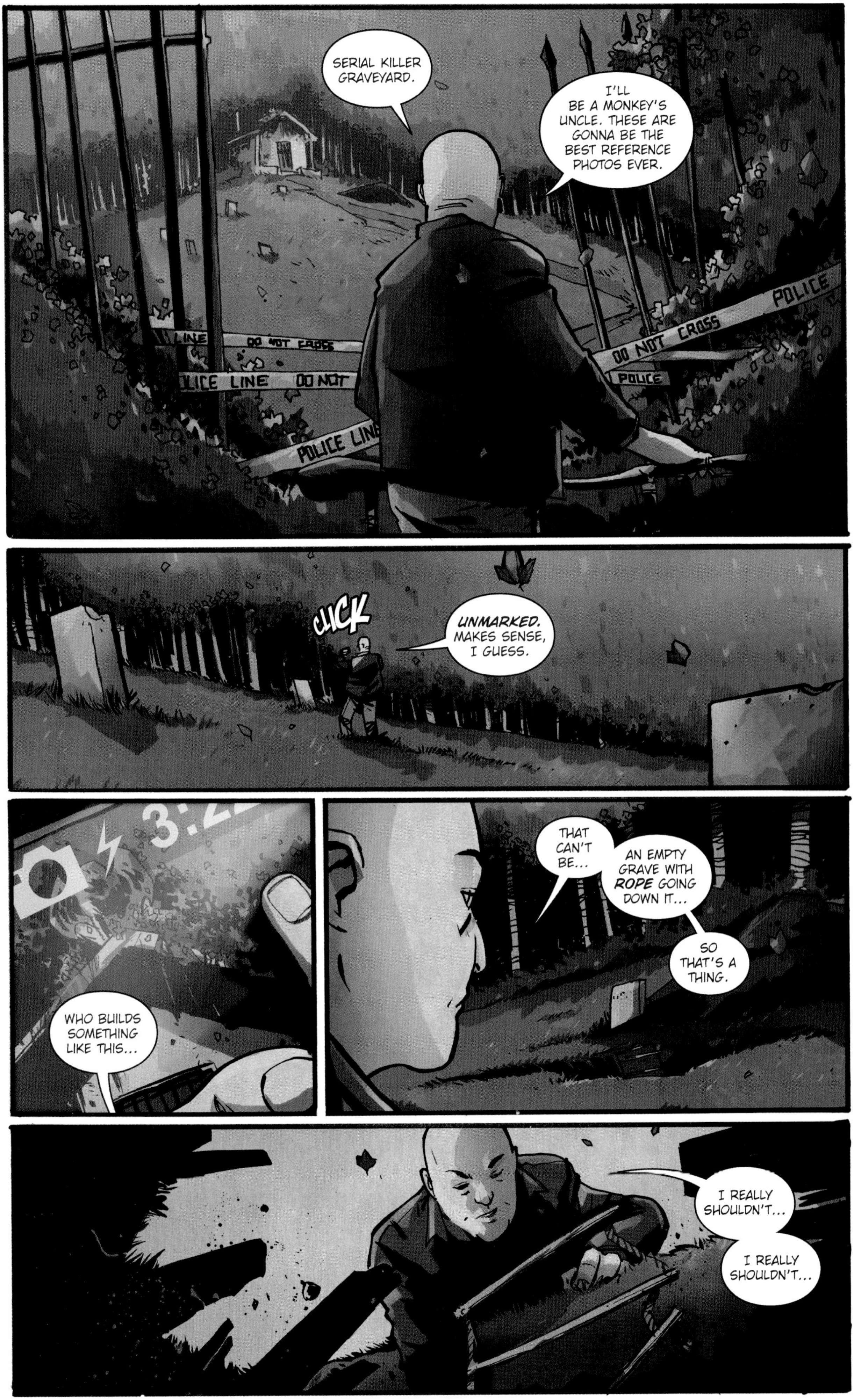
SERIAL KILLER GRAVEYARD.
I'LL BE A MONKEY'S UNCLE. THESE ARE GONNA BE THE BEST REFERENCE PHOTOS EVER.
POLICE LINE DO NOT CROSS
POLICE LINE DO NOT
POLICE LINE
DO NOT CROSS POLICE
POLICE
CLICK
UNMARKED. MAKES SENSE, I GUESS.
WHO BUILDS SOMETHING LIKE THIS...
THAT CAN'T BE...
AN EMPTY GRAVE WITH ROPE GOING DOWN IT...
SO THAT'S A THING.
I REALLY SHOULDN'T...
I REALLY SHOULDN'T...

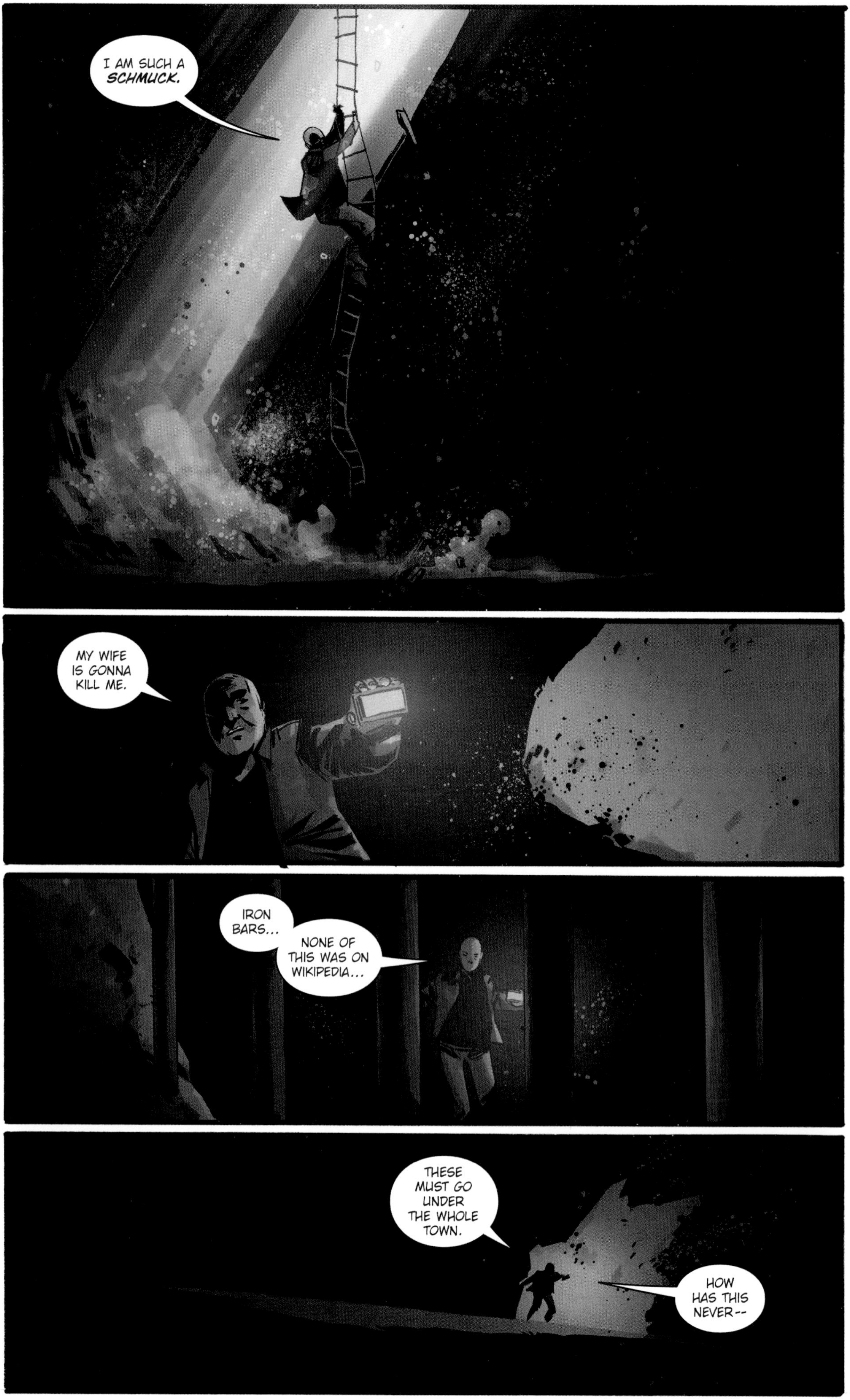
I AM SUCH A SCHMUCK.
MY WIFE IS GONNA KILL ME.
IRON BARS...
NONE OF THIS WAS ON WIKIPEDIA...
THESE MUST GO UNDER THE WHOLE TOWN.
HOW HAS THIS NEVER--

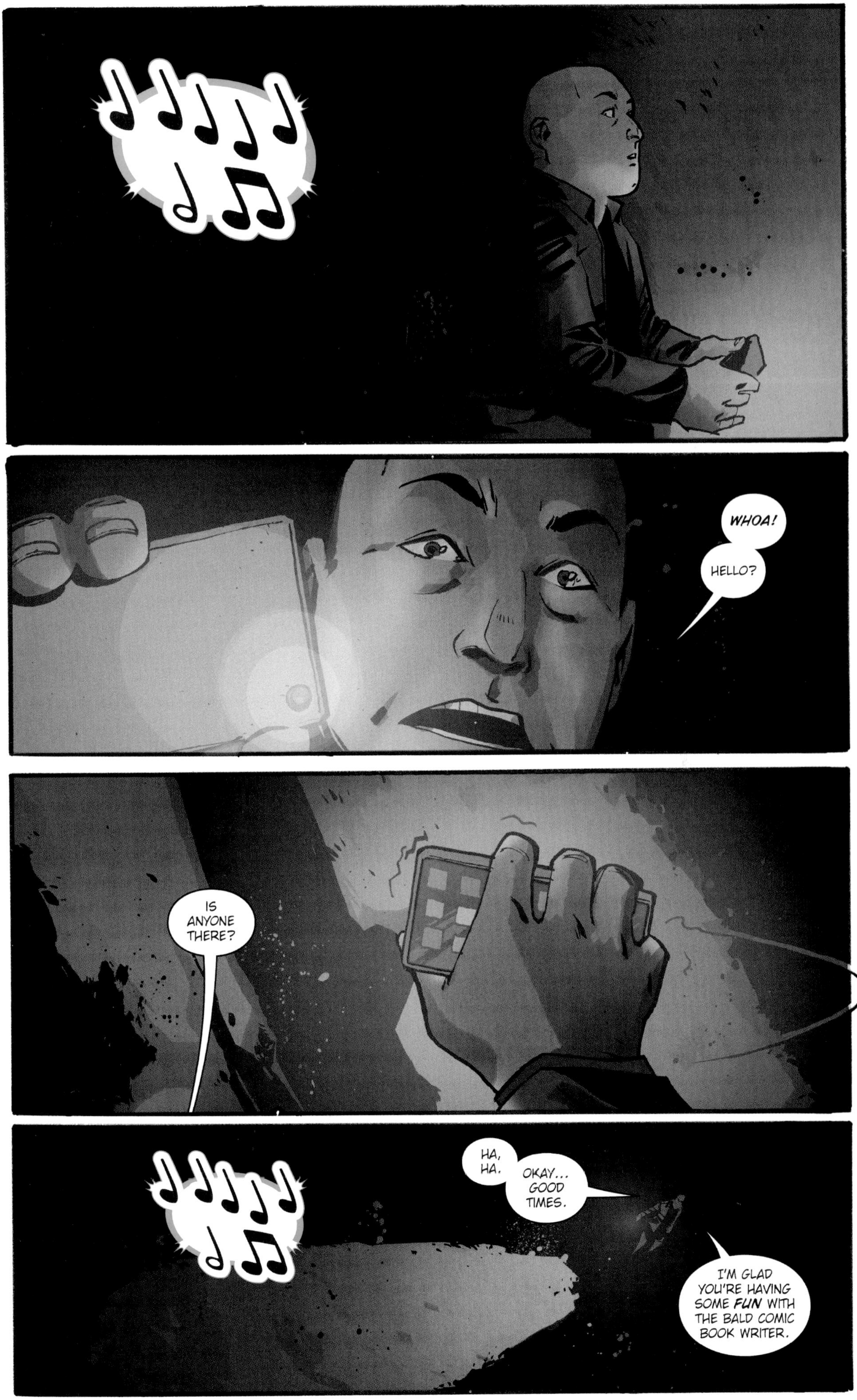
WHOA!
HELLO?
IS ANYONE THERE?
HA, HA.
OKAY... GOOD TIMES.
I'M GLAD YOU'RE HAVING SOME FUN WITH THE BALD COMIC BOOK WRITER.

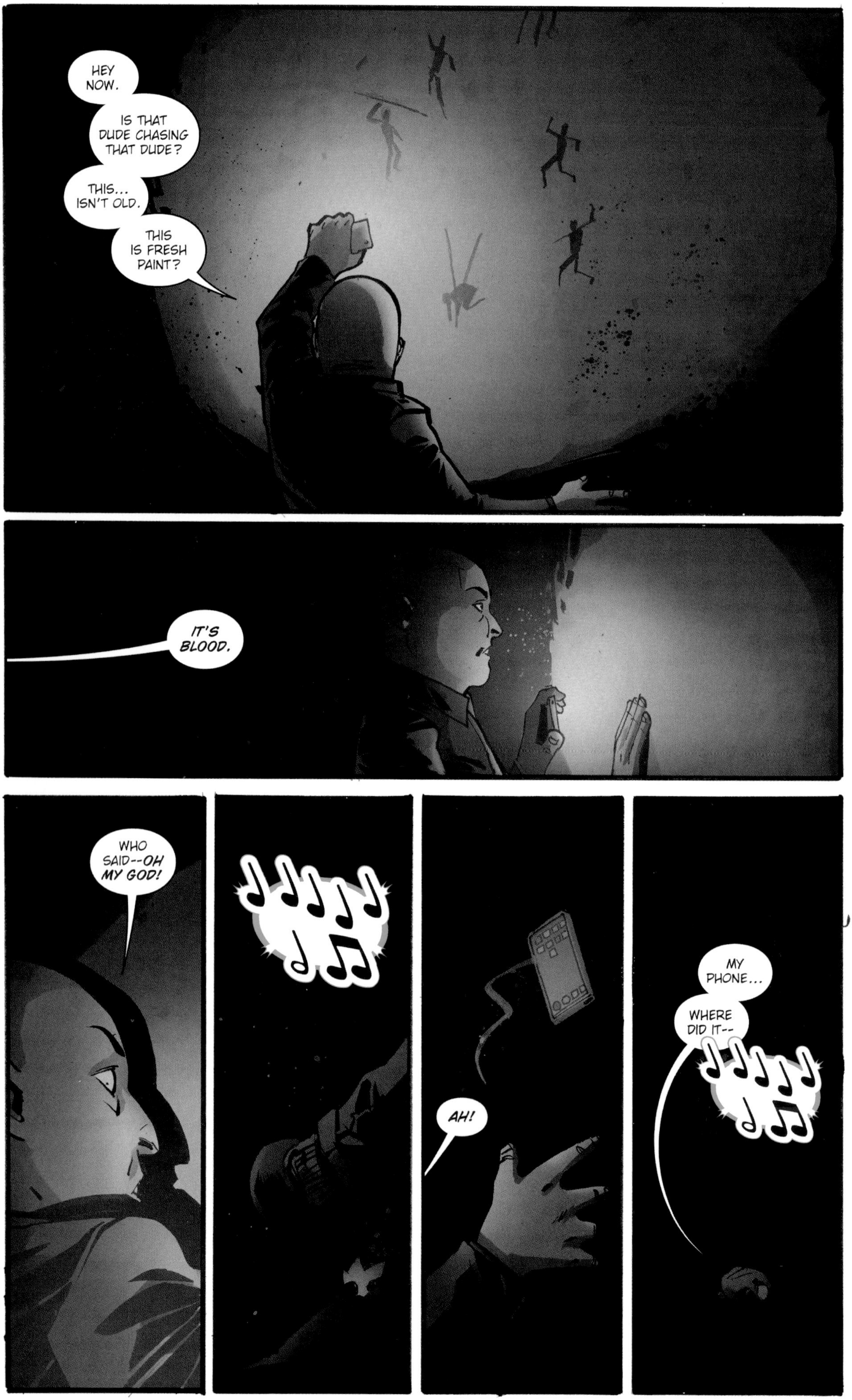
HEY NOW.
IS THAT DUDE CHASING THAT DUDE?
THIS... ISN'T OLD.
THIS IS FRESH PAINT?
IT'S BLOOD.
WHO SAID--OH MY GOD!
AH!
MY PHONE...
WHERE DID IT--

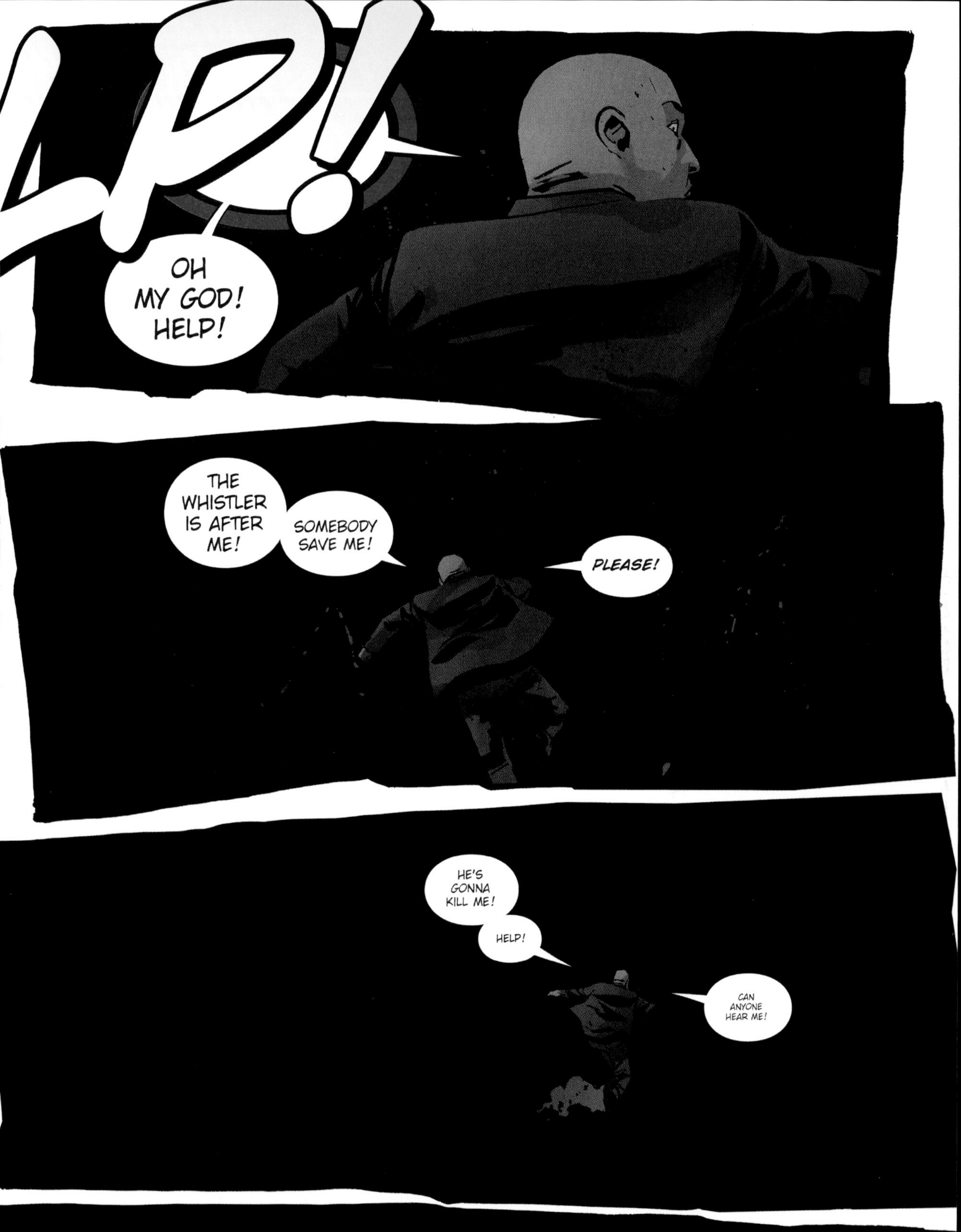
LP!
OH MY GOD! HELP!
THE WHISTLER IS AFTER ME!
SOMEBODY SAVE ME!
PLEASE!
HE'S GONNA KILL ME!
HELP!
CAN ANYONE HEAR ME!

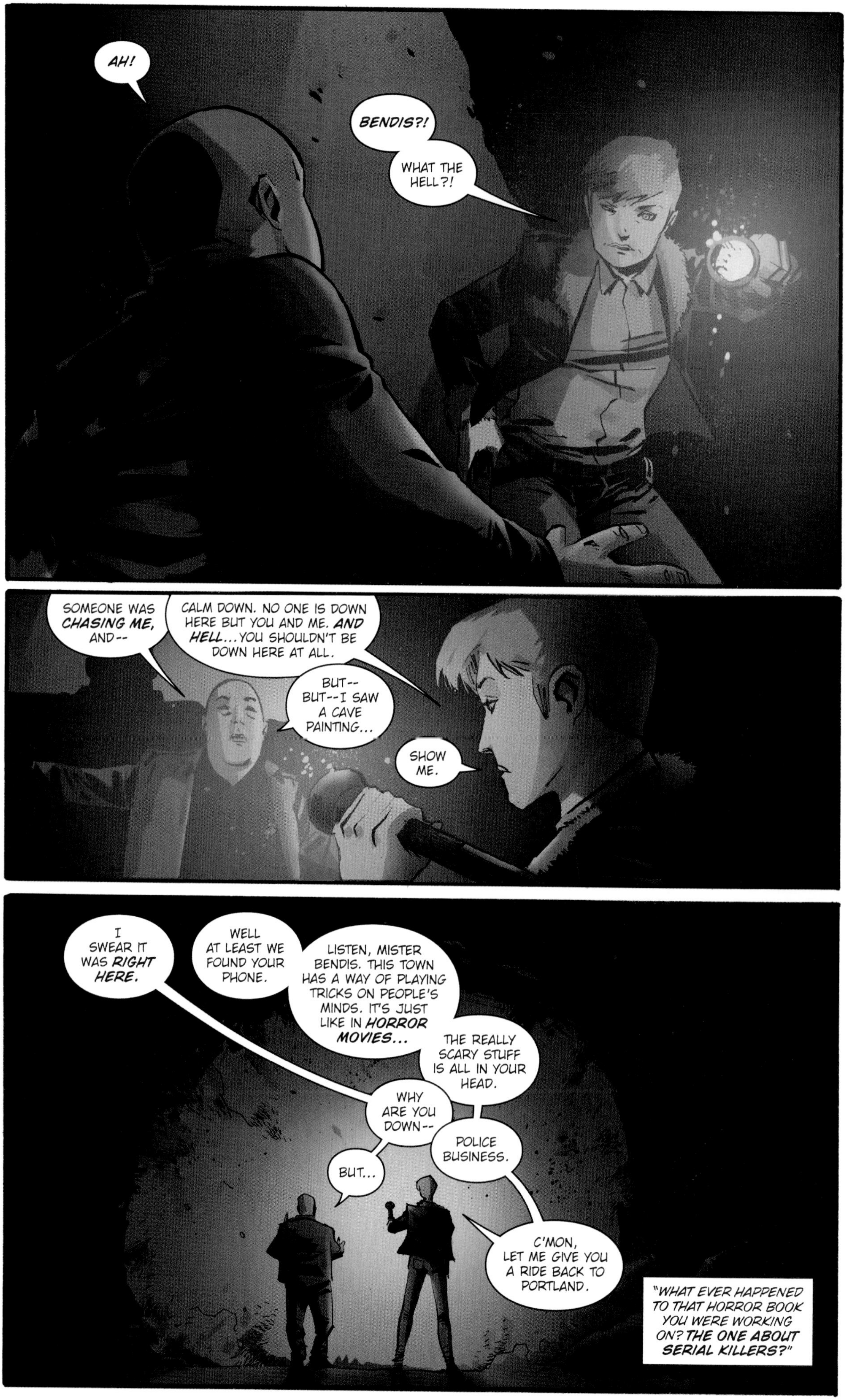
AH!
BENDIS?!
WHAT THE HELL?!
SOMEONE WAS CHASING ME, AND--
CALM DOWN. NO ONE IS DOWN HERE BUT YOU AND ME. AND HELL... YOU SHOULDN'T BE DOWN HERE AT ALL.
BUT-- BUT--I SAW A CAVE PAINTING...
SHOW ME.
I SWEAR IT WAS RIGHT HERE.
WELL AT LEAST WE FOUND YOUR PHONE.
LISTEN, MISTER BENDIS. THIS TOWN HAS A WAY OF PLAYING TRICKS ON PEOPLE'S MINDS. IT'S JUST LIKE IN HORROR MOVIES...
THE REALLY SCARY STUFF IS ALL IN YOUR HEAD.
WHY ARE YOU DOWN--
BUT...
POLICE BUSINESS.
C'MON, LET ME GIVE YOU A RIDE BACK TO PORTLAND.
"WHAT EVER HAPPENED TO THAT HORROR BOOK YOU WERE WORKING ON? THE ONE ABOUT SERIAL KILLERS?"

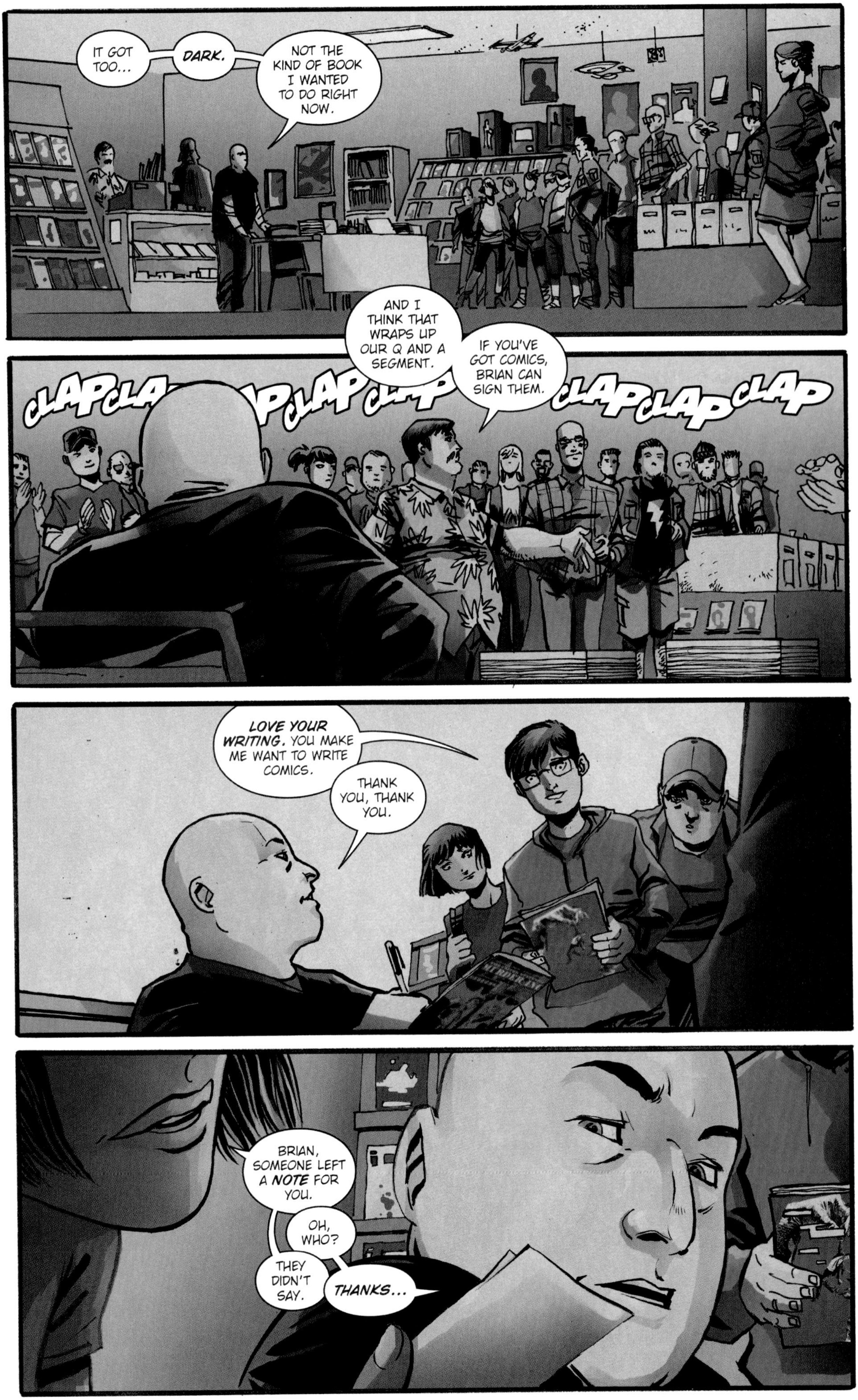

IT GOT TOO...
DARK.
NOT THE KIND OF BOOK I WANTED TO DO RIGHT NOW.
CLAP CLAP CLAP CLAP CLAP
AND I THINK THAT WRAPS UP OUR Q AND A SEGMENT.
IF YOU'VE GOT COMICS, BRIAN CAN SIGN THEM.
CLAP CLAP CLAP
LOVE YOUR WRITING. YOU MAKE ME WANT TO WRITE COMICS.
THANK YOU, THANK YOU.
BRIAN, SOMEONE LEFT A NOTE FOR YOU.
OH, WHO?
THEY DIDN'T SAY.
THANKS...

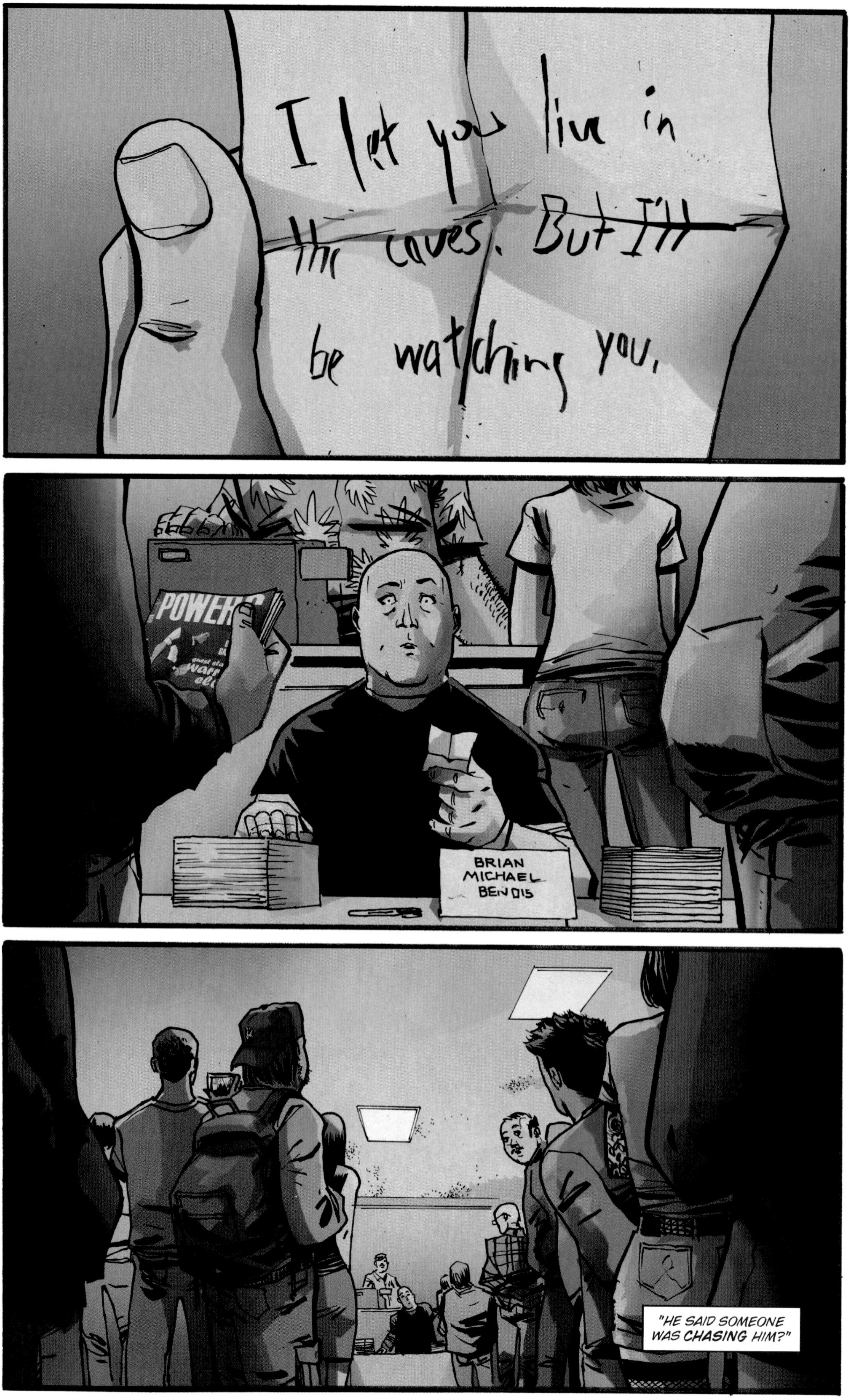
I let you live in the caves. But I'll be watching you.
BRIAN MICHAEL BENDIS
"HE SAID SOMEONE WAS CHASING HIM?"

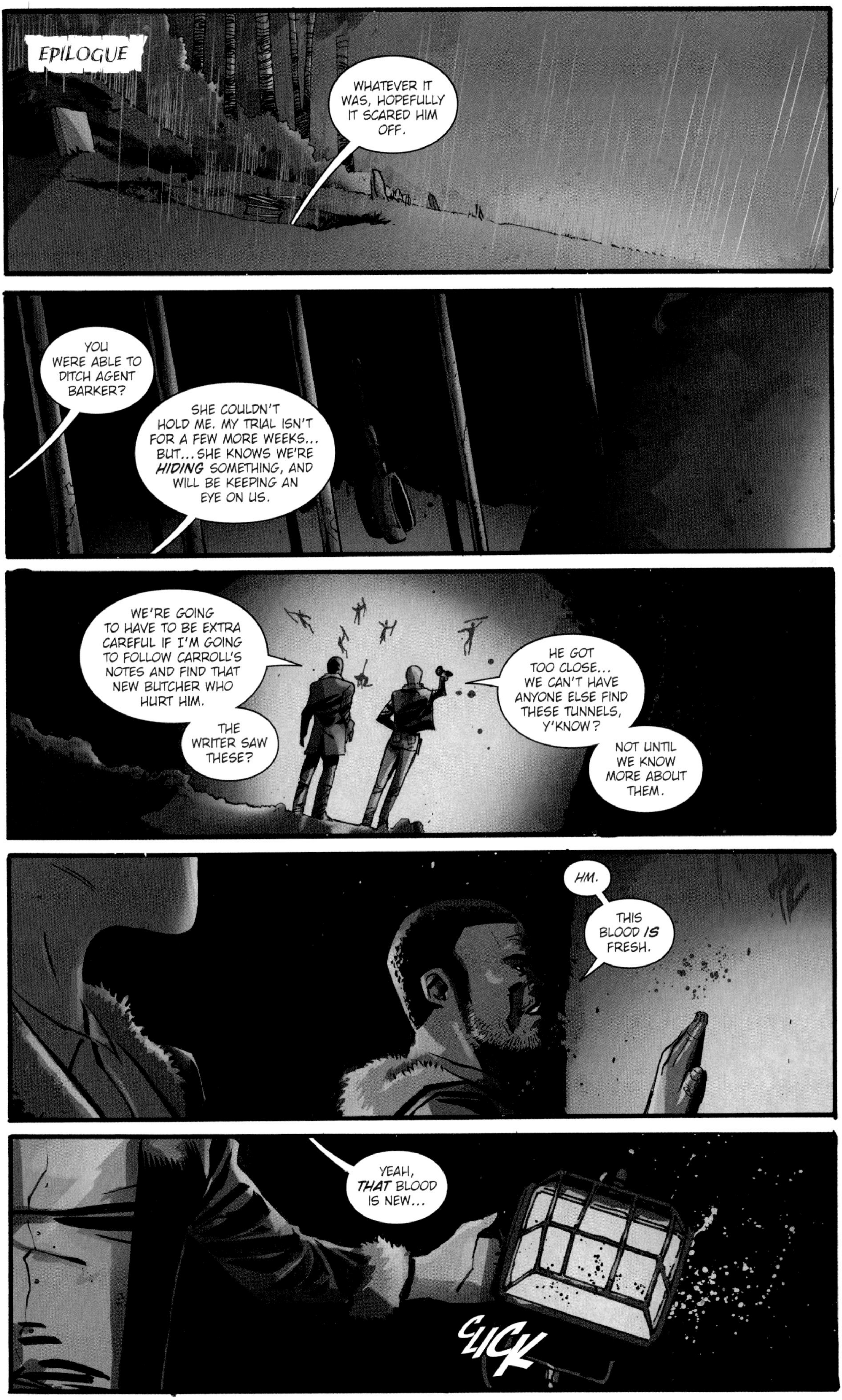
EPILOGUE
WHATEVER IT WAS, HOPEFULLY IT SCARED HIM OFF.
YOU WERE ABLE TO DITCH AGENT BARKER?
SHE COULDN'T HOLD ME. MY TRIAL ISN'T FOR A FEW MORE WEEKS... BUT...SHE KNOWS WE'RE HIDING SOMETHING, AND WILL BE KEEPING AN EYE ON US.
WE'RE GOING TO HAVE TO BE EXTRA CAREFUL IF I'M GOING TO FOLLOW CARROLL'S NOTES AND FIND THAT NEW BUTCHER WHO HURT HIM.
THE WRITER SAW THESE?
HE GOT TOO CLOSE... WE CAN'T HAVE ANYONE ELSE FIND THESE TUNNELS, Y'KNOW?
NOT UNTIL WE KNOW MORE ABOUT THEM.
HM.
THIS BLOOD IS FRESH.
YEAH, THAT BLOOD IS NEW...
CLICK

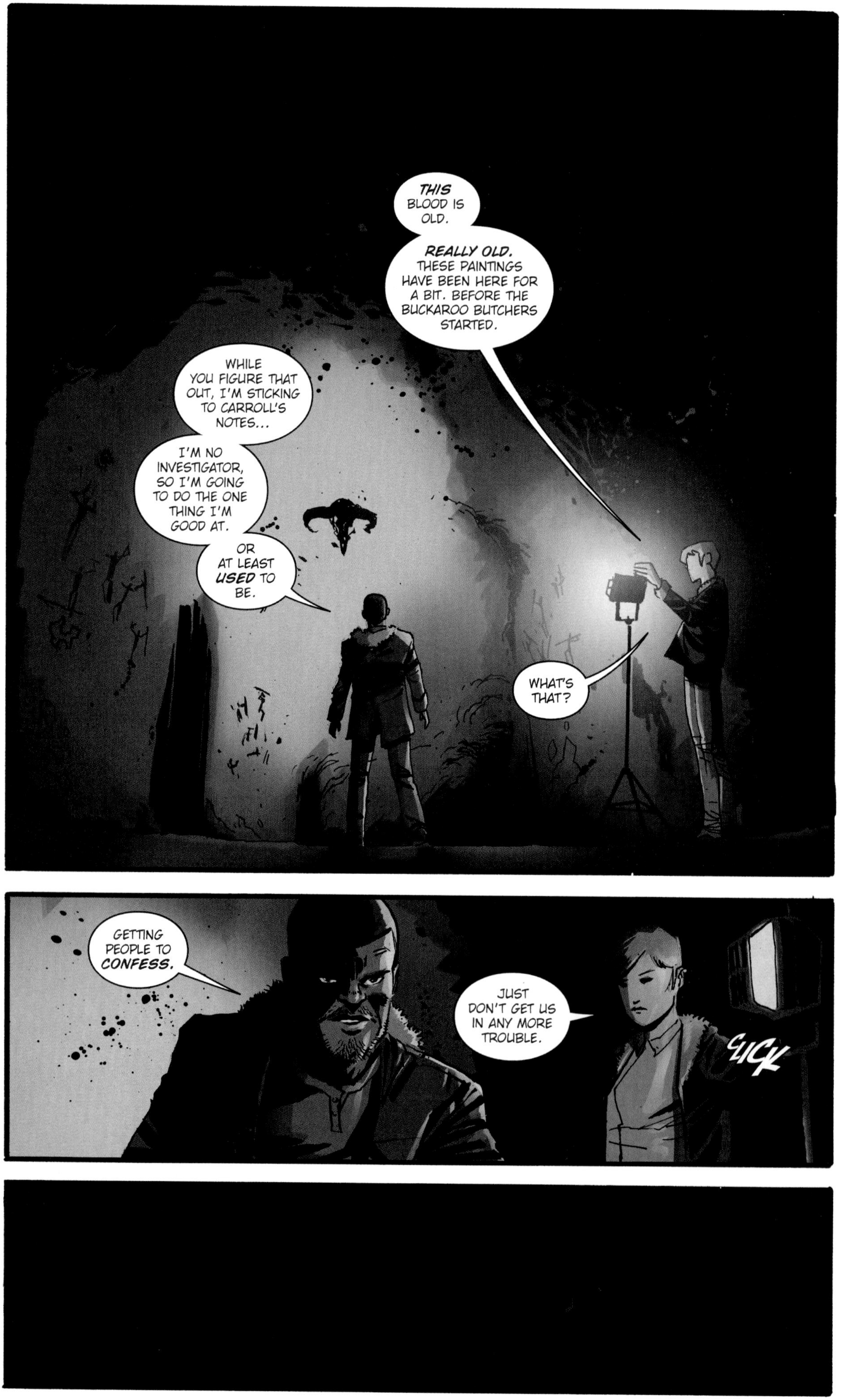
THIS BLOOD IS OLD.
REALLY OLD. THESE PAINTINGS HAVE BEEN HERE FOR A BIT. BEFORE THE BUCKAROO BUTCHERS STARTED.
WHILE YOU FIGURE THAT OUT, I'M STICKING TO CARROLL'S NOTES...
I'M NO INVESTIGATOR, SO I'M GOING TO DO THE ONE THING I'M GOOD AT.
OR AT LEAST USED TO BE.
WHAT'S THAT?
GETTING PEOPLE TO CONFESS.
JUST DON'T GET US IN ANY MORE TROUBLE.
CLICK

EIGHT

"What kind of predator would
sacrifice itself so that it could kill another?"

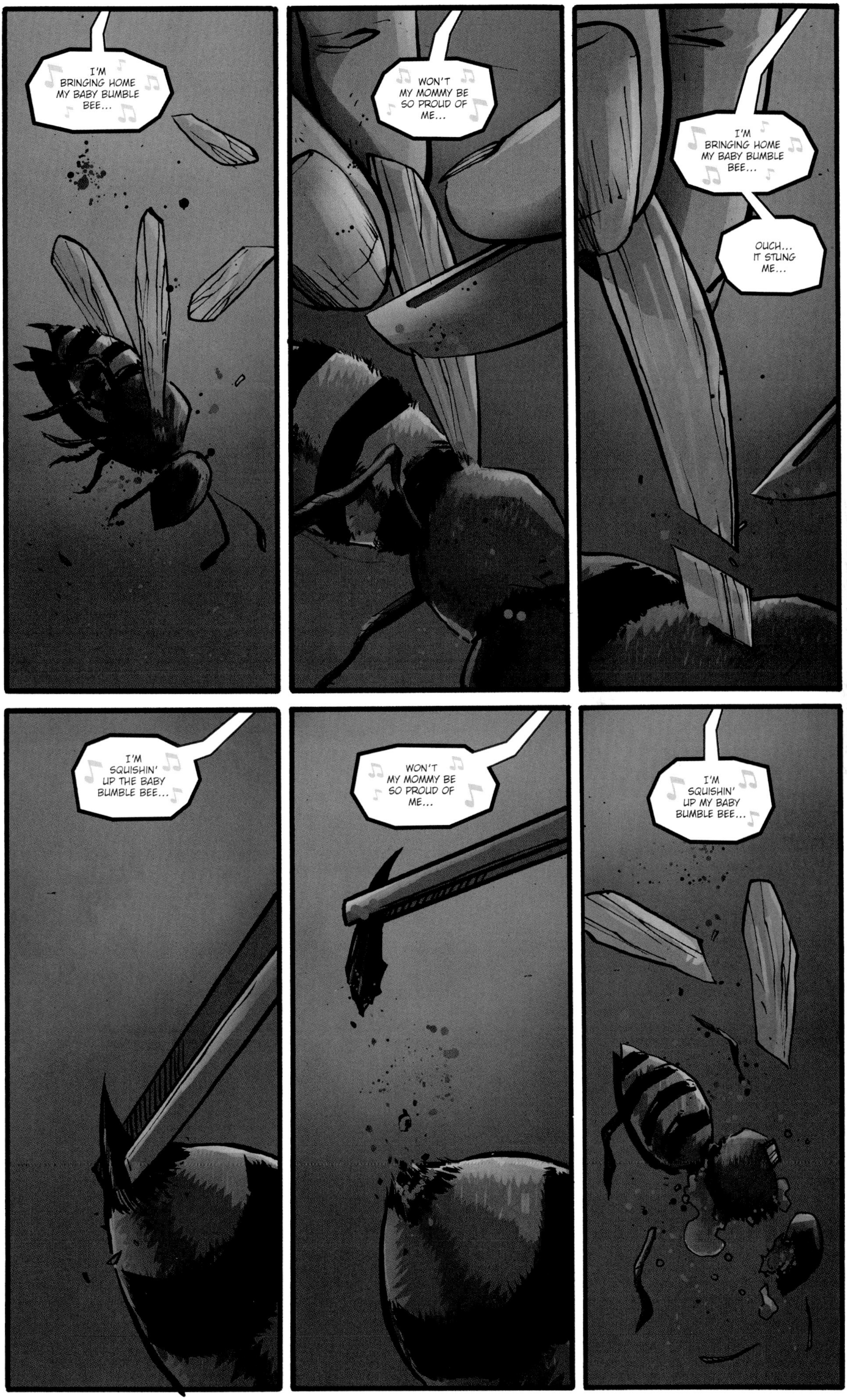
I'M BRINGING HOME MY BABY BUMBLE BEE...
WON'T MY MOMMY BE SO PROUD OF ME...
I'M BRINGING HOME MY BABY BUMBLE BEE...
OUCH... IT STUNG ME...
I'M SQUISHIN' UP THE BABY BUMBLE BEE...
WON'T MY MOMMY BE SO PROUD OF ME...
I'M SQUISHIN' UP MY BABY BUMBLE BEE...

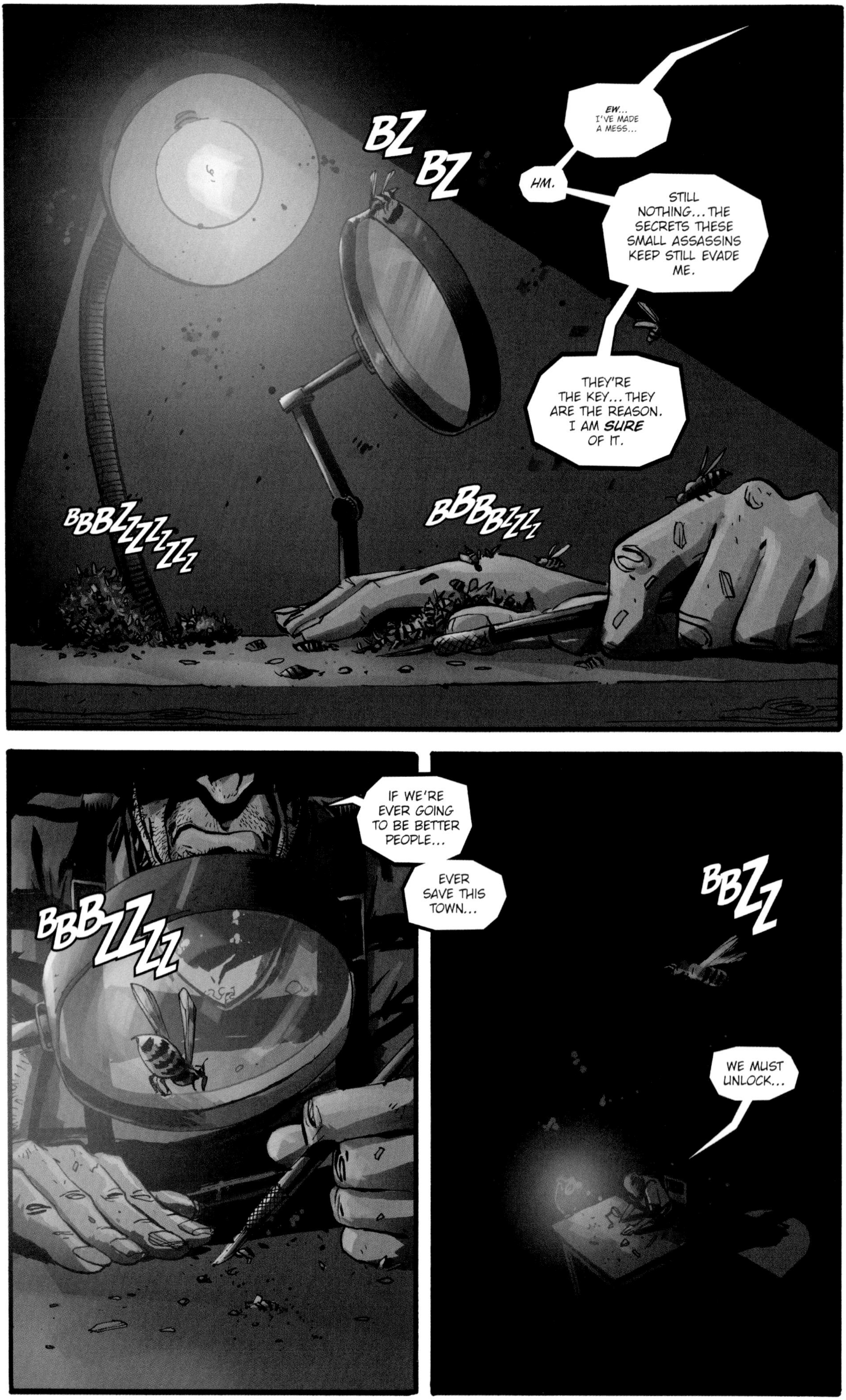
BZ BZ
EW... I'VE MADE A MESS...
HM.
STILL NOTHING... THE SECRETS THESE SMALL ASSASSINS KEEP STILL EVADE ME.
THEY'RE THE KEY... THEY ARE THE REASON. I AM SURE OF IT.
BBBZZZZZZZZ
BBBBZZZZ
IF WE'RE EVER GOING TO BE BETTER PEOPLE...
EVER SAVE THIS TOWN...
BBBZZZZ
BBZZ
WE MUST UNLOCK...

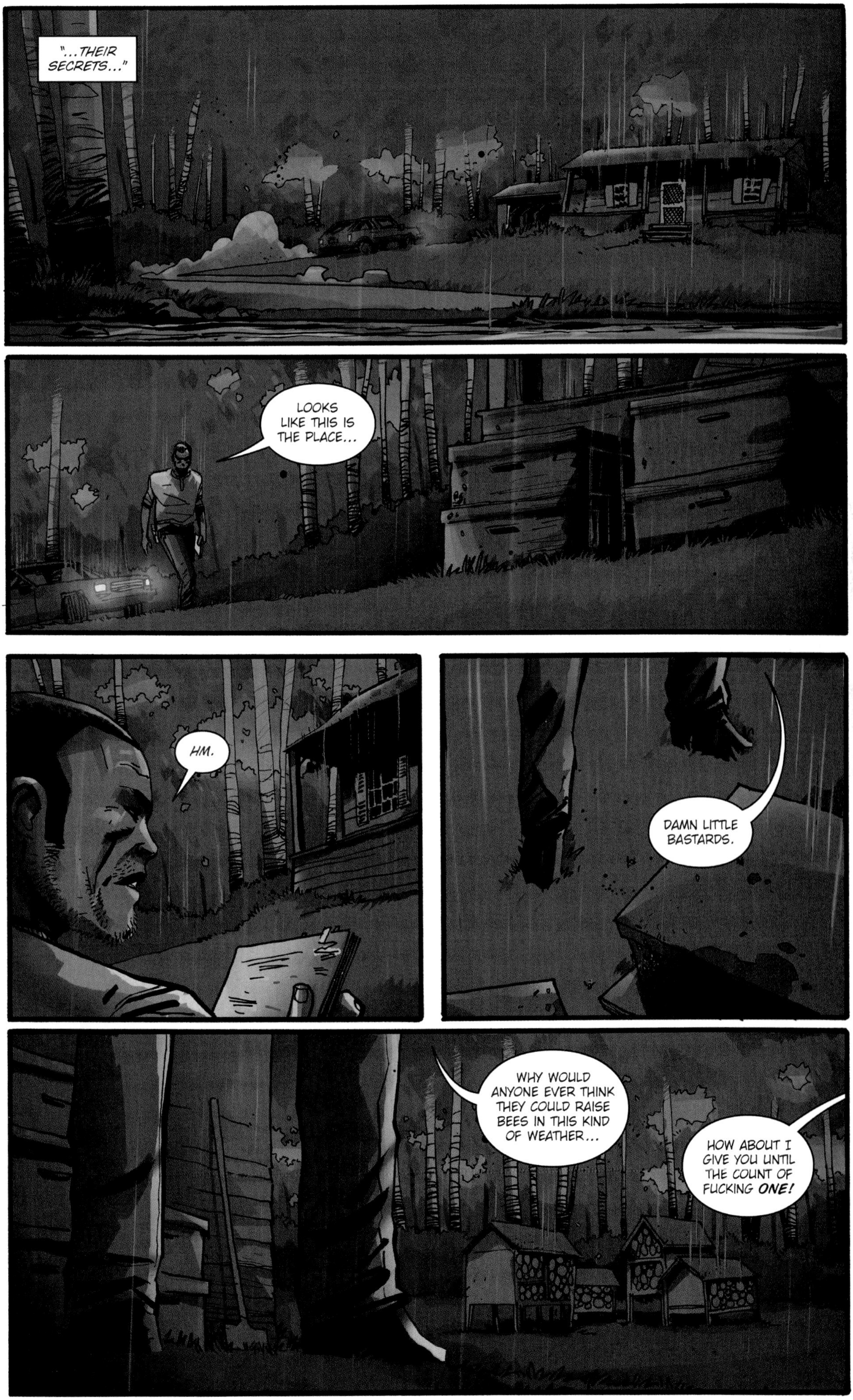
"...THEIR SECRETS..."
LOOKS LIKE THIS IS THE PLACE...
HM.
DAMN LITTLE BASTARDS.
WHY WOULD ANYONE EVER THINK THEY COULD RAISE BEES IN THIS KIND OF WEATHER...
HOW ABOUT I GIVE YOU UNTIL THE COUNT OF FUCKING ONE!

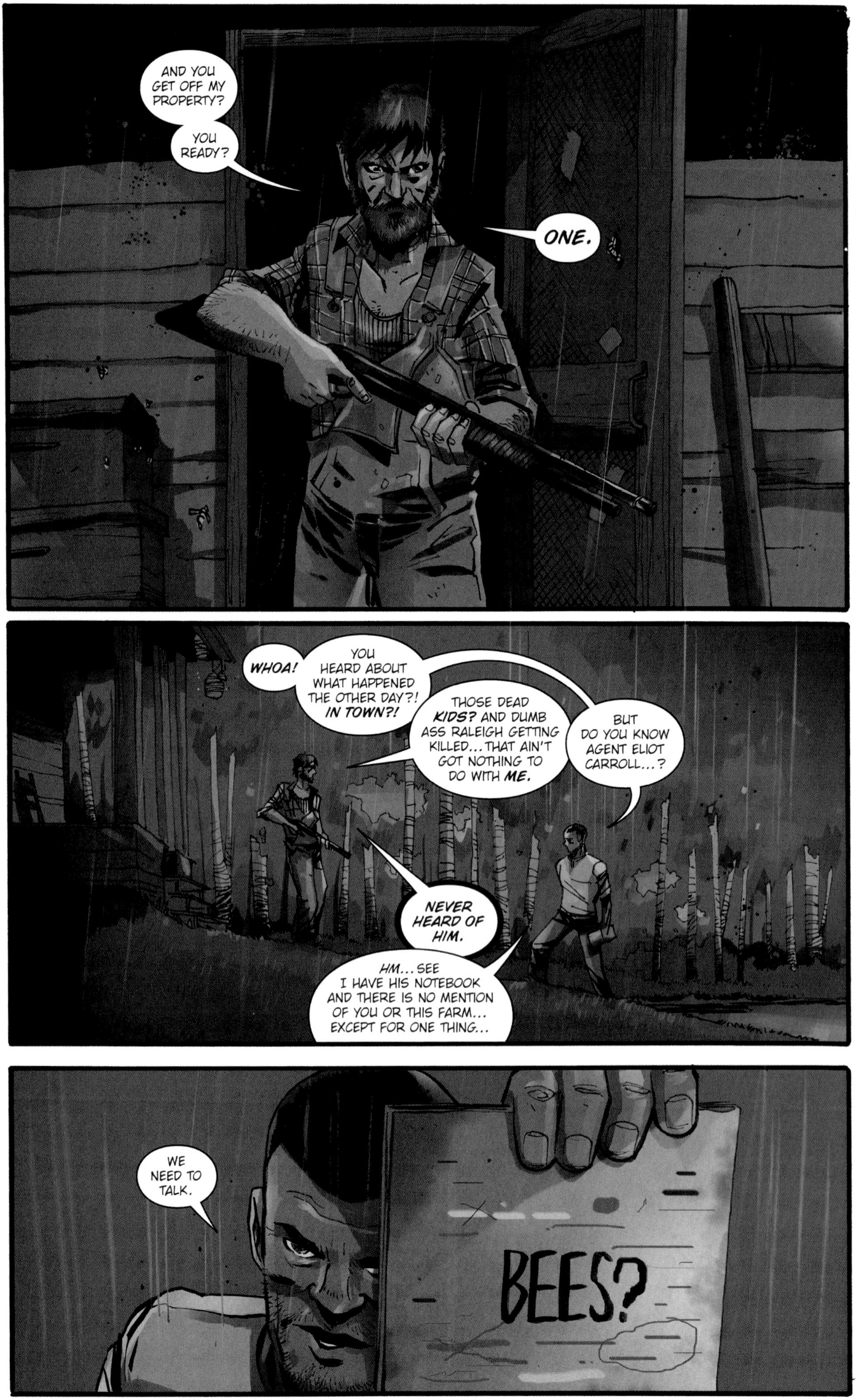
AND YOU GET OFF MY PROPERTY?
YOU READY?
ONE.
WHOA!
YOU HEARD ABOUT WHAT HAPPENED THE OTHER DAY?! IN TOWN?!
THOSE DEAD KIDS? AND DUMB ASS RALEIGH GETTING KILLED... THAT AIN'T GOT NOTHING TO DO WITH ME.
BUT DO YOU KNOW AGENT ELIOT CARROLL...?
NEVER HEARD OF HIM.
HM... SEE I HAVE HIS NOTEBOOK AND THERE IS NO MENTION OF YOU OR THIS FARM... EXCEPT FOR ONE THING...
WE NEED TO TALK.
BEES?

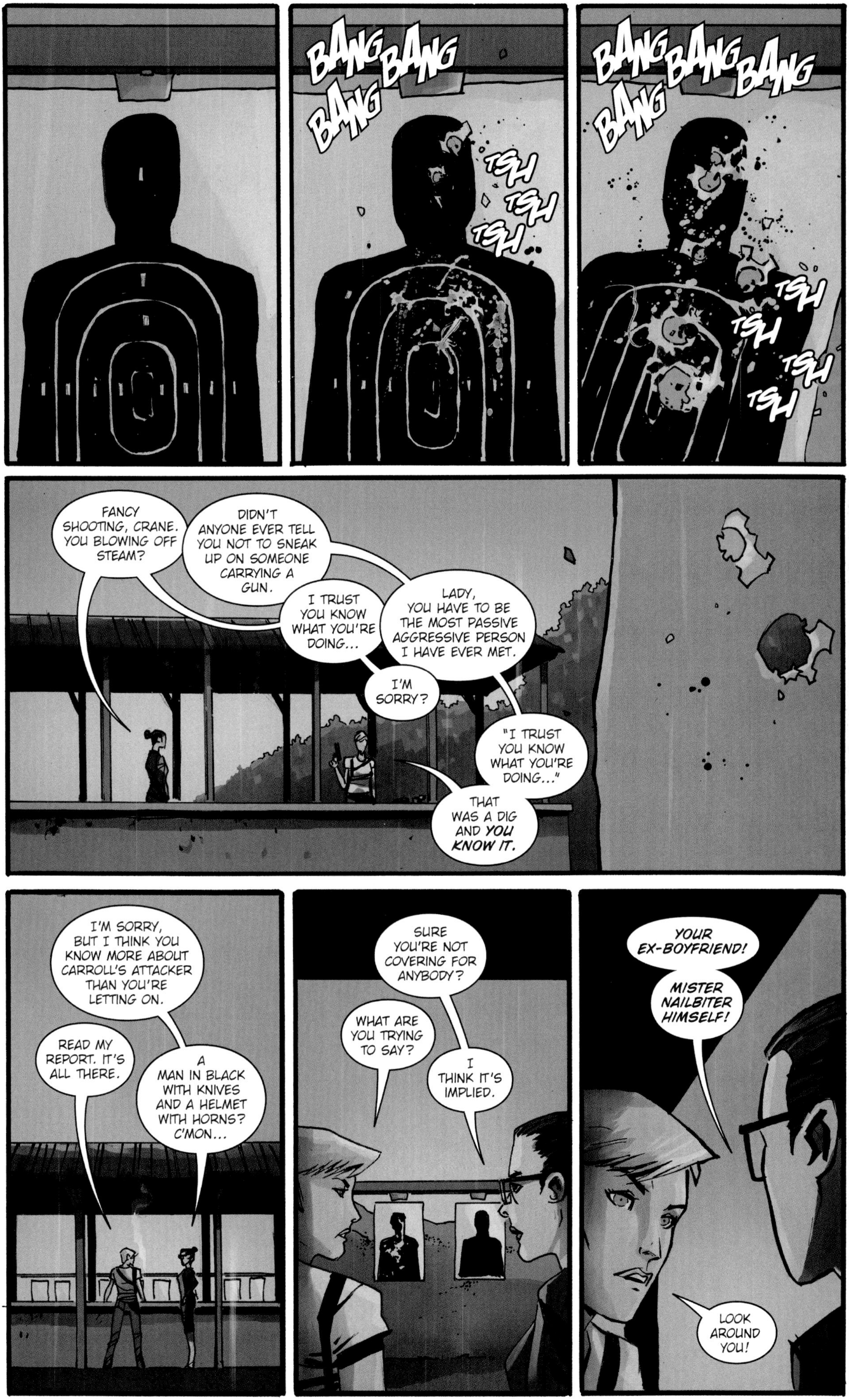
BANG BANG BANG
TSH TSH TSH
BANG BANG BANG BANG
TSH TSH TSH TSH
FANCY SHOOTING, CRANE. YOU BLOWING OFF STEAM?
DIDN'T ANYONE EVER TELL YOU NOT TO SNEAK UP ON SOMEONE CARRYING A GUN.
I TRUST YOU KNOW WHAT YOU'RE DOING...
LADY, YOU HAVE TO BE THE MOST PASSIVE AGGRESSIVE PERSON I HAVE EVER MET.
I'M SORRY?
"I TRUST YOU KNOW WHAT YOU'RE DOING..."
THAT WAS A DIG AND *YOU KNOW IT.*
I'M SORRY, BUT I THINK YOU KNOW MORE ABOUT CARROLL'S ATTACKER THAN YOU'RE LETTING ON.
READ MY REPORT. IT'S ALL THERE.
A MAN IN BLACK WITH KNIVES AND A HELMET WITH HORNS? C'MON...
SURE YOU'RE NOT COVERING FOR ANYBODY?
WHAT ARE YOU TRYING TO SAY?
I THINK IT'S IMPLIED.
YOUR EX-BOYFRIEND!
MISTER NAILBITER HIMSELF!
LOOK AROUND YOU!

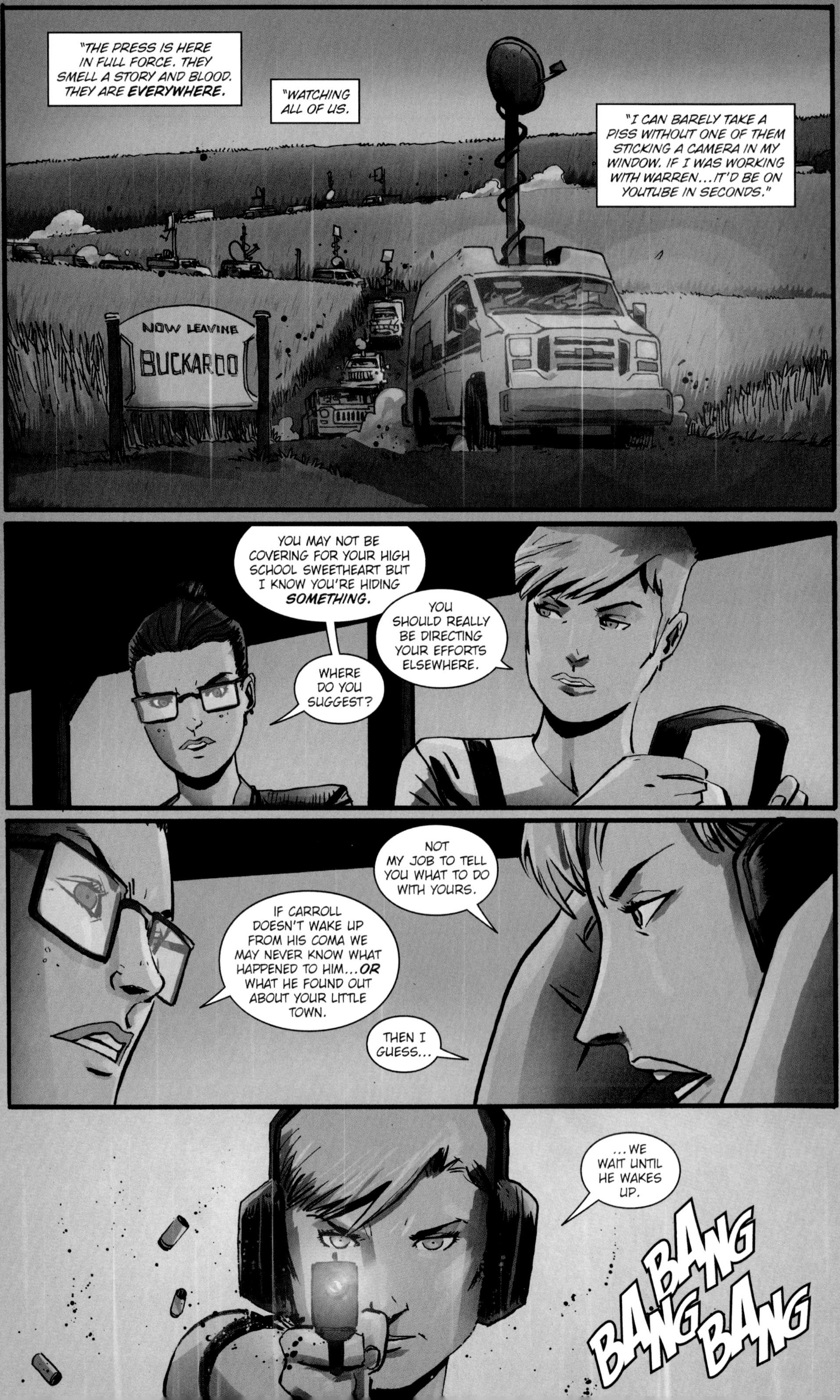
"THE PRESS IS HERE IN FULL FORCE. THEY SMELL A STORY AND BLOOD. THEY ARE EVERYWHERE.
"WATCHING ALL OF US.
"I CAN BARELY TAKE A PISS WITHOUT ONE OF THEM STICKING A CAMERA IN MY WINDOW. IF I WAS WORKING WITH WARREN...IT'D BE ON YOUTUBE IN SECONDS."
NOW LEAVING BUCKAROO
YOU MAY NOT BE COVERING FOR YOUR HIGH SCHOOL SWEETHEART BUT I KNOW YOU'RE HIDING SOMETHING.
YOU SHOULD REALLY BE DIRECTING YOUR EFFORTS ELSEWHERE.
WHERE DO YOU SUGGEST?
NOT MY JOB TO TELL YOU WHAT TO DO WITH YOURS.
IF CARROLL DOESN'T WAKE UP FROM HIS COMA WE MAY NEVER KNOW WHAT HAPPENED TO HIM...OR WHAT HE FOUND OUT ABOUT YOUR LITTLE TOWN.
THEN I GUESS...
...WE WAIT UNTIL HE WAKES UP.
BANG BANG BANG

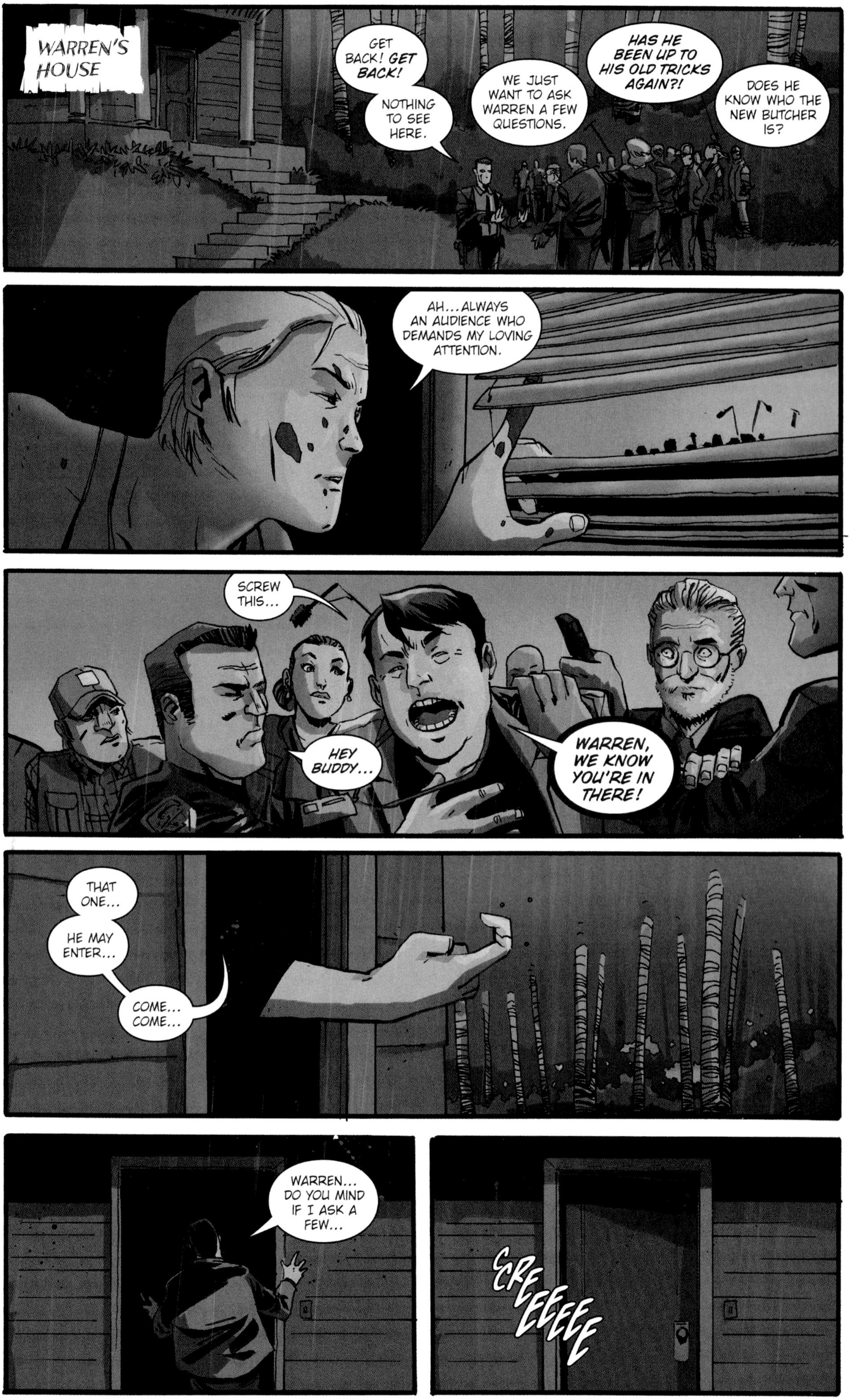
WARREN'S HOUSE
GET BACK! GET BACK!
NOTHING TO SEE HERE.
WE JUST WANT TO ASK WARREN A FEW QUESTIONS.
HAS HE BEEN UP TO HIS OLD TRICKS AGAIN?!
DOES HE KNOW WHO THE NEW BUTCHER IS?
AH... ALWAYS AN AUDIENCE WHO DEMANDS MY LOVING ATTENTION.
SCREW THIS...
HEY BUDDY...
WARREN, WE KNOW YOU'RE IN THERE!
THAT ONE...
HE MAY ENTER...
COME... COME...
WARREN... DO YOU MIND IF I ASK A FEW...
SCREEEEEE

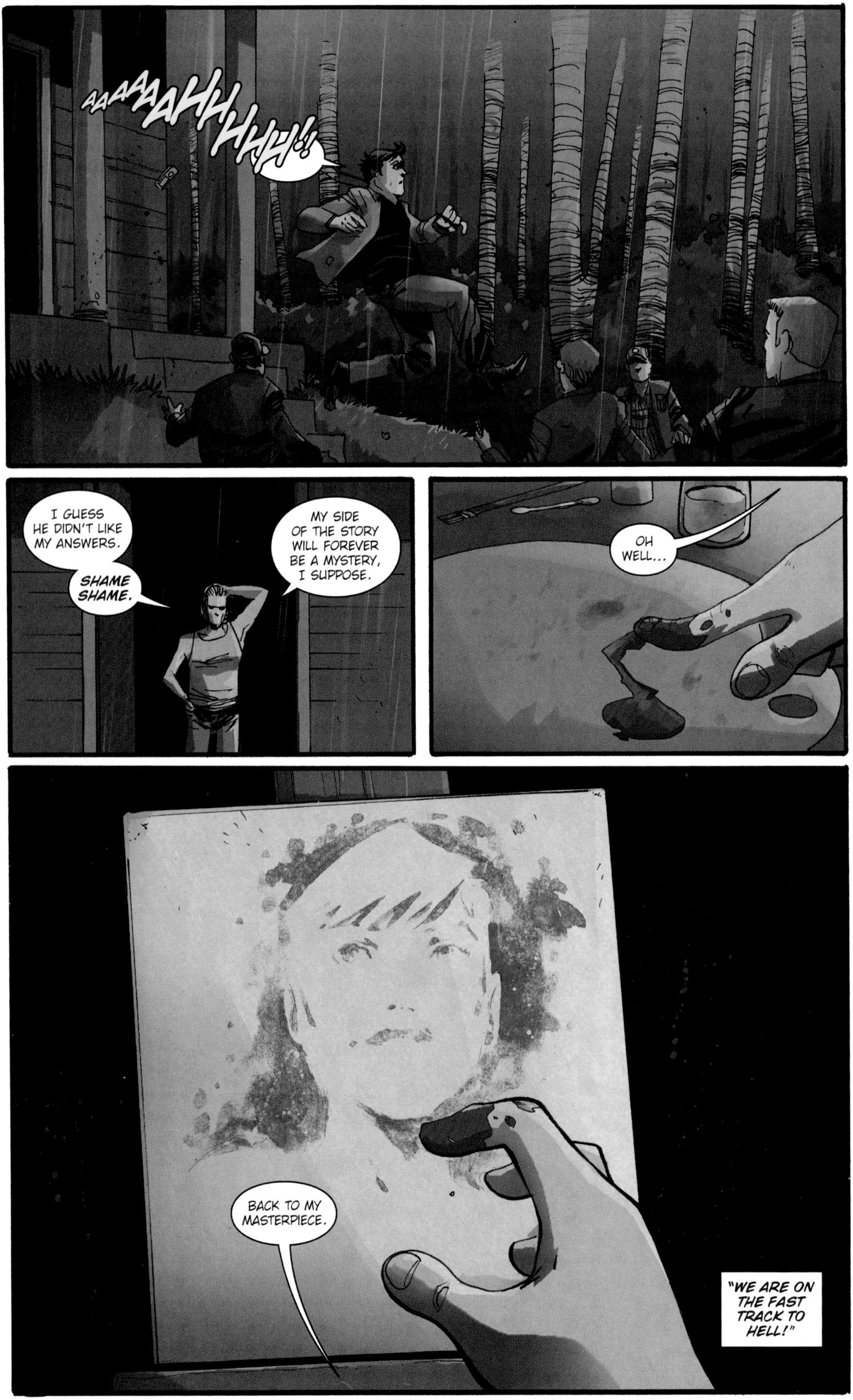
AAAAAAHHHHHH!!
I GUESS HE DIDN'T LIKE MY ANSWERS.
SHAME SHAME.
MY SIDE OF THE STORY WILL FOREVER BE A MYSTERY, I SUPPOSE.
OH WELL...
BACK TO MY MASTERPIECE.
"WE ARE ON THE FAST TRACK TO HELL!"

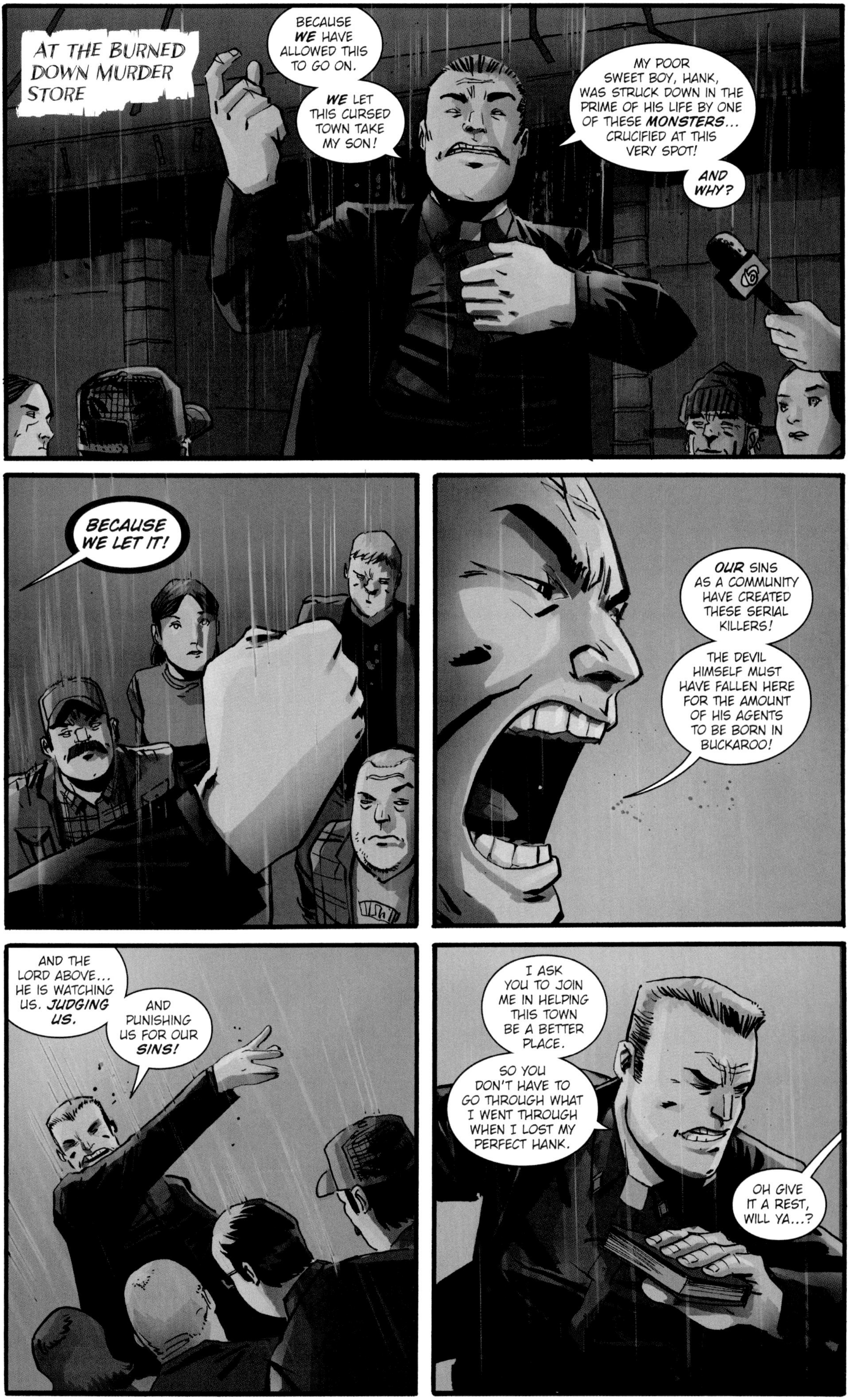

AT THE BURNED DOWN MURDER STORE
MY POOR SWEET BOY, HANK, WAS STRUCK DOWN IN THE PRIME OF HIS LIFE BY ONE OF THESE MONSTERS... CRUCIFIED AT THIS VERY SPOT!
AND WHY?
BECAUSE WE HAVE ALLOWED THIS TO GO ON.
WE LET THIS CURSED TOWN TAKE MY SON!
BECAUSE WE LET IT!
OUR SINS AS A COMMUNITY HAVE CREATED THESE SERIAL KILLERS!
THE DEVIL HIMSELF MUST HAVE FALLEN HERE FOR THE AMOUNT OF HIS AGENTS TO BE BORN IN BUCKAROO!
AND THE LORD ABOVE... HE IS WATCHING US. JUDGING US.
AND PUNISHING US FOR OUR SINS!
I ASK YOU TO JOIN ME IN HELPING THIS TOWN BE A BETTER PLACE.
SO YOU DON'T HAVE TO GO THROUGH WHAT I WENT THROUGH WHEN I LOST MY PERFECT HANK.
OH GIVE IT A REST, WILL YA...?

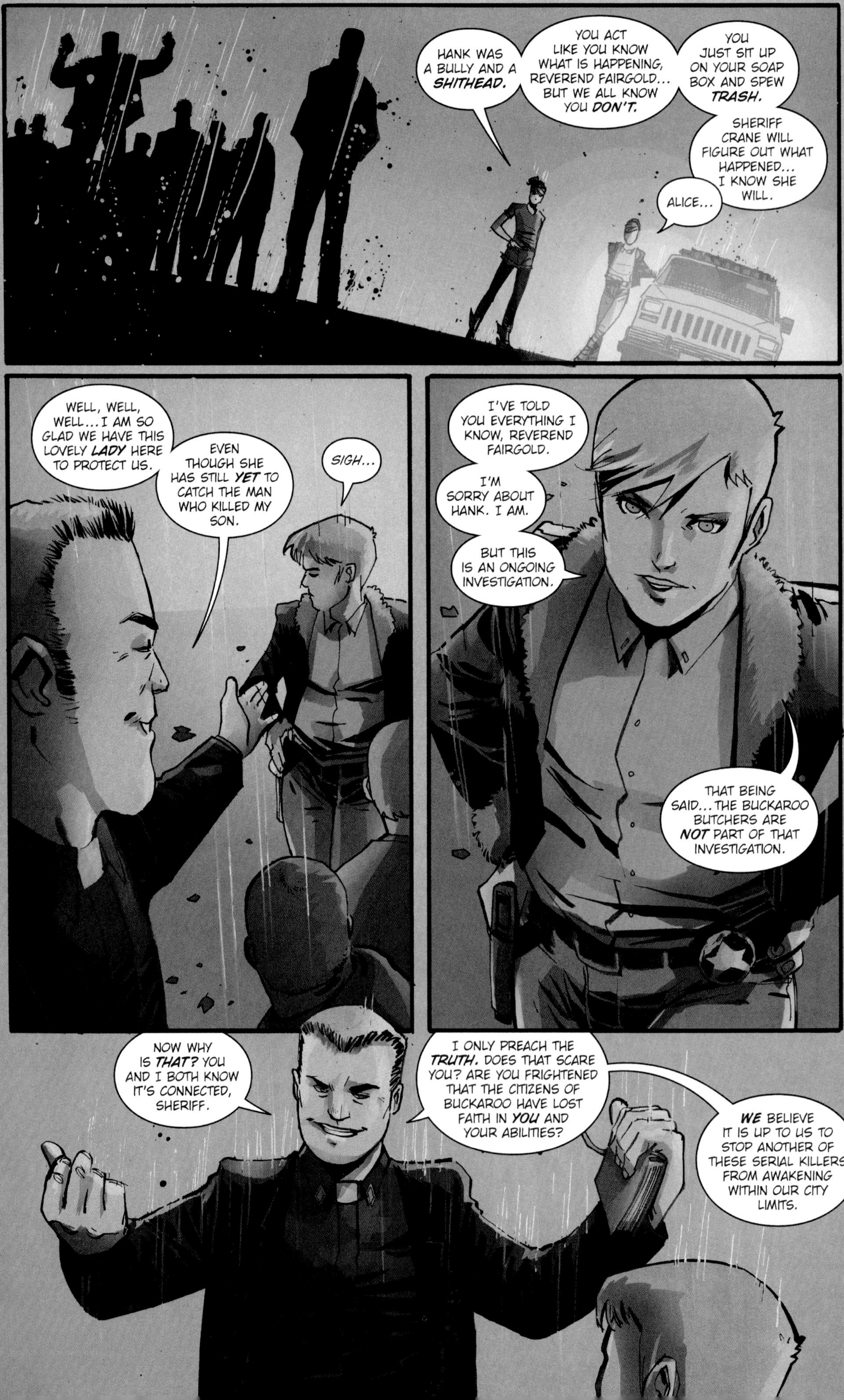
HANK WAS A BULLY AND A SHITHEAD.
YOU ACT LIKE YOU KNOW WHAT IS HAPPENING, REVEREND FAIRGOLD... BUT WE ALL KNOW YOU DON'T.
YOU JUST SIT UP ON YOUR SOAP BOX AND SPEW TRASH.
SHERIFF CRANE WILL FIGURE OUT WHAT HAPPENED... I KNOW SHE WILL.
ALICE...
WELL, WELL, WELL... I AM SO GLAD WE HAVE THIS LOVELY LADY HERE TO PROTECT US.
EVEN THOUGH SHE HAS STILL YET TO CATCH THE MAN WHO KILLED MY SON.
SIGH...
I'VE TOLD YOU EVERYTHING I KNOW, REVEREND FAIRGOLD.
I'M SORRY ABOUT HANK. I AM.
BUT THIS IS AN ONGOING INVESTIGATION.
THAT BEING SAID... THE BUCKAROO BUTCHERS ARE NOT PART OF THAT INVESTIGATION.
NOW WHY IS THAT? YOU AND I BOTH KNOW IT'S CONNECTED, SHERIFF.
I ONLY PREACH THE TRUTH. DOES THAT SCARE YOU? ARE YOU FRIGHTENED THAT THE CITIZENS OF BUCKAROO HAVE LOST FAITH IN YOU AND YOUR ABILITIES?
WE BELIEVE IT IS UP TO US TO STOP ANOTHER OF THESE SERIAL KILLERS FROM AWAKENING WITHIN OUR CITY LIMITS.

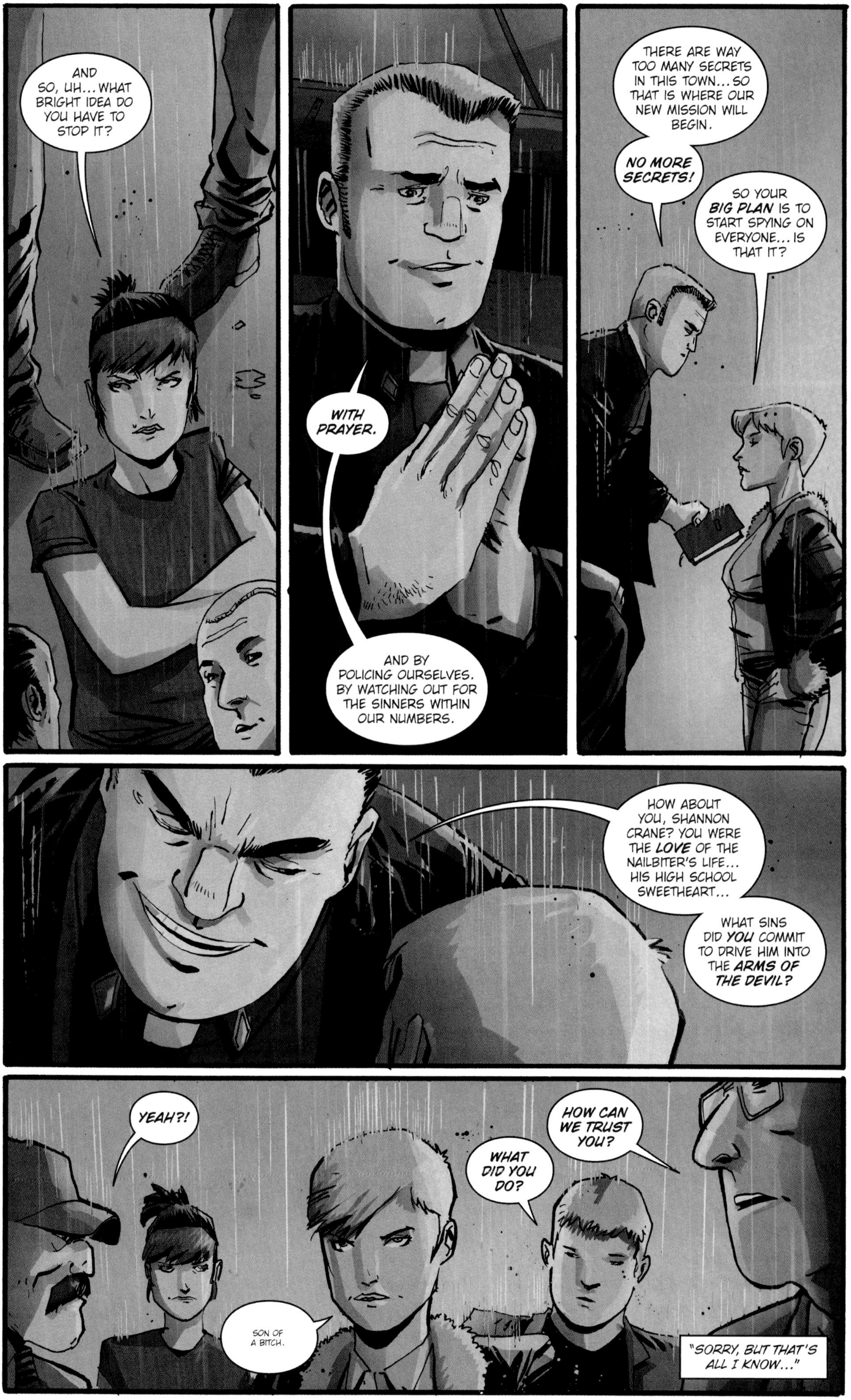
AND SO, UH... WHAT BRIGHT IDEA DO YOU HAVE TO STOP IT?
WITH PRAYER.
AND BY POLICING OURSELVES. BY WATCHING OUT FOR THE SINNERS WITHIN OUR NUMBERS.
THERE ARE WAY TOO MANY SECRETS IN THIS TOWN... SO THAT IS WHERE OUR NEW MISSION WILL BEGIN.
NO MORE SECRETS!
SO YOUR BIG PLAN IS TO START SPYING ON EVERYONE... IS THAT IT?
HOW ABOUT YOU, SHANNON CRANE? YOU WERE THE LOVE OF THE NAILBITER'S LIFE... HIS HIGH SCHOOL SWEETHEART...
WHAT SINS DID YOU COMMIT TO DRIVE HIM INTO THE ARMS OF THE DEVIL?
YEAH?!
HOW CAN WE TRUST YOU?
WHAT DID YOU DO?
SON OF A BITCH.
"SORRY, BUT THAT'S ALL I KNOW..."

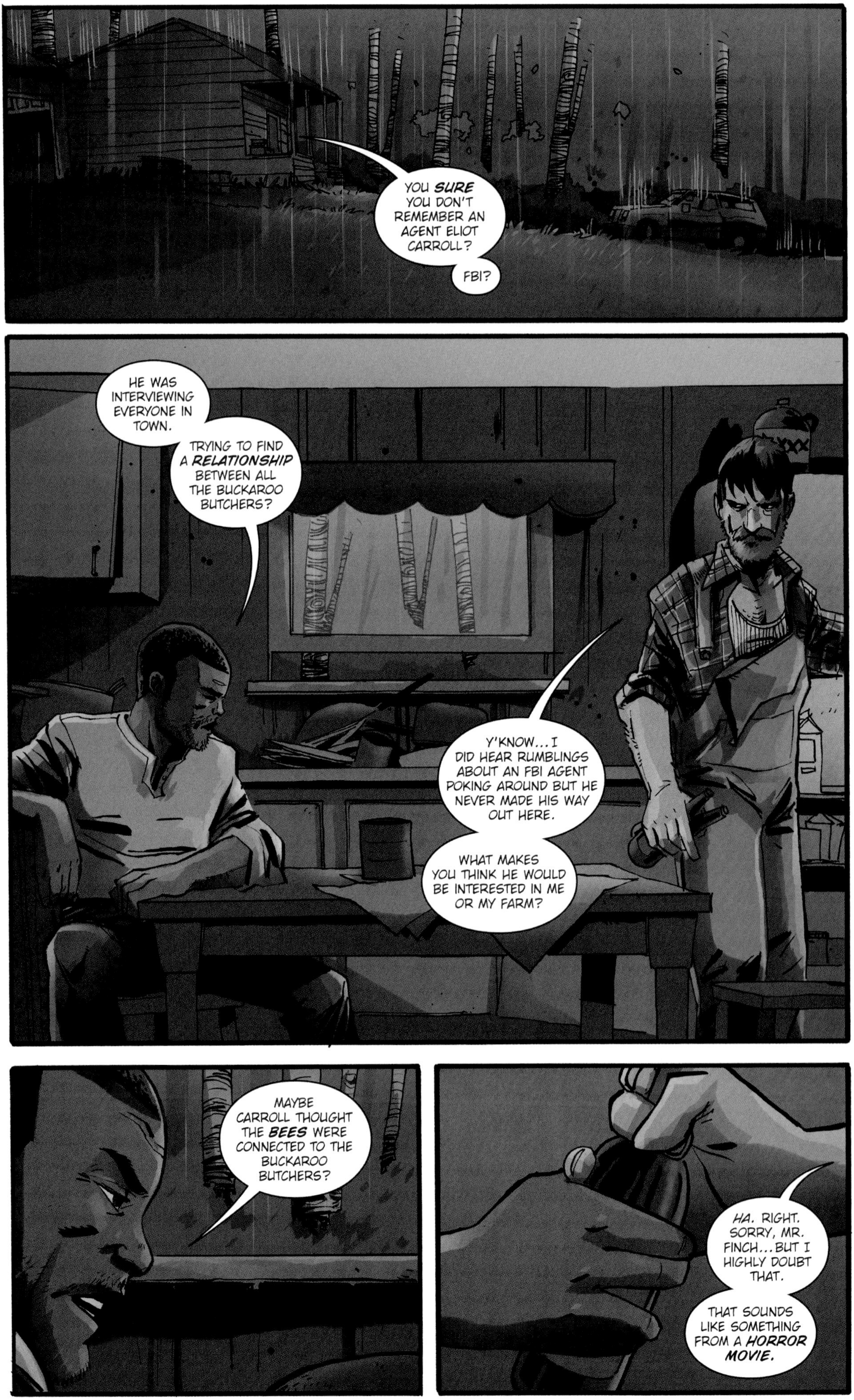
YOU SURE YOU DON'T REMEMBER AN AGENT ELIOT CARROLL?
FBI?
HE WAS INTERVIEWING EVERYONE IN TOWN.
TRYING TO FIND A RELATIONSHIP BETWEEN ALL THE BUCKAROO BUTCHERS?
Y'KNOW... I DID HEAR RUMBLINGS ABOUT AN FBI AGENT POKING AROUND BUT HE NEVER MADE HIS WAY OUT HERE.
WHAT MAKES YOU THINK HE WOULD BE INTERESTED IN ME OR MY FARM?
MAYBE CARROLL THOUGHT THE BEES WERE CONNECTED TO THE BUCKAROO BUTCHERS?
HA. RIGHT. SORRY, MR. FINCH... BUT I HIGHLY DOUBT THAT.
THAT SOUNDS LIKE SOMETHING FROM A HORROR MOVIE.

HM.

LET ME ASK YOU THIS.

WHY *DO* YOU THINK CARROLL WAS INTERESTED IN THE BEES?

DAMN, YOU DON'T QUIT, DO YOU? HOW MANY TIMES WE GOTTA GO OVER THIS...?

LIKE I SAID... THAT COULD BE ANY NUMBER OF THINGS. THIS WHOLE TOWN USED TO RELY ON THE *HONEY FARMS*. IT WAS *BIG BUSINESS* FOR US.

BUT...ABOUT TWENTY YEARS AGO THE BEES JUST STARTED TO *DIE*.

"NO ONE KNOWS WHY...

"THEY JUST SLOWLY STARTED TO DROP DEAD.

"IT KILLED THIS TOWN. A *LOT* OF PEOPLE GOT LAID OFF.

"IT'S A SORE SUBJECT AROUND HERE.

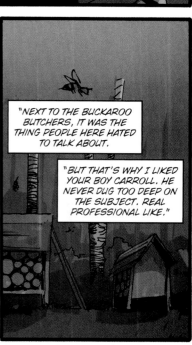

"NEXT TO THE BUCKAROO BUTCHERS, IT WAS THE THING PEOPLE HERE HATED TO TALK ABOUT.

"BUT THAT'S WHY I LIKED YOUR BOY CARROLL. HE NEVER DUG TOO DEEP ON THE SUBJECT. REAL PROFESSIONAL LIKE."

YOU SAID YOU NEVER TALKED TO CARROLL.

OH, UH...

BEFORE ALL THIS I WAS AN *ARMY INTERROGATOR*. AND THE NUMBER ONE THING WE LOOKED FOR WAS *CHANGES* IN THE STORY. TRY TO FIND A LIE.

AND SIR... I JUST CAUGHT YOU IN A *LIE*.

NOW YOU WANT TO TELL ME WHAT YOU AND CARROLL TALKED ABOUT?

UH... WELL... UH...

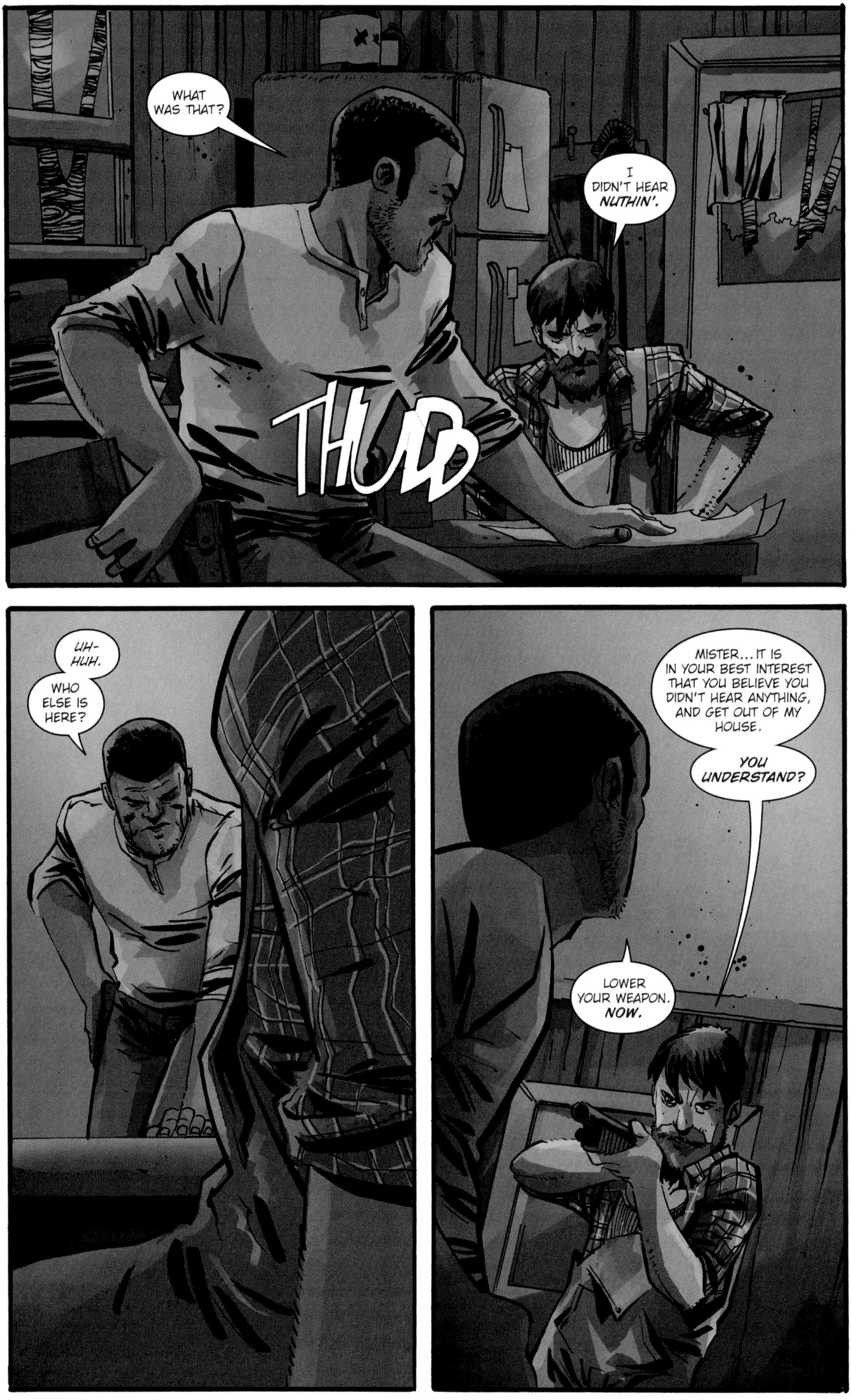
WHAT WAS THAT?
I DIDN'T HEAR NUTHIN'.
THUDD
UH-HUH.
WHO ELSE IS HERE?
MISTER... IT IS IN YOUR BEST INTEREST THAT YOU BELIEVE YOU DIDN'T HEAR ANYTHING, AND GET OUT OF MY HOUSE.
YOU UNDERSTAND?
LOWER YOUR WEAPON. NOW.

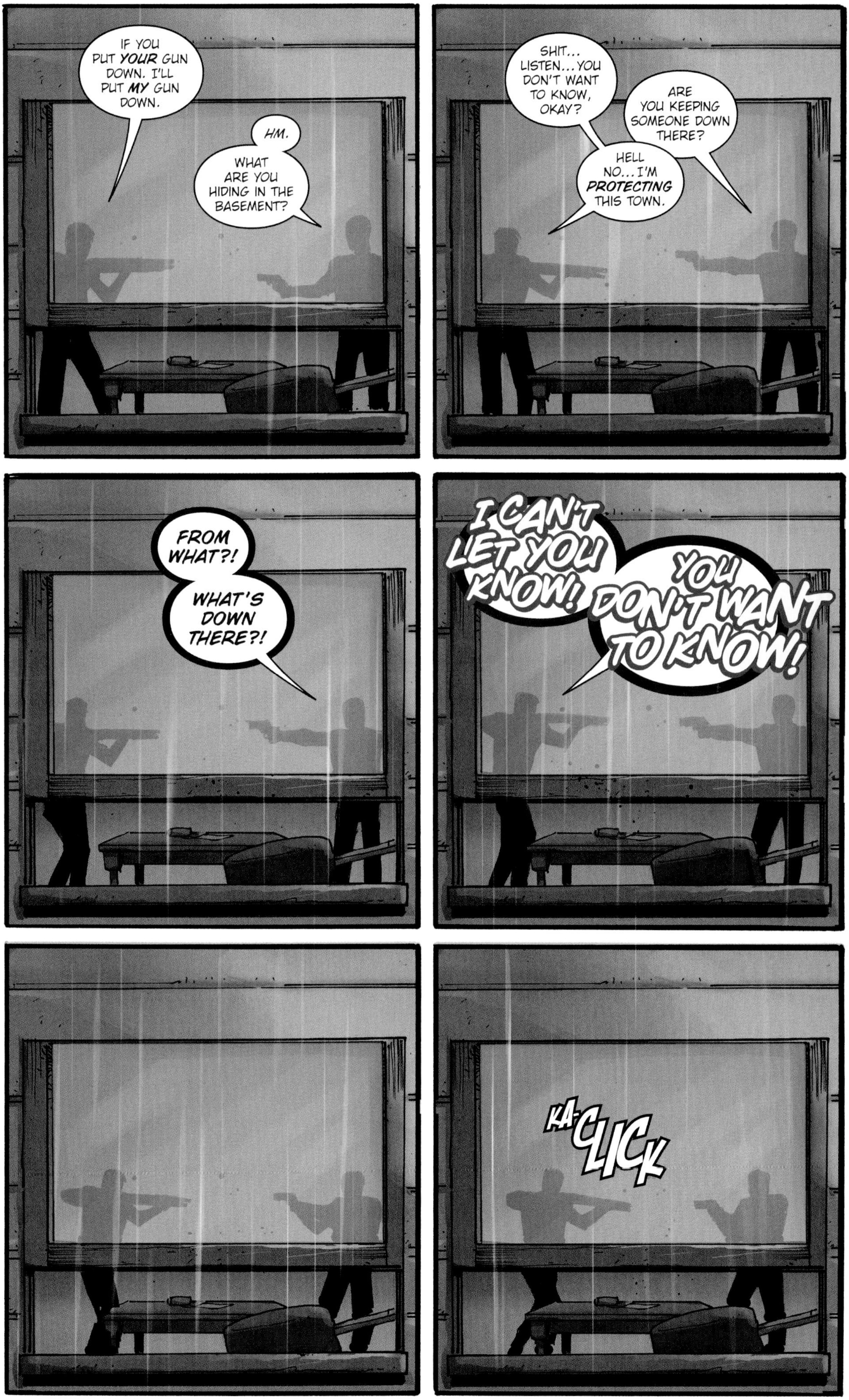
IF YOU PUT YOUR GUN DOWN. I'LL PUT MY GUN DOWN.
HM.
WHAT ARE YOU HIDING IN THE BASEMENT?
SHIT... LISTEN... YOU DON'T WANT TO KNOW, OKAY?
ARE YOU KEEPING SOMEONE DOWN THERE?
HELL NO... I'M PROTECTING THIS TOWN.
FROM WHAT?!
WHAT'S DOWN THERE?!
I CAN'T LET YOU KNOW!
YOU DON'T WANT TO KNOW!
KA-CLICK

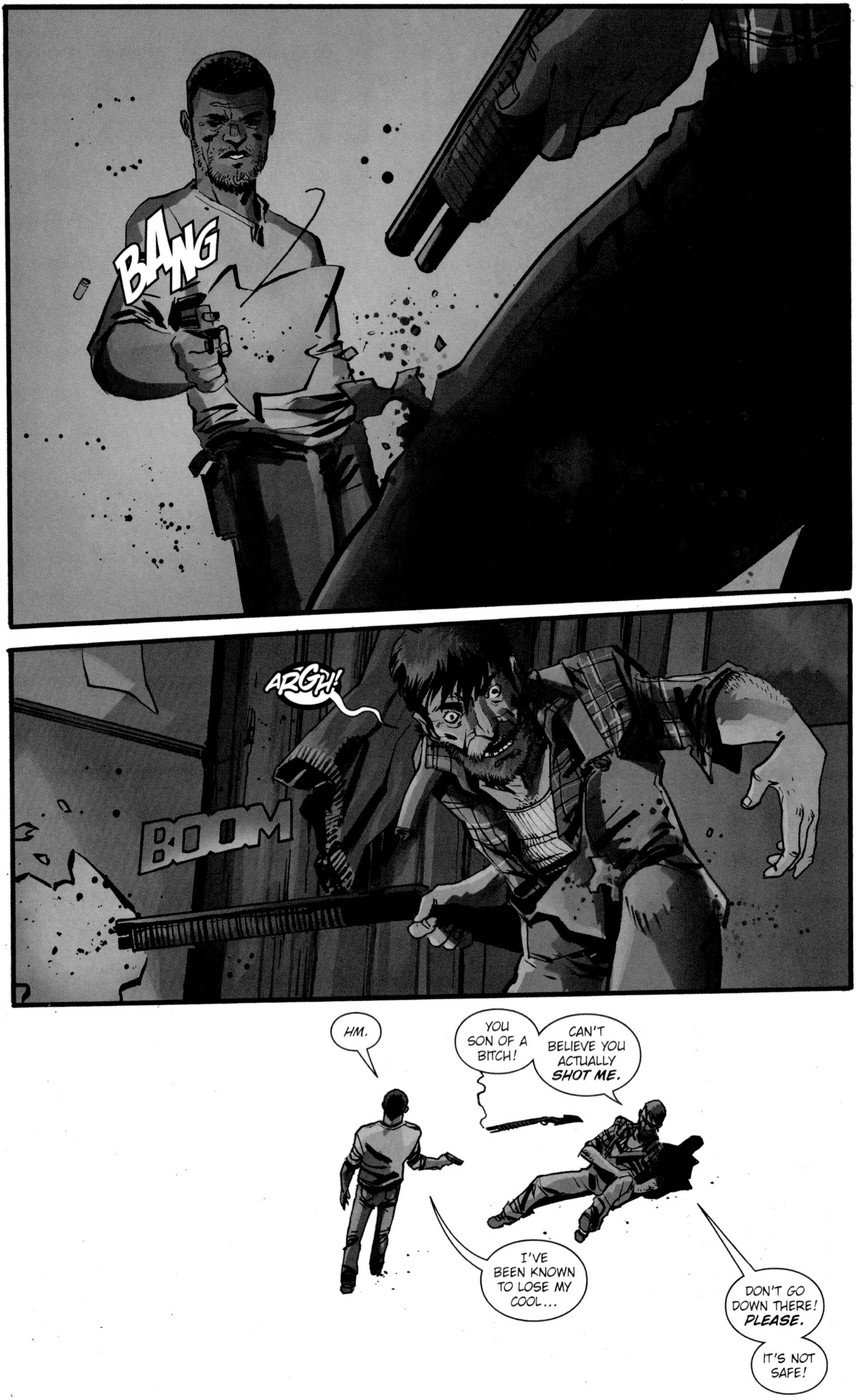
BANG
ARGH!
BOOM
HM.
YOU SON OF A BITCH!
CAN'T BELIEVE YOU ACTUALLY SHOT ME.
I'VE BEEN KNOWN TO LOSE MY COOL...
DON'T GO DOWN THERE! PLEASE.
IT'S NOT SAFE!

DON'T GO DOWN THERE!
BBBZZZZ
BZZ
SHIT...
I'M BRINGING HOME MY BABY BUMBLE BEE...
WON'T MY MOMMY BE SO PROUD OF ME...
I'M BRINGING HOME MY BABY BUMBLE BEE...

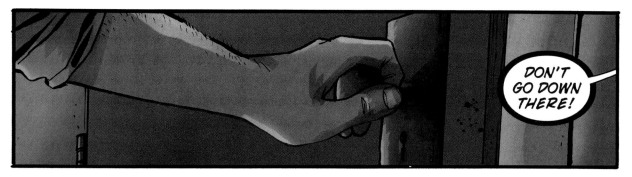

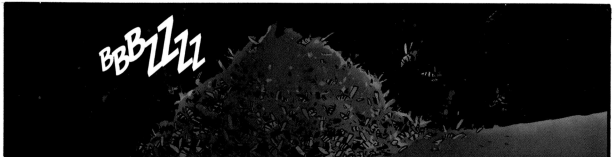

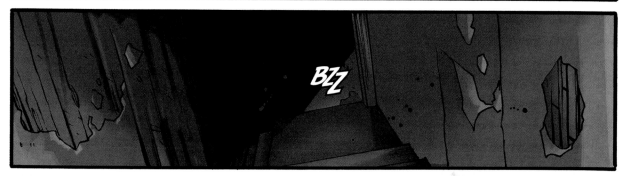

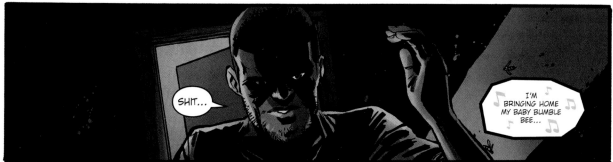

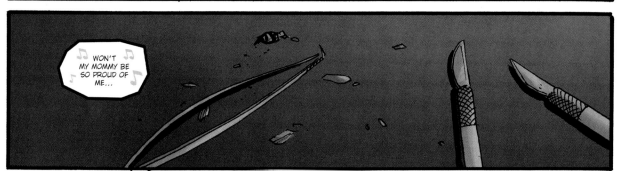

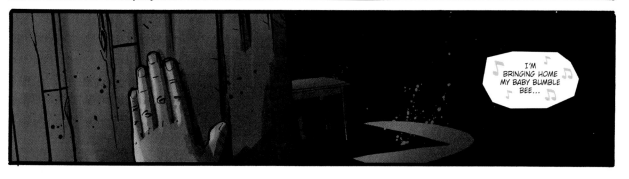

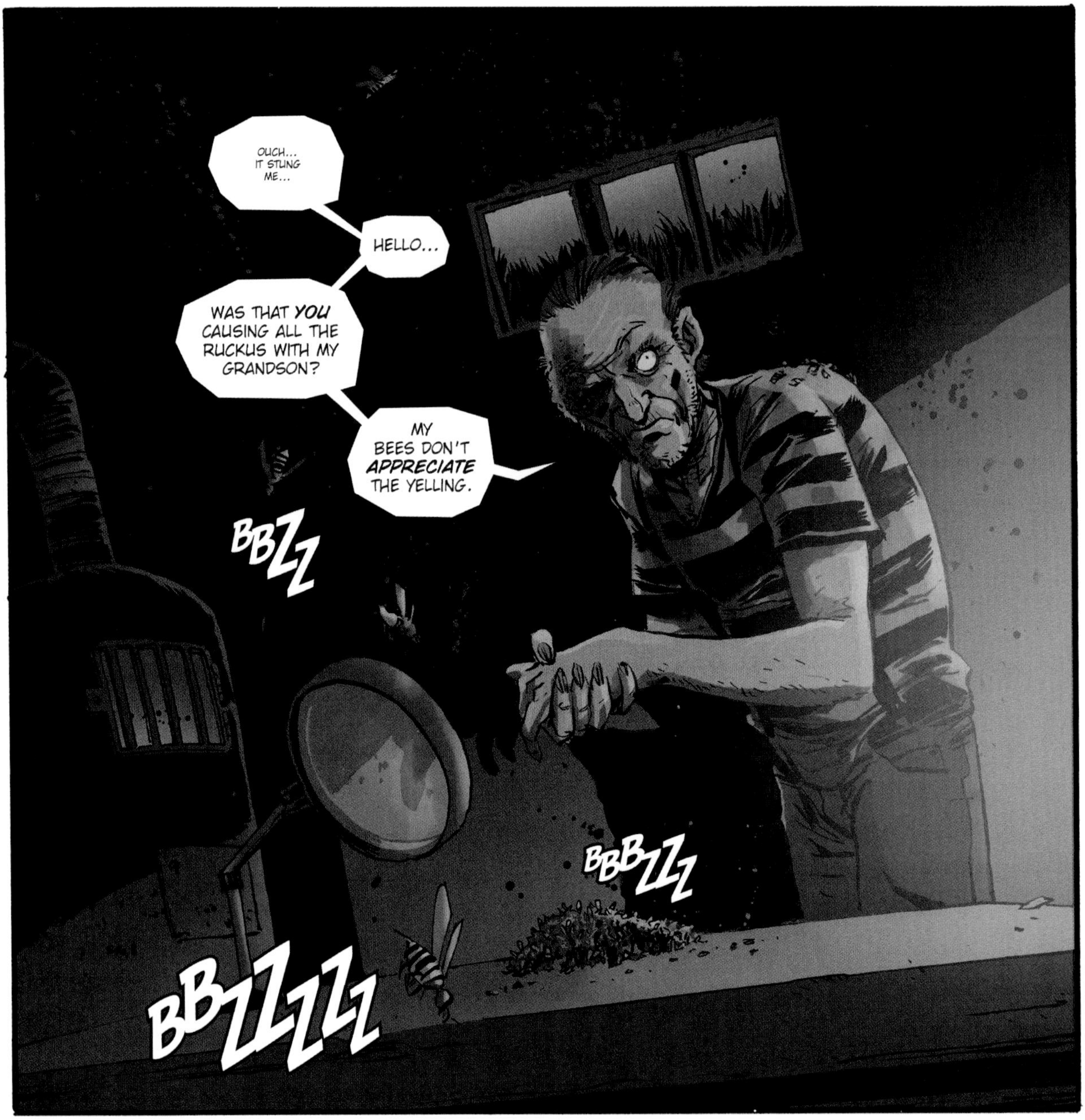
OUCH... IT STUNG ME...
HELLO...
WAS THAT *YOU* CAUSING ALL THE RUCKUS WITH MY GRANDSON?
MY BEES DON'T *APPRECIATE* THE YELLING.
BBZZ
BBBZZZ
BBZZZZZ

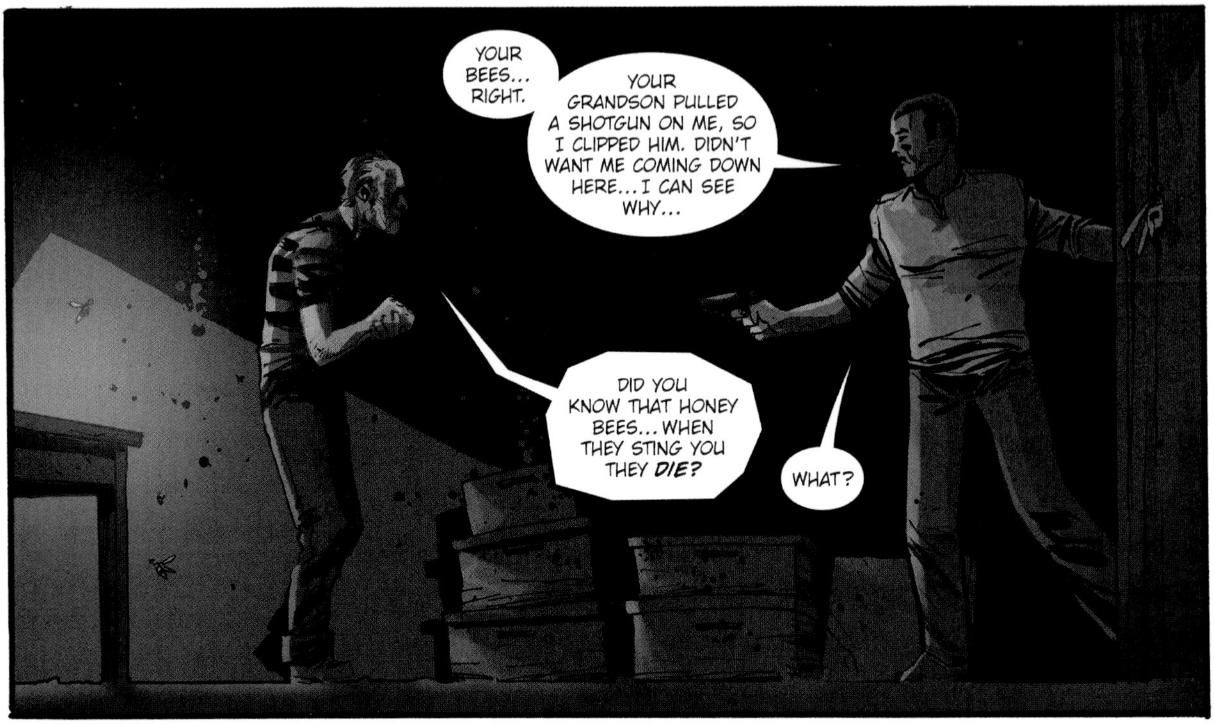
YOUR BEES... RIGHT.
YOUR GRANDSON PULLED A SHOTGUN ON ME, SO I CLIPPED HIM. DIDN'T WANT ME COMING DOWN HERE... I CAN SEE WHY...
DID YOU KNOW THAT HONEY BEES... WHEN THEY STING YOU THEY *DIE?*
WHAT?

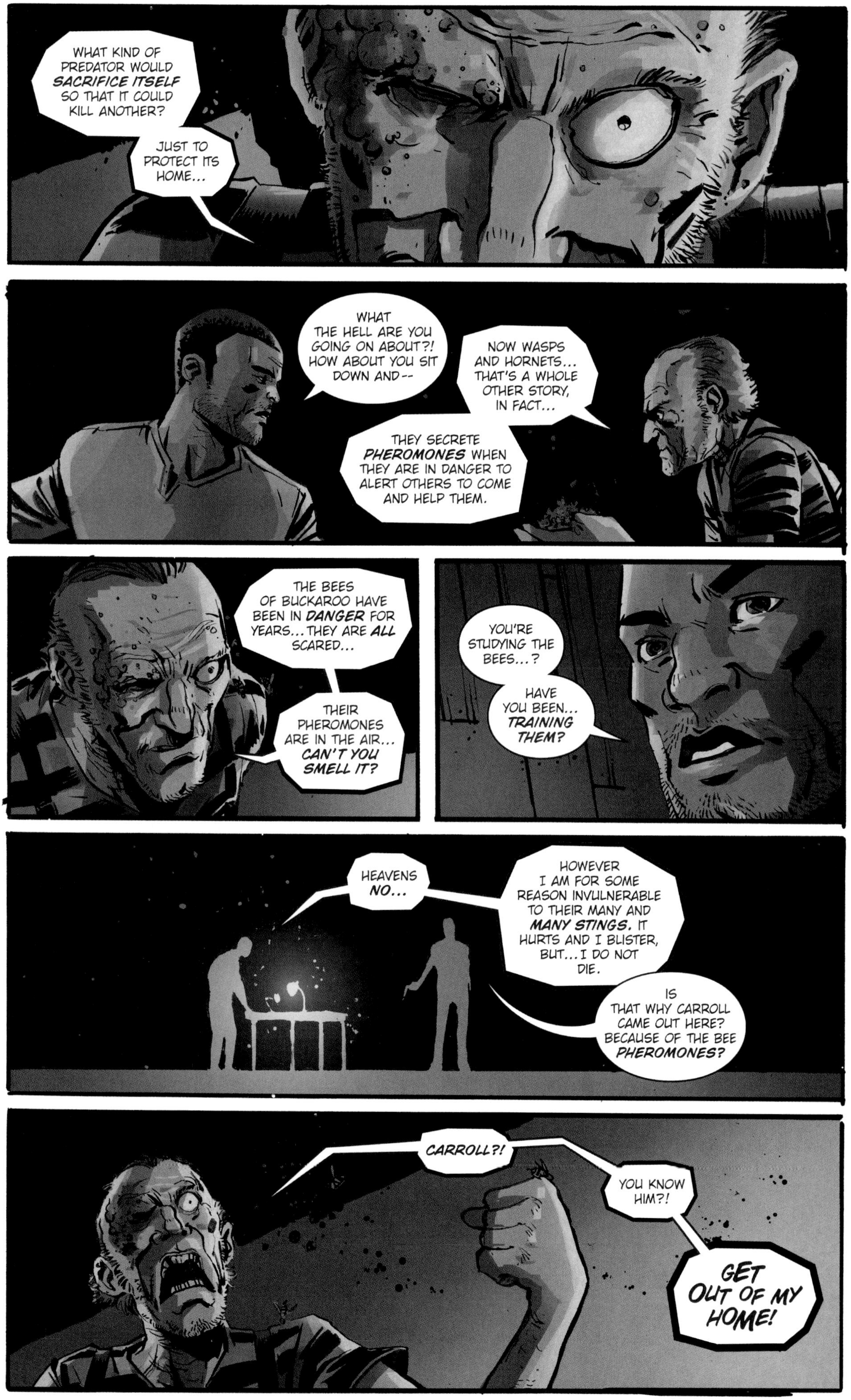
WHAT KIND OF PREDATOR WOULD SACRIFICE ITSELF SO THAT IT COULD KILL ANOTHER?
JUST TO PROTECT ITS HOME...
WHAT THE HELL ARE YOU GOING ON ABOUT?! HOW ABOUT YOU SIT DOWN AND--
NOW WASPS AND HORNETS... THAT'S A WHOLE OTHER STORY, IN FACT...
THEY SECRETE PHEROMONES WHEN THEY ARE IN DANGER TO ALERT OTHERS TO COME AND HELP THEM.
THE BEES OF BUCKAROO HAVE BEEN IN DANGER FOR YEARS...THEY ARE ALL SCARED...
THEIR PHEROMONES ARE IN THE AIR... CAN'T YOU SMELL IT?
YOU'RE STUDYING THE BEES...?
HAVE YOU BEEN... TRAINING THEM?
HEAVENS NO...
HOWEVER I AM FOR SOME REASON INVULNERABLE TO THEIR MANY AND MANY STINGS. IT HURTS AND I BLISTER, BUT...I DO NOT DIE.
IS THAT WHY CARROLL CAME OUT HERE? BECAUSE OF THE BEE PHEROMONES?
CARROLL?!
YOU KNOW HIM?!
GET OUT OF MY HOME!

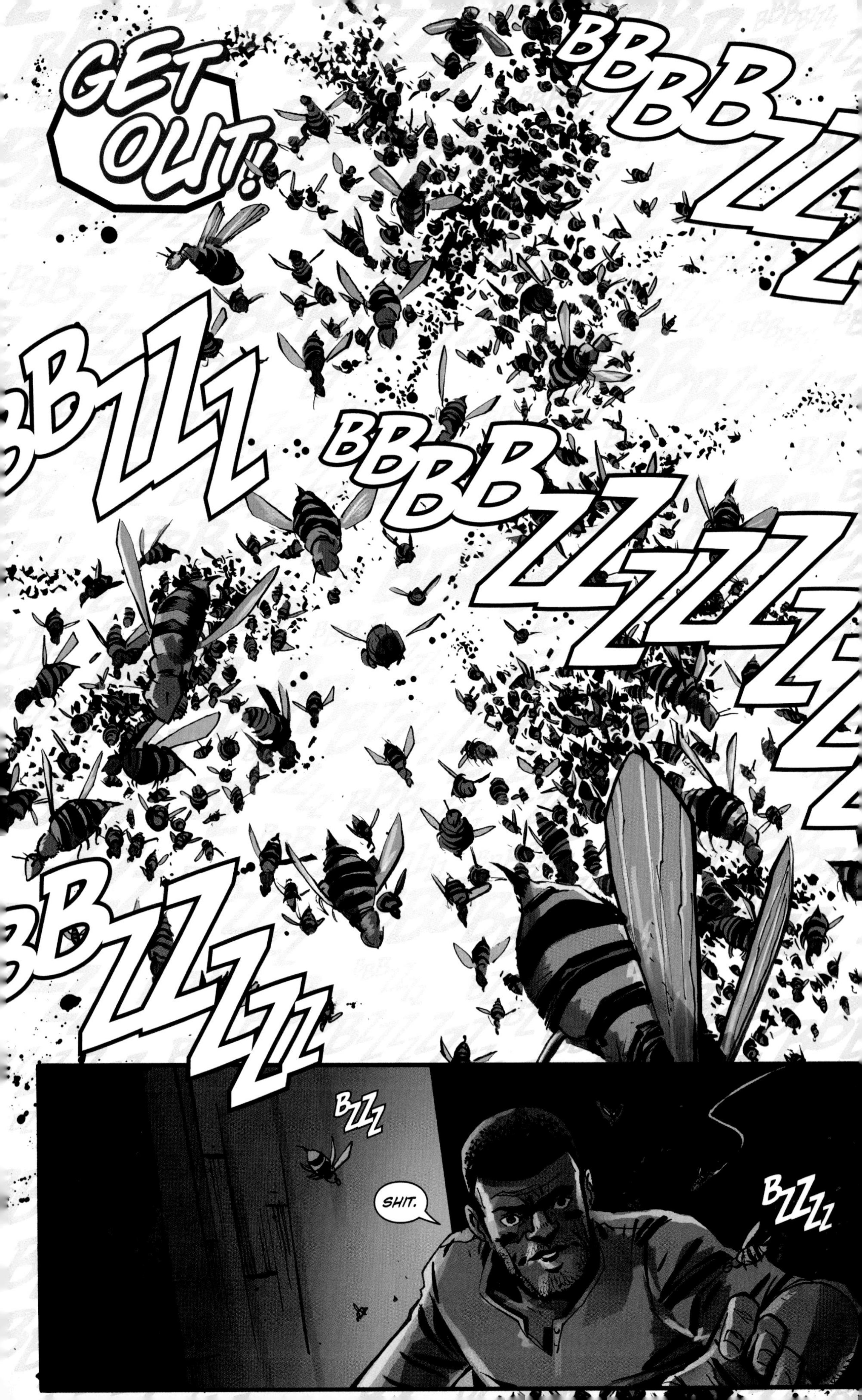
GET OUT!
BBBBBZZZ
BZZZ
BBBBZZZZZZZZ
BZZZZ
BZZZ
SHIT.
BZZZZ

NINE

"This is the only way."

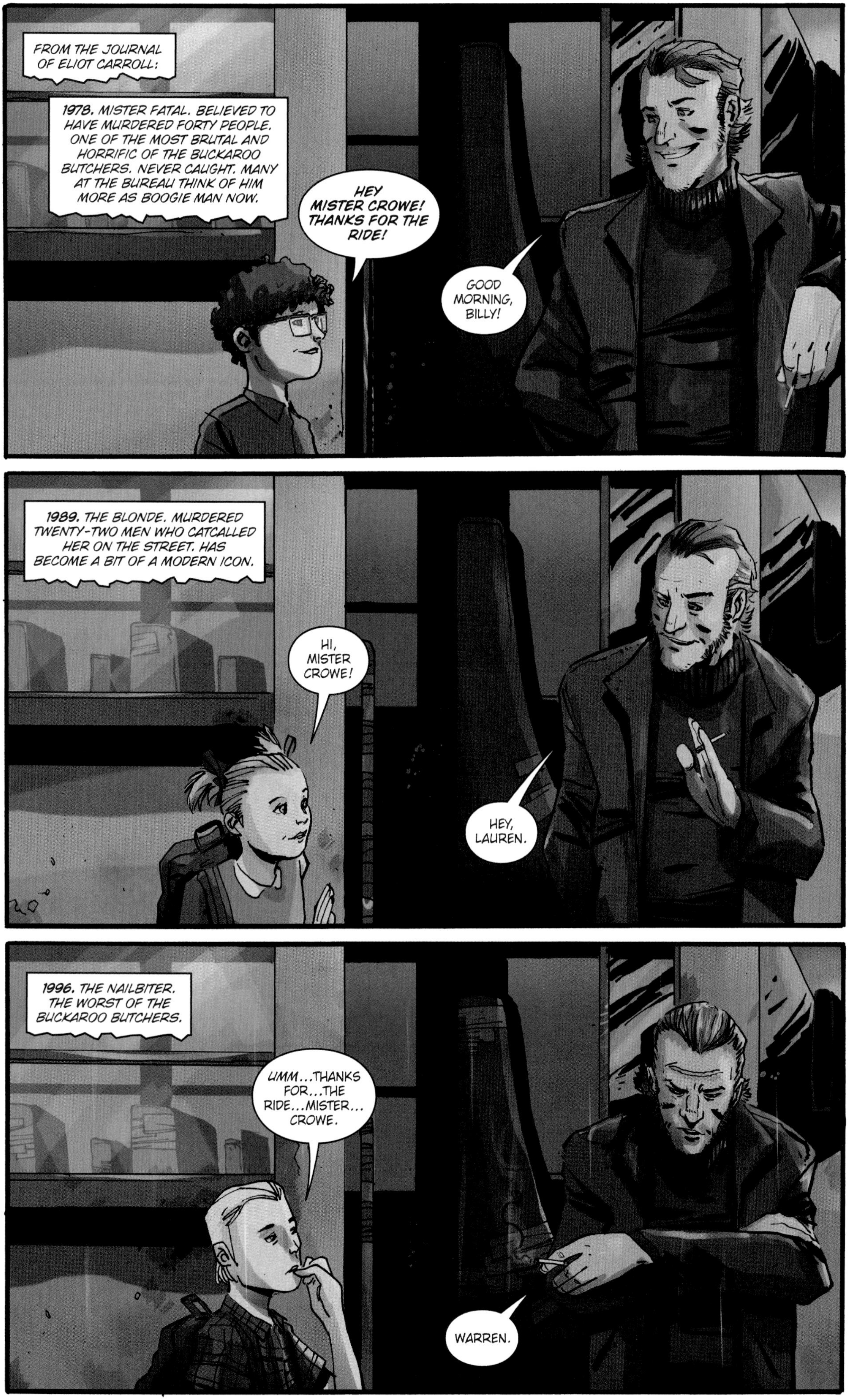
FROM THE JOURNAL OF ELIOT CARROLL:
1978. MISTER FATAL. BELIEVED TO HAVE MURDERED FORTY PEOPLE. ONE OF THE MOST BRUTAL AND HORRIFIC OF THE BUCKAROO BUTCHERS. NEVER CAUGHT. MANY AT THE BUREAU THINK OF HIM MORE AS BOOGIE MAN NOW.
HEY MISTER CROWE! THANKS FOR THE RIDE!
GOOD MORNING, BILLY!
1989. THE BLONDE. MURDERED TWENTY-TWO MEN WHO CATCALLED HER ON THE STREET. HAS BECOME A BIT OF A MODERN ICON.
HI, MISTER CROWE!
HEY, LAUREN.
1996. THE NAILBITER. THE WORST OF THE BUCKAROO BUTCHERS.
UMM...THANKS FOR...THE RIDE...MISTER... CROWE.
WARREN.

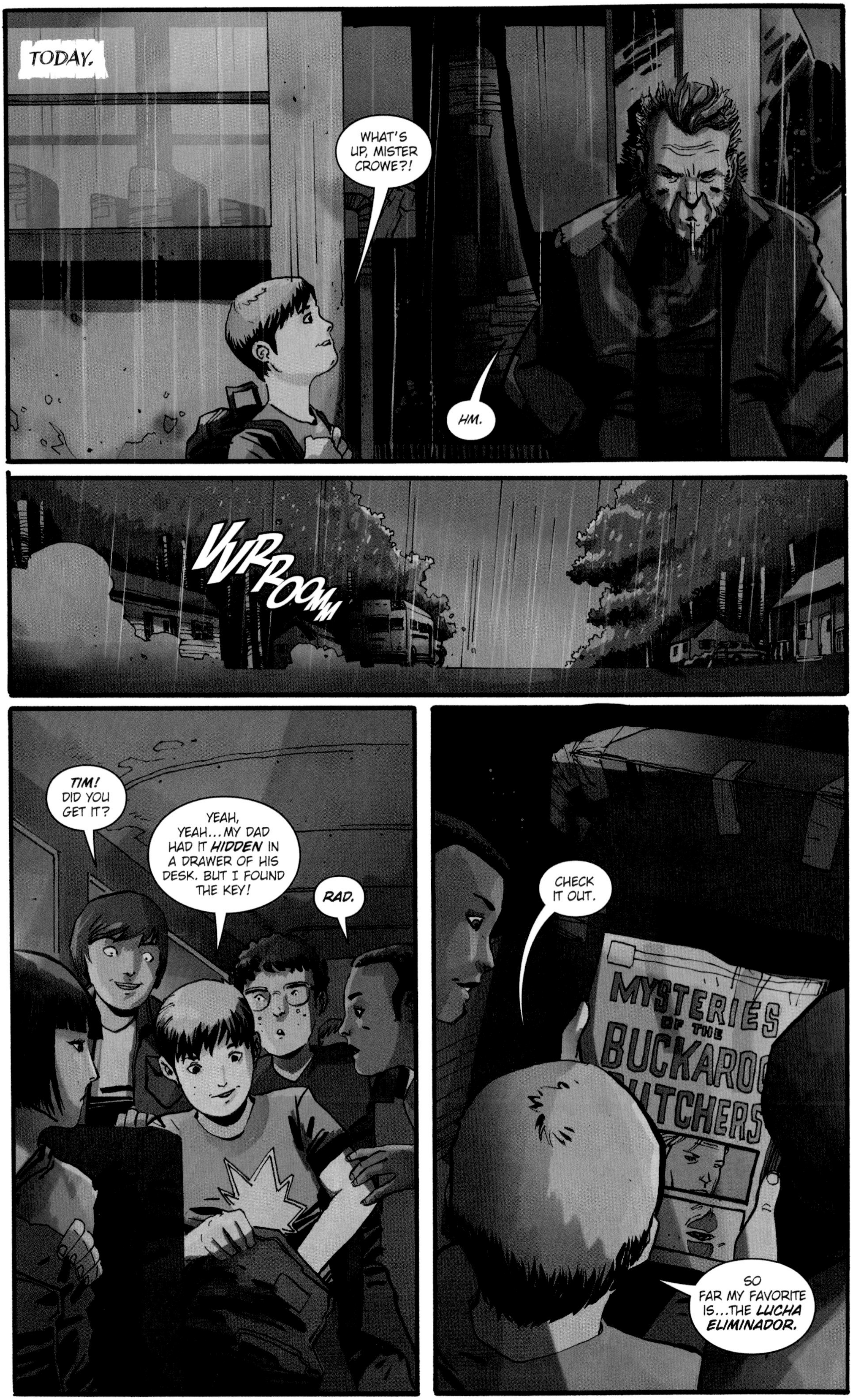
TODAY.
WHAT'S UP, MISTER CROWE?!
HM.
VVRROOMM
TIM! DID YOU GET IT?
YEAH, YEAH... MY DAD HAD IT HIDDEN IN A DRAWER OF HIS DESK. BUT I FOUND THE KEY!
RAD.
CHECK IT OUT.
MYSTERIES OF THE BUCKAROO BUTCHERS
SO FAR MY FAVORITE IS... THE LUCHA ELIMINADOR.

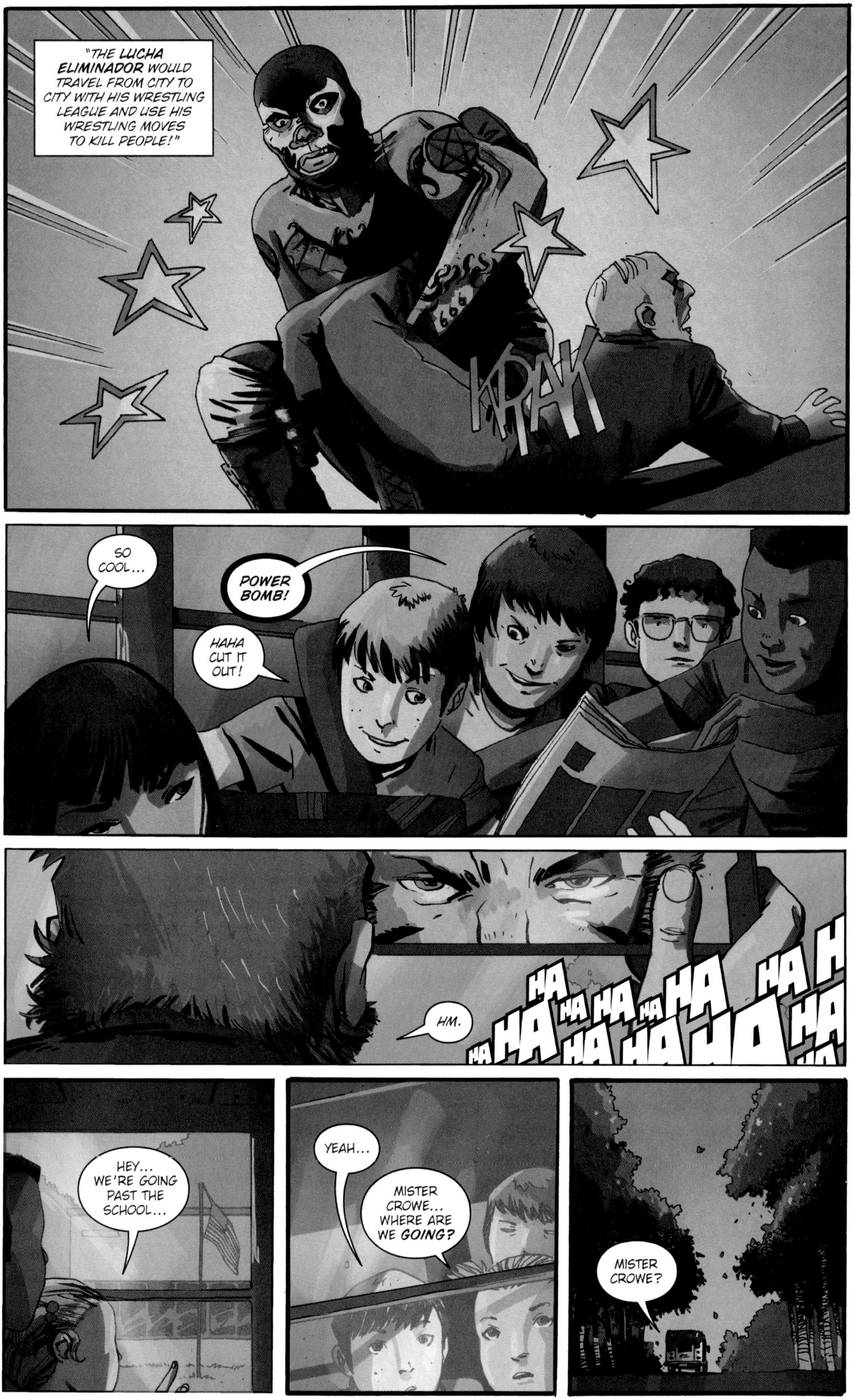
"THE LUCHA ELIMINADOR WOULD TRAVEL FROM CITY TO CITY WITH HIS WRESTLING LEAGUE AND USE HIS WRESTLING MOVES TO KILL PEOPLE!"
KRAK
SO COOL...
POWER BOMB!
HAHA CUT IT OUT!
HM.
HA HA HA HA HA HA HA HA HA HA HA HA HA HA
HEY... WE'RE GOING PAST THE SCHOOL...
YEAH...
MISTER CROWE... WHERE ARE WE GOING?
MISTER CROWE?

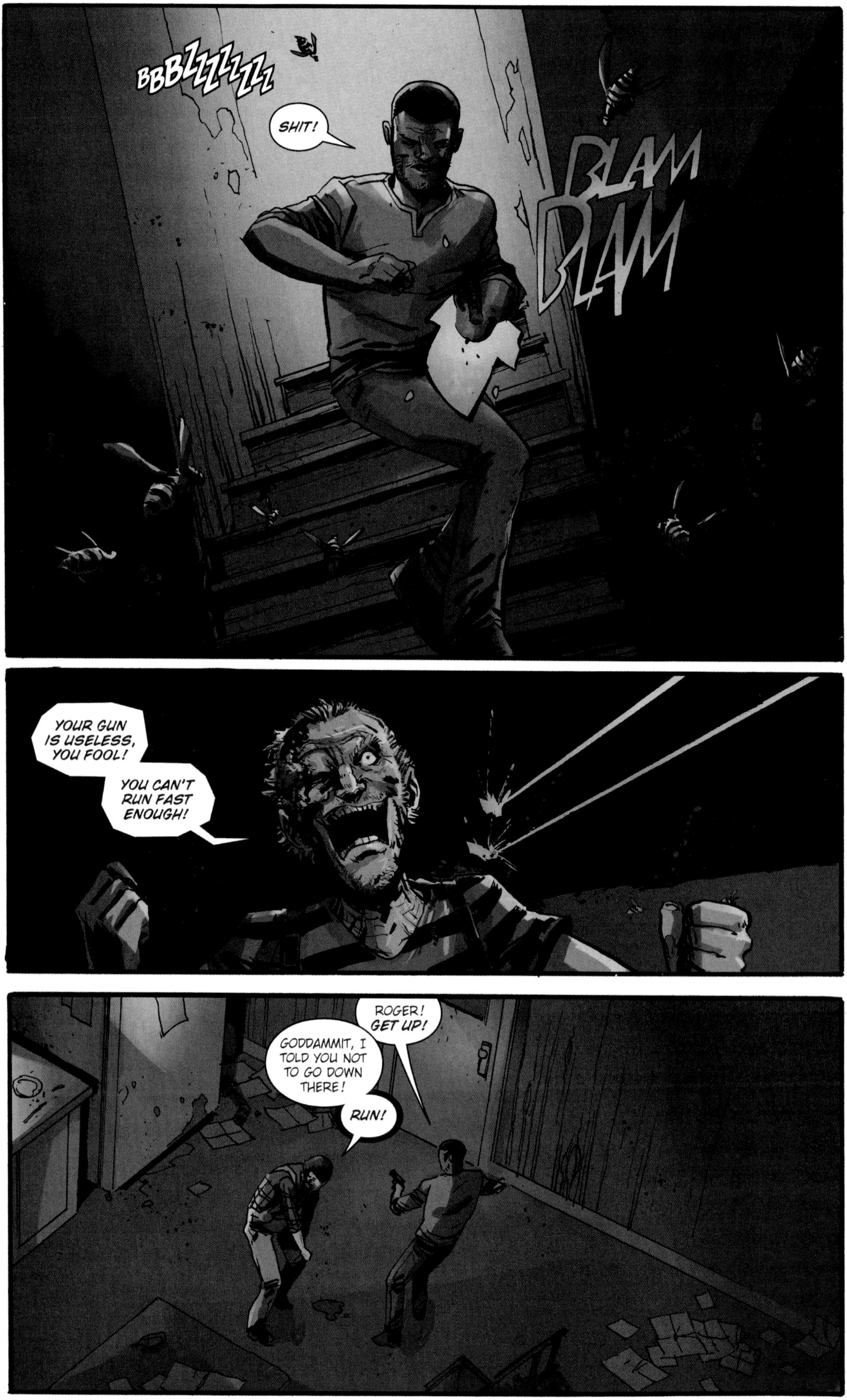
BBBZZZZZZZZ
SHIT!
BLAM BLAM
YOUR GUN IS USELESS, YOU FOOL!
YOU CAN'T RUN FAST ENOUGH!
ROGER! GET UP!
GODDAMMIT, I TOLD YOU NOT TO GO DOWN THERE!
RUN!

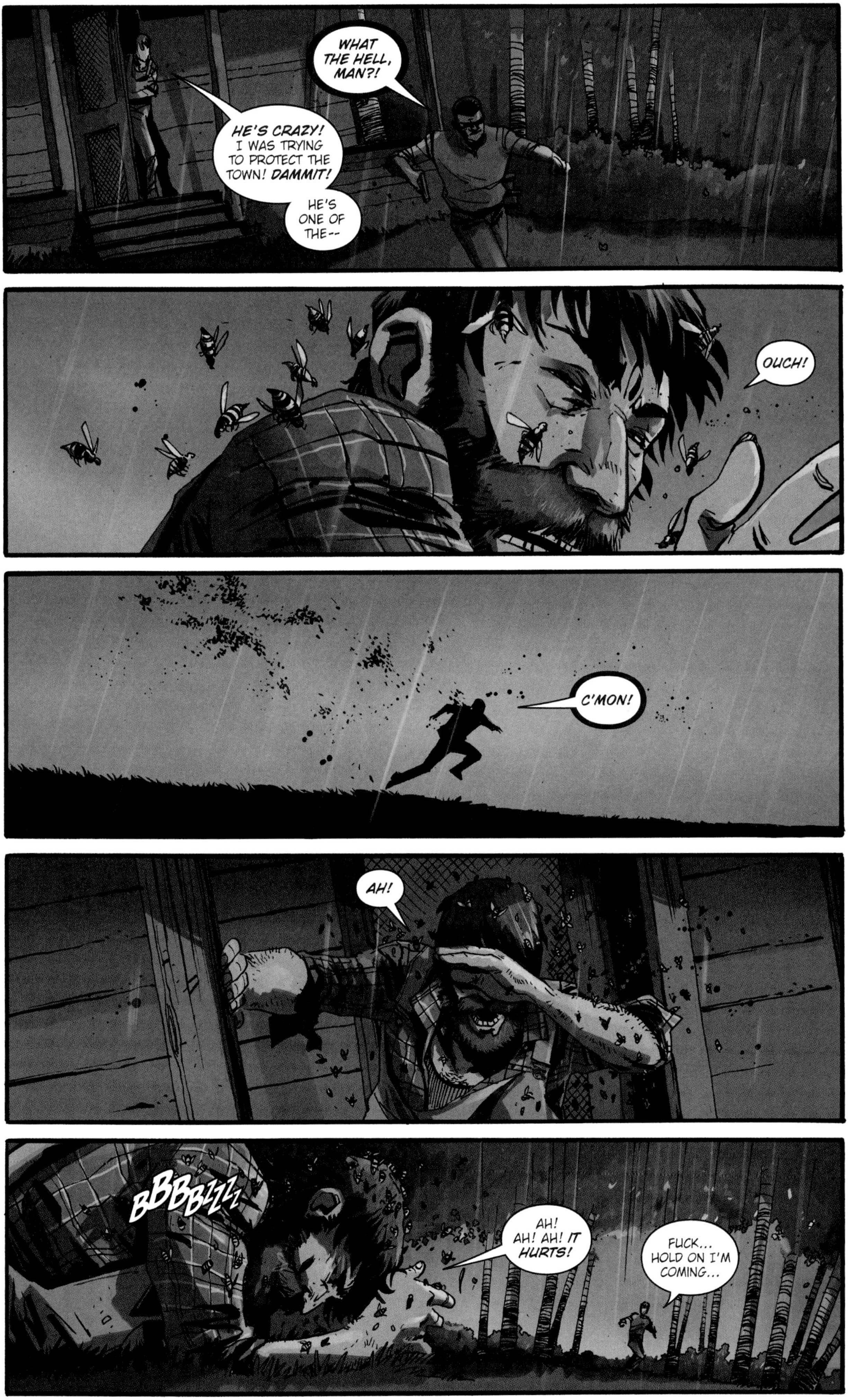
WHAT THE HELL, MAN?!
HE'S CRAZY! I WAS TRYING TO PROTECT THE TOWN! DAMMIT!
HE'S ONE OF THE--
OUCH!
C'MON!
AH!
BBBBZZZZ
AH! AH! AH! IT HURTS!
FUCK... HOLD ON I'M COMING...

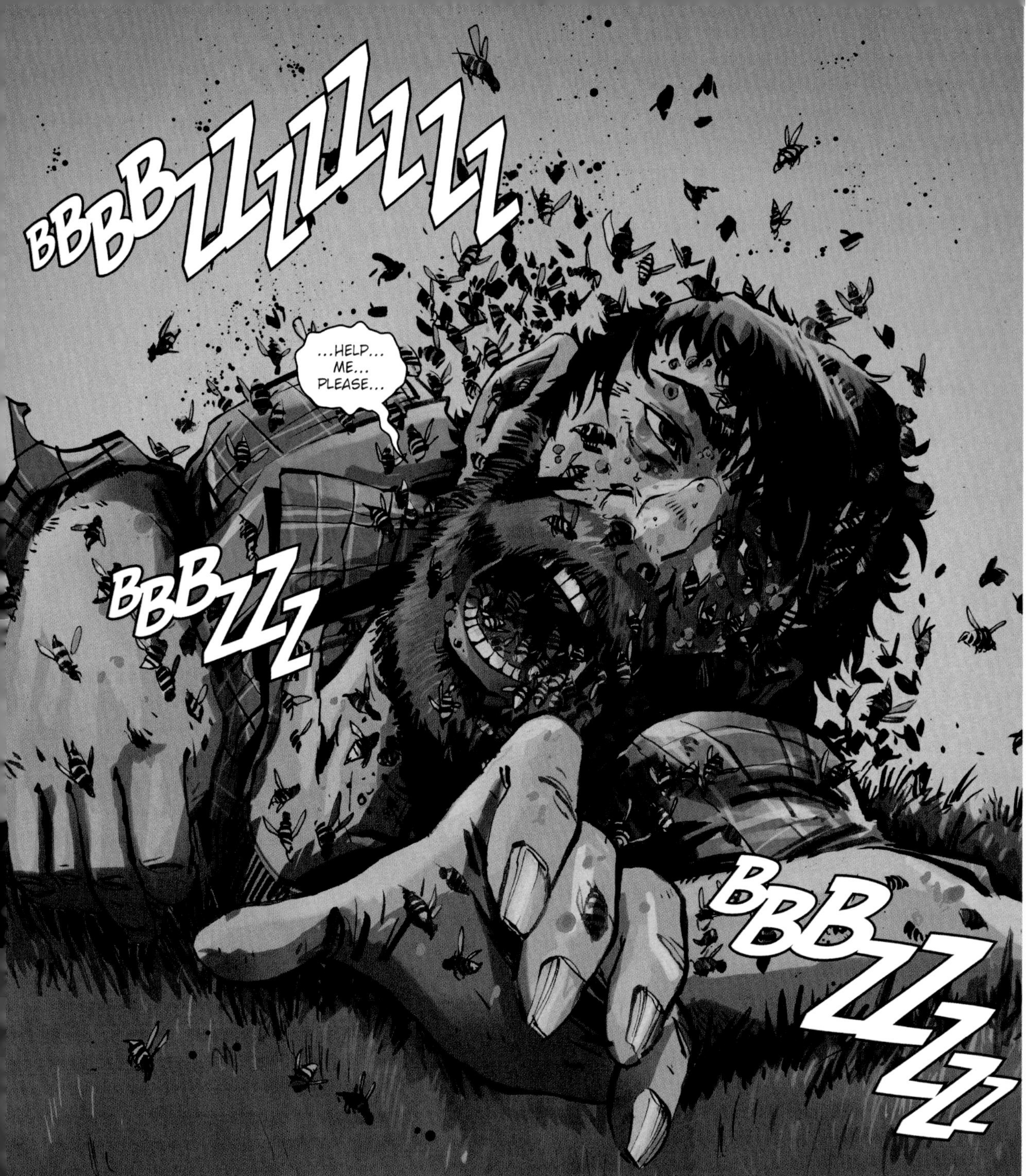
BBBBZZZZZZZZZ
...HELP... ME... PLEASE...
BBBZZZ
BBBZZZZ

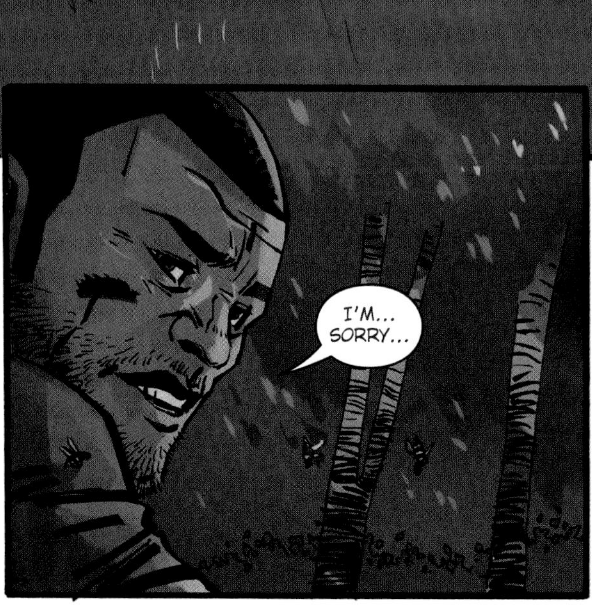
I'M... SORRY...

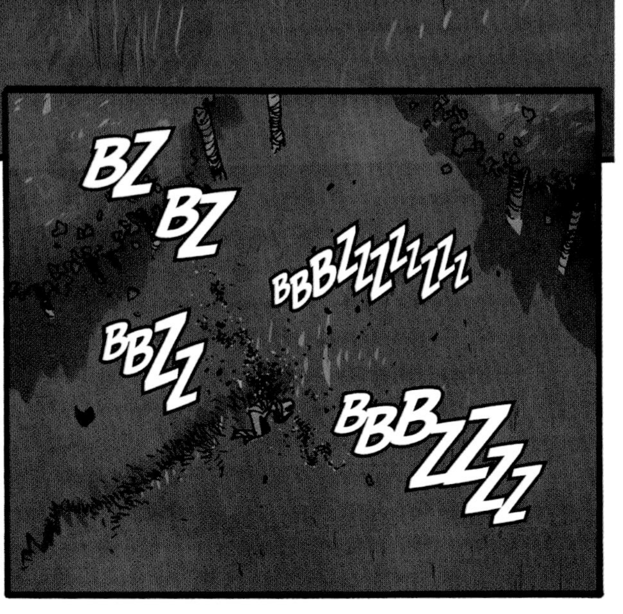
BZ
BZ
BBBZZZZZZZZ
BBZZ
BBBZZZZ

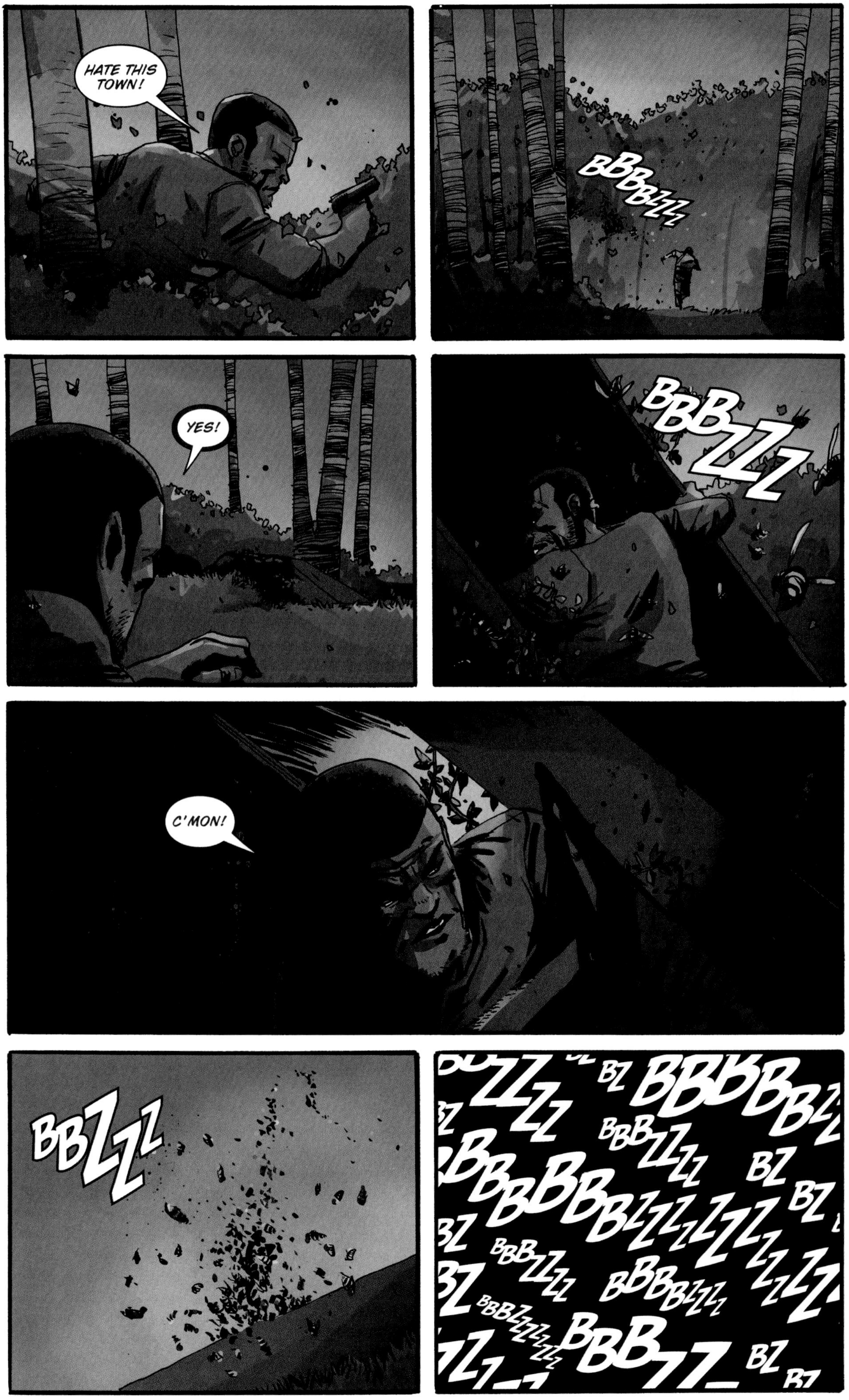
HATE THIS TOWN!
BBBBZZZZ
YES!
BBBZZZ
C'MON!
BBZZZ
BBBBBBZZ
BZ
BBBZZZZ
BBBBBBZZZZZZZ
BBBZZZZ
BBBBZZZZ
BBBZZZZZZZ
BBBZZ
BZ

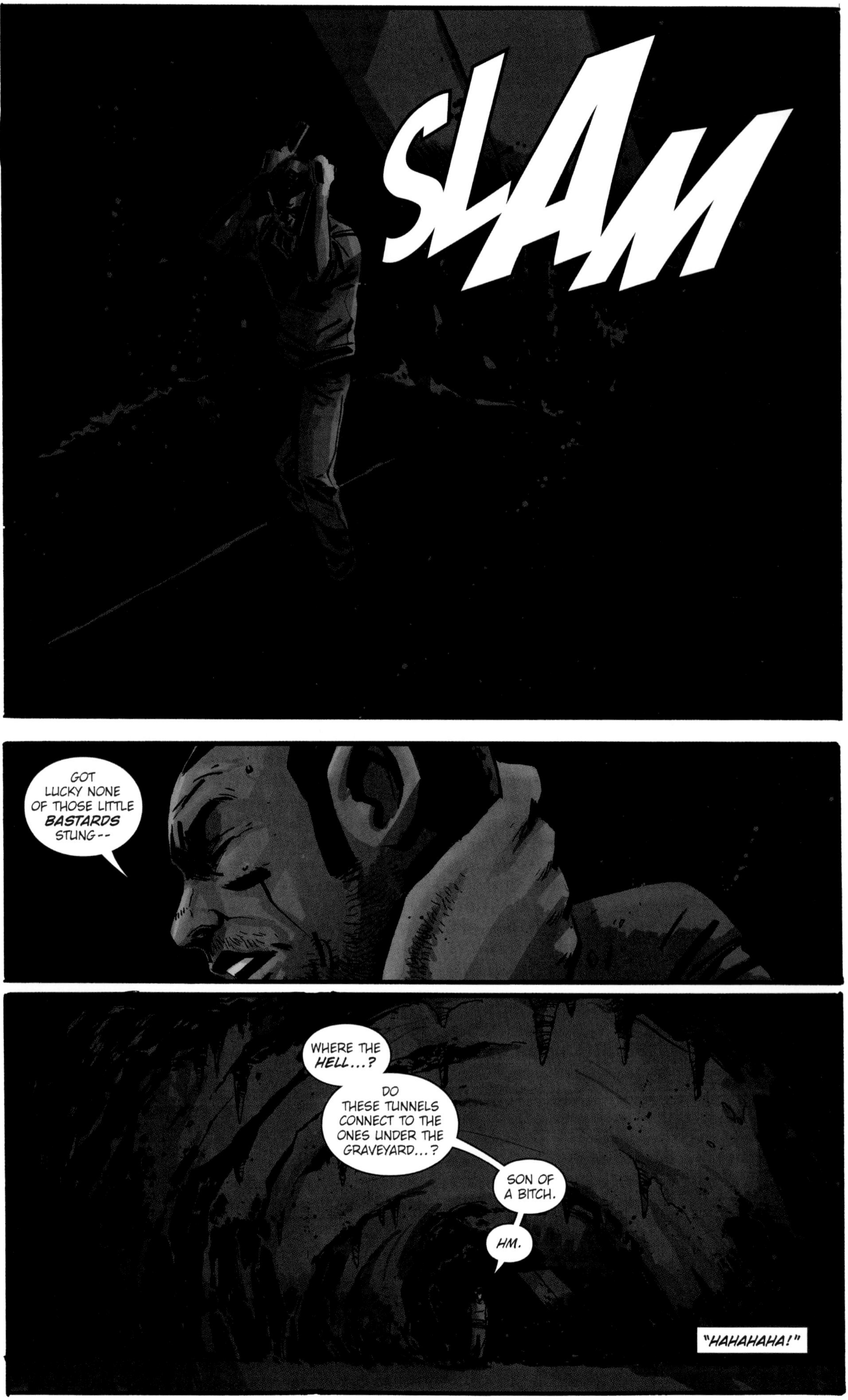
SLAM
GOT LUCKY NONE OF THOSE LITTLE **BASTARDS** STUNG--
WHERE THE **HELL...?**
DO THESE TUNNELS CONNECT TO THE ONES UNDER THE GRAVEYARD...?
SON OF A BITCH.
HM.
"HAHAHAHA!"

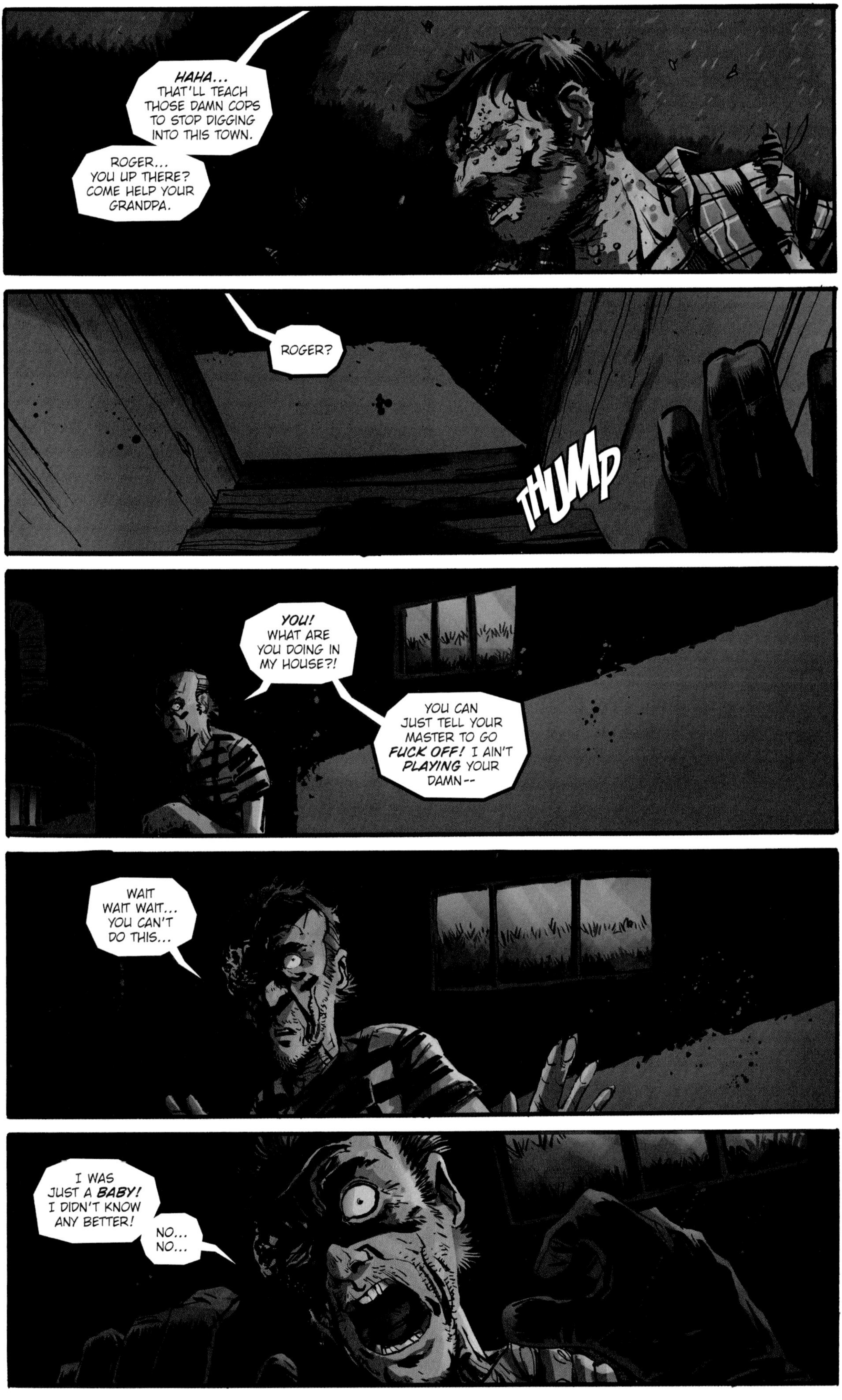
HAHA... THAT'LL TEACH THOSE DAMN COPS TO STOP DIGGING INTO THIS TOWN.
ROGER... YOU UP THERE? COME HELP YOUR GRANDPA.
ROGER?
THUMP
YOU! WHAT ARE YOU DOING IN MY HOUSE?!
YOU CAN JUST TELL YOUR MASTER TO GO FUCK OFF! I AIN'T PLAYING YOUR DAMN--
WAIT WAIT WAIT... YOU CAN'T DO THIS...
I WAS JUST A BABY! I DIDN'T KNOW ANY BETTER!
NO... NO...

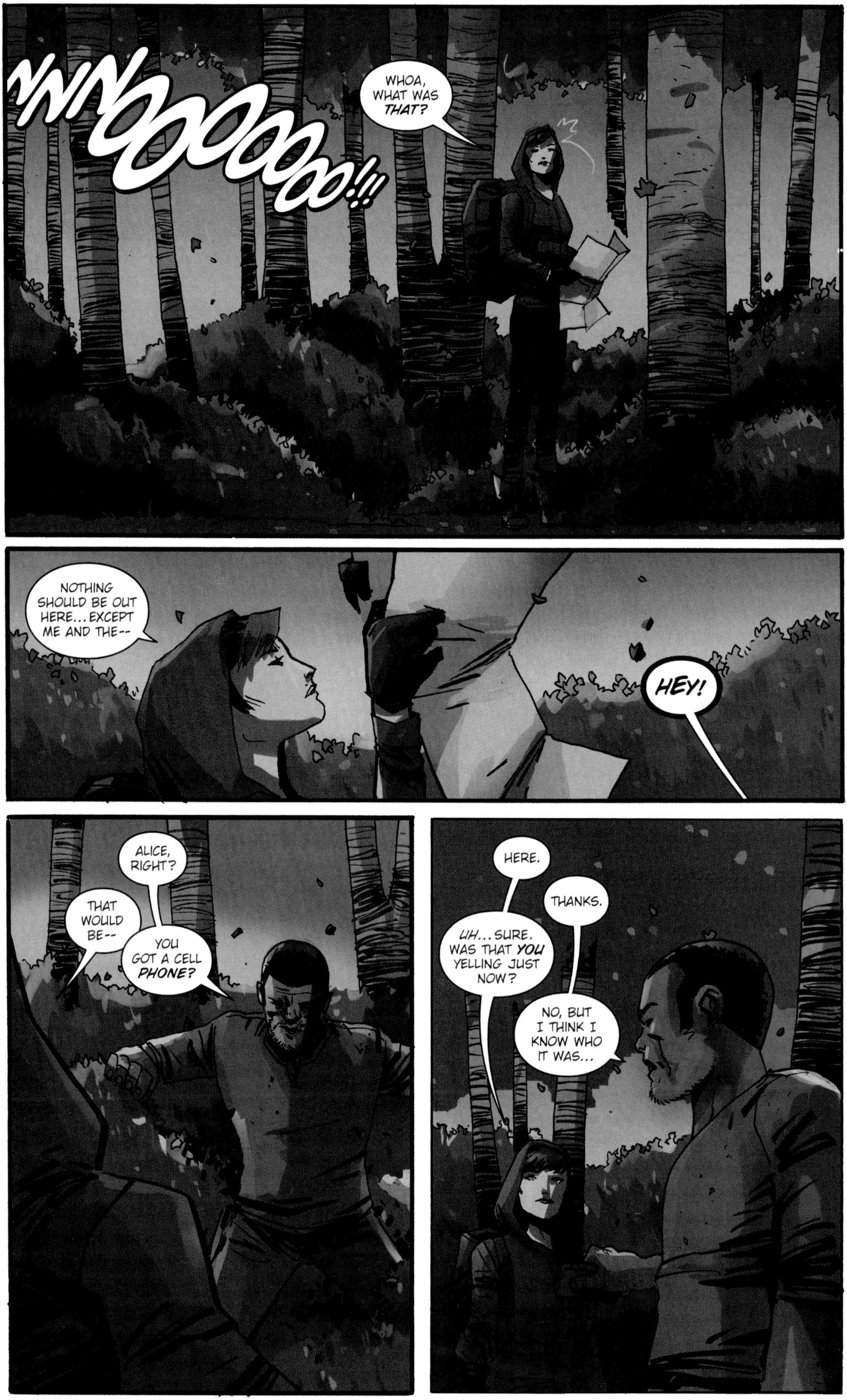
NNOOOOOOOO!!!
WHOA, WHAT WAS *THAT?*
NOTHING SHOULD BE OUT HERE... EXCEPT ME AND THE--
HEY!
ALICE, RIGHT?
THAT WOULD BE--
YOU GOT A CELL ***PHONE?***
HERE.
THANKS.
UH... SURE. WAS THAT ***YOU*** YELLING JUST NOW?
NO, BUT I THINK I KNOW WHO IT WAS...

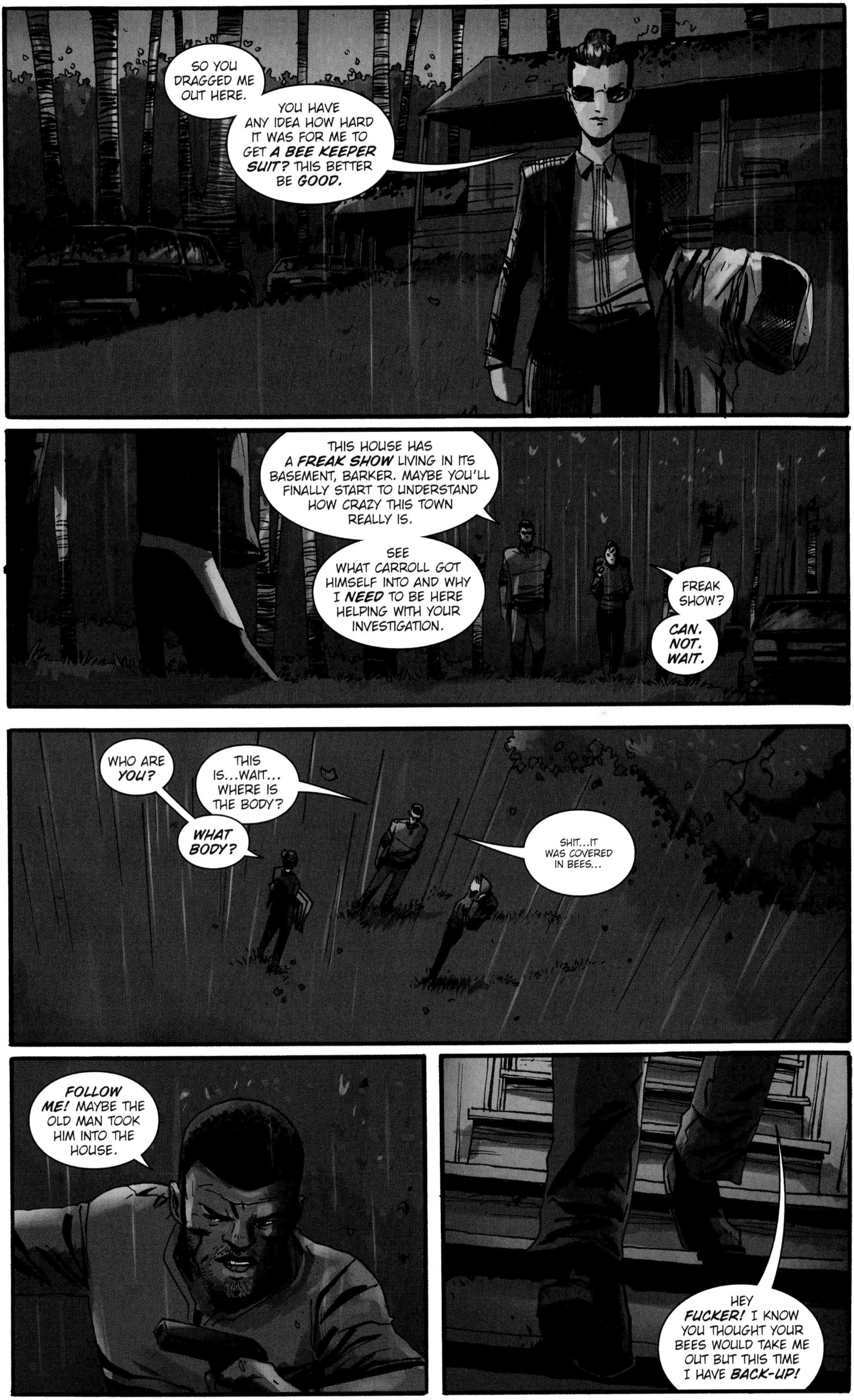
SO YOU DRAGGED ME OUT HERE.
YOU HAVE ANY IDEA HOW HARD IT WAS FOR ME TO GET **A BEE KEEPER SUIT?** THIS BETTER BE **GOOD.**
THIS HOUSE HAS A **FREAK SHOW** LIVING IN ITS BASEMENT, BARKER. MAYBE YOU'LL FINALLY START TO UNDERSTAND HOW CRAZY THIS TOWN REALLY IS.
SEE WHAT CARROLL GOT HIMSELF INTO AND WHY I **NEED** TO BE HERE HELPING WITH YOUR INVESTIGATION.
FREAK SHOW?
CAN. NOT. WAIT.
WHO ARE **YOU?**
THIS IS...WAIT... WHERE IS THE BODY?
WHAT BODY?
SHIT...IT WAS COVERED IN BEES...
FOLLOW ME! MAYBE THE OLD MAN TOOK HIM INTO THE HOUSE.
HEY **FUCKER!** I KNOW YOU THOUGHT YOUR BEES WOULD TAKE ME OUT BUT THIS TIME I HAVE **BACK-UP!**

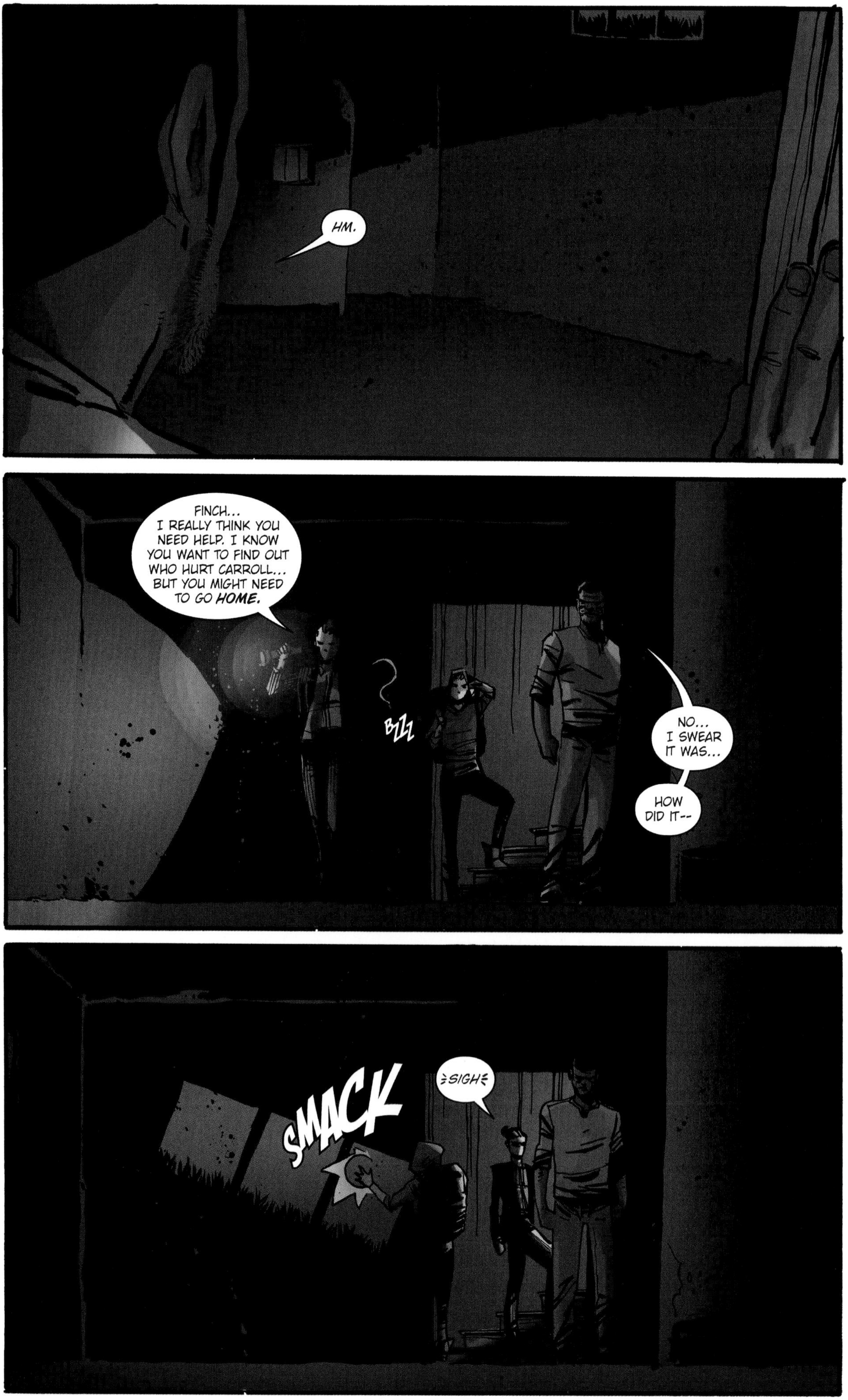
HM.
FINCH... I REALLY THINK YOU NEED HELP. I KNOW YOU WANT TO FIND OUT WHO HURT CARROLL... BUT YOU MIGHT NEED TO GO **HOME.**
BZZZ
NO... I SWEAR IT WAS...
HOW DID IT--
SMACK
SIGH

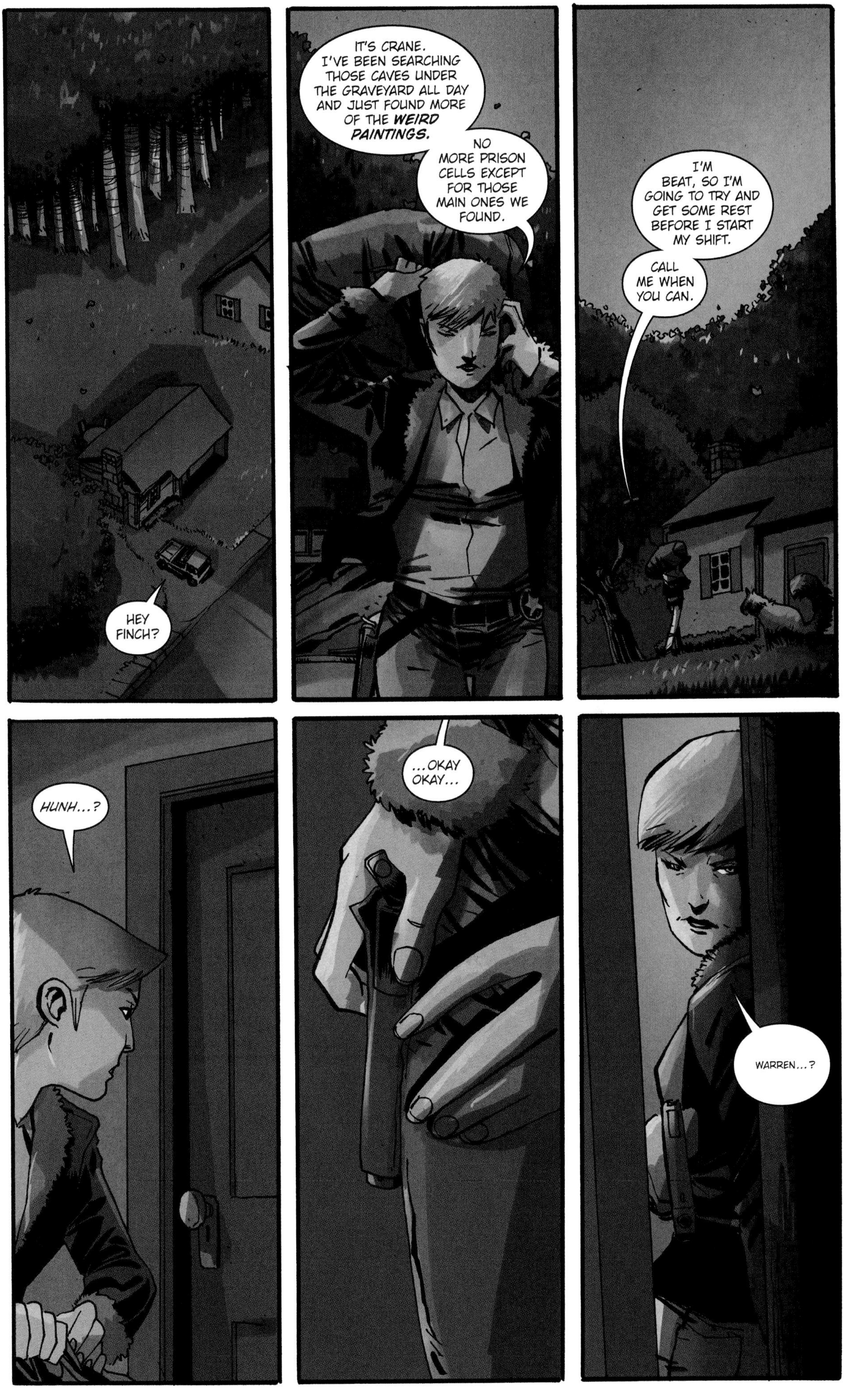
HEY FINCH?
IT'S CRANE. I'VE BEEN SEARCHING THOSE CAVES UNDER THE GRAVEYARD ALL DAY AND JUST FOUND MORE OF THE WEIRD PAINTINGS.
NO MORE PRISON CELLS EXCEPT FOR THOSE MAIN ONES WE FOUND.
I'M BEAT, SO I'M GOING TO TRY AND GET SOME REST BEFORE I START MY SHIFT.
CALL ME WHEN YOU CAN.
HUNH...?
...OKAY OKAY...
WARREN...?

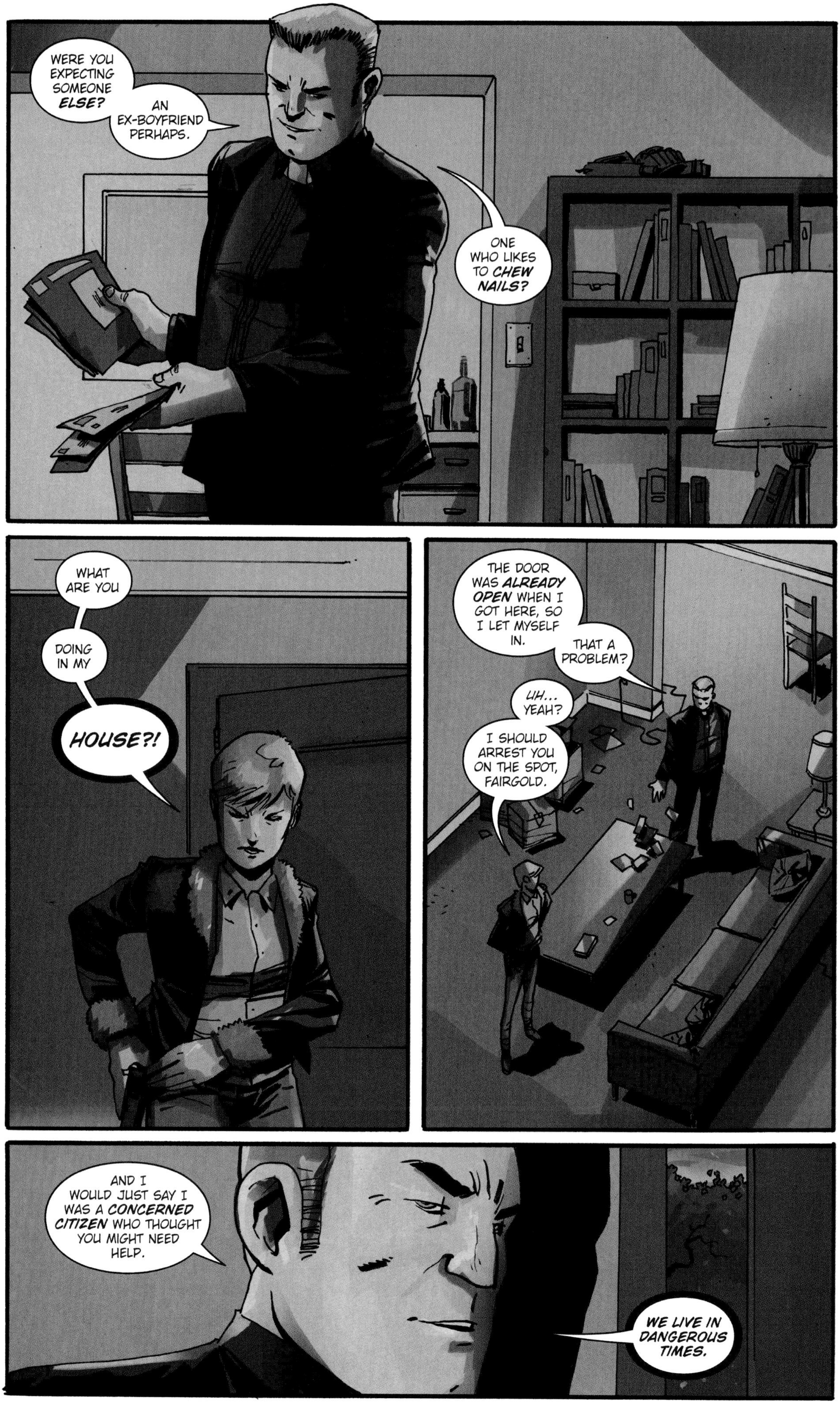
WERE YOU EXPECTING SOMEONE ELSE?
AN EX-BOYFRIEND PERHAPS.
ONE WHO LIKES TO CHEW NAILS?
WHAT ARE YOU
DOING IN MY
HOUSE?!
THE DOOR WAS ALREADY OPEN WHEN I GOT HERE, SO I LET MYSELF IN.
THAT A PROBLEM?
UH... YEAH?
I SHOULD ARREST YOU ON THE SPOT, FAIRGOLD.
AND I WOULD JUST SAY I WAS A CONCERNED CITIZEN WHO THOUGHT YOU MIGHT NEED HELP.
WE LIVE IN DANGEROUS TIMES.

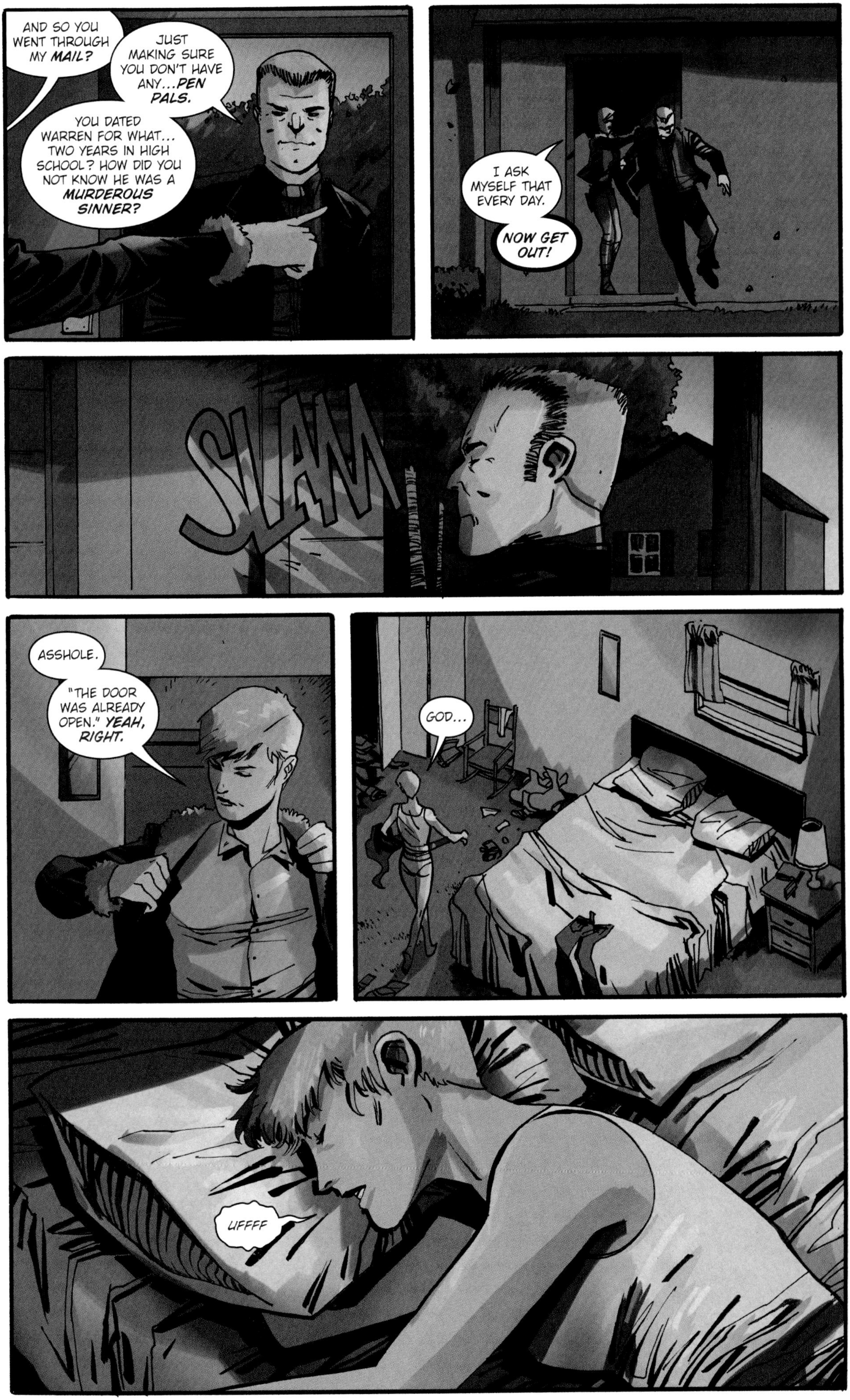
AND SO YOU WENT THROUGH MY *MAIL?*
JUST MAKING SURE YOU DON'T HAVE ANY...*PEN PALS.*
YOU DATED WARREN FOR WHAT... TWO YEARS IN HIGH SCHOOL? HOW DID YOU NOT KNOW HE WAS A *MURDEROUS SINNER?*
I ASK MYSELF THAT EVERY DAY.
NOW GET OUT!
SLAM
ASSHOLE.
"THE DOOR WAS ALREADY OPEN." *YEAH, RIGHT.*
GOD...
UFFFF

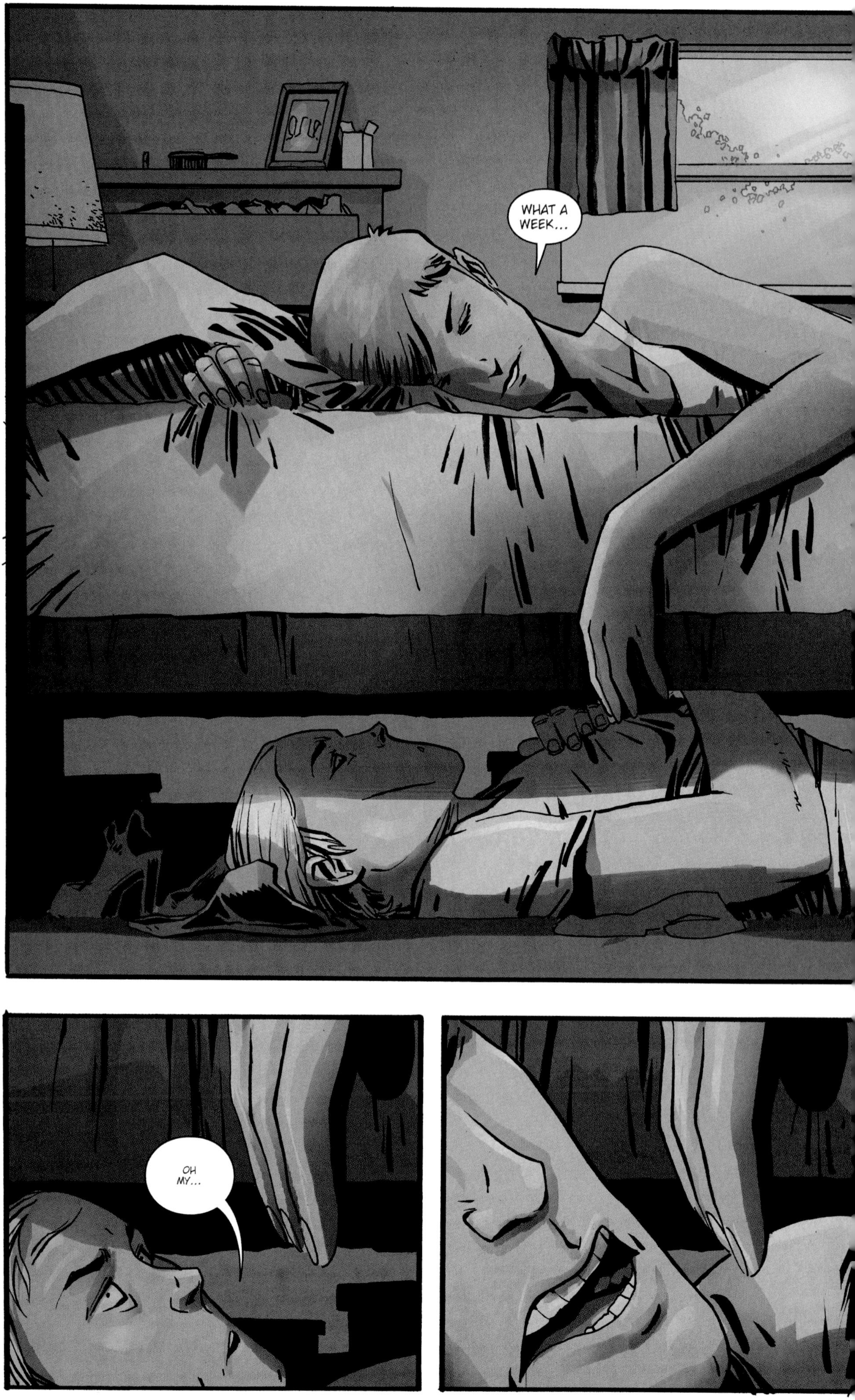
WHAT A WEEK...
OH MY...

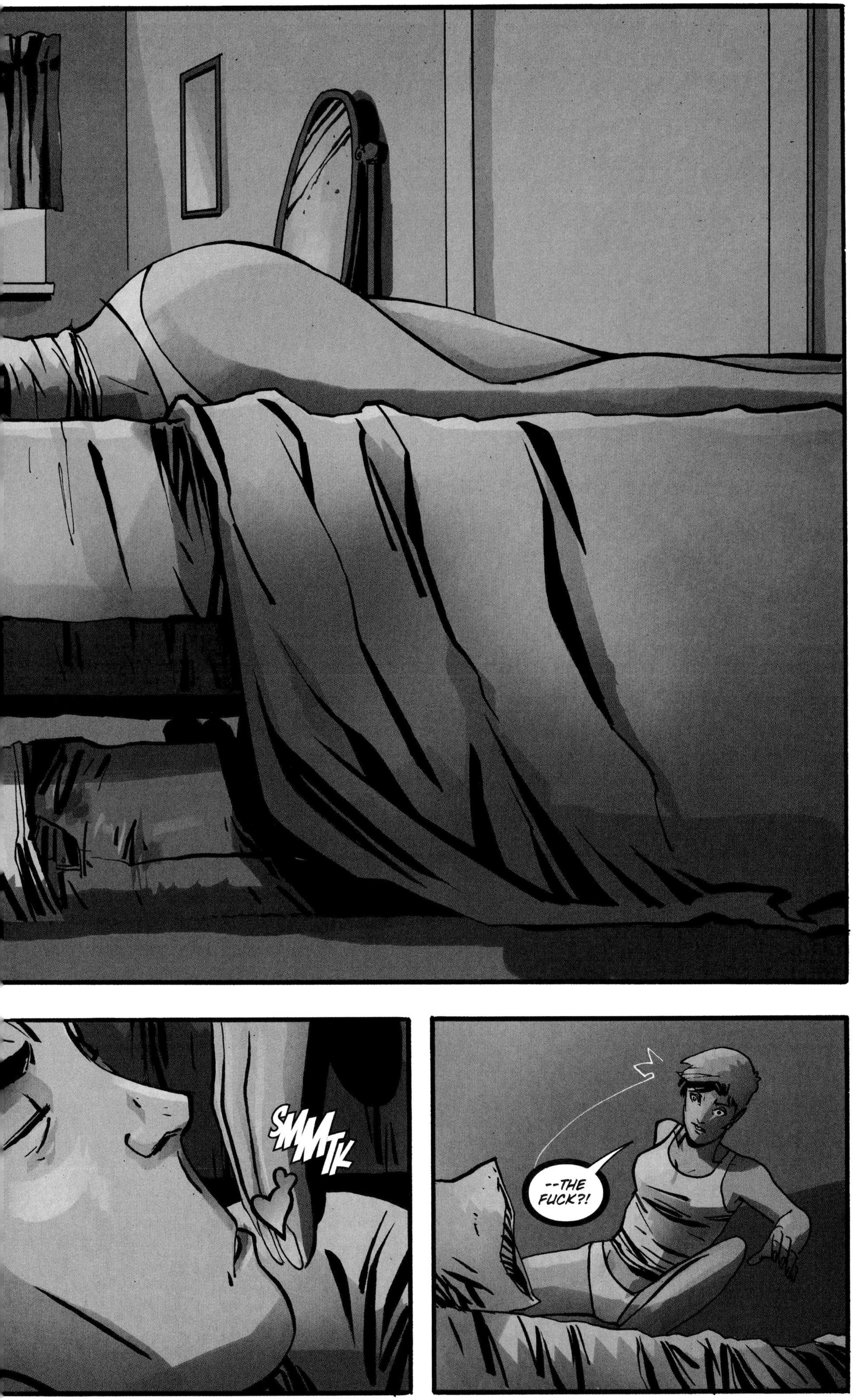
SMMTK
--THE FUCK?!

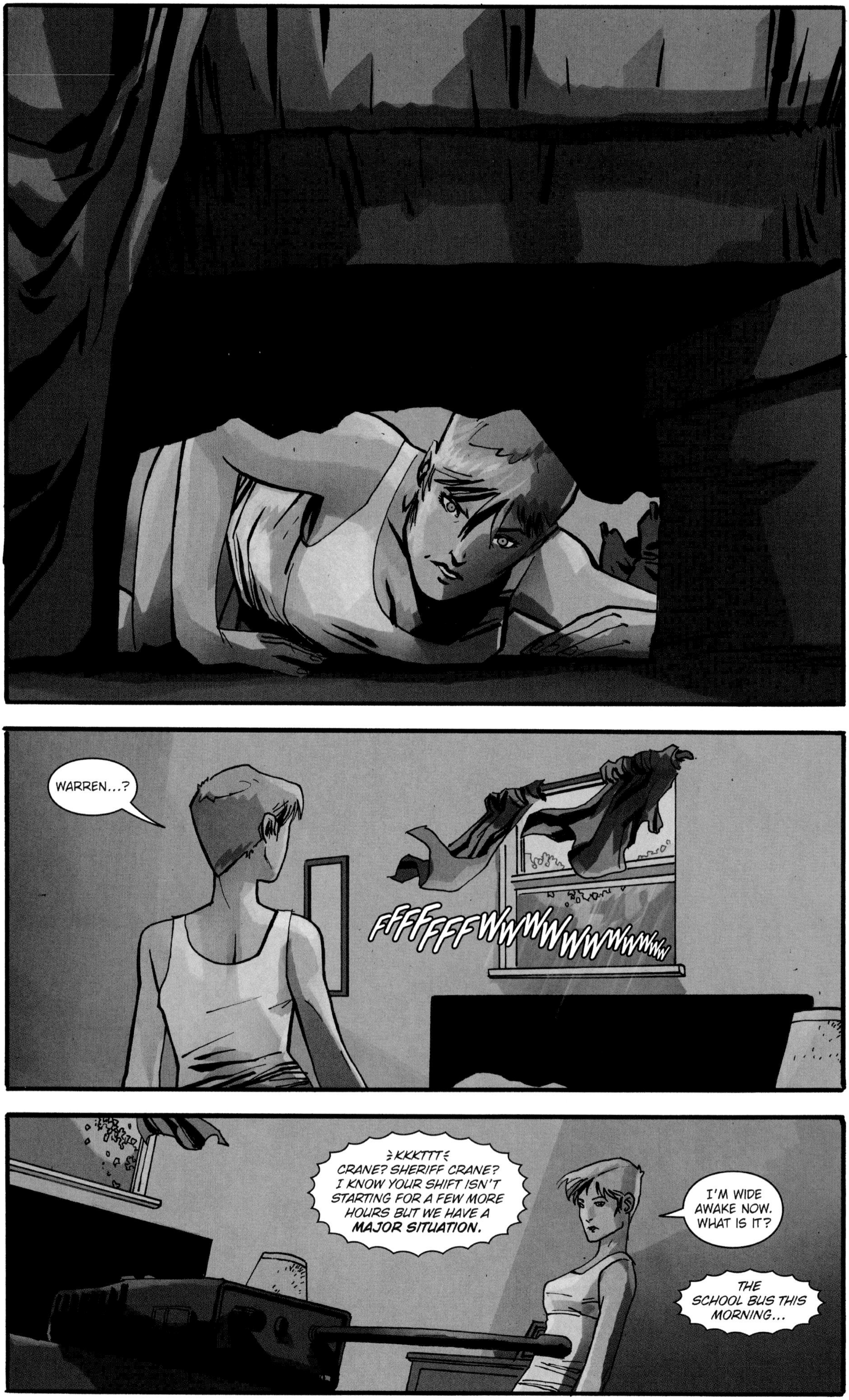
WARREN...?
FFFFFFFWWWWWWWWWWWW
KKKTTT
CRANE? SHERIFF CRANE? I KNOW YOUR SHIFT ISN'T STARTING FOR A FEW MORE HOURS BUT WE HAVE A MAJOR SITUATION.
I'M WIDE AWAKE NOW. WHAT IS IT?
THE SCHOOL BUS THIS MORNING...

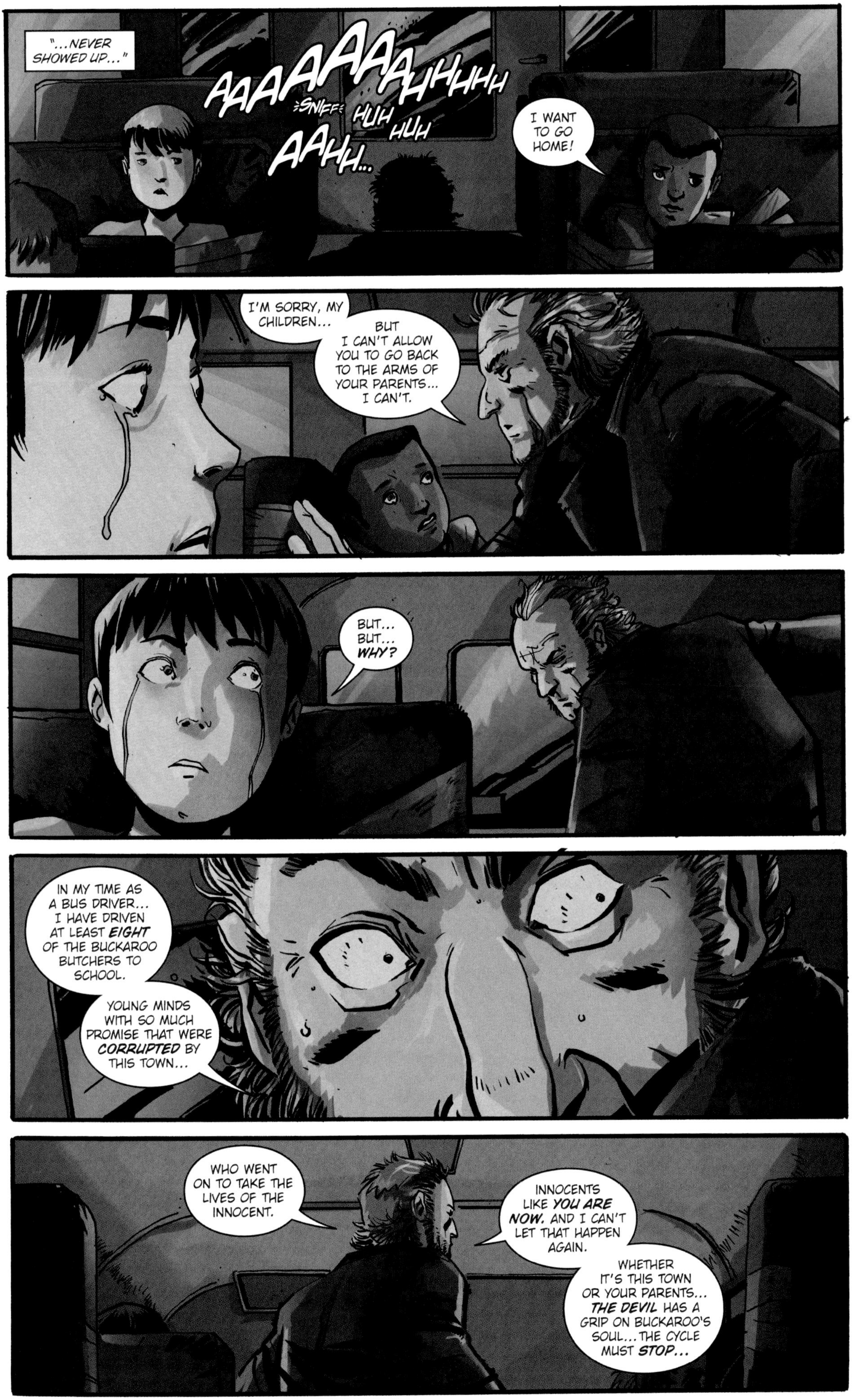
"...NEVER SHOWED UP..."
AAAAAAAAHHHHH
SNIFF HUH HUH
AAHH...
I WANT TO GO HOME!
I'M SORRY, MY CHILDREN...
BUT I CAN'T ALLOW YOU TO GO BACK TO THE ARMS OF YOUR PARENTS... I CAN'T.
BUT... BUT... WHY?
IN MY TIME AS A BUS DRIVER... I HAVE DRIVEN AT LEAST EIGHT OF THE BUCKAROO BUTCHERS TO SCHOOL.
YOUNG MINDS WITH SO MUCH PROMISE THAT WERE CORRUPTED BY THIS TOWN...
WHO WENT ON TO TAKE THE LIVES OF THE INNOCENT.
INNOCENTS LIKE YOU ARE NOW. AND I CAN'T LET THAT HAPPEN AGAIN.
WHETHER IT'S THIS TOWN OR YOUR PARENTS... THE DEVIL HAS A GRIP ON BUCKAROO'S SOUL... THE CYCLE MUST STOP...

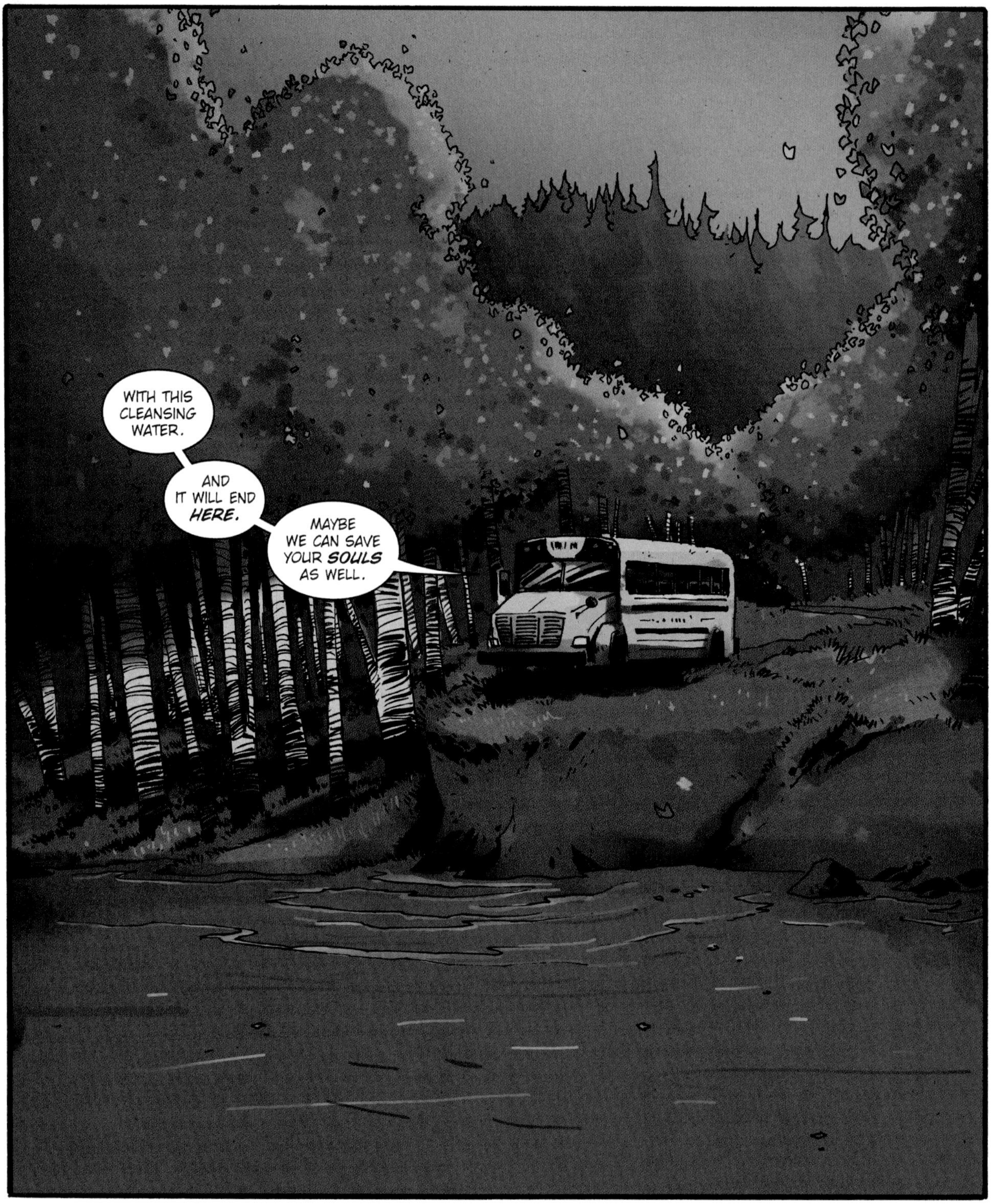
WITH THIS CLEANSING WATER.
AND IT WILL END *HERE.*
MAYBE WE CAN SAVE YOUR *SOULS* AS WELL.

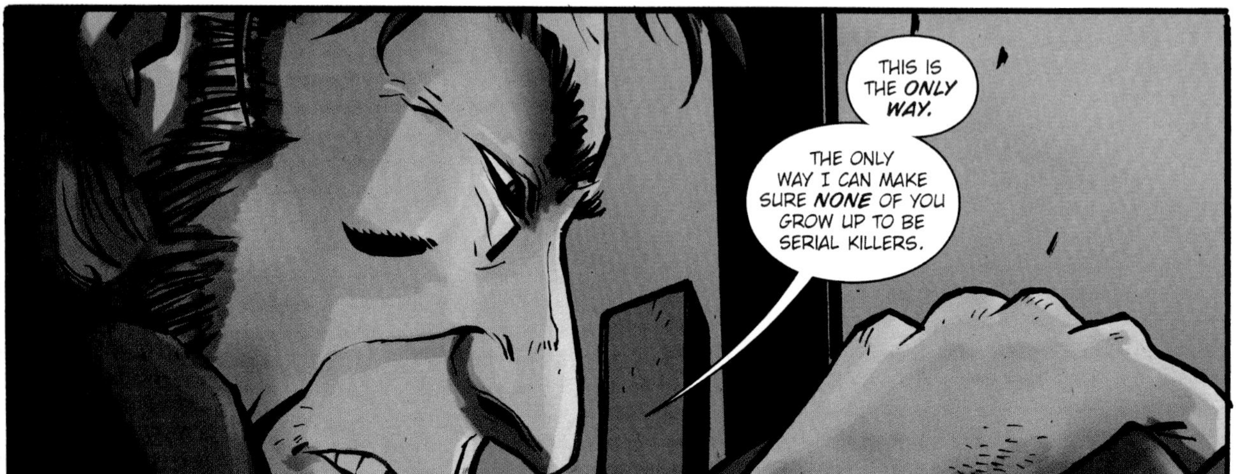
THIS IS THE *ONLY WAY.*
THE ONLY WAY I CAN MAKE SURE *NONE* OF YOU GROW UP TO BE SERIAL KILLERS.

TEN

"I was only trying to stop them
from becoming killers!"

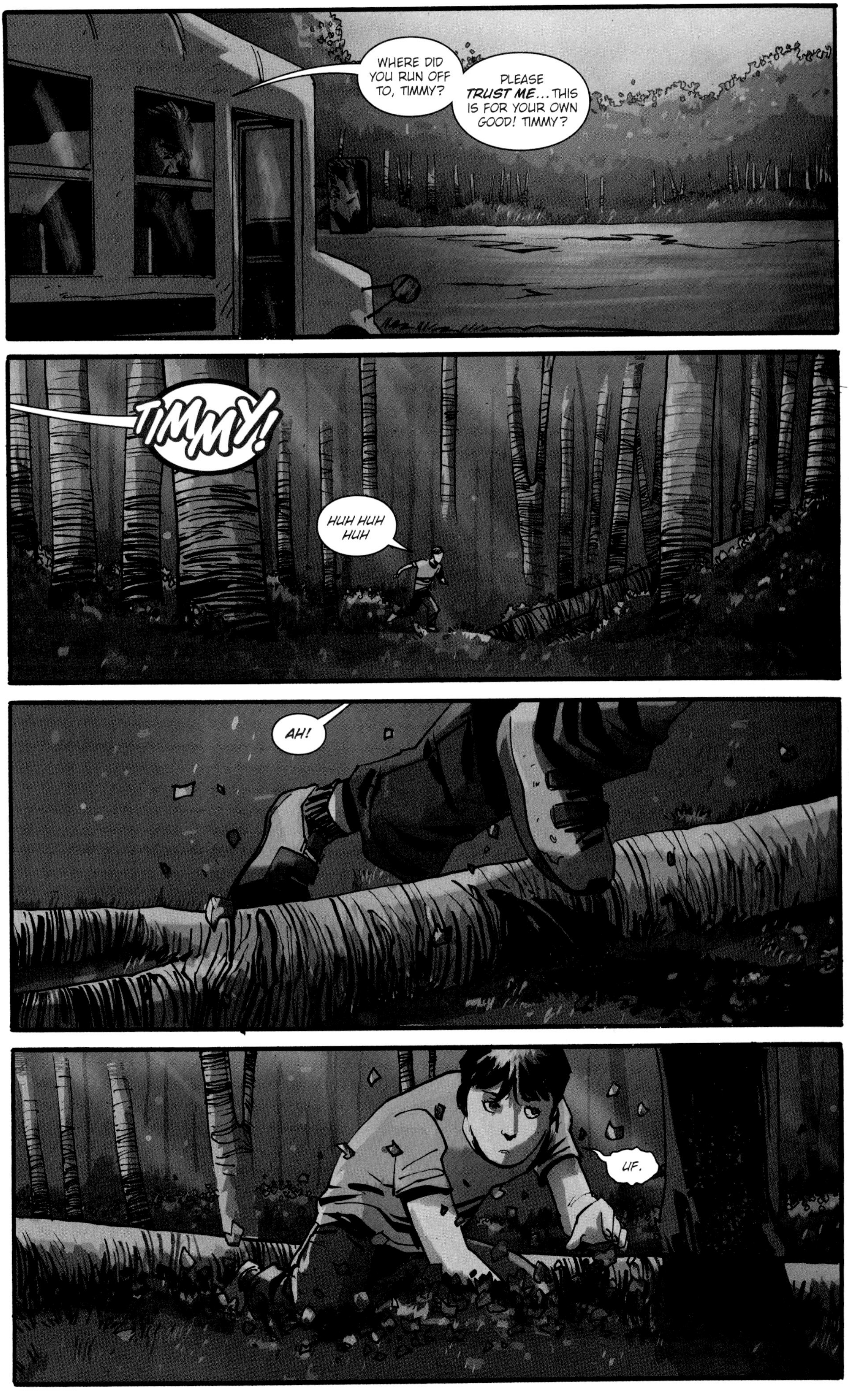
WHERE DID YOU RUN OFF TO, TIMMY?
PLEASE TRUST ME... THIS IS FOR YOUR OWN GOOD! TIMMY?
TIMMY!
HUH HUH HUH
AH!
UF.

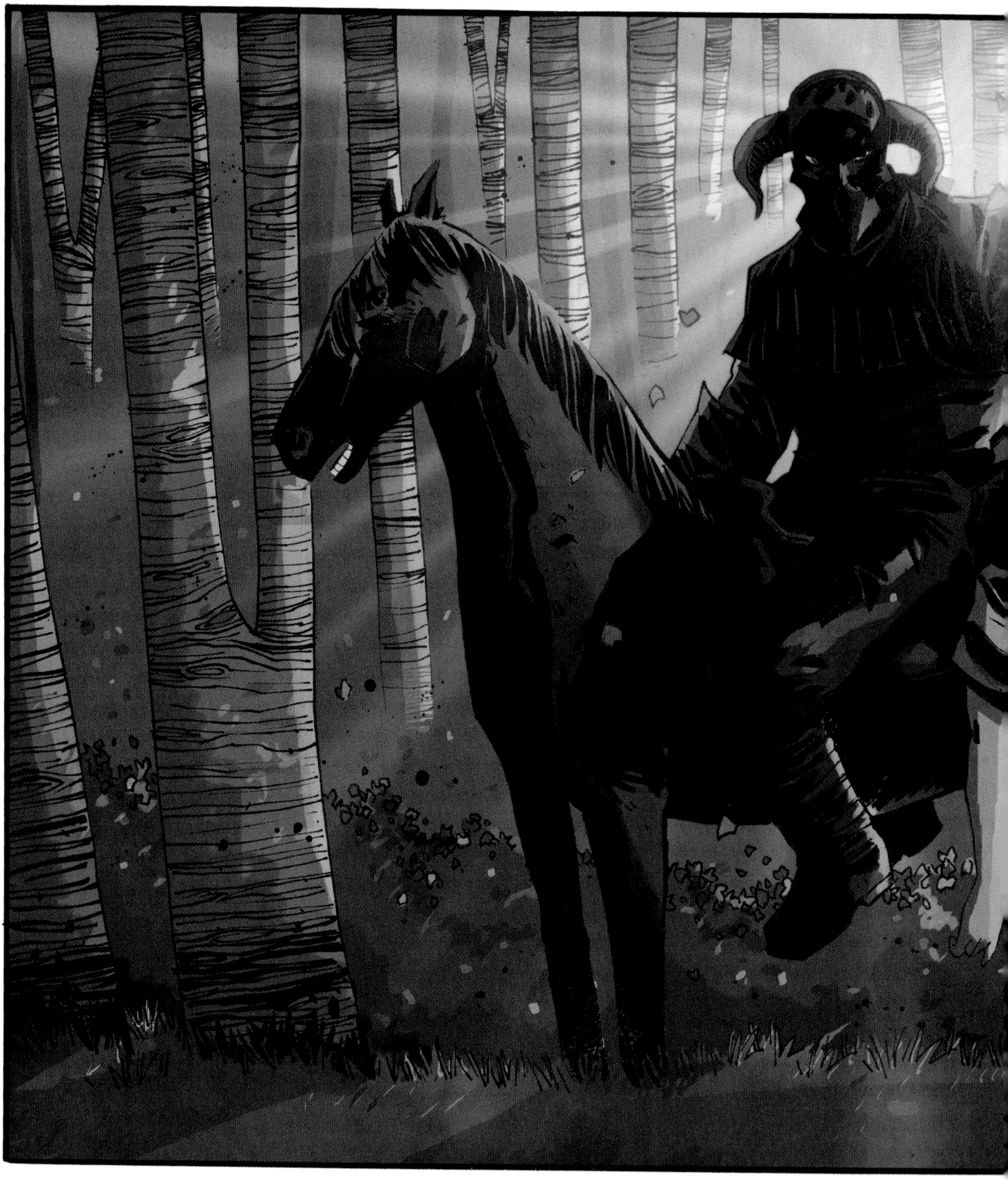

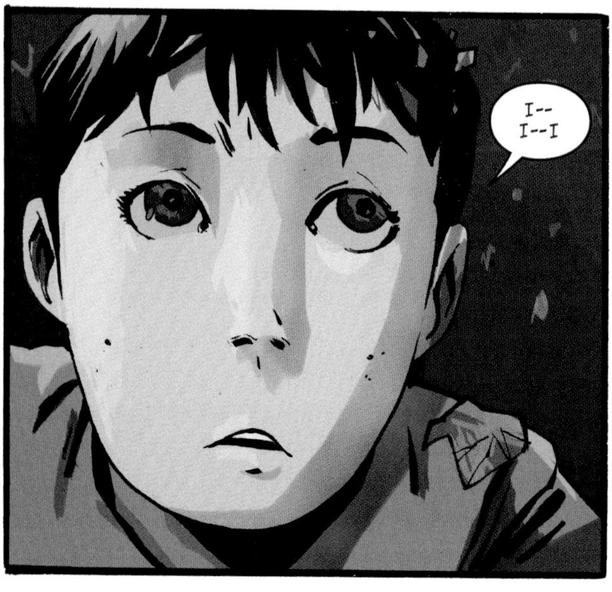
I--
I--I

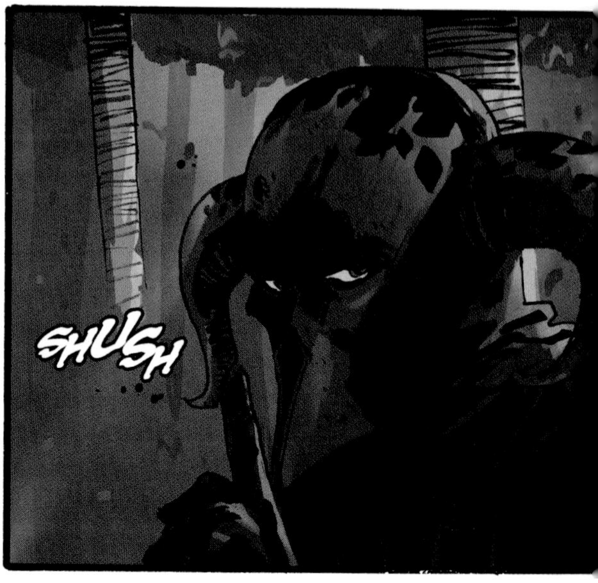
SHUSH

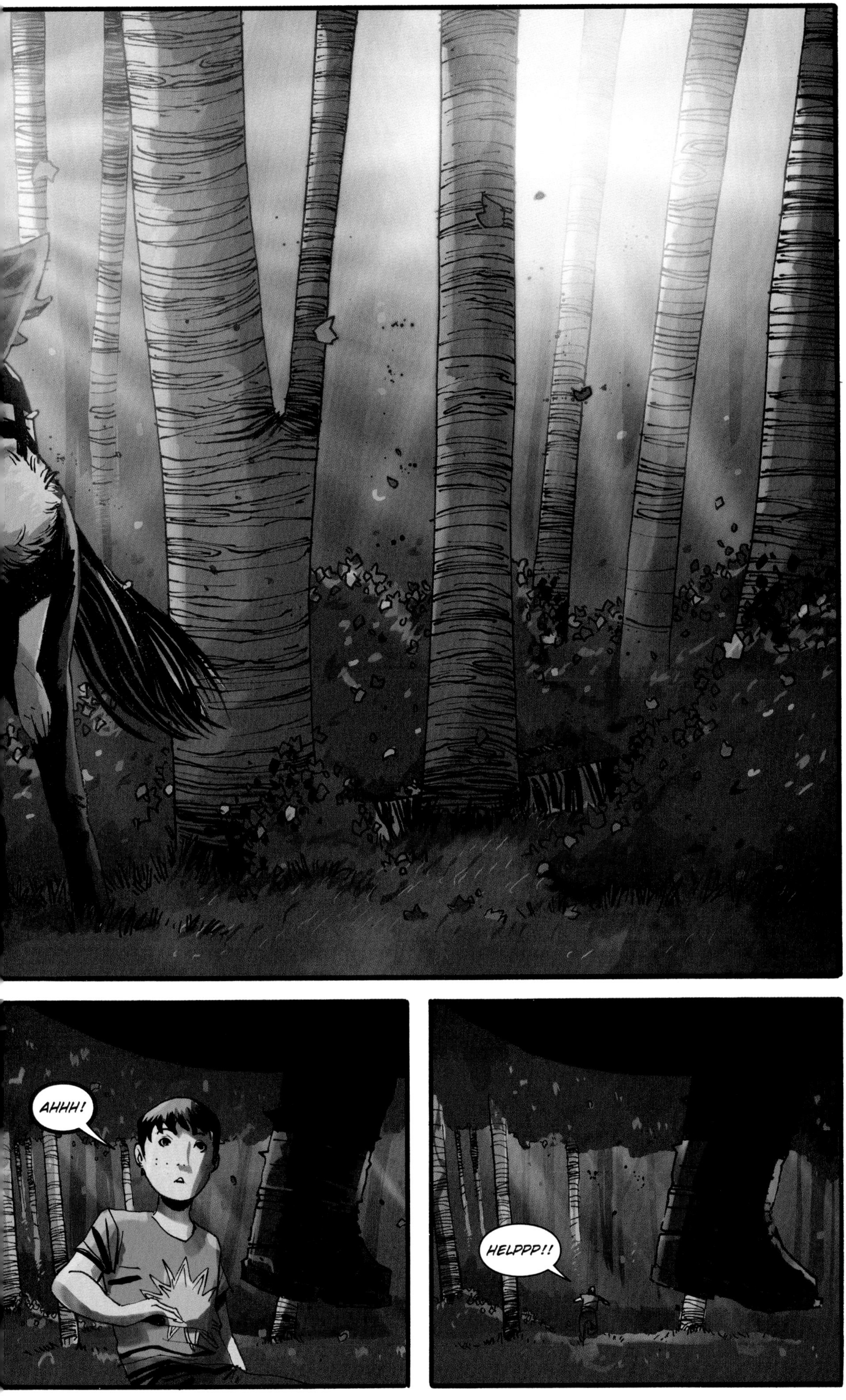
AHHH!
HELPPP!!

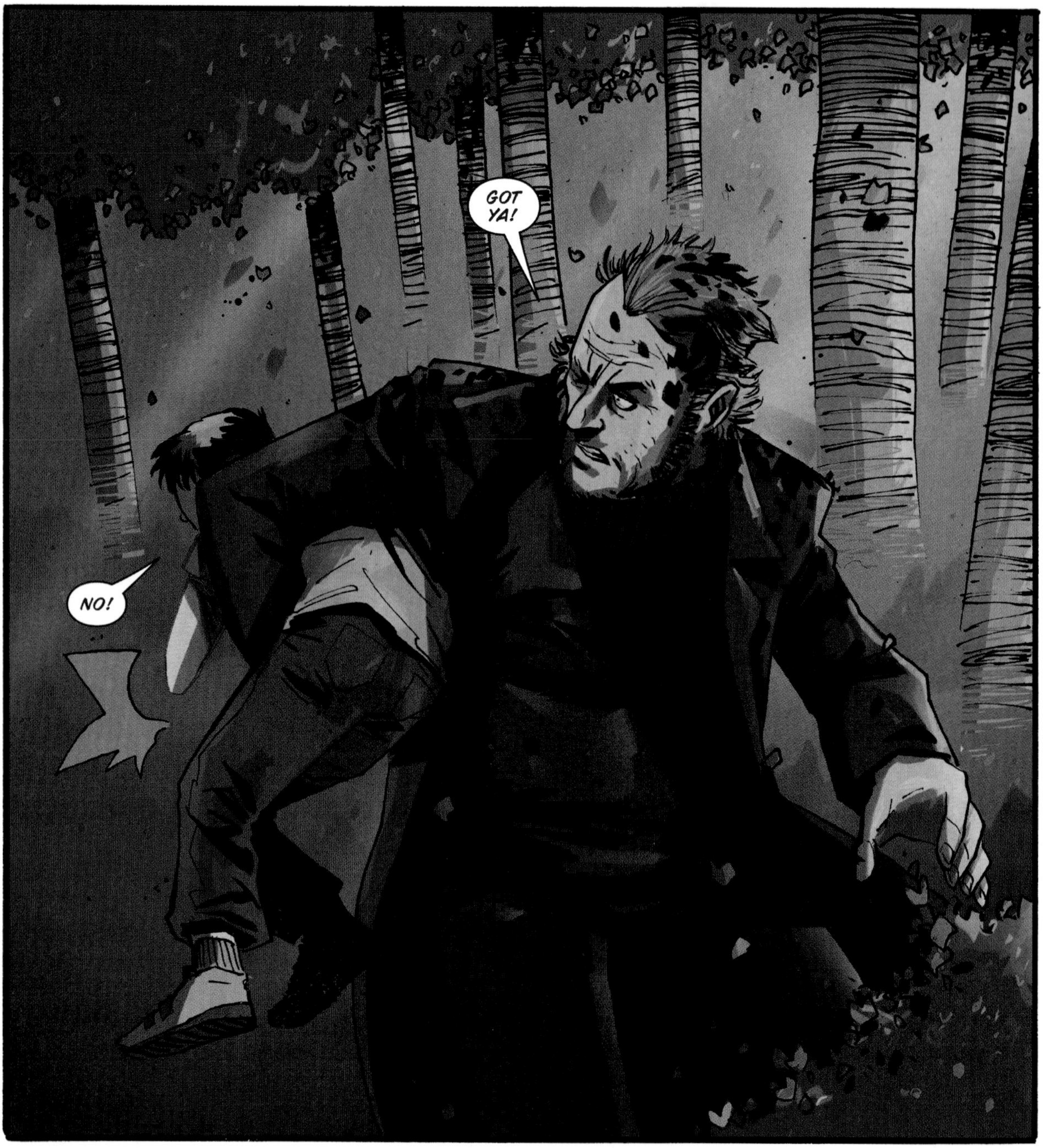
GOT YA!
NO!

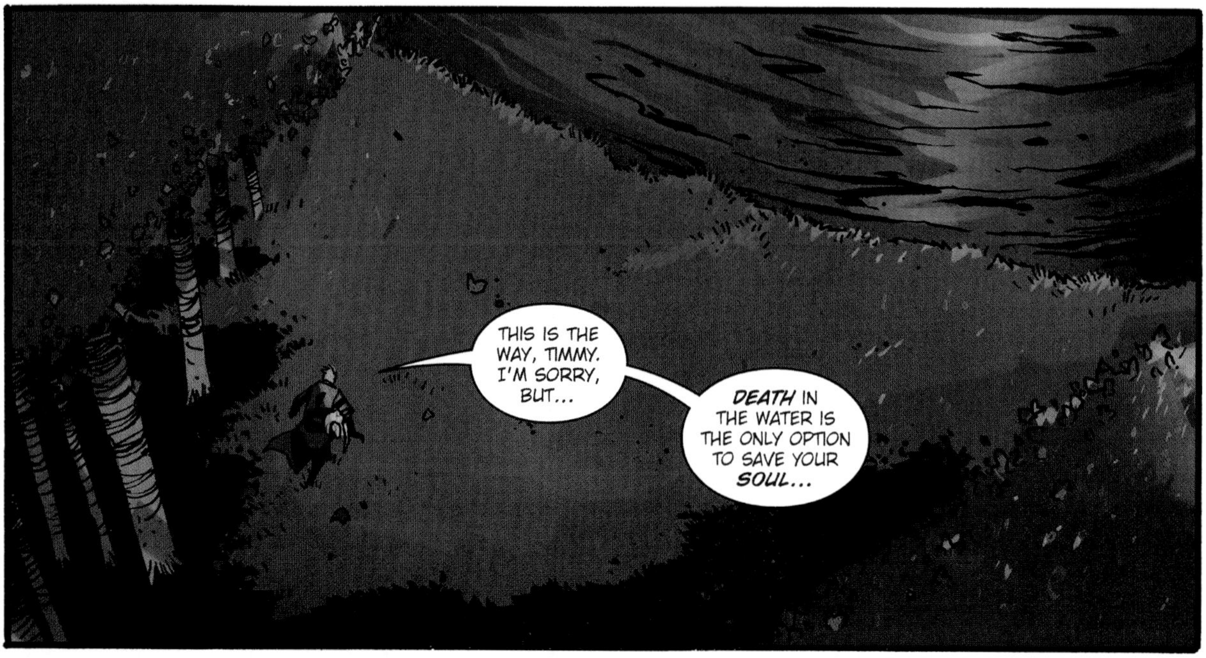
THIS IS THE WAY, TIMMY. I'M SORRY, BUT...
DEATH IN THE WATER IS THE ONLY OPTION TO SAVE YOUR SOUL...

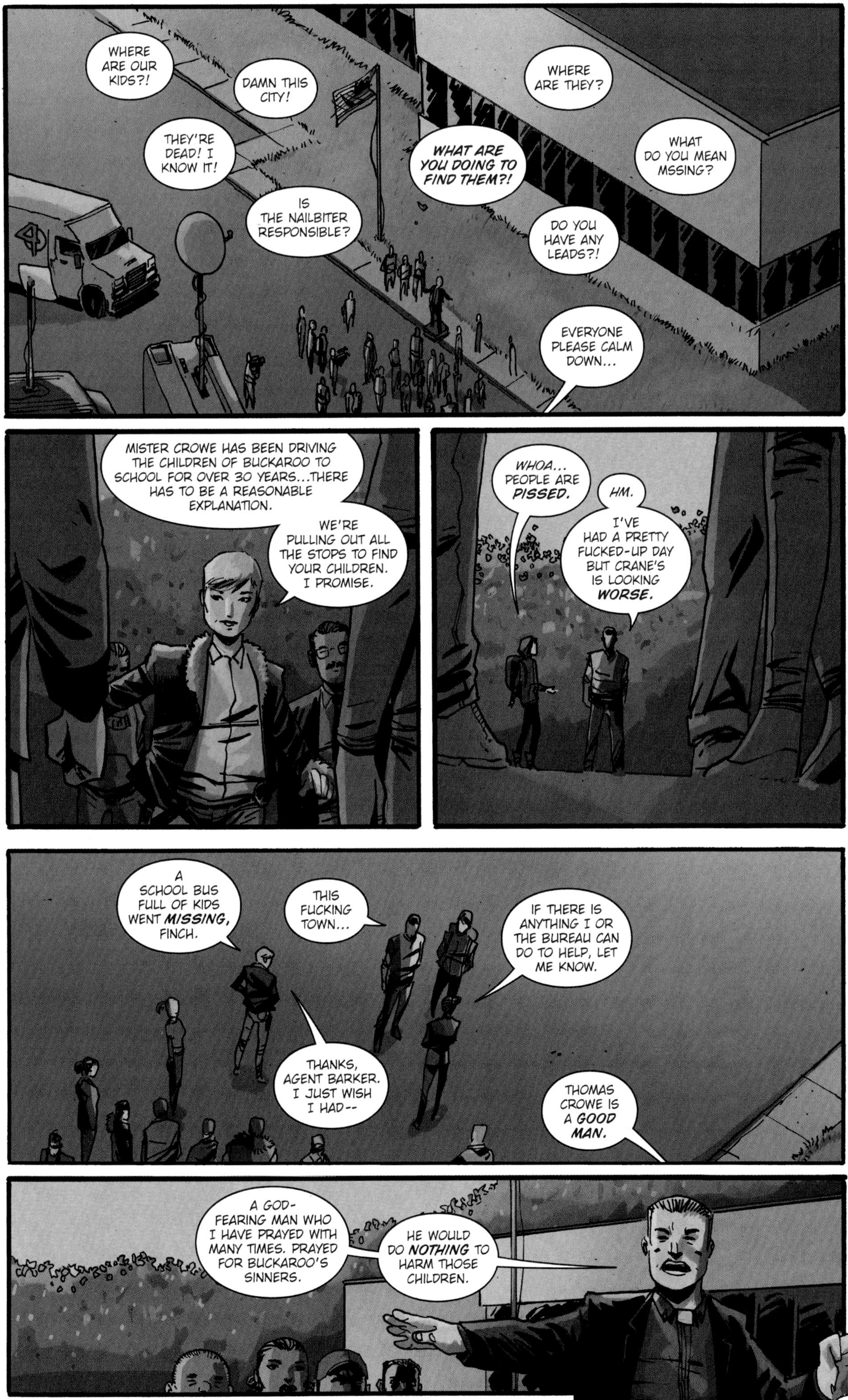
WHERE ARE OUR KIDS?!
DAMN THIS CITY!
THEY'RE DEAD! I KNOW IT!
IS THE NAILBITER RESPONSIBLE?
WHAT ARE YOU DOING TO FIND THEM?!
WHERE ARE THEY?
WHAT DO YOU MEAN MSSING?
DO YOU HAVE ANY LEADS?!
EVERYONE PLEASE CALM DOWN...
MISTER CROWE HAS BEEN DRIVING THE CHILDREN OF BUCKAROO TO SCHOOL FOR OVER 30 YEARS...THERE HAS TO BE A REASONABLE EXPLANATION.
WE'RE PULLING OUT ALL THE STOPS TO FIND YOUR CHILDREN. I PROMISE.
WHOA... PEOPLE ARE PISSED.
HM.
I'VE HAD A PRETTY FUCKED-UP DAY BUT CRANE'S IS LOOKING WORSE.
A SCHOOL BUS FULL OF KIDS WENT MISSING, FINCH.
THIS FUCKING TOWN...
IF THERE IS ANYTHING I OR THE BUREAU CAN DO TO HELP, LET ME KNOW.
THANKS, AGENT BARKER. I JUST WISH I HAD--
THOMAS CROWE IS A GOOD MAN.
A GOD-FEARING MAN WHO I HAVE PRAYED WITH MANY TIMES. PRAYED FOR BUCKAROO'S SINNERS.
HE WOULD DO NOTHING TO HARM THOSE CHILDREN.

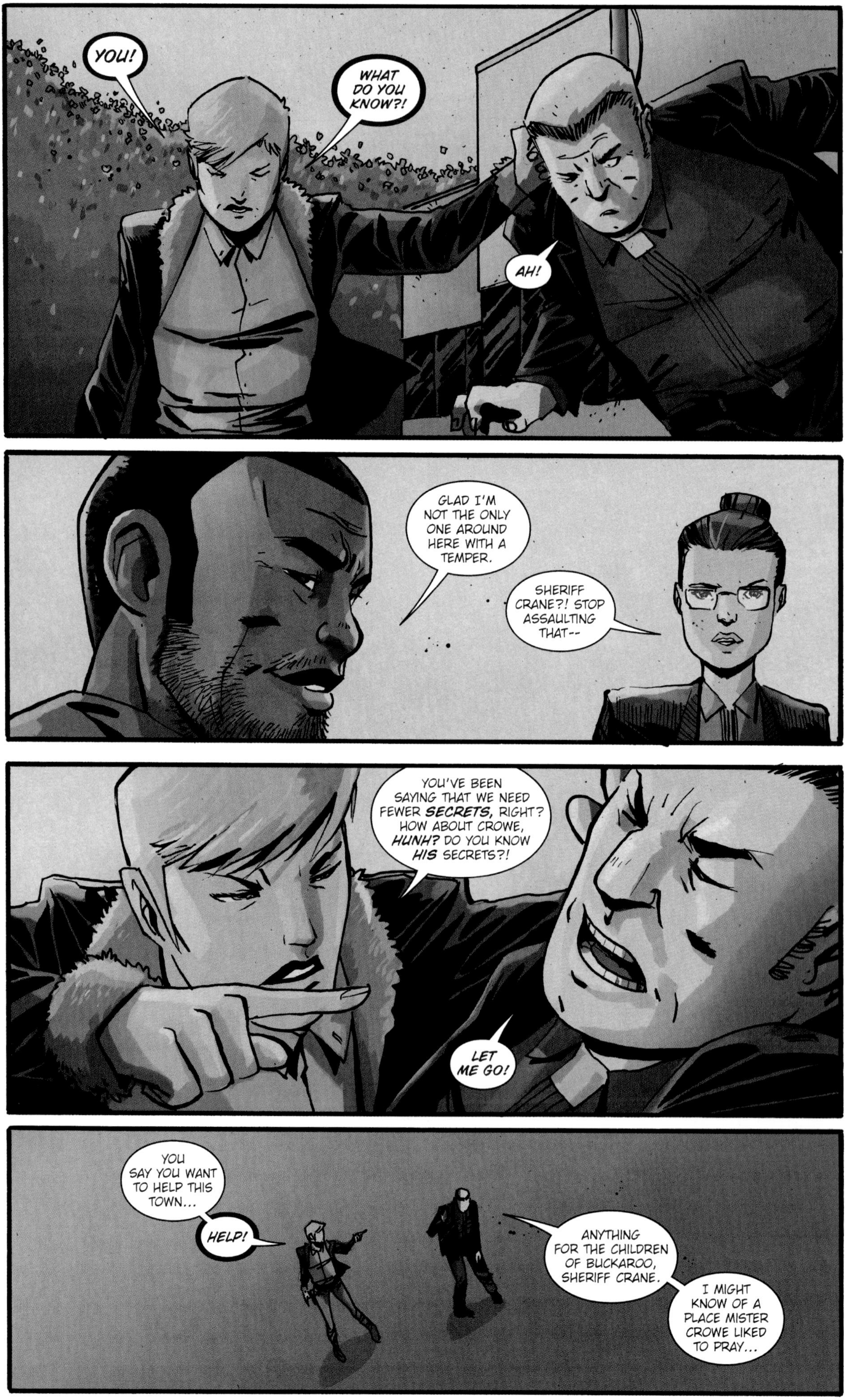
YOU!
WHAT DO YOU KNOW?!
AH!
GLAD I'M NOT THE ONLY ONE AROUND HERE WITH A TEMPER.
SHERIFF CRANE?! STOP ASSAULTING THAT--
YOU'VE BEEN SAYING THAT WE NEED FEWER SECRETS, RIGHT? HOW ABOUT CROWE, HUNH? DO YOU KNOW HIS SECRETS?!
LET ME GO!
YOU SAY YOU WANT TO HELP THIS TOWN...
HELP!
ANYTHING FOR THE CHILDREN OF BUCKAROO, SHERIFF CRANE.
I MIGHT KNOW OF A PLACE MISTER CROWE LIKED TO PRAY...

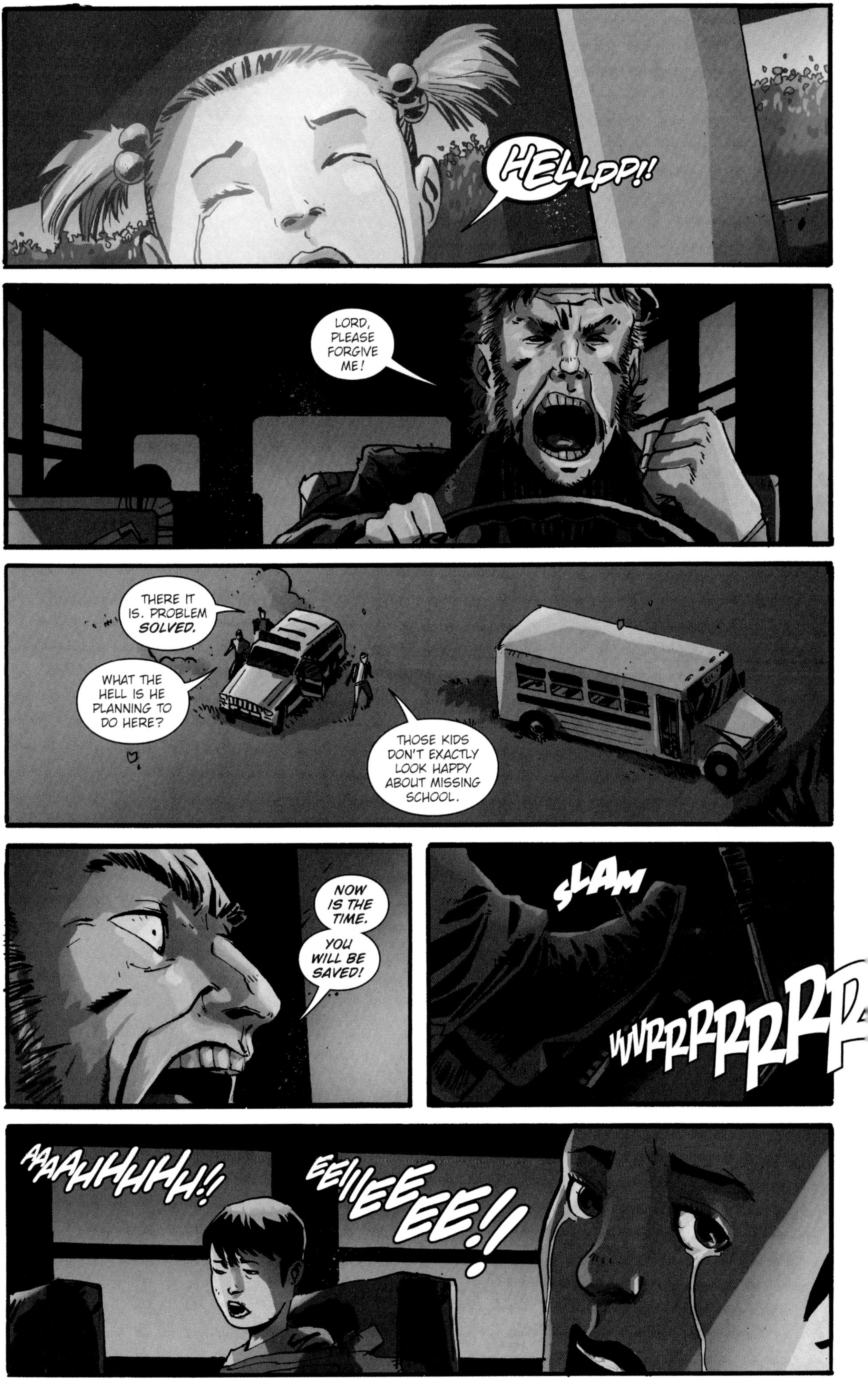
HELLPP!!
LORD, PLEASE FORGIVE ME!
THERE IT IS. PROBLEM SOLVED.
WHAT THE HELL IS HE PLANNING TO DO HERE?
THOSE KIDS DON'T EXACTLY LOOK HAPPY ABOUT MISSING SCHOOL.
NOW IS THE TIME.
YOU WILL BE SAVED!
SLAM
WRRRRRRR
AAAAHHHHH!!
EEIIIEEEEE!!

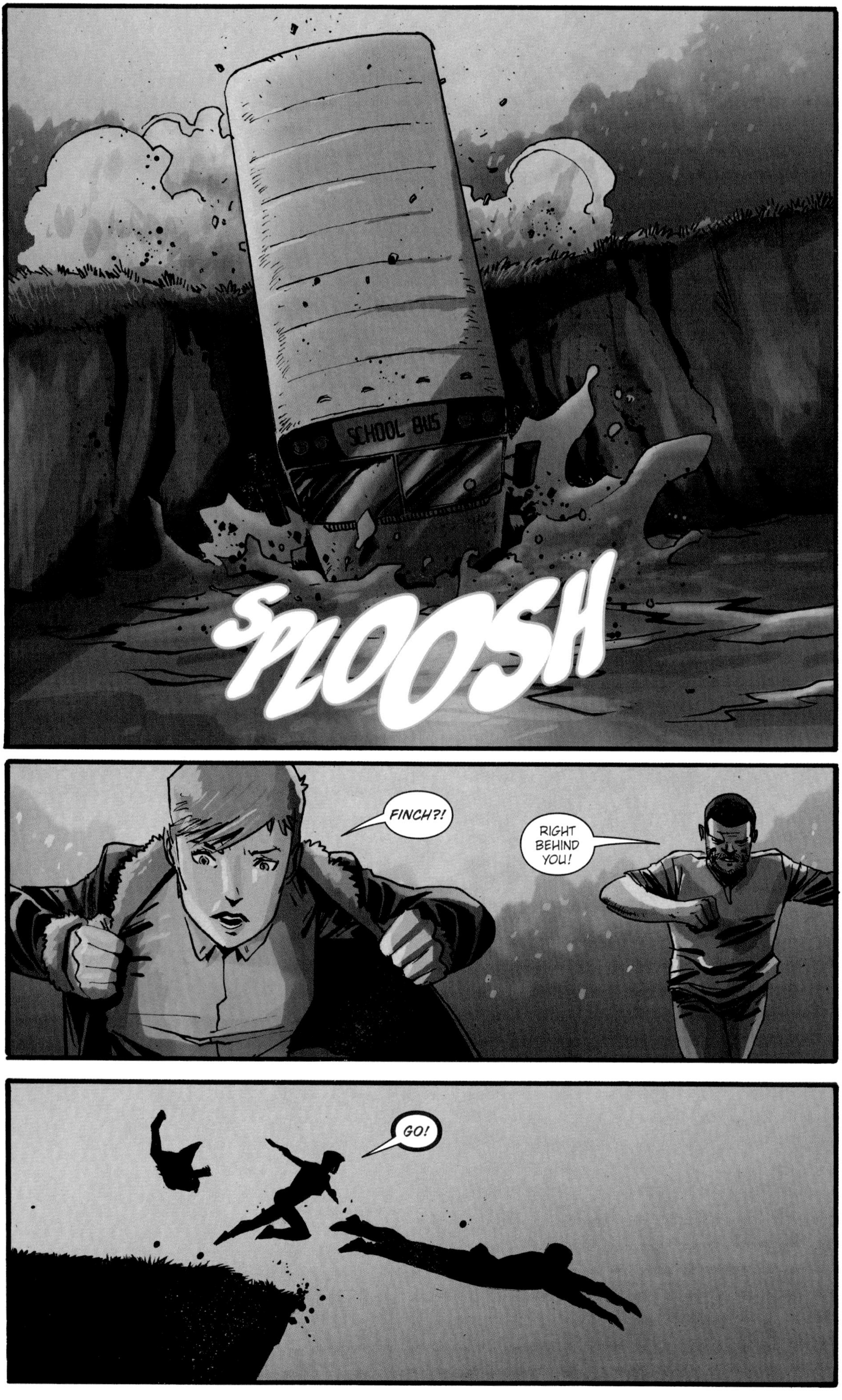
SCHOOL BUS
SPLOOSH
FINCH?!
RIGHT BEHIND YOU!
GO!

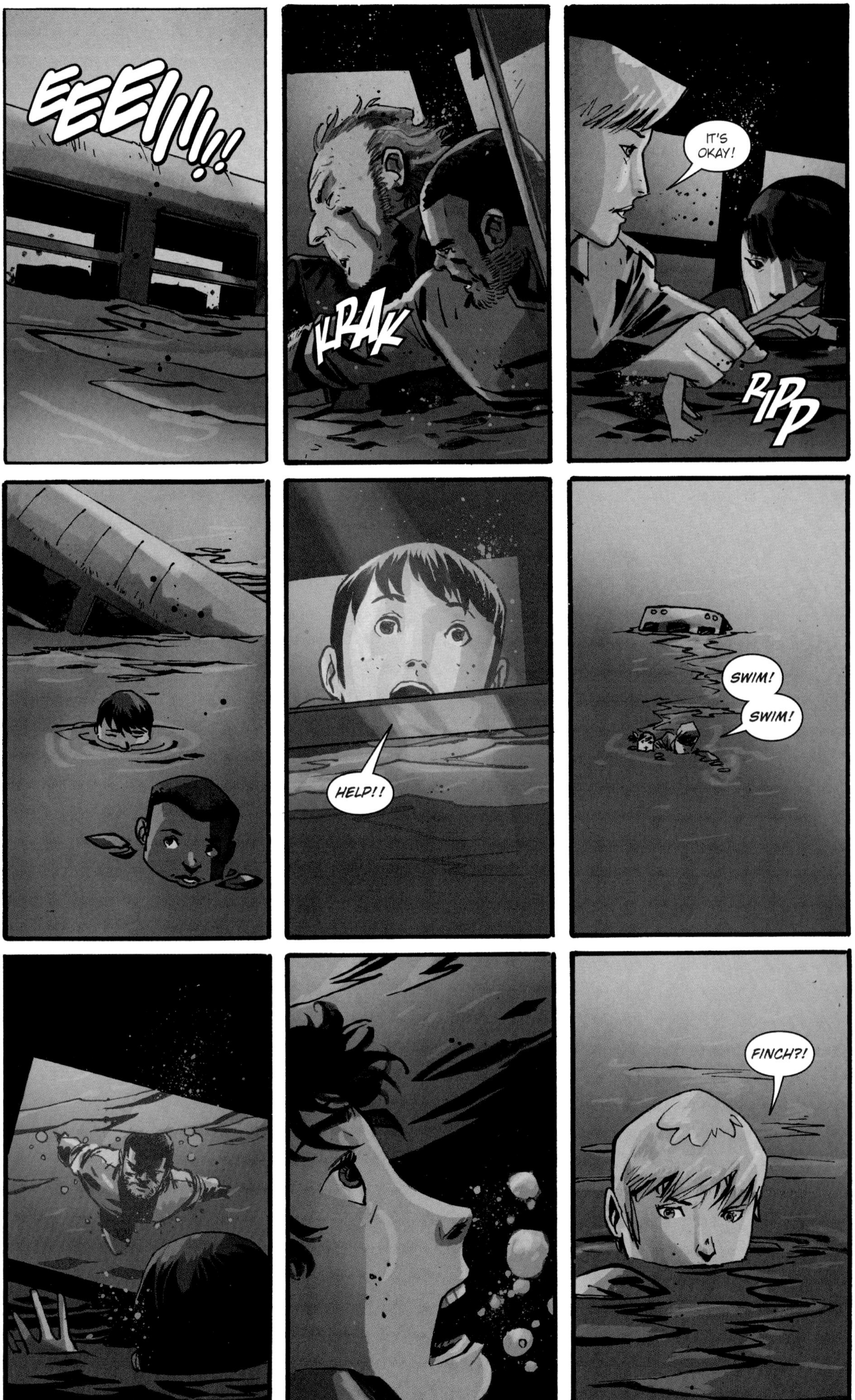
EEEIII!!!
KRAK
IT'S OKAY!
RIPP
HELP!!
SWIM!
SWIM!
FINCH?!

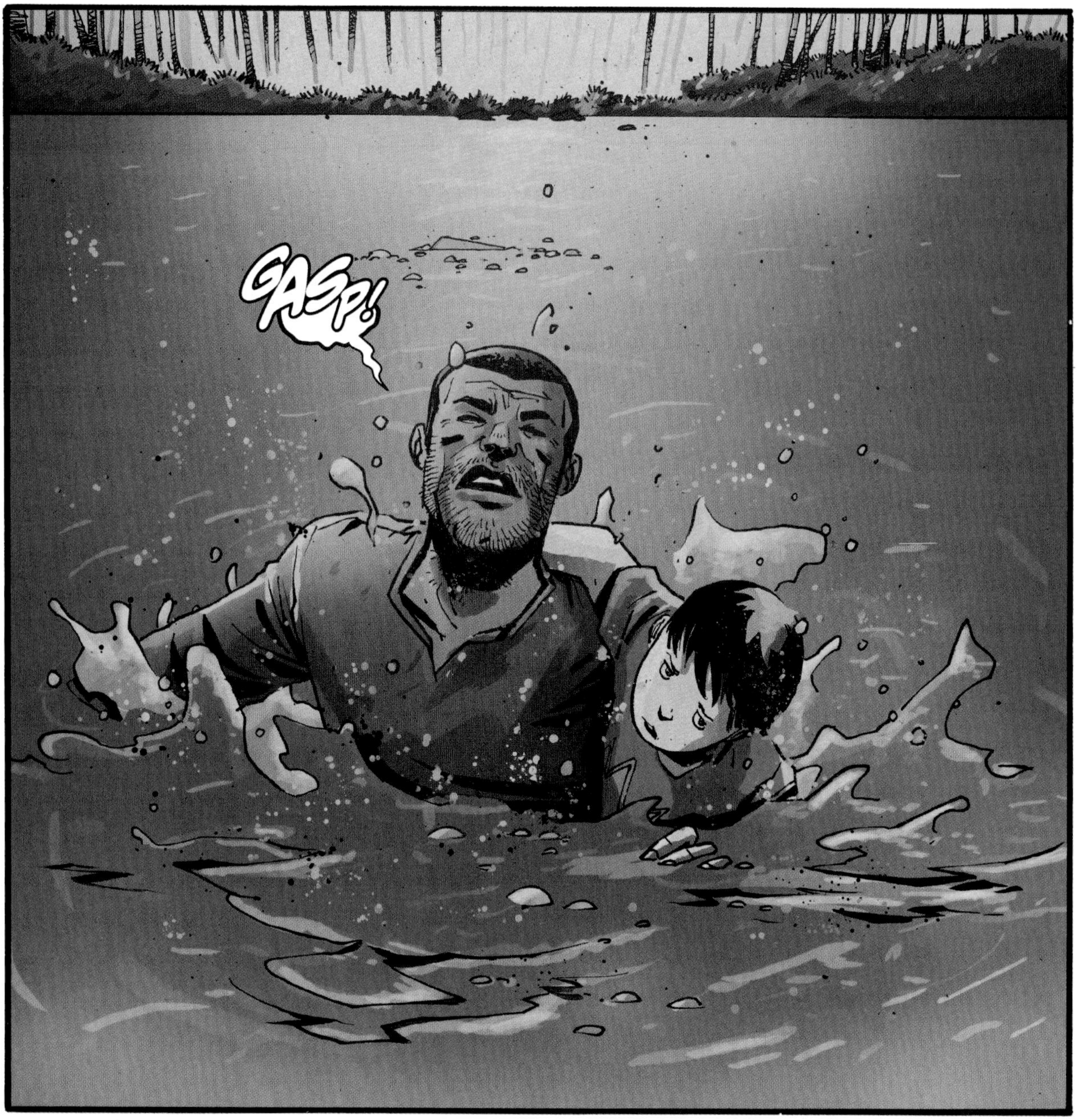
GASP!

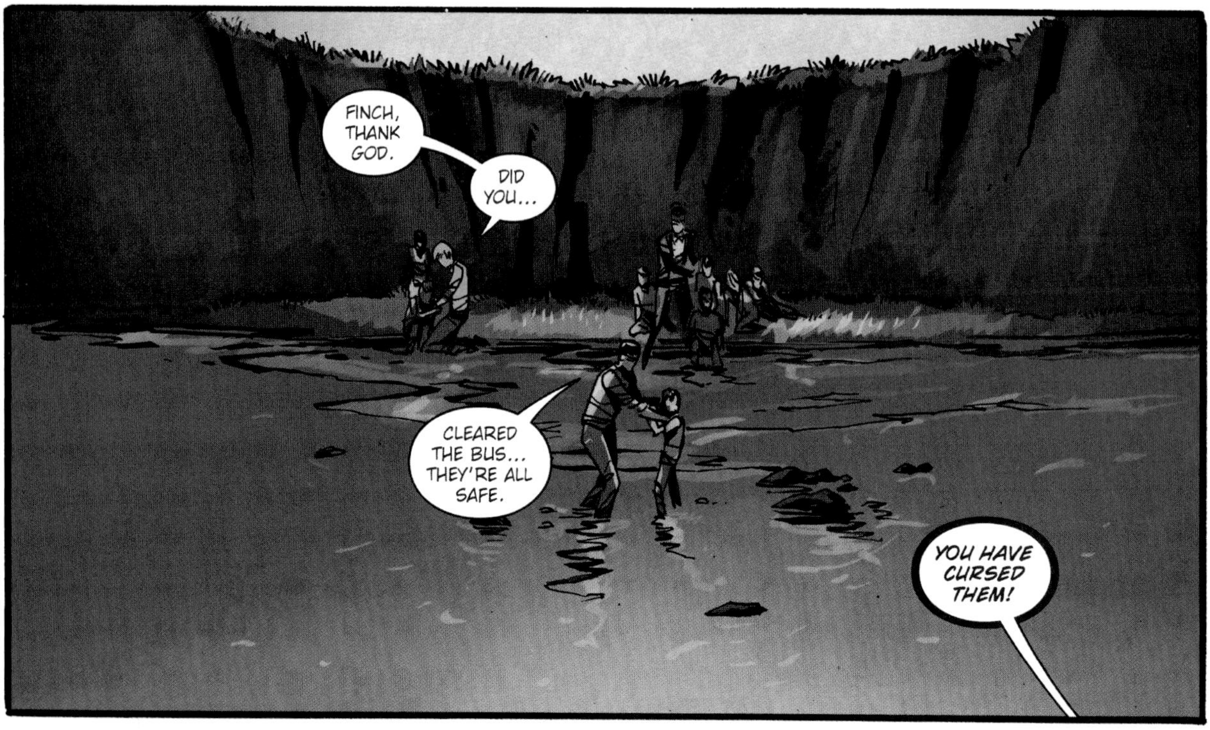
FINCH, THANK GOD.
DID YOU...
CLEARED THE BUS... THEY'RE ALL SAFE.
YOU HAVE CURSED THEM!

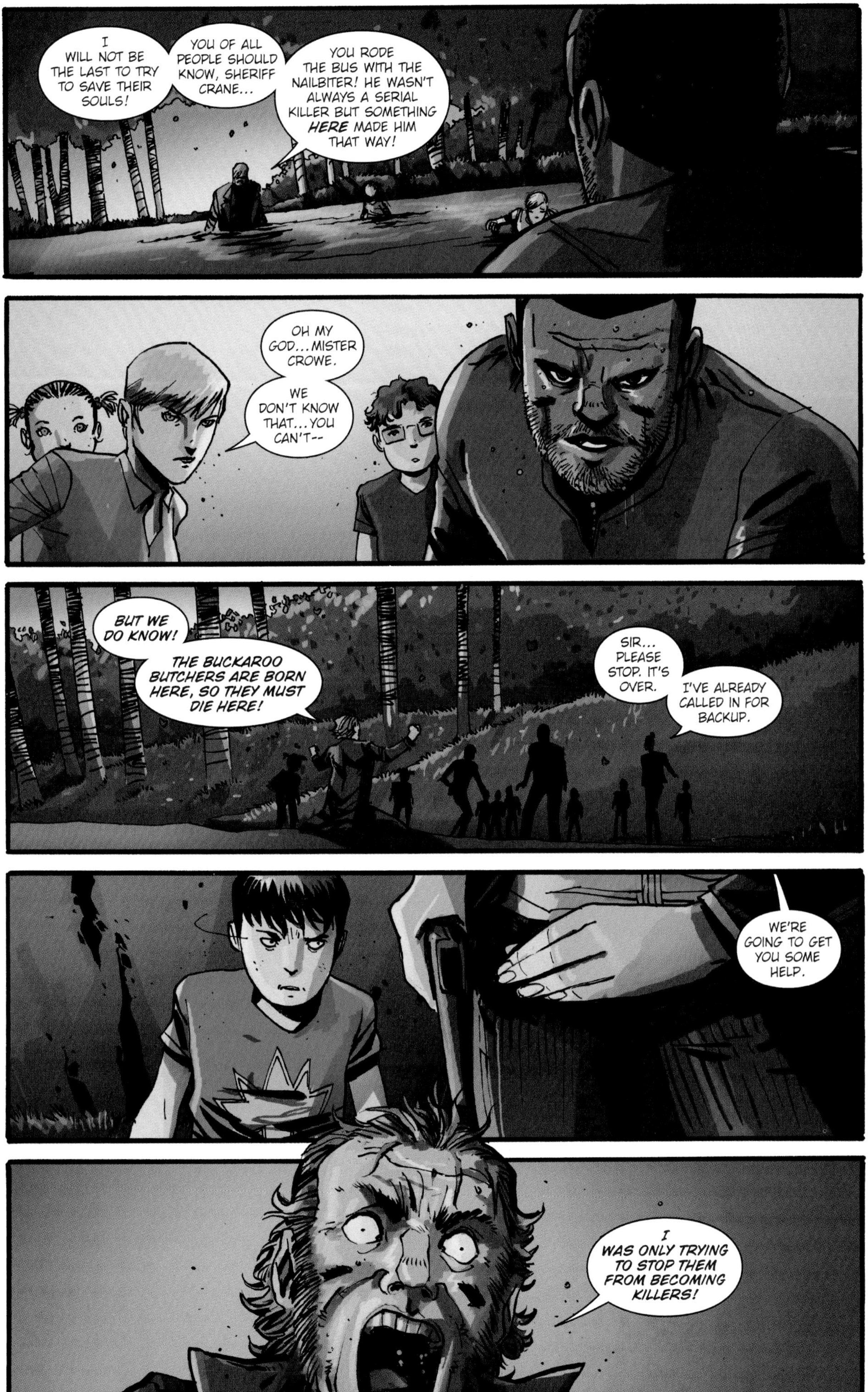
I WILL NOT BE THE LAST TO TRY TO SAVE THEIR SOULS!
YOU OF ALL PEOPLE SHOULD KNOW, SHERIFF CRANE...
YOU RODE THE BUS WITH THE NAILBITER! HE WASN'T ALWAYS A SERIAL KILLER BUT SOMETHING HERE MADE HIM THAT WAY!
OH MY GOD...MISTER CROWE.
WE DON'T KNOW THAT...YOU CAN'T--
BUT WE DO KNOW!
THE BUCKAROO BUTCHERS ARE BORN HERE, SO THEY MUST DIE HERE!
SIR... PLEASE STOP. IT'S OVER.
I'VE ALREADY CALLED IN FOR BACKUP.
WE'RE GOING TO GET YOU SOME HELP.
I WAS ONLY TRYING TO STOP THEM FROM BECOMING KILLERS!

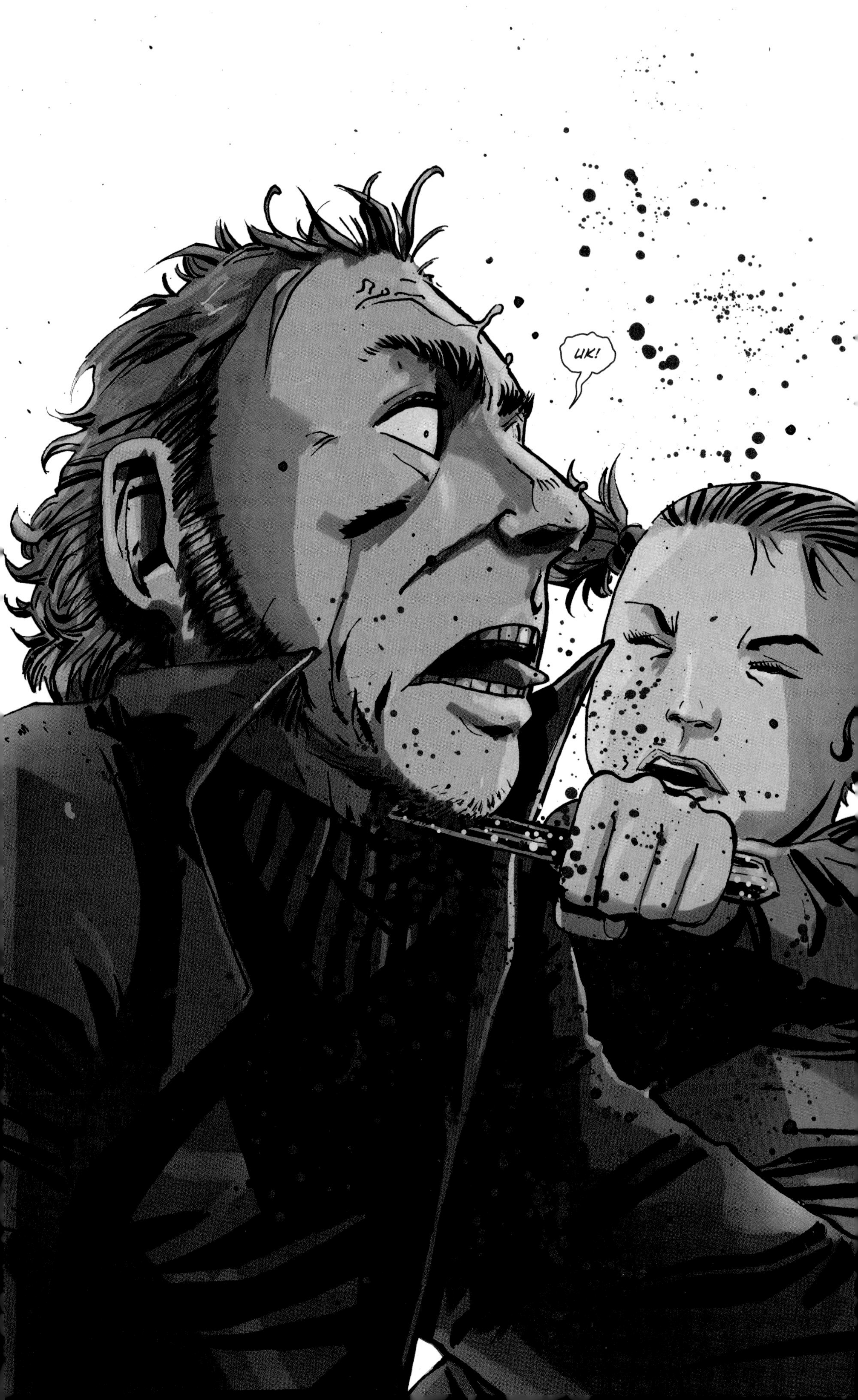
UK!

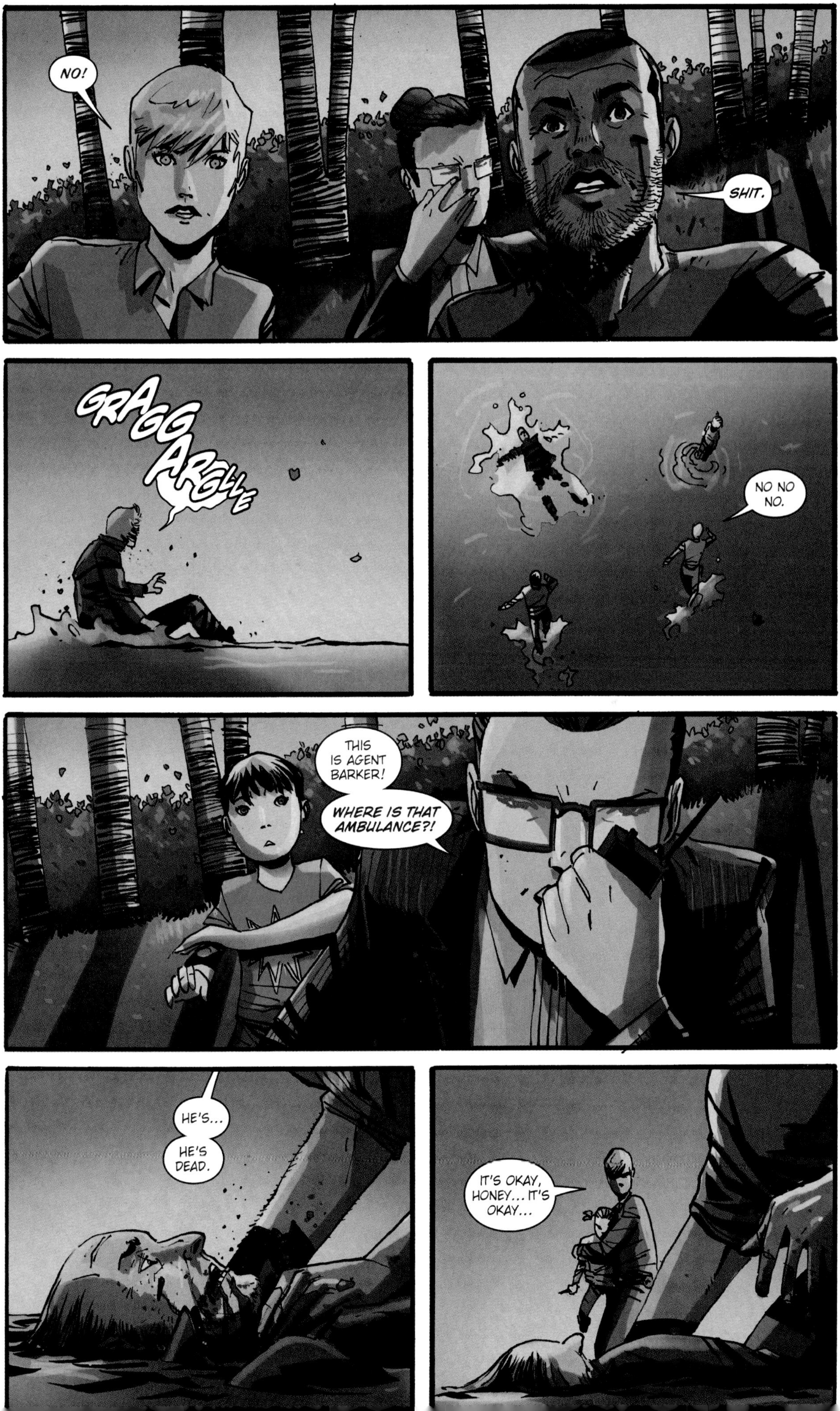
NO!
SHIT.
GRAGGARGLLE
NO NO NO.
THIS IS AGENT BARKER!
WHERE IS THAT AMBULANCE?!
HE'S...
HE'S DEAD.
IT'S OKAY, HONEY... IT'S OKAY...

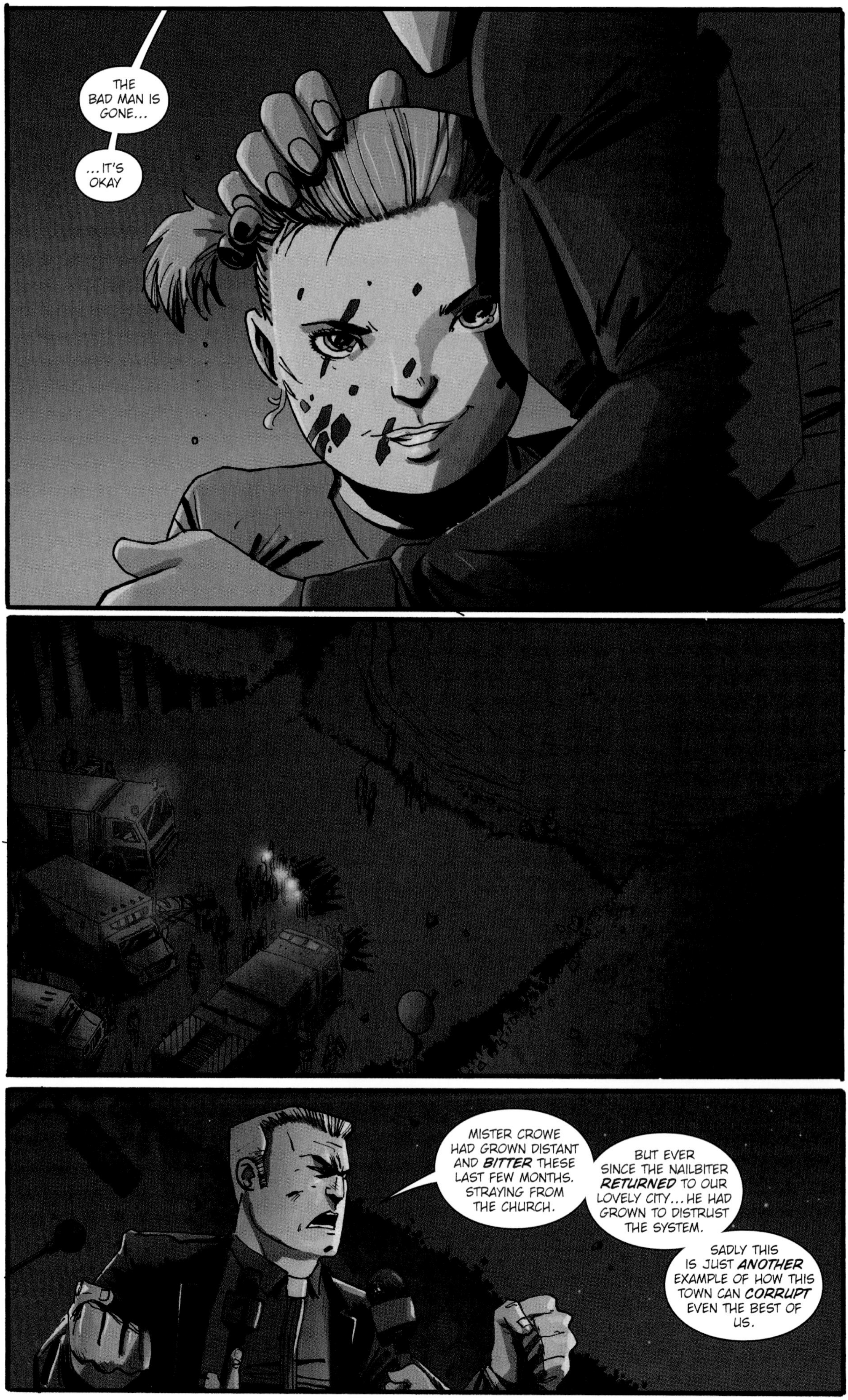
THE BAD MAN IS GONE...
...IT'S OKAY
MISTER CROWE HAD GROWN DISTANT AND BITTER THESE LAST FEW MONTHS. STRAYING FROM THE CHURCH.
BUT EVER SINCE THE NAILBITER RETURNED TO OUR LOVELY CITY... HE HAD GROWN TO DISTRUST THE SYSTEM.
SADLY THIS IS JUST ANOTHER EXAMPLE OF HOW THIS TOWN CAN CORRUPT EVEN THE BEST OF US.

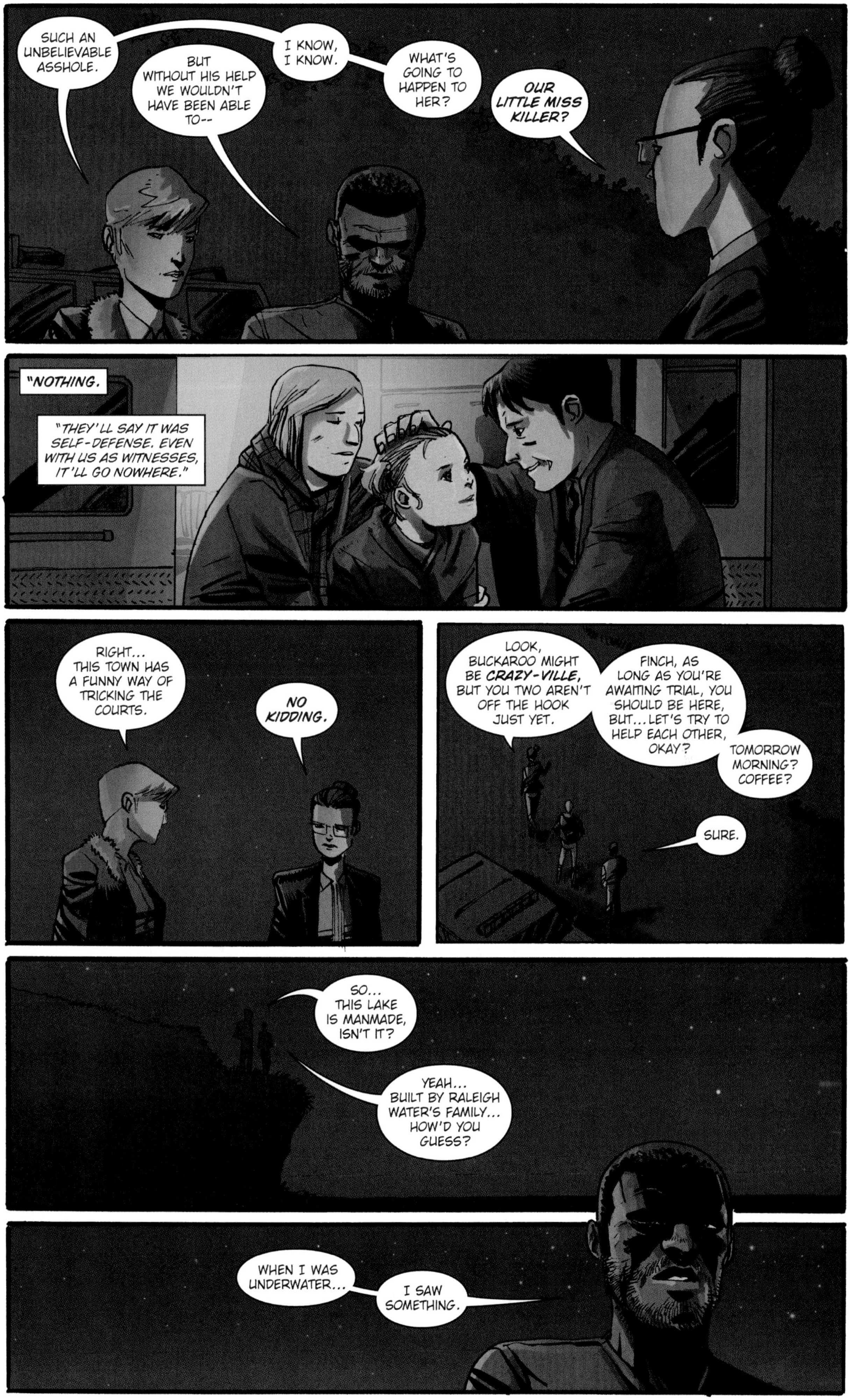
SUCH AN UNBELIEVABLE ASSHOLE.
BUT WITHOUT HIS HELP WE WOULDN'T HAVE BEEN ABLE TO--
I KNOW, I KNOW.
WHAT'S GOING TO HAPPEN TO HER?
OUR LITTLE MISS KILLER?
"NOTHING.
"THEY'LL SAY IT WAS SELF-DEFENSE. EVEN WITH US AS WITNESSES, IT'LL GO NOWHERE."
RIGHT... THIS TOWN HAS A FUNNY WAY OF TRICKING THE COURTS.
NO KIDDING.
LOOK, BUCKAROO MIGHT BE CRAZY-VILLE, BUT YOU TWO AREN'T OFF THE HOOK JUST YET.
FINCH, AS LONG AS YOU'RE AWAITING TRIAL, YOU SHOULD BE HERE, BUT... LET'S TRY TO HELP EACH OTHER, OKAY?
TOMORROW MORNING? COFFEE?
SURE.
SO... THIS LAKE IS MANMADE, ISN'T IT?
YEAH... BUILT BY RALEIGH WATER'S FAMILY... HOW'D YOU GUESS?
WHEN I WAS UNDERWATER...
I SAW SOMETHING.

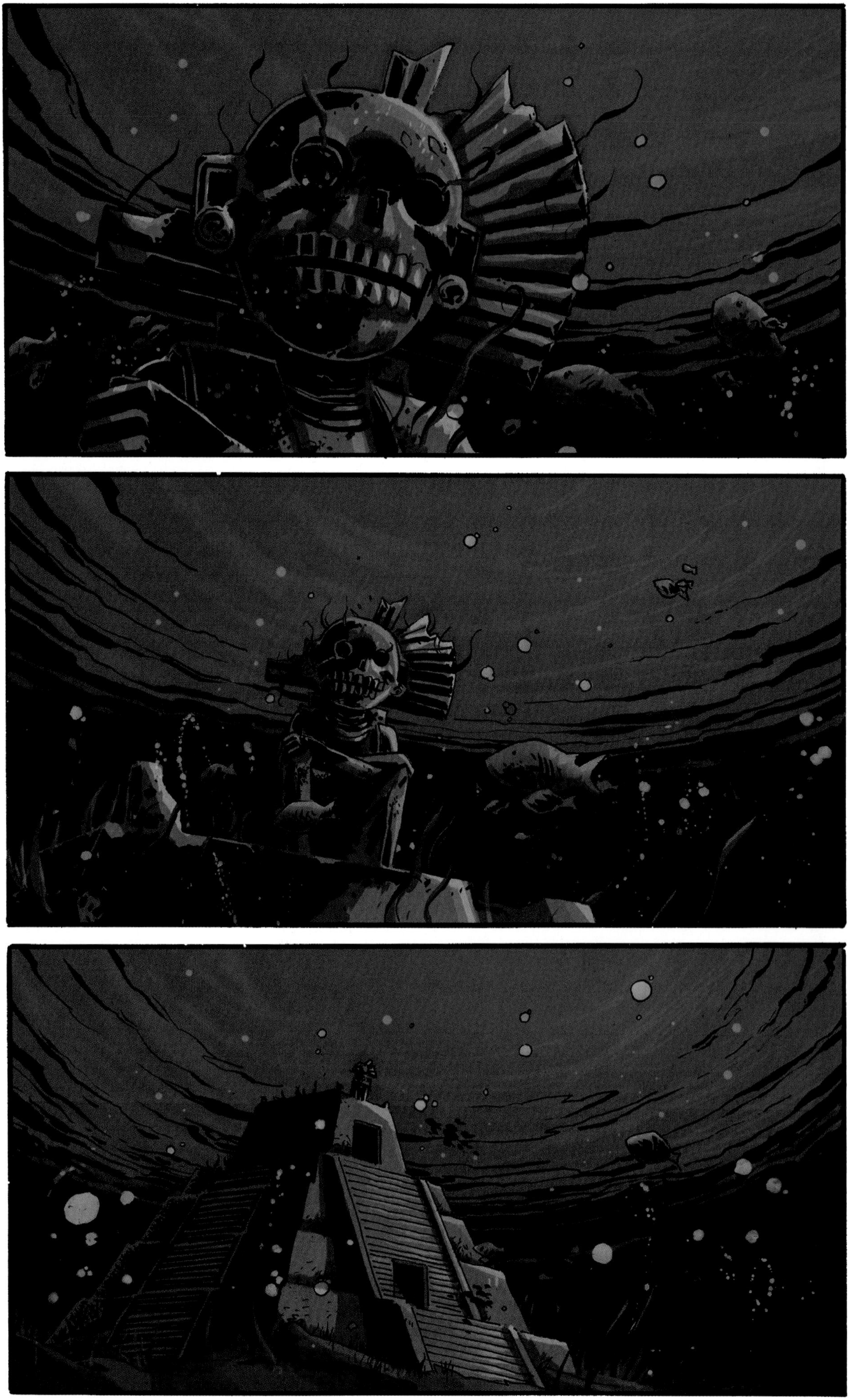

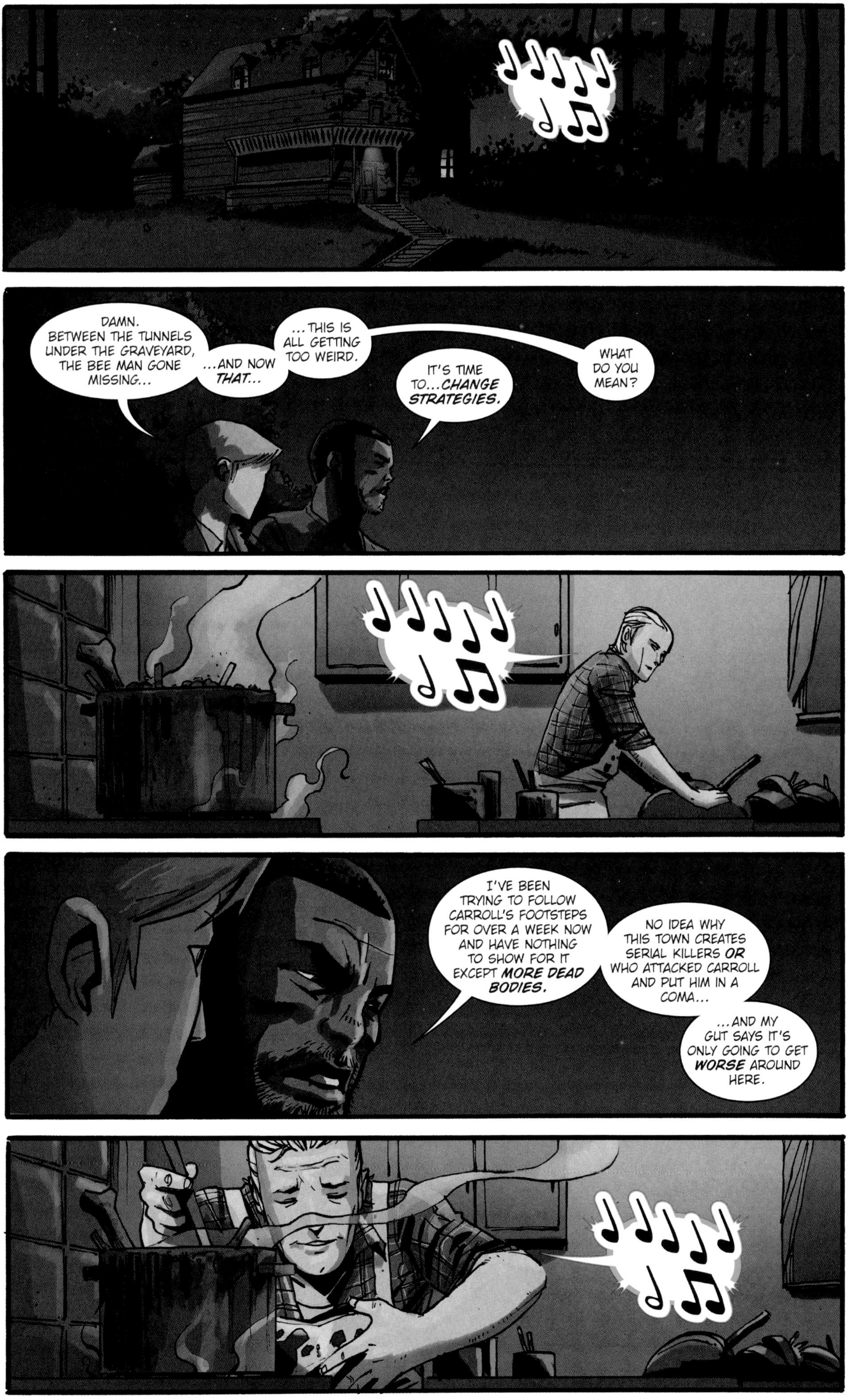
DAMN. BETWEEN THE TUNNELS UNDER THE GRAVEYARD, THE BEE MAN GONE MISSING...
...AND NOW *THAT*...
...THIS IS ALL GETTING TOO WEIRD.
IT'S TIME TO...*CHANGE STRATEGIES.*
WHAT DO YOU MEAN?
I'VE BEEN TRYING TO FOLLOW CARROLL'S FOOTSTEPS FOR OVER A WEEK NOW AND HAVE NOTHING TO SHOW FOR IT EXCEPT *MORE DEAD BODIES.*
NO IDEA WHY THIS TOWN CREATES SERIAL KILLERS *OR* WHO ATTACKED CARROLL AND PUT HIM IN A COMA...
...AND MY GUT SAYS IT'S ONLY GOING TO GET *WORSE* AROUND HERE.

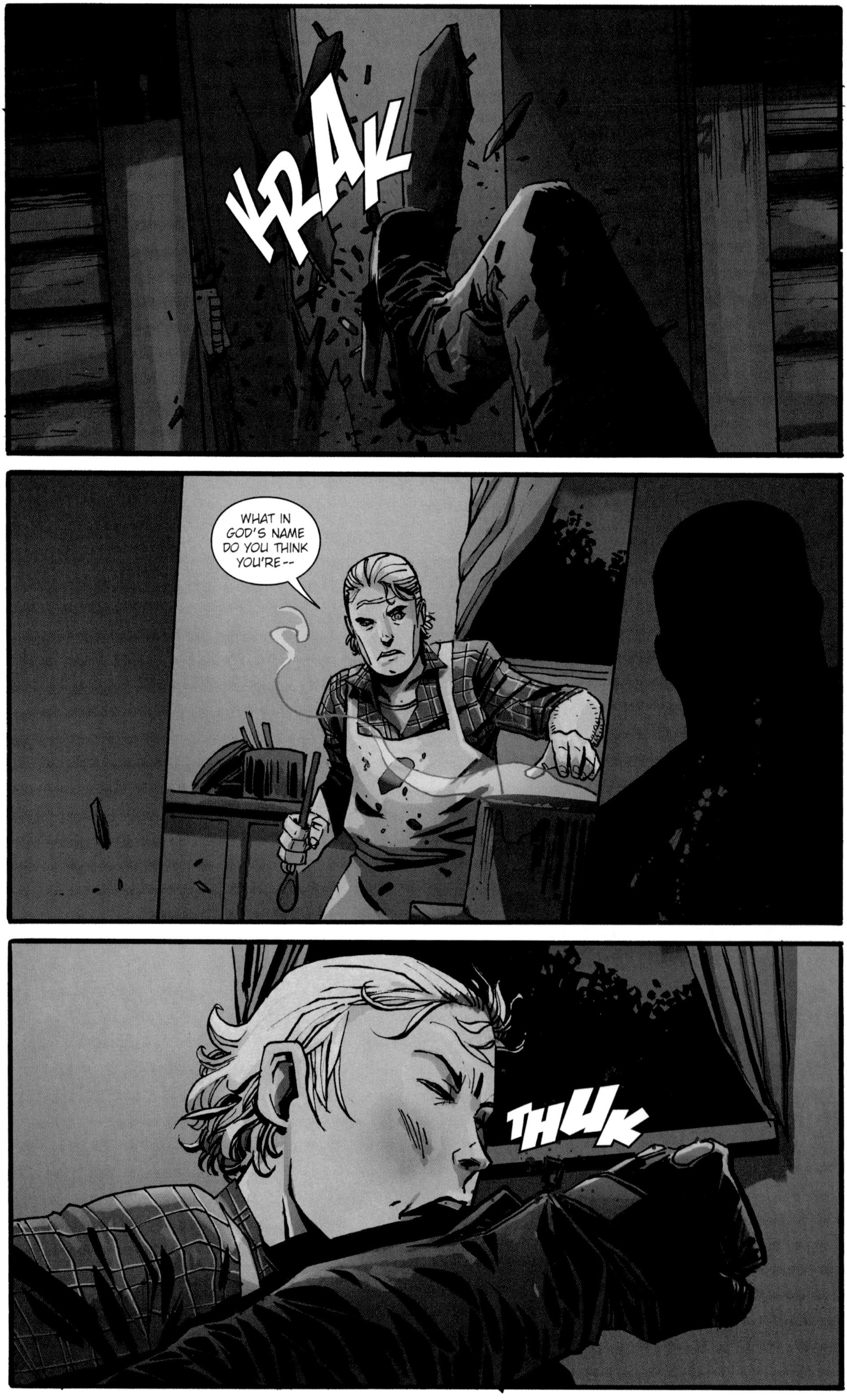
KRAK
WHAT IN GOD'S NAME DO YOU THINK YOU'RE--
THUK

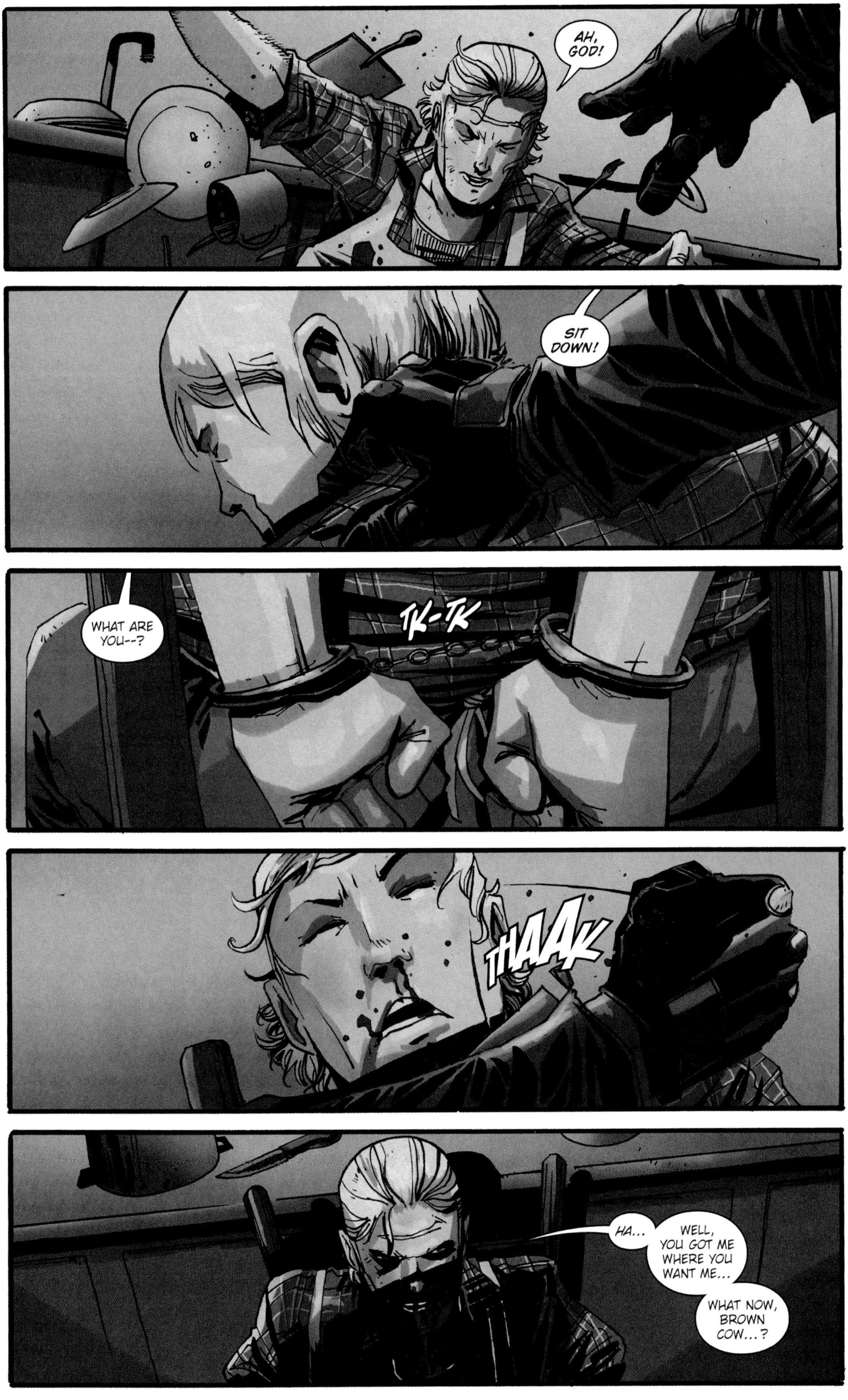
AH, GOD!
SIT DOWN!
WHAT ARE YOU--?
TK-TK
THAAK
HA...
WELL, YOU GOT ME WHERE YOU WANT ME...
WHAT NOW, BROWN COW...?

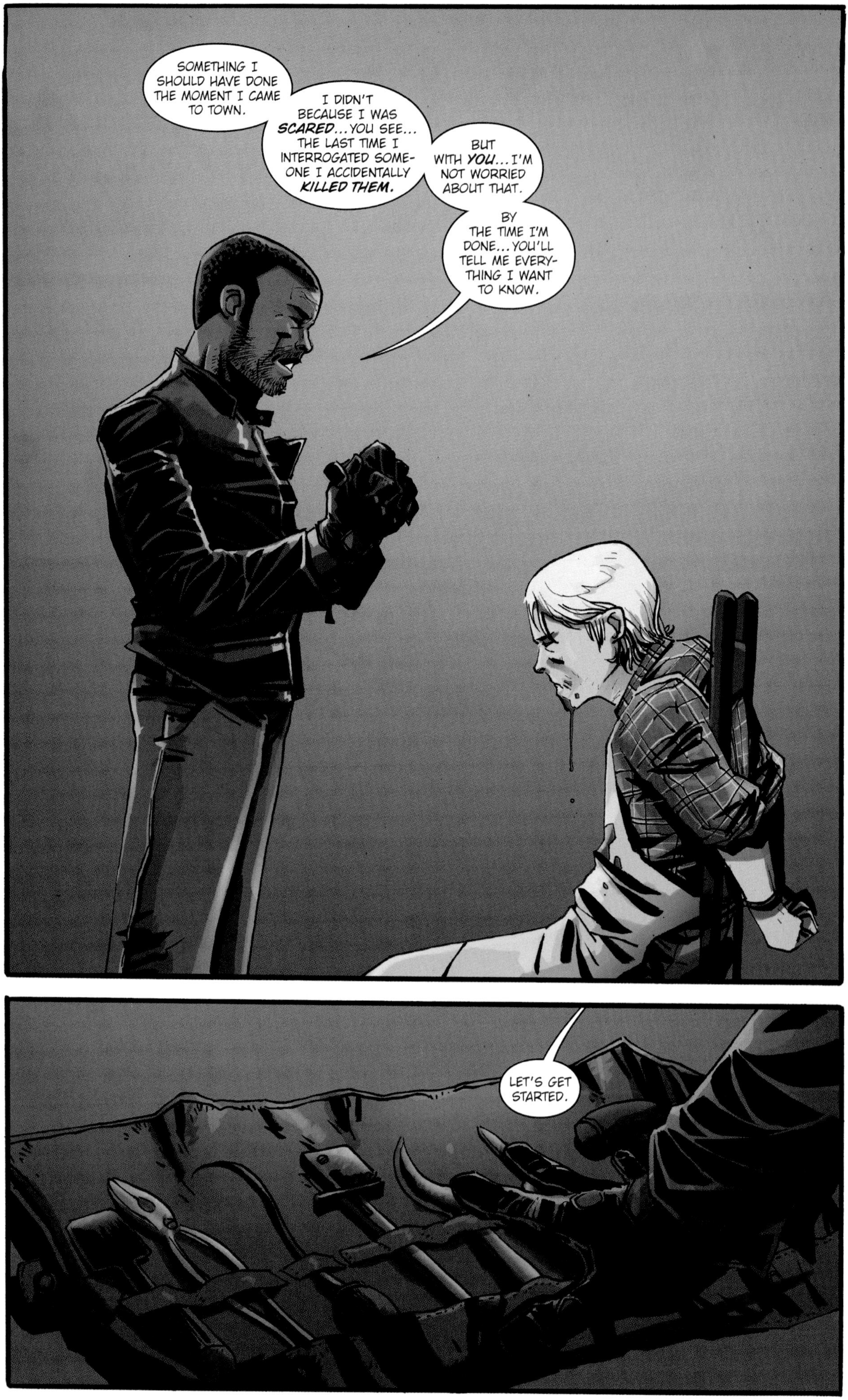
SOMETHING I SHOULD HAVE DONE THE MOMENT I CAME TO TOWN.
I DIDN'T BECAUSE I WAS SCARED... YOU SEE... THE LAST TIME I INTERROGATED SOME-ONE I ACCIDENTALLY KILLED THEM.
BUT WITH YOU... I'M NOT WORRIED ABOUT THAT.
BY THE TIME I'M DONE... YOU'LL TELL ME EVERY-THING I WANT TO KNOW.
LET'S GET STARTED.

TO BE CONTINUED...

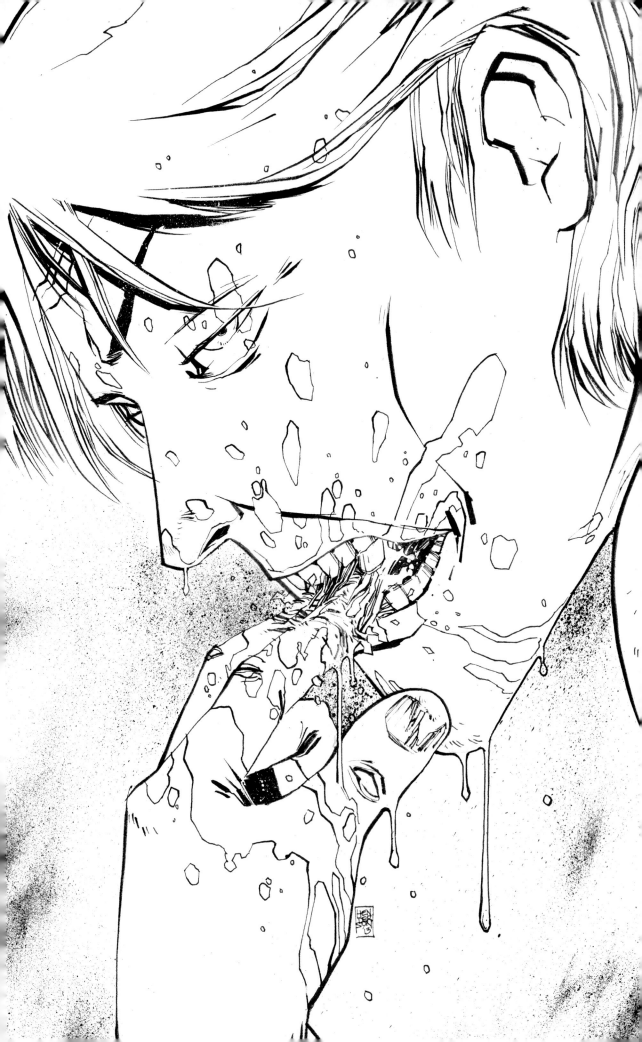

EXTRAS

I

COVER GALLERY

NUMBERS 1-10 + VARIANTS
COLLECTIONS VOLUME 1 & 2

NAILBITER #1 COVER VARIANT ARTISTS:
CHARLIE ADLARD · CHIP ZDARSKY
WES CRAIG · MIKE ROOTH

II

SCRIPT

NUMBER ONE

III

ORIGINAL PITCH

IV

PROCESS

NUMBER ONE PAGES 12-19

V

SKETCHBOOK

MIKE HENDERSON

VI

BIOGRAPHIES

I - COVER GALLERY

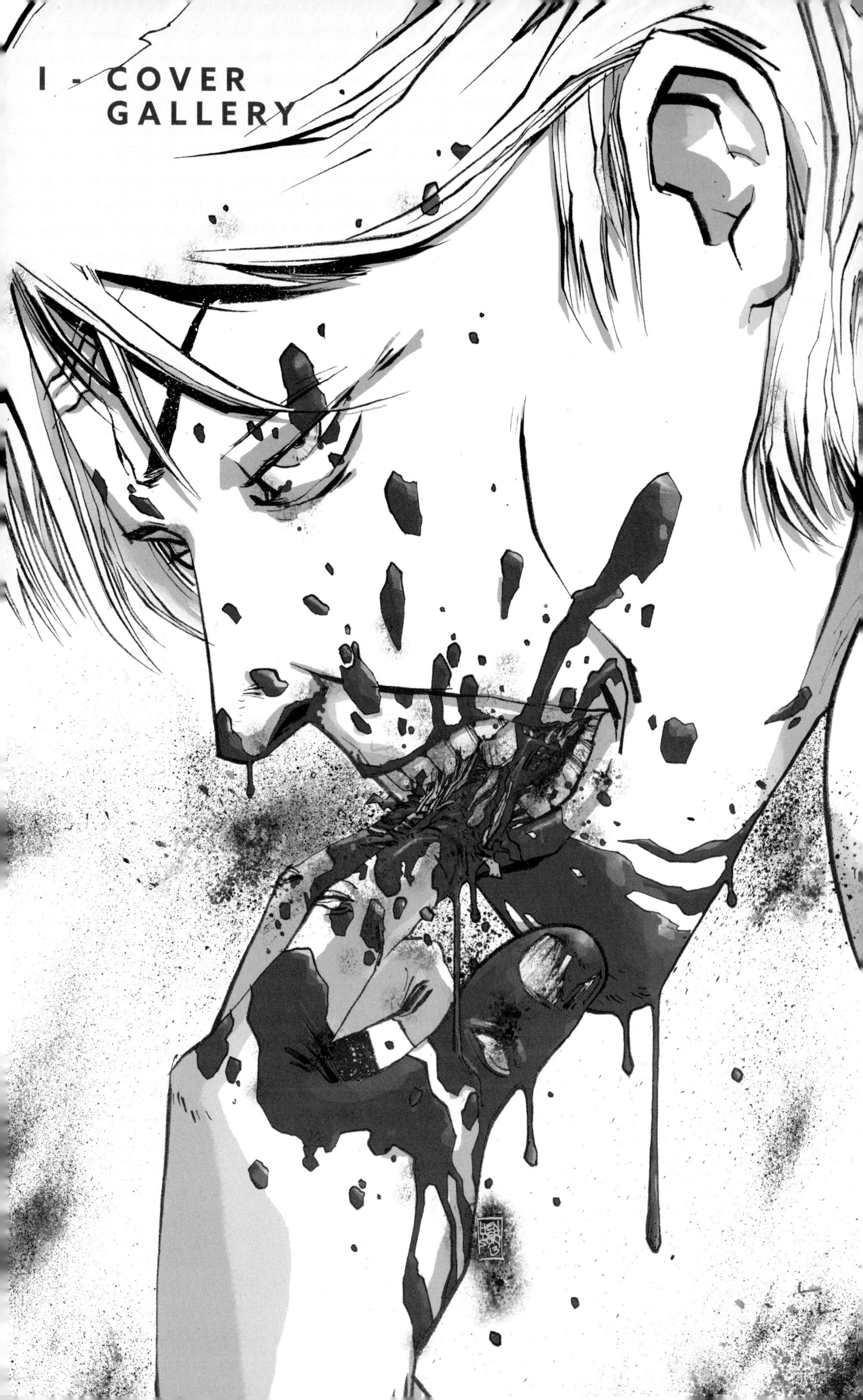

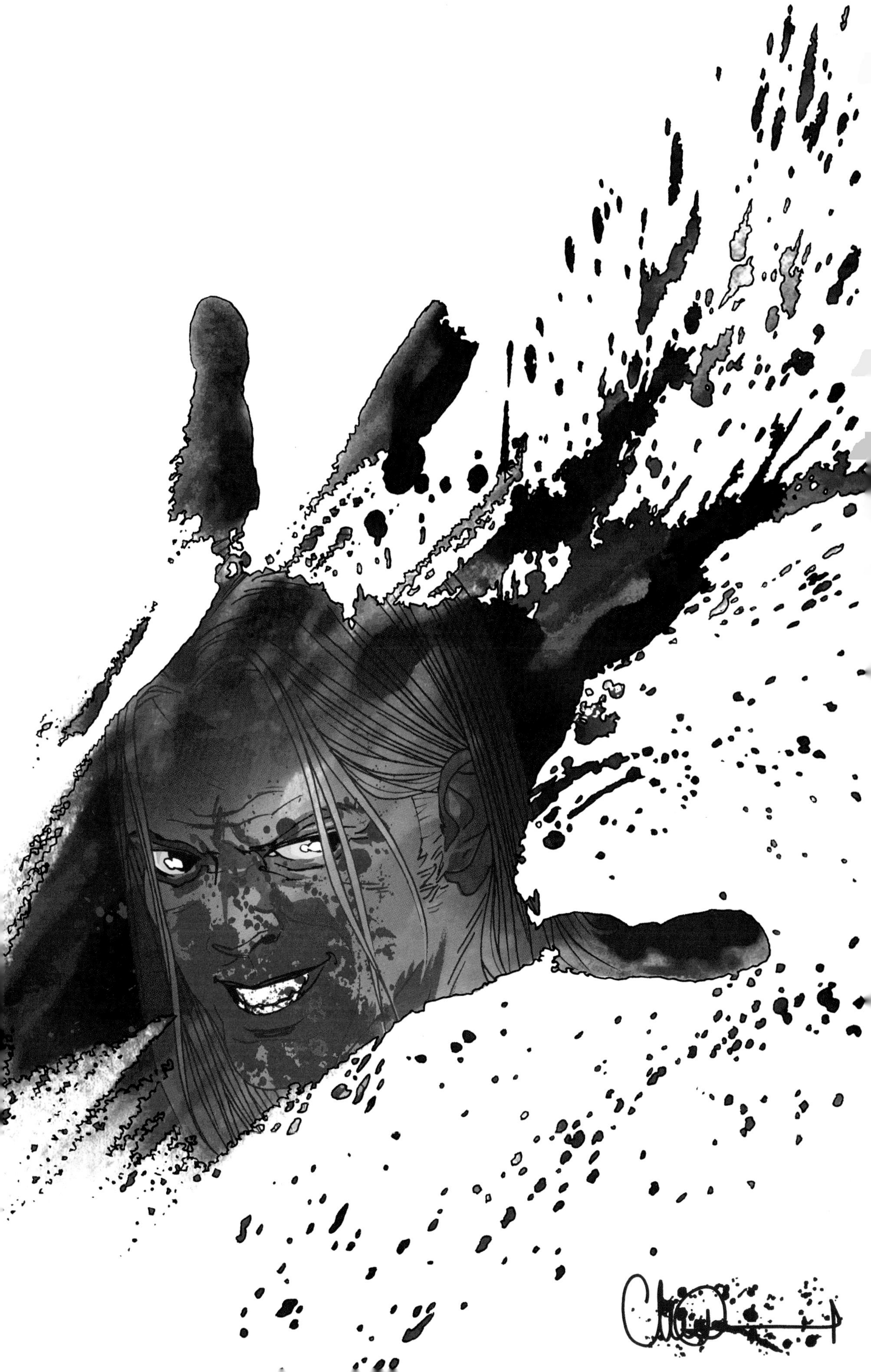

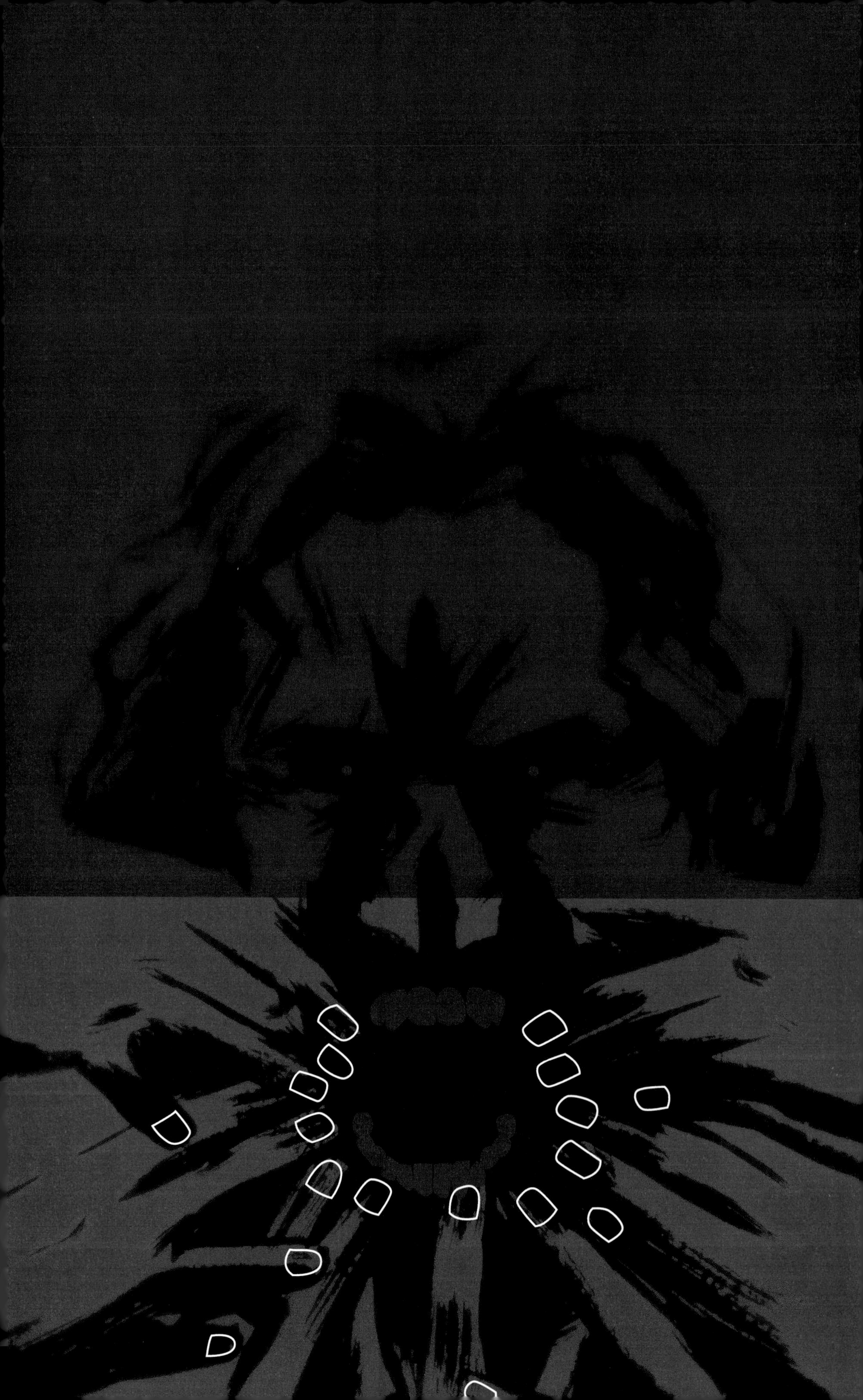

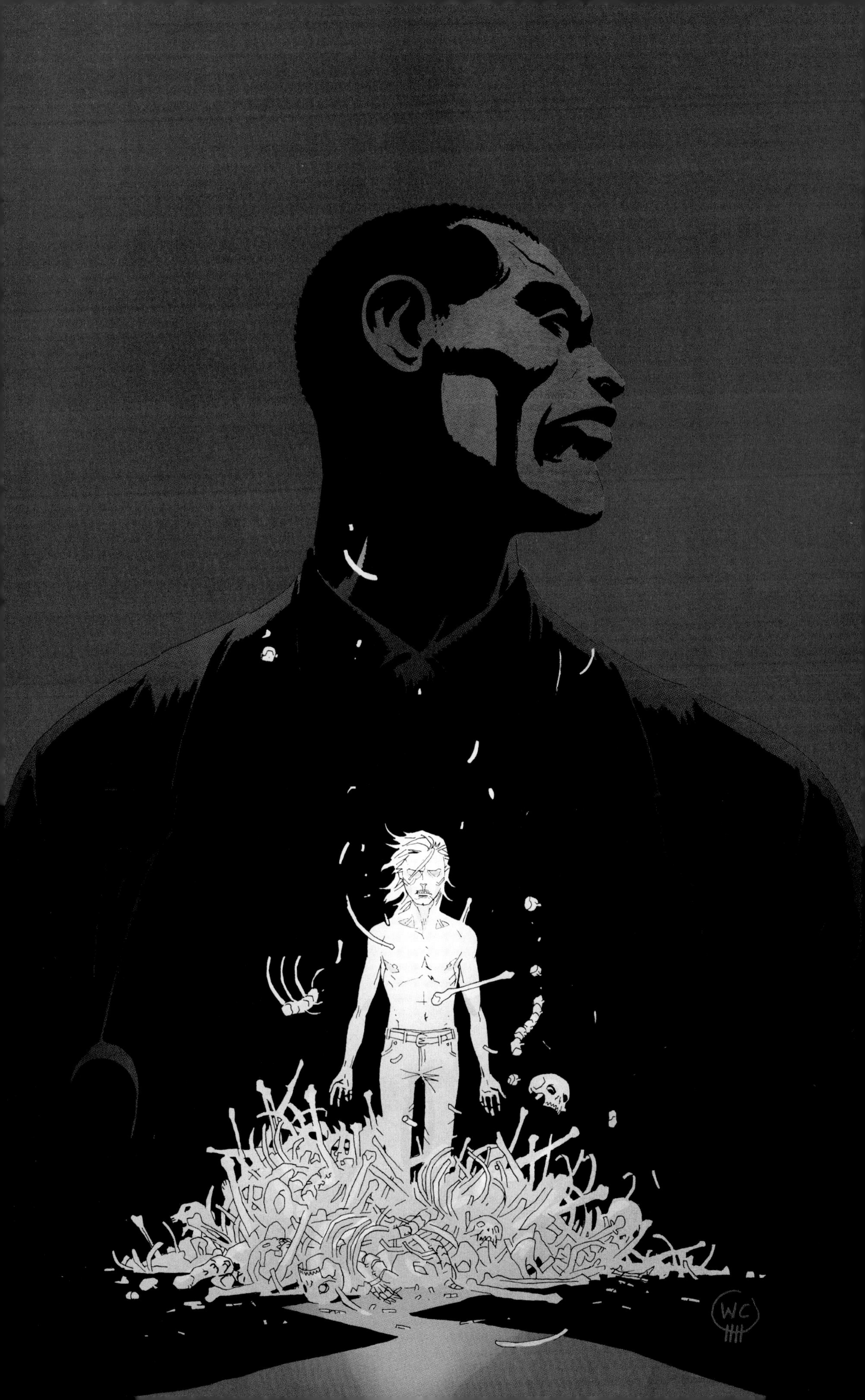

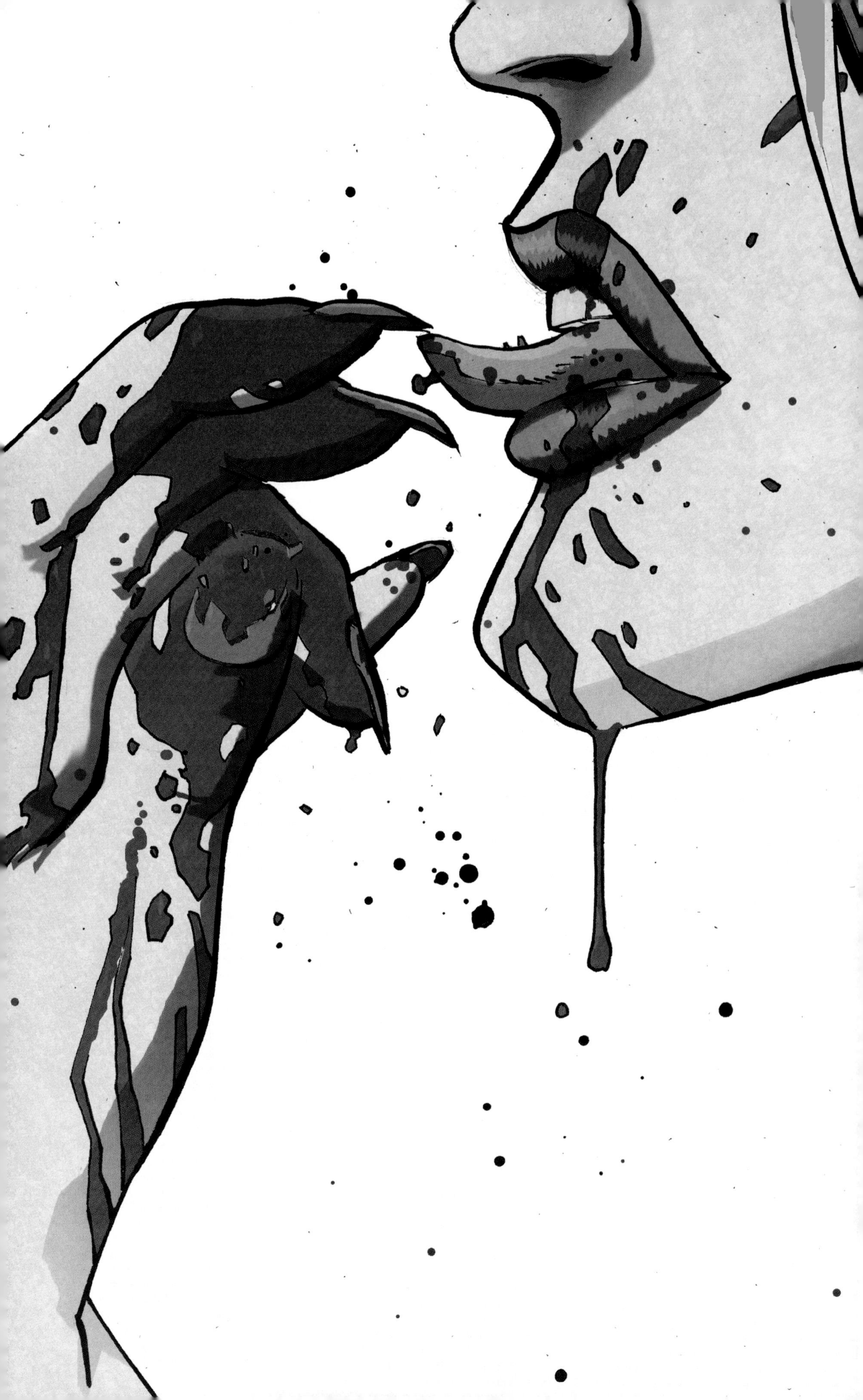

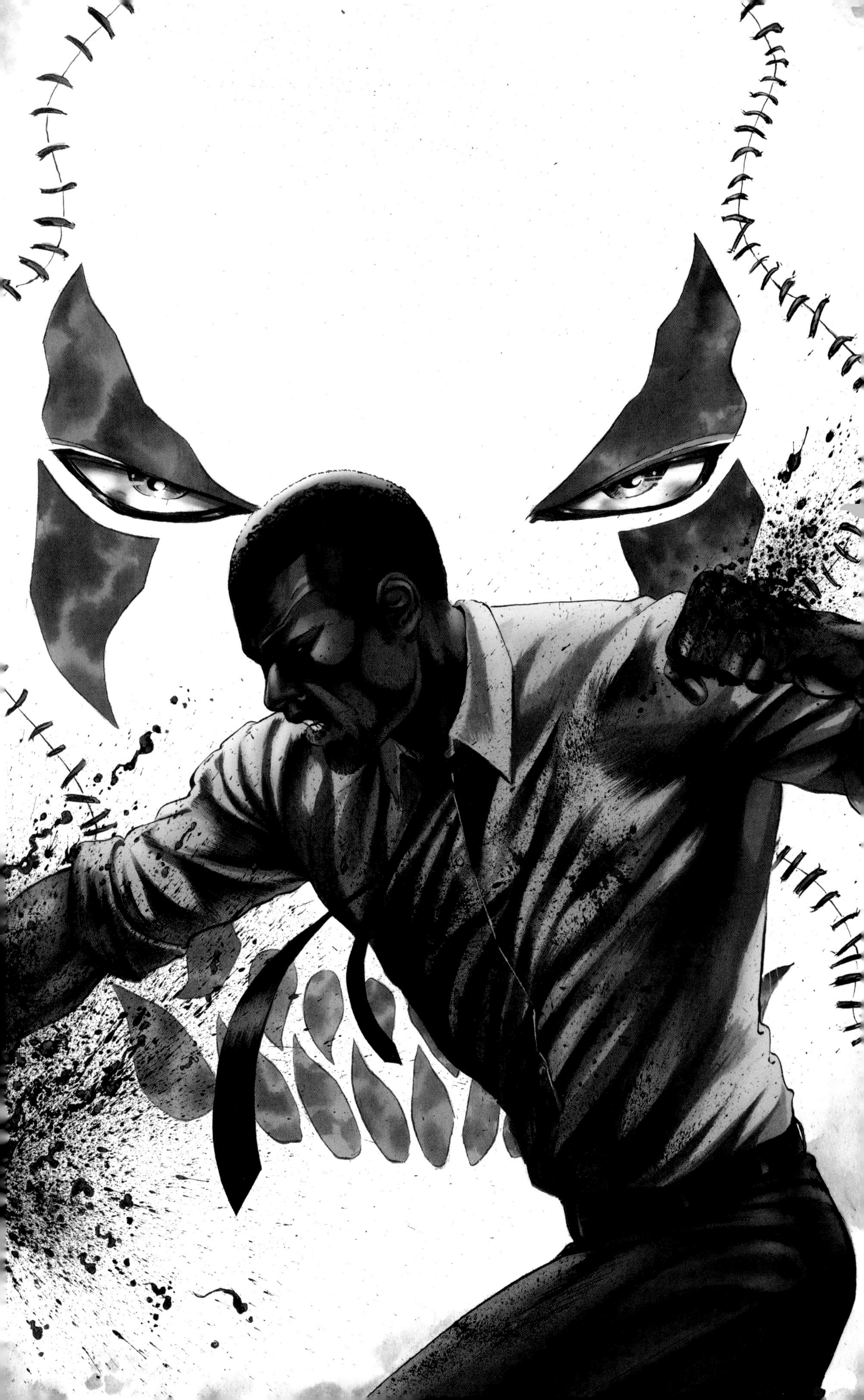

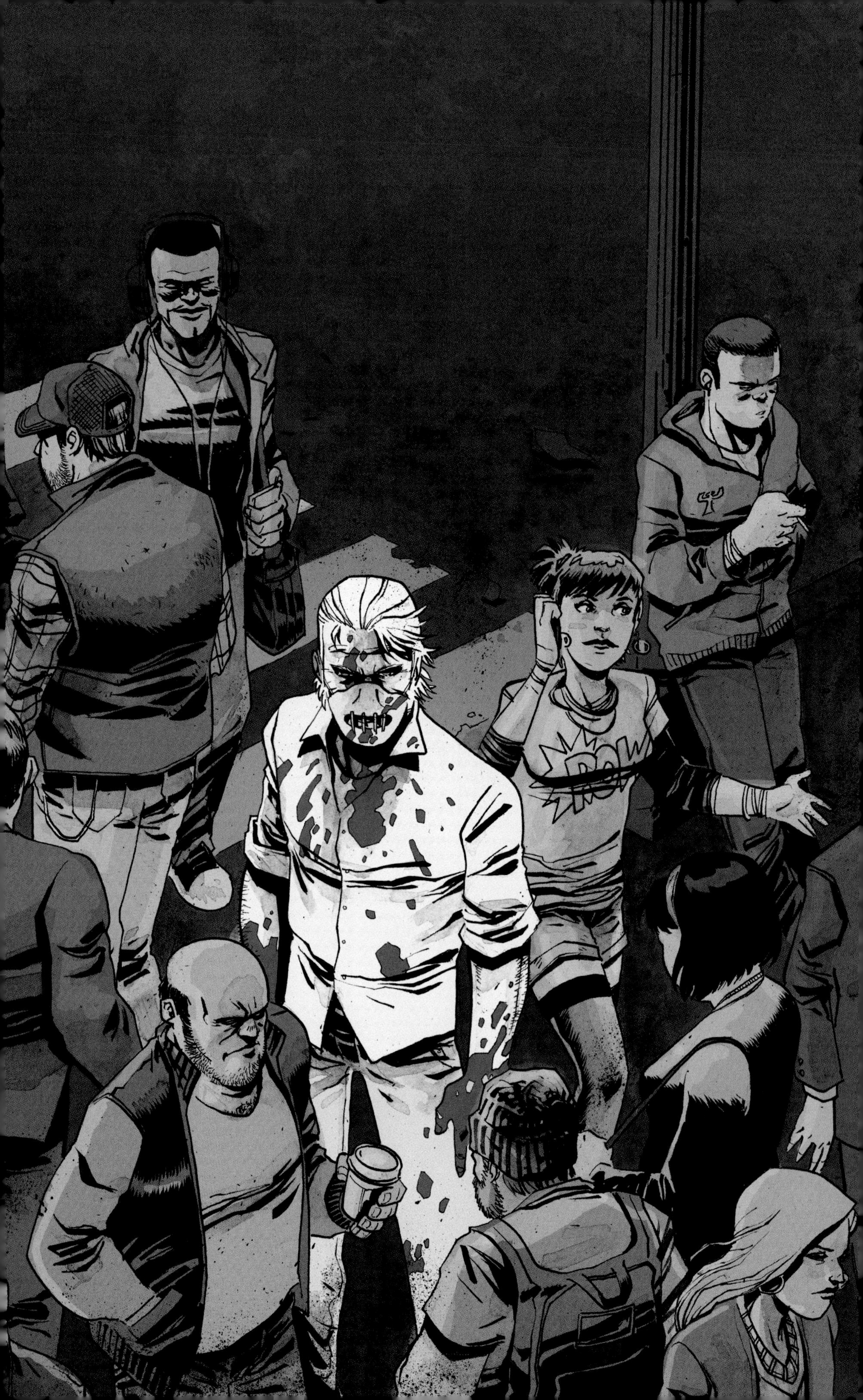

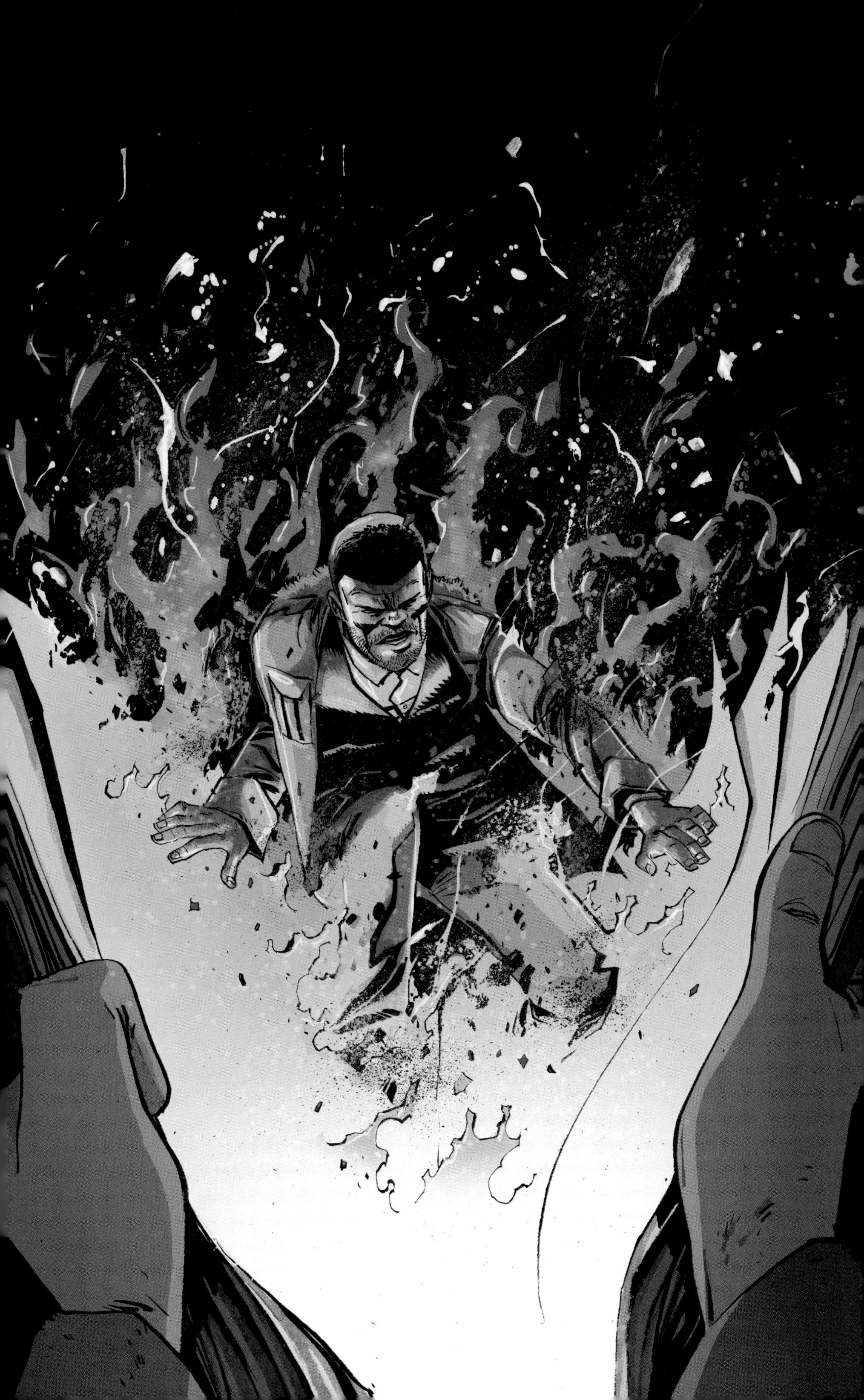

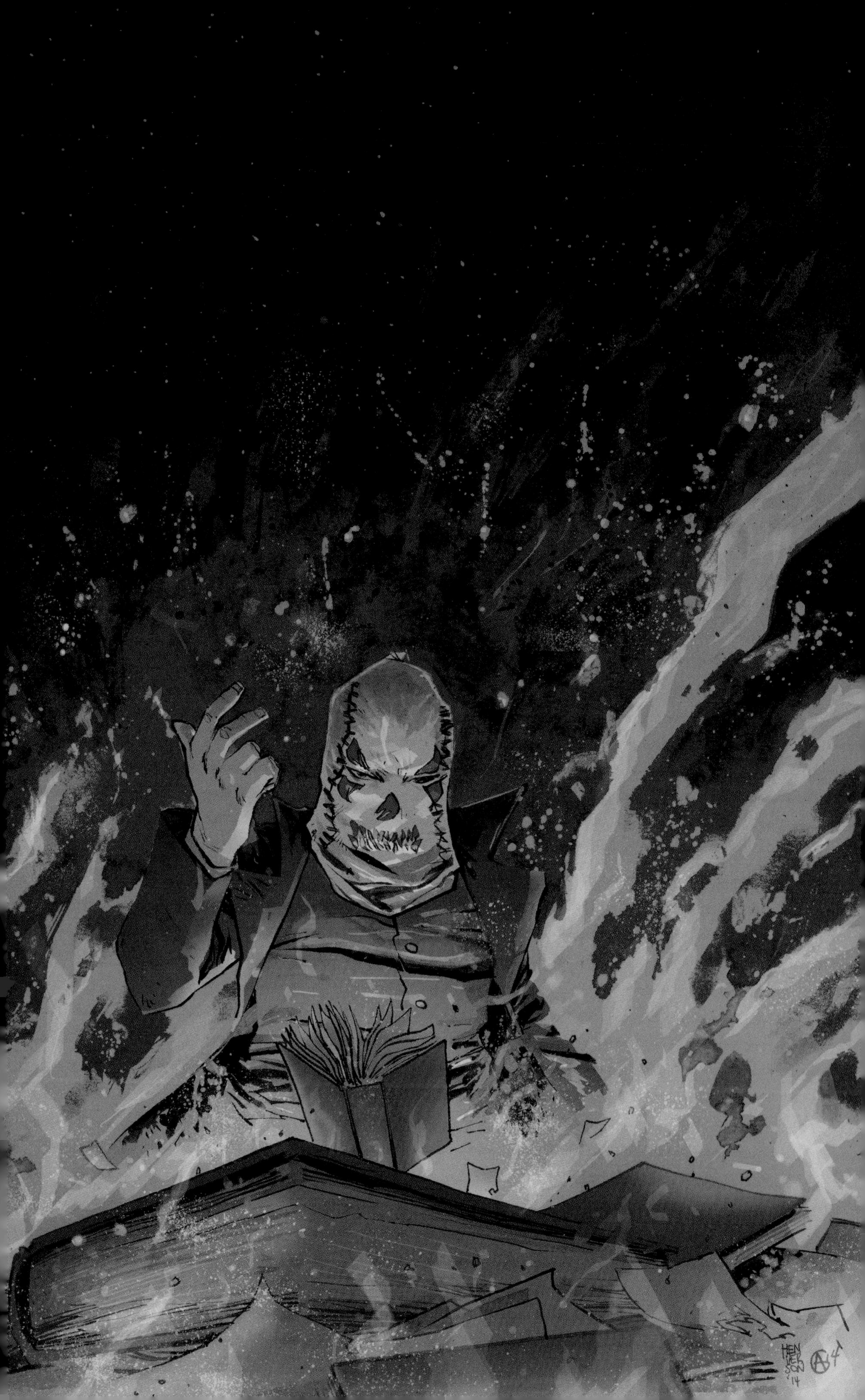

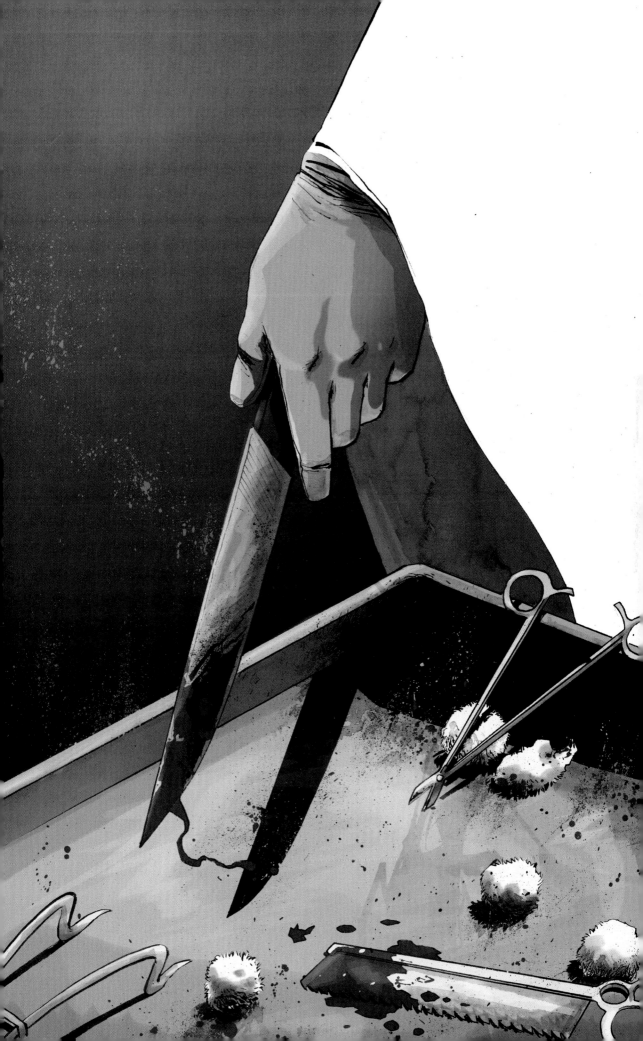

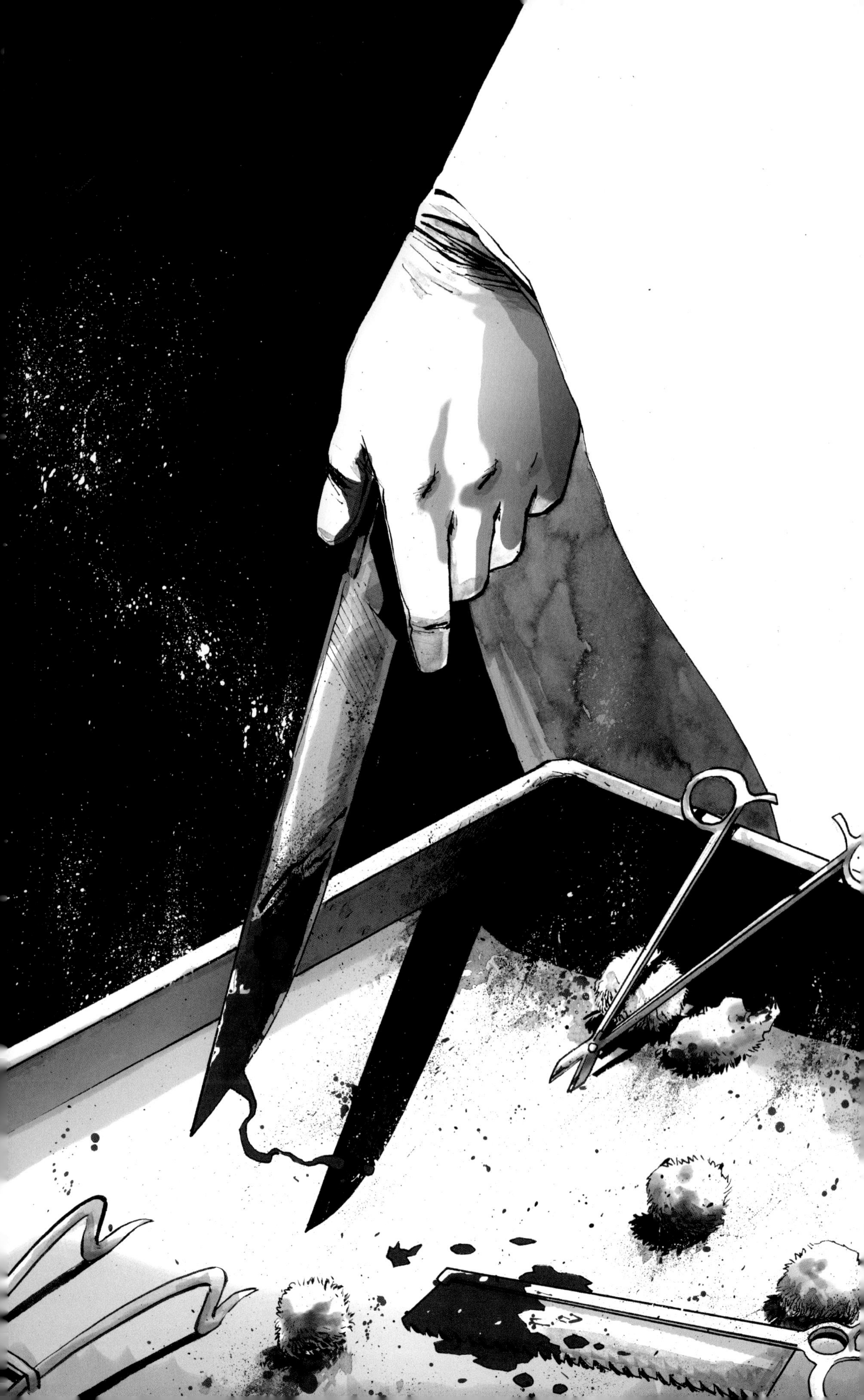

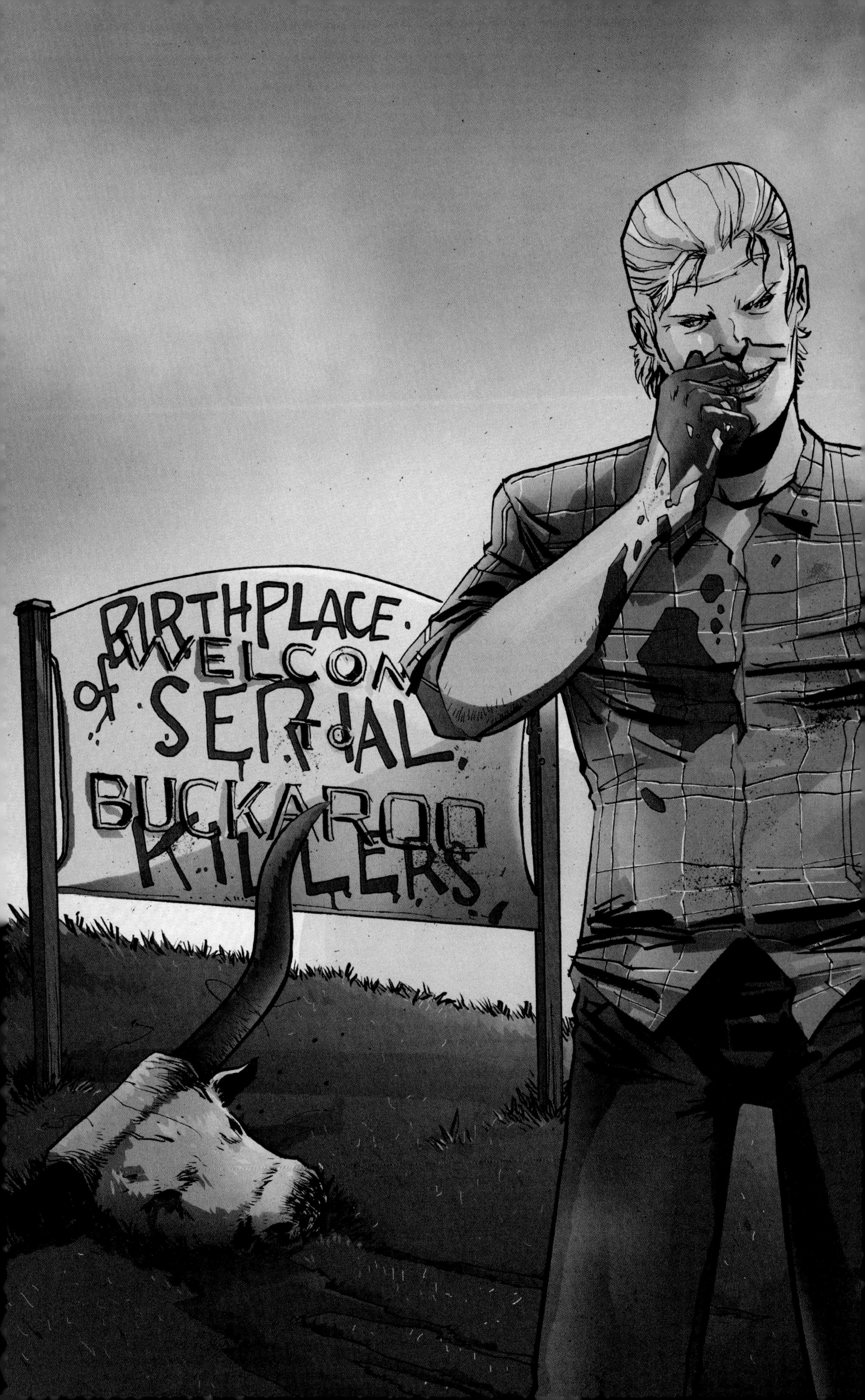
BIRTHPLACE
of WELCOM
SERIAL
BUCKAROO
KILLERS

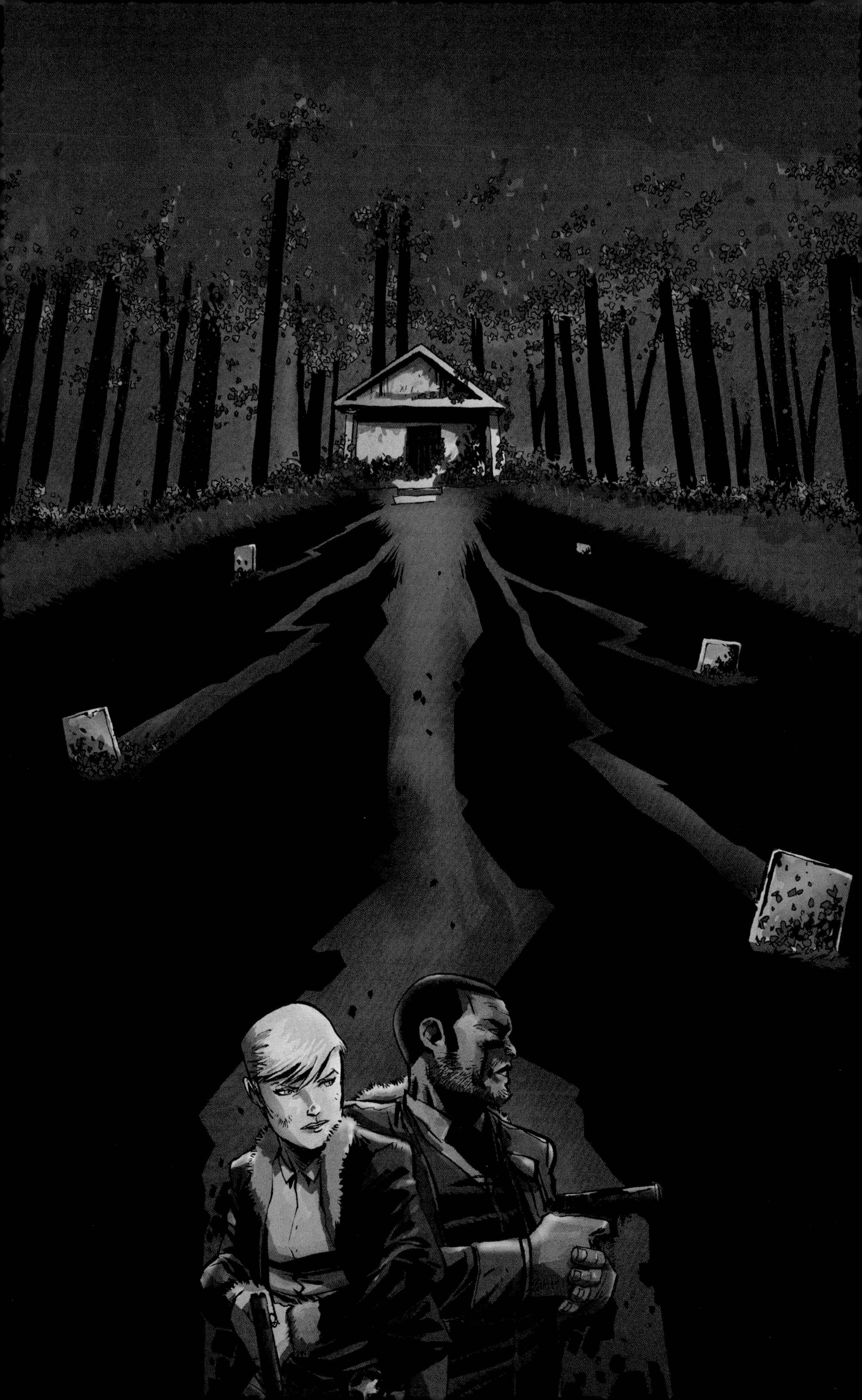

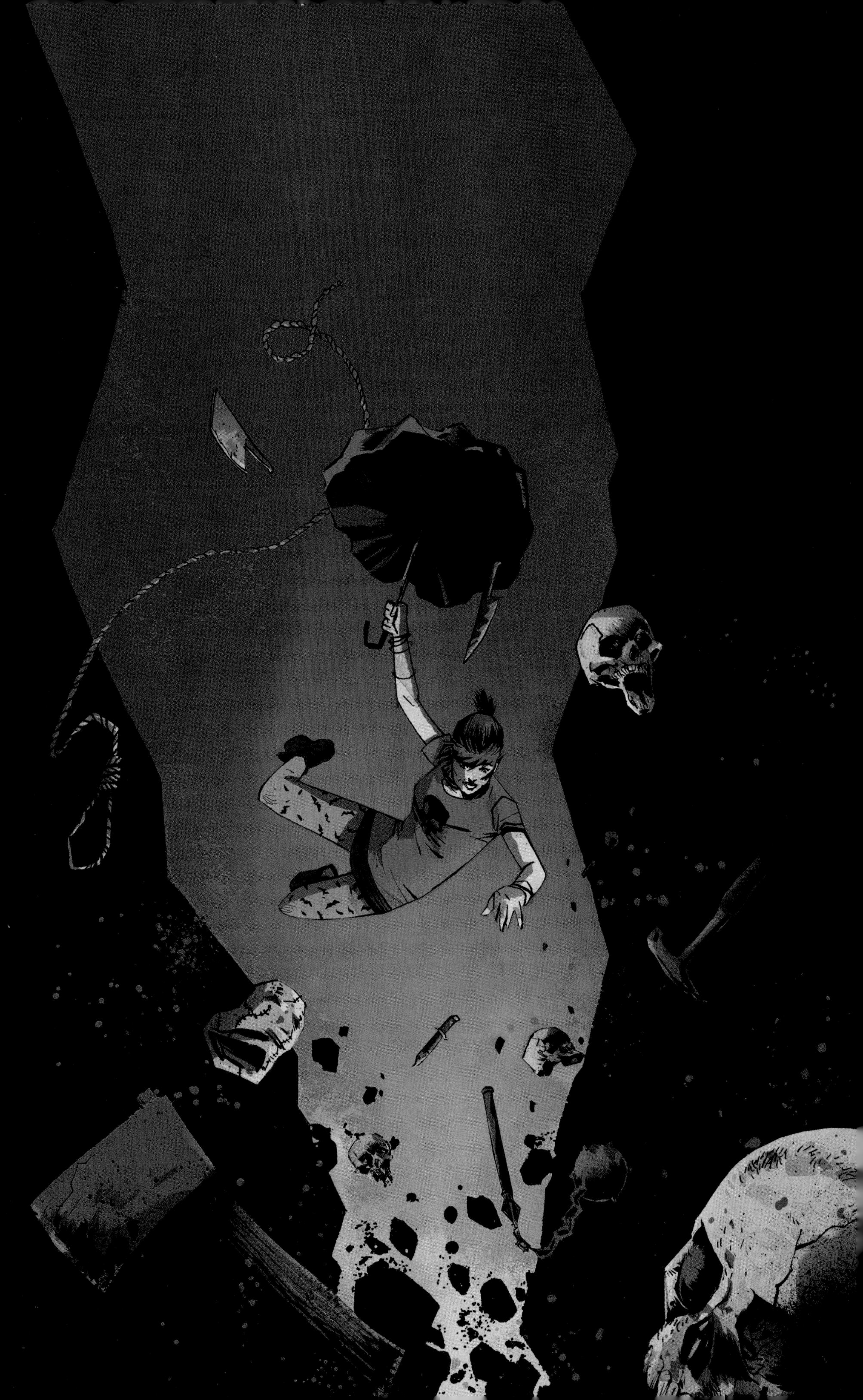

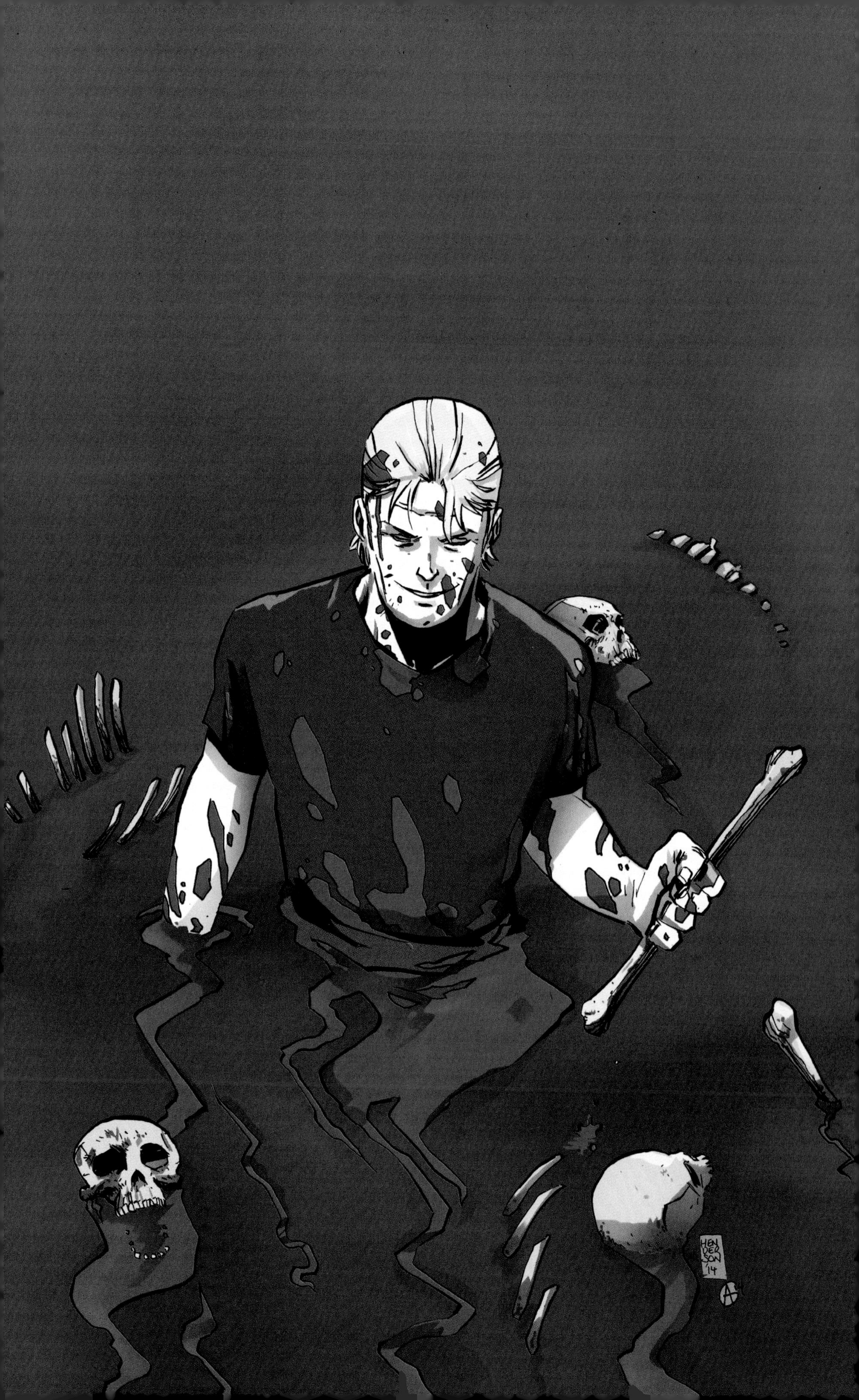

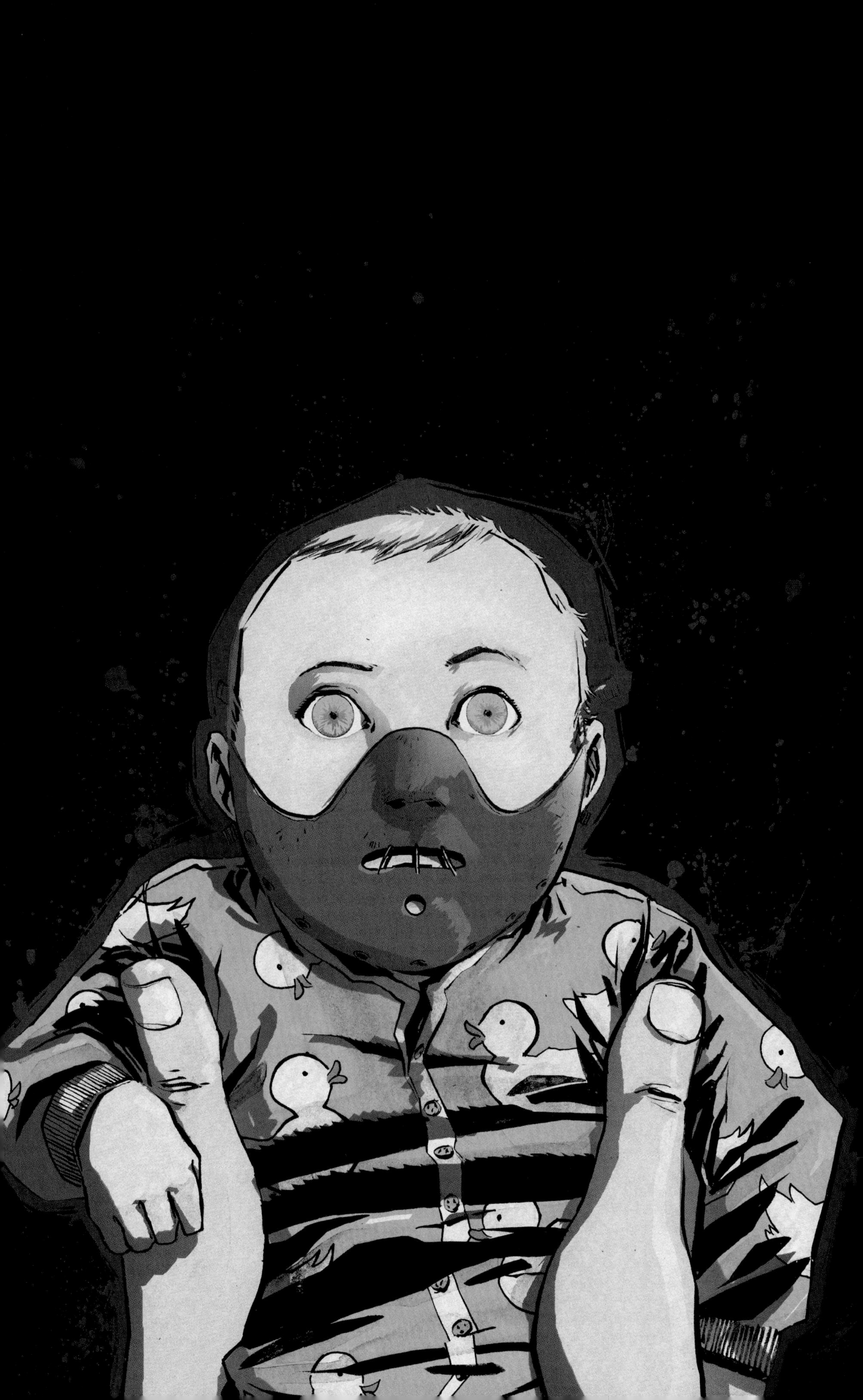

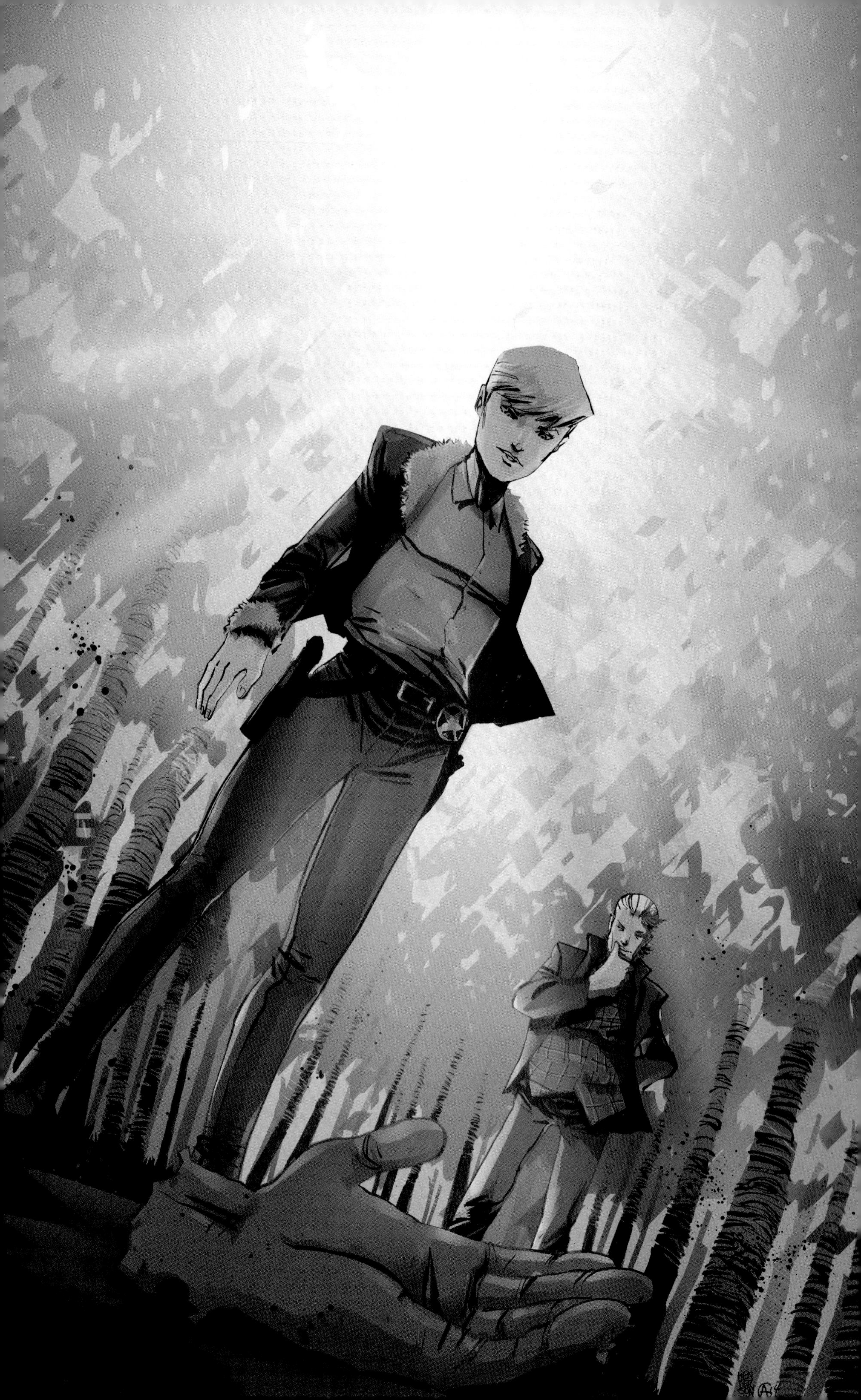

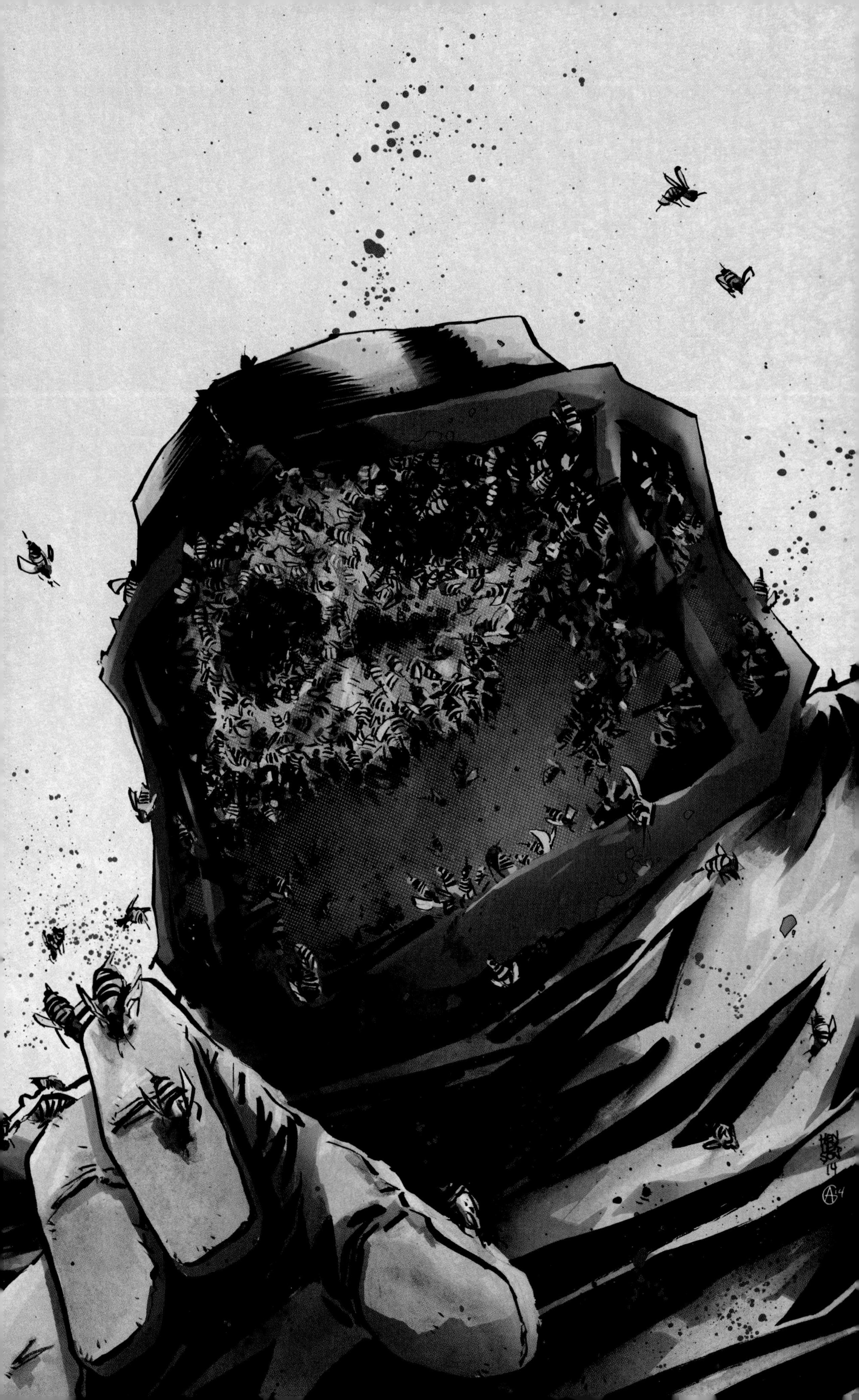

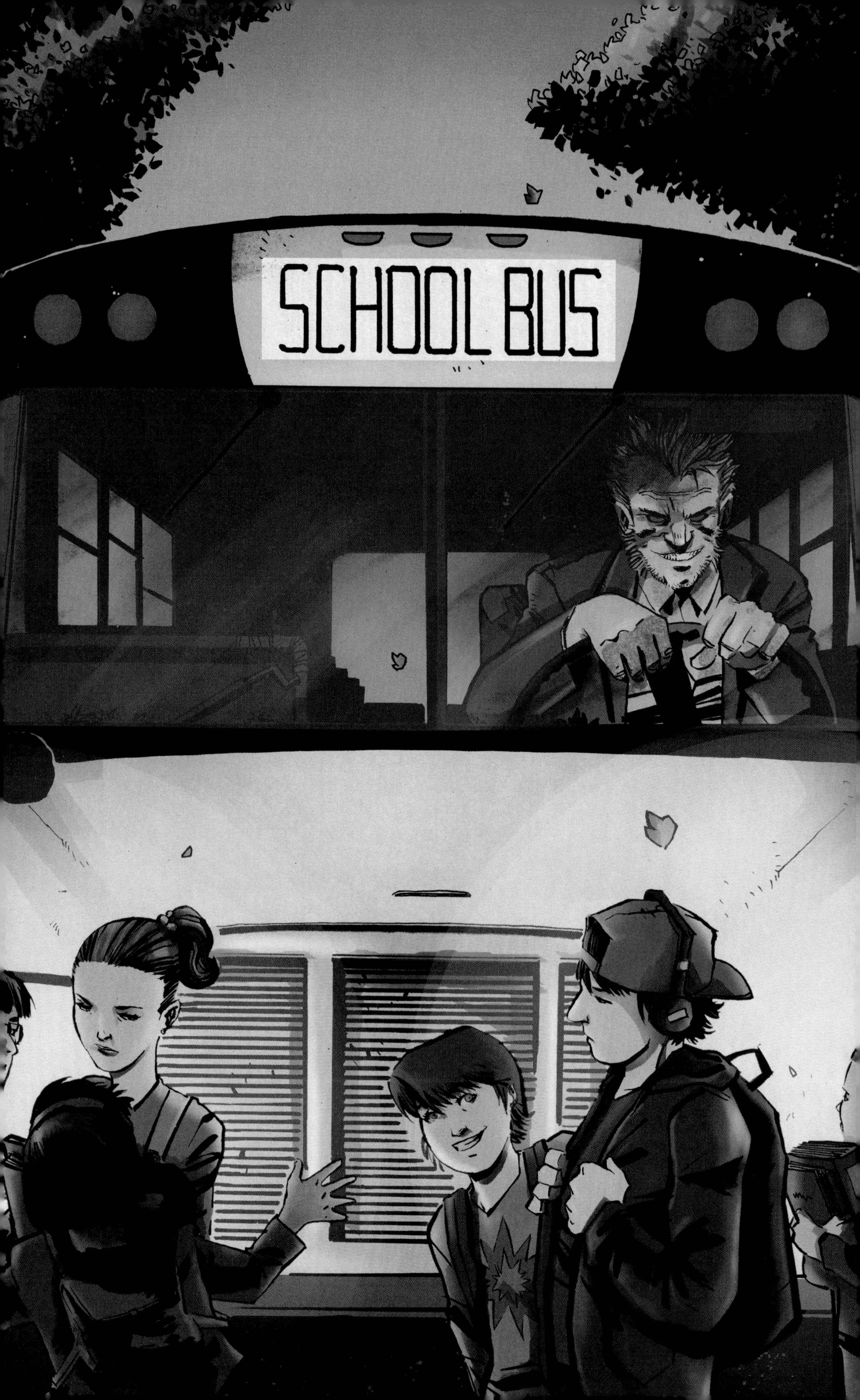
SCHOOL BUS

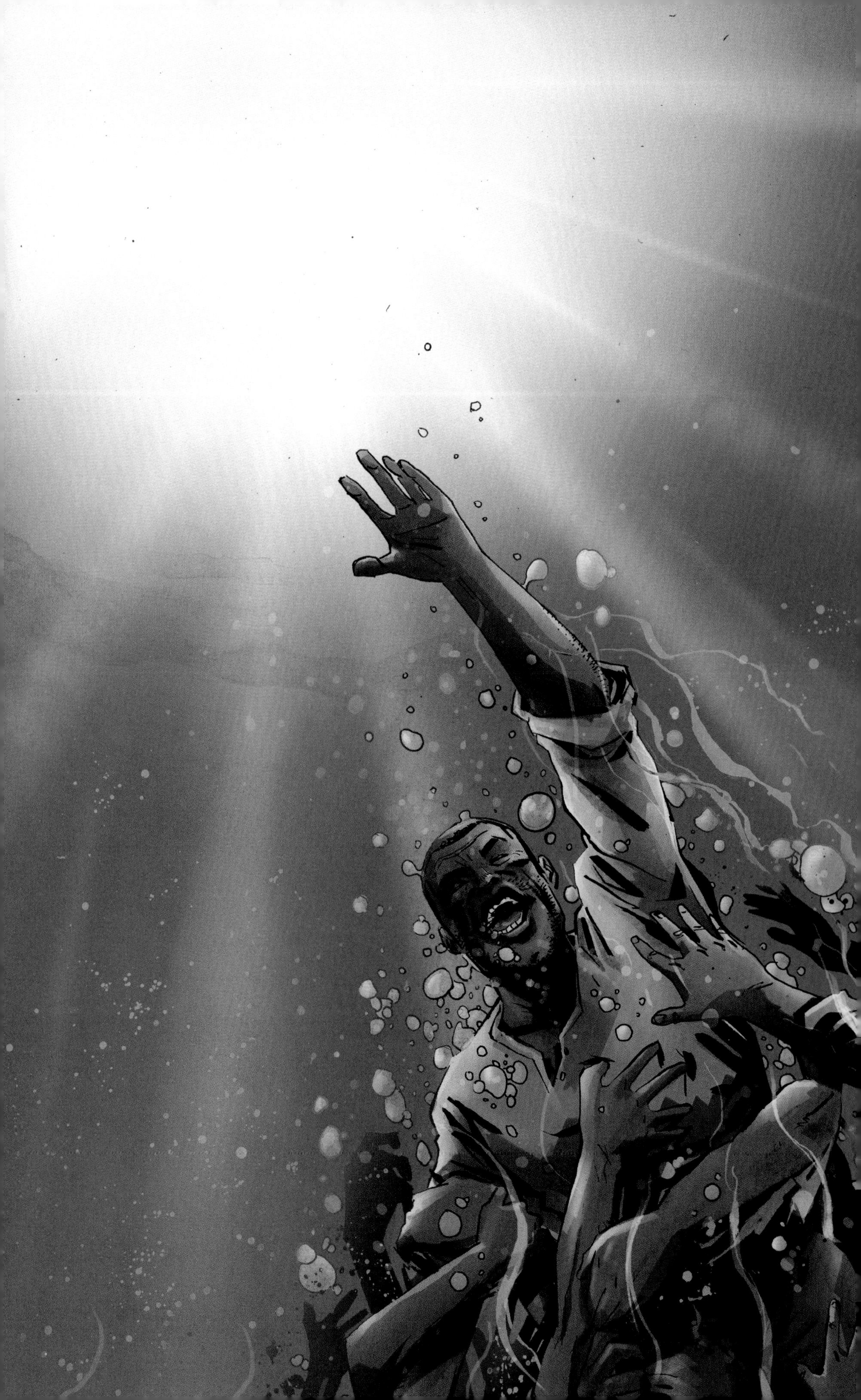

HENDERSON '14

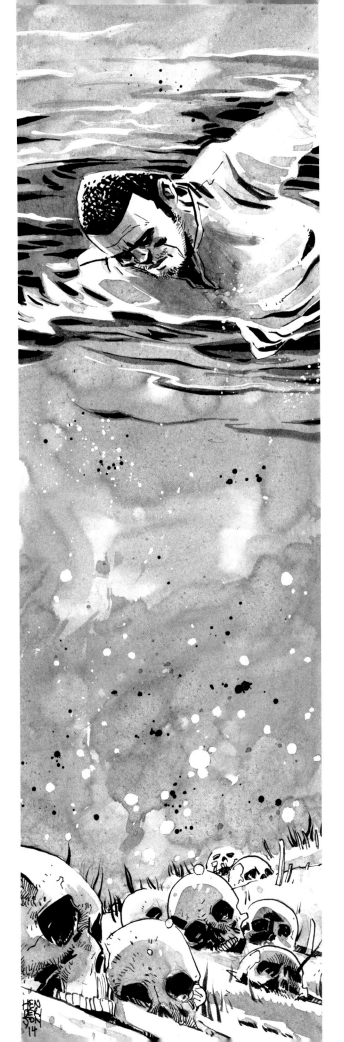

II - SCRIPT
NAILBITER NUMBER ONE

NOTE FROM THE AUTHOR:

A few changes were made to this version of the script for the hardcover collection.

-I removed any spoilers for the series as a whole.

-There were a lot of web links embedded in this script that lead to references online but I cut them all out. Mostly because it would be pointless here.

-You'll notice a lot of names changed and so did a bunch of dialogue. At the lettering stage we made a lot of changes. This is pretty standard for the comic book process. But for this edition, I left those.

-You'll even notice that not everything is exactly as described including the last page. This is because as Mike and I work together we often make changes at the rough art stage. Just like with the dialogue.

Otherwise this is exactly as the script was given to Mike.

NAILBITER #1

Joshua Williamson & Mike Henderson

PAGE ONE

Four page wide panels stacked on to top of each other.
There will be "thump thump" SFX effects on the first five pages that should be tied into the art, into the panel gutters, almost like they bridge the panels together.
As with most of the SFX, I'd like it to be drawn into the page. We should talk about color and how there will be visual cues for colors and how certain characters will need to have color cues. If you think you have room to add a few beats here and there, go for it.

PANEL ONE
PAGE WIDE
A small suburban house late at night. It's your standard small, one level house.
There are five cops running up to the house. Two police patrols have just pulled up to the house. It's all very sudden and urgent. Two of the police officers look like they are in heavier SWAT gear while the rest are in regular patrol uniforms.
Be sure to set the scene. The house is smaller and the cops are all there.

> CAPTION: Riverside, California

> COP (walkie talkie): House is secure, sir! We are LOCKED AND LOADED.

> COP: (walkie talkie): What're your orders, Kohl?!

> SFX: thump thump

PANEL TWO
PAGE WIDE
A very serious looking Agent Kohl is talking into a walkie talkie as he leans on the roof of a police squad car. The red sirens on the car are flashing on his face.

> KOHL: TAKE HIM.

> KOHL: But remember we need Warren ALIVE!

> SFX: thump thump

PANEL THREE
PAGE WIDE
A heavily booted SWAT officer kicks in the front door.

> COP: DO IT!

> SFX: THOOM

> SFX: thump thump thump thump

PANEL FOUR
PAGE WIDE
The door feels packed as the cops and SWAT storm inside the door. Cops are all yelling and aiming guns at the reader. The bright light from outside and the guns are shining in the readers' eyes. This should feel intense, almost like there is a bottleneck in the door filled with cops.

> COPS: FREEZE, WARREN!

> COP: HANDS IN THE AIR, YOU SICK--!

> SFX: thump thump thump thump thump thump

PAGE TWO-THREE

TWO PAGE SPREAD OF THE PLACE
We reveal Nailbiter Warren as he sits on the ground eating the fingers of one of his victims.
The reader is seeing the inside of a murder house. The Nailbiter is eating fingers. Enjoying the taste of them. The fingers are still connected to a dead body on the floor.
It's a large living room with only a few pieces of furniture.
Warren is sitting cross-legged on the tattered, stained carpet. Dead bodies everywhere. Needs to feel gross. In the corner, there are skeletons piled up. Maybe even have a dead body chained to the wall. Nailbiter Warren has the sweetest blue eyes - shining baby blue crystals. Blond hair. Very good looking man. It's important for our last page to reveal that Warren has a very unique and distant look. We need to make sure that his eyes are stunning. He is smiling as he looks up at the police officers.
Really set the scene. Eye level. Full body. Direct shot.
The cops are in the doorway aiming their guns at him.
Behind him, we see newspaper clippings taped to the walls of the "NAILBITER SERIAL KILLER CLAIMS ITS 43RD VICTIM." That one should be visible.

This two page spread is in no way a close up of anything. It might feel complicated but can also be super simple. This will probably be the hardest page of the book to draw.

Everything has a drab feel to it, lots of grays the only color is coming from the blood on the carpet and the blue of Warren's eyes. The light sources are from the cops guns and a few candles around the room.

    COP: FREAK!

    WARREN: Wasn't expecting VISITORS. But don't worry.

    WARREN: There's enough for EVERYONE.

LETTERS: In the upper right corner on this page is a file card stating info about the serial killers. We will do this as the series continues. This might be better suited on the far right of the page.

    FILE: *Buckaroo Butcher. #16*
    Edward Charles Warren. Warren's modus operandi was to kidnap innocent men and women who had the habit of chewing their finger nails. Warren would keep them captive until his victim's nails grew back, and then chew their fingers down to the bone before ultimately killing them. Suspected of forty-six deaths in California alone, this peculiar appetite had the press give Warren the nickname of the -(cont on next card.)

PAGE FOUR-FIVE

TITLE PAGE

This is our design and title page. Imagine if Saul Bass designed this page.

The thumps are getting bigger.
Across the top of the page, we see the words "Nailbiter" in a creepy font. Our names are underneath that, written out. Leave room for the colorist and letterer.

Have the page be full of the Thumps SFX connecting, almost like they continue from the last two page spread. Maybe even have one that bridges the gaps. With each Thump they get more and more chaotic, like the beating is getting louder.

On the far right, we are inside the last THUMP. It's the frame of a panel.
And inside the THUMP frame, we can fully see FINCH's chest, tie, and part of his face. His face looking stressed. It's pretty much a cut out from the next page, but we can't see that he is holding a gun to his head yet. This is almost as though it's a shot coming into focus.

I know all of this might sound complicated but it can be simple. Let's talk when you start the roughs.

TITLE (across the top in a creepy font.)

    Nailbiter. Chapter One. "There Will Be Blood."

PAGE SIX

Five panels stacked on top of each other. Mostly repeats.

PANEL ONE
PAGE WIDE
Eye Level. Direct shot.
FINCH about to kill himself with a small handgun. Finch is sitting on the edge of the bed, stressed out and obviously about to shoot himself in the head.
The page before this is pretty much a cut out from this panel. It's like it was cropped on the last page, but now we get to see the whole thing. For this first panel, let's just show him from the waist up. No panel. Just his chest, his head, and the gun to his head. No bed yet.
Finch is wearing a white tank top under a plain white dress shirt. The dress shirt is open and loose, like he is exhausted from his day.

PANEL TWO
Now we zoom out to reveal that he is sitting on the edge of a bed in a small dingy hotel room. Same pose as the last panel, but now we can see his waist and part of his legs.
Next to his knees on the right side of the panel, we see a small nightstand with a lone lamp. Next to that lamp, we can see a cell iphone. Just resting there, but not in focus.

    CAPTION: THREE YEARS LATER

PANEL THREE
SAME AS PANEL TWO.
No movement. Finch is still thinking about killing himself. His gun aimed right at his head.
    CAPTION: SAN ANTONIO, TEXAS

PANEL FOUR
SAME AS PANEL TWO.

PANEL FIVE
SAME ANGLE EXCEPT… The cell phone buzzes. Finch looks over at it, his eyes and head tilt to see who is calling as he slightly starts to lower his gun. The stress of the scene breaks just a little bit.

    SFX: BBBZZZ

PAGE SEVEN

This page will have one large panel across the top with six underneath it. Like a Nine panel

grid with one full tier. This page is mostly a bunch of back and forth on the phone. Go with
lots of room for dialogue. No background except for with the first panel. This might be hard to
pull off, so let's take a look at the layouts.

PANEL ONE
PAGE WIDE
Finch is looking down at his phone with disappointment. He knows that on the other line is his
buddy Kohl, but you'd think it was an overbearing mother calling.
Show Finch from the waist up. Still holding the gun in his other hand, but now at his side. He
is standing and looking down at his phone. Leave a lot of open space in the panel.

    SFX: BBZZZZ

    FINCH: Shit.

    FINCH: *Sigh*

    SFX: BEEP.

STARTING THE SIX PANEL GRID
PANEL TWO
Finch has answered his cell phone. He looks annoyed.

    FINCH: Are you in trouble, Kohl?

PANEL THREE
Cut to Kohl talking on his phone. Make sure we can tell this is the same guy from page one. He
is outside, with a blue sky.

    KOHL: There you are! Damn, Finch. I've been trying to reach you all day. You too
    busy to check your messages now?

PANEL FOUR
Back to Finch looking up, unhappy.

    FINCH: I'm going to go ahead and ask AGAIN… Are you in TROUBLE?

    KOHL (PHONE): No, of course not. Why do you always jump to that conclusion?

    FINCH: Did you forget that I can always sense a LIAR?

PANEL FIVE
Kohl's face with a smile.

    KOHL: Haha. EXACTLY. And that's why I need you to bring your skills out here.

    FINCH (PHONE): HERE being WHERE?

    KOHL: Buckaroo, Oregon, buddy.

    KOHL: TODAY. Like now. ASAP. First flight, rent a car, WHATEVER. Just get on the road.

PANEL SIX
Finch's face. Annoyed.

    FINCH: Now why would I want to do that?

    KOHL (PHONE): Because… I figured it out.

    FINCH: Figured WHAT out?

PANEL SEVEN
Kohl's face with a mischievous smile.

    KOHL: Ha.

    KOHL: What do you THINK?

PAGE EIGHT

PANEL ONE
LARGE PANEL-PAGE WIDE
Kohl is standing in a graveyard. Pull back so we can see that it's a crazy massive graveyard
with many tall, bizarre looking grave stones and crosses. Keep Kohl small in the shot.

    KOHL: The Buckaroo Butchers.

    KOHL: THE SECRET. I cracked it.

    KOHL: But you need to come and see this. You won't BELIEVE it unless you do.

PANEL TWO
Back to Finch in the hotel room. Now he is pacing around the room. Frustrated. Scratching the
side of his head with his gun. It should feel tense.

    FINCH: That's not exactly my EXPERTISE, Kohl, and I don't have time for your SCOOBY
    DOO BULLSHIT.

KOHL (PHONE): Listen, I know about your SUSPENSION and the trial doesn't start for nine weeks. Until then they--

FINCH: You recognize that I have ZERO authority to--

PANEL THREE
Kohl is looking up at the stone face of one of the creepy statues in the graveyard.

KOHL: You're HIDING with your tail between your legs. I'm sorry, but… this will help you get your mind off of it.

FINCH (PHONE): Kohl-- I…

PANEL FOUR
Kohl's face looking desperate. He knows that he needs Finch.

KOHL: You're the only one I can trust.

PANEL FIVE
FINCH is rubbing his eyes as he accepts the deal. Frustrated, but he knows that Kohl is right.

FINCH: You're such an asshole.

FINCH: E-mail me the address and I'll be there tomorrow morning.

FINCH: What's the name of the town again?

PAGE NINE

PANEL ONE
LARGE PANEL-PAGE WIDE
CUT TO: a "Welcome to Buckaroo!" Very much the sign from Jaws. But now someone has spray painted "Birthplace of Serial Killers" on the sign.
It's raining with storm clouds coming over the hills. It's pouring rain, the sky full of dark clouds.

It should look dark, scary and very Twin Peaks. It's our first real look at the town.

A small car is driving past the sign. It's a small road heading into town. Finch is in the car but don't show that until the next panel.

CAPTION: Buckaroo, Oregon

PANEL TWO
Finch is inside the car. The windshield wipers are going crazy. Focus on the windshield wipers, and the car from the outside.

FINCH: Rain.

FINCH: Stupid, STUPID RAIN.

PANEL THREE
Finch is parking his car at a small diner with one of those large "Diner" signs on top.

PANEL FOUR
Finch is running away from his car. Trying to avoid the rain. Pull back a bit so we can see him in full body running. The car is parked in a diner parking lot. Have Finch stepping into a big puddle that is splashing up on his legs and clothes.

FINCH: SHIT!

PANEL FIVE
Finch is leaning against a wall and looking at his watch, waiting for Kohl. Avoiding the rain.

FINCH: Where are you, Kohl?

PANEL SIX
PAGE WIDE
The bored and inpatient Finch is starting to chew on his nails as he is lost in thought.
Focus on his chewing his nails.

CAPTION: "He's dead!"

PAGE TEN

PANEL ONE
PAGE WIDE
FLASHBACK
Straight eye-level shot.
Finch is leaving a room with blood on his hands. He is looking down at his hands.
Behind him, we see an open door to an interrogation room.
A man in a suit is yelling at Finch. The door behind him is just cracked enough so that we can see a man sitting in a chair with paramedics trying to attend him. This might sound complicated but could be rad if we pulled it off.
Finch is wearing a white dress shirt and a nice tie. His sleeves are rolled up, but there is

Have the boss and Finch on the left side of the panel with the open door on the right.
This panel needs to have a different vibe than the rest. Like the past is smashing into the
present.
COLOR NOTE: BLACK AND WHITE AND RED. Only color the blood red.

     MAN: What the HELL happened in there, Finch?!

     FINCH: I-- I don't know. I--

     ALICE (off panel): You don't want to do that here, dude.

PANEL TWO
BACK TO PRESENT DAY:
Finch is still chewing on his nails. Lost in thought. Pull back for this panel so that we can
see both Alice and Finch in full body. Alice is still standing in the rain. We can zoom in on
them in the next few panels.
Alice, the town weirdo is standing a few feet away.
For this first panel, we can't see Alice's face. It's blocked by the umbrella she is holding but
she is walking toward Finch.

     ALICE: HEY!

     FINCH: Excuse me?

PANEL THREE
Now we see Alice removing Finch's hand from his mouth, stopping him from chewing his nails.

     ALICE: Your NAILS?

     ALICE: You don't want to CHEW your fingernails in Buckaroo.

     FINCH: Hunh?

PANEL FOUR
Finch is wiping his nails on his chest. Embarrassed that he was chewing them.

     FINCH: Oh sure. Didn't even think that might a bit UNCOMFORTABLE around here.

     FINCH: Sorry, it's a bad HABIT. Had it since I was a kid.

     FINCH: Better than SMOKING, right?

PANEL FIVE
Alice is walking away holding her umbrella up to block the rain. Finch is watching her walk
away.

     ALICE: Both make you look like an IDIOT.

     FINCH: Shouldn't you be in school or--?

PANEL ONE
LARGE PANEL
A bee is stinging Finch in the side of his neck. Go in close on the bee as it stings him in the
neck. Focus on the bee and the sting.

     SFX: STING!

PANEL TWO
Finch is swatting and trying to wave the bee away with one hand while he rubs the back of his
neck with the other.

     FINCH: Ow, Damn.

     FINCH: Something just got me

PANEL THREE
The bee is dying on the ground. Now missing its stinger.

PANEL FOUR
Finch and Alice are talking as bus driver drives past them in the background. Alice is standing
on the street corner. Finch has his hands on his hips looking annoyed.

     ALICE: Probably a BEE.

     ALICE: It's the honey farms out in the woods. Sometimes the bees escape.

     FINCH: A bee? Flying in this RAIN?

PANEL FIVE
Alice is still holding up her umbrella, but is now pulling it back so she can look out at the
sky. Her hand is out as she tries to see if any rain hits her hand.

     ALICE: The rain is STOPPING.

     ALICE: Look.

ALICE: First time it's stopped all day.

PANEL SIX
Finch sees something across the street that surprises him. In the background, Alice has closed her umbrella and is shaking it.

FINCH: You're right it's…

FINCH: Um, is that what I THINK it is?

PAGE TWELVE

PANEL ONE
LARGE PANEL- PAGE WIDE
The Murder Store from the outside. Big sign on the front of a small souvenir shop. This should just look outrageous and almost out of place. The entrance should look creepy with two large metal doors. It should look like a Haunted House Souvenir shop. Like a Halloween store but with a horrible twist. It might also have a weird image of a man with a giant knife on top.

We can see a bit of Alice and Finch in the foreground.

ALICE: Yeah and wait'll you meet the CREEPY OLD GUY who owns it.

PANEL TWO
Close up of a door bell ringing from inside the store as a door hits it, showing that a customer has entered.

SFX: DING DING

PANEL THREE
Finch has entered the Murder Store. Pull back so we can see the door open and Finch stepping in. Pull back down an aisle, so that we can get the feeling that it's empty.
At first, this just appears to be a dark and creepy souvenir shop. Full of supernatural items. Skulls, coffins.
It's dark inside with low light from candles and from lamps.

FINCH: Hello?

PAGE THIRTEEN

This page is full of odd things within the store, but we want to build a sort of odd presence, like someone is watching him. So every other panel will change up the camera distance. Break into far away shots and closer in. This page is mostly to build tension and make the reader feel nervous and excited.

Another thing with this page and the last page. If you want to throw in small close up panels of any of the items, feel free, just make sure it doesn't feel too cluttered.

PANEL ONE
FAR AWAY
Finch has started to walk past the shelves of weird shit. Have the stuff be in the foreground and Finch in the background, like we are looking at Finch through the shelves.

FINCH: Hello?

PANEL TWO
CLOSE
Finch is looking at a shelf of items on the counter. It's full of skulls, mini coffins, graveyard items, bones, creepy doll heads that are missing eye balls. Ouija board. A day of the dead doll. Have the creepy doll head be in the center of it all.

PANEL THREE
FAR AWAY
Finch is walking past an insect frame full of moths, and a few other items hanging on the walls. He is drawn to something hanging on a far wall.

PANEL FOUR
CLOSE
Finch is looking at a series of small figures that are reenacting murder scenes from horror movies. Have fun with this but don't go too much into the movies. Just focus on making it seem like it's a series of small freaking action figures with knives and guns.

PANEL FIVE
FAR AWAY
Pull back far, so again we can see that Jackson is walking toward a wall with a mask on it. It should again feel like someone is watching him from within the store.

PANEL SIX
PAGE WIDE
Finch is holding a very creepy mask in his hand.
It's the mask that belongs to the town Boogie Man, and the first Butcher. The "Book Burner."
This is Raleigh's grandfather's mask. Make it as creepy as possible.

Now for a bit of a scare for the next page, let's have the big hand of Raleigh reaching for Finch from behind. About to grab Finch's shoulder. We can only see the hand and part of the wrist, but it's mostly a silhouette.

FINCH: Hm.

PAGE FOURTEEN

PANEL ONE
LARGE PANEL-PAGE WIDE
Suddenly, we see Raleigh with his hand on Finch's shoulder. His large imposing figure overtaking the panel and the store. Hopefully, Raleigh's look surprises the reader. Not what they were expecting. Raleigh is holding a giant cup of soda. Make him look a bit like a classy redneck.

     RALEIGH: HOWDY!

PANEL TWO
Finch is still holding the mask. Unafraid. But is now looking over at Raleigh/the reader.

     FINCH: You trying to SCARE me?

     RALEIGH: Well, SHOOT! You got me! I sure was.

PANEL THREE
Raleigh is excited as he walks behind the counter. Lots of product around him. Skulls, hanging skeletons. He almost seems out of place around all that horror. Raleigh has a big smile on his face.

     RALEIGH: Just wanted to give you a proper welcome to the world's first SERIAL KILLER SOUVENIR SHOP!

     RALEIGH: The name is Raleigh. Raleigh Woods and if you're a fan of the gruesome and the macabre my MURDER STORE is the right place for you!

PANEL FOUR
Finch is standing in the middle of the store looking around. Amazed at what he is seeing. He can't believe that someone would actually create a place to sell souvenirs from killers.

     FINCH: hunh hunh.

PANEL FIVE
Raleigh is super excited to have a customer and is leaning on a shelf near Finch and pointing to the Book Burner's mask in his hands.

     RALEIGH: That mask in your hands right there is a replica of the very mask worn by the infamous "BOOK BURNER."

PAGE FIFTEEN

PANEL ONE
PAGE WIDE- FLASHBACK
The Booker Burner as a little kid. Being picked on at school for not being able to read. He is in a classroom as a bunch of kids point and laugh at him.

     RALEIGH (CAPTION): After being picked on as a kid for his TRAGIC inability to read or write…

PANEL TWO
PAGE WIDE- FLASHBACK
Books being burned with skeletons on top of them. We can see the Book Burner as a young man standing in the background. Further in the background, we can see a library on fire.

     RALEIGH (CAPTION): …the Book Burner went on a murder spree, burning down libraries all over Washington and Idaho.

     RALEIGH (CAPTION): With people TRAPPED INSIDE!

PANEL THREE
PAGE WIDE- FLASHBACK
A close up of just the creepy mask. The Book Burner's face, as the fire reflects and burns around him.

     RALEIGH (CAPTION): This made the Booker Burner the first of the Buckaroo Butchers. The Book Burner then started killing all those poor authors in the seventies and THEN--

PANEL FOUR
Finch is stopping Raleigh from going on with the story and putting the Book Burner mask back up on the wall.

     FINCH: I know what happened next.

PANEL FIVE
Raleigh is excited as he chats with Finch. Finch is trying to blow him off.

     RALEIGH: Ha. I KNEW IT! You're a serial killer fan! Caught a little bit of the Buckaroo Butcher mania, am I right?

     FINCH: Not quite.

     RALEIGH: How could you NOT?

PAGE SIXTEEN

PANEL ONE
Raleigh is presenting a shelf of the store. It's covered with knick knacks and souvenirs of death and destruction. A big car sales man smile spread across his face.

RALEIGH: Sixteen of the world's worst SERIAL KILLERS were all BORN AND RAISED right here in Buckaroo, Oregon. The last, of course, being the infamous Edward "The Nailbiter" Warren.

RALEIGH: If it's a curse, a coincidence, or an act of the DEVIL himself, it is not for us to know, but--

PANEL TWO
Finch is interrupting Raleigh as he looks at a toy electric chair. He just can't believe he i seeing all of this. Focus on Finch looking at the chair.

FINCH: You don't think it's a bit insensitive to gain from… THIS.

PANEL THREE
Raleigh is pulling his pants up as he comes around the counter. A little bit frustrated.

RALEIGH: Somebody oughta.

RALEIGH: My grandfather, Norman Woods, WAS the Book Burner. Ruined our good family name. Can't hurt to try to turn a negative to a POSITIVE, now does it?

PANEL FOUR
Raleigh is tapping a petition that he has on the counter. There's a stack of paper attached.

RALEIGH: My next goal is bring one of those HORROR CONVENTIONS out here. Just need everyone in town to sign this here PETITION.

SFX: Tap. Tap. Tap.

RALEIGH: Gonna call it "KILLER-CON." Catchy name, isn't it?

PANEL FIVE
Finch is looking down at the petition with an apprehensive look on his face. His eye cocked. Almost in awe of what he sees.

FINCH: A convention for fans… OF SERIAL KILLERS?

PANEL SIX
Raleigh is standing near a window making a "whoa" face. Like he wants Finch to calm down.

RALEIGH: Listen here. Don't you go judging me. There are a lot of SICK FREAKS out there who would PAY to be close to pure evil.

RALEIGH: And it would bring a lot of much needed dinero into this town. People are hurting and--

ALICE (off panel): Hey baby! Are you DEAF?

PAGE SEVENTEEN

PANEL ONE
Across the street, we can see Alice is getting picked on by two jock boys wearing letterman jackets. They are harassing her, but she is doing a good job of ignoring them. Her headphones in place. These two shit-for-brains jocks are named Hank and Bobby. Hank is the bigger of the two.

BOBBY: C'mon, Alice. Why won't you share your umbrella with me? It might rain again soon and the only person around here that I want to get wet is YOU.

HANK: OHH NICE!

PANEL TWO
Raleigh and Finch are standing in the doorway to the Murder Store. Raleigh has a shitty grin while Finch looks annoyed. They are both watching the fight.

RALEIGH: Aw, stay out of it. Just kids being KIDS.

FINCH: Hm.

PANEL THREE
Hank rudely pulls one of Alice's headphones from her ear.

HANK: Listen up, WEIRDO!

HANK: Everybody knows YOU'RE going to grow up to be the NEXT Buckaroo Butcher, Alice. Just a matter of time.

PANEL FOUR
Alice yanks the headphone back from Hank and gives him the evil eye. If this were a cartoon, we'd see little daggers coming from her eyes aimed at Hank.

ALICE: If I am, I know who my first VICTIM is going to be, Hank.

PANEL FIVE
Hank has taken a step back to open his arms and brag to his buddies. Trying to act like a tough guy. Zoom out a bit for this shot so we can see a bit of the street and them in full body.

>HANK: You hear that, Bobby?

>HANK: "ALICE IN HORRORLAND" here just THREATENED me. But that's okay…

PANEL SIX
Hank grabs Alice's ass as he tries to pull her in. Hank looks excited, like he feels he can get away with anything. Alice looks angry, frustrated, and we can already see that she is pissed. Make sure to draw attention to the ass grab and also to both of their faces.

>HANK: I like BAD girls.

>SFX: GRAB!

PAGE EIGHTEEN

PANEL ONE
LARGE PANEL-PAGE WIDE
Alice knees Hank right in the nuts.

>HANK: DOH!

>SFX: THUK!

PANEL TWO
As Hank falls to his knees, grabbing his crotch, Bobby tries to grab Alice. Looks like he might hurt her. This should all feel very violent.

>BOBBY: FUCKING BITCH!

PANEL THREE
But Alice scratches his face.

>BOBBY: AH!

PANEL FOUR
Finch starts to pull Alice off Bobby.

>FINCH: Whoa, whoa, whoa. It's OVER.

PANEL FIVE
Finch is talking to Alice and making sure that she is okay.

>FINCH: You okay?

>ALICE: I didn't need your help.

>FINCH: I can see that.

PANEL SIX
Hank is getting up and yelling at Finch and Alice. Finch has turned his attention back to Hank.

>HANK: WHAT THE HELL?! We were just joking around!

>FINCH: We'll talk about the definition of "JOKING" later.

>HANK: Fuck you, she was practically begging for it, homie.

PAGE NINETEEN

PANEL ONE
PAGE WIDE
Finch is walking up to Hank and the jock, who are standing and trying to act tough. Finch is calm as he walks up.

>FINCH: I have two rules. Number one—no women. And…

>FINCH: How old are you?

>HANK: TWENTY-ONE!

>FINCH: You're LYING.

>HANK: Eighteen.

>FINCH: And number two…

PANEL TWO
Finch decks Hank in the face. It's a good solid punch that knocks him out.

>SFX: KRAK!

>FINCH: NO KIDS.

PANEL THREE
Bobby is trying to punch Finch. Finch is dodging it and grabbing the guy's arm.

      BOBBY: I'm going to kick your--

PANEL FOUR
Finch tosses the guy into the Murder Store window, cracking the glass. He doesn't go through but he still cracks the glass.
Raleigh looks pissed as he yells in the background. We can see Hank is getting up and pissed.

      RALEIGH: Jesus Christ Almighty, did you have to do that!

      SFX: CRACK!

PANEL FIVE
Hank's face.

      HANK: You are fucking DEAD, man. You know who my DAD is?!

PANEL SIX
Finch has grabbed Hank by his collar and is about to punch his face again.

      FINCH: Nope.

      FINCH: And I don't care.

      CRANE (off panel): WHOA!

PAGE TWENTY

PANEL ONE
LARGE PANEL-PAGE WIDE
Meet Officer Crane. Crane has her gun aimed at Finch. Make her look bad ass with her small town police cruiser behind her.

      CRANE: You mind NOT BEATING on my citizens?

PANEL TWO
Finch is letting Hank go.

      FINCH: Uh, sorry I let my … ah…TEMPER get the better of me sometimes.

PANEL THREE
Bobby and Hank look angry as they yell. Have Hank be wiping the blood away from his nose. They look a little worse for wear but angry at the same time.

      BOBBY: This loser just came outta NOWHERE and--

PANEL FOUR
Alice's face back under her umbrella. She is calm, but is pointing to Hank and Bobby.

      ALICE: That is totally NOT what happened, Sheriff Crane.

      ALICE: I was handing Hank and Bobby their ASSES when tall, dark and handsome started defending my HONOR or something.

      ALICE: True story.

PANEL FIVE
Crane is looking at Hank and Bobby.

      CRANE: That right? You two were getting beat up by a girl and this good SAMARITAN bailed you out? That what I'm going to put in the report?

      HANK: Not… EXACTLY.

      CRANE: Right.

PANEL SIX
Crane is motioning for her partner to take in the three men.

      CRANE: Officer Link, take Hank and Bobby to the STATION to cool down for a bit. Call their parents, and tell them I'll meet them in a few hours.

PAGE TWENTY-ONE

PANEL ONE
Alice's face looking annoyed and a bit angry.

      ALICE: That's IT? What about…

PANEL TWO
Crane is putting her gun away as Alice quickly walks away in the background.

      CRANE: School. NOW.

      ALICE: Yes, ma'am.

RALEIGH: You letting this BUM go, too? I want to press CHARGES. Throw the damn book at—

CRANE: Shut the fuck up, Raleigh.

PANEL FOUR
Crane is walking toward Finch. Crane looks stern as she walks over. Finch is dusting off his shoulder.

FINCH: Everyone in this town is so POLITE.

CRANE: So you a cop or a reporter?

FINCH: What now?

PANEL FIVE
Crane's face with a bit of a know-it-all smile.

CRANE: New people that come strolling into Buckaroo are always reporters looking for the BIG SCORE, or cops… looking for the BIG SCORE.

CRANE: Your shoulders tell me COP. You in the habit of coming to the rescue of teenage girls or was today SPECIAL?

PANEL SIX
Finch flashes his badge. It has an Army Intelligence logo in the sleeve.

FINCH: Officer Nicholas Finch.

FINCH: Army Intelligence.

FINCH: I'm looking for a friend… CHARLES KOHL?

PANEL SEVEN
Crane is motioning for Finch to follow her.

CRANE: DAMN. Yeah.

CRANE: You better come with me.

PAGE TWENTY-TWO AND TWENTY- THREE

TWO PAGE SPREAD OVER THE TOP PART OF TWO PAGES
FOUR PANELS ACROSS THE BOTTOM

Crane and Finch are standing in a ransacked studio hotel room. The bed is a mess and a lamp has been knocked over. Try to make the room look like a big mess. It should look a bit like a crime scene. Not the same as pages 2-3, but its own unique thing.
There are books, magazines, and newspapers all over the place. Pull back with the character in small full body and go for broke with the detail.

On the back wall is a murder wall of pictures and newspaper articles. A map of the town, with lots and lots of little red strings going from picture to picture.
The Murder Wall. Finch and Crane are standing in front of a wall full of pictures of murder victims. A map of the town, red lines everywhere.
(We might actually need to work on this wall together and figure out what it all means since it will be important later.)

Lots of dialogue on this page. It's a Bendis page.

CRANE: Ever since he came to town, Kohl and I meet every Monday morning for coffee. NEVER MISSED.

CRANE: When he didn't SHOW, I got worried. Was on my way to the station to report this and call the feds when I ran into you.

FINCH: I'm guessing you know why Kohl was here? What he was INVESTIGATING?

CRANE: You kidding? It's all he ever talked about.

CRANE: Kohl thought that there had to be a connection between all the Buckaroo Butchers.

CRANE: No way sixteen serial killers born in our small town was a COINCIDENCE. Something so random. He was just so… so…

FINCH: OBSESSED? Been that way ever since Nailbiter Warren. He had to know why.

FINCH: Why THIS town.

FOUR PANELS ACROSS THE BOTTOM:

PANEL ONE
Finch is taking a look at the murder wall. Looking closely at the red strings, maybe tugging on one of them.

FINCH: Kohl always loved his PUZZLES. And this one HAUNTED him.

FINCH: He called me yesterday saying that he… pieced it together.

PANEL TWO
Crane and Finch are looking at the wall. Pull back so we can see the room again. They are small within the panel.

CRANE: Looks like someone wanted that secret kept HIDDEN.

FINCH: You're the LAW around here…

FINCH: Did anyone have a PROBLEM with Kohl?

PANEL THREE
Crane has walked out of the hotel room leaving Finch standing in the doorway. Crane looks annoyed, while Finch looks a bit confused.

It's started to rain again, and will rain for the rest of this issue.

CRANE (whispering): Stupid rain.

CRANE: Aside from the obvious, no. Everybody around town thought he was a NICE GUY and didn't mind him snooping a bit.

FINCH: Wait… who was the "OBVIOUS?"

PANEL FOUR
Crane turns her head around to look over her shoulder. Crane has that no bullshit look on her face.

CRANE: Who do you think?

PAGE TWENTY-FOUR

PANEL ONE
CUT TO:
Crane and Finch are driving in Crane's police squad car together. She is looking ahead while he is looking out the window. It's started to rain again.

FINCH: That sick of sonofabitch just came HOME after he was ACQUITTED? Just like that?

CRANE: Yup. Can't trust a jury to do anything right nowadays. Jury of peers, my ass.

CRANE: Moved into his parents' old place like it was NOTHING.

PANEL TWO
FROM FINCH'S POV: We see the Book Burner off in the woods. A man standing next to an old gross tree that looks like something people would be hung from. His mask can clearly be seen.

CRANE (off panel): A publisher paid him a hefty advance for him to write a BOOK.

CRANE (off panel): But most of the money is going to CIVIL SUITS and PROTECTION.

PANEL THREE
Somewhat the same panelas panel two. This gets Finch's attention and he starts to jump up. He is surprised by what he just saw.

CRANE: We keep an officer on the freak at ALL times in case he ever…

PANEL FOUR
Same POV as Panel Three, but now the Book Burner is gone. The whole point of this was to just scare the reader a bit. Nearly a duplicate panel but minus the Booker Burner.

CRANE (OFF PANEL): Starts up again.

PANEL FIVE
Finch's face full of confusion. Still looking back and surprised by what he did or didn't see.

FINCH: That's ah… that's understandable.

PAGE TWENTY-FIVE

PANEL ONE
Crane and the police car have pulled up to a small cabin in the woods. There is an unmarked car parked in front.

PANEL TWO
Crane is leaning into the unmarked car, the cop inside is reading a book

CRANE: He home?

COP: Yup.

PANEL THREE
Crane is walking up the steps of the house. Pull back a bit so we can see them almost in full body walking up the steps and a bit of the house. FINCH is walking up the steps behind her. He

has no idea what is happening and is sort of looking around.

      CRANE: You really think Kohl might have figured out why so many serial killers came from Buckaroo?

      FINCH: Doesn't matter to me. I just want to know WHERE my FRIEND is. Make sure he's
SAFE.

PANEL FOUR
Crane knocks on the door.

      CRANE: Well, maybe Kohl's good old BUDDY here will have some ANSWERS.

      SFX: KNOCK KNOCK

PANEL FIVE
CUT TO: The inside of the house, Warren, grabbing a towel. His hands look dirty. Maybe even bloody. Just a close up of his hands. No face. We don't want to give it away just yet. Again focus on his hands as he washes what looks like blood from them.

      WARREN: One moment, please!

PANEL SIX
Crane is outside knocking again. Same angle as panel 2. She looks a bit frustrated.

      CRANE: Aw, c'mon.

      SFX: KNOCK KNOCK.

PANEL SEVEN
The front door is opening. We can see one of Warrens hand's holding the door knob as he opens the door, but let's make sure that we can't see who it is. We want to save the reveal until the next page.

      WARREN: Hold you're horses. Hold your HORSES, I'm comin', I'm COMIN'.

PANEL EIGHT
PAGE WIDE
Crane is cold, while Finch looks surprised. He can't believe his eyes. Go with a straight shot of them looking at the reader.

      WARREN (off panel): Got a pot roast in the oven.

      WARREN (off panel): Wasn't expecting visitors. But don't worry.

PAGE TWENTY-SIX

PANEL ONE
SPLASH PAGE

Nailbiter Warren is standing in the open doorway. It's eye level POV of him from the waist up. He looks normal. It's clearly him in regular clothes.

Warren is wearing an apron that looks like it has a bit of blood splatter on it, but that could be food.
His smile and his blue eyes are shining brightly. This is man is creepy. Welcome to the star of the show.

Oh yeah, and Warren is chewing on his nails a bit. No blood and like he is being gentle with it. But make sure that the reader can tell he is chewing on his nail.

There is also a small hornet flying around near his shoulder.

      WARREN: There's enough for everyone.

PANEL TWO
Along the bottom of the page, we have a panel that isn't quite page wide but is nearly there. Close up of the bee flying in the air.

It's a hornet flying in the air. Its wings flying fast.

      SFX (from the wings): THUMP THUMP.

      END CAP: "To be continued..."

NAILBITER
A Proposal for an ongoing series by Joshua Williamson

"Did you know that more serial killers have been born in Buckaroo, Oregon than any other city in the world?"

Since 1969, sixteen serial killers were born and grew up in Buckaroo, Oregon; and now an obsessed NSA agent wants to know why a small town is giving birth to some of the most vile human beings America has ever seen.

Friday Night Lights crossed with Twin Peaks and Dexter in a small town thriller with a large cast of characters and a hint of the supernatural. In most small town mysteries, residents are shaken up by a murder or supernatural occurrence. What sets NAILBITER apart is that Buckaroo, Oregon has already been dealing with investigations for years, creating unique small town politics that haven't been explored before. What creates a serial killer? Is it nature or nurture? Does where you come from dictate your future?

THE PITCH:
"The Buckaroo Butchers" are sixteen people who, at different times since 1969, left Buckaroo and went on to became serial killers. Their only connection? Being born in Buckaroo. The thing is... there hasn't been a single murder in Buckaroo since 1969. FBI criminal profiler Charles Kohl is obsessed with finding out why this small town is producing so many serial killers, and feels like he is close to the answer. He calls for his friend and the only person he can trust, NSA agent Nicholas Finch, to help him. When Nick gets into town, Kohl has gone missing. Nick stays in Buckaroo to find his friend and pick up the pieces of the investigation. What causes the serial killers to be born in Buckaroo? Is it a freak coincidence? Does Buckaroo have some kind of supernatural secret... or is it something even more sinister?

Why "Nailbiter?
The worst and most infamous of the Buckaroo Butchers was Edward "Nailbiter" Warren. Warren would kidnap people who chewed their nails, keep them captive until they grew back, and then chew their fingers down to the bone before ultimately killing them. When he was captured after claiming sixty four victims, Warren's trial and connections to Buckaroo shined a light on the small town, revealing the common origin of the Buckaroo Butchers. Buckaroo, Oregon has its own legends and tall tales stories based on Buckaroo's dark history—stories of monsters, local historical figures, cults, and black magic.

THE TWIST: Then the worst possible thing happens: After a long and controversial trial, Edward Warren is acquitted. The history of the town caused doubt in the mind of the jury, and so Edward Warren was set free. Warren has returned home to Buckaroo, watched by all towns' inhabitants. What would you do if you knew a serial killer lived next door? Unlike Hannibal and Dexter, this killer isn't a secret but out in the open for the world to see.

What's Nick's secret? (Main character and our ticking clock)
Nick Finch is a NSA interrogator who at one time served in Afghanistan as a specialist in "coercive information extraction from resistant sources"... better known as a torture expert. But now Nick has been placed on indefinite leave after using excessive force and accidentally killing a suspect. Accustomed to using violence to get his way, Nick has to find other methods to get answers in Buckaroo. Hoping to find Kohl and solve the mystery before anyone learns that he has no official jurisdiction to be investigating the strange goings-on in Buckaroo.

The Appeal: The possibilities of NAILBITER are endless, opening the door to explore the dark mind of a killer and will appeal to fans of crime mysteries and horror. America's obsession with serial killers and the book's large cast can fuel years worth of storylines as the readers keep asking "Why this town?" and "Who's next?"

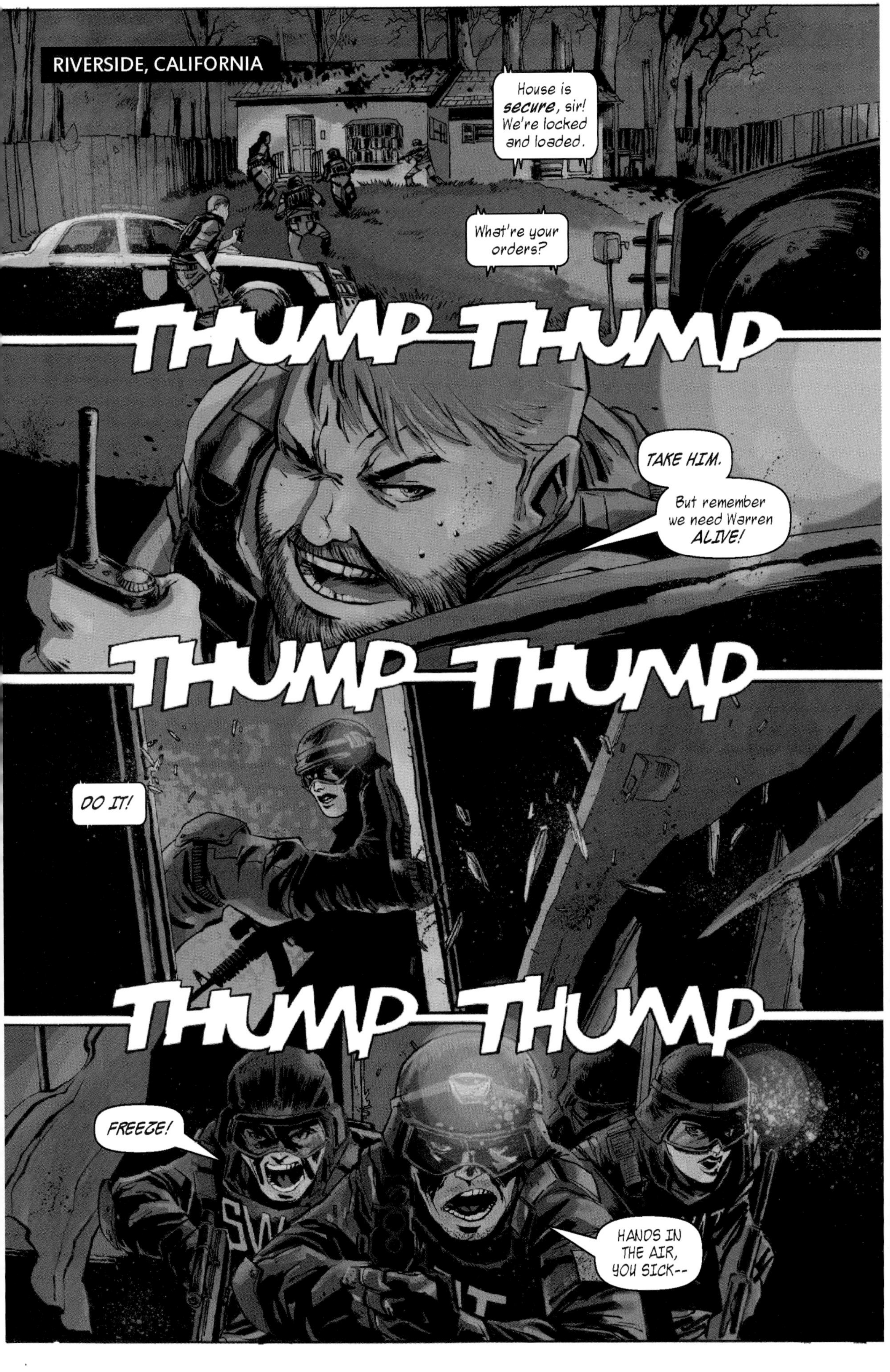
RIVERSIDE, CALIFORNIA
House is secure, sir! We're locked and loaded.
What're your orders?
THUMP THUMP
TAKE HIM.
But remember we need Warren ALIVE!
THUMP THUMP
DO IT!
THUMP THUMP
FREEZE!
HANDS IN THE AIR, YOU SICK--

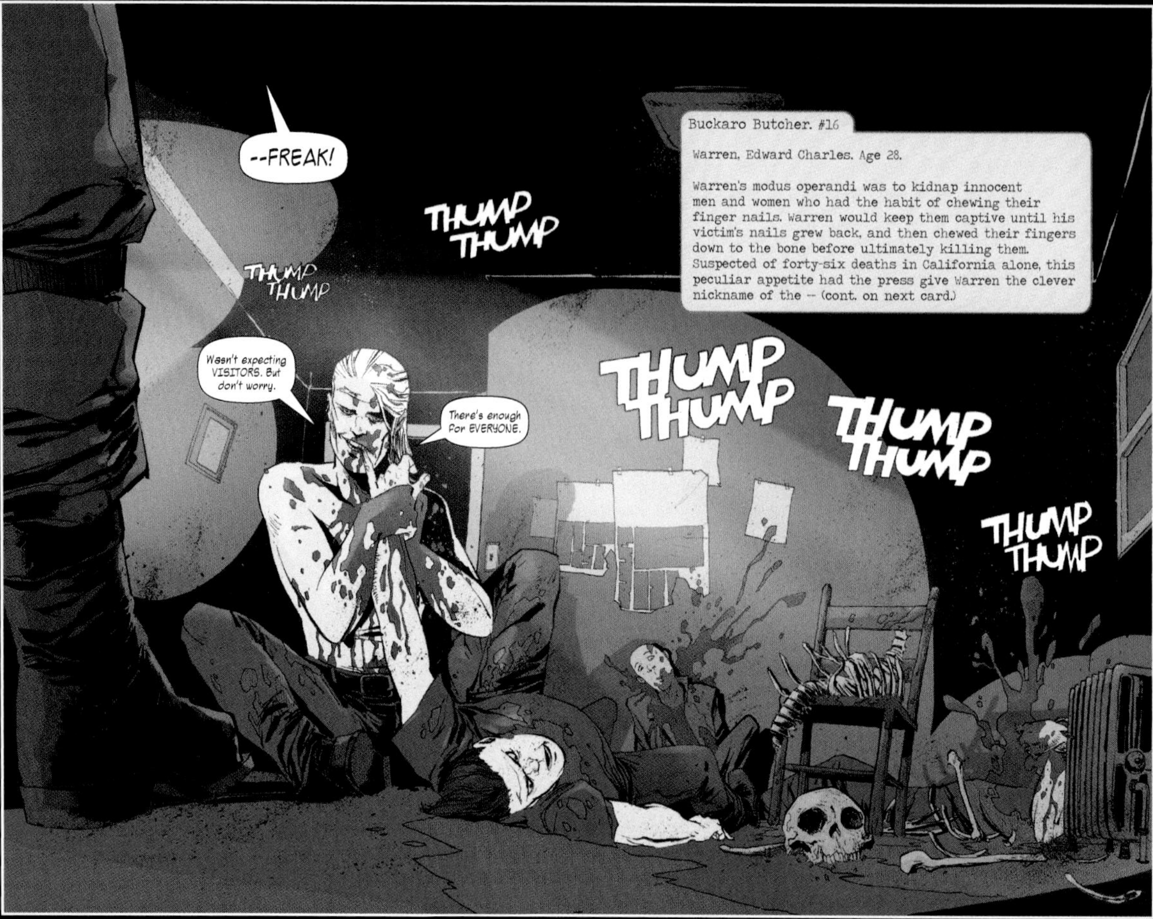
--FREAK!
THUMP THUMP
THUMP THUMP
Buckaro Butcher. #16
Warren, Edward Charles. Age 28.
Warren's modus operandi was to kidnap innocent men and women who had the habit of chewing their finger nails. Warren would keep them captive until his victim's nails grew back, and then chewed their fingers down to the bone before ultimately killing them. Suspected of forty-six deaths in California alone, this peculiar appetite had the press give Warren the clever nickname of the -- (cont. on next card.)
Wasn't expecting VISITORS. But don't worry.
There's enough for EVERYONE.
THUMP THUMP
THUMP THUMP
THUMP THUMP

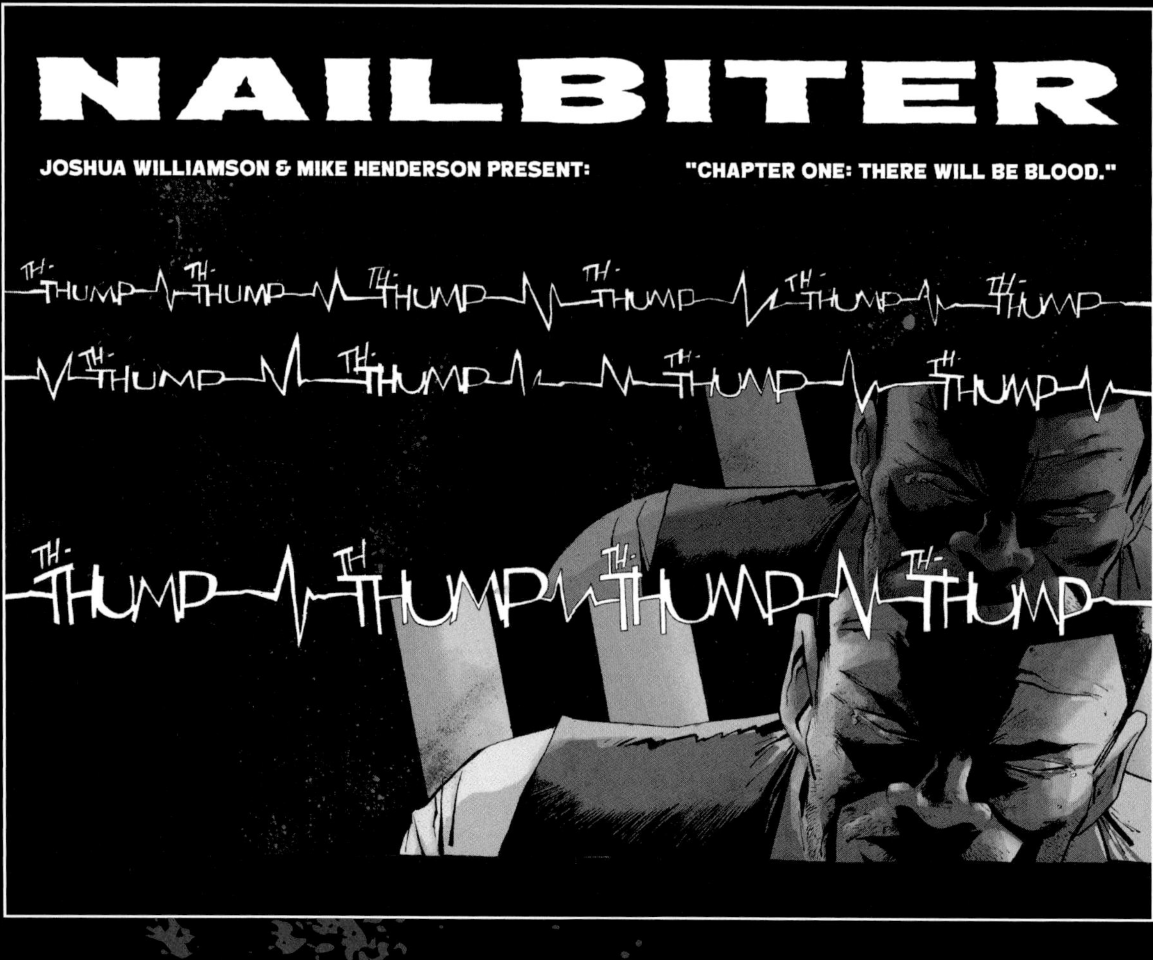
NAILBITER
JOSHUA WILLIAMSON & MIKE HENDERSON PRESENT:
"CHAPTER ONE: THERE WILL BE BLOOD."
TH-THUMP TH-THUMP TH-THUMP TH-THUMP TH-THUMP TH-THUMP
TH-THUMP TH-THUMP TH-THUMP TH-THUMP
TH-THUMP TH-THUMP TH-THUMP TH-THUMP

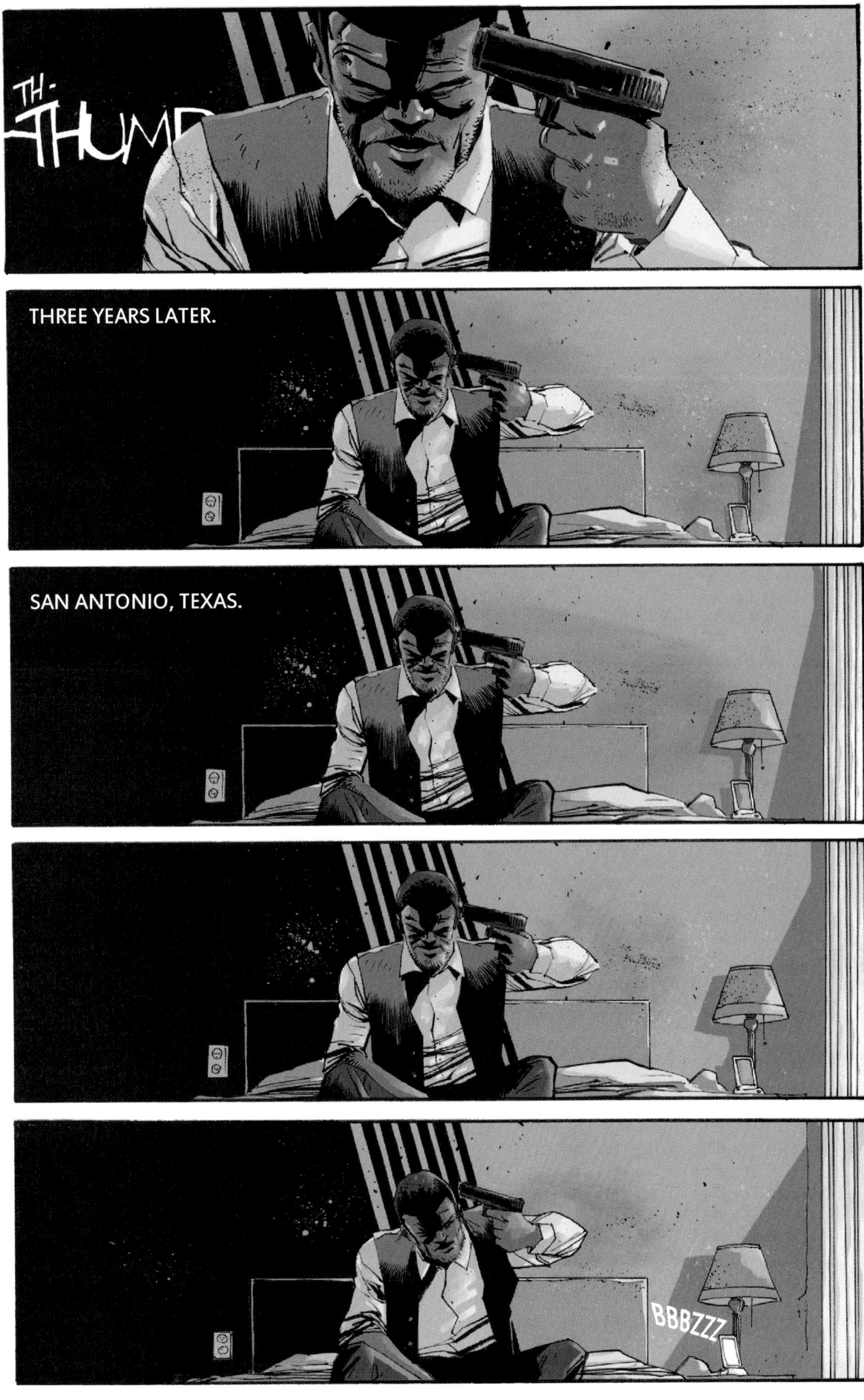
TH-THUMP
THREE YEARS LATER.
SAN ANTONIO, TEXAS.
BBBZZZ

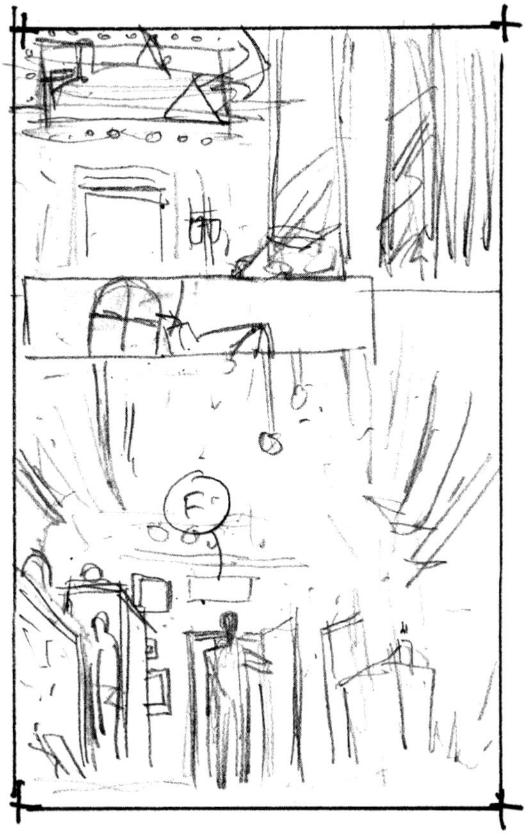
F

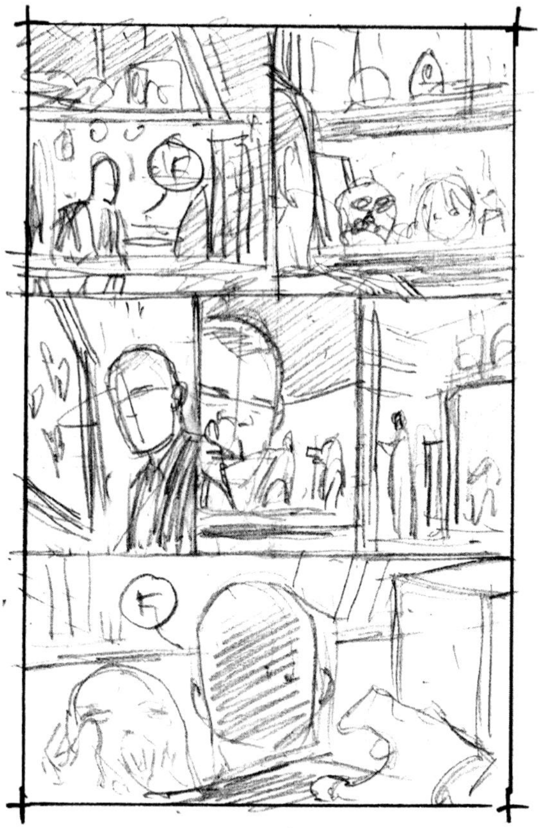
F
F

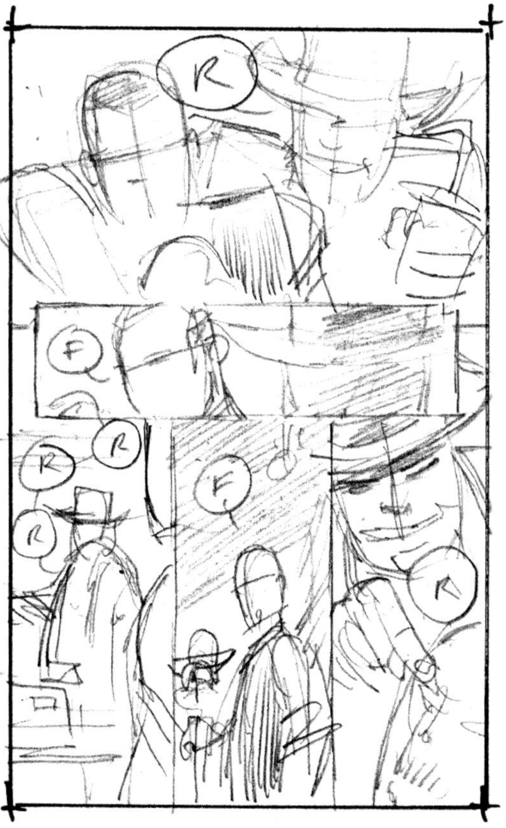
R
F
R
R
R
F
R

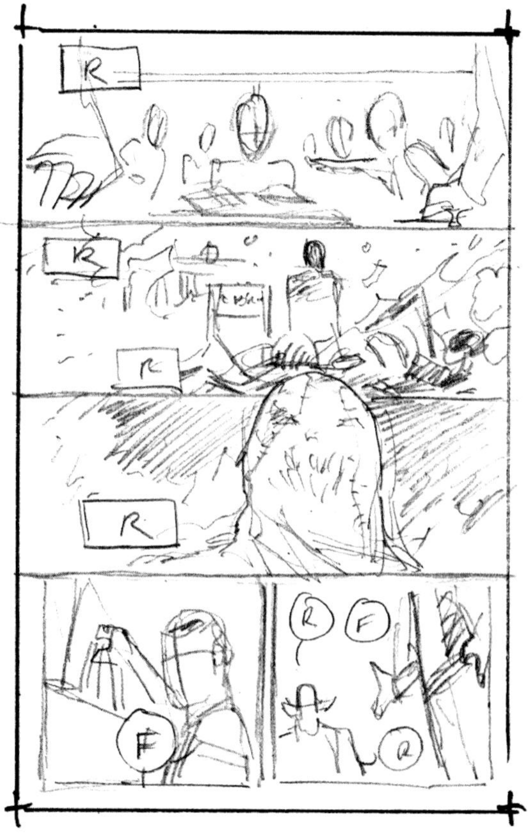
R
R
R
R
R
F
F
R

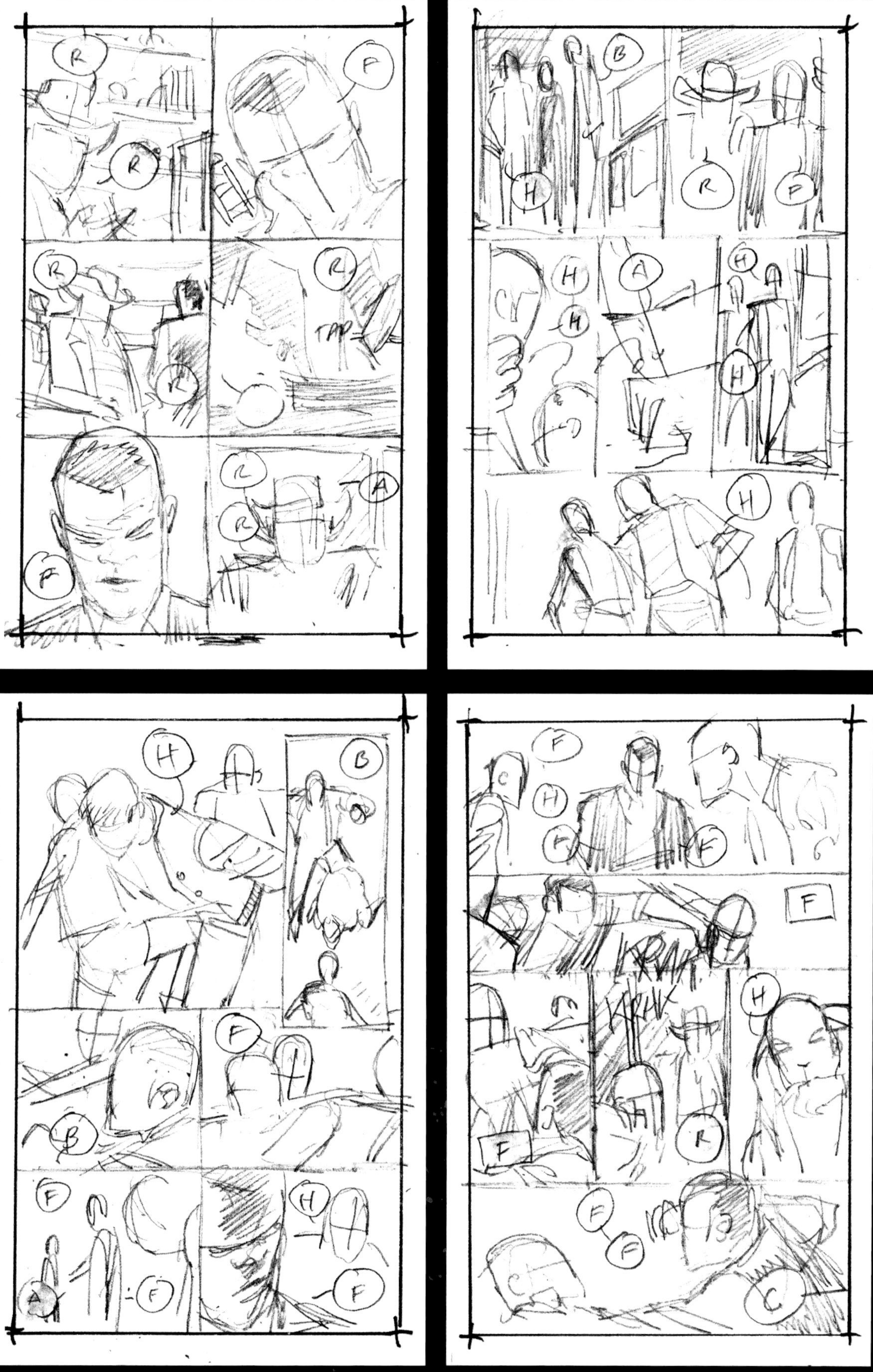
TAP

Nailbiter number one, pages 12-19 - Roughs by MIKE HENDERSON

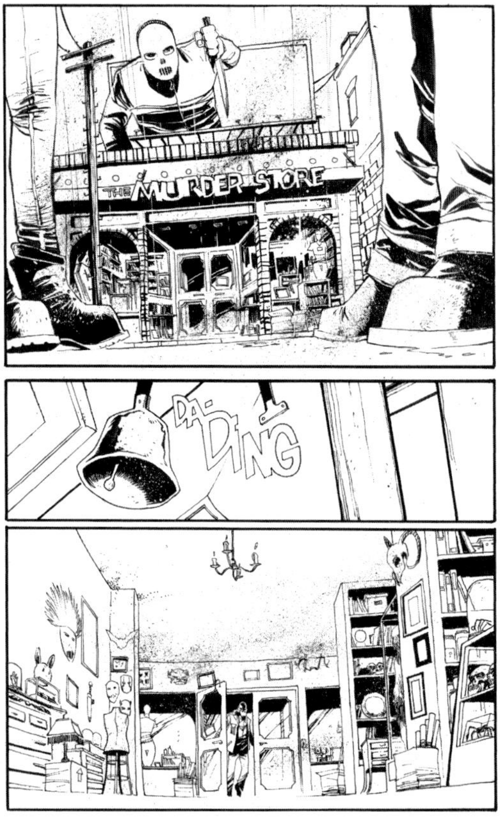
THE MURDER STORE
DA-DING

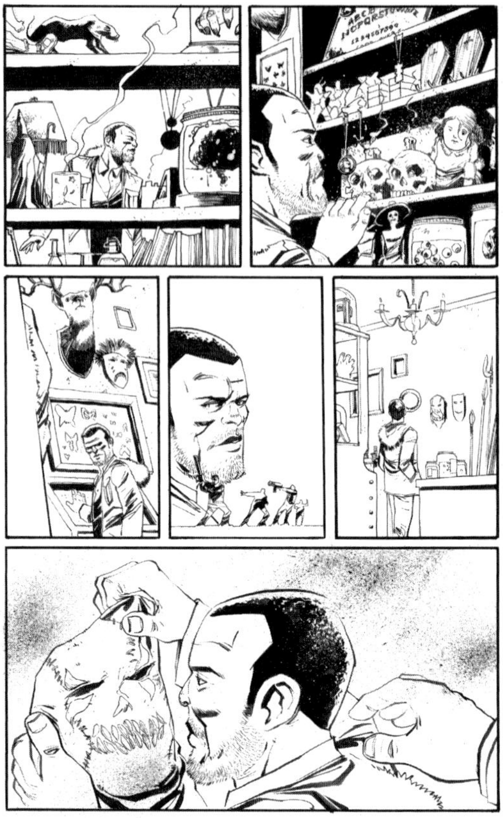

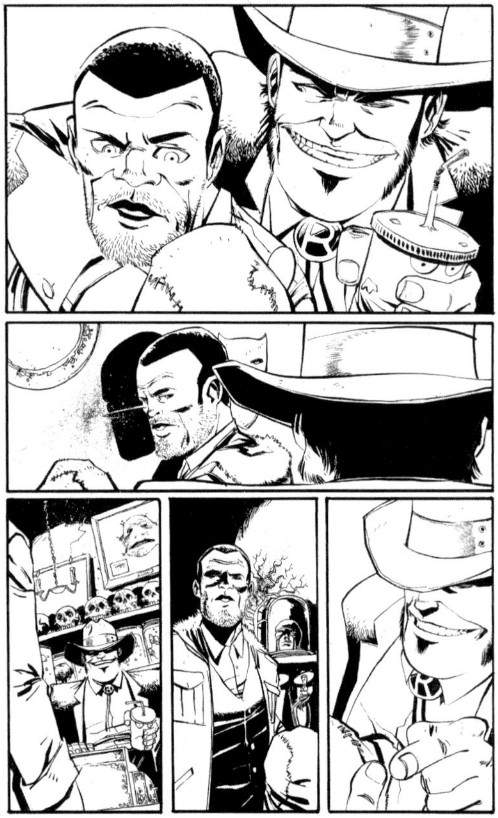

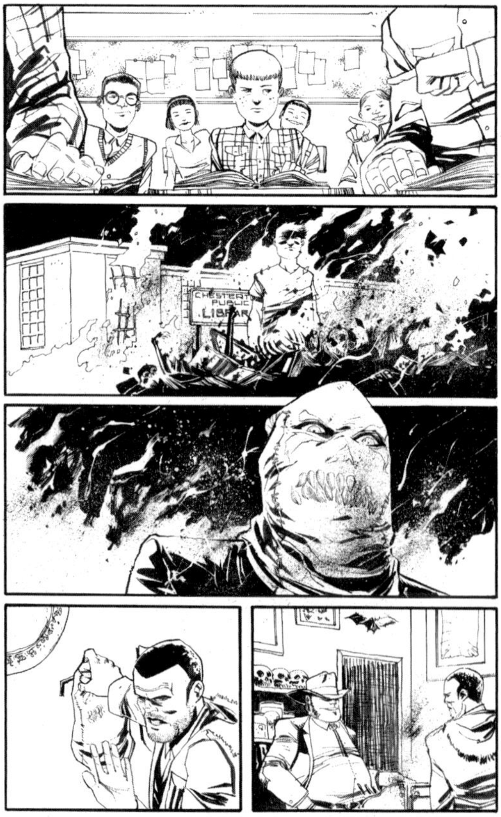

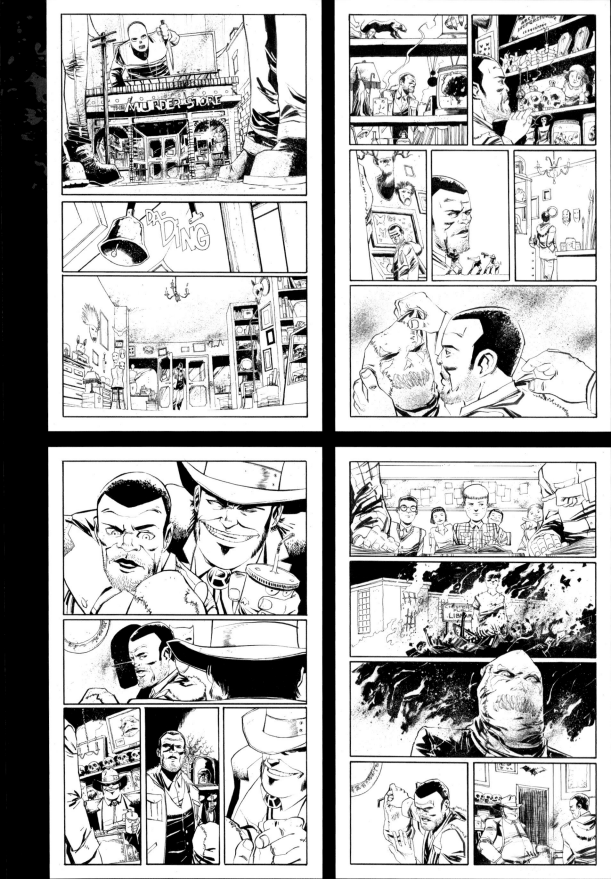

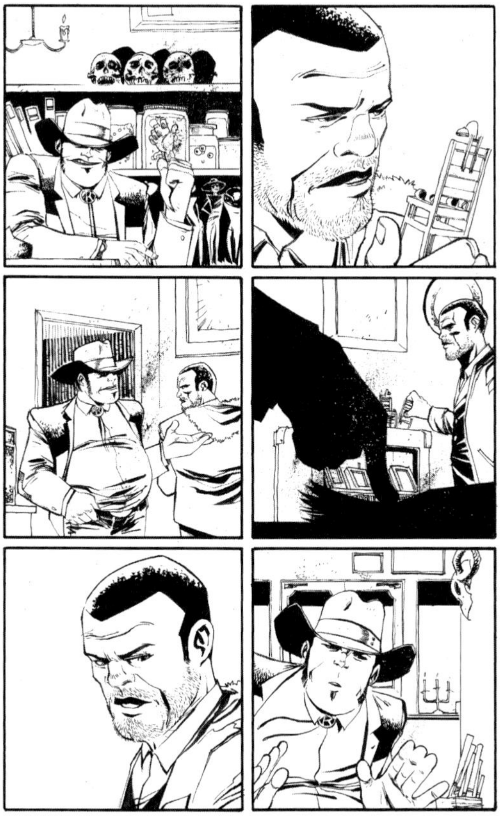

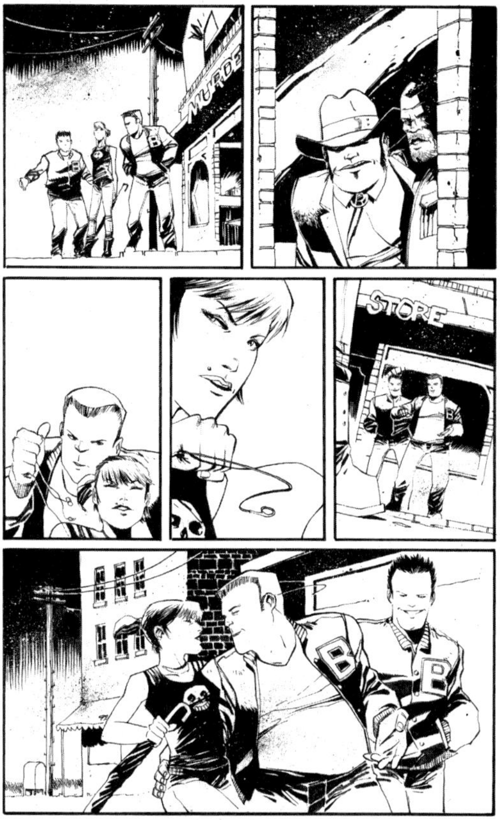
STORE

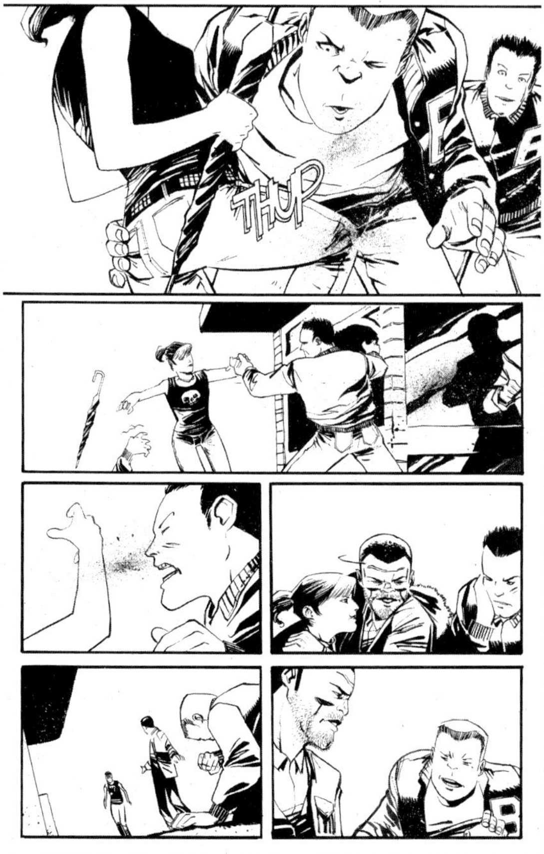
THUP

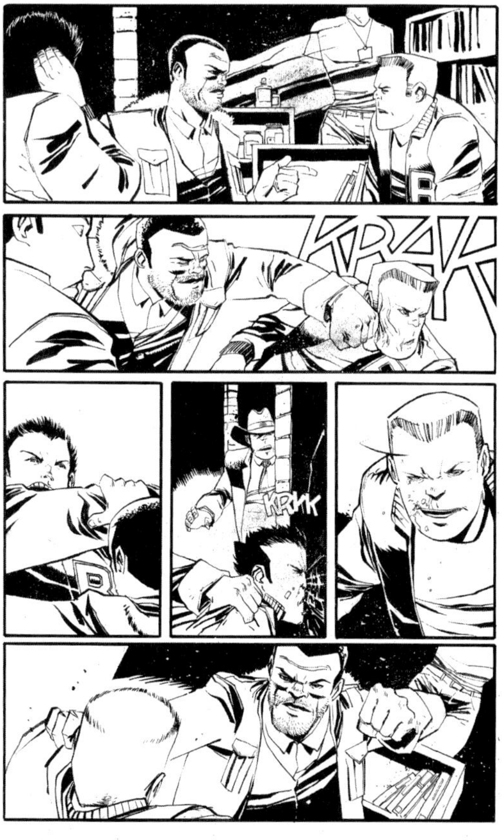
KRAK
KRAK

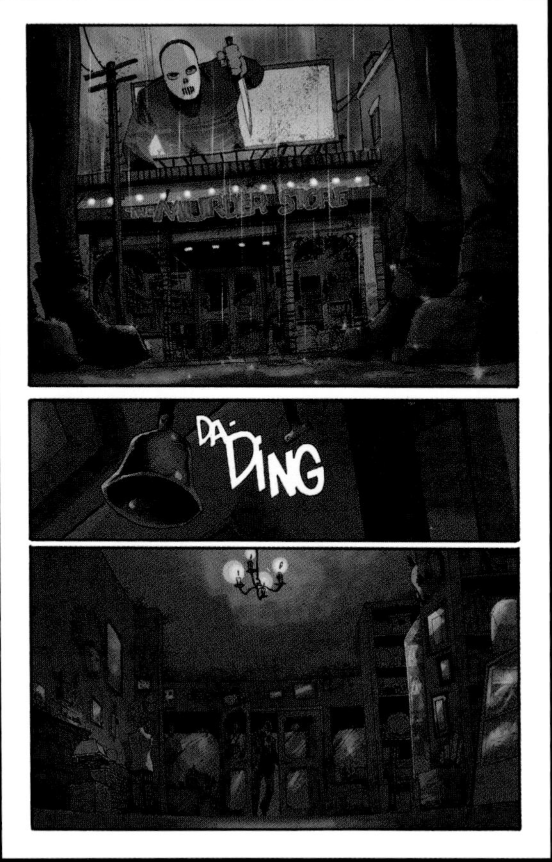
MURDER STORE
DA-DING

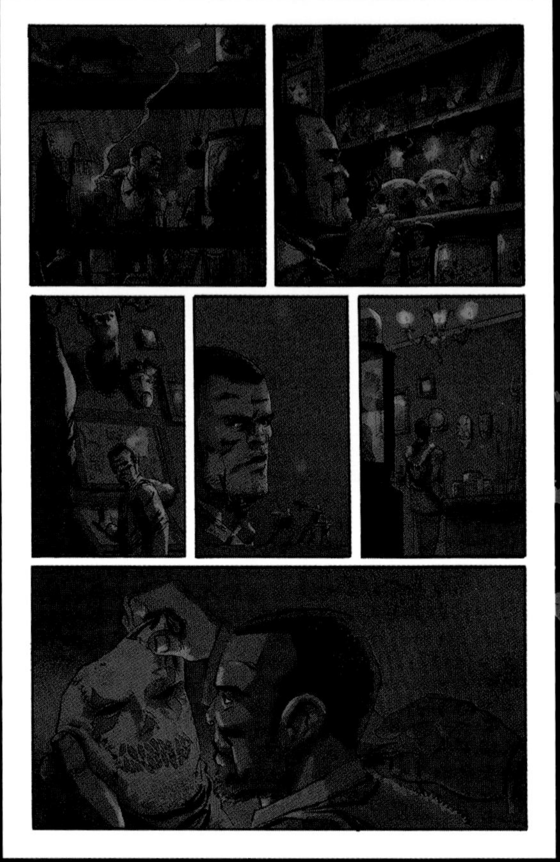

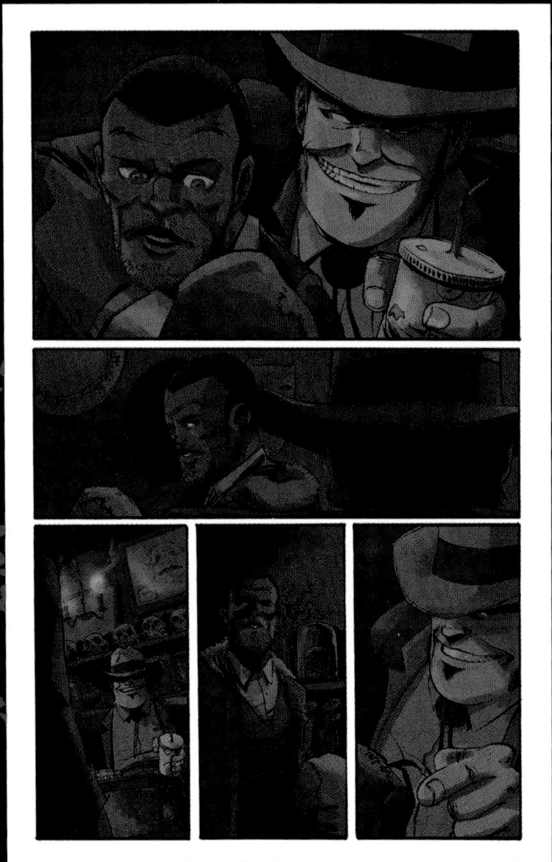

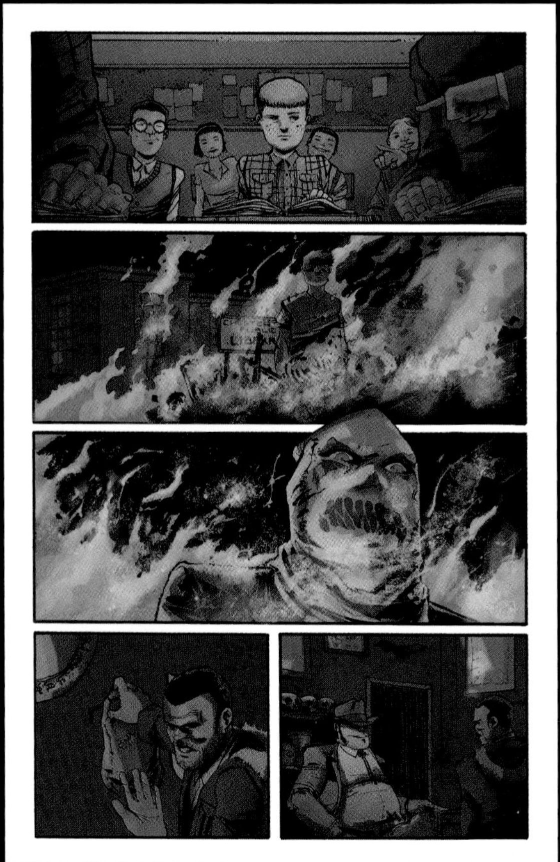

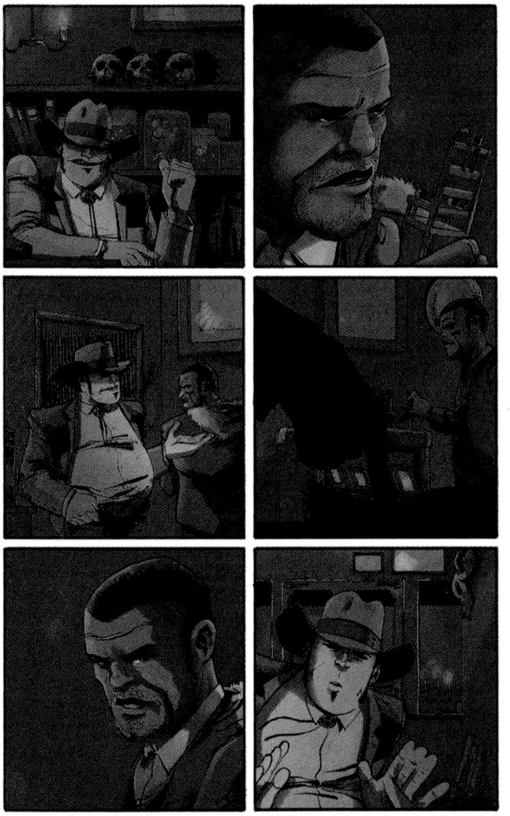

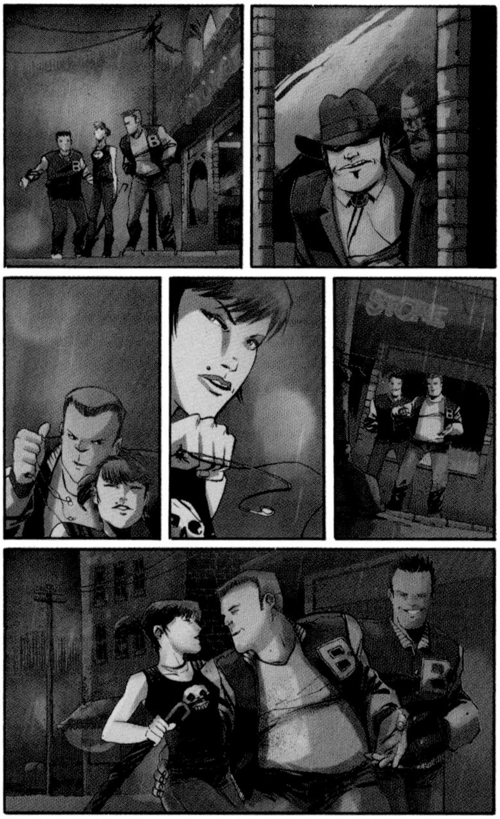
STORE

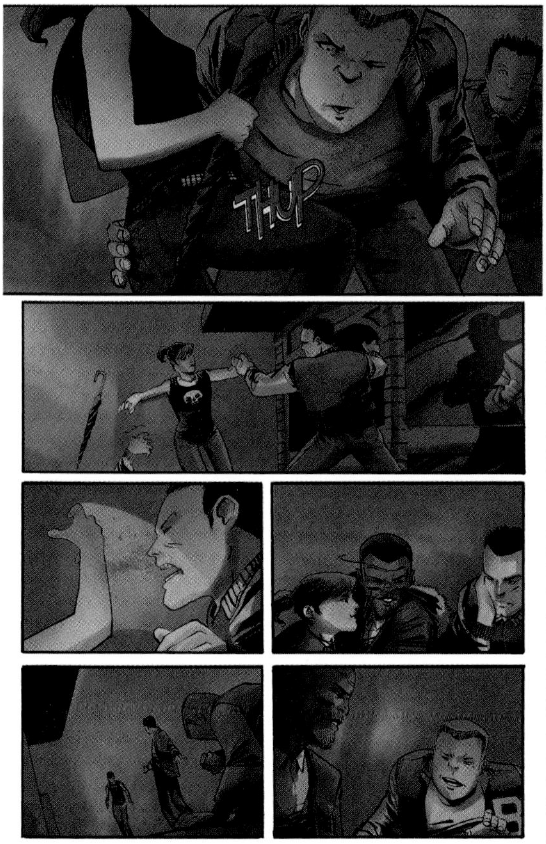
THUP

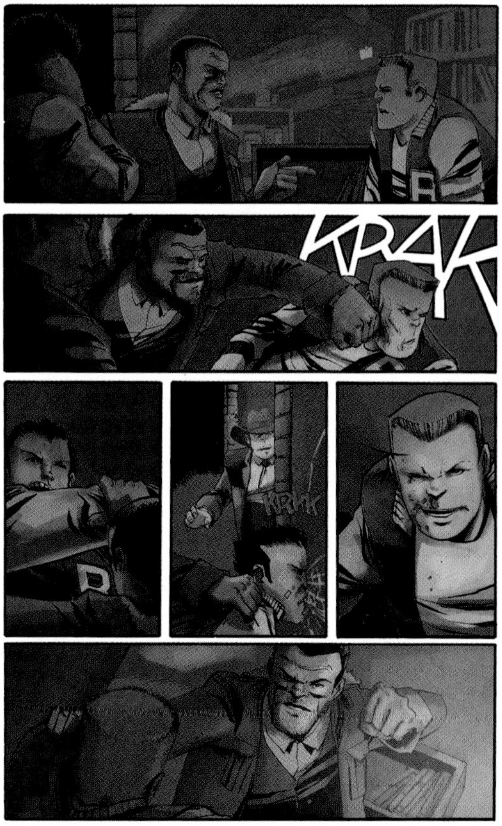
KRAK
KRAK

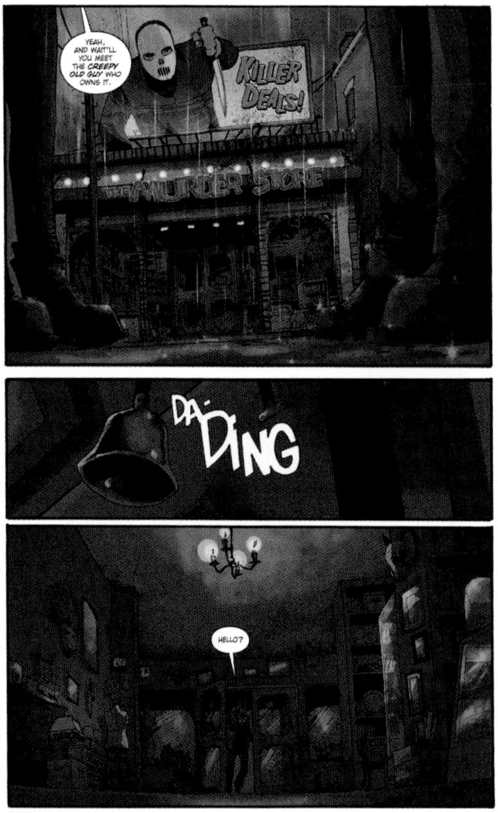
YEAH, AND WAIT'LL YOU MEET THE CREEPY OLD GUY WHO OWNS IT.
KILLER DEALS!
MURDER STORE
DA-DING
HELLO?

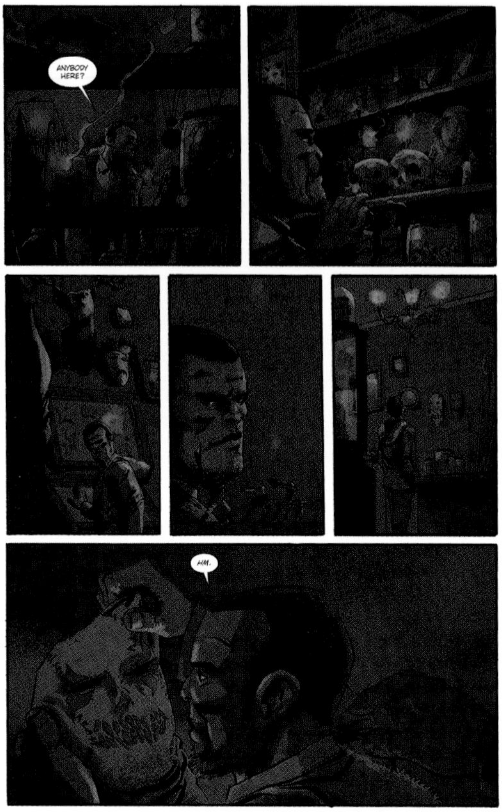
ANYBODY HERE?
HM.

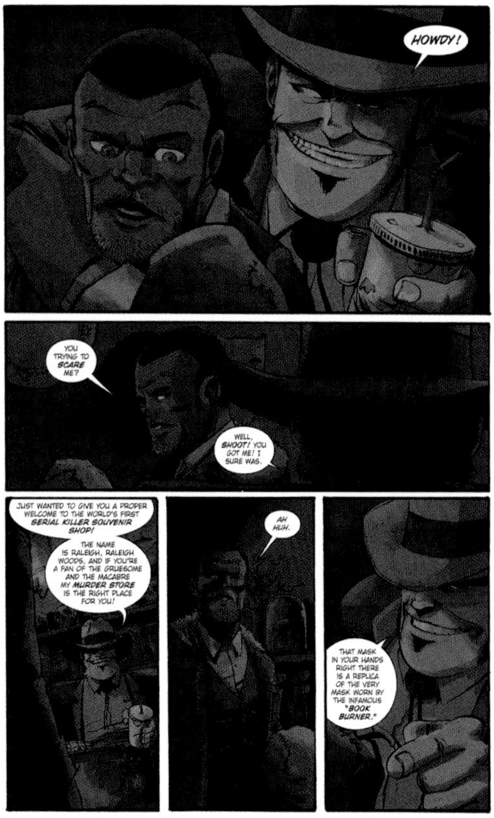
HOWDY!
YOU TRYING TO SCARE ME?
WELL, SHOOT! YOU GOT ME! I SURE WAS.
JUST WANTED TO GIVE YOU A PROPER WELCOME TO THE WORLD'S FIRST SERIAL KILLER SOUVENIR SHOP!
THE NAME IS RALEIGH, RALEIGH WOODS, AND IF YOU'RE A FAN OF THE GRUESOME AND THE MACABRE MY MURDER STORE IS THE RIGHT PLACE FOR YOU!
AH HUH.
THAT MASK IN YOUR HANDS RIGHT THERE IS A REPLICA OF THE VERY MASK WORN BY THE INFAMOUS "BOOK BURNER."

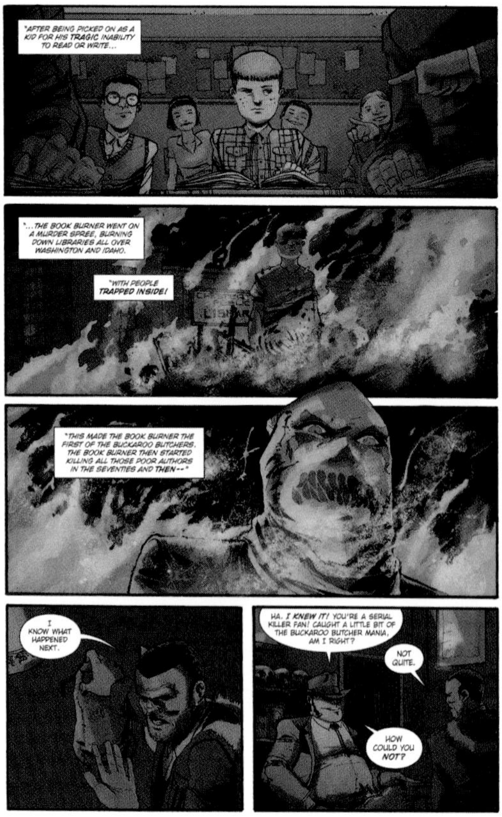
"AFTER BEING PICKED ON AS A KID FOR HIS TRAGIC INABILITY TO READ OR WRITE...
"...THE BOOK BURNER WENT ON A MURDER SPREE, BURNING DOWN LIBRARIES ALL OVER WASHINGTON AND IDAHO.
"WITH PEOPLE TRAPPED INSIDE!
"THIS MADE THE BOOK BURNER THE FIRST OF THE BUCKAROO BUTCHERS. THE BOOK BURNER THEN STARTED KILLING ALL THOSE POOR AUTHORS IN THE SEVENTIES AND THEN--"
I KNOW WHAT HAPPENED NEXT.
HA. I KNEW IT! YOU'RE A SERIAL KILLER FAN! CAUGHT A LITTLE BIT OF THE BUCKAROO BUTCHER MANIA, AM I RIGHT?
NOT QUITE.
HOW COULD YOU NOT?

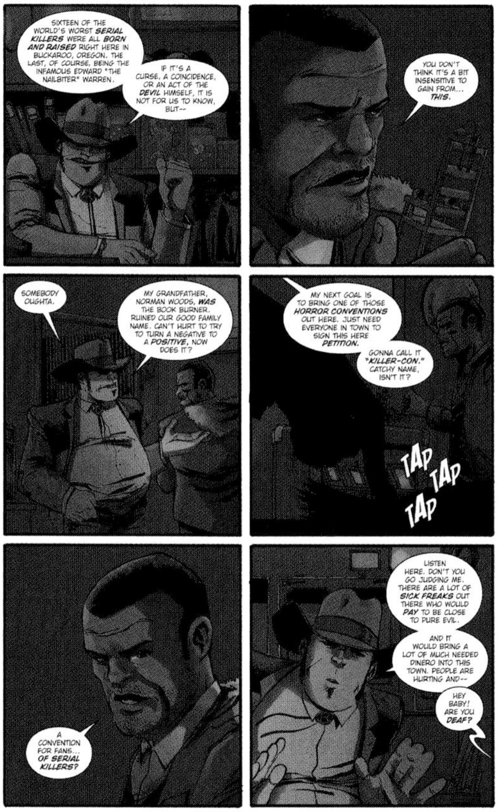
SIXTEEN OF THE WORLD'S WORST SERIAL KILLERS WERE ALL BORN AND RAISED RIGHT HERE IN BUCKAROO, OREGON. THE LAST, OF COURSE, BEING THE INFAMOUS EDWARD "THE NAILBITER" WARREN.
IF IT'S A CURSE, A COINCIDENCE, OR AN ACT OF THE DEVIL HIMSELF, IT IS NOT FOR US TO KNOW, BUT--
YOU DON'T THINK IT'S A BIT INSENSITIVE TO GAIN FROM... THIS.
SOMEBODY OUGHTA.
MY GRANDFATHER, NORMAN WOODS, WAS THE BOOK BURNER. RUINED OUR GOOD FAMILY NAME. CAN'T HURT TO TRY TO TURN A NEGATIVE TO A POSITIVE, NOW DOES IT?
MY NEXT GOAL IS TO BRING ONE OF THOSE HORROR CONVENTIONS OUT HERE. JUST NEED EVERYONE IN TOWN TO SIGN THIS HERE PETITION.
GONNA CALL IT "KILLER-CON." CATCHY NAME, ISN'T IT?
TAP TAP TAP
A CONVENTION FOR FANS... OF SERIAL KILLERS?
LISTEN HERE. DON'T YOU GO JUDGING ME. THERE ARE A LOT OF SICK FREAKS OUT THERE WHO WOULD PAY TO BE CLOSE TO PURE EVIL.
AND IT WOULD BRING A LOT OF MUCH NEEDED DINERO INTO THIS TOWN. PEOPLE ARE HURTING AND--
HEY BABY! ARE YOU DEAF?

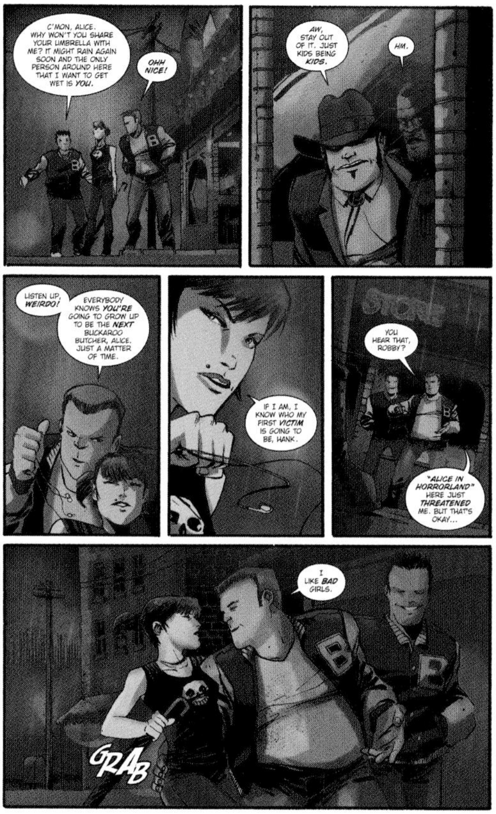
C'MON, ALICE. WHY WON'T YOU SHARE YOUR UMBRELLA WITH ME? IT MIGHT RAIN AGAIN SOON AND THE ONLY PERSON AROUND HERE THAT I WANT TO GET WET IS YOU.
OHH NICE!
AW, STAY OUT OF IT. JUST KIDS BEING KIDS.
HM.
LISTEN UP, WEIRDO!
EVERYBODY KNOWS YOU'RE GOING TO GROW UP TO BE THE NEXT BUCKAROO BUTCHER, ALICE. JUST A MATTER OF TIME.
IF I AM, I KNOW WHO MY FIRST VICTIM IS GOING TO BE, HANK.
STORE
YOU HEAR THAT, ROBBY?
"ALICE IN HORRORLAND" HERE JUST THREATENED ME. BUT THAT'S OKAY...
I LIKE BAD GIRLS.
GRAB

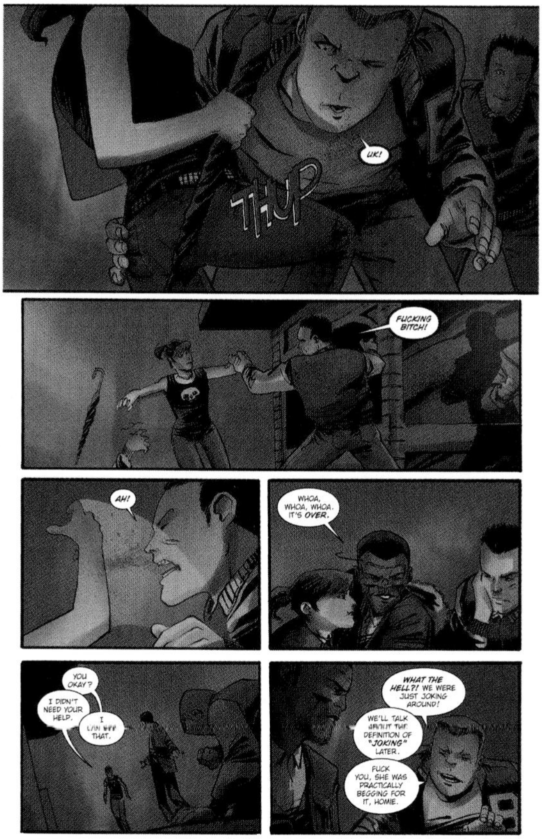
UK!
THUP
FUCKING BITCH!
AH!
WHOA, WHOA, WHOA. IT'S OVER.
YOU OKAY?
I DIDN'T NEED YOUR HELP.
I THAT.
WHAT THE HELL?! WE WERE JUST JOKING AROUND!
WE'LL TALK ABOUT THE DEFINITION OF "JOKING" LATER.
FUCK YOU, SHE WAS PRACTICALLY BEGGING FOR IT, HOMIE.

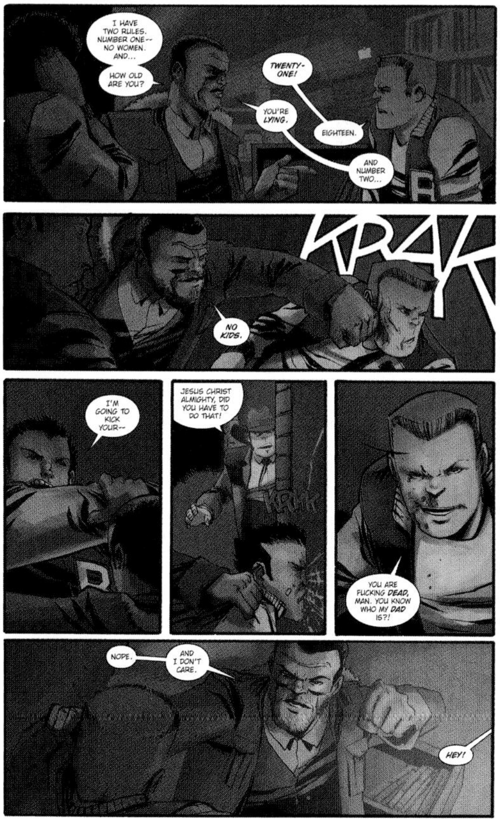
I HAVE TWO RULES. NUMBER ONE-- NO WOMEN. AND...
HOW OLD ARE YOU?
TWENTY-ONE!
YOU'RE LYING.
EIGHTEEN.
AND NUMBER TWO...
KRAK
NO KIDS.
I'M GOING TO KICK YOUR--
JESUS CHRIST ALMIGHTY, DID YOU HAVE TO DO THAT!
YOU ARE FUCKING DEAD, MAN. YOU KNOW WHO MY DAD IS?!
NOPE.
AND I DON'T CARE.
HEY!

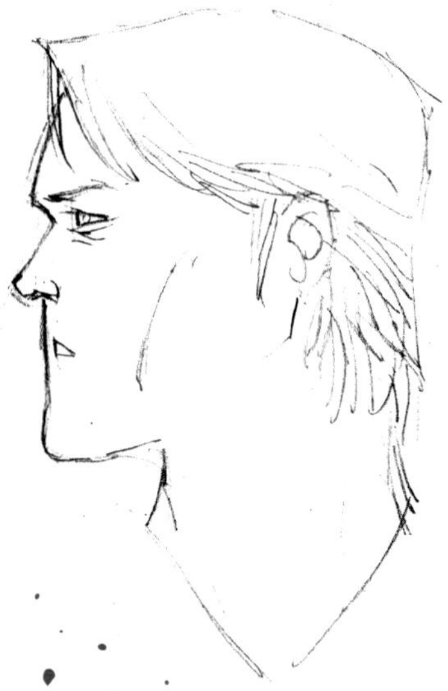

V - SKETCHBOOK

MIKE HENDERSON

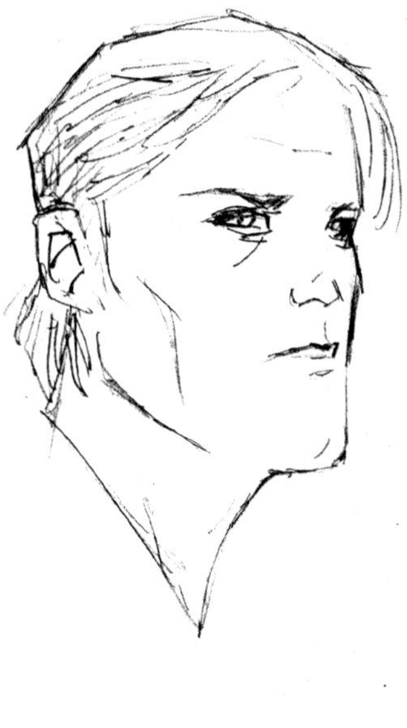

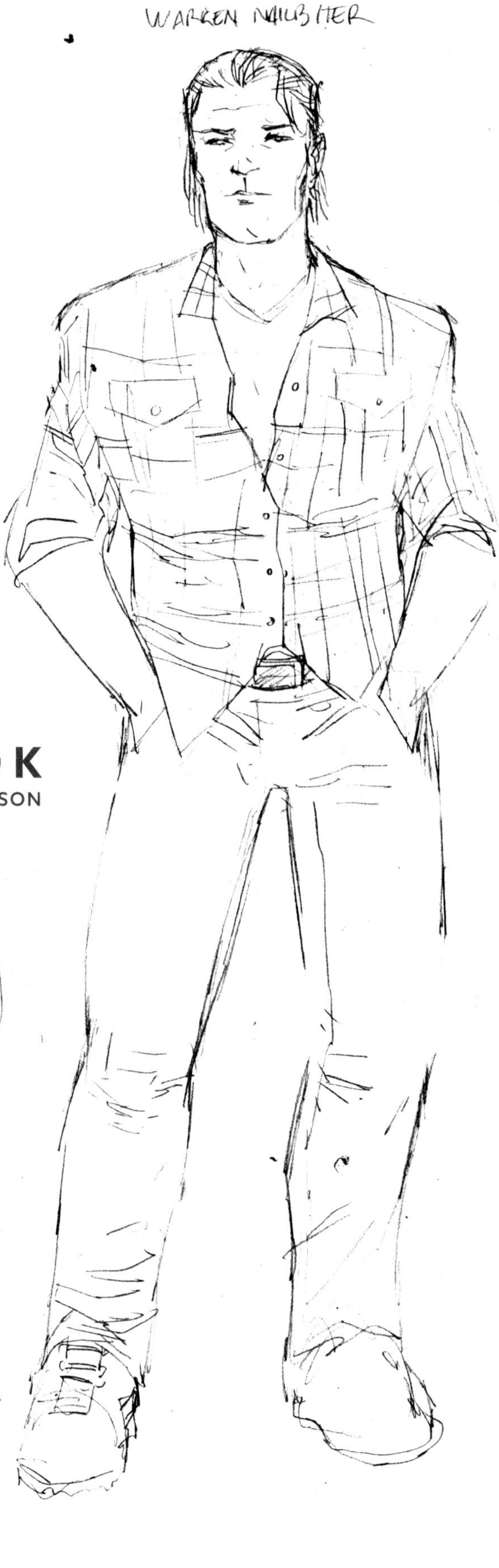
WARREN NAILBITER

NICKOLAS FINCH

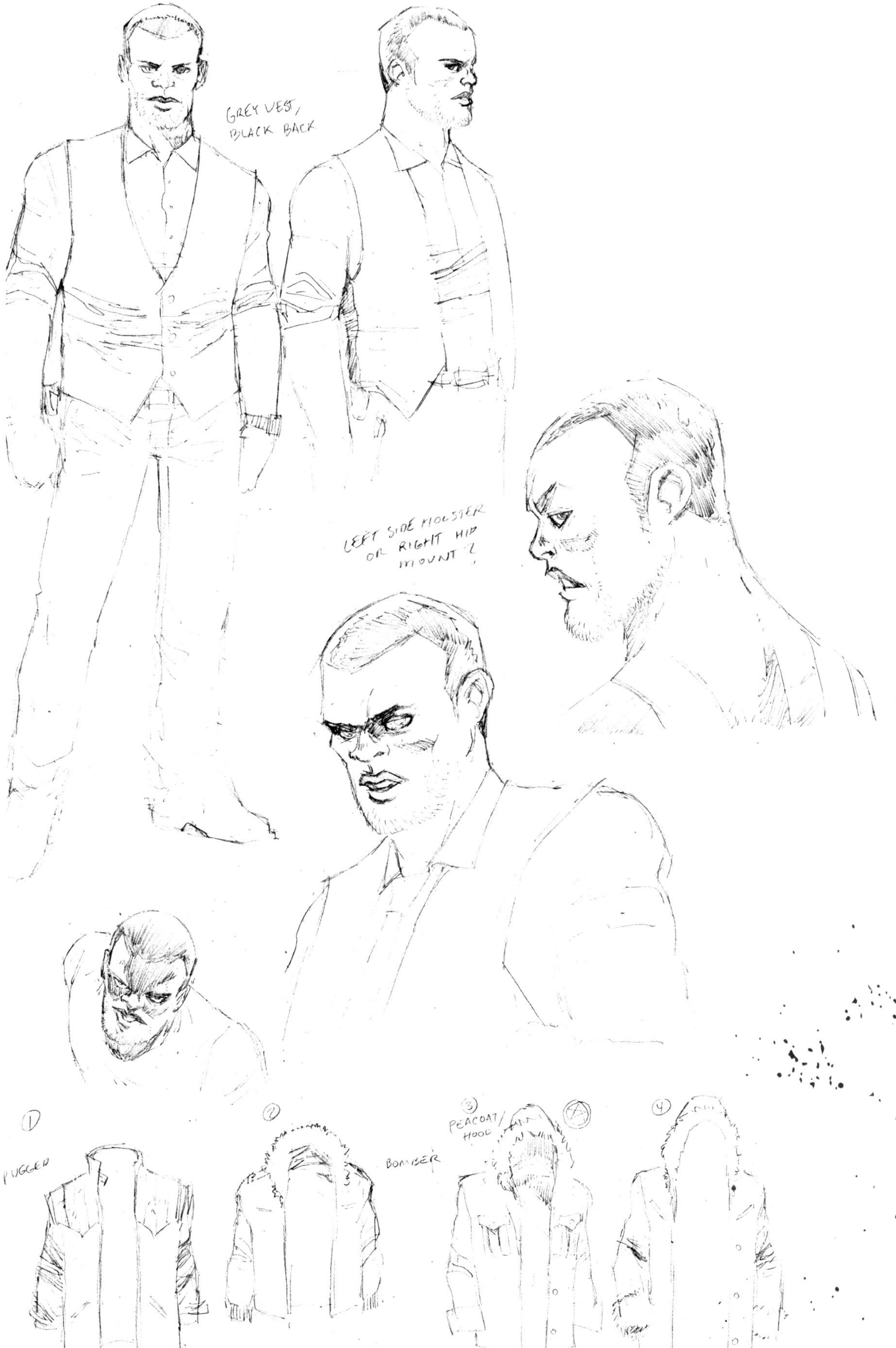
GREY VEST, BLACK BACK
LEFT SIDE HOLSTER OR RIGHT HIP MOUNT?
1
RUGGED
2
BOMBER
3
PEACOAT/ HOOD
4

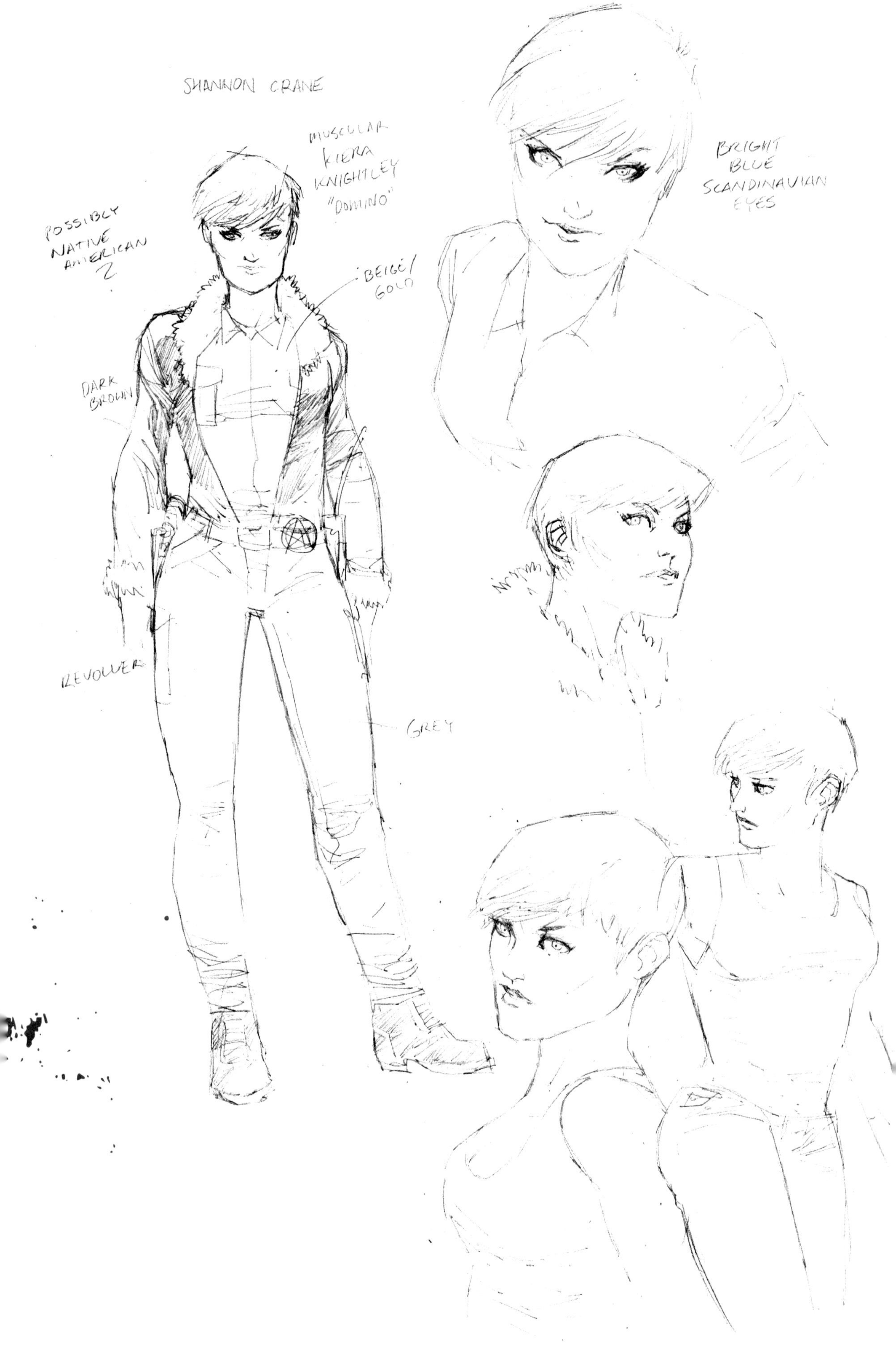
SHANNON CRANE
MUSCULAR
KIERA
KNIGHTLEY
"DOMINO"
POSSIBLY
NATIVE
AMERICAN
?
BEIGE/
GOLD
DARK
BROWN
REVOLVER
GREY
BRIGHT
BLUE
SCANDINAVIAN
EYES

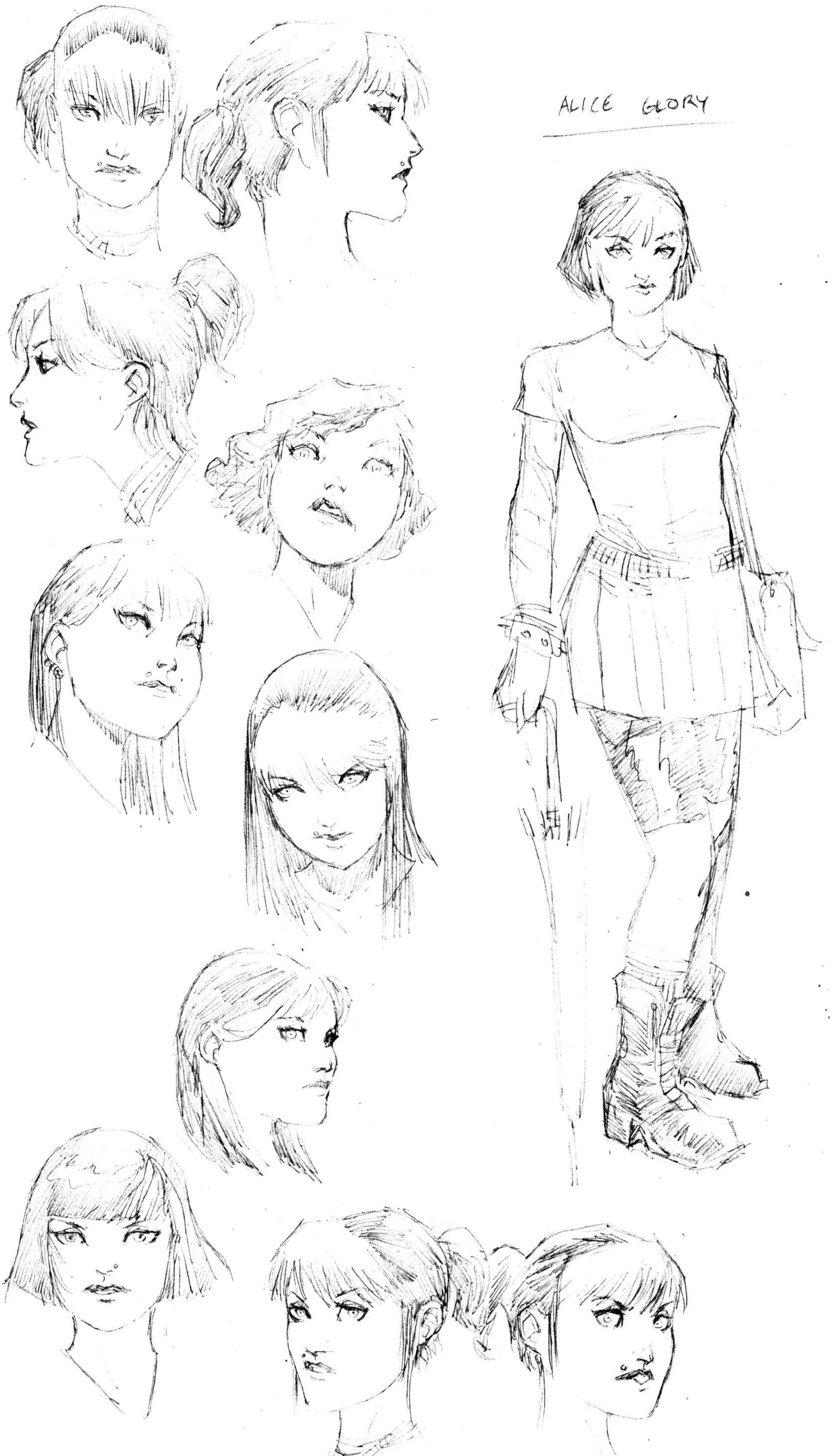
ALICE GLORY

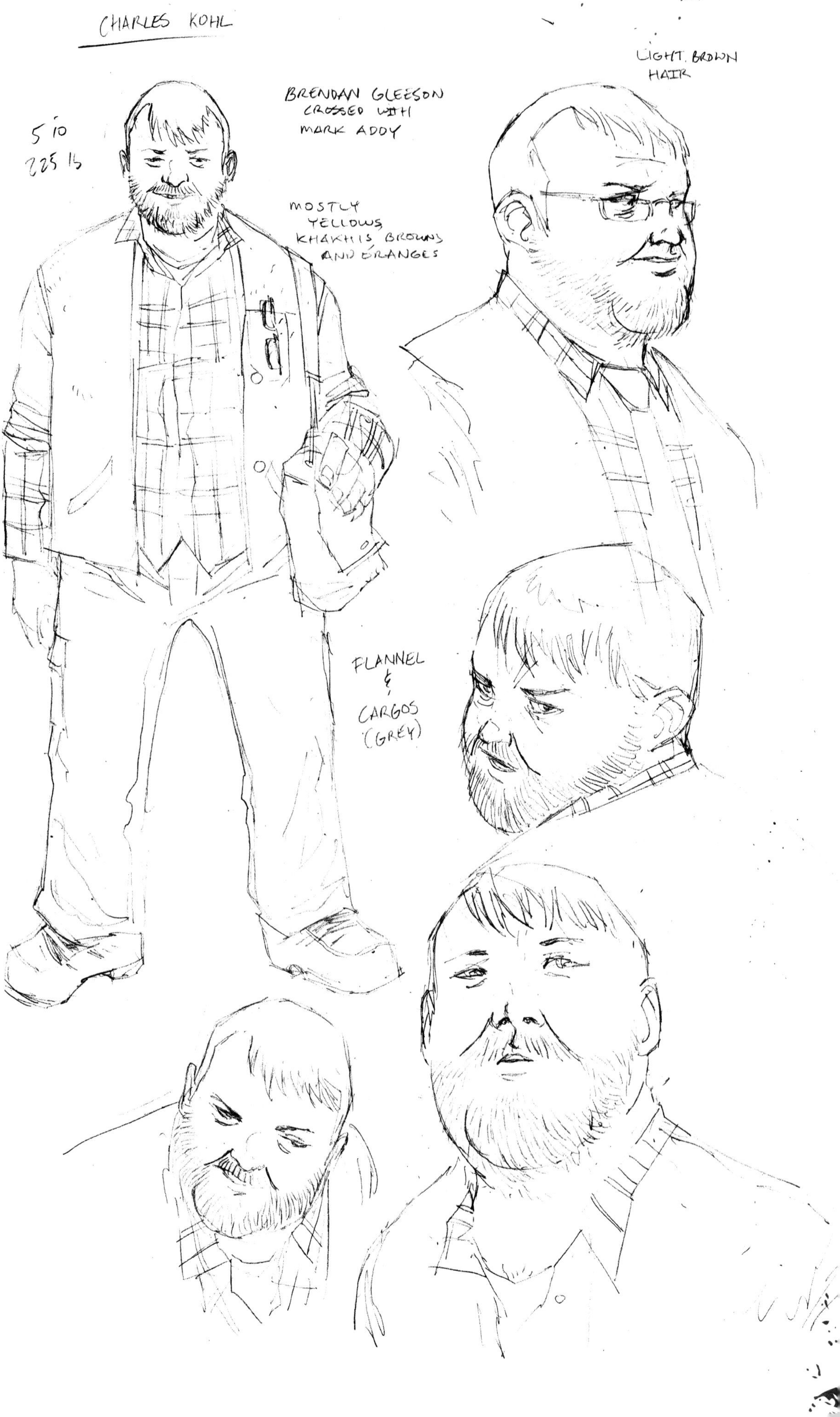
CHARLES KOHL
5'10
225 lb
BRENDAN GLEESON CROSSED WITH MARK ADDY
MOSTLY YELLOWS KHAKHIS BROWNS AND ORANGES
LIGHT BROWN HAIR
FLANNEL & CARGOS (GREY)

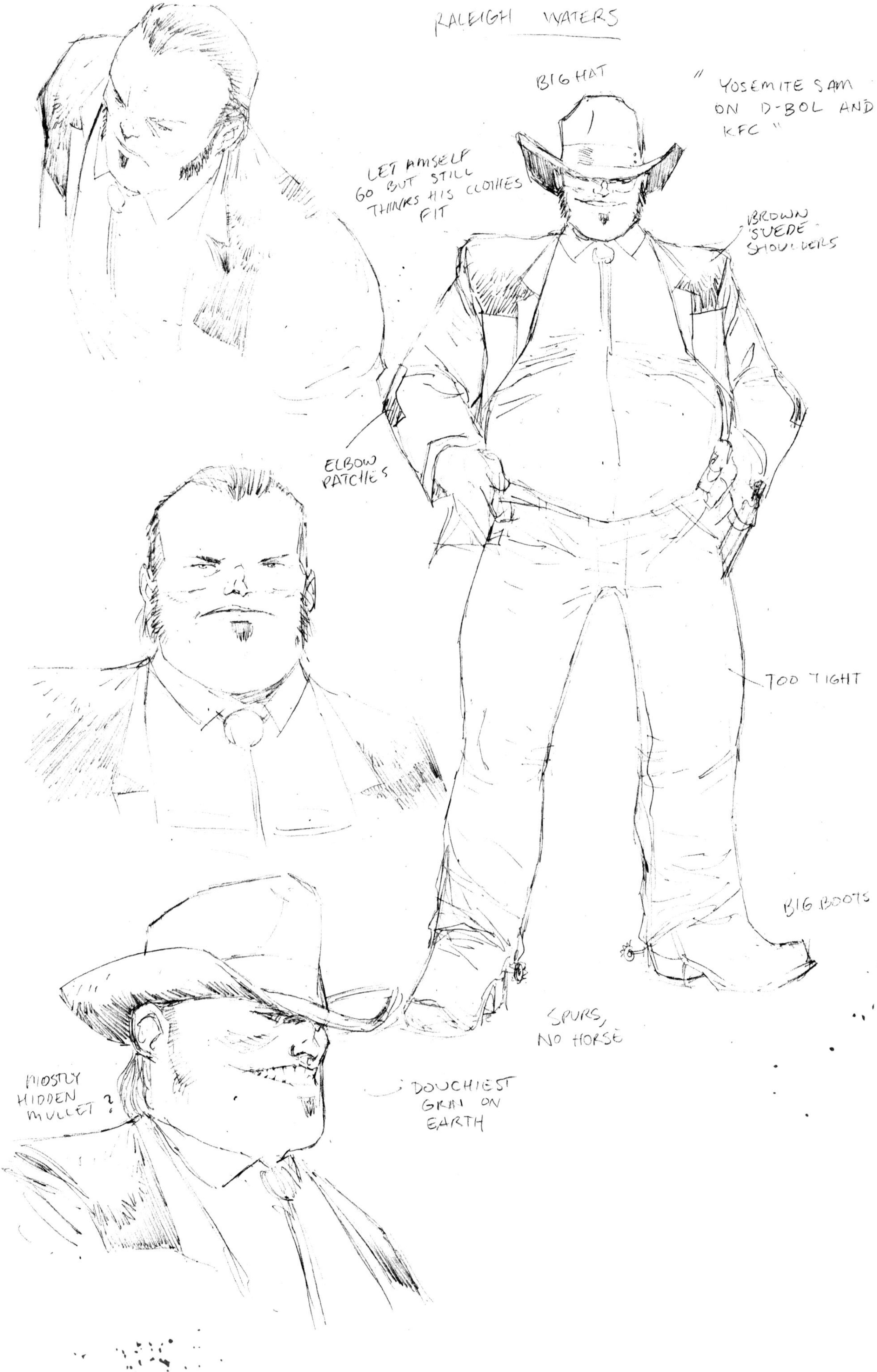
RALEIGH WATERS
BIG HAT
" YOSEMITE SAM ON D-BOL AND KFC "
LET HIMSELF GO BUT STILL THINKS HIS CLOTHES FIT
BROWN 'SUEDE' SHOULDERS
ELBOW PATCHES
TOO TIGHT
BIG BOOTS
SPURS, NO HORSE
MOSTLY HIDDEN MULLET ?
DOUCHIEST GRIN ON EARTH

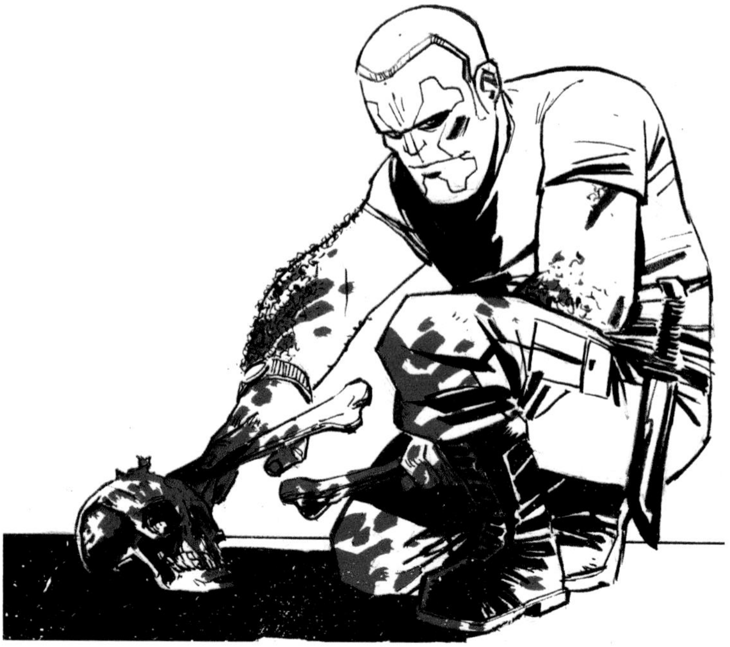

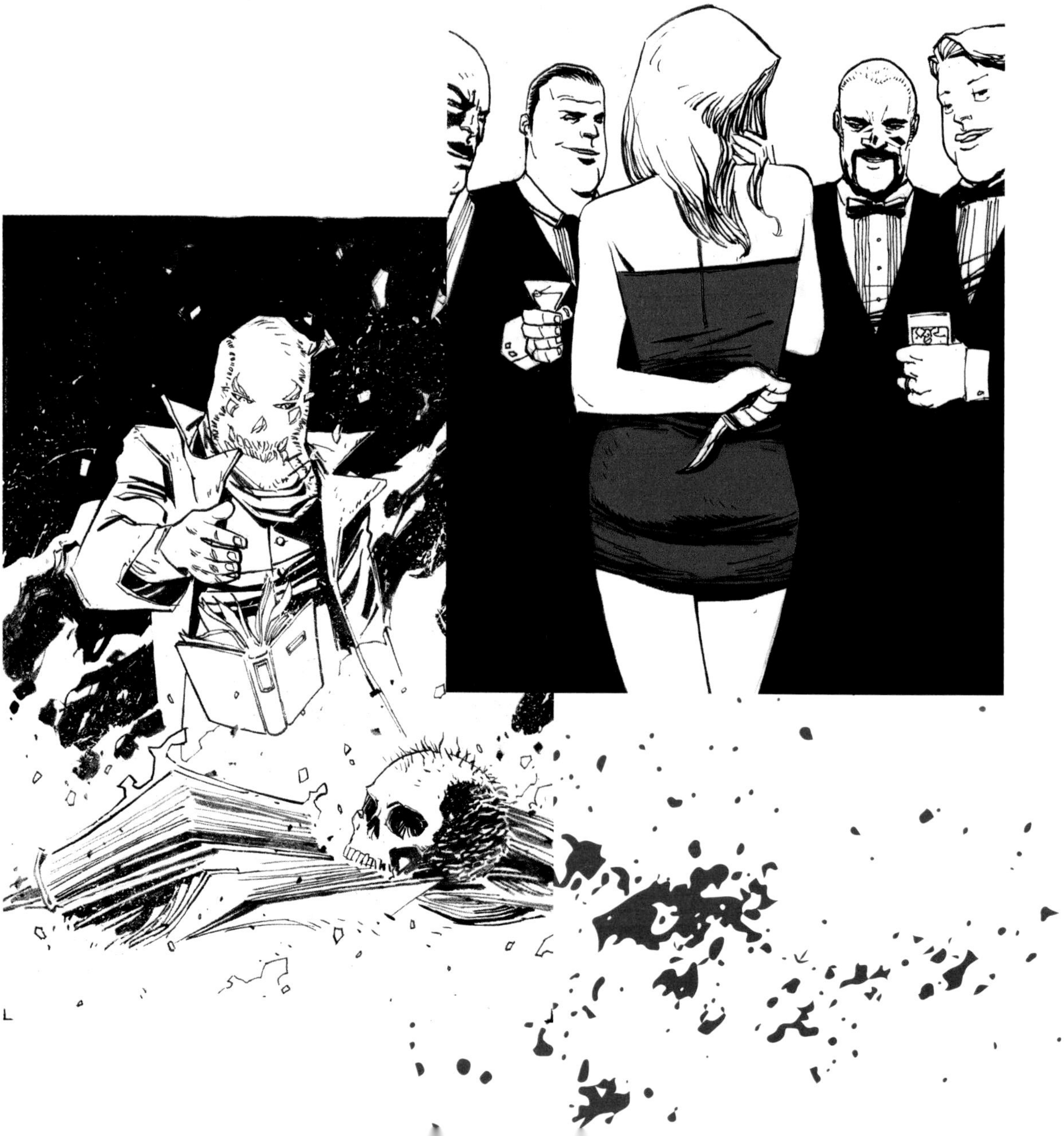

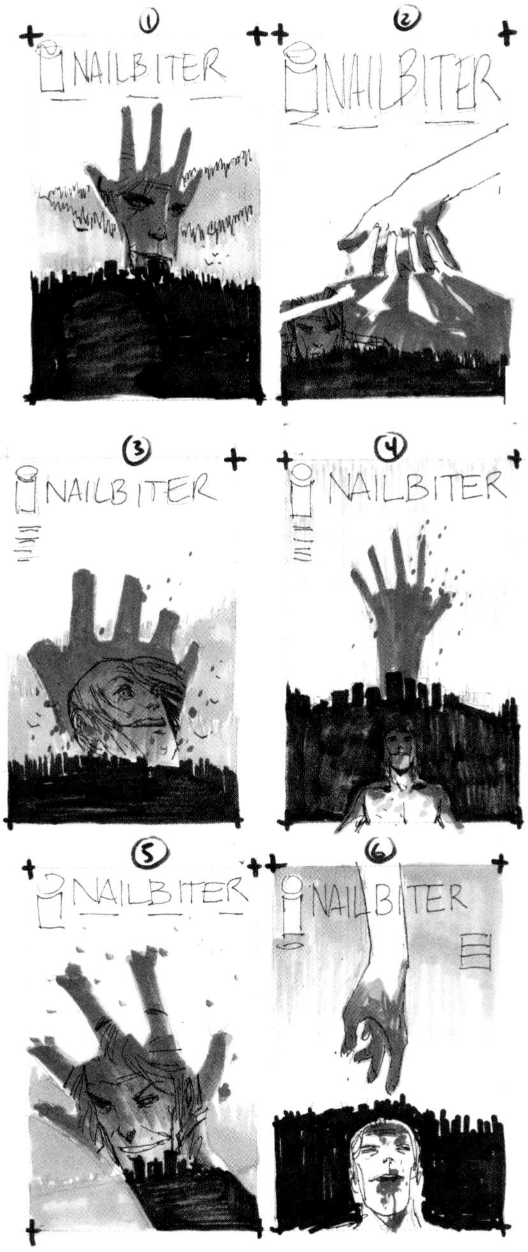
1
NAILBITER
2
NAILBITER
3
NAILBITER
4
NAILBITER
5
NAILBITER
6
NAILBITER

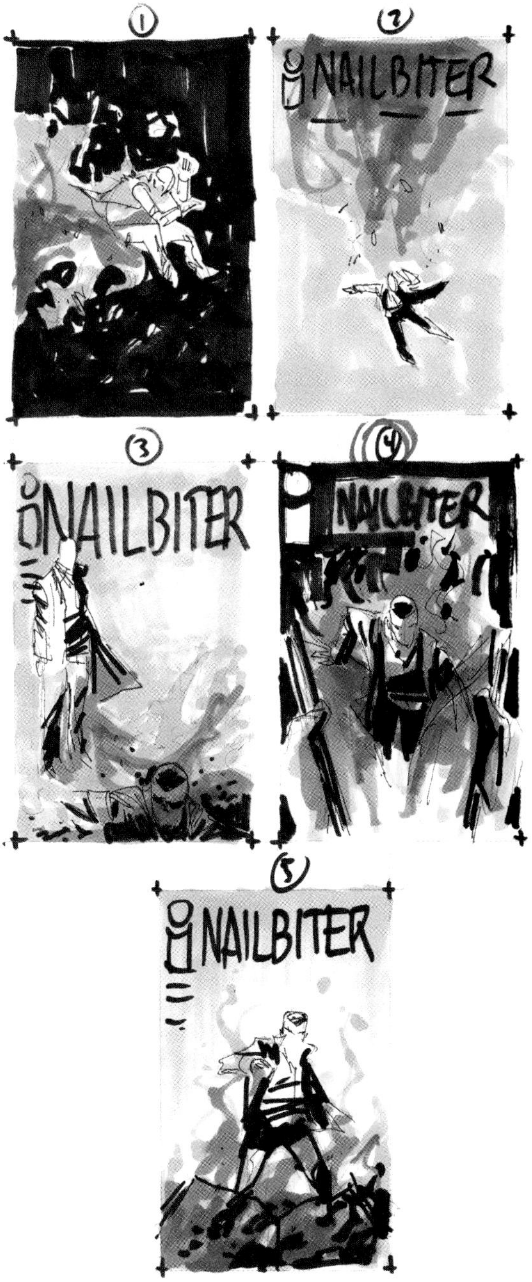
1
2
NAILBITER
3
NAILBITER
4
NAILBITER
5
NAILBITER

VI - BIOGRAPHIES

JOSHUA WILLIAMSON is a workaholic who resides in Portland OR, home of big trees, rain, great beer and half the comic industry. Joshua has written for nearly every comic publisher there is mostly on creator owned works such as *Ghosted, Dear Dracula* and *Masks and Mobsters*. He is currently writing *Birthright* and *Nailbiter* for Image Comics and Skybound along with a few other books you might have heard of...

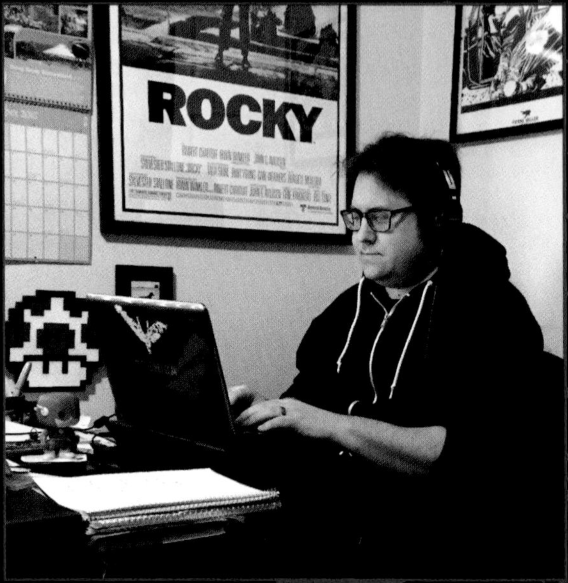
ROCKY

MIKE HENDERSON is an artist in the comic book industry and co-creator of *Nailbiter* with Joshua Williamson, and freelancer of Marvel, DC, IDW and BOOM! Studios' comics. A freelancer since 2006, he operates out of the pacific northwest and knows more about Hobbits than he has a right to.

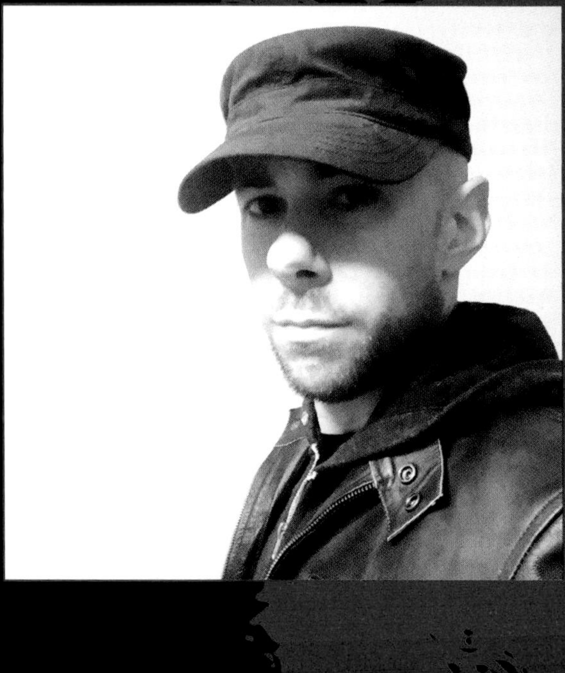

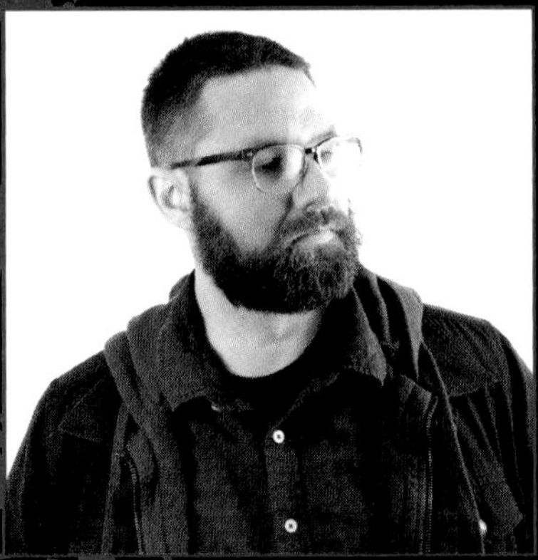

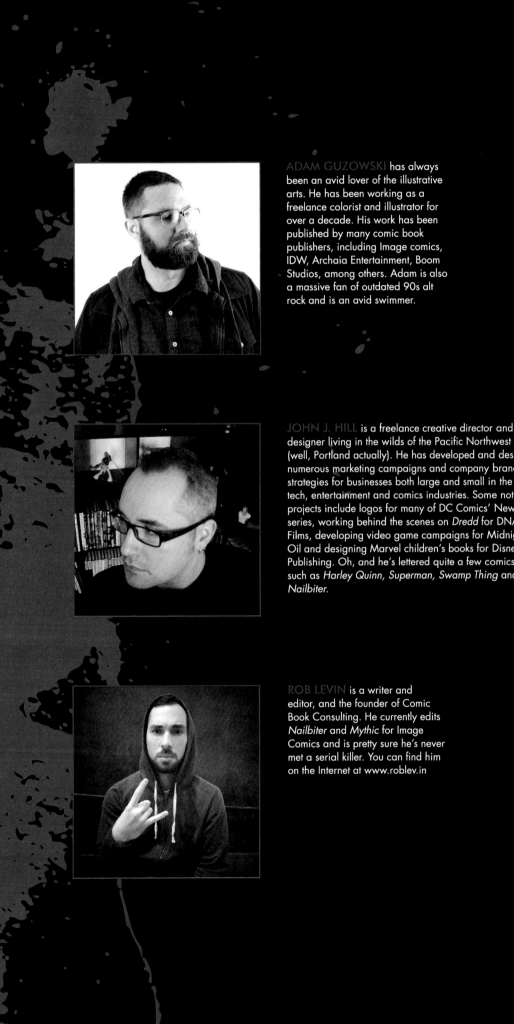

ADAM GUZOWSKI has always been an avid lover of the illustrative arts. He has been working as a freelance colorist and illustrator for over a decade. His work has been published by many comic book publishers, including Image comics, IDW, Archaia Entertainment, Boom Studios, among others. Adam is also a massive fan of outdated 90s alt rock and is an avid swimmer.

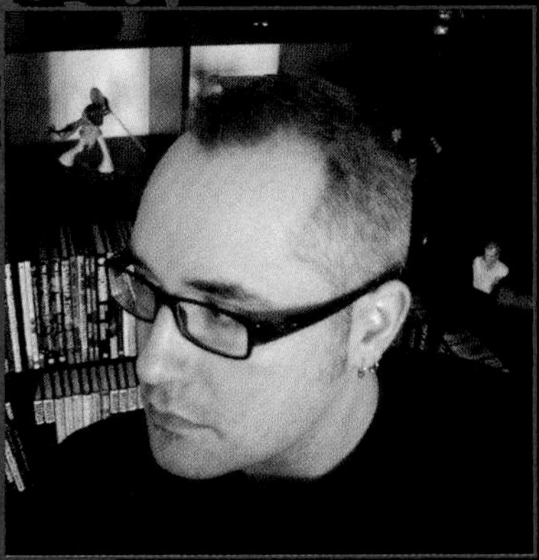

JOHN J. HILL is a freelance creative director and designer living in the wilds of the Pacific Northwest (well, Portland actually). He has developed and designed numerous marketing campaigns and company branding strategies for businesses both large and small in the tech, entertainment and comics industries. Some notable projects include logos for many of DC Comics' New 52 series, working behind the scenes on *Dredd* for DNA Films, developing video game campaigns for Midnight Oil and designing Marvel children's books for Disney Publishing. Oh, and he's lettered quite a few comics too, such as *Harley Quinn, Superman, Swamp Thing* and *Nailbiter.*

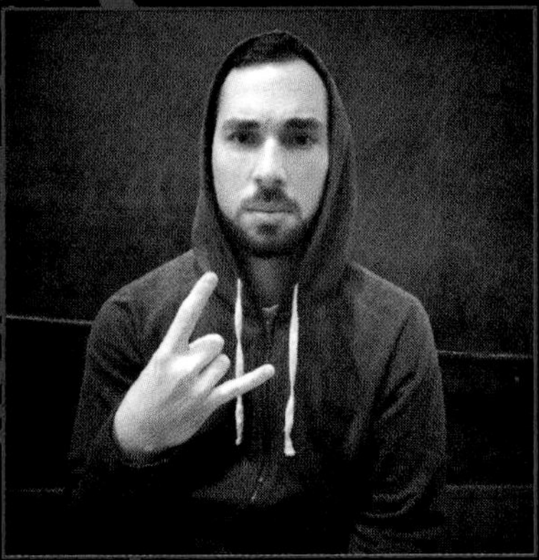

ROB LEVIN is a writer and editor, and the founder of Comic Book Consulting. He currently edits *Nailbiter* and *Mythic* for Image Comics and is pretty sure he's never met a serial killer. You can find him on the Internet at www.roblev.in

SPECIAL THANKS

JOSHUA: My lovely wife, Lauren, who knows more about serial killers than I do.

Joshua Fialkov, Dennis Culver, Joe Keatinge, Eric Stephenson, Robert Kirkman, Sean Mackiewicz, Jim Valentino, Jeremy Barlow, Tim Daniel, John Layman, Mark Doyle, Brian Michael Bendis, Scott Snyder, Rob Levin, Jason Ho, Vinny Navarrete, Riley Rossmo, Dustin Nguyen, Ben Abernathy, Brian K. Vaughan, John Carpenter, Alfred Hitchcock and everyone working hard at the Image Comics offices.

And of course, Mike Henderson, Adam Guzowski and John J. Hill. It's been a blast scaring people with you, gentleman.

MIKE: Josh and Adam for keeping me going on what has turned out to be a pretty long, pretty great ride on *Nailbiter*, and John for always making the book look great. And to my friend D, for pushing me and serving our country for the better part of these last 15 years.

ADAM: Mom, Dad, Aron, Alli, Megan, Kneeko Constantino, Jared Fletcher, John J. Hill, Josh Williamson and a special thanks to Mike Henderson for making me stick with my art.

JOHN: Jack "King" Kirby, whose creativity and independence throughout his life and career continues to be an inspiration every day.

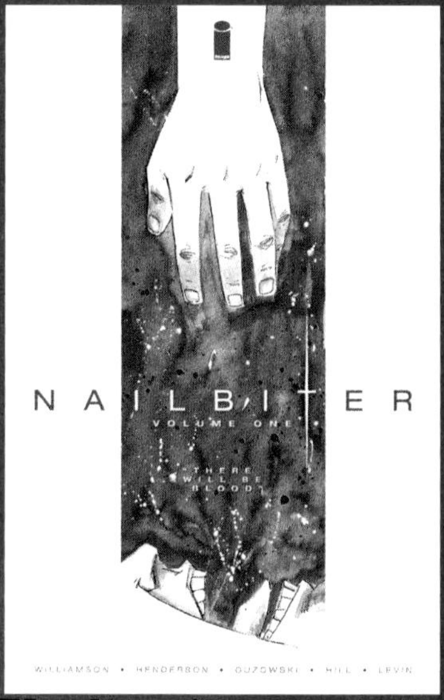
NAILBITER
VOLUME ONE
THERE WILL BE BLOOD
WILLIAMSON • HENDERSON • GUZOWSKI • HILL • LEVIN

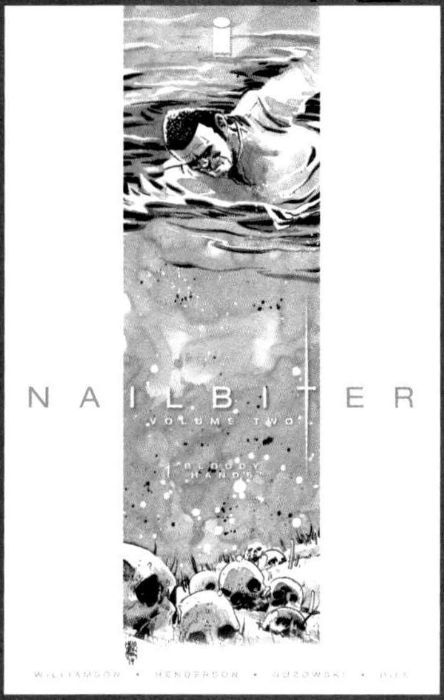
NAILBITER
VOLUME TWO
WILLIAMSON • HENDERSON • GUZOWSKI • HILL

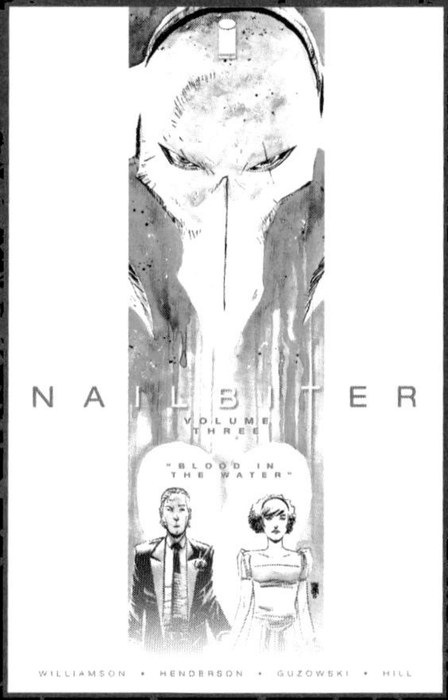
NAILBITER
VOLUME THREE
"BLOOD IN THE WATER"
WILLIAMSON • HENDERSON • GUZOWSKI • HILL

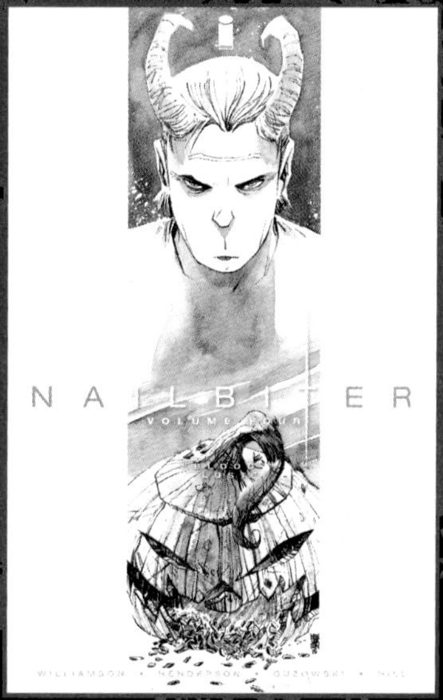
NAILBITER

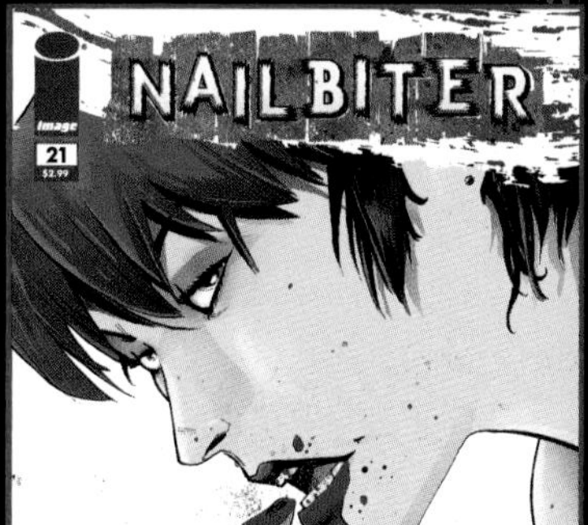
NAILBITER
21
$2.99
BOUND BY BLOOD
CHAPTER 1
WILLIAMSON • HENDERSON • GUZOWSKI • HILL • LEVIN

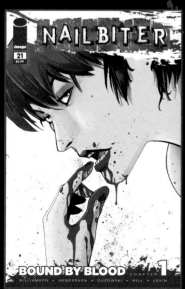

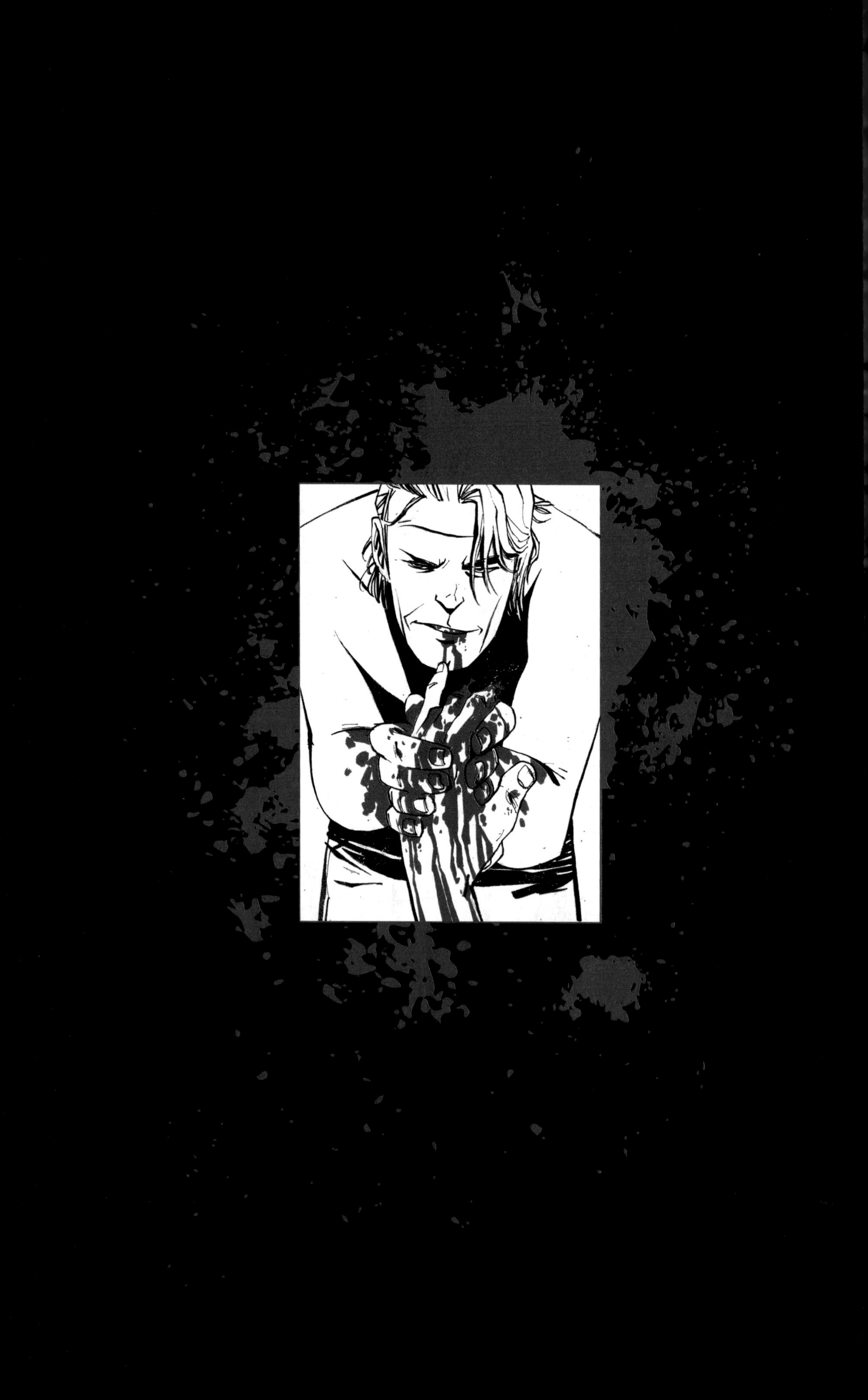